TH...

JUGGERNAUT

Desmond Bagley was born in 1923 in Kendal, Westmorland, and brought up in Blackpool. He began his working life, aged 14, in the printing industry and then did a variety of jobs until going into an aircraft factory at the start of the Second World War.

When the war ended, he decided to travel to southern Africa, going overland through Europe and the Sahara. He worked en route, reaching South Africa in 1951.

Bagley became a freelance journalist in Johannesburg and wrote his first published novel, *The Golden Keel*, in 1962. In 1964 he returned to England and lived in Totnes, Devon, for twelve years. He and his wife Joan then moved to Guernsey in the Channel Islands. Here he found the ideal place for combining his writing and his other interests, which included computers, mathematics, military history, and entertaining friends from all over the world.

Desmond Bagley died in April 1983, having become one of the world's top-selling authors, with his 16 books – two of them published after his death – translated into more than 30 languages.

'I've read all Bagley's books and he's marvellous, the best.'
ALISTAIR MACLEAN

By the same author

Flyaway AND *Windfall*

The Golden Keel AND *The Vivero Letter*

High Citadel AND *Landslide*

Running Blind AND *The Freedom Trap*

The Snow Tiger AND *Night of Error*

The Tightrope Men AND *The Enemy*

Wyatt's Hurricane AND *Bahama Crisis*

DESMOND BAGLEY

The Spoilers

AND

Juggernaut

HARPER

HARPER
an imprint of HarperCollins*Publishers*
77-85 Fulham Palace Road
Hammersmith, London W6 8JB
www.harpercollins.co.uk

This omnibus edition 2009
1

The Spoilers first published in Great Britain by Collins 1969
Juggernaut first published in Great Britain by Collins 1985
The House of the Lions first published by Harper 2009

Desmond Bagley asserts the moral right to
be identified as the author of these works

Copyright © Brockhurst Publications 1969, 1985, 2009

ISBN 978 0 00 730480 6

Printed and bound in Great Britain by
Clays Ltd, St Ives plc

Mixed Sources
Product group from well-managed
forests and other controlled sources
www.fsc.org Cert no. SW-COC-1806
© 1996 Forest Stewardship Council

FSC is a non-profit international organisation established
to promote the responsible management of the world's forests.
Products carrying the FSC label are independently certified
to assure consumers that they come from forests that are managed
to meet the social, economic and ecological needs
of present and future generations.

Find out more about HarperCollins and the environment at
www.harpercollins.co.uk/green

CONTENTS

The Spoilers
1

Juggernaut
323

The House of the Lions
667

THE SPOILERS

This one is for Pat and Philip Bawcombe
and, of course, Thickabe

ONE

She lay on the bed in an abandoned attitude, oblivious of the big men crowding the room and making it appear even smaller than it was. She had been abandoned by life, and the big men were there to find out why, not out of natural curiosity but because it was their work. They were policemen.

Detective-Inspector Stephens ignored the body. He had given it a cursory glance and then turned his attention to the room, noting the cheap, rickety furniture and the threadbare carpet which was too small to hide dusty boards. There was no wardrobe and the girl's few garments were scattered, some thrown casually over a chair-back and others on the floor by the side of the bed. The girl herself was naked, an empty shell. Death is not erotic.

Stephens picked up a sweater from the chair and was surprised at its opulent softness. He looked at the maker's tab and frowned before handing it to Sergeant Ipsley. 'She could afford good stuff. Any identification yet?'

'Betts is talking to the landlady.'

Stephens knew the worth of that. The inhabitants of his manor did not talk freely to policemen. 'He won't get much. Just a name and that'll be false, most likely. Seen the syringe?'

'Couldn't miss it, sir. Do you think it's drugs?'

'Could be.' Stephens turned to an unpainted whitewood chest of drawers and pulled on a knob. The drawer opened an inch and then stuck. He smote it with the heel of his hand. 'Any sign of the police surgeon yet?'

'I'll go and find out, sir.'

'Don't worry; he'll come in his own sweet time.' Stephens turned his head to the bed. 'Besides, she's not in too much of a hurry.' He tugged at the drawer which stuck again. 'Damn this confounded thing!'

A uniformed constable pushed open the door and closed it behind him. 'Her name's Hellier, sir – June Hellier. She's been here a week – came last Wednesday.'

Stephens straightened. 'That's not much help, Betts. Have you seen her before on your beat?'

Betts looked towards the bed and shook his head. 'No, sir.'

'Was she previously known to the landlady?'

'No, sir; she just came in off the street and said she wanted a room. She paid in advance.'

'She wouldn't have got in otherwise,' said Ipsley. 'I know this old besom here – nothing for nothing and not much for sixpence.'

'Did she make any friends – acquaintances?' asked Stephens. 'Speak to anyone?'

'Not that I can find out, sir. From all accounts she stuck in her room most of the time.'

A short man with an incipient pot belly pushed into the room. He walked over to the bed and put down his bag. 'Sorry I'm late, Joe; this damned traffic gets worse every day.'

'That's all right, Doctor.' Stephens turned to Betts again. 'Have another prowl around and see what you can get.' He joined the doctor at the foot of the bed and looked down at the body of the girl. 'The usual thing – time of death and the reason therefore.'

Doctor Pomray glanced at him. 'Foul play suspected?'

Stephens shrugged. 'Not that I know of – yet.' He indicated the syringe and the glass which lay on the bamboo bedside table. 'Could be drugs; an overdose, maybe.'

Pomray bent down and sniffed delicately at the glass. There was a faint film of moisture at the bottom and he was just about to touch it when Stephens said, 'I'd rather you didn't, Doctor. I'd like to have it checked for dabs first.'

'It doesn't really matter,' said Pomray. 'She was an addict, of course. Look at her thighs. I just wanted to check what her particular poison was.'

Stephens had already seen the puncture marks and had drawn his own conclusions, but he said, 'Could have been a diabetic.'

Pomray shook his head decisively. 'A trace of phlebothrombosis together with skin sepsis – no doctor would allow that to happen to a diabetic patient.' He bent down and squeezed the skin. 'Incipient jaundice, too; that shows liver damage. I'd say it's drug addiction with the usual lack of care in the injection. But we won't really know until after the autopsy.'

'All right, I'll leave you to it.' Stephens turned to Ipsley and said casually, 'Will you open that drawer, Sergeant?'

'Another thing,' said Pomray. 'She's very much underweight for her height. That's another sign.' He gestured towards an ashtray overflowing untidily with cigarette-stubs. 'And she was a heavy smoker.'

Stephens watched Ipsley take the knob delicately between thumb and forefinger and pull open the drawer smoothly. He switched his gaze from the smug expression on Ipsley's face, and said, 'I'm a heavy smoker too, Doctor. That doesn't mean much.'

'It fills out the clinical picture,' argued Pomray.

Stephens nodded. 'I'd like to know if she died on that bed.'

Pomray looked surprised. 'Any reason why she shouldn't have?'

Stephens smiled slightly. 'None at all; I'm just being careful.'

'I'll see what I can find,' said Pomray.

There was not much in the drawer. A handbag, three stockings, a pair of panties due for the wash, a bunch of keys, a lipstick, a suspender-belt and a syringe with a broken needle. Stephens uncapped the lipstick case and looked inside it; the lipstick was worn right down and there was evidence that the girl had tried to dig out the last of the wax, which was confirmed by the discovery of a spent match with a reddened end caught in a crack of the drawer. Stephens, an expert on the interpretation of such minutiae, concluded that June Hellier had been destitute.

The panties had a couple of reddish-brown stains on the front, stains which were repeated on one of the stocking tops. It looked very much like dried blood and was probably the result of inexpert injection into the thigh. The key-ring contained three keys, one of which was a car ignition key. Stephens turned to Ipsley. 'Nip down and see if the girl had a car.'

Another key fitted a suitcase which he found in a corner. It was a de-luxe elaborately fitted case of the type which Stephens had considered buying as a present for his wife – the idea had been rejected on the grounds of excessive expense. It contained nothing.

He could not find anything for the third key to fit so he turned his attention to the handbag, which was of fine-grained leather. He was about to open it when Ipsley came back. 'No car, sir.'

'Indeed!' Stephens pursed his lips. He snapped open the catch of the handbag and looked inside. Papers, tissues, another lipstick worn to a nubbin, three shillings and fourpence in coins and no paper money. 'Listen carefully, Sergeant,' he said. 'Good handbag, good suitcase, car key but no car, good clothes except the stockings which are cheap, gold lipstick case in drawer, Woolworth's lipstick in bag – both worn out. What do you make of all that?'

'Come down in the world, sir.'

Stephens nodded as he pushed at the few coins with his forefinger. He said abruptly. 'Can you tell me if she was a virgin, Doctor?'

'She wasn't,' said Pomray. 'I've checked that.'

'Maybe she was on the knock,' offered Ipsley.

'Possibly,' said Stephens. 'We can find out – if we have to.'

Pomray straightened. 'She died on this bed all right; there's the usual evidence. I've done all I can here. Is there anywhere I can wash?'

'There's a bathroom just along the hall,' said Ipsley. 'It's not what I'd call hygienic, though.'

Stephens was sorting the few papers. 'What did she die of, Doctor?'

'I'd say an overdose of a drug – but what it was will have to wait for the autopsy.'

'Accidental or deliberate?' asked Stephens.

'That will have to wait for the autopsy too,' said Pomray. 'If it was a really massive overdose then you can be pretty sure it was deliberate. An addict usually knows to a hair how much to take. If it's not too much of an overdose then it could be accidental.'

'If it's deliberate then I have a choice between suicide and murder,' said Stephens musingly.

'I think you can safely cut out murder,' said Pomray. 'Addicts don't like other people sticking needles into them.' He shrugged. 'And the suicide rate among addicts is high once they hit bottom.'

A small snorting noise came from Stephens as he made the discovery of a doctor's appointment card. The name on it rang a bell somewhere in the recesses of his mind. 'What do you know about Dr Nicholas Warren? Isn't he a drug man?'

Pomray nodded. 'So she was one of his girls, was she?' he said with interest.

'What kind of a doctor is he? Is he on the level?'

Pomray reacted with shock. 'My God! Nick Warren's reputation is as pure as the driven snow. He's one of the top boys in the field. He's no quack, if that's what you mean.'

'We get all kinds,' said Stephens levelly. 'As you know very well.' He gave the card to Ipsley. 'He's not too far from here. See if you can get hold of him, Sergeant; we still haven't any positive identification of the girl.'

'Yes, sir,' said Ipsley, and made for the door.

'And, Sergeant,' called Stephens. 'Don't tell him the girl's dead.'

Ipsley grinned. 'I won't.'

'Now look here,' said Pomray. 'If you try to pressure Warren you'll get a hell of a surprise. He's a tough boy.'

'I don't like doctors who hand out drugs,' said Stephens grimly.

'You know damn-all about it,' snapped Pomray. 'And you won't fault Nick Warren on medical ethics. If you go on that tack he'll tie you up in knots.'

'We'll see. I've handled tough ones before.'

Pomray grinned suddenly. 'I think I'll stay and watch this. Warren knows as much – if not more – about drugs and drug addicts as anyone in the country. He's a bit of a fanatic about it. I don't think you'll get much change out of him. I'll be back as soon as I've cleaned up in this sewer of a bathroom.'

Stephens met Warren in the dimly lit hall outside the girl's room, wanting to preserve the psychological advantage he had gained by not informing the doctor of the girl's death. If he was surprised at the speed of Warren's arrival he did not show it, but studied the man with professional detachment as he advanced up the hall.

Warren was a tall man with a sensitive yet curiously immobile face. In all his utterances he spoke thoughtfully, sometimes pausing for quite a long time before he answered. This gave Stephens the impression that Warren had not heard or was ignoring the question, but Warren always answered just as a repetition was on Stephens's tongue. This deliberateness irritated Stephens, although he tried not to show it.

'I'm glad you were able to come,' he said. 'We have a problem, Doctor. Do you know a young lady called June Hellier?'

'Yes, I do,' said Warren, economically.

Stephens waited expectantly for Warren to elaborate, but Warren merely looked at him. Swallowing annoyance, he said, 'Is she one of your patients?'

'Yes,' said Warren.

'What were you treating her for, Doctor?'

There was a long pause before Warren said, 'That is a matter of patient-doctor relationship which I don't care to go into.'

Stephens felt Pomray stir behind him. He said stiffly, 'This is a police matter, Doctor.'

Again Warren paused, holding Stephens's eye with a level stare. At last he said, 'I suggest that if Miss Hellier needs treatment we are wasting time standing here.'

'She will not be requiring treatment,' said Stephens flatly.

Again Pomray stirred. 'She's dead, Nick.'

'I see,' said Warren. He seemed indifferent.

Stephens was irritated at Pomray's interjection, but more interested in Warren's lack of reaction. 'You don't seem surprised, Doctor.'

'I'm not,' said Warren briefly.

'You were supplying her with drugs?'

'I have prescribed for her – in the past.'

'What drugs?'

'Heroin.'

'Was that necessary?'

Warren was as immobile as ever, but there was a flinty look in his eye as he said, 'I don't propose to discuss the medical treatment of any of my patients with a layman.'

A surge of anger surfaced in Stephens. 'But you are not surprised at her death. Was she a dying woman? A terminal case?'

Warren looked at Stephens consideringly, and said, 'The death rate among drug addicts is about twenty-eight times that of the general population. That is why I am not surprised at her death.'

'She was a heroin addict?'

'Yes.'

'And you have supplied her with heroin?'

'I have.'

'I see,' said Stephens with finality. He glanced at Pomray, then turned back to Warren. 'I don't know that I like that.'

'I don't care whether you like it or not,' said Warren equably. 'May I see my patient – you'll be wanting a death certificate. It had better come from me.'

Of all the bloody nerve, thought Stephens. He turned abruptly and threw open the door of the bedroom. 'In there,' he said curtly.

Warren walked past him into the room, followed closely by Pomray. Stephens jerked his head at Sergeant Ipsley, indicating that he should leave, then closed the door behind him. When he strode to the bed Warren and Pomray were already in the midst of a conversation of which he understood about one word in four.

The sheet with which Pomray had draped the body was drawn back to reveal again the naked body of June Hellier.

Stephens butted in. 'Dr Warren: I suggested to Dr Pomray that perhaps this girl was a diabetic, because of those puncture marks. He said there was sepsis and that no doctor would allow that to happen to his patient. This girl was your patient. How do you account for it?'

Warren looked at Pomray and there was a faint twitch about his mouth that might have been a smile. 'I don't have to account for it,' he said. 'But I will. The circumstances of the injection of an anti-diabetic drug are quite different from those attendant on heroin. The social ambience is different and there is often an element of haste which can result in sepsis.'

In an aside to Pomray he said, 'I taught her how to use a needle but, as you know, they don't take much notice of the need for cleanliness.'

Stephens was affronted. 'You *taught* her how to use a needle! By God, you make a curious use of ethics!'

Warren looked at him levelly and said with the utmost deliberation, 'Inspector, any doubts you have about my ethics should be communicated to the appropriate authority, and if you don't know what it is I shall be happy to supply you with the address.'

The way he turned from Stephens was almost an insult. He said to Pomray, 'I'll sign the certificate together with the pathologist. It will be better that way.'

'Yes,' said Pomray thoughtfully. 'It might be better.'

Warren stepped to the head of the bed and stood for a moment looking down at the dead girl. Then he drew up the sheet very slowly so that it covered the body. There was something in that slow movement which puzzled Stephens; it was an act of . . . of tenderness.

He waited until Warren looked up, then said, 'Do you know anything of her family?'

'Practically nothing. Addicts resent probing – so I don't probe.'

'Nothing about her father?'

'Nothing beyond the fact that she had a father. She mentioned him a couple of times.'

'When did she come to you for drugs?'

'She came to me for treatment about a year and a half ago. For treatment, Inspector.'

'Of course,' said Stephens ironically, and produced a folded sheet of paper from his pocket. 'You might like to look at this.'

Warren took the sheet and unfolded it, noting the worn creases. 'Where did you get it?'

'It was in her handbag.'

It was a letter typed in executive face on high quality paper and bore the embossed heading: REGENT FILM COMPANY, with a Wardour Street address. It was dated six months earlier, and ran:

Dear Miss Hellier,

   On the instructions of your father I write to tell you that he will be unable to see you on Friday next because he is leaving for America the same afternoon. He expects to be away for some time, how long exactly I am unable to say at this moment.

   He assures you that he will write to you as soon as his more pressing business is completed, and he hopes you will not regret his absence too much.

                                Yours sincerely,

                                          D. L. Walden

Warren said quietly, 'This explains a lot.' He looked up. 'Did he write?'

'I don't know,' said Stephens. 'There's nothing here.'

Warren tapped the letter with a finger-nail. 'I don't think he did. June wouldn't keep a secondhand letter like this and destroy the real thing.' He looked down at the shrouded body. 'The poor girl.'

'You'd better be thinking of yourself, Doctor,' said Stephens sardonically. 'Take a look at the list of directors at the head of that letter.'

Warren glanced at it and saw: Sir Robert Hellier (Chairman). With a grimace he passed it to Pomray.

'My God!' said Pomray. '*That* Hellier.'

'Yes, *that* Hellier,' said Stephens. 'I think this one is going to be a stinker. Don't you agree, Dr Warren?' There was an unconcealed satisfaction in his voice and a dislike in his eyes as he stared at Warren.

II

Warren sat at his desk in his consulting-room. He was between patients and using the precious minutes to catch up on the mountain of paperwork imposed by the Welfare State. He disliked the bureaucratic aspect of medicine as much as any doctor and so, in an odd way, he was relieved to be interrupted by the telephone. But his relief soon evaporated when he heard his receptionist say, 'Sir Robert Hellier wishes to speak to you, Doctor.'

He sighed. This was a call he had been expecting. 'Put him through, Mary.'

There was a click and a different buzz on the line. 'Hellier here.'

'Nicholas Warren speaking.'

The tinniness of the telephone could not disguise the rasp of authority in Hellier's voice. 'I want to see you, Warren.'

'I thought you might, Sir Robert.'

'I shall be at my office at two-thirty this afternoon. Do you know where it is?'

'That will be quite impossible,' said Warren firmly. 'I'm a very busy man. I suggest I find time for an appointment with you here at my rooms.'

There was a pause tinged with incredulity, then a splutter. 'Now, look here . . .'

'I'm sorry, Sir Robert,' Warren cut in. 'I suggest you come to see me at five o'clock today. I shall be free then, I think.'

Hellier made his decision. 'Very well,' he said brusquely, and Warren winced as the telephone was slammed down at the other end. He laid down his handset gently and flicked a switch on his intercom. 'Mary, Sir Robert Hellier will be seeing me at five. You might have to rearrange things a bit. I expect it to be a long consultation, so he must be the last patient.'

'Yes, Doctor.'

'Oh, Mary: as soon as Sir Robert arrives you may leave.'

'Thank you, Doctor.'

Warren released the switch and gazed pensively across the room, but after a few moments he applied himself once more to his papers.

Sir Robert Hellier was a big man and handled himself in such a way as to appear even bigger. The Savile Row suiting did not tone down his muscular movements by its suavity, and his voice was that of a man unaccustomed to brooking opposition. As soon as he entered Warren's room he said curtly and without preamble, 'You know why I'm here.'

'Yes; you've come to see me about your daughter. Won't you sit down?'

Hellier took the chair on the other side of the desk. 'I'll come to the point. My daughter is dead. The police have given me information which I consider incredible. They tell me that she was a drug addict – that she took heroin.'

'She did.'

'Heroin which you supplied.'

'Heroin which I prescribed,' corrected Warren.

Hellier was momentarily taken aback. 'I did not expect you to admit it so easily.'

'Why not?' said Warren. 'I was your daughter's physician.'

'Of all the bare-faced effrontery!' burst out Hellier. He leaned forward and his powerful shoulders hunched under his suit. 'That a doctor should prescribe hard drugs for a young girl is disgraceful.'

'My prescription was . . .'

'I'll see you in jail,' yelled Hellier.

'. . . entirely necessary in my opinion.'

'You're nothing but a drug pedlar.'

Warren stood up and his voice cut coldly through Hellier's tirade. 'If you repeat that statement outside this room I shall sue you for slander. If you will not listen to what I have to say then I must ask you to leave, since further communication on your part is pointless. And if you want to complain about my ethics you must do so to the Disciplinary Committee of the General Medical Council.'

Hellier looked up in astonishment. 'Are you trying to tell me that the General Medical Council would condone such conduct?'

'I am,' said Warren wryly, and sat down again. 'And so would the British Government – they legislated for it.'

Hellier seemed out of his depth. 'All right,' he said uncertainly. 'I suppose I should hear what you have to say. That's why I came here.'

Warren regarded him thoughtfully. 'June came to see me about eighteen months ago. At that time she had been taking heroin for nearly two years.'

Hellier flared again. 'Impossible!'

'What's so impossible about it?'

'I would have known.'

'How would you have known?'

'Well, I'd have recognized the . . . the symptoms.'

'I see. What are the symptoms, Sir Robert?'

Hellier began to speak, then checked himself and was silent. Warren said, 'A heroin addict doesn't walk about with palsied hands, you know. The symptoms are much subtler than that – and addicts are adept at disguising them. But you might have noticed something. Tell me, did she appear to have money troubles at that time?'

Hellier looked at the back of his hands. 'I can't remember the time when she didn't have money troubles,' he said broodingly. 'I was getting pretty tired of it and I put my foot down hard. I told her I hadn't raised her to be an idle spend-thrift.' He looked up. 'I found her a job, installed her in her own flat and cut her allowance by half.'

'I see,' said Warren. 'How long did she keep the job?'

Hellier shook his head. 'I don't know – only that she lost it.' His hands tightened on the edge of the desk so that the knuckles showed white. 'She robbed me, you know – she stole from her own father.'

'How did that happen?' asked Warren gently.

'I have a country house in Berkshire,' said Hellier. 'She went down there and looted it – literally looted it. There was a lot of Georgian silver, among other things. She had the nerve to leave a note saying that she was responsible – she even gave me the name of the dealer she'd sold the stuff to. I got it all back, but it cost me a hell of a lot of money.'

'Did you prosecute?'

'Don't be a damned fool,' said Hellier violently. 'I have a reputation to keep up. A fine figure I'd cut in the papers if I prosecuted my own daughter for theft. I have enough trouble with the Press already.'

'It might have been better for her if you had prosecuted,' said Warren. 'Didn't you ask yourself why she stole from you?'

Hellier sighed. 'I thought she'd just gone plain bad – I thought she'd taken after her mother.' He straightened his shoulders. 'But that's another story.'

'Of course,' said Warren. 'As I say, when June came to me for treatment, or rather, for heroin, she had been addicted for nearly two years. She said so and her physical condition confirmed it.'

'What do you mean by that?' asked Hellier. 'That she came to you for heroin and not for treatment.'

'An addict regards a doctor as a source of supply,' said Warren a little tiredly. 'Addicts don't want to be treated – it scares them.'

Hellier looked at Warren blankly. 'But this is monstrous. Did you give her heroin?'

'I did.'

'And no treatment?'

'Not immediately. You can't treat a patient who won't be treated, and there's no law in England which allows of forcible treatment.'

'But you pandered to her. You gave her the heroin.'

'Would you rather I hadn't? Would you rather I had let her go on the streets to get her heroin from an illegal source at an illegal price and contaminated with God knows what filth? At least the drug I prescribed was clean and to British Pharmacopoeia Standard, which reduced the chance of hepatitis.'

Hellier looked strangely shrunken. 'I don't under-stand,' he muttered, shaking his head. 'I just don't understand.'

'You don't,' agreed Warren. 'You're wondering what has happened to medical ethics. We'll come to that later.' He tented his fingers. 'After a month I managed to persuade June to take treatment; there are clinics for cases like hers. She was in for twenty-seven days.' He stared at Hellier with hard eyes. 'If I had been her I doubt if I could have lasted a week. June was a brave girl, Sir Robert.'

'I don't know much about the . . . er . . . the actual treatment.'

Warren opened his desk drawer and took out a cigarette-box. He took out a cigarette and then pushed the open box across the desk, apparently as an afterthought. 'I'm sorry; do you smoke?'

'Thank you,' said Hellier, and took a cigarette. Warren leaned across and lit it with a flick of his lighter, then lit his own.

He studied Hellier for a while, then held up his cigarette. 'There's a drug in here, you know, but nicotine isn't particularly powerful. It produces a psychological dependency. Anyone who is strong-minded enough can give it up.' He leaned forward. 'Heroin is different; it produces a physiological dependency – the *body* needs it and the mind has precious little say about it.'

He leaned back. 'If heroin is withheld from an addicted patient there are physical withdrawal symptoms of such a nature that the chances of death are about one in five – and that is something a doctor must think hard about before he begins treatment.'

Hellier whitened. 'Did she suffer?'

'She suffered,' said Warren coldly. 'I'd be only too pleased to tell you she didn't, but that would be a lie. They all suffer. They suffer so much that hardly one in a hundred will see the treatment through. June stood as much of it as she could take and then walked out. I couldn't stop her – there's no legal restraint.'

The cigarette in Hellier's fingers was trembling noticeably. Warren said, 'I didn't see her for quite a while after that, and then she came back six months ago. They usually come back. She wanted heroin but I couldn't prescribe it. There had been a change in the law – all addicts must now get their prescriptions from special clinics which have been set up by the government. I advised treatment, but she wouldn't hear of it, so I took her to the clinic. Because I knew her medical history – and because I took an interest in her – I was able to act as consultant. Heroin was prescribed – as little as possible – until she died.'

'Yet she died of an overdose.'

'No,' said Warren. 'She died of a dose of heroin dissolved in a solution of methylamphetamine – and that's a cocktail with too much of a kick. The amphetamine was not prescribed – she must have got it somewhere else.'

Hellier was shaking. 'You take this very calmly, Warren,' he said in an unsteady voice. 'Too damned calmly for my liking.'

'I have to take it calmly,' said Warren. 'A doctor who becomes emotional is no good to himself or his patients.'

'A nice, detached, professional attitude,' sneered Hellier. 'But it killed my June.' He thrust a trembling finger under Warren's nose. 'I'm going to have your hide, Warren. I'm not without influence. I'm going to break you.'

Warren looked at Hellier bleakly. 'It's not my custom to kick parents in the teeth on occasions like this,' he said tightly. 'But you're asking for it – so don't push me.'

'Push you!' Hellier grinned mirthlessly. 'Like the Russian said – I'm going to bury you!'

Warren stood up. 'All right – then tell me this: do you usually communicate with your children at second hand by means of letters from your secretary?'

'What do you mean?'

'Six months ago, just before you went to America, June wanted to see you. You fobbed her off with a form letter from your secretary, for God's sake!'

'I was very busy at the time. I had a big deal impending.'

'She wanted your help. You wouldn't give it to her, so she came to me. You promised to write from America. Did you?'

'I was busy,' said Hellier weakly. 'I had a heavy schedule – a lot of flights . . . conferences . . .'

'So you didn't write. When did you get back?'

'A fortnight ago.'

'Nearly six months away. Did you know where your daughter was? Did you try to find out? She was still alive then, you know.'

'Good Christ, I had to straighten out things over here. Things had gone to hell in my absence.'

'They had, indeed!' said Warren icily. 'You say that you found June a job and set her up in a flat. It sounds very nice when put that way, but I'd say that you threw her out. In the preceding years did you try to find out why her behaviour had changed? Why she needed more and more money? In fact I'd like to know how often you saw your daughter. Did you supervise her activities? Check on the company she was keeping? Did you act like a father?'

Hellier was ashen. 'Oh, my God!'

Warren sat down and said quietly, 'Now I'm really going to hurt you, Hellier. Your daughter hated your guts. She told me so herself, although I didn't know who you were. She kept that damned patronizing secretary's letter to fuel her hatred, and she ended up in a sleazy doss-house in Notting Hill with cash resources of three shillings and fourpence. If, six months ago, you'd have granted your daughter fifteen minutes of your precious time she'd have been alive now.'

He leaned over the desk and said in a rasping voice, 'Now tell me, Hellier; who was responsible for your daughter's death?'

Hellier's face crumpled and Warren drew back and regarded him with something like pity. He felt ashamed of himself; ashamed of letting his emotions take control in such an unprofessional way. He watched Hellier grope for a handkerchief, and then got up and went to a cupboard where he tipped a couple of pills from a bottle.

He returned to the desk and said, 'Here, take these – they'll help.' Unresistingly, Hellier allowed him to administer the pills and. gulped them down with the aid of a glass of water. He became calmer and presently began to speak in a low, jerky voice.

'Helen – that's my wife – June's mother – my ex-wife – we had a divorce, you know. I divorced her – June was fifteen then. Helen was no good – no good at all. There were other men – I was sick of it. Made me look a fool. June stayed with me, she said she wanted to. God knows Helen didn't want her around.'

He took a shaky breath. 'June was still at school then, of course. I had my work – my business – it was getting bigger and more involved all the time. You have no idea how big and complicated it can get. International stuff, you know. I travelled a lot.' He looked blindly into the past. 'I didn't realize. . . .'

Warren said gently, 'I know.'

Hellier looked up. 'I doubt it, Doctor.' His eyes flickered under Warren's steady gaze and he dropped his head again. 'Maybe you do. I suppose I'm not the only damned fool you've come across.'

In an even voice, trying to attune himself to Hellier's mood, Warren said, 'It's hard enough to keep up with the younger generation even when they're underfoot. They seem to have a different way of thought – different ideals.'

Hellier sighed. 'But I could have *tried*.' He squeezed his hands together tightly. 'People of my class tend to think that parental neglect and juvenile delinquency are prerogatives of the lower orders. Good Christ!'

Warren said briskly. 'I'll give you something to help you sleep tonight.'

Hellier made a negating gesture. 'No, thanks, Doctor, I'll take my medicine the hard way.' He looked up. 'Do you know how it started? How did she . . .? How could she . . .?'

Warren shrugged. 'She didn't say much. It was hard enough coping with present difficulties. But I think her case

was very much the standard form; cannabis to begin with –
taken as a lark or a dare – then on to the more potent drugs,
and finally heroin and the more powerful amphetamines. It
all usually starts with running with the wrong crowd.'

Hellier nodded. 'Lack of parental control,' he said bitterly.
'Where do they get the filthy stuff?'

'That's the crux. There's a fair amount of warehouse looting by criminals who have a ready market, and there's smuggling, of course. Here in England, where clinics prescribe
heroin under controlled conditions to Home Office registered
addicts, it's not so bad compared with the States. Over there,
because it's totally illegal, there's a vast illicit market with
consequent high profits and an organized attempt to push
the stuff. There's an estimated forty thousand heroin addicts
in New York alone, compared with about two thousand in
the whole of the United Kingdom. But it's bad enough here –
the number is doubling every sixteen months.'

'Can't the police do anything about illegal drugs?'

Warren said ironically, 'I suppose Inspector Stephens told
you all about me.'

'He gave me a totally wrong impression,' mumbled
Hellier. He stirred restlessly.

'That's all right; I'm used to that kind of thing. The police
attitude largely coincides with the public attitude – but it's
no use chivvying an addict once he's hooked. That only
leads to bigger profits for the gangsters because the addict
on the run must get his dope where he can. And it adds to
crime because he's not too particular where he gets the
money to pay for the dope.' Warren studied Hellier, who
was becoming noticeably calmer. He decided that this was
as much due to the academic discussion as to the sedation,
so he carried on.

'The addicts are sick people and the police should leave
them alone,' he said. 'We'll take care of them. The police
should crack down on the source of illegal drugs.'

'Aren't they doing that?'

'That's not so easy. It's an international problem. Besides, there's the difficulty of getting information – this is an illegal operation and people don't talk.' He smiled. 'Addicts don't like the police and so the police get little out of them. On the other hand, I don't like addicts – they're difficult patients most doctors won't touch – but I understand them, and they tell me things. I probably know more about what's going on than the official police sources.'

'Then why don't you tell the police?' demanded Hellier.

Warren's voice went suddenly hard. 'If any of my patients knew that I was abusing their confidence by blabbing to the police, I'd lose the lot. Trust between patient and doctor must be absolute – especially with a drug addict. You can't help them if they don't trust you enough to come to you for treatment. So I'd lose them to an illicit form of supply; either an impure heroin from the docks at an inflated price, or an aseptic heroin with no treatment from one of my more unethical colleagues. There are one or two bad apples in the medical barrel, as Inspector Stephens will be quick enough to tell you.'

Hellier hunched his big shoulders and looked broodingly down at the desk. 'So what's the answer? Can't you do anything yourself?'

'Me!' said Warren in surprise. 'What could I do? The problem of supply begins right outside England in the Middle East. I'm no story-book adventurer, Hellier; I'm a medical doctor with patients, who just makes ends meet. I can't just shoot off to Iran on a crazy adventure.'

Hellier growled deep in his throat, 'You might have fewer patients if you were as crazy as that.' He stood up. 'I'm sorry about my attitude when I first came in here, Dr Warren. You have cleared up a lot of things I didn't understand. You have told me my faults. You have told me of your ethics in this matter. You have also pointed out a possible solution which you refuse to countenance. What about *your* faults, Dr Warren, and where are your ethics now?'

He strode heavily to the door. 'Don't bother to see me out, Doctor; I'll find my own way.'

Warren, taken wrong-footed, was startled as the door closed behind Hellier. Slowly he returned to the chair behind his desk and sat down. He lit a cigarette and remained in deep thought for some minutes, then shook his head irritably as though to escape a buzzing fly.

Ridiculous! he thought. Absolutely ridiculous!

But the maggot of doubt stirred and he could not escape its irritation in his mind no matter how hard he tried.

That evening he walked through Piccadilly and into Soho, past the restaurants and strip joints and night clubs, the chosen haunt of most of his patients. He saw one or two of them and they waved to him. He waved back in an automatic action and went on, almost unaware of his surroundings, until he found himself in Wardour Street outside the offices of the Regent Picture Company.

He looked up at the building. 'Ridiculous!' he said aloud.

III

Sir Robert Hellier also had a bad night.

He went back to his flat in St James's and was almost totally unaware of how he got there. His chauffeur noted the tight lips and lowering expression and took the precaution of ringing the flat from the garage before he put away the car. 'The old bastard's in a mood, Harry,' he said to Hellier's man, Hutchins. 'Better keep clear of him and walk on eggs.'

So it was that when Hellier walked into his penthouse flat Hutchins put out the whisky and made himself scarce. Hellier ignored both the presence of the whisky and the

absence of Hutchins and sank his bulk into a luxurious arm-
chair, where he brooded deep in thought.

Inside he writhed with guilt. It had been many more
years than he could remember since anyone had had the
guts to hold up a mirror wherein he could see himself, and
the experience was harrowing. He hated himself and, perhaps, he hated Warren even more for rubbing his nose into
his shortcomings. Yet he was basically honest and he
recognized that his final remarks and abrupt exit from
Warren's rooms had been the sudden crystallization of his
desire to crack Warren's armour of ethics – to find the feet
of clay and to pull Warren down to his own miserable
level.

And what about June? Where did she come into all this?
He thought of his daughter as he had once known her – gay,
light-hearted, carefree. There was nothing he had not been
prepared to give her, from the best schools to good clothes
by fashionable designers, parties, continental holidays and
all the rest of the good life.

Everything, except myself, he thought remorsefully.

And then, unnoticed in the interstices of his busy life, a
change had come. June developed an insatiable appetite for
money; not, apparently, for the things money can buy, but
for money itself. Hellier was a self-made man, brought up in
a hard school, and he believed that the young should earn
their independence. What started out to be calm discussions
with June turned into a series of flaming rows and, in the
end, he lost his temper and then came the break. It was true
what Warren had said; he had thrown out his daughter
without making an attempt to find the root cause of the
change in her.

The theft of the silver from his home had only confirmed
his impression that she had gone bad, and his main worry
had been to keep the matter quiet and out of the press. He
suddenly realized, to his shame, that the bad press he was

likely to get because of the inquest had been uppermost in
his mind ever since he had seen Inspector Stephens.

How had all this happened? How had he come to lose
first a wife and then a daughter?

He had worked – by God, how he had worked! The
clapperclawing to the top in an industry where knives are
wielded with the greatest efficiency; the wheedling and dealing with millions at stake. The American trip, for instance –
he had got on top of those damned sharp Yanks – but at
what cost? An ulcer, a higher blood pressure than his doctor
liked and a nervous three packets of cigarettes a day as
inheritance of those six months.

And a dead daughter.

He looked around the flat, at the light-as-air Renoir on
the facing wall, at the blue period Picasso at the end of the
room. The symbols of success. He suddenly hated them and
moved to another chair where they were at his back and
where he could look out over London towards the Tudor
crenellations of St James's Palace.

Why had he worked so hard? At first it had been for
Helen and young June and for the other children that were
to come. But Helen had not wanted children and so June
was the only one. Was it about then that the work became
a habit, or perhaps an anodyne? He had thrown himself
whole-heartedly into the curious world of the film studios
where it is a toss-up which is the more important, money or
artistry; and not a scrap of his heart had he left for his wife.

Perhaps it was his neglect that had forced Helen to look
elsewhere – at first surreptitiously and later blatantly – until
he had got tired of the innuendoes and had forced the
divorce.

But where, in God's name, had June come into all this?
The work was there by then, and had to be done; decisions
had to be taken – by him and by no one else – and each
damned decision led to another and then another, filling his

time and his life until there was no room for anything but the work.

He held out his hands and looked at them. Nothing but a machine, he thought despondently. A mind for making the right decisions and hands for signing the right cheques.

And somewhere in all this, June, his daughter, had been lost. He was suddenly filled with a terrible shame at the thought of the letter Warren had told him about. He remembered the occasion now. It had been a bad week; he was preparing to carry a fight to America, and everything had gone wrong so he was rushed off his feet. He remembered being waylaid by Miss Walden, his secretary, in a corridor between offices.

'I've a letter for you from Miss Hellier, Sir Robert. She would like to see you on Friday.'

He had stopped, somewhat surprised, and rubbed his chin in desperation, wanting to get on but still wanting to see June. 'Oh, damn; I have that meeting with Matchet on Friday morning – and that means lunch as well. What do I have after lunch, Miss Walden?'

She did not consult an appointment book because she was not that kind of secretary, which was why he employed her. 'Your plane leaves at three-thirty – you might have to leave your lunch early.'

'Oh! Well, do me a favour, Miss Walden. Write to my daughter explaining the situation. Tell her I'll write from the States as soon as I can.'

And he had gone on into an office and from there to another office and yet another until the day was done – the 18-hour working day. And in two more days it was Friday with the conference with Matchet and the expensive lunch that was necessary to keep Matchet sweet. Then the quick drive to Heathrow – and New York in no time at all – to be confronted by Hewling and Morrin with their offers and propositions, all booby-trapped.

The sudden necessity to fly to Los Angeles and to beat the Hollywood moguls on their own ground. Then back to New York to be inveigled by Morrin to go on that trip to Miami and the Bahamas, an unsubtle attempt at corruption by hospitality. But he had beaten them all and had returned to England with the fruits of victory and at the high point of his career, only to be confronted by the devil of a mess because no one had been strong enough to control Matchet.

In all that time he had never once thought of his daughter. The dimming light concealed the greyness of his face as he contemplated that odious fact. He sought to find excuses and found none. And he knew that this was not the worst – he knew that he had *never* given June the opportunity of communicating with him on the simple level of one human being to another. She had been something in the background of his life, and the knowledge hurt him that she had been *something* and not *someone*.

Hellier got up and paced the room restlessly, thinking of all the things Warren had said. Warren had seemed to take drug addiction as a matter of course, a normal fact of life to be coped with somehow. Although he had not said so outright, he had implied it was his task to clear up the mess left by the negligence of people like himself.

But surely someone else was to blame. What about the profit-makers? The pushers of drugs?

Hellier paused as he felt a spark of anger flash into being, an anger which, for the first time, was not directed against himself. His was a sin of omission, although not to be minimized on that account. But the sin of commission, the deliberate act of giving drugs to the young for profit, was monstrous. He had been thoughtless, but the drug pedlars were evil.

The anger within him grew until he thought he would burst with the sheer agony of it, but he deliberately checked himself in order to think constructively. Just as he had not allowed his emotions to impede his negotiations with Matchet, Hewling and Morrin,, so he brought his not inconsiderable intellect to bear unclouded on this new problem. Hellier, as an efficient machine, began to swing smoothly into action.

He first thought of Warren who, with his special knowledge, was undoubtedly the key. Hellier was accustomed to studying closely the men with whom he dealt because their points of strength and weakness showed in subtle ways. He went over in his mind everything Warren had said and the way in which he had said it, and seized upon two points. He was certain Warren *knew* something important.

But he had to make sure that his chosen key would not break in his hand. Decisively he picked up the telephone and dialled a number. A moment later he said, 'Yes, I know it's late. Do we have that firm of investigators still on our books? They helped us on the Lowrey case . . . Good! I want them to investigate Dr Nicholas Warren MD. Repeat that. It must be done discreetly. Everything there is to know about him, damn it! As fast as possible . . . a report in three days . . . oh, damn the expense! . . . charge it to my private account.'

Absently he picked up the decanter of whisky. 'And another thing. Get the Research Department to find out all they can about drug smuggling – the drug racket in general. Again, a report in three days . . . Yes, I'm serious . . . it might make a good film.' He paused. 'Just one thing more; the Research Department mustn't go near Dr Warren . . . Yes, they're quite likely to, but they must steer clear of him – is that understood? Good!'

He put down the telephone and looked at the decanter in some surprise. He laid it down gently and went into his bedroom. For the first time in many years he ignored his

normal meticulous procedure of hanging up his clothes and
left them strewn about the floor.

Once in bed the tensions left him and his body relaxed.
It was only then that the physical expression of his grief
came to him and he broke down. Waves of shudders racked
his body and this man of fifty-five wet the pillow with his
tears.

TWO

Warren was – and was not – surprised to hear from Hellier again. In the forefront of his mind he wondered what Hellier was after and was almost inclined to refuse to see him. In his experience prolonged post-mortems with the survivors did no one any good in the long run; they merely served to turn guilt into acceptance and, as a moral man, he believed that the guilty should be punished and that self-punishment was the most severe form.

But in the remote recesses of his mind still lurked the nagging doubt which had been injected by Hellier's final words and so, somewhat to his surprise, he found himself accepting Hellier's invitation to meet him in the St James's flat. This time, oddly enough, he was not averse to meeting Hellier on his own ground – that battle had already been won.

Hellier greeted him with a conventional, 'It's very good of you to come, Doctor,' and led him into a large and softly luxurious room where he was waved courteously to a chair. 'Drink?' asked Hellier. 'Or don't you?'

Warren smiled. 'I have all the normal vices. I'd like a Scotch.'

He found himself sipping a whisky so good that it was almost criminal to dilute it with water, and holding one of Hellier's monogrammed cigarettes. 'We're a picturesque lot,

we film people,' said Hellier wryly. 'Self-advertisement is
one of our worst faults.'

Warren looked at the intertwined R H stamped in gold on
the handmade cigarette, and suspected that it was not Hellier's
normal style and that he went about it coldbloodedly in what
was a conformist industry. He said nothing and waited for
Hellier to toss a more reasonable conversational ball.

'First, I must apologize for the scene I made in your
rooms,' said Hellier.

'You have already done so,' said Warren gravely. 'And in
any case, no apology is necessary.'

Hellier settled in a chair facing Warren and put his glass
on a low table. 'I find you are very well thought of in your
profession.'

Warren twitched an eyebrow. 'Indeed!'

'I've been finding out things about the drug racket – I
think I have it pretty well taped.'

'In three days?' said Warren ironically.

'In the film industry, by its very nature, there must be an
enormous fund of general knowledge. My Research
Department is very nearly as good as, say, a newspaper
office. If you put enough staff on to a problem you can do a
lot in three days.'

Warren let that go and merely nodded.

'My research staff found that in nearly one-third of their
enquiries they were advised to consult you as a leading
member of the profession.'

'They didn't,' said Warren succinctly.

Hellier smiled. 'No, I told them not to. As you said the
other day, you're a very busy man. I didn't want to disturb
you.'

'I suppose I should thank you,' said Warren with a
straight face.

Hellier squared his shoulders. 'Dr Warren, let us not
fence with each other. I'm putting all my cards on the table.
I also had you independently investigated.'

Warren sipped whisky and kept steady eyes on Hellier over the glass. 'That's a damned liberty,' he observed mildly. 'I suppose I should ask you what you found.'

Hellier held up his hand. 'Nothing but good, Doctor. You have an enviable reputation both as a man and as a physician, besides being outstanding in the field of drug addiction.'

Warren said satirically, 'I should like to read that dossier some time – it would be like reading one's obituary, a chance which comes to few of us.' He put down his glass. 'And to what end is all this . . . this effort on your part?'

'I wanted to be sure that you are the right man,' said Hellier seriously.

'You're talking in riddles,' said Warren impatiently. He laughed. 'Are you going to offer me a job? Technical adviser to a film, perhaps?'

'Perhaps,' said Hellier. 'Let me ask you a question. You are divorced from your wife. Why?'

Warren felt outrage, surprise and shock. He was outraged at the nature of the question; surprised that the urbane Hellier should have asked it; shocked because of the intensive nature of Hellier's investigation of him. 'That's my affair,' he said coldly.

'Undoubtedly,' Hellier studied Warren for a moment. I'll tell you why your wife divorced you. She didn't like your association with drug addicts.'

Warren put his hands on the arms of the chair preparatory to rising, and Hellier said sharply, 'Sit down, man; listen to what I've got to say.'

'It had better be good,' said Warren, relaxing. 'I don't take kindly to conversations of this nature.'

Hellier stubbed out his cigarette and lit another. 'That tells me more about you than it does about your wife, whom I am not interested in. It tells me that the interests of your profession come ahead of your personal relationships. Are you aware that you are considered to be a fanatic on the subject of drugs?'

'It has been brought to my attention,' said Warren stiffly.

Hellier nodded. 'As you pointed out – and as I have found in my brief study – drug addicts are not the most easy patients. They're conceited, aggressive, deceitful, vicious, crafty and any other pejorative term you care to apply to them. And yet you persist against all the odds in trying to help them – even to the extent of losing your wife. That seems to me to show a great deal of dedication.'

Warren snorted. 'Dedication my foot! It's just what goes with the job. All those vices you've just mentioned are symptoms of the general drug syndrome. The addicts are like that because of the drugs, and you can't just leave them to stew because you don't like the way they behave.' He shook his head. 'Come to the point. I didn't come here to be admired – especially by you.'

Hellier flushed. 'I was making a point in my own peculiar way,' he said. 'But I'll come to the nub of it. When I came to see you, you said that the problem was in stopping the inflow of illicit drugs and you said it was an international problem. You were also damned quick to say that you weren't prepared to jump off to Iran on a crazy adventure.' He stuck out his finger. 'I think you know something, Dr Warren; and I think it's something definite.'

'My God!' said Warren. 'You jump to a fast conclusion.'

'I'm used to it,' said Hellier easily. 'I've had a lot of experience – and I'm usually right. I get paid for being right and I'm highly paid. Now, why Iran? Heroin is ultimately derived from opium, and opium comes from many places. It could come from the Far East – China or Burma – but you said the problem of illegal supply begins in the Middle East. Why the Middle East? And why pick Iran in particular? It could come from any of half a dozen countries from Afghanistan to Greece, but you took a snap judgment on Iran without a second thought.' He set down his glass with a tiny click. 'You know something definite, Dr Warren.'

Warren stirred in his chair. 'Why this sudden interest?'

'Because I've decided to do something about it,' said Hellier. He laughed briefly at the expression on Warren's face. 'No, I haven't gone mad; neither do I have delusions of grandeur. You pointed out the problem yourself. What the devil's the good of patching up these damned idiots if they can walk out and pick up a fresh supply on the nearest corner? Cutting off the illegal supply would make your own job a lot easier.'

'For God's sake!' exploded Warren. 'There are hundreds of policemen of all nationalities working on this. What makes you think you can do any better?'

Hellier levelled a finger at him. 'Because you have information which for reasons of your own – quite ethical reasons, I am sure – you will not pass on to the police.'

'And which I will pass on to you – is that it?'

'Oh, no,' said Hellier. 'You can keep it to yourself if you wish.' He stabbed a finger towards Warren again. 'You see, *you* are going to do something about it.'

'Now I know you're crazy,' said Warren in disgust. 'Hellier, I think you've been knocked off balance; you're set on some weird kind of expiation and you're trying to drag me into it.' His lips twisted. 'It's known as shutting the stable door after the horse has gone, and I want no part of it.'

Unperturbedly, Hellier lit another cigarette, and Warren suddenly said, 'You smoke too much.'

'You're the second doctor to tell me that within a fortnight.' Hellier waved his hand. 'You see, you can't help being a doctor, even now. At our last meeting you said something else – "I'm a doctor who just makes ends meet".' He laughed. 'You're right; I know your bank balance to a penny. But suppose you had virtually unlimited funds, and suppose you coupled those funds with the information I'm certain you have and which, incidentally, you don't deny having. What then?'

Warren spoke without thinking. 'It's too big for one man.'

'Who said anything about one man? Pick your own team,' said Hellier expansively,

Warren stared at him. 'I believe you mean all this,' he said in wonder.

'I might be in the business of spinning fairy tales for other people,' said Hellier soberly. 'But I don't spin them for myself. I mean every word of it.'

Warren knew he had been right; Hellier *had* been pushed off balance by the death of his daughter. He judged that Hellier had always been a single-minded man, and now he had veered off course and had set his sights on a new objective. And he would be a hard man to stop.

'I don't think you know what's involved,' he said.

'I don't *care* what's involved,' said Hellier flatly. 'I want to hit these bastards. I want blood.'

'Whose blood – mine?' asked Warren cynically. 'You've picked the wrong man. I don't think the man exists, anyway. You need a combination of St George and James Bond. I'm a doctor, not a gang-buster.'

'You're a man with the knowledge and qualifications I need,' said Hellier intensely. He saw he was on the edge of losing Warren, and said more calmly, 'Don't make a snap decision now, Doctor; just think it over.' His voice sharpened. 'And pay a thought to ethics.' He looked at his watch. 'Now what about a bite to eat?'

II

Warren left Hellier's flat comfortable in stomach but uneasy in mind. As he walked up Jermyn Street towards Piccadilly Circus he thought of all the aspects of the odd proposition Hellier had put to him. There was no doubt that Hellier meant it, but he did not know what he was getting into – not by half; in the vicious world of the drug trade no quarter was given – the stakes were too high.

He pushed his way through the brawling crowds of Piccadilly Circus and turned off into Soho. Presently he stopped outside a pub, looked at his watch, and then went in. It was crowded but someone companionably made room for him at a corner of the bar and he ordered a Scotch and, with the glass in his hand, looked about the room. Sitting at a table on the other side were three of his boys. He looked at them speculatively and judged they had had their shots not long before; they were at ease and conversation between them flowed freely. One of them looked up and waved and he raised his hand in greeting.

In order to get to his patients, to acquire their unwilling trust, Warren had lived with them and had, at last, become accepted. It was an uphill battle to get them to use clean needles and sterile water; too many of them had not the slightest idea of medical hygiene. He lived in their half-world on the fringes of crime where even the Soho prostitutes took a high moral tone and considered that the addicts lowered the gentility of the neighbourhood. It was enough to make a man laugh – or cry.

Warren made no moral judgments. To him it was a social and medical problem. He was not immediately concerned with the fundamental instability in a man which led him to take heroin; all he knew was that when the man was hooked he was hooked for good. At that stage there was no point in recrimination because it solved nothing. There was a sick man to be helped, and Warren helped him, fighting society at large, the police and even the addict himself.

It was in this pub, and in places like it, that he had heard the three hard facts and the thousand rumours which con-stituted the core of the special knowledge which Hellier was trying to get from him. To mix with addicts was to mix with criminals. At first they had been close-mouthed when he was around, but later, when they discovered that his lips were equally tight, they spoke more freely. They knew who – and what – he was, but they accepted it, although to a few he was just another 'flaming do-gooder' who ought to keep his long nose out of other people's affairs. But generally he had become accepted.

He turned back to the bar and contemplated his glass. Nick Warren – do-it-yourself Bond! he thought. Hellier is incredible! The trouble with Hellier was that he did not know the magnitude of what he had set out to do. Millionaire though he was, the prizes offered in the drug trade would make even Hellier appear poverty-stricken, and with money like that at stake men do not hesitate to kill.

A heavy hand smote him on the back and he choked over his drink. 'Hello, Doc; drowning your sorrows?'

Warren turned. 'Hello, Andy. Have a drink.'

'Most kind,' said Andrew Tozier. 'But allow me.' He pulled out a wallet and peeled a note from the fat wad.

'I wouldn't think of it,' said Warren drily. 'You're still unemployed.' He caught the eye of the barman and ordered two whiskies.

'Aye,' said Tozier, putting away his wallet. 'The world's becoming too bloody quiet for my liking.'

'You can't be reading the newspapers,' observed Warren. 'The Russians are acting up again and Vietnam was still going full blast the last I heard.'

'But those are the big boys,' said Tozier. 'There's no room for a small-scale enterprise like mine. It's the same every-where – the big firms put the squeeze on us little chaps.' He lifted his glass. 'Cheers!'

Warren regarded him with sudden interest. Major Andrew Tozier; profession – mercenary soldier. A killer for hire. Andy would not shoot anyone indiscriminately – that would be murder. But he was quite prepared to be employed by a new government to whip into line a regiment of half-trained black soldiers and lead them into action. He was a walking symptom of a schizophrenic world.

'Cheers!' said Warren absently. His mind was racing with mad thoughts.

Tozier jerked his head towards the door. 'Your consulting-room is filling up, Doc.' Warren looked over and saw four young men just entering; three were his patients but the fourth he did not know. 'I don't know how you stand those cheap bastards,' said Tozier.

'Someone has to look after them,' said Warren. 'Who's the new boy?'

Tozier shrugged. 'Another damned soul on the way to hell,' he said macabrely. 'You'll probably meet up with him when he wants a fix.'

Warren nodded. 'So there's still no action in your line.'

'Not a glimmer.'

'Maybe your rates are too high. I suppose it's a case of supply and demand like everything else.'

'The rates are never too high,' said Tozier, a little bleakly. 'What price would you put on *your* skin, Doc?'

'I've just been asked that question – in an oblique way,' said Warren, thinking of Hellier. 'What is the going rate, anyway?'

'Five hundred a month plus a hell of a big bonus on completion.' Tozier smiled. 'Thinking of starting a war?'

Warren looked him in the eye. 'I just might be.'

The smile faded from Tozier's lips. He looked at Warren closely, impressed by the way he had spoken. 'By God!' he said. 'I think you're serious. Who are you thinking of tackling? The Metropolitan Police?' The smile returned and grew broader.

Warren said, 'You've never gone in for really private enterprise, have you? I mean a private war as opposed to a public war.'

Tozier shook his head. 'I've always stayed legal or, at any rate, political. Anyway, there are precious few people financing private brawls. I take it you don't mean carrying a gun for some jumped-up Soho "businessman" busily engaged in carving out a private empire? Or bodyguarding?'

'Nothing like that,' said Warren. He was thinking of what he knew of Andrew Tozier. The man had values of a sort. Not long before, Warren had asked why he had not taken advantage of a conflict that was going on in a South American country.

Tozier had been scathingly contemptuous. 'Good Christ! That's a power game going on between two gangs of top-class cut-throats. I have no desire to mow down the poor sons of bitches of peasants who happen to get caught in the middle.' He had looked hard at Warren. 'I choose my fights,' he said.

Warren thought that if he did pick up Hellier's ridiculous challenge then Andy Tozier would be a good man to have around. Not that there was any likelihood of it happening.

Tozier was waving to the barman, and held up two fingers. He turned to Warren, and said, 'You have something on your mind, Doctor. Is someone putting the pressure on?'

'In a way,' said Warren wryly. He thought Hellier had not really started yet; the next thing to come would be the moral blackmail.

'Give me his name,' said Tozier. 'I'll lean on him a bit. He won't trouble you any more.'

Warren smiled. 'Thanks, Andy; it's not that sort of pressure.'

Tozier looked relieved. 'That's all right, then. I thought some of your mainliners might have been ganging up on you. I'd soon sort *them* out.' He put a pound note on the counter and accepted the change. 'Here's mud in your eye.'

'Supposing *I* needed bodyguarding,' said Warren carefully. 'Would you take on the job – at your usual rates?'

Tozier laughed loudly. 'You couldn't afford me. I'd do it for free, though, if it isn't too long a job.' A frown creased his forehead. 'Something really is biting you, Doc. I think you'd better tell me what it is.'

'No,' said Warren sharply. If – and it was a damned big 'if' – he went deeper into this then he could not trust anyone, not even Andy Tozier who seemed straight enough. He said slowly, 'If it ever happens it will take, perhaps, a few months, and it will be in the Middle East. You'd get paid your five hundred a month plus a bonus.'

Tozier put down his glass gently. 'And it's not political?'

'As far as I know, it isn't,' said Warren thoughtfully.

'And I bodyguard *you*?' Tozier seemed bewildered.

Warren grinned. 'Perhaps there'd be a bit of fetching and carrying in a fierce sort of way.'

'Middle East and not political – maybe,' mused Tozier. He shook his head. 'I usually like to know more about what I'm getting into.' He shot Warren a piercing glance. 'But you I trust. If you want me – just shout.'

'It may never happen,' warned Warren. 'There's no firm commitment.'

'That's all right,' said Tozier. 'Let's just say you have a free option on my services.' He finished his drink with a flourish and bumped down the glass, looking at Warren expectantly. 'Your round. Anyone who can afford my rates can afford to buy me drinks.'

Warren went home and spent a long time just sitting in a chair and gazing into space. In an indefinable way he somehow felt committed, despite what he had said to Andy Tozier. The mere act of meeting the man had put ideas into his head, ideas that were crazy mad but becoming more real and solid with every tick of the clock. At one point he got up restlessly and paced the room.

'Damn Hellier!' he said aloud.

He went to his desk, drew out a sheet of paper, and began writing busily. At the end of half an hour he had, perhaps, twenty names scribbled down. Thoughtfully he scanned his list and began to eliminate and in another fifteen minutes the list was reduced to five names,

ANDREW TOZIER
JOHN FOLLET
DAN PARKER
BEN BRYAN
MICHAEL ABBOT

III

Number 23, Acacia Road, was a neat, semi-detached house, indistinguishable from the hundreds around it. Warren pushed open the wooden gate, walked the few steps necessary to get to the front door and past the postage-stamp-sized front garden, and rang the bell. The door was opened by a trim, middle-aged woman who greeted him with pleasure.

'Why, Dr Warren; we haven't seen you for a long time.' Alarm chased across her face. 'It's not Jimmy again, is it? He hasn't been getting into any more trouble?'

Warren smiled reassuringly. 'Not that I know of, Mrs Parker.'

He almost felt her relief. 'Oh!' she said. 'Well, that's all right, then. Do you want to see Jimmy? He's not in now – he went down to the youth club.'

'I came to see Dan,' said Warren. 'Just for a friendly chat.'

'What am I thinking of,' said Mrs Parker. 'Keeping you on the doorstep like this. Come in, Doctor. Dan just got home – he's upstairs washing.'

Warren was quite aware that Dan Parker had just reached home. He had not wanted to see Parker at the garage where he worked so he had waited in his car and followed him home. Mrs Parker ushered him into the front room. 'I'll tell him you're here,' she said.

Warren looked about the small room; at the three pottery ducks on the wall, at the photographs of the children on the sideboard and the other photograph of a much younger Dan Parker in uniform. He did not have to wait long. Parker came into the room and held out his hand. 'This is a pleasure we didn't expect, Doctor.' Warren, grasping the hand, felt the hardness of callouses. 'I was only sayin' to Sally the other day that it's a pity we don't see more of you.'

'Perhaps it's just as well,' said Warren ruefully. 'I'm afraid I put the breeze up Mrs Parker just now.'

'Aye,' said Parker soberly. 'I know what you mean. But we'd still like to see you, sociable like.' The warm tones of the Lancastrian were still heard, although Parker had lived in London for many years. 'Sit down, Doctor; Sally'll be bringing in tea any minute.'

'I've come to see you on . . . a matter of business.'

'Oh, aye,' said Parker comfortably. 'We'll get down to it after tea, then, shall we? Sally has to go out, anyway; her younger sister's a bit under the weather, so Sally's doin' a bit o' baby-sitting.'

'I'm sorry to hear that,' said Warren. 'How's Jimmy these days?'

'He's all right now,' said Parker. 'You straightened him out, Doctor. You put the fear o' God into him – an' I keep it there.'

'I wouldn't be too hard on him.'

'Just hard enough,' said Parker uncompromisingly. 'He'll not get on that lark again.' He sighed. 'I don't know what kids are comin' to these days. It weren't like that when I were a lad. If I'd a' done what young Jimmy did, me father would a' laid into me that hard with his strap. He had a heavy hand, had me dad.' He shook his head. 'But it wouldn't a' entered our heads.'

Warren listened to this age-old plaint of the parents without a trace of a smile. 'Yes,' he agreed gravely. 'Things have changed.'

Sally Parker brought in the tea – a cut down, southern version of the traditional northern high tea. She pressed homemade cakes and scones on Warren, and insisted on refilling his cup. Warren studied Parker unobtrusively and tried to figure out how to broach the delicate subject in such a way as to ensure the greatest co-operation.

Daniel Parker was a man of forty. He had joined the Navy during the last few months of the war and had elected to make a career of it. In the peacetime Navy he had forged ahead in his stubborn way despite the inevitably slow rate of promotion. He had fought in Korean waters during that war and had come out of it a petty officer with the heady prospect of getting commissioned rank. But in 1962 a torpedo got loose and rolled on his leg, and that was the end of his naval career.

He had come out of the Navy with one leg permanently shortened, a disability pension and no job. The last did not worry him because he knew he was good with his hands. Since 1963 he had been working as a mechanic in a garage, and Warren thought his employer was damned lucky.

Mrs Parker looked at her watch and made an exclamation. 'Oh, I'll be late. You'll have to excuse me, Doctor.'

'That's all right, Mrs Parker,' said Warren, rising.

'You get off, lass,' said Parker. 'I'll see to the dishes, an' the doctor an' me will have a quiet chat.' Mrs Parker left, and Parker produced a stubby pipe which he proceeded to fill. 'You said you wanted to see me on business, Doctor.' He looked up in a puzzled way, and then smiled. 'Maybe you'll be wantin' a new car.'

'No,' said Warren. 'How are things at the garage, Dan?'

Parker shrugged. 'Same as ever. Gets a bit monotonous at times – but I'm doin' an interestin' job now on a Mini-Cooper.' He smiled slowly. 'Most o' the time I'm dealin' wi' the troubles o' maiden ladies. I had one come in the other day – said the car was usin' too much petrol. I tested it an' there was nothin' wrong, so I gave it back. But she was back in no time at all wi' the same trouble.'

He struck a match. 'I still found nothin' wrong, so I said to her, "Miss Hampton, I want to drive around a bit with you just for a final check," so off we went. The first thing she did was to pull out the choke an' hang her bag on it – said she thought that was what it was for.' He shook his head in mild disgust.

Warren laughed. 'You're a long way from the Navy, Dan.'

'Aye, that's a fact,' said Parker, a little morosely. 'I still miss it, you know. But what can a man do?' Absently, he stroked his bad leg. 'Still, I daresay it's better for Sally an' the kids even though she never minded me bein' away.'

'What do you miss about it, Dan?'

Parker puffed at his pipe contemplatively. 'Hard to say. I think I miss the chance o' handling fine machinery. This patching up o' production cars doesn't stretch a man – that's why I like to get something different, like this Mini-Cooper I'm workin' on now. By the time I'm finished wi' it Issigonis wouldn't recognize it.'

Warren said carefully, 'Supposing you were given the chance of handling naval equipment again. Would you take it?'

Parker took the pipe out of his mouth. 'What are you gettin' at, Doctor?'

'I want a man who knows all about torpedoes,' Warren said bluntly.

Parker blinked. 'I know as much as anyone, I reckon, but I don't see . . .' His voice tailed off and he looked at Warren in a baffled way.

'Let me put it this way. Supposing I wanted to smuggle something comparatively light and very valuable into a country that has a seaboard. Could it be done by torpedo?'

Parker scratched his head. 'It never occurred to me,' he said, and grinned. 'But it's a bloody good idea. What are you thinkin' o' doin' the Excise with? Swiss watches?'

'What about heroin?' asked Warren quietly.

Parker went rigid and stared at Warren as though he had suddenly sprouted horns and a tail. The pipe fell from his fingers to lie unregarded as he said, 'Are you serious? I'd a' never believed it.'

'It's all right, Dan,' said Warren. 'I'm serious, but not in the way you mean. But could it be done?'

There was a long moment before Parker groped for his pipe. 'It could be done all right,' he said. 'The old Mark XI carried a warhead of over seven hundred pounds. You could pack a hell of a lot o' heroin in there.'

'And the range?'

'Maximum five thousand, five hundred yards if you pre-heat the batteries,' said Parker promptly.

'Damn!' said Warren disappointedly. 'That's not enough. You said batteries. Is this an electric torpedo?'

'Aye. Ideal for smugglin' it is. No bubbles, you see.'

'But not nearly enough range,' said Warren despondently. 'It was a good idea while it lasted.'

'What's your problem?' asked Parker, striking a match.

'I was thinking of a ship cruising outside the territorial waters of the United States and firing a torpedo inshore. That's twelve miles – over twenty-one thousand yards.'

'That's a long way,' said Parker, puffing at his pipe. It did not ignite and he had to strike another match and it was some time before he got the pipe glowing to his satisfaction. 'But maybe it could be done.'

Warren ceased to droop and looked up alertly. 'It could?'

'The Mark XI came out in 1944 an' things have changed since then,' said Parker thoughtfully. He looked up. 'Where would you be gettin' a torpedo, anyway?'

'I haven't gone into that yet,' said Warren. 'But it shouldn't be too difficult. There's an American in Switzerland who has enough war surplus arms to outfit the British forces. He should have torpedoes.'

'Then they'd be Mark XIs,' said Parker. 'Or the German equivalent. I doubt if anythin' more modern has got on the war surplus market yet.' He pursed his lips. 'It's an interestin' problem. You see, the Mark XI had lead-acid batteries – fifty-two of 'em. But things have changed since the war an' you can get better batteries now. What I'd do would be to rip out the lead-acid batteries an' replace with high-power mercury cells.' He stared at the ceiling dreamily. 'All the circuits would need redesignin' an' it would be bloody expensive, but I think I could do it.'

He leaned forward and tapped his pipe against the fireplace, then looked Warren firmly in the eye. 'But not for smugglin' dope.'

'It's all right, Dan; I haven't switched tracks.' Warren rubbed his chin. 'I want you to work with me on a job. It will pay twice as much as you're getting at the garage, and there'll be a big bonus when you've finished. And if you don't want to go back to the garage there'll be a guaranteed steady job for as long as you want it.'

Parker blew a long plume of smoke. 'There's a queer smell to this one, Doctor. It sounds illegal to me.'

'It's not illegal,' said Warren quickly. 'But it could be dangerous.'

Parker pondered. 'How long would it take?'

'I don't know. Might be three months – might be six. It wouldn't be in England, either, you'd be going out to the Middle East.'

'And it could be dangerous. What sort o' danger?'

Warren decided to be honest. 'Well, if you put a foot wrong you could get yourself shot.'

Parker laid down his pipe in the hearth. 'You're askin' a bloody lot, aren't you? I have a wife an' three kids – an' here you come wi' a funny proposition that stinks to high heaven an' you tell me I could get shot. Why come to me, anyway?'

'I need a good torpedo man – and you're the only one I know.' A slight smile touched Warren's lips. 'It's not the most crowded trade in the world.'

Parker nodded his agreement. 'No, it's not. I don't want to crack meself up, but I can't think of another man who can do what you want. It 'ud be a really bobby-dazzler of a job, though – wouldn't it? Pushin' the old Mark XI out to over twenty thousand yards – just think of it.'

Warren held his breath as he watched Parker struggle against temptation, then he sighed as Parker shook his head and said, 'No, I couldn't do it. What would Sally say?'

'I know it's a dangerous job, Dan.'

'I'm not worried about that – not for meself. I could have got killed in Korea. It's just that . . . well, I've not much insurance, an' what would she do with three kids if anythin' happened to me?'

Warren said, 'I'll tell you this much, Dan. I don't think the worst will happen, but if it does I'll see that Sally gets a life pension equal to what you're getting now. No strings attached – and you can have it in writing.'

'You're pretty free wi' your money – or is it your money?' asked Parker shrewdly.

'It doesn't matter where it comes from. It's in a good cause.'

Parker sighed. 'I'd trust you that far. I know you'd never be on the wrong side. When is this lark startin'?'

'I don't know,' said Warren. 'It might not even start at all. I haven't made up my mind yet. But if we do get going it will be next month.'

Parker chewed the stem of his pipe, apparently unaware it had gone out. At last he looked up, bright-eyed. 'All right, I'll do it. Sally'll give me hell, I expect.' He grinned. 'Best not to tell her, Doctor. I'll cook up a yarn for her.' He scratched his head. 'I must see me old Navy mates an' see if I can get hold of a service manual for the Mark XI – there ought to be some still knockin' around. I'll need that if I'm goin' to redesign the circuits.'

'Do that,' said Warren. 'I'd better tell you what it's all about.'

'No!' said Parker. 'I've got the general drift. If this is goin' to be dangerous then the less I know the better for you. When the time comes you tell me what to do an' I'll do it – if I can.'

Warren asked sharply, 'Any chance of failure?'

'Could be – but if I get all I ask for then I think it can be done. The Mark XI's a nice bit o' machinery – it shouldn't be too hard to make it do the impossible.' He grinned. 'What made you think o' goin' about it this way? Tired of treatin' new addicts?'

'Something like that,' said Warren.

He left Parker buzzing happily to himself about batteries and circuits and with a caution that this was not a firm commitment. But he knew that in spite of his insistence that the arrangements were purely tentative the commitment was hardening.

IV

He telephoned Andrew Tozier. 'Can I call on you for some support tonight, Andy?'

'Sure. Doc; moral or muscular?'

'Maybe a bit of both. I'll see you at the Howard Club – know where that is?'

'I know,' said Tozier. 'You could choose a better place to lose your money, Doc; it's as crooked as a dog's hind leg.'

'I'm gambling, Andy,' said Warren. 'But not with money. Stick in the background, will you? I'll call on you if I need you. I'll be there at ten o'clock.'

'I get the picture; you just want some insurance.'

'That's it,' said Warren, and rang off.

The Howard Club was in Kensington, discreetly camouflaged in one of the old Victorian terraced houses. Unlike the Soho clubs, there were no flashing neon signs proclaiming blackjack and roulette because this was no cheap operation. There were no half-crown chips to be bought in the Howard Club.

Just after ten o'clock Warren strolled through the gambling rooms towards the bar. He was coolly aware of the professional interest aroused by his visit; the doorkeeper had picked up an internal telephone as he walked in and the news would be quick in reaching the higher echelons. He watched the roulette for a moment, and thought sardonically, *If I were James Bond I'd be in there making a killing.*

At the bar he ordered a Scotch and when the barman placed it before him a flat American voice said, 'That will be on the house, Dr Warren.'

Warren turned to find John Follet, the manager of the club, standing behind him. 'What are you doing so far west?' asked Follet, 'If you're looking for any of your lost sheep you won't find them here. We don't like them.'

Warren understood very well that he was being warned. It had happened before that some of his patients had tried to make a quick fortune to feed the habit. They had not succeeded, of course, and things had got out of hand, ending in a brawl. The management of the Howard Club did not like brawls – they lowered the plushy tone of the place – and word had been passed to Warren to keep his boys in line.

He smiled at Follet. 'Just sightseeing, Johnny.' He lifted the glass. 'Join me?'

Follet nodded to the barman, and said, 'Well, it's nice to see you, anyway.'

He would not feel that way for long, thought Warren. He said, 'These are patients you're talking about, Johnny;

they're sick people. I don't rule them – I'm not a leader or anything like that.'

'That's as may be,' said Follet. 'But once your hopheads go on a toot they can do more damage than you'd believe possible. And if anyone can control them, it's you.'

'I've passed around the word that they're not welcome here,' said Warren. 'That's all I can do.'

Follet nodded shortly. 'I understand, Doctor. That's good enough for me.'

Warren looked about the room and saw Andrew Tozier standing at the nearest blackjack table. He said casually, 'You seem to be doing well.'

Follet snorted. 'You can't do well in this crazy country. Now we're having to play the wheel without a zero and that's goddam impossible. No club can operate without an edge.'

'I don't know,' said Warren. 'It's an equal chance for you and the customer, so that's square. And you make your profit on the club membership, the bar and the restaurant.'

'Are you crazy?' demanded Follet. 'It just doesn't work that way. In any game of equal chances a lucky rich man will beat hell out of a lucky poor man any time. Bernoulli figured that out back in 1713 – it's called the St Petersburg paradox.' He gestured towards a roulette table. 'That wheel carries a nut of fifty thousand pounds – but how much do you think the customers are worth? We're in the position of playing a game of equal chances against the public – which can be regarded as infinitely rich. In the long run we get trimmed but good.'

'I didn't know you were a mathematician,' said Warren.

'Any guy in this racket who doesn't understand mathematics goes broke fast,' said Follet. 'And it's about time your British legislators employed a few mathematicians.' He scowled. 'Another thing – take that blackjack table; at one time it was banned because it was called a game of chance.

Now that games of chance are legal they still want to ban it because a good player can beat a bad player. They don't know what in hell they want.'

'Can a good player win at blackjack?' asked Warren interestedly.

Follett nodded. 'It takes a steeltrap memory and nerves of iron, but it can be done. It's lucky for the house there aren't too many of those guys around. We'll take that risk on blackjack but on the wheel we've got to have an edge.' He looked despondently into his glass. 'And I don't see much chance of getting one – not with the laws that are in the works.'

'Things are bad all round,' said Warren unfeelingly. 'Maybe you'd better go back to the States.'

'No, I'll ride it out here for a while.' Follet drained his glass.

'Don't go,' said Warren. 'I had a reason for coming here. I wanted to talk to you.'

'If it's a touch for your clinic I'm already on your books.'

Warren smiled. 'This time I want to give *you* money.'

'This I must stick around to hear,' said Follet. Tell me more.'

'I have a little expedition planned,' said Warren. 'The pay isn't much – say, two-fifty a month for six months. But there'll be a bonus at the end if it all works out all right.'

'Two-fifty a month!' Follet laughed. 'Look around you and figure how much I'm making right now. Pull the other one, Doctor.'

'Don't forget the bonus,' said Warren calmly.

'All right; what's the bonus?' asked Follet, smiling.

'That would be open to negotiation, but shall we say a thousand?'

'You kill me, Warren, you really do – the way you make jokes with a straight face.' He began to turn away. 'I'll be seeing you, Doctor.'

'Don't go, Johnny. I'm confident you'll join me. You see, I know what happened to that Argentinian a couple of months ago – and I know how it was done. It was a little over two hundred thousand pounds you rooked him of, wasn't it?'

Follet stopped dead and turned his head to speak over his shoulder. 'And how did you learn about that?'

'A good story like that soon gets around, Johnny. You and Kostas were very clever.'

Follet turned back to Warren and said seriously, 'Dr Warren: I'd be very careful about the way you talk – especially about Argentinian millionaires. Something might happen to you.'

'I dare say,' agreed Warren. 'And something might happen to you too, Johnny. For instance, if the Argentinian were to find out how he'd been had, he'd raise a stink, wouldn't he? He'd certainly go to the police. It's one thing to lose and quite another to be cheated, so he'd go to the police.' He tapped Follet on the chest. 'And the police would come to you, Johnny. The best that could happen would be that they'd deport you – ship you back to the States. Or would it be the best? I hear that the States is a good place for Johnny Follet to keep away from right now. It was something about certain people having long memories.'

'You hear too damn' much,' said Follet coldly.

'I get around,' said Warren with a modest smile.

'It seems you do. You wouldn't be trying to put the bite on me, would you?'

'You might call it that.'

Follet sighed. 'Warren, you know how it is. I have a fifteen per cent piece of this place – I'm not the boss. Whatever was done to the Argentinian was done by Kostas. Sure, I was around when it happened, but it wasn't my idea – I wasn't in on it, and I got nothing out of it. Kostas did everything.'

'I know,' said Warren. 'You're as pure as the driven snow. But it won't make much difference when they put you on a VC-10 and shoot you back to the States.' He paused and said contemplatively. 'It might even be possible to arrange for a reception committee to meet you at Kennedy Airport.'

'I don't think I like any of this,' said Follet tightly. 'Supposing I told Kostas you were shooting your mouth. What do you suppose would happen to you? I've never had a beef against you, and I don't see why you're doing this. Just watch it.'

As he turned away, Warren said, 'I'm sorry, Johnny; it seems as though you'll be back in the States before the month's out.'

'That does it,' said Follet violently. 'Kostas is a bad guy to cross. Watch out for your back, Warren.' He snapped his fingers and a man who was lounging against the wall suddenly tautened and walked over to the bar. Follet said, 'Dr Warren is just leaving.'

Warren glanced over at Andy Tozier and held up a finger. Tozier strolled over and said pleasantly, 'Evening, all.'

'Johnny Follet wants to throw me out,' said Warren.

'Does he?' said Tozier interestedly. 'And how does he propose to do that? Not that it matters very much.'

'Who the hell's this?' snapped Follet.

'Oh, I'm a friend of Dr Warren,' said Tozier. 'Nice place you've got here, Follet. It should be an interesting exercise.'

'What are you talking about? What exercise?'

'Oh, just to see how quickly it could be taken apart. I know a couple of hearty sergeant types who could go through here like a dose of salts in less than thirty minutes. The trouble about that, though, is that you'd have a hell of a job putting back the pieces.' His voice hardened. 'My advice to you is that if Dr Warren wants to talk to you, then you pin back your hairy ears and listen.'

Follet took a deep breath and blew out his cheeks. 'All right, Steve; I'll sort this out,' he said to the man next to him. 'But stick around – I might need you fast.' The man nodded and returned to his position against the wall.

'Let's all have a nice, soothing drink,' suggested Tozier.

'I don't get any of this,' protested Follet. 'Why are you pushing me, Warren? I've never done anything to you.'

'And you won't, either,' observed Warren. 'In particular you won't say anything about this to Kostas because if anything happens to me all my information goes directly to the places where it will do most good.'

Tozier said, 'I don't know what this is all about, but if anything happens to Dr Warren then a certain Johnny Follet will wish he'd never been born, whatever else happens to him.'

'What the hell are you ganging up on me for?' said Follet desperately.

'I don't know,' said Tozier. 'Why are we ganging up on him, Doc?'

'All you have to do is to take a holiday, Johnny,' said Warren. 'You come with me to the Middle East, help me out on a job, and then come back here. And everything will be as it was. Personally, I don't care how much money you loot from Argentinian millionaires. I just want to get a job done.'

'But why pick on me?' demanded Follet.

'I didn't pick on you,' said Warren wearily. 'You're all I've got, damn it! I have an idea I can use a man of your peculiar talents, so you're elected. And you don't have much say about it, either – you daren't take the chance of being pushed back to the States. You're a gambler, but not that much of a gambler.'

'Okay, so you've whipsawed me,' said Follet sourly. 'What's the deal?'

'I'm running this on the "need to know" principle. You don't have to know, you just have to do – and I'll tell you when to do it.'

'Now, wait a goddam minute. . . .'

'That's the way it is,' said Warren flatly.

Follet shook his head in bewilderment. 'This is the screwiest thing that ever happened to me.'

'If it's any comfort, brother Jonathan, I don't know what's going on, either,' said Tozier. He eyed Warren thoughtfully. 'But Doc here is showing unmistakable signs of acting like a boss, so I suppose he is the boss.'

'Then I'll give you an order,' said Warren with a tired grin. 'For God's sake, stop calling me "Doc". It could be important in the future.'

'Okay, boss,' said Tozier with a poker face,

V

Warren did not have to go out to find Mike Abbot because Mike Abbot came to him. He was leaving his rooms after a particularly hard day when he found Abbot on his doorstep. 'Anything to tell me, Doctor?' asked Abbot.

'Not particularly,' said Warren. 'What are you looking for?'

'Just the usual – all the dirt on the drug scene.' Abbot fell into step beside Warren. 'For instance, what about Hellier's girl?'

'Whose girl?' said Warren with a blank face.

'Sir Robert Hellier, the film mogul – and don't go all po-faced. You know who I mean. The inquest was bloody uninformative – the old boy had slammed down the lid and screwed it tight. It's amazing what you can do if you have a few million quid. Was it accidental or suicide – or was she pushed?'

'Why ask me?' said Warren. 'You're the hotshot reporter.'

Abbot grinned. 'All I know is what I write for the papers – but I have to get it from somewhere or someone. This time the someone is you.'

'Sorry, Mike – no comment.'

'Oh well; I tried,' said Abbot philosophically. 'Why are we passing this pub? Come in and I'll buy you a drink.'

'All right,' said Warren. 'I could do with one. I've had a hard day.'

As they pushed open the door Abbot said, 'All your days seem to be hard ones, judging by the way you've been knocking it back lately.' They reached the counter, and he said, 'What'll you have?'

'I'll have a Scotch,' said Warren. 'And what the devil do you mean by that crack?'

'No harm meant,' said Abbot, raising his hands in mock fright. 'Just one of my feebler non-laughter-making jokes. It's just that I've seen you around inhaling quite a bit of the stuff. In a pub in Soho and a couple of nights later in the Howard Club.'

'Have you been following me?' demanded Warren.

'Christ, no!' said Abbot. 'It was just coincidental.' He ordered the drinks. 'All the same, you seem to move in rum company. I ask myself – what is the connection between a doctor of medicine, a professional gambler and a mercenary soldier? And you know what? I get no answer at all.'

'One of these days that long nose of yours will get chopped off at the roots.' Warren diluted his whisky with Malvern water.

'Not as bad as losing face,' said Abbot. 'I make my reputation by asking the right questions. For instance, why should the highly respected Dr Warren have a flaming row with Johnny Follet? It was pretty obvious, you know.'

'You know how it is,' said Warren tiredly. 'Some of my patients had been cutting up ructions at the Howard Club. Johnny didn't like it.'

'And you had to take your own private army to back you up?' queried Abbot. 'Tell me another fairy tale.' The barman was looking at him expectantly so Abbot paid him, and said, 'We'll have another round.' He turned back to Warren, and said, 'It's all right, Doctor; it's on the expense account – I'm working.'

'So I see,' said Warren drily. Even now he had not made up his mind about Hellier's proposition. All the moves he had made so far had been tentative and merely to ensure that he could assemble a team if he had to. Mike Abbot was a putative member of the team – Warren's choice – but it seemed that he was dealing himself in, anyway.

'I know this is a damnfool question to ask a pressman,' he said. 'But how far can you keep a secret?'

Abbot cocked an eyebrow. 'Not very far. Not so far as to allow someone to beat me to a story. You know how cut-throat Fleet Street is.'

Warren nodded. 'But how independent are you? I mean, do you have to report on your investigations to anyone on your paper? Your editor, perhaps?'

'Usually,' said Abbot. 'After all, that's where my pay cheque comes from.' Wise in the way of interviews, he waited for Warren to make the running.

Warren refused to play the game. 'That's a pity,' he said, and fell silent.

'Oh, come now,' said Abbot. 'You can't just leave it at that. What's on your mind?'

'I'd like you to help me – but not if it's going to be noised about the newspaper offices. You know what a rumour factory your crowd is. You'll know what the score is, but no one else must – or we'll come a cropper.'

'I can't see my editor buying that,' observed Abbot. 'It's too much like that character in the South Sea Bubble who was selling shares in a company – "but nobody to know what it is." I suppose it's something to do with drugs?'

'That's right,' said Warren. 'It will involve a trip to the Middle East.'

Abbot brightened. 'That sounds interesting.' He drummed his fingers on the counter. 'Is there a real story in it?'

'There's a story. It might be a very big one indeed,'

'And I get an exclusive?'

'It'll be yours,' said Warren. 'Full right.'

'How long will it take?'

'That is something I don't know.' Warren looked him in the eye. 'I don't even know if it's going to start. There's a lot of uncertainty. Say, three months.'

'A hell of a long time,' commented Abbot, and brooded for a while. Eventually he said, 'I've got a holiday coming up. Supposing I talk to my editor and tell him that I'm doing a bit of private enterprise in my own time. If I think it's good enough I'll stay on the job when my holiday is up. He might accept that.'

'Keep my name out of it,' warned Warren.

'Sure.' Abbot drained his glass. 'Yes, I think he'll fall for it. The shock of my wanting to work on my holiday ought to be enough.' He put down the glass on the counter. 'But I'll need convincing first.'

Warren ordered two more drinks. 'Let's sit at a table, and I'll tell you enough to whet your appetite.'

VI

The shop was in Dean Street and the neatly gold-lettered sign read: SOHO THERAPY CENTRE. Apart from that there was nothing to say what was done on the premises; it looked like any Dean Street shop with the difference that the windows were painted over in a pleasant shade of green so that it was impossible to see inside.

Warren opened the door, found no one in sight, and walked through into a back room which had been turned into an office. He found a dishevelled young man sitting at a desk and going through the drawers, pulling everything out and piling the papers into an untidy heap on top of the desk. As Warren walked in, he said, 'Where have you been, Nick? I've been trying to get hold of you.'

Warren surveyed the desk. 'What's the trouble, Ben?'

'You'd never believe it if I told you,' said Ben Bryan. He scrabbled about in the papers, 'I'll have to show you. Where the devil is it?'

Warren dumped a pile of books off a chair and sat down. 'Take it easy,' he advised. 'More haste, less speed.'

'Take it easy? Just wait until you see this. You won't be taking it as easy as you are now.' Bryan rummaged some more and papers scattered.

'Perhaps you'd better just tell me,' suggested Warren.

'All right . . . no, here it is. Just read that.'

Warren unfolded the single sheet of paper. What was written on it was short and brutally to the point. 'He's throwing you out?' Warren felt a rage growing within him. 'He's throwing *us* out!' He looked up. 'Can he break the lease like that?'

'He can – and he will,' said Bryan. 'There's a line of fine print our solicitor didn't catch, damn him.'

Warren was angrier than he had ever been in his life. In a choked voice he said, 'There's a telephone under all that junk – dig it out.'

'It's no good,' said Bryan. 'I've talked to him. He said he didn't realize the place would be used by drug addicts; he says his other tenants are complaining – they say it lowers the tone of the neighbourhood.'

'God Almighty!' yelled Warren. 'One's a strip joint and the other sells pornography. What the hell have they to complain of? What stinking hypocrisy!'

'We're going to lose our boys, Nick. If they don't have a place to come to, we'll lose the lot.'

Ben Bryan was a psychologist working in the field of drug addiction. Together with Warren and a couple of medical students he had set up the Soho Therapy Centre as a means of getting at the addicts. Here the addicts could talk to people who understood the problem and many had been referred to Warren's clinic. It was a place off the streets where they could relax, a hygienic place where they could take their shots using sterile water and aseptic syringes.

'They'll be out on the streets again,' said Bryan. 'They'll be taking their shots in the Piccadilly lavatories, and the cops will chase them all over the West End.'

Warren nodded. 'And the next thing will be another outbreak of hepatitis. Good God, that's the last thing we want.'

'I've been trying to find another place,' said Bryan. 'I was on the telephone all day yesterday. Nobody wants to know our troubles. The word's got around, and I think we're blacklisted. It must be in this area – you know that.'

Something exploded within Warren. 'It will be,' he said with decision. 'Ben, how would you like a really good place here in Soho? Completely equipped, regardless of expense, down to hot and cold running footmen?'

'I'd settle for what we have now,' said Bryan.

Warren found an excitement rising within him. 'And, Ben – that idea you had – the one about a group therapy unit as a self-governing community on the line of that Californian outfit. What about that?'

'Have you gone off your little rocker?' asked Bryan. 'We'd need a country house for that. Where would we get the funds?'

'We'll get the funds,' said Warren with confidence. 'Excavate that telephone.'

His decision was made and all qualms gone. He was tired of fighting the stupidity of the public, of which the queasiness of this narrow-gutted landlord was only a single example. If the only way to run his job was to turn into a synthetic James Bond, then a James Bond he'd be.

But it was going to cost Hellier an awful lot of money.

THREE

Warren was ushered into Hellier's office in Wardour Street after passing successfully a hierarchy of secretaries, each more svelte than the last. When he finally penetrated into the inner sanctum, Hellier said, 'I really didn't expect to see you, Doctor. I expected I'd have to chase you. Sit down.'

Warren came to the point abruptly. 'You mentioned unlimited funds, but I take that to be a figure of speech. How unlimited?'

'I'm pretty well breeched,' said Hellier with a smile. 'How much do you want?'

'We'll come to that. I'd better outline the problem so that you can get an idea of its magnitude. When you've absorbed that you might decide you can't afford it.'

'Well see,' said Hellier. His smile broadened.

Warren laid down a folder. 'You were right when you said I had particular knowledge, but I warn you I don't have much – two names and a place – and all the rest is rumour.' He smiled sourly. 'It isn't ethics that has kept me from going to the police – it's the sheer lack of hard facts.'

'Leaving aside your three facts, what about the rumour? I've made some damned important decisions on nothing but rumour, and I've told you I get paid for making the right decisions.'

Warren shrugged. 'It's all a bit misty – just stuff I've picked up in Soho. I spend a lot of time in Soho – in the West End generally – it's where most of my patients hang out. It's convenient for the all-night chemist in Piccadilly,' he said sardonically.

'I've seen them lining up,' said Hellier.

'In 1968 a drug ring was smashed in France – a big one. You must realize that the heroin coming into Britain is just a small leakage from the more profitable American trade. This particular gang was smuggling to the States in large quantities, but when the ring was smashed we felt the effects here. The boys were running around like chickens with their heads chopped off – the illegal supply had stopped dead.'

'Wait a minute,' said Hellier. 'Are you implying that to stop the trade into Britain it would be necessary to do the same for the States?'

'That's virtually the position if you attack it at the source, which would be the best way. One automatically implies the other. I told you the problem was big.'

'The ramifications are more extensive than I thought,' admitted Hellier. He shrugged. 'Not that I'm chauvinistic about it; as you say, it's an international problem.'

Hellier still did not seem to be disturbed about the probable cost to his pocket, so Warren went on: 'I think the best way of outlining the current rumours is to look at the problem backwards, so to speak – beginning at the American end. A typical addict in New York will buy his shot from a pusher as a "sixteenth" – meaning a sixteenth of an ounce. He must buy it from a pusher because he can't get it legally, as in England. That jerks up the price, and his sixteenth will cost him somewhere between six and seven dollars. His average need will be two shots a day.'

Hellier's mind jerked into gear almost visibly. After a moment he said, 'There must be a devil of a lot of heroin going into the States.'

'Not much,' said Warren. 'Not in absolute bulk. I daresay the illegal intake is somewhere between two and three tons a year. You see, the heroin as sold to the addict is diluted with an inert soluble filler, usually lactose – milk sugar. Depending on whether he's being cheated – and he usually is – the percentage of heroin will range from one-half to two per cent. I think you could take a general average of one per cent.'

Hellier was figuring again. He drew forward a sheet of paper and began to calculate. 'If there's a sixteen-hundredth of an ounce of pure heroin in a shot, and the addict pays, say, $6.50 . . .' He stopped short. 'Hell, that's over $10,000 an ounce!'

'Very profitable,' agreed Warren. 'It's big business over there. A pound of heroin at the point of consumption is worth about $170,000. Of course, that's not all profit – the problem is to get it to the consumer. Heroin is ultimately derived from the opium poppy, *papaver somniferum*, which is not grown in the States for obvious reasons. There's a chain of production – from the growing of the poppy to raw opium; from the opium to morphine; from morphine to heroin.'

'What's the actual cost of production?' asked Hellier.

'Not much,' said Warren. 'But that's not the issue. At the point of consumption in the States a pound of heroin is worth $170,000; at the point of the wholesaler inside the States it's worth $50,000; at any point outside the States it's worth $20,000. And if you go right back along the chain you can buy illicit raw opium in the Middle East for $50 a pound.'

'That tells me two things,' said Hellier thoughtfully. 'There are high profits to be made at each stage – and the cost at any point is directly related to the risks involved in smuggling.'

'That's it,' said Warren. 'So far the trade has been fragmented, but rumour has it that a change is on the way. When the French gang was busted it left a vacuum and someone else is moving in – and moving in with a difference. The idea seems to be that this organization will cut out the middlemen – they'll start with the growing of the poppy and end up with delivery *inside* the States of small lots in amy given city. A guaranteed delivery on that basis should net them $50,000 a pound after expenses have been met. That last stage – getting the stuff into the States – is a high risk job.'

'Vertical integration,' said Hellier solemnly. 'These people are taking hints from big business. Complete control of the product.'

'If this comes off, and they can sew up the States, we can expect an accelerated inflow into Britain. The profits are much less, but they're still there, and the boys won't neglect the opportunity.' Warren gestured with his hand. 'But this is all rumour. I've put it together from a hundred whispers on the grapevine.'

Hellier laid his hands flat on the desk. 'So now we come to your facts,' he said intently.

'I don't know if you could dignify them by that name,' said Warren tiredly. 'Two names and a place. George Speering is a pharmaceutical chemist with a lousy reputation. He got into trouble last year in a drug case, and the Pharmaceutical Society hammered him. He was lucky to escape a jail sentence.'

'They . . . er . . . unfrocked him?'

'That's right. This crowd will need a chemist and I heard his name mentioned. He's still in England and I'm keeping an eye on him as well as I can, but I expect him to go abroad soon.'

'Why soon? And how soon?'

Warren tapped the desk calendar. 'The opium crop isn't in yet, and it won't be for a month. But morphine is best extracted from fresh opium, so as soon as this gang have enough of the stuff to work on then Speering will get busy.'

'Perhaps we should keep a closer watch on Speering.'

Warren nodded. 'He still seems to be taking it pretty easy at the moment. And he's in funds, so he's probably on a retainer. I agree he should be watched.'

'And the other name?' enquired Hellier.

'Jeanette Delorme. I've never heard of her before. She sounds as though she could be French, but that doesn't mean much in the Middle East, if that's where she hangs out. But I don't even know that. I don't know anything about her at all. It was just a name that came up in connection with Speering.'

Hellier scribbled on a piece of paper. 'Jeanette Delorme.' He looked up. 'And the place?'

'Iran,' said Warren briefly.

Hellier looked disappointed. 'Well, that's not much.'

'I never said it was,' said Warren irritatedly. 'I thought of giving it to the police but, after all, what had I to give them?'

'They could pass it on to Interpol. Maybe they could do something.'

'You've been making too many television pictures,' said Warren abrasively. 'And believing them, at that! Interpol is merely an information centre and doesn't initiate any executive work. Supposing the word was passed to the Iranian police. No police force is incorruptible, and I wouldn't take any bets at all on the cops in the Middle East – although I hear the Iranians are better than most.'

'I appreciate your point.' Hellier was silent for a moment. 'Our best bet would appear to be this man, Speering.'

'Then you're willing to go on with it on the basis of the little information I have?'

Hellier was surprised. 'Of course!'

Warren took some papers from his file. 'You might change your mind when you see these. It's going to cost you a packet. You said I could pick a team. I've been making commitments on your behalf which you'll have to honour.' He pushed two sheets across the desk. 'You'll find the details there – who the men are, what they'll cost, and some brief biographical details.'

Hellier scanned the papers rapidly and said abruptly, 'I agree to these rates of pay. I also agree to the bonus of £5,000 paid to each man on the *successful* completion of the venture.' He looked up. 'No success – no bonus. Fair enough?'

'Fair enough – but it depends on what you mean by success.'

'I want this gang smashed,' said Hellier in a harsh voice. 'Smashed totally.'

Warren said wryly, 'If we're going to do anything at all that is implied.' He pushed another paper across the desk. 'But we haven't come to my price.'

Hellier picked it up and, after a moment, said 'Humph! What the devil do you want with a property in Soho? They come damned expensive.'

Warren explained, with feeling, the trouble the Soho Therapy Centre had run into. Hellier chuckled. 'Yes, people are damned hypocrites. I'd have probably been the same before . . . well, never mind that.' He got up and went to the window. 'Would a place in Wardour Street do?'

'That would be fine.'

'The company has a place just across the road here. We were using it as a warehouse but that's been discontinued. It's empty now and a bit run down, but it may suit you.' He returned to his desk. 'We were going to sell it, but I'll let you have it at a peppercorn rent and reimburse the company out of my own funds.'

Warren, who had not yet finished with him, nodded briefly and pushed yet another paper across the desk. 'And that's my bonus on the *successful* completion of the job.' Ironically he emphasized the operative word in mockery of Hellier.

Hellier glanced at the wording and nearly blew up. 'A *twenty-bedroomed country house*! What the devil's this?' He glared at Warren. 'Your services come high, Doctor.'

'You asked for blood,' said Warren. 'That's a commodity with a high price. When we go into this we'll come smack into opposition with a gang who'll fight because the prize could run into millions. I think there'll be blood shed somewhere along the line – either ours or theirs. You want the blood – you pay for it.'

'By making you Lord of the Manor?' asked Hellier cynically.

'Not me – a man called Ben Bryan. He wants to establish a self-governing community for addicts; to get them out of circulation to start with, and to get them to act in a responsible manner. It's an idea which has had fair results in the States.'

'I see,' said Hellier quietly. 'All right; I accept that.'

He began to read the brief biographies of the team, and Warren said casually, 'None of those people really know what they're getting into. Suppose we come into possession of, say, a hundred pounds of heroin – that would be worth a lot of money. I don't know whether I'd trust Andy Tozier with it – probably not. I certainly wouldn't trust Johnny Follet.'

Hellier turned a page and, after a while, lifted his head. 'Are you *serious* about this – about these men you've picked? Good God, half of them are villains and the other half incomprehensible.'

'What kind of men did you expect?' asked Warren. 'This can't be done by a crowd of flag-waving saints. But not one of those men is in it for the money – except Andy Tozier. They all have their own reasons.' He took a sour look at himself and thought of Follet. 'I discover I have an unexpected talent for blackmail and coercion.'

'I can understand you picking Tozier – the professional soldier,' said Hellier. 'But Follet – a gambler?'

'Johnny is a man of many parts. Apart from being a gambler he's also a successful con man. He can think up ways of pulling money from your pocket faster than you can think up ways of stopping him. It seems to me that his talents could be used on other things than money.'

'If you put it that way I suppose it seems reasonable,' said Hellier in an unconvinced voice. 'But this man, Abbot – a newspaperman, for God's sake! I won't have that.'

'Yes, you will,' said Warren flatly. 'He's on to us, anyway, and I'd rather have him working for us than against us. He was on my original list, but he dealt himself in regardless and it would be too risky to leave him out now. He's got a good nose, better than any detective, and that's something we need.'

'I suppose that seems reasonable, too,' said Hellier glumly. 'But what doesn't seem reasonable is this man, Parker. I can't see anything here that's of use to us.'

'Dan's the only really honest man among the lot of them,' said Warren. He laughed. 'Besides, he's my insurance policy.'

II

Hellier propounded some of the philosophy of the film business. 'Most countries – especially the poorer ones – like film companies. The boys at the top like us because we're not too stingy with our bribes. The man in the street likes us because on location we pay exceptionally high rates, by local standards, for colourfully-dressed extras. We don't mind because, when all's said and done, we're paying a damned sight less than we would at home.'

He hefted a large book, foolscap size and neatly bound. 'This is a screen play we've had on the shelf for some time. About half the scenes are set in Iran. I've decided to resurrect it, and we're going to make the film. You and your team will be employed by us. You'll be an advance team sent out to Iran by us to scout out good locations – that gives you an excuse for turning up everywhere and anywhere. How does that suit you?'

'I like it,' said Warren. 'It's a good cover.'

'You'll be provided with vehicles and all the usual junk that goes with an advance team,' said Hellier. 'Give me a list of anything else you might need.' He flicked through the pages of the script. 'Who knows? We might even make the picture,' he said sardonically.

Andy Tozier approached Warren. 'You're keeping me too much in the dark,' he complained. 'I'd like to know what I'm getting into. I don't know what to prepare for.'

'Prepare for the worst,' said Warren unhelpfully.

'That's no bloody answer. Is this going to be a military thing?'

Warren said carefully, 'Let's call it paramilitary.'

'I see. A police action – with shooting.'

'But unofficial,' said Warren. 'There might be shooting.'

Tozier stroked the edge of his jaw. 'I don't like that unofficial bit. And if I'm going to be shot at I'd like to have something handy to shoot back with. How do we arrange that?'

'I don't know,' said Warren. 'I thought I'd leave that to you. You're the expert.' Tozier made a rude noise, and Warren said, 'I don't really know what we're going to get into at the other end. It's all a bit difficult.'

Tozier pondered. 'What vehicles are they giving us?'

'A couple of new Land-Rovers. They'll be flown out to Iran with us. The country out there is pretty rough.'

'And the equipment we're getting. What does it consist of?'

'It's all part of our cover. There are some still cameras with a hell of a lot of lenses. A couple of 16-millimetre movie cameras. A video-tape outfit. A hell of a lot of stuff I can't put a name to.'

'Are there tripods with the movie cameras?' Warren nodded, and Tozier said, 'Okay, I'd like to have the Land-Rovers and all the equipment delivered to me as soon as possible. I might want to make a few modifications.'

'You can have them tomorrow.'

'And I'd like some boodle from this money mine you seem to have discovered – at least a thousand quid. My modifications come expensive.'

'I'll make it two thousand,' said Warren equably. 'You can have that tomorrow, too.'

'Johnny Follet might be more useful than I thought,' said Tozier thoughtfully. 'He knows his weapons – he was in Korea.'

'Was he? Then he'll get on well with Dan Parker.'

Tozier jerked his head. 'And who is Dan Parker?'

Warren grinned. 'You'll meet him sometime,' he promised.

'I'm coming with you,' said Ben Bryan when Warren told him of what was happening.

'And why would we need a psychiatrist?' asked Warren.

Bryan grinned. 'To inject a modicum of sanity. This is the craziest thing I've heard.'

'If you join us you'll be as mad as we are. Still, you might come in useful.' He looked at Bryan speculatively, then said, 'I think you'd better be in the main party. Mike Abbot can go with Parker.'

'What's he going to do?'

'He's our Trojan Horse – if we can find the Delorme woman – and that's proving to be a hell of a problem. Hellier has a team in Paris going through birth certificates, pulling out all the Jeanette Delormes and running them down. They've found eight already. On the off-chance she was born in Switzerland he has another team there.'

'Supposing she was born in Martinique?' asked Bryan.

'We can only try the obvious first,' said Warren. 'Hellier's investigators are good – I know because they did a bang-up job on me. Anyway, he's spending money as though he has his own printing press. We're already into him for over £70,000.' He grinned. 'Still, that's only a couple of years' upkeep on his yacht'

'I've never heard of a rich man really keen to part with his money,' said Bryan. 'You must have knocked the props clean from under him. You made him take a look at himself – a good, clear-eyed look – and he didn't like what he saw. I wish I could do the same to some of my patients. Perhaps you should change your profession.'

'I have – I'm in the business of raising private armies.'

Everything seemed to happen at once.

It may have been luck or it may have been good investigative practice, but the Delorme woman was traced, not through the patient sifting of birth certificates, but from a pipeline into the French Sûreté. It seemed that Mike Abbot had a friend who had a friend who . . .

Hellier tossed a file over to Warren. 'Read that and tell me what you think.'

Warren settled back in his chair and opened the folder.

Jeanette Véronique Delorme: Born April 12, 1937 at Chalons. Parents . . .

He skipped the vital statistics in order to come to the meat of it.

'. . . three months' imprisonment in 1955 for minor fraud; six months' imprisonment in 1957 for smuggling over Franco-Spanish border; left France in 1958.'

Then followed what could only be described as a series of hypotheses.

Believed to have been involved in smuggling from Tangier to Spain, 1958-1960; smuggling arms to Algeria, 1961-1963; smuggling drugs into Italy and Switzerland, 1963-1967. Believed to have been implicated in the murders of Henry

Rowe (American) 1962; Kurt Schlesinger (German), Ahmed ben Bouza (Algerian) and Jean Fouget (French) 1963; Kamer Osman (Lebanese) and Pietro Fuselli (Italian) 1966.

Operational Characteristics: Subject is good organizer and capable of controlling large groups; is ruthless and intolerant of errors; is careful not to become personally involved in smuggling activities, but may have been director of large-scale jewel thefts, south of France, 1967. This, however, may be considered doubtful.

Present Whereabouts: Beirut, Lebanon.

Present Status: Not wanted for crime in Metropolitan France.

There were a couple of smudgy photographs which had not survived the copying process at all well, but which showed a blonde of indeterminate age.

Warren blew out his cheeks. 'What a hell-cat she must be.' He tapped the folder. 'I think this is the one – everything fits.'

'I think so, too,' said Hellier. 'I've stopped everything else and narrowed it down to her. A man has already flown out to Beirut to pinpoint her.'

'I hope someone has told him to be careful,' said Warren.

'He just has to find out where she lives and . . . er . . . her standing in the community. That shouldn't be too risky. Then he pulls out and you take over.'

'I'll get Dan Parker out there as soon as we know something definite. Mike Abbot will support him – I'm not sure Dan could pull it off on his own. This might need the sophisticated touch. Oh, and we have a volunteer – Ben Bryan will be joining the Iran group.'

'I'm glad to hear that Mr Bryan is going to earn his manor house,' said Hellier, a shade acidly. 'There's still nothing on your man, Speering.'

'He'll make a move soon,' said Warren with certainty. His confidence had risen because the dossier on Jeanette Delorme fitted in so tidily.

'Well, the same thing applies. There'll be an investigator with him all the way – probably on the same plane if he flies. Then you'll take over.'

Speering moved two days later, and within twelve hours Warren, Tozier, Follet and Bryan were in the air in a chartered aircraft which also carried the two Land-Rovers. Parker and Abbot were already on their way to the Lebanon.

III

It was snowing in Tehran.

Follet shivered as the sharp wind cut through his jacket. 'I thought this place was supposed to be hot.' He looked out across the airport at the sheer wall of the Elburz Mountains and then up at the cold grey sky from which scudded a minor blizzard. 'This is the Middle East?' he asked doubtfully.

'About as Middle as you can get,' said Tozier. 'Still, it's March and we're nearly five thousand feet above sea level.'

Follet turned up his collar and pulled the lapels close about his throat. 'Where the hell is Warren?'

'He's clearing the vehicles and the gear through customs.' He smiled grimly. The modifications he had made to the Land-Rovers were such that if they were discovered then all hell would break loose in the customs shed, and Warren and Bryan would find themselves tossed into jail without a quibble. But he had not told Warren what the modifications were, which was all to the good. True innocence is better than bluff when faced with the X-ray eye of the experienced customs official.

All the same he breathed more easily when Follet touched him on the shoulder and pointed. 'Here they come,' he said, and Tozier saw with relief a Land-Rover bearing down upon them. On its side it bore the neat legend: *Regent Film Company. Advance Unit.* The tension left him.

Warren poked his head through the side window. 'Ben's just behind me,' he said. 'One of you jump in.'

'Did you have any trouble?' asked Tozier.

Warren looked surprised. 'No trouble at all.'

Tozier smiled and said nothing. He walked around to the back of the vehicle and stroked one of the metal struts which held up the canopy. Follet said, 'Let me get in and out of this goddam wind. Where are we going?'

'We're booked in at the Royal Tehran Hilton. I don't know where it is but it shouldn't be too difficult to find.' He pointed to a minibus filling up with passengers, which had the name of the hotel on its side. 'We just follow that.'

Follet got in and slammed the door. He looked broodingly at the alien scene, and said abruptly, 'Just what in hell are we doing here, Warren?'

Warren glanced at the rear view mirror and saw that the other Land-Rover had arrived. 'Following a man.'

'Jeeze, you're as close-mouthed as that strongarm man of yours. Or are you keeping him in the dark, too?'

'You just do as you're told, Johnny, and you'll be all right,' advised Warren.

'I'd feel a hell of a lot better if I knew what I was supposed to do,' grumbled Follet.

'Your turn will come.'

Follet laughed unexpectedly. 'You're a funny one, Warren. Let me tell you something; I like you – I really do. You had me over a barrel; you offered me a thousand when you knew I'd take peanuts. Then you raised the bonus to five thousand when you didn't have to. Why did you do that?'

Warren smiled. 'The labourer is worthy of his hire. You'll earn it.'

'Maybe I will, but I don't see how right now. Anyway, I just wanted to say I appreciated the gesture. You can depend on me – for anything reasonable, that is,' he added hastily. 'Tozier was talking about unreasonable things – like being shot at.'

'You ought to have got used to that in Korea.'

'You know,' said Follet. 'I never did. Funny the things a man can never get used to, isn't it?'

The Royal Tehran Hilton was on the outskirts of the city, a caravanserai designed specifically for the oilmen and businessmen flocking into Iran under the impetus of the booming economy underwritten by the reforming regime of Mohammad Rezi Pahlevi, King of Kings and Light of the Aryans. It had not been an easy drive from the airport because of the propensity of the local inhabitants to regard a road as a race track. Several times Warren had been within an ace of serious trouble and when they reached the hotel he was sweating in spite of the cold.

They registered, and Warren found a message awaiting him. He waited until he was in his room before ripping open the envelope, and found but a single inscrutable line of writing: *Your room – 7.30 p.m. Lane.* He looked at his watch and decided he had just time to unpack.

At 7.29 there was a discreet knock. He opened the door and a man said, 'Mr Warren? I believe you're expecting me. My name is Lane.'

'Come in, Mr Lane,' said Warren, and held open the door wider. He studied Lane as he took off his coat; there was not much to the man – he could have been anybody – a virtue in a private detective.

Lane sat down. 'Your man is staying here at the Hilton – his reservation is for a week. He's here right now, if you want him.'

'Not alone, I trust,' said Warren.

'That's all right, Mr Warren; there are two of us on the job. He's being watched.' Lane shrugged. 'But he won't move – he likes to stay close to where the bottles are.'

'He drinks a lot?'

'He may not be an alcoholic, but he's pushing it. He lives in the bar until it closes, then has a bottle sent to his room.'

Warren nodded. 'What else can you tell me about Mr Speering?'

Lane took a notebook from his pocket. 'He's been getting around. I have a list of all this stuff written up which I'll let you have, but I can tell it to you in five minutes.' He flipped open the notebook. 'He was met at the airport by one of the locals – an Iranian, I think – and brought here to the hotel. I wasn't able to nail down the Iranian; we'd just arrived and we weren't equipped,' he said apologetically.

'That's all right.'

'Anyway, we haven't seen the Iranian since. Speering went out next day to a place on Mowlavi, near the railway station. I have the address here. He came out of there with a car or, rather, an American jeep. It isn't a hire car, either – I've been trying to check on the registration, but that's a bit difficult in a strange city like this one.'

'Yes, it must be,' said Warren.

'He went from there to a firm of wholesale pharmaceutical chemists – name and address supplied – where he spent an hour and a half. Then back to the Hilton where he spent the rest of the day. That was yesterday. This morning he had a visitor – an American called John Eastman; that was up in his room. Eastman stayed all morning – three hours – then they had lunch in the Hilton dining-room.'

'Any line on Eastman?'

Lane shook his head. 'A full-time check on a man really takes four operatives – there are only two of us. We couldn't do anything about Eastman without the risk of losing Speering. Our instructions were to stick to Speering.' Lane consulted his notebook again. 'Eastman left soon after lunch today, and Speering hasn't moved since. He's down in the bar right now. That's the lot, Mr Warren.'

'I think you've done well under the circumstances,' said Warren. 'I have some friends here; I'd like to let them get a look at Speering for future reference. Can that be arranged?'

'Nothing easier,' said Lane. 'All you have to do is have a drink.' He took out an envelope which he gave to Warren. 'That's all we have on Speering; registration number of his jeep, names and addresses of the places he's been to in Tehran.' He paused. 'I understand that finishes our job – after I've pointed the man out.'

'That's right. That's all you were asked to do.'

Lane seemed relieved. 'This one's been tricky,' he confided. 'I don't have any trouble in London, and I've done jobs in Paris and Rome. But a Westerner here stands out like a sore thumb in some parts of the city and that makes following a man difficult. When do you want to see Speering?'

'Why not now?' said Warren. 'I'll collect my chaps.'

Before going into the bar Warren paused and said, 'We're here on business. Mr Lane will indicate unobtrusively the man we've come to see – and the operative word is see. Take a good look at him so that you'll recognize him again anywhere – but don't make it obvious. The idea is to see and not be seen. I suggest we split up.'

They crossed the foyer and went into the bar. Warren spotted Speering immediately and veered away from him. He had seen Speering on several occasions in London and, although he did not think he was known to Speering, it was best to make sure he was not observed. He turned his back on the room, leaned on the bar counter and ordered a drink.

The man next to him turned. 'Hi, there!'

Warren nodded politely. 'Good evening.'

'You with IMEG?' The man was American.

'IMEG?'

The man laughed. 'I guess not. I saw you were British and I guessed you might be with IMEG.'

'I don't even know what IMEG is,' said Warren. He looked into the mirror at the back of the bar and saw Tozier sitting at a table and ordering a drink.

'It's just about the biggest thing to hit this rathole of a country,' said the American. He was slightly drunk. 'We're reaming a forty-inch gas line right up the middle – Abadan right to the Russian border. Over six hundred million bucks' worth. Money's flowing like . . . like money.' He laughed.

'Indeed!' said Warren. He was not very interested.

'IMEG's bossing the show – that's you British. Me – I'm with Williams Brothers, who are doing the goddam work. Call that a fair division of labour?'

'It sounds like a big job,' said Warren evasively. He shifted his position and saw Follet at the other end of the bar.

'The biggest.' The American swallowed his drink. 'But the guys who are going to take the cream are the Russkis. Christ, what a set-up! They'll take Iranian gas at under two cents a therm, and they've pushed a line through to Trieste so they can sell Russian gas to the Italians at over three cents a therm. Don't tell me those Bolshevik bastards aren't good capitalists.' He nudged Warren. 'Have a drink.'

'No, thanks,' said Warren. 'I'm expecting a friend.'

'Aw, hell!' The American looked at his watch. 'I guess I've gotta eat, anyway. See you around.'

As he left, Tozier came up to the bar with his drink in his hand. 'Who's your friend?'

'A lonely drunk.'

'I've seen your man,' said Tozier. 'He looks like another drunk. What now?'

'Now we don't lose him.'

'And then?'

Warren shrugged. 'Then we find out what we find out.'

Tozier was silent for a while. He pulled out his cigarette case, lit a cigarette and blew out a long plume of smoke. 'It's not good enough, Nick. I don't like acting in the dark.'

'Sorry to hear it.'

'You'll be even sorrier when I pull out tomorrow.' Warren turned his head sharply, and Tozier said, 'I don't know what you're trying to do, but you can't run this operation by keeping everything under wraps. How the hell can I do a job if I don't know what I'm doing?'

'I'm sorry you feel that way about it, Andy. Don't you trust me?'

'Oh, I trust you. The trouble is that you don't trust me. So I'm pulling out, Nick – I'll be back in London tomorrow night. You've got something on Johnny Follet, and you might have something on Ben Bryan for all I know. But I'm clean, Nick; I'm in this for honest reasons – just for the money.'

'So stay and earn it.'

Tozier shook his head gently. 'Not without knowing what I'm getting into – and why. I told you once that I like to have something to shoot back with if someone shoots at me. I also like to know why he's shooting at me. Hell, I might approve of his reasons – I might even be on his side if I knew the score.'

Warren's hand tightened on his glass. He was being pushed into a decision. 'Andy, you do jobs for money. Would you smuggle dope for money?'

'The problem has never come up,' said Tozier reflectively. 'Nobody has ever made the proposition. Are you asking me, Nick?'

'Do I look like a dope smuggler?' said Warren in disgust.

'I don't know,' said Tozier. 'I don't know how a dope smuggler behaves. I do know that the straightest people get bent under pressure. You've been under pressure for quite some time, Nick; I've watched you struggling against it.' He drained his glass. 'Now that the question has arisen,' he said, 'the answer is no. I wouldn't smuggle dope for money. And I think you've turned into a right son of a bitch, Nick; you've tried to con me into this thing and it hasn't worked, has it?'

Warren blew out his cheeks and let the air escape in a long sigh. Internally he was cheering to the sound of trumpets. He grinned at Tozier. 'You've got the wrong end of the stick, Andy. Let me tell you about it – around the corner out of the sight of Speering.'

He took Tozier by the arm and steered him to a table and in five minutes had given him the gist of it. Tozier listened and a slightly stupefied expression appeared on his face. He said, 'And that's all you have to go on? Have you gone out of your mind?'

'It's not much,' admitted Warren. 'But it's all we have.'

Suddenly, Tozier chuckled. 'It's just mad enough to be interesting. I'm sorry if I got things wrong just now, Nick; but you were being so bloody mysterious.' He nodded ruefully. 'I can see the position you were in – you can't trust anyone in this racket. Okay, I'm with you.'

'Thanks, Andy,' said Warren quietly.

Tozier called up a waiter and ordered drinks. 'Let's get practical,' he said. 'You were right in one thing – I wouldn't let a breath of this leak out to Johnny Follet. If there's any money in it Johnny will want to cut his share, and he won't be too particular how he does it. But all the same, he's a good man to have along, and we can use him as long as you keep that stranglehold tight. What have you got on him, anyway?'

'Does it matter?'

Tozier shrugged. 'I suppose not. Now, what are your ideas on Speering?'

'He's come here to extract morphine from opium, I'm fairly sure of that,' said Warren. 'That's why he went to a wholesale pharmaceutical firm yesterday. He was ordering supplies.'

'What would he need?'

'Pharmaceutical quality lime, methylene chloride, benzene, amyl alcohol and hydrochloric acid, plus a quantity of glassware.' Warren paused. 'I don't know if he intends transforming the morphine into heroin here. If he does he'll need acetic acid as well.'

Tozier frowned. 'I don't quite understand this. What's the difference between morphine and heroin?'

The drinks arrived and Warren did not reply until the waiter had gone. 'Morphine is an alkaloid extracted from opium by a relatively simple chemical process. Heroin is morphine with its molecular structure altered by an even simpler process.' He grimaced. 'That job could be done in a well-equipped kitchen.'

'But what's the difference?'

'Well, heroin is the acetylated form of morphine. It's soluble in water, which morphine is not, and since the human body mostly consists of water it gets to the spot faster. Various properties are accentuated and it's a damned sight more addictive than morphine.'

Tozier leaned back. 'So Speering is going to extract the morphine. But where? Here in Iran? And how is the morphine – or heroin – going to get to the coast? South to the Persian Gulf? Or across Iraq and Syria to the Mediterranean? We have to find out one hell of a lot of things, Nick.'

'Yes,' said Warren gloomily. 'And there's one big problem I can't see past at all. It's something I haven't even discussed with Hellier.'

'Oh! Well, you'd better spit it out.'

Warren said flatly, 'There's no opium in Iran.'

Tozier stared at him. 'I thought all these Middle East countries were rotten with the stuff.'

'They are – and so was Iran under the old Shah. But this new boy is a reformer.' Warren leaned his elbows on the table. 'Under the old Shah things went to hell in a bucket. He was running Iran on the lines of the old Roman Empire – in order to keep in sweet with the populace he kept the price of grain down to an artificial low level. That was a self-defeating policy because the farmers found they couldn't make a living growing grain, so they planted poppies instead – a much more profitable crop. So there was less and less grain and more and more opium.' He grimaced. 'The old Shah didn't mind because he created the Opium Monopoly; there was a government tax and he got a rake-off from every pound collected.'

'A sweet story,' said Tozier.

'You haven't heard the half of it. In 1936 Iranian opium production was 1,350 metric tons. World requirements of medicinal opium were 400 tons.'

Tozier jerked. 'You mean the old bastard was smuggling the stuff.'

'He didn't need to,' said Warren. 'It wasn't illegal. He was the law in Iran. He just sold the stuff to anyone who had the money to pay for it. He was on to a good thing, but all good things come to an end. He pushed his luck too far and was forced to abdicate. There was a provisional government for a while, and then the present Shah took over. Now, he was a really bright boy. He wanted to drag this woebegone country into the twentieth century by the scruff of its neck, but he found that you can't have industrialism in a country where seventy-five per cent of the population are opium addicts. So he clamped down hard and fast, and I doubt if you can find an ounce of illegal opium in the country today.'

Tozier looked baffled. 'Then what is Speering doing here?'

'That's the problem,' said Warren blandly. 'But I don't propose asking him outright.'

'No,' said Tozier pensively. 'But we stick to him closer than his shirt.'

A waiter came and and said enquiringly, 'Mistair Warren?'

'I'm Warren.'

'A message for you, sair.'

'Thank you,' Warren raised his eyebrows at Tozier as he tipped the waiter. A minute later he said, 'It's from Lane. Speering has given up his reservation – he's leaving tomorrow. Lane doesn't know where he's going, but his jeep has been serviced and there are water cans in the back. What do you suppose that means?'

'He's leaving Tehran,' said Tozier with conviction. 'I'd better get back to check on the trucks; I'd like to see if the radios are still in working order. We'll leave separately – give me five minutes.'

Warren waited impatiently for the time to elapse, then got up and walked out of the bar. As he passed Speering he almost stopped out of sheer surprise. Speering was sitting with Johnny Follet and they were both tossing coins.

IV

Speering headed north-west from Tehran on the road to Qazvin. 'You get ahead of him and I'll stick behind,' said Tozier to Warren. 'We'll have him like the meat in a sandwich. If he turns off the road I'll get on to you on the blower.'

They had kept an all night watch on Speering's jeep but it had been a waste of time. He had a leisurely breakfast and did not leave Tehran until ten, and with him was a sharp-featured Iranian as chauffeur. They trailed the jeep through thick traffic out of the city and once they were on the main road Warren put on a burst of speed, passed Speering, and then slowed down to keep a comfortable distance ahead.

Follet, in the passenger seat, kept a sharp eye astern, using the second rear view mirror which was one of Tozier's modifications.

To the right rose the snow-capped peaks of the Elburz Mountains but all around was a featureless plain, dusty and monotonous. The road was not particularly good as far as Warren could judge, but he had been educated to more exacting standards than the Iranian driver and he reflected that by Iranian standards it was probably excellent. After all, it was the main arterial highway to Tabriz.

As soon as he became accustomed to driving the Land-Rover he said to Follet abruptly, 'You were talking to Speering last night. What about?'

'Just passing the time of day,' said Follet easily.

'Don't make a mistake, Johnny,' said Warren softly. 'You could get hurt – badly.'

'Hell, it was nothing,' protested Follet. 'It wasn't even my doing. He came over to me – what else was I expected to do besides talk to him?'

'What did you talk about?'

'This and that. Our jobs. I told him I was with Regent Films. You know – all this crap about the film we're making. He said he worked for an oil company.' He laughed. 'I took some of his money off him, too.'

'I saw you,' said Warren acidly. 'What did you use – a two-headed penny?'

Follet raised his hands in mock horror. 'As God is my judge, I didn't cheat him. You know that's not my style. I didn't have to, anyway; he was pretty near blind drunk.' His eyes flicked up to the mirror. 'Slow down a bit – we're losing him.'

From Tehran to Qazvin was nearly a hundred miles and it was almost one o'clock when they neared the outskirts of the town. As they were driving through the loudspeaker crackled into life. 'Calling Regent Two. Calling Regent Two. Over.'

Follet picked up the microphone and thumbed the switch. 'You're coming in fine, Regent One. Over.'

Tozier's voice was thin and distorted. 'Our man has stopped at a hotel. I think he's feeding his face. Over.'

'That's a damned good idea; I'm hungry myself,' said Follet, and raised an eyebrow at Warren.

'We'll pull off the road at the other side of town,' said Warren. 'Tell him that.' He carried on until he was well past the outskirts of Qazvin and then pulled up on a hard shoulder. 'There's a hamper in the back,' he said. 'I gave Ben the job of quartermaster; let's see how good he is.'

Warren felt better after chicken sandwiches and hot coffee from a flask, but Follet seemed gloomy. 'What a crummy country,' he said. 'We've travelled a hundred miles and those goddam mountains haven't changed an inch.' He pointed to a string of laden camels coming down the road. 'What's the betting we end up on the back of a thing like that?'

'We could do worse,' said Warren thoughtfully. 'I have the idea that these Land-Rovers are a shade too conspicuous for a shadowing job like this.' He picked up a map. 'I wonder where Speering is going.'

Follet looked over his shoulder. 'The next town is Zanjan – another hundred goddam miles.' He looked around. 'Christ, isn't this country horrible? Worse than Arizona.'

'You've been there?'

'Hell, I was born there. I got out by the time I was old enough to run away. I'm a city boy at heart. The bright lights for me.' He hummed a phrase of *Broadway Melody* and reached forward and took a pack of cards from the dash shelf. 'I'll be going back, too, so I'd better keep in practice.'

Warren heard the crisp flick of the cards and glanced sideways to see Follet riffle-shuffle with unbelievable dexterity, something far removed from the amateur's awkwardness. 'I thought you said you didn't cheat.'

'I don't – but I can if I have to. I'm a pretty fair card mechanic when I want to be.' He grinned engagingly. 'It's like this; if you have a piece of a casino like I have back in London, you don't have to cheat – as long as the house has an edge. It's the edge that counts, you see. You don't suppose Monte Carlo gets by because of cheating, do you?'

'It's supposed to be an honest game.'

'It's one hundred per cent honest,' said Follet stoutly. 'As long as you have the percentages going for you then you're all right and cheating isn't necessary. I'll show you what I mean because right now I feel lucky. On this road we've been meeting about twenty cars an hour – I'll give you even money that in the next hour two of those cars will have the same last two digits in the registration number. Just a game to pass the time.'

Warren thought it out. There were a hundred possible numbers – 00 to 99. If Follet restricted it to twenty cars then it seemed that the odds were on Warren's side. He said carefully, 'For the first twenty cars you're on.'

'For a hundred pounds,' said Follet calmly. 'If I win you can add it to my bonus – if and when. Okay?'

Warren breathed hard, then said, 'All right.'

The quiet hum from the loudspeaker altered as a carrier wave came on, and then Ben Bryan said, 'Calling Regent Two. Our man is getting ready to move. Over.'

Warren unhooked the microphone. 'Thanks, Regent One. We'll get moving slowly and let him catch up. The grub was pretty good, Ben; you're elected caterer for the duration. Over.'

The loudspeaker made a rude squawk and lapsed into silence. Warren grinned and pressed the self-starter. 'Keep an eye to the rear, Johnny, and tell me when Speering shows up.'

Follet produced a pen. 'You call the numbers – I'll write them down. Don't worry; I'll keep an eye on Speering.'

The game served to while away the time. It was a monotonous drive on a monotonous road and it was something for Warren to do. With Follet keeping watch to the rear there was nothing for him to do except drive and to speed up or slow down at Follet's instruction so as to keep a safe distance ahead of Speering. Besides he was tending to become sleepy and the game kept him awake.

He called out the numbers as the oncoming cars passed, and Follet scribbled them down. Although Follet's attention was, in the main, directed towards Speering, Warren noticed that once in a while he would do a spot check of a number called. He smiled – Follet would never trust anyone. When fifteen numbers had been called without duplication Warren had high hopes of winning his hundred pounds and he became more interested – this was more than a way of passing the time.

On the eighteenth number Follet suddenly said, 'That's it – number five and number eighteen are the same – thirty-nine. You lose, Warren. You've just raised my bonus by a hundred.' He put the pen back into his shirt pocket. 'That was what is known as a proposition. Another name for it is a sucker bet. You didn't have much of a chance.'

'I don't see it,' said Warren.

Follet laughed. 'That's because you're a mathematical ignoramus. You figured that because there were a hundred possibles and only twenty chances that the odds were four to one in your favour, and that I was a chump for offering evens. You were the chump because the odds were actually in my favour – no less than seven to one. It pays to understand mathematics.'

Warren thought it over. 'I still don't see it.'

'Look at it this way. If I'd bet that a *specific* number would come up twice in the first twenty then I would have been a chump. But I didn't. I said *any two numbers* in the first twenty would match.'

Warren frowned. He still did not get the point, but he had always been weak in mathematics. Follet said, 'A proposition can be defined as a bet which looks good to the sucker but which is actually in favour of the smart guy who offers it. You dig into the holes and corners of mathematics – especially probability theory – and you'll find dozens of propositions which the suckers fall for every time.'

'You won't catch me again,' said Warren.

Follet chuckled. 'Want to bet on it? It's surprising how often a sucker comes back for more. Andy Tozier fell for that one, too. He'll fall again – I'll take the whole of his bonus from him before we're through with this caper.' He glanced at the mirror. 'Slow down, will you? This road's becoming twisty.'

They drove on and on until they came to Zanjan, and Follet said, 'I see the jeep – I think he's coming through.' Two minutes later he said, 'I've lost him.'

The radio broke into life with a crackle of mid-afternoon static caused, presumably, by the stormy weather over the mountains to the west. '. . . turned off to left . . . hotel . . . follow . . . Got that? Over.'

Follet clicked a switch 'Speering turned off to the left by the hotel and you want us to follow. Is that it, Andy? Over.'

'That's it . . . quickly . . . out.'

Warren pulled to a halt, and Follet said, 'I'll take over – you look a bit beat.'

'All right,' said Warren. They changed seats and Warren stretched his shoulders and slumped in the passenger seat. He had been driving all day and the Land-Rover was a bit harder to handle than his saloon car. They went back into Zanjan and by the hotel found a road leading off to the west; it was signposted in Arabic script which Warren could make no sense of. Follet wheeled around and Warren grabbed the maps.

The new road deteriorated rapidly and, because it was heading into the mountains, became more sinuous and tricky. Follet drove a shade faster than was absolutely safe in an effort to catch up with Tozier and Bryan, and the vehicle bumped and shuddered. At last they caught a glimpse of a dust cloud ahead. 'That should be Andy.' After a while he said, 'It's Andy, all right.' He eased the speed a little. 'I'll drop back a bit – we don't want to eat his dust from here to hell-and-gone.'

As they drove deeper into the mountains their speed dropped. The road surface was very bad, ridged in bone-jarring corrugations and washed out in places where storm-swelled freshets had swept across. The gradients became steeper and the bends tighter, so much so that Follet was forced to use the extra-low gearing that is the speciality of the Land-Rover. The day wore on to its end.

Warren had the maps on his knee attached to a clipboard and kept his eye on the compass. They were heading west-ward all the time and, after checking the map again, he said, 'We're heading into Kurdistan.' He knew that this was the traditional route for smuggling opium out of Iran into Syria and Jordan, and again he felt confident that he was right – this was more than a coincidence.

Follet turned another corner and drove down one of the few straight stretches of road. At this point the road clung to the side of a mountain with a sheer cliff on the right and an equally sheer drop on the left. 'Look at that,' he said jerkily and nodded across the valley.

The road crossed the valley and rose again to climb the side of the mountain on the other side. In the far distance a cloud of brick-red dust picked out by the sun indicated a speeding car. 'That's Speering,' said Follet. 'Andy is still in the valley bottom. If we can see Speering then he can see us. If he doesn't know we're following him then he's blind or dead drunk.'

'It can't be helped,' said Warren grimly. 'That's the way it is.'

'You can tell me something,' said Follet. 'What the hell happens at sunset? Have you thought of that?'

Warren had thought of it and it had been worrying him. He looked at his watch and estimated that there was less than an hour to go. 'We'll keep going as far as we can,' he said with no expression in his voice.

Which was not very far. Within half an hour they came upon the other Land-Rover parked by the roadside with Ben Bryan flagging them down. Just beyond him Tozier was standing, looking over the mountains. Follet halted and Warren leaned from the window. 'What's up, Ben?'

Bryan's teeth showed white against his dusty face and the mountain wind whipped his hair. 'He's beaten us, Nick. Take a look over there where Andy is.'

Warren stepped down and followed him towards Tozier who turned and said, 'You tell me which way he went.'

There were five possible exits from the rocky area on top of the plateau. 'Five roads,' said Tozier. 'You tell me which one he picked.'

'No tracks?'

'The ground is hard where it isn't naked rock.' Tozier looked about. 'This seems to be a main junction, but it isn't on the map.'

'The road we've been travelling on isn't on the map, either,' said Warren. He squatted and balanced the clipboard on his knee. 'I reckon we're about there.' He made a small cross on the map. 'About thirty miles inside Kurdistan.' He stood up and walked to the edge of the road and gazed westward to where the setting sun fitfully illuminated the storm clouds over the red mountains. 'Speering could be heading clear to the Iraqi border.'

'He won't make it tonight,' said Tozier. 'Not on these roads in these mountains. What do we do, Nick?'

'What the devil can we do?' said Warren violently. 'We've lost him right at the start of the game. It's four to one against us that we pick the right road – a sucker bet.' He suppressed his futile rage. 'We can't do much now. It's nearly dark so we'd better make camp.'

Tozier nodded. 'All right; but let's do it out of sight of any of these roads.'

'Why? What's the point?'

'No point, really.' Tozier shrugged. 'Just on general security principles. It gets to be a habit in my game.'

He walked towards the trucks leaving Warren in a depressed mood. We've blown it at this end, he thought; I hope to God that Mike and Dan have better luck. But he did not feel like betting on it – that would be another sucker bet.

FOUR

'This is the life,' said Michael Abbot. He sipped from a tall frosted glass and watched with more than idle interest as a nubile girl clad in the briefest of brief bikinis stepped on to the diving-board. She flexed her knees, stood poised for a moment, and then cleft the air in a perfect swallow dive to plunge with minimum splash into the Mediterranean.

Dan Parker was unimpressed. 'We're wastin' time.'

'It can't be hurried,' said Abbot. He had talked this over with Parker before, and Dan had reluctantly agreed that this was the best way. There were two possible approaches that could be made; the approach direct, which was to introduce themselves to the Delorme woman as potential allies. The trouble with that was that if it failed then it was a complete failure with nothing to fall back upon. The approach indirect was to somehow make Delorme come to them. If it did not work within a reasonable period of time then the direct approach was indicated.

Abbot leaned forward to watch the girl who was now climbing out of the water. 'We'll get there in time.'

'So we sit around in this fancy hotel while you get pissed on those fancy drinks. Is that it?' Parker was feeling edgy. He was out of place in the Hotel Saint-Georges and he knew it.

'Take it easy, Dan,' said Abbot calmly. 'It's early days. If we can't approach her then we have to find out who her friends are – and that's what we're doing now.'

Jeanette Delorme moved in the highest Lebanese society; she lived in a de luxe villa in the mountains at Hammana, and she could afford to eat two days running at the Hotel Saint-Georges. Getting close to her was the problem. Somehow they had to snuggle up to her and that, thought Abbot, was like snuggling up to a rattlesnake. He had read the dossier on her.

The only approach, as he saw it, was to find out who her associates were – her more disreputable associates – and then to lay out some ground bait. It was going to be very slow – much too slow for the liking of Dan Parker – but it was the only way. And so they were sitting in a discreet corner of the Hotel Saint-Georges while Delorme lunched with an unknown friend who would be checked on as soon as they parted. The previous day had been a repetition – and a bust. Her companion then had proved to be a paunchy Lebanese banker of pristine reputation and decidedly not disreputable enough for their purpose.

Abbot watched the girl step on to the diving-board again. He said suddenly, 'Do you know why this hotel is called the Saint-Georges, Dan?'

'No,' said Parker briefly in a tone which indicated that he could not care less.

Abbot waved his glass largely. 'Saint George killed the dragon right here in Beirut. So they tell me. Probably here in Saint George's Bay. But I've always thought the Christians pinched that bit from Greek mythology – Perseus and Andromeda, you know.' He gestured towards the girl on the diving-board. 'I wouldn't mind slaying a dragon myself if she were the prize.'

Parker moved restlessly in his chair, and Abbot thought he would have to do something about him. Dan would be all right once he had something to do with his hands, but this alien environment tended to unnerve him. He said, 'What's on your mind, Dan?'

'I still think this is a waste o' time.' Parker took out a handkerchief and mopped his brow. 'I wish I could have a beer. What wouldn't I give for a pint?'

'I don't see why you shouldn't have that,' said Abbot, and looked about for a waiter. 'Why didn't you order one?'

'What! In this place?' Parker was surprised. He associated English beer with the Edwardian glass of a London pub or the low beams of a country inn. 'I didn't think they'd serve it in a place as posh as this.'

'They make a living by serving what people want,' said Abbot drily. 'There's a Yank behind us drinking his Budweiser, so I don't see why you shouldn't have your pint.' He caught the eye of a waiter who responded immediately. 'Have you any English beer?'

'Certainly, sair, what would you like? Bass, Worthington, Watney's . . .'

'Watney's'll do fine,' said Parker.

'And I'll have another of these.' Abbot watched the waiter depart. 'See, Dan, it's easy.'

'I'd never 'a' thought it,' said Dan in wonder.

Abbot said, 'If an English millionaire comes here and can't get his favourite tipple he raises the roof, and that's bad for business. We'll probably have to pay a millionaire's price, but it's on the old expense account.'

Dan's wonder increased even more when he was presented with a pewter tankard into which he promptly disappeared. He came up for air with froth on his upper lip. 'It's a bit o' right stuff,' he said. 'Cold but in good condition.'

'Maybe it'll lighten your day,' said Abbot. He glanced at the bar check, winced, and turned it over so Dan would not see it. That would certainly take the edge off his simple pleasure, even though Hellier was paying for it. He slid his eyes sideways at Parker and saw that the familiar taste of the beer had eased him. 'Are you sure you're right about this torpedo thing? I mean, it can be done.'

'Oh, aye; I can do it. I can make those fish do tricks.'

'We don't want it to do tricks. We just want it to go a hell of a long way – five times further than it was designed to go.'

'Don't you worry yourself about that,' said Dan comfortably. 'I can do it. What I want to know is, can these people find a torpedo? They're not the easiest thing to come by, you know.'

That had been worrying Abbot, too, although he had not admitted it. It was one thing for Warren to come up with the nutty idea of smuggling by torpedo and another thing to implement it. If Delorme could not lay her hands on a torpedo then the whole scheme was a bust. He said, 'We'll worry about that when we come to it.'

They indulged in idle conversation while Abbot surveyed the procession to the diving-board with the air of a caliph at the slave market. But he still kept an eye on the restaurant entrance, and after half an hour had passed, he said quietly, 'Here she is. Drink up, Dan.'

Parker knocked back his second pint with the ease of long practice. 'Same as yesterday, then?'

'That's right. We follow the man – we know where we can pick her up.' Abbot paid the check while Parker sauntered out in the wake of Jeanette Delorme and her companion. He caught up just as Parker was unlocking the car.

'Fourth car along,' said Parker. 'It should be a doddle. But I hope this isn't another bloody banker.'

'I'll drive,' said Abbot, and slid behind the wheel. He watched the big Mercedes pull away, then engaged gear and drifted into the traffic stream three cars behind. 'I don't think this one's a banker. He has no paunch, for one thing; and he certainly doesn't look Lebanese.'

'I noticed you watchin' all those naked popsies paradin' up an' down in front of the hotel,' said Parker. 'But what do you think of that one ahead of us?'

'Our Jeanette?' Abbot concentrated on piloting the car out of the Rue Minet El Hosn. 'I've never thought of her in *that* way,' he said satirically. 'Come to think of it, she's not bad-looking but I've never had the chance of giving her a real slow and loving once-over. It's a bit hard to assess a woman when you're not supposed to be looking at her.'

'Come off it,' scoffed Parker.

'Oh, all right. She's a bit long in the tooth for me.' Abbot was twenty-six. 'But trim – very trim – very beddable.' He grimaced. 'But I think it would be like getting into bed with a spider.'

'What the hell are you talkin' about?'

'Didn't you know – female spiders eat their mates after they've had their bit of fun.' He turned into the Avenue Bliss, following the Mercedes at a discreet distance. As they passed the American University he said, 'I wonder why they're going this way; there's nothing at the end of here but the sea.'

'We'll see soon enough,' said Parker stolidly.

The Avenue Bliss gave way to the Rue Manarah and still the Mercedes carried on. As they rounded a bend the sea came into view, and Parker said warningly, 'Watch it! He's pullin' in.'

Abbot went by and rigidly prevented himself from look-ing sideways. He turned the corner and parked on the Corniche. 'That was a hotel,' he said, and pondered. He made up his mind. 'I'm going in there. As soon as that Mercedes takes off you follow it if the man is in it. Don't wait for me.'

'All right,' said Parker.

'And, Dan; be unobtrusive.'

'That goes for you too,' said Parker. He watched Abbot turn the corner into the Rue Manarah and then swung the car round to where he could get a view of the hotel entrance and still be in a position to follow the Mercedes which was still parked outside. Presently Delorme and the man came out together with a page who packed a lot of luggage in the boot.

The Mercedes took off smoothly and he followed, and soon found himself going along a familiar road – past the Lebanese University and Khaldeh Airport on the way to Hammana. He was almost tempted to turn back but he went on all the way until he saw Jeanette Delorme safely home with her guest. Then he drove back to Beirut, running into heavy traffic on the way back to the hotel.

Abbot was taking it easy when Parker walked in. 'Where the devil have you been, Dan?'

'The traffic's bloody awful at this time o' day,' said Parker irascibly. 'She took him home an' you know what the road out o' town is like. She took him home – bags an' all. Stayin' with her as a house guest, like.' He grinned. 'If he disappears then you'll know she really is a bloody spider. Did you get anythin'?'

'I did,' said Abbot. 'By exerting my famous charm on a popsy in that hotel I found that he is an American, his name is John Eastman, and he flew in from Tehran yesterday. Did you hear that, Dan? *Tehran*. It's the first link.'

II

It may have been the first link but it wasn't the last because Eastman proved to be almost as inaccessible as Delorme herself. 'A snooty lot, these heroin smugglers,' observed Abbot. 'They don't mix with the common herd.'

So they applied the same technique to Eastman. It was a painfully slow task to keep him under observation and then to tag his associates and they would have given up had they not known with certainty that they were on the right track. For Abbot received a letter from Hellier who was acting as a clearing house for information.

'Good news and bad,' said Abbot after he had read it.

'Let's have the bad news first,' said Parker. 'I might need to be cheered up after hearin' it.'

'Warren has lost Speering. He disappeared into the blue in the middle of Kurdistan. It's up to us now, Dan. I bet Nick's climbing the wall,' he said reflectively.

'We're not much forrarder,' said Parker gloomily.

'Oh, but we are. That's the good news. Eastman saw Speering the day before he gave Nick the slip. That directly links Speering with Delorme. This is the first bit of concrete evidence we've had yet. Everything else was just one of Nick Warren's hunches.'

Parker brightened. 'Aye, that's so. Well, let's get on wi' it.'

So they got on with it, but it was a long time before Abbot made the decision. 'This is the man,' he said. 'This is where we cast our bread upon the waters and hope it'll come back buttered on both sides.'

'Picot?'

Picot was a long way down the line. He knew a man who knew a man who knew Eastman. He was accessible and, Abbot hoped, receptive to new ideas if they were cast his way. He was also, to a keen and observant eye, a crook, which further raised Abbot's hopes.

'How do we tackle him?' asked Parker.

'The first thing is to move into a cheaper hotel.' He looked at Parker consideringly. 'We're not rolling in cash – but we're not dead broke. We're hungry for loot, but careful. We have something to sell and we want the best price, so we're cagey. Got the picture?'

Parker smiled sombrely. 'That bit about not rollin' in cash'll come easy to me; I've never had much money. How do we broach the subject to Picot?'

'We play it by ear,' said Abbot easily.

Picot frequented a cafe in the old town near the Port, and when Abbot and Parker strolled in the next evening he was sitting at a table reading a newspaper. Abbot selected a table just in front and to the side of him, and they sat down. Abbot wrinkled his nose as he looked at the food-spotted menu and ordered for both of them.

Parker looked about the place and said in a low voice, 'What now?'

'Take it easy,' said Abbot softly. 'Let it come naturally.' He turned and looked at the little pile of newspapers and magazines on Picot's table, obviously there for the use of the customers. In English, he said, 'Excuse me, monsieur; do you mind?'

Picot looked up and nodded shortly. 'Okay with me.' His English was incongruously tinged with a mixed French and American accent.

Abbot took a magazine and flipped the pages idly until the waiter served them, putting down many plates, two drinks and a jug of water. Abbot poured a little water into his glass and there was a swirl of milkiness. 'Cheers, Dan.'

Hesitantly Parker did the same, drank and spluttered. He banged down the glass. 'What is this stuff? Cough mixture?'

'The local white lightning – arak.'

Parker investigated his palate with his tongue. 'I haven't tasted anything like this since I were a boy.' He looked surprised as he made the discovery. 'Aniseed balls!' He sniffed the glass. 'It's no drink for a grown man. Any chance of a Watney's in here?'

Abbot grinned. 'I doubt it. If you want beer you have a choice of Lebanese French and Lebanese German.'

'Make it the German,' said Parker, so Abbot ordered him a Henninger Byblos and turned back to find him regarding the contents of the plates with deep suspicion.

'For God's sake, stop acting like a tourist, Dan,' he said with irritation. 'What do you expect here – fish and chips?'

'I like to know what I'm eatin',' said Parker, unmoved.

'It's *mezza*, said Abbot loudly. 'It's filling and it's cheap. If you want anything better go to the Saint-Georges – but I'm not paying. I'm getting fed up with you. I have a good mind to call the whole thing off.'

Parker looked startled but subsided as Abbot winked. The beer arrived and Parker tasted it and put down the glass. 'It'll do, I suppose.'

Abbot said quietly, 'Do you think you could . . . er . . . get pissed?'

Parker flicked the glass with his fingernail. 'It 'ud take more than this stuff. It's like maiden's water.'

'But you could try, couldn't you? You might even become indiscreet.'

'Then buy me another,' said Parker, and drained the glass with one mighty swallow.

Abbot made a good meal but Parker picked at his food fastidiously and drank more than was apparently good for him. His voice became louder and his words tended to slur together, and he seemed to be working up to a grievance. '*You* want to call it off – how do you suppose I feel? I get this idea – a bloody good idea – an' what are you doin' about it? Nothin' but sittin' on your upper-class bottom, that's what.'

'Quiet, Dan!' urged Abbot.

'I won't be bloody quiet! I'm gettin' tired o' your snipin', too.' His voice took on an ugly mimicry. '"Don't do this, Dan; don't do that, Dan; don't eat wi' your mouth open, Dan.' Who the hell do you think you are?'

'Oh, for God's sake!' said Abbot.

'You said you could help me wi' what I've got – an' what ha' you done? Sweet Fanny Adams!'

'It takes time to make the contact,' said Abbot wearily.

'You said you *had* the contacts,' said Parker venomously.

'What have you got to complain about,' said Abbot in a high voice. 'You're not paying for all this, are you? If it wasn't for me you'd still be on your arse in London fiddling around with beat-up cars and dreaming of how to make a quick fortune. I've laid out nearly a thousand quid on this, Dan – doesn't that count for anything?'

'I don't care whose money it is. You're still doin' nothin' an' you're wastin' my time.' Parker gestured largely towards the open door. 'That harbour's full o' ships, an' I bet half of 'em are in the smugglin' racket. They'd go for what I have in me noggin an' they'd pay big for it, too. You talk about me sittin' on me arse; why don't you get up off yours?'

Abbot was trying – unsuccessfully – to quiet Parker. 'For God's sake, shut up! Do you want to give everything away? How do you know this place isn't full of police?'

Parker struggled to his feet drunkenly. 'Aw, hell!' He looked around blearily. 'Where is it?'

Abbot looked at him resignedly. 'Through there.' He indicated a door at the back of the cafe. 'And don't get talking to any strange men.' He watched Parker stagger away, shrugged, and picked up the magazine.

A voice behind him said, 'Monsieur?'

He turned and found Picot looking at him intently. 'Yes?'

'Would I be right if I said that you and your friend are looking for . . . employment?'

'No,' said Abbot shortly, and turned away. He hesitated perceptibly and turned back to face Picot. 'What makes you think that?'

'I thought maybe you were out of work. Sailors, perhaps?'

'Do I look like a sailor?' demanded Abbot.

Picot smiled. 'No, monsieur. But your friend . . .'

'My friend's business is his.'

'And not yours, monsieur?' Picot raised his eyebrows. 'Then you are definitely not interested in employment?'

'What kind of employment?'

'Any man, particularly a sailor who has . . . ingenious ideas . . . there is always an opening for him in the right place.'

'I'm not a sailor. My friend was at one time. There'd have to be a place for me. We're great friends – inseparables, you know.'

Picot examined his finger-nails and smiled. 'I understand, monsieur. A great deal would depend on the ideas your friend has in mind. If you could enlighten me then it could be worth your while.'

'If I told you then you'd know as much as me, wouldn't you?' said Abbot cunningly. 'Nothing doing. Besides, I don't know who you are. I don't go a bundle on dealing with total strangers.'

'My name is Jules Fabre,' said Picot with a straight face.

Abbot shook his head. 'Means nothing to me. You *could* be a big-timer for all I know – and then again, you could be a cheap crook.'

'That's not very nice, monsieur,' said Picot reproachfully.

'I didn't intend it to be,' said Abbot.

'You are making things difficult,' said Picot. 'You can hardly expect me to buy something unknown. That is not good business. You would have to tell me sooner or later.'

'I'm not too worried about that. What Dan – my friend – has can only be made to work by him. He's the expert.'

'And you?'

Abbot grinned cheekily. 'You can say I'm his manager. Besides, I've put up the money so far.' He looked Picot up and down insultingly. 'And talking about money – what we've got would cost a hell of a lot, and I don't think a cheap chiseller like you has it, so stop wasting my time.' He turned away.

'Wait,' said Picot. 'This secret you have – how much do you expect to sell it for?'

Abbot swung around and stared at Picot. 'Half a million American dollars. Have you got that much?' he asked ironically.

Picot's lips twitched and he lowered his voice. 'And this is for smuggling?'

'What the hell do you think we've been talking about all this time?' demanded Abbot.

Picot became animated. 'You want to get in touch with someone at the top? I can help you, monsieur; but it will cost money.' He rubbed his finger and thumb together meaningfully and shrugged. 'My expenses, monsieur.'

Abbot hesitated, then shook his head. 'No. What we have is so good that the man at the top will pay you for finding us. Why should I grease your palm?'

'Because if you don't, the man at the top will never hear of you. I'm just trying to make a living, monsieur.'

Parker came back and sat down heavily. He picked up an empty bottle and banged it down. 'I want another beer.'

Abbot half-turned in his seat. 'Well, buy one,' he said irritably.

'Got no money,' said Parker. 'Besides,' he added belligerently, 'you're Mr Moneybags around here.'

'Oh, for Christ's sake!' Abbot took out his wallet, peeled off a note from the thin wad, and threw it on the table. 'Buy yourself a bucketful and swill in it. You can drown in the stuff for all I care.' He turned to Picot. 'All right – how much, you bloody twister?'

'A thousand pounds – Lebanese.'

'Half now and the other half when contact has been made.' He counted out notes and dropped them in front of Picot. 'All right?'

Picot put out his hand and delicately took the money. 'It will do, monsieur. What is your name and where can I find you?'

'My name doesn't matter and I'll be in here most evenings,' said Abbot. 'That's good enough.'

Picot nodded. 'You had better not be wasting time,' he warned. 'The man at the top has no use for fools.'

'He'll be happy with what we have,' said Abbot confidently.

'I hope so.' Picot looked at Parker who had bis nose deep in a glass. 'Your friend drinks too much – and talks too loudly. That is not good.'

'He's all right. He's just become edgy because of the waiting, that's all. Anyway, I can control him.'

'I understand your position – exactly,' said Picot drily. He stood up. 'I will be seeing you soon.'

Abbot watched him leave, then said, 'You wcrc great, Dan. Thc stage lost a great actor somewhere along the line.'

Parker put down his glass and looked at it without enthusiasm. 'I was pretty good at amateur theatricals at one time,' he said complacently. 'You paid him something. How much?'

'He gets a thousand pounds; I paid half.' Abbot laughed. 'Keep your hair on, Dan; they're Lebanese pounds – worth about half-a-crown each.'

Parker grunted and swirled the beer in his glass. 'It's still too much. This stuff is full of piss and wind. Let's go somewhere we can get a real drink, and you can tell me all about it.'

III

Nothing happened next day. They went to the café at the same time in the evening but Picot was not there, so they had a meal, chatted desultorily and went away. Despite his confident attitude Abbot was wondering whether Picot was genuine or whether he had paid over £60 to a smooth grafter he would never see again.

They were just about to leave for the café the next evening when there was a knock at the door. Abbot raised his eyebrows at Parker and went to open it. 'Who's there?'

'Fabre.'

He opened up. 'How did you know we were here?'

'That does not matter, Monsieur Abbot. You wish to speak to someone – he is here.' He jerked his eyes sideways. 'That will be five hundred pounds.'

Abbot glanced to where a tall man stood in the shadowed corridor. 'Don't try to con me, Fabre. How do I know it's the man I want? It could be one of your put-up jobs. I'll talk to him first, then you'll get your money.'

'All right,' said Picot. 'I'll be in the usual place tomorrow.'

He walked away down the corridor and Abbot waited at the door. The tall man moved forward and, as his face came out of shadow, Abbot knew he had hit the jackpot. It was Eastman. He stepped on one side to let him enter, and Eastman said in a flat mid-western accent, 'Was Picot trying to shake you down?'

Abbot closed the door. 'Who?' he said blankly. 'He said his name was Fabre.'

'His name is Picot and he's a chiselling nogoodnik,' said Eastman without rancour.

'Talking about names,' said Abbot. 'This is Dan Parker and I'm Mike Abbot. And you are . . . ?' He let the question hang in the air.

'The name is Eastman.'

Abbot smiled. 'Sit down, Mr Eastman. Dan, pull up a chair and join the congregation.'

Eastman sat down rigidly on the chair offered. 'I'm told you have something to sell me. Start selling.'

'I'll start off, Dan,' said Abbot. 'You can chip in when things become technical.' He looked at Eastman. 'I'm told there's a fair amount of smuggling goes on around here. Dan and I have got an idea – a good idea. The trouble is we don't have the capital to pull it off ourselves, so we're open to offers – on a participation basis, of course.'

'You don't get offered a cent until I know what you're talking about.'

'This is where the conversation gets tricky,' said Abbot. 'However, Dan tells me it doesn't matter very much if you know the secret. He thinks he's the only one around who can make it work. Of course, it wouldn't work with too much weight or bulk. What are you interested in smuggling?'

Eastman hesitated. 'Let's say gold.'

'Let's say gold,' agreed Abbot. 'Dan, how much could you carry – in weight?'

'Up to five hundred pounds.'

'Interested?' asked Abbot.

'Maybe. What's the gimmick?'

'This works when coming in from the sea. You shoot it in by torpedo.' Abbot looked at Eastman as though expecting a round of applause.

Eastman sighed and put his hands on the table as though to. lever himself up. 'You're wasting my time,' he said. 'Sorry.'

'Wait a minute,' said Abbot. 'Why are we wasting your time?'

Eastman stared at him and shook his head sadly. 'It's been tried before and it doesn't work very well. You're out of luck, boys.'

'Perhaps you were using the wrong torpedoes.'

'Perhaps.' Eastman looked at Abbot with renewed interest. 'What have you got?'

'You tell me what you want, then maybe we can get together.'

Eastman smiled thinly. 'Okay, I'll play ball; I've got ten minutes spare. A torpedo has only worked well once. That was on the Austrian-Italian border; a few smart-alick amateurs got hold of a torpedo and started smuggling across one of the little lakes up there. Booze one way and tobacco the other. They had the customs cops going nuts trying to figure out how it worked. Then some jerk shot off at the mouth and that was the end of it.'

'So?' said Abbot. 'It worked, didn't it?'

'Oh, it worked – but only across a half-assed pond. A torpedo doesn't have the range for what I want.'

'Can you get hold of a torpedo?'

'Sure – but for what? Those we can get hold of don't have the range, and those we could use are on the secret lists. Boy, if I could get hold of one of the modern underwater guided missile babies I'd be made.'

Parker broke in. 'What kind of torpedo can you get?'

Eastman shrugged. 'Those on the international arms market – models of the 'forties and 'fifties. Nothing really up to date.'

'What about the British Mark XI?'

'Those are available, sure. With a maximum range of three miles – and what the hell's the good of that?'

'Fifty-five hundred yards wi' batteries brought up to heat,' corrected Parker.

Abbot grinned. 'I think you'd better tell him, Dan.'

Parker said deliberately, 'I can get fifteen miles out o' a Mark XI.'

Eastman sat up straight. 'Are you on the level?'

'He is,' said Abbot. 'Danny boy can make a Mark XI sit up and do tricks. Meet Mr Parker, the best petty officer and torpedo mechanic the Royal Navy ever had.'

'You interest me,' said Eastman. 'Are you sure about that fifteen miles?'

Parker smiled slowly. 'I can pep up a Mark XI so you can stay safely outside the legal twelve mile limit an' shoot her ashore at thirty knots. No bubbles, either.'

'And carrying five hundred pounds' weight?'

'That's right.'

Eastman pondered. 'What about accuracy?'

'That depends on the fish you give me – some o' the guidance gear is a bit rough sometimes. But I can doctor it up if you let me have sea trials.' Parker scratched his jaw. 'I reckon

I could give an accuracy o' three inches in a hundred yards –
that's less than seventy yards out either way at fifteen miles.'

'Jesus!' said Eastman. 'That's not too bad.'

'You should be able to find a quiet beach that big,' said
Abbot. 'You'll have to find one that slopes pretty shallowly,
but that shouldn't be too difficult.'

'Wait a minute,' said Parker. 'That's the accuracy o' the
fish I'm talkin' about. Currents are somethin' else. You shoot
across a current an' the fish is goin' to be carried sideways,
an' don't forget it'll be in the water for half an hour. If you
have a cross-current of as little as half a knot then the fish
will get knocked five hundred yards off course. Still, if you
can plot the current you can compensate, an' you might
avoid the problem altogether if you shoot at slack water.'

'Yeah, that can be gotten around.' Eastman nibbled at a
joint of his thumb thoughtfully. 'You seem pretty certain
about this.'

'I am,' said Parker. 'But it's goin' to cost you a hell of a
lot. There's a torpedo in the first place an' a tube to go wi'
it; there's high-power mercury cells to be bought an' they
don't come cheap, an' there's . . .'

'. . .the cost of our services,' said Abbot smoothly. 'And
we don't come cheap, either.'

'If you can pull it off you'll get taken care of,' said
Eastman. 'If you don't you'll get taken care of another way.'
His eyes were chilling.

Parker was unperturbed. 'I'll show you that it can be
done first. You'll have sea trials.'

'Right,' said Eastman. 'I'll have to see the boss about this
first.'

'The boss!' said Abbot in surprise. 'I thought you were
the boss.'

'There are a lot of things you don't know,' said Eastman.
'Stick around and stay available.' He stood up. 'Where are
you guys from?'

'London,' said Abbot.

Eastman nodded. 'Okay – I'll be seeing you soon.'

'I don't want to seem too pushing,' said Abbot, 'but what about a retainer? Or shall we say you've just taken an option on our services which has to be paid for.'

'You've got a nerve.' Eastman pulled out his wallet. 'How much did Picot stick you for?'

'A thousand Lebanese pounds. Half down, half later.'

'Okay – here's two-five; that gives you two thousand clear profit so far – and you haven't done anything yet. If Picot asks you for the other five hundred tell him to see me.' He smiled thinly. 'He won't, though.' He turned abruptly and walked out of the room.

Abbot sat down slowly and turned to Parker. 'I hope to God you can handle your end. We've hooked them at last, but they've also hooked us. If we can't deliver we'll be in trouble.'

Parker filled his pipe with steady hands. 'They'll get what they want – an' maybe a bit more.' He paused. 'Do you think he'll check back to London?'

'He's sure to. You're all right, Dan; there's nothing in your background to worry him.' Abbot stretched. 'As for me – I had a flaming row with my editor just before I left, specially laid on. I'll bet the echoes are still reverberating down Fleet Street.' He grinned. 'I was fired, Dan – out on my can for unprofessional conduct unbefitting a journalist and a gentleman. I only hope it'll satisfy Eastman and company.'

IV

Eastman did not keep them waiting long. Three days later he rang up and said, 'Hello, Abbot; put on your best bib and tucker – you're going on the town tonight.'

'Where to?'

'Le Paon Rouge. If you don't have decent clothes, buy some out of the dough I gave you.'

'Who's paying for the night out?' asked Abbot in his character as a man on the make.

'It'll be paid for,' said Eastman. 'You're meeting the boss. Be on your best behaviour. I'll send a car for you at nine-thirty.'

Abbot put the phone on the hook slowly and turned to find Parker regarding him with interest. 'Have you got a dinner-jacket, Dan?'

Parker nodded. 'I packed it on the off-chance I'd need it.'

'You'll need it tonight. We've been invited to the Paon Rouge.'

'That'll be the third time I've worn it, then,' said Parker. He put his hand on his belly. 'Might be a bit tight. What's the Paon Rouge?'

'A night-club in the Hotel Phoenicia. We're meeting the boss, and if it's who I think it is, we've got it made. We've just been told tactfully to shave and brush our teeth nicely.'

'The Hotel Phoenicia – isn't that the big place near the Saint-Georges?'

'That's it. Do you know what a five-star hotel is, Dan?'

Parker blinked. 'The Saint-Georges?' he hazarded.

'Right! Well, there aren't enough stars in the book to classify the Phoenicia. Dope-smuggling must be profitable.'

They were picked up by the black Mercedes and driven to the Phoenicia by an uncommunicative Lebanese. Parker was unhappy because his doubts about his evening wear had been confirmed; his dress shirt had taken a determined grip on his throat and was slowly throttling him, and his trousers pinched cruelly at waist and crotch. He made a mental note to start a course of exercises to conquer his middle-age spread.

The name of Eastman dropped to an impressively-dressed major-domo brought them to Eastman's table with remarkable alacrity. The Paon Rouge was fashionably dark in the night-club manner, but not so dark that Abbot could not spot his quarry; Eastman was sitting with Jeanette Delorme and rose at their approach. 'Glad you could make it,' he said conventionally.

'Delighted, Mr Eastman,' said Abbot. He looked down at the woman. 'Is *this* the boss?'

Eastman smiled. 'If you cross her you'll find out.' He turned to her. 'This is Abbot, the other is Parker. Gentlemen – Miss Delorme.'

Abbot inclined his head and studied her. She was dressed in a simple sheath which barely covered her upperworks and she appeared to be, at the most, twenty-five years old. He knew for a fact that she was thirty-two, but it was wonderful what money would do. A very expensive proposition was Miss Delorme.

She crooked a finger at him. 'You – sit here.' There was a minor flurry as flunkies rearranged chairs and Abbot found himself sitting next to her and facing Parker, with a glass of champagne in his fingers. She studied Parker for a moment, then said, 'If what Jack tells me is true, I may be willing to employ you. But I need proof.' Her English was excellent and almost unaccented.

'You'll get your proof,' said Abbot. 'Dan will give you that.'

Parker said, 'There's plenty of sea out there. You can have trials.'

'Which torpedo would be most suitable?'

'Doesn't really matter,' said Parker. 'As long as it's an electric job.'

She twirled her glass slowly in her fingers. 'I have a friend,' she said. 'He was a U-boat captain during the war. His opinion of the British torpedo was very low. He said that on half the firings the British torpedo went wild.' Her voice became sharp. 'That would not be permissible.'

'Christ, no!' said Eastman. 'We can't lose a torpedo – not with what it will be carrying. It would be too goddam expensive.'

'Ah, you're talking about the early British torpedoes,' said Parker. 'The Mark XI was different. Your U-boat skipper was dead right – the early British fish were bloody awful. But the Mark XI was a Chinese copy o' the German fish an' it was very good when it came into service in '44. We pinched it from the Jerries, an' the Yanks pinched it from us. Any o' those torpedoes would be good enough but I'd rather have the old Mark XI – it's more familiar, like. But they're all pretty much the same an' just differ a bit in detail.'

'On what basis will you get the extra performance?'

'Look,' said Parker, leaning forward earnestly. 'The Mark XI came out in '44 an' it had lead-acid batteries – that was all they had in them days. Twenty-five years have gone by since then, an' things have changed. The new kalium cells – that's mercury oxide-zinc – pack a hell o' a lot more power, an' you can use that power in two ways. You can either increase the range or the speed. I've designed circuits for both jobs.'

'We're interested in increasing range,' said Eastman.

Parker nodded. 'I know. It's goin' to cost you a packet,' he warned. 'Mercury cells ain't cheap.'

'How much?' asked Delorme.

Parker scratched his head. 'Every time you shoot a fish it'll cost you over a thousand quid just for the power.'

She looked at Eastman, who interpreted, 'A thousand pounds sterling.'

Abbot sipped his champagne. 'The cost of everything is going up,' he observed coolly.

'That's a fact,' said Parker with a grin, 'Back in '44 the whole bloody torpedo only cost six hundred quid. I dunno what they cost now, though.'

'Fifteen hundred pounds,' said Eastman. 'That's the going rate on the surplus market.'

'There you are,' said Parker. 'Another thousand for a trial an' another for the real job, plus, say, five hundred for conversion. That's four thousand basic. Then there's our share on top o' that.'

'And what is your share?' asked Jeanette Delorme.

'A percentage of the profits,' said Abbot.

She turned to him. 'Indeed! And where do you come in on this? It seems that Parker is doing all the work.'

Abbot smiled easily. 'Let's say I'm his manager.'

'There are no passengers in the organization,' she said flatly.

Parker broke in. 'Me an' Mike are mates – I go where he goes, an' vicey-versey. Besides, I'll see he works hard – I can't do it all meself.'

'It's a package deal, you see,' said Abbot. 'And you talk business to me.'

'The profits on smuggling gold are not very big,' she said doubtfully.

'Oh, come off it,' said Abbot in disgust. 'You're not smuggling gold – you're running dope.'

She looked at Eastman and then back at Abbot. 'And how do you know that?' she asked softly.

'Just putting two and two together. There was a whisper in London – that's why we came out here.'

'That was one whisper too many,' she snapped.

Abbot smiled. 'I wouldn't worry too much about it. I was a professional in the whisper-listening business. It was just a matter of chance, and coming out here was a hell of a long shot.' He shrugged. 'But it's paid off.'

'Not yet,' she said pointedly. 'How much do you want?'

Twenty per cent of the take,' said Abbot promptly.

She laughed. 'Oh, what a stupid man we have here. Don't you think so, Jack?' Eastman grinned, and she said seriously, 'You will get one per cent and that will make you very rich, Monsieur Michael Abbot.'

'I may be stupid,' said Abbot, 'but I'm not crazy enough to take one per cent.'

Eastman said, 'I think you are crazy if you expect to get any kind of a percentage. We're not going to work that way.'

'That's right,' said Delorme. 'We'll give you a flat rate for the work. What would you say to a hundred thousand American dollars?'

Abbot raised his eyebrows. 'Each?'

She hesitated fractionally. 'Of course.'

'I'd say it's not on,' said Abbot, shaking his head. 'We'd want at least double that. Do you think I don't know what the profits are in this racket?'

Eastman chuckled raspingly. 'You're both stupid and crazy. Hell, you've given us the idea anyway. What's to prevent us going ahead without you?'

'Now who's being stupid?' asked Abbot. He pointed to Parker. 'Torpedo mechanics aren't easy to come by, and those who can do a conversion like this are even rarer. But a mechanic who can and is willing to run dope is as rare as a hen's tooth. You can't do it without us – and you know it.'

'So you figure you've got us over a barrel.' said Eastman ironically. 'Look, buster; a week ago we didn't even know you existed. We don't *need* you, you know.'

'But it's still a good idea, Jack,' said Delorme thoughtfully. 'Maybe Abbot will meet us half way.' She turned to him. 'This is final – take it or leave it. Three hundred thousand dollars for the two of you. One hundred thousand deposited in a bank here on the successful completion of trials – the rest when the job is done.'

Abbot said, 'What do you think, Dan?'

Parker's mouth was open. He closed it, and said, 'You have the business head; I'll leave it to you, Mike.' He swallowed convulsively.

Abbot pondered for a long time. 'All right; we'll take it.'

'Good!' said Delorme, and smiled radiantly. 'Order some more champagne, Jack.'

Abbot winked at Parker. 'Satisfied, Dan?'

'I'm happy,' said Parker faintly.

'I think payment by result is the best way,' said Abbot, and looked sideways at Eastman. 'If we'd have stuck to a percentage, Jack here would have cheated the pants off us. He wouldn't have shown us the books, that's for certain.'

Eastman grinned. 'What books?' He held up a finger and the sommelier came running.

Delorme said, 'I'd like to dance.' She looked at Abbot who began to rise, and said, 'I think I'll dance with . . . Mr Parker.'

Abbot subsided and watched her allow the bemused Parker to take her on to the floor. His lips quirked into a smile. 'So that's the boss. Something I hadn't expected.'

'If you're thinking what I think you're thinking – forget it,' advised Eastman. 'Jeanette isn't a girl to be monkeyed around with. I'd just as soon fight a buzz-saw with my bare hands.' He nodded towards the dance floor. 'Is Parker as good as he says he is?'

'He'll do the job. What's the cargo?'

Eastman hesitated briefly, then said, 'You'll get to know, I guess. It's heroin.'

'A full cargo – the whole five hundred pounds?'

'Yeah.'

Abbot whistled and calculated briefly. He laughed. 'That's worth about twenty-five million dollars, at least. I topped Jeanette's one per cent, anyway.'

'You're in the big time now,' said Eastman. 'But don't forget – you're still only a hired hand.' He lit a cigarette. 'That whisper you heard in London. Who did it come from?'

Abbot shrugged. 'You know how it is – a piece comes from here and another from there. You put them all together and get some sort of picture. I've had experience at it – I was a reporter.'

'I know,' said Eastman calmly. 'You've been checked out. We've got nothing on Parker yet, though.' He stared at

Abbot with hard eyes. 'You'd better not still be a reporter, Abbot.'

'I couldn't get a job on the *Tolpuddle Gazette*,' said Abbot bitterly. 'Not with the reputation I've got now. If you've been checking on me you know I was given the bum's rush. That's why I decided to come on this lark and make some real money.'

'Just a penny ante blackmailer,' agreed Eastman.

'They couldn't prove anything,' said Abbot defensively.

'Just keep your nose clean while you're with us,' said Eastman. 'Now, what can you tell us about Parker? The boss wants him checked out, too. She's very security-minded.'

Abbot obligingly gave him a run-down on Parker, sticking entirely to the known facts. There was no harm in that because the truth was exactly what would serve best. He had just finished when Jeanette and Parker returned to the table, Parker pink in the face.

Jeanette said, 'I don't think Dan is accustomed to modern dancing. What about you, Mike Abbot?'

Abbot stood up. 'Would you like to test me on a trial run?'

In reply she opened her arms as the opening bars of music started and he stepped forward. It was a slow and rather old-fashioned number so he took her in his arms and said, as they stepped on to the floor, 'What's a nice girl like you doing in a business like this?'

'I like the money,' she said. 'Just as you do.'

'You must be making quite a lot,' he said thoughtfully. 'It's not everyone who can lay hands on a hundred thousand dollars' loose cash – that's the boodle for the successful trial, in case you've forgotten. I take it this isn't a one-shot venture?'

'What do you care?'

'I like to stick where the money is. It would be nice if this built up into a regular income.'

She moved closer to him. 'There is no reason why not. All that is required is that you do your work and keep your mouth shut. Both are essential to your general health.'

'Would that be a threat?' asked Abbot lightly.

She snuggled up to him, pressing her body against his. 'It would. Nobody plays tricks with me, Monsieur Abbot.'

'No tricks intended,' said Abbot, chilled at the disparity between her words and her present actions. He had seen her dossier and it chimed in exactly with Eastman's description. A buzz-saw, he had said. Anyone laying a hand on Delorme or any of her dubious enterprises would draw back a bloody stump at best. And there was a list of six names of varied nationality to demonstrate the worst. He danced with five-foot-six of warm womanhood pressed vibrantly against him and thought that perhaps she was a spider, after all.

She breathed into his ear, 'You dance very well, Mike.' He winced as her teeth nipped his earlobe.

'Thanks, but there's no need to be so enthusiastic,' he said drily.

She giggled. 'Dan was shocked. He kept talking about his wife and children. Does he really have a wife and children?'

'Of course. Three kids, I think.'

'He is a peasant type,' she said. 'His brains are in his hands. You are different.'

Abbot chuckled internally at the outrage Parker would show at being described as a peasant. 'How am I different?'

'You know very well,' she said. 'Welcome to the organization, Mike. We'll try to keep you very happy.'

He grinned in the semi-darkness. 'Does that include Jack Eastman?'

'Never mind Jack Eastman,' she said, her voice suddenly sharp. 'Jack will do what I tell him. He doesn't . . .' She stopped speaking and made a sinuous movement so that her breasts nuzzled his chest. '*I'll* keep you very happy,' she whispered.

The music stopped and she stepped away from him after a lingering moment. He escorted her back to the table and thought he saw a satirical gleam in Eastman's eye.

'I'm not tired yet,' she said. 'It's nice having three escorts. Come on, Jack.'

Eastman took her on to the floor again and Abbot dropped into the chair next to Parker. He found he was sweating slightly. Must be the heat, he thought, and picked up his newly refilled champagne glass.

Parker looked at the throng on the dance floor. 'That woman scares mc,' he said gloomily.

'What did she do – try to rape you on the floor?'

'Bloody near.' Parker's brow turned pink again. 'By God, if my missus could have seen me there'd be a divorce tomorrow.' He tugged at his collar. 'She's a man-eater, all right.'

'It seems as though our jobs are neatly allocated,' said Abbot. 'You look after the torpedo and I look after Jeanette.' He sipped his champagne. 'Or she looks after me, if I understood her correctly.'

He found he was smiling.

They stayed for quite a while at the Paon Rouge, dining and watching the cabaret. They left at about two in the morning to find the Mercedes waiting outside. Eastman got in the front next to the driver, and Abbot found himself rubbing shoulders and legs with Jeanette who wore a shimmering silver cape.

The car moved away, and after a while he looked out of the window at the sea and said, 'It would be helpful if I knew where we were going.'

'You'll find out,' she said, and opened her cigarette case. 'Give me a light.'

He flicked his lighter and saw Parker sitting on the other side of Jeanette, easing his tight collar. 'You're the boss.'

The car proceeded smoothly on the road out of Beirut towards Tripoli and he wondered where it was taking them – and why. He did not wonder long because presently it swung off the road and drew up in front of a large wooden gate which was swung open by an Arab. The car rolled into a large yard and stopped.

They got out and Abbot looked around. As far as he could see in the darkness it seemed to be some sort of factory. A large shed loomed against the night sky, and beyond the moon sparkled on the sea. 'This way,' said Eastman, and Abbot followed him into an office.

The first thing he saw when the lights snapped on was his own suitcase against the wall. 'What the hell . . .?'

'You'll be staying here,' said Eastman. 'There are two beds in the next room. No bathroom, I'm afraid – but there's a wash-basin.' He glanced at Jeanette and then his gaze came back to Abbot. 'You should be quite comfortable,' he said sardonically. 'Ali will do your cooking.'

Jeanette said, 'You'll stay here until after the trials of the torpedo. How long you stay depends on yourselves.' She smiled and said lightly, 'But I'll come to see you – often.' She turned to Parker and said abruptly, 'How long to make the conversion?'

Parker shrugged. 'Two weeks – with the right equipment. A hell of a long time, or never, without it. But I'll have to have a torpedo first.'

She nodded. 'Come with me.' They followed her from the office and across the yard to the big shed. Ali, the Arab, produced a big key and unlocked the door, then stood back to allow them to enter. The shed was on two levels and they came out on a platform overlooking the main workshop. A flight of wooden stairs led down to ground level.

Abbot looked over the rail, and said, 'Well, I'm damned! You were pretty sure of us, weren't you?'

Illumined under harsh lighting was a sleek and deadly-looking torpedo set up on trestles, gleaming because of the thin film of protective oil which covered it. To Abbot it looked enormous, and the first thought that came into his head was: How in hell did this bitch lay her hands on a torpedo at three days' notice?

FIVE

Warren checked the maps again, and his pen traced out the record of their journeys. The two weeks they had spent in Kurdistan had been wasted, but he did not see how they could have done differently. There had been a chance, admittedly a slim one, of running across Speering, and they could not have passed it by. But it had been a futile two weeks.

So they had returned to Tehran in the hope of finding something, what he did not know. All he knew was that he had failed, and failed dismally. Every time he had to write to Hellier confessing failure he cursed and fretted. The only bright spot was that Abbot and Parker seemed to be making good in the Lebanon – it seemed that his 'insurance policy' might pay off in the end. But now they had dropped out of sight and he did not know what to make of it.

Johnny Follet took it all phlegmatically. He did not know what Warren was looking for so assiduously, nor did he care so long as he was paid. He had long ago written off his resentment against Warren and was quite enjoying himself in Tehran, and took it as a pleasant and exotic holiday. He wandered the streets and saw the sights, and presently found himself some congenial companions.

Ben Bryan was also uneasy, if not as much as Warren, but that may have been because he did not have Warren's overall responsibility. He and Warren pored over the maps of northwest Iran trying to figure out where Speering could have gone to ground. 'It's no use,' said Ben. 'If these maps were up to the standard of British Ordnance Survey we might have a hope, but half the damned roads up there aren't even shown here.'

'So what do we do?' asked Warren.

Ben did not know, and they all idled in low gear.

Andy Tozier had a problem – a minor problem, true – but still a problem, and it puzzled him mightily. He was losing money steadily to Johnny Follet and he could not see how the trick was worked. The money he lost was not much when considered against the number of games played, but the steady trickle annoyed him.

He spoke to Warren about it. 'On the face of it, it's a fair game – I can't see how he does it.'

'I wouldn't trust Johnny to play a fair game,' said Warren. 'What is it this time?'

'It goes like this. We each have a coin, and we match coins. We don't toss them, so the element of chance is eliminated as far as that goes – we each have control as to whether we show a head or a tail. Got that?'

'It seems all right so far,' said Warren cautiously.

'Yes,' said Tozier. 'Now, if I show heads and he shows tails he pays me thirty pounds. If I show tails and he shows heads he pays me ten pounds.'

Warren thought about it. 'Those are two of the four possible occurrences.'

'Right!' said Tozier. 'The other two occurrences are both heads or both tails. If either of those happen I pay him twenty pounds.'

'Wait a minute,' said Warren, and scribbled on a piece of paper. 'There are four possible cases of which you can win two and he can win two. Taking all four cases as equal – which they are – if they all happen you will win forty pounds – and so will he. It seems a fair game to me.' It also seemed a childish game but that he did not say.

'Then why the hell is he winning?' demanded Tozier. 'I'm nearly a hundred pounds down already.'

'You mean to say that you never win?'

'Oh, no. I win games and so does he – but he wins more often. It's a sort of see-saw, but he seems to have more weight than I have and my money tends to roll towards him. The thing that makes me wild is that I can't figure the gimmick.'

'Perhaps you'd better stop playing.'

'Not until I find out how he does it,' said Tozier determinedly. 'The thing that gets me is that it isn't as though he could ring in a double-headed penny – that wouldn't help him. Hell, it would make it worse for him because then I'd *know* what he was calling and I'd act accordingly.' He grinned. 'I'm willing to go another hundred just to find the secret. It's a profitable game – I could use it myself if I knew how.'

'It seems as though you'll have plenty of time to play,' said Warren acidly. 'We're getting nowhere here.'

'I've been thinking about that,' said Tozier. 'I've had an idea. What about that pharmaceutical place where Speering ordered his supplies? They'd deliver the stuff, wouldn't they? So they must have an address somewhere in their records. All we have to do is to extract it somehow.'

Warren looked at him wearily. 'Are you suggesting a burglary?'

'Something like that.'

'I've thought of it, too,' admitted Warren. 'But just tell me one thing. How the devil are we going to recognize what we want even if we see it? These people keep records in Persian, which is a foreign language to begin with, and in Arabic script which none of us can read. Could you sort it out, Andy?'

'Hell, I hadn't thought of that,' said Tozier. 'My colloqui-
al Arabic isn't bad but I can't read the stuff.' He looked up.
'Do you mind if I talk to Johnny about this?'

Warren hesitated. 'Not as long as you stick to generalities. I don't want him knowing too much.'

'I won't tell him more than he ought to know. But it's
about time he was put to work. He's a good con man and if
we can't get the information in any other way then perhaps
we can get it by Johnny's fast talk.'

So Tozier talked to Johnny Follet and Johnny listened.
'Okay,' he said. 'Give me a couple of days and I'll see what
I can come up with.' He disappeared into the streets of
Tehran and they did not see him for four days. When he
came back he reported to Tozier, 'It can be done. It'll take a
bit of fooling around, but it can be done. You can have the
information in less than a week.'

II

Follet's plan was so diabolical that it raised the hairs on the
back of Warren's head. He said, 'You've got an evil mind,
Johnny.'

'I guess so,' said Follet insouciantly. 'There's a part for
everyone – the more the merrier. But for Christ's sake take
it seriously; it's got to look good and real.'

Tell me more about this man.'

'He's assistant to the Chief Clerk in the Stores Department
of the company. That means he issues goods against indents
and keeps the books on quantities. He's just the guy to have
the information you need – or to be in a position to get it.
There's no money involved because he never handles it; all
that is done by the main office. That's a pity in a way because
we lose a chance of really hooking him.'

'Why don't we just bribe him?' asked Tozier.

'Because the guy's honest, that's why – or a reasonable facsimile. Suppose we tried to bribe him and it didn't take? He'd report to his bosses and the information would be whisked out of that office so fast that we wouldn't get another chance at it. And they might tell the police and then we'd be in trouble.'

'They might not tell the police,' said Warren. 'We don't know how much this firm is involved with Speering, but it's my guess that it's in on the whole thing. It must be. Any firm issuing certain chemicals and equipment has a damned good idea of what they'll be used for. It's my guess that this crowd is in it up to its collective neck.'

'What thing?' asked Follet alertly.

'Never mind, Johnny; carry on with what you were saying.'

Follet shrugged. 'This guy – Javid Raqi – is a bright boy. He speaks English well, he's had a good education and he's ambitious. I guess that chief clerk won't last long with friend Javid on his heels. He has only one flaw – he's a gambler.'

Tozier smiled. 'Your flaw, Johnny?'

'Not mine,' said Follet promptly. 'He's a sucker gambler. Now, that doesn't mean he's a fool. He's learned to play poker – the guys working on the gas line taught him – and he's a good player. I know because he's gotten some of my dough right now, and I didn't have to let him win it, either – he gouged it out of me like a pro. But it means he can be got at – he can be had; and once he's been got at then we squeeze him goddam hard.'

Warren wrinkled his nose distastefully. 'I wish there were some other way of doing this.'

'Never give a sucker an even break,' said Follet, and turned to Tozier. 'The whole scheme hinges on that video-tape gadget. How well does it work?'

'I have it set up in my room; it works very well.'

'That I have to see for myself,' said Follet. 'Let's all go up there.'

They all went up to Tozier's room and Tozier switched on the TV and pointed to the videotape machine. 'There it is. It's already connected to the TV set.'

The machine looked very much like an ordinary tape recorder, although bulkier than most. The tape, however, was an inch wide and the reels were oversized. Follet bent down and examined it interestedly. 'I'd like to get this just right; this gadget will take in everything – sight and sound both?'

'That's it,' said Tozier.

'How's the quality?'

'If you use the video-camera there's a bit of blurring, particularly on movement, but if you take a taping of a TV programme then the reproduction is indistinguishable from the original.' He looked at the TV screen. 'I'll show you now.'

A man was speaking and his voice was heard as Tozier turned up the volume. Warren did not know the language but it seemed to be a news broadcast because the man disappeared and a street scene replaced him, although his voice continued. Tozier bent down and flicked a switch and the reels began to turn, much faster than a normal recording machine. 'We're recording now.'

'That tape's fairly whipping through,' commented Follet. 'How long can you record?'

'An hour.'

'Hell, that's plenty.' He regarded the television screen for a while, then said, 'Okay, let's have a repeat.'

Tozier ran the tape back and switched the television set to a previously selected unused channel. He stopped the recorder and set it to playback, then snapped the starting switch. On the television screen appeared the street scene they had just witnessed, together with the voice of the announcer.

Follet bent forward with a critical eye on the screen. 'Hey, this quality's fine. It's just about as good as the original, like you said. This is going to work.'

He straightened. 'Now, look, the action starts on Saturday and you've got to get it right. Not only have you got to get every word right, but the way you say the word. No false notes.' He looked at them appraisingly. 'You're amateurs at this game, so we'll have some rehearsals. Imagine we're putting on a play and I'm the producer. You only have to play to an audience of one.'

'I can't act,' said Bryan. 'I never could.'

'That's okay – you can work this television gadget. As for the rest of us – I'll play the easy guy, Andy does the hard-nosed stuff, and Warren can be the boss.' Follet grinned as he saw the expression on Warren's face. 'You don't say much and you say it quietly. The way I figure it the less acting you do the better. An ordinary conversational tone can sound real menacing in some situations.'

He looked about the room. 'Now, where do we put Ben and the videotape?'

Tozier went to the window, opened it and looked out. 'I think I can run a line into your room, Johnny. We can settle Ben in there.'

'Good enough,' said Follet. He slapped his hands together, 'Okay, first rehearsal – beginners, please.'

III

At twelve-thirty on Saturday they waited in a lounge just off the foyer of the hotel, not exactly in hiding but certainly concealed from casual inspection. Follet nudged Warren. 'There he is – I told him to wait for me in the bar. You go in first; Andy will give you time to settle, and I'll be in right after. Get going.'

As Warren left, he said a little worriedly to Tozier, 'I hope Ben doesn't ball up his bit with the television.'

Warren crossed the foyer and entered the bar where he ordered a drink. Javid Raqi was seated at a table and appeared to be somewhat nervous, although probably not as nervous as Warren as he steeled himself to play his part in the charade. Raqi was a young man of about twenty-five, smartly dressed in European fashion from top to toe. He was darkly handsome if you like Valentino looks, and probably had a great future. Warren felt sorry for him.

Tozier appeared at the door, his jacket draped carelessly over his arm. He walked forward, past Raqi, and something apparently dropped from a pocket to plop right at Raqi's feet. It was a fat wallet of brown leather. Raqi looked down and stooped, then straightened with the wallet in his hand. He looked towards Tozier who had walked on without missing a pace, then followed him to the bar.

Warren heard the murmur of voices and then the louder tones of Tozier. 'Well, thank you. That was very careless of me. Allow me to buy you a drink.'

Johnny Follet was now in the room, on Raqi's heels. 'Hi, Javid; I didn't know you two knew each other.' There was surprise in his voice.

'We don't, Mr Follet,' said Raqi.

'Oh!' said Tozier. 'So this is who you were talking about, Johnny. Mr Raqi – that's the name, isn't it? – just rescued my wallet.' He opened it to display a thick wad of notes. 'He could have taken the lot without winning it.'

Follet chuckled. 'He'll probably take it anyway. He's a right sharp poker-player.' He looked around. 'There's Nick. It'll be a foursome, Javid; does that suit you?'

Raqi said a little shyly, 'That's all right, Mr Follet.'

'The hell with Mr Follet. We're all friends here. I'm Johnny and this is Andy Tozier – and coming over is Nick

Warren. Gentlemen, Javid Raqi, the best poker-player I've come across in Tehran – and I'm not kidding.'

Warren smiled stiffly at Raqi and murmured something conventional. Follet said, 'Don't buy a drink, Andy; let's go where the action is. I have everything laid on – booze and food both.'

They all went up to Tozier's room, where the television set had been moved over to the window. Follet had laid on quite a spread; there was cold chicken, sausages of various sorts and salads, together with some unopened bottles of whisky. Everything was set for a long session. Unobtrusively, Warren looked at his watch – it read just after twelve – exactly half an hour slow. He wondered how Follet would doctor the expensive-looking watch he saw on Raqi's slim brown wrist without Raqi knowing it had been done.

Follet opened a drawer and tossed a sealed pack of cards on to the table. 'There you are, Javid; you have first deal. Stranger's privilege – but you won't be a stranger long. Go easy on the water in mine, Nick.'

Warren poured four drinks and brought them to the table. Raqi was shuffling the cards. He seemed to do it expertly enough, although Warren was no judge of that. He was not as good as Follet, of that he was sure.

Follet looked about the table. 'We'll be confining our-selves to draw poker, gentlemen – there'll be none of your fancy wild hands here; this is a serious game for serious gamblers. Let's play poker.'

Raqi dealt the cards, five to each, and said in a quiet voice, 'Jacks or better open.'

Warren looked at his cards. He was not a good poker-player, although he knew the rules. 'That doesn't matter,' Follet had said. 'You don't want to win, anyway.' But he had schooled Warren in a couple of intensive lessons all the same.

At the end of the first hour he was losing – about four thousand rials to the bad – say twenty-two pounds. Tozier had lost a little, too, but not nearly as much. Follet had won a little and Raqi was on top, winning about five thousand rials.

Follet riffled the cards. 'What did I tell you? This boy can play poker,' he said jovially. 'Say, that's a nice watch you have there, Javid. Mind if I have a look at it?'

Raqi was flushed with success and was not nearly as shy and nervous as he had been at first. 'Of course,' he said easily, and slipped it from his wrist.

As Follet took it, Warren said, 'You speak very good English, Javid. Where did you learn it?'

'I studied at school, Nick; then I went to night classes.' He smiled. 'This is where I practise it – at the poker table.'

'You're doing very well.'

Tozier counted his money. 'Play poker,' he said. 'I'm losing.'

Follet grinned. 'I warned you Javid would take your wad.' He held out the watch on his forefinger, but somehow it seemed to slip and it dropped to the floor. Follet pushed back his chair and there was a crunch. 'Oh, hell!' he exclaimed in disgust, and picked up the watch. 'I've bust the dial.' He held it to his ear. 'It's still going, though.'

Raqi held out his hand, 'It does not matter, Johnny.'

'It matters to me,' said Follet. 'I'll have it fixed for you.' He dropped it into his shirt pocket. 'No, I insist,' he said over Raqi's expostulations. 'I did the damage – I'll pay for the fixing. Whose deal is it?' Raqi subsided.

They continued to play and Raqi continued to win. As far as Warren could judge he was a good natural poker-player and he did not think Follet was discreetly assisting him, although he did not have the special knowledge to know if this was correct. He did know that he himself was losing steadily, although he played as best he could. Tozier recouped his earlier losses and stood about even, but Follet was on the losing side.

The haze of cigarette smoke in the room grew thicker and Warren began to get a slight headache. This was not his idea of a pleasant Saturday afternoon's entertainment. He glanced at his watch and saw that it read half-past-two. Ben Bryan, in the next room, ought to be busy taping the television programme.

At quarter to three Tozier threw in his hand with an expression of disgust. 'Hey !' he said in alarm. 'You'd better make that call.'

Follet looked at his watch. 'Christ, I nearly forgot. It's quarter to three already.' He stood up and walked over to the telephone.

'I thought it would be later than that,' said Raqi in mild surprise.

Warren uncovered his watch with the dial turned towards Raqi. 'No – that's all it is. It might be a bit late for us, though.'

Follet had his hand on the telephone when Tozier said curtly, 'Not that one, Johnny. Make the call from the lobby.' He jerked his head at Raqi meaningly.

'Javid's all right,' said Follet easily.

'I said make it from the lobby.'

'Don't be so hard-nosed, Andy. Here you have a guy who was honest enough to give you back your wallet when he didn't know who the hell you were. Why cut him out?'

Warren said quietly, 'You always were a hard case, Andy.'

Raqi was looking from face to face, not understanding what was going on. Tozier shrugged with ill-grace. 'No skin off my nose – but I thought you wanted to keep it quiet.'

'It doesn't matter,' said Warren indifferently. 'Javid's all right – we know that. Make the call, Johnny; it's getting late. If we argue over it any more we'll miss post time.'

'Okay,' said Follet and began to dial. His body screened the telephone from view. There was a pause. 'Is that you, Jamshid? . . . Yeah, I know; things are bad all round . . . this time I'm going to win, I promise you . . . I'm still in time for the three o'clock race – make it twenty thousand rials on Al Fahkri.' He turned and grinned at Raqi. 'Yeah, on the nose . . . and, say, put on another two thousand for a friend of mine.'

He put down the telephone. 'The bet's on, boys; the odds are eight to one. And there's two thousand on for you, Javid.'

'But, Johnny, I don't bet the horses,' protested Raqi. 'Two thousand rials is a lot of money.'

'Have it on the house,' said Follet generously. 'Andy's putting up the stake as a penance. Aren't you, Andy?'

'Go to hell,' said Tozier morosely.

'Quit worrying, Javid,' said Follet. 'I'll stake you.' He turned to Warren. 'The kid can stay and watch. None of us can speak the lingo, so he can tell us which horse wins – as if we didn't know.'

'Why don't you keep your big mouth shut?' said Tozier in exasperation.

'It's all right, Andy,' said Warren. 'Johnny's right; you're a mean, ungrateful bastard. How much did you have in your wallet when you dropped it?'

'About a hundred thousand rials,' said Tozier reluctantly.

Follet was outraged. 'And you're being hard-nosed about giving the kid a reward,' he cried. 'Hell, you don't even have to pay it yourself. Jamshid will do the paying.' He turned to Raqi. 'You know Jamshid, kid?'

Raqi gave a small smile. He was embarrassed because he was unaccountably the centre of an argument. 'Who doesn't in Tehran? Anyone who bets the horses goes to Jamshid.'

'Yeah, he's got quite a reputation,' agreed Follet. 'He pays out fast when you win, but God help you if you don't pay him equally fast when you lose. A real tough baby.'

'What about watching us win our money?' suggested Warren. He nodded towards the television set. 'The race should be corning on soon.'

'Yeah,' said Follet and stepped over to the set. Warren crossed his fingers, hoping that Ben had done his job. He had already got the name of the winner of the three o'clock race and transmitted it to Follet during the fake telephone call to Jamshid, but if he had fumbled the recording then the whole scheme was a dead loss.

A voice swelled in volume, speaking Persian, and then the screen filled with a view of a racecourse crowd. Follet looked at the screen appraisingly, and said, 'About five minutes to go.' Warren let out his pent-up breath silently.

'What's he saying?' asked Tozier.

'Just talking about the horses,' said Raqi. He listened for a while. 'That's Al Fahkri – your horse – number five.'

'Our horse, Javid,' said Follet jovially. 'You're in on this.' He got up and went to the impromptu bar at the sideboard. 'I'll pour the drinks for the celebration now. This race will be fast.'

'You seem certain you'll win,' said Raqi.

Follet turned and winked largely. 'Certain isn't the word for it. This one's blue chip – a gilt-edged security.' He took his time pouring the drinks.

Tozier said, 'They're coming up to the post, Johnny.'

'Okay, okay; it doesn't really matter, does it?'

The commentator's voice rose as the race started, and Warren thought that it did not matter whether you understood the language or not, you could never mistake a horse race for anything else. Raqi was tense as Al Fahkri forged ahead of the pack on the heels of the leading horse. 'He stands a chance.'

'More than that,' said Follet unemotionally. 'He's going to win.'

Al Fahkri swept ahead to win by two lengths.

Warren got up and switched off the set. 'That's it,' he said calmly.

'Here, kid; have a drink on Jamshid,' said Follet, thrusting a glass into Raqi's hand. 'The honest bookie who never welshes. You're a bit richer than you were this morning.'

Raqi looked at the three of them in turn. Warren had produced a notebook and was methodically jotting down figures; Tozier was gathering up the cards scattered on the table; Follet was beaming in high good humour. He said, hesitantly. 'The race was . . . arranged?'

'Fixed is the word, kid. We've bought a couple of good jockeys. I told you it was a gilt-edged investment.'

Guilt-edged would be more like it, thought Warren.

Follet took a wallet from his jacket which was draped over the back of a chair and counted out notes. 'You don't have to wait to collect from Jamshid,' he said. 'I'll do that when I collect ours.' He tossed a roll of currency on the table before Raqi. 'It was eight to one – there's your sixteen thousand.' He grinned. 'You don't get your stake back because it wasn't yours. Okay, kid?'

Raqi took the money in his hands and gazed at it in wonder. 'Go ahead,' said Follet. 'Take it – it's yours.'

'Thanks,' said Raqi, and put the money away quickly.

Tozier said briefly, 'Let's play poker.'

'That's an idea,' said Follet. 'Maybe we can win that sixteen thousand from Javid.' He sat down as Warren put away the notebook. 'What's the score so far, Nick?'

'Just under two million,' said Warren. 'I think we ought to give it a rest for a while.'

'When we're hitting the big time? You must be crazy.'

'Jamshid will be getting worried,' said Warren. 'I know we've played it clever – he doesn't know the three of us are a syndicate – but he'll tumble to it if we don't watch it. Knowing Jamshid, I wouldn't like that to happen. I'd like to stay in one piece for a while longer.'

'Okay,' said Follet resignedly. 'Next Saturday is the last – for a while. But why not make it a really big hit this time.'

'No!' said Tozier abruptly.

'Why not? Supposing we put on a hundred thousand at ten to one. That's another quick million.' Follet spread his hands. 'Makes the arithmetic easier, too – a million each.'

'It's too risky,' Warren insisted.

'Say, I have an idea,' said Follet excitedly. 'Jamshid doesn't know Javid here. Why can't Javid lay the bet for us? It's good for us and it's good for him. He can add his own dough and make a killing for himself. How about that, Javid?'

'Well, I don't know,' said Raqi uncertainly.

Tozier looked interested. 'It *could* work,' he said thoughtfully.

'You could be a rich man, Javid,' said Follet. 'You take that sixteen thousand you just won and you could turn it into a hundred and sixty thousand – that's as much as the three of us made today. And you can't miss – that's the beauty of it.'

Raqi took the hire as a trout takes a fly. 'All right,' he said suddenly. 'I'll do it.'

'Very well,' said Warren, capitulating. 'But this is the last time this year. Is that understood?'

Follet nodded, and Tozier said, 'Let's play poker.'

'Until six o'clock,' said Warren. 'I have a date tonight. Win or lose we stop at six.'

He won back most of his losses during the rest of the afternoon. Some of it was made by a big pot won on an outrageous bluff, but he seemed to have much better hands. At six o'clock he was down a mere thousand rials. He had unobtrusively put his watch right, too.

'That's it,' said Follet. 'See you next week, Javid.' He winked. 'You'll be in the big time then.'

When Raqi had gone Warren got up and stretched. 'What a way to pass a day,' he said.

'Our boy's very happy,' said Follet. 'He's broken into the big time and it hasn't cost him a cent. Let's figure out how much he's into us for. What did you lose, Warren?'

'A thousand as near as damn it.'

'Andy?'

'Close on three thousand. He can play poker.'

'That he can,' said Follet. 'I had to cut into him after the race – I didn't want him to think he can make more playing poker than playing the horses.' He looked up at Warren. 'You're no poker player. Now, let's see – I'm out a thousand, so he's taken a total of twenty-one thousand, including that dough I gave him for the race. He'll be back next week.'

'Greedy for more,' said Tozier. 'I thought you said he was honest.'

'There's a bit of larceny in all of us,' said Follet. 'Cheating a bookie is considered respectable by a lot of upright citizens – like smuggling a bottle of whisky through customs.' He picked up the pack of cards and riffled them. 'There's an old saying among con men – you can't cheat an honest man. If Javid was really honest this thing wouldn't work. But he's as honest as most.'

'Can you really take money off him at poker?' asked Warren. 'A lot depends on that.'

'I was doing it this afternoon, wasn't I?' demanded Follet. 'You ought to know that better than anyone. You don't think you started winning by your own good play.' He extended the pack to Warren. 'Take the top card.'

Warren took it. It was the nine of diamonds.

Follet was still holding the pack. 'Put it back. Now I'm going to deal that top card on to the table. Watch me carefully.' He picked up the top card and spun it smoothly on to the table in front of Warren. 'Now turn it over.'

Warren turned over the ace of clubs.

Follet laughed. 'I'm a pretty good second dealer. I dealt the second card, not the top card, but you didn't spot it.' He held up his hand. 'If you see any guy holding a pack of cards like this, don't play with him. That's the mechanic's grip, and he'll second deal you, bottom deal you, and strip your pockets. I'll take Javid Raqi all right.'

IV

It was a long week. Warren understood the necessity for inaction but it still irked him. Tozier and Follet played their coin-matching game interminably and Tozier steadily lost, much to his annoyance. 'I'll figure this out if it's the last thing I do,' he said, and Follet chuckled comfortably.

Warren could not see the fascination the game held for Tozier. It seemed to be a childish game although there *was* the problem of why Follet won so consistently in what seemed to be an even game in which there was no possibility of cheating.

Bryan was as restless as Warren. 'I feel out of it,' he said. 'Like a spare wheel. I feel as though I'm doing nothing and going nowhere.'

'You're not the only one who feels that way,' said Warren irritably.

'Yes, but I was stuck playing with that bloody video recorder while you three were having all the fun.'

'That's the most important part, Ben.'

'Maybe – but it's over now. You won't need the recorder this time. So what do I do – twiddle my thumbs?'

Follet looked up. 'Wait a minute.' He eyed Ben speculatively. 'Maybe we're passing up a chance here. I think we can use you, Ben, but it'll need a bit of rehearsal with me and Andy. It'll be important, too. Are you game for it?'

'Of course,' said Bryan eagerly.

So the three of them went to Follet's room with Follet saying, 'Nothing to trouble you with, Nick; it's best you don't know what's going to happen. You're a lousy actor, anyway, and I want this to come as a real surprise.'

Came Saturday and Javid Raqi arrived early. Follet had tele-phoned him and suggested a lengthened session starting in the morning, and Raqi had eagerly agreed. 'We've got to have time to strip the little bastard,' said Follet cynically.

They started to play poker at ten-thirty and, to begin with, Raqi won as he had the previous week. But then things seemed to go against him. His three kings were beaten by Warren's three aces; his full house was beaten by Tozier's four threes; his ace-high flush was beaten by Follet's full house. Not that this seemed to happen often but when it did the pots were big and Raqi lost heavily. His steady trickle of winning hands was more than offset by his few occasional heavy losses.

By midday he had exhausted the contents of his wallet and hesitantly drew out an envelope. Impatiently he ripped it open and spilled a pile of money on to the table.

'Are you sure you want to do that?' asked Follet gently.

'I still have money – plenty money,' said Raqi tensely.

'No offence,' said Follet as he gathered the cards. 'I guess you know what you're doing. You're a big boy now.' He dealt cards. Javid Raqi lost again.

By two in the afternoon Raqi was almost cleaned out. He had been holding his own for about half an hour and the money in front of him – about a thousand rials – ebbed and flowed across the table but, in the main, stayed steady. Warren guessed that Follet was organizing that and he felt a little sick. He did not like this cat and mouse game.

At last Tozier looked at his watch. 'We'd better switch to the horses,' he said. 'There's not much time.'

'Sure,' said Follet. 'Put up the stake, Nick; you're the banker. Javid, you know what to do?'

Raqi looked a little pale. 'Just make the phone call,' he said listlessly as Warren counted out large denomination notes on to the table.

'Hell, no !' said Follet. 'Jamshid doesn't accept credit bets over twenty-five thousand, and we three are putting up a hundred thousand. You have to stake it at Jamshid's place – cash on the barrel head. How much are you putting in, Javid?'

Raqi swallowed. 'I don't know.' He made a feeble gesture at the table. 'I've . . . I've lost it,' he said plaintively.

'Too bad,' said Tozier evenly. 'Better luck next time.'

Warren patted the notes together. 'A hundred thousand,' he said, and pushed the stack across the table.

'You'll still put this on for us, won't you?' said Follet, pushing the money across to Raqi. 'You said you would.'

Raqi nodded. He hesitated, then said, 'Could . . . could you . . . er . . . could you lend me some – until it's over?'

Follet looked at him pityingly. 'Hey, kid; you're in the big time now. You play with your own dough. You might swap nickels and dimes in a penny-ante school but not here.'

Tozier's snort of disgust seemed to unnerve Raqi and he flinched as though someone had hit him. 'But . . . but . . .' he stammered.

Warren shook his head. 'Sorry, Javid; but I thought you understood. Everybody here stands his own racket.' He paused. 'I suppose you could say it's not good form – not good etiquette – to borrow.'

Raqi was sweating. He looked at the backs of his hands which were trembling, and thrust them into his pockets. He swallowed. 'When do I have to go to Jamshid's?'

'Any time before the nags go to the post,' said Follet. 'But we'd like to get the dough in fairly early. We don't want to miss out on this – it's the big one.'

'Do you mind if I go out for a few minutes?' asked Raqi.

'Not so long as you're back in time,' said Follet. 'This is the big one, like I told you.'

Raqi got up. 'I'll be back soon,' he said in a husky voice. 'Not more than half an hour.' He went out and seemed to stumble at the door.

Follet listened for the click of the latch, then said softly. 'He's hooked.'

'But *will* he come back?' asked Warren.

'He'll be back. When you put a sucker on the send he *always* comes back,' said Follet with cynical certitude.

'How much did we take him for?' asked Tozier.

Follet counted money and did a calculation. 'I make it just over forty-eight thousand. He must have drawn out his savings for the big kill, but we got to it first. He'll be sweating blood right now, wondering where to raise the wind.'

'Where will he get it?' asked Warren.

'Who cares? But he'll get it – that's a certainty. He *knows* he's on to a good thing and he won't pass up the chance now. He won't be able to resist cheating Jamshid, so he'll find the dough somehow.'

Tozier and Follet matched coins while they waited for Raqi to come back – a sheep to the slaughter – and Follet came out the worse for a change. He shrugged. 'It doesn't matter – the percentages are still on my side.'

'I wish I knew how,' said Tozier venomously. 'I'll get to the bottom of this one yet. I think I can see a way.'

There was a soft knock at the door. 'That's our boy,' said Follet.

Javid Raqi came into the room quietly when Follet opened the door. He came up to the table and looked at the hundred thousand rials, but he made no move to touch the money. Warren said, 'All right, Javid?'

Slowly Raqi put out his hands and took the wad of notes. 'Yes,' he said. 'I'm ready.' He turned suddenly to

Follet. 'This horse *will* be all right – it *will* win?' he asked urgently.

'Christ !' said Follet. 'You're holding a hundred thousand of our money and you ask that? Of course it will win. It's all set up.'

'Then I'm ready to go,' said Raqi, and swiftly put away the money.

'I'll go with you,' said Follet. He grinned. 'It's not that we don't trust you, but I'd hate some smart guy to knock you off when you're carrying our dough. Consider me a body-guard.' He put on his jacket. 'We'll be back to watch the race,' he said as he left, shepherding Raqi before him.

Warren sighed. 'I feed sorry for that boy.'

'So do I,' said Tozier. 'But it's as Johnny said – if he were honest this would never be happening to him.'

'I suppose so,' said Warren, and fell silent. Presently he stirred and said, 'Supposing the horse wins?'

'It won't,' said Tozier positively. 'Johnny and I picked the sorriest screw we could find. It *might* win,' he conceded, 'if every other horse in the race breaks a leg.'

With what might have been a chuckle Warren said, 'But what if it does win? Someone must have faith in it.'

'Then we'll have won a hell of a lot of money – and so will Raqi, depending on how much of a stake he's been able to raise. We'll have to go through the whole business of breaking him again. But it won't happen.'

He began to match coins with himself and Warren paced up and down restlessly. Follet and Raqi were away for quite a long time and arrived back just as Warren switched on the set to get the race. Raqi sat at his place at the table; a slight, self-contained figure. Follet was jovial. 'Javid has the jitters. I keep telling him it'll be okay, but he can't stop worrying. He's been plunging, too – I reckon this is a bit too rich for his blood.'

'How much did you back the nag for?' asked Tozier curiously.

Raqi did not answer, but Follet gave a booming laugh. 'Fifty thousand,' he said. 'And the odds are fifteen to one. Our boy stands to make three-quarters of a million rials. I keep telling him it's okay, but he doesn't seem to believe me.'

Tozier whistled. Three-quarters of a million rials was about £4,000 – a fortune for a young Iranian clerk. Even his fifty thousand stake was a bit rich – about £260 – approximating to a sizeable bite of Raqi's annual income. He said, 'Where did you get that much? Did you go home and break open your piggy bank?'

Warren said sharply, 'Shut up! The race is about to start.'

'I'll pour the drinks for the celebration,' said Follet, and went over to the sideboard. 'You guys can cheer for me – the nag's name is Nuss el-leil.'

'I don't get the lingo,' said Tozier. 'What's that mean, Javid?'

Raqi opened bloodless lips. He did not take his eyes off the screen as he answered, 'Midnight.'

'A good name for a black horse,' commented Tozier. 'There they go.'

Warren glanced sideways at Raqi who was sitting tensely on the edge of his chair, the bluish gleam of the television screen reflected in his eyes. His hands were clasped together in a knuckle-whitening grip.

Tozier jerked irritably. 'Where the blazes is that horse? Can you see it, Javid?'

'It's lying fourth,' said Raqi. A moment later he said, 'It's dropped back to fifth – no, sixth.' A tremor developed in his hands.

'What's that bloody jockey up to?' demanded Tozier. 'He's throwing it away, damn him!'

Fifteen seconds later the race ended. Nuss el-leil was not even placed.

Follet stood transfixed at the sideboard. 'The little bastard double-crossed us,' he breathed. In a moment of savagery he hurled a full glass of whisky at the wall where it smashed explosively. 'I'll fix his goddam wagon come tomorrow,' he yelled.

Warren switched off the set. 'Calm down, Johnny. I told you it couldn't last forever.'

'Yeah, but I didn't reckon it would end this way,' said Follet bellicosely. 'I thought Jamshid would cotton on to us. I didn't think I'd be gypped by that little monkey on the horse. Wait until I get my hands around his scrawny neck.'

'You'll leave him alone,' said Warren sharply. In a more placatory tone he said, 'So we've lost a hundred thousand – that's only five per cent of our winnings up to now. We're all right.' He sat at the table and gathered the cards. 'Who's for a game?'

'I reckon Johnny's right,' said Tozier in a hard voice. 'We can't let this pass. No jock is going to get the better of me, I tell you that. When I buy a jockey, he bloody well stays bought.'

'Forget it,' said Warren curtly. 'That particular game is over – we move on to something else. I told you this was the last time, didn't I?' He looked over his shoulder. 'For God's sake, come over here and sit down, Johnny. The world hasn't come to an end. Besides, it's your deal.'

Follet sighed as he took his seat. 'Okay – but it goes against the grain – it really does. Still, you're the boss.' He riffle-shuffled the pack and pushed it across the table. 'Your cut.'

Javid Raqi sat frozen and did not move.

'Hey!' said Follet. 'What's the matter, kid? You look as though you've seen a ghost.'

Two big tears squeezed from Raqi's eyes and rolled down his cheeks.

'For God's sake!' said Tozier in disgust. 'We've got a crybaby on our hands.'

'Shut up, Andy!' said Warren savagely.

'What's the matter, Javid?' asked Follet. 'Couldn't you stand the racket? Couldn't you afford the fifty thousand?'

Raqi seemed to be staring at an inward scene of horror. His olive complexion had turned a dirty green and he was trembling uncontrollably. He moistened his lips, and whispered, 'It wasn't mine.'

'Oh, that's bad,' said Follet commiseratingly. 'But remember what I told you – you should always play with your own money. I did tell you that, you know – and so did Nick.'

'I'll lose my job,' said Raqi. His voice was filled with desperation. 'What will my wife say? What will she say?' His voice rose and cracked. Suddenly he was babbling in Persian and none of them could understand what he was saying.

Follet's hand came out sharply and cracked Raqi across the cheek, shocking him into silence. 'Sorry about that, Javid; but you were becoming hysterical. Now, calm down and talk sense. Where did you get the dough?'

'From the place I work,' said Raqi, swallowing hard. 'The chief clerk has a safe – and I have a key. He keeps money for out-of-hand expenses. I went back to the office and . . . and . . .'

'Stole the money,' said Tozier flatly.

Raqi nodded dejectedly. 'He'll know as soon as he opens the safe on Monday. He'll know it's . . .'

'Take it easy, kid,' said Follet. 'You're not in jail yet.'

That was an aspect that had not hit Raqi, and he stared at Follet with renewed horror. Follet said, 'Maybe we can help you.'

'Count me out,' said Tozier uncompromisingly. 'I'm not going to subsidise a freeloading kid who's still wet behind the ears. If he can't stand the heat, let him get out of the kitchen. He should never have come into this game, anyway. I told you that in the first place.'

Warren looked at Follet who just shrugged, and said, 'I guess that's so. You've gotta learn by your mistakes, kid. If we bail you out now, you'll do it again some time else.'

'Oh, no; I promise – I promise.' Raqi spread his arms wide on the table, grovelling before Follet. 'Help me – please help me – I promise . . .'

'Oh, for Christ's sake, stand up and be a man!' barked Tozier. He stood up. 'I can't stand scenes like this. I'm getting out.'

'Wait a minute,' said Follet. 'I think I've got something.' He pointed his finger at Tozier. 'Weren't you telling me about a guy who wanted to get something from the company this kid works for? Something about some chemicals?'

Tozier thought for a moment, then nodded. 'What about it?'

'How much would he pay?'

'How the hell do I know?' said Tozier in a pained voice. 'This chap was working an angle in which I wasn't interested.'

'You could always ask him. There's a telephone there.'

'Why should I? There's nothing in it for me.'

'For Pete's sake, can't you be human for once in your goddam life?' asked Follet in an exasperated voice.

Warren's voice was quiet but it cut through the room with authority. 'Use the phone, Andy.'

'Oh, all right.' Tozier picked up his jacket. 'I think I have the number here somewhere.'

Follet patted Raqi on the shoulder. 'Bear up, Javid; we'll get you out of this jam somehow.' He sat next to him and began to talk to him quietly.

Tozier mumbled to someone on the telephone. At last he put it down and crossed the room with a paper in his hand. 'This man wants to know who's been ordering these chemicals – especially in quantity. He wants to know where they were despatched to. He also wants to know of any transactions concerning a man called . . .' He peered at the paper. '. . . Speering. That's it.' He rubbed the side of his jaw. 'I screwed him up to forty thousand but he wouldn't go higher for the information.'

'Why does he want it?' asked Warren.

'I reckon he's in industrial espionage.'

Follet took the sheet of paper. 'Who cares why he wants it so long as Javid can deliver?' He gave the paper to Raqi. 'Can you get that stuff?'

Raqi wiped his eyes and looked carefully. He nodded, and whispered, 'I think so. All this is in the stock ledgers.'

'But the guy will only go to forty thousand, damn him,' said Follet. 'For crying out loud, I'm game to help make up the difference.'

'Count me out on that,' said Tozier grimly. 'I've done my bit.'

'Nick?'

'All right, Johnny; we'll split it between us.' Warren sorted out five thousand rials from the money on the table and passed it to Follet.

'There, you see, Javid; we've got ten thousand here. All you have to do to get the other forty thousand is to go back to the office. You have the key?'

Raqi nodded, and allowed Follet to help him to his feet. 'It will take time,' he said.

'Half an hour. That's all it took to loot the safe this afternoon,' said Tozier brutally.

Follet saw Raqi to the door and closed it gently. He turned, and said, 'We're nearly there. There's just one thing more to be done.'

Warren sighed. 'It can't be any dirtier than what we've done already. What is it?'

'You're not concerned in it, so rest easy,' said Follet. 'Now, all we have to do is wait. I'm going to see Ben – I'll be back in ten minutes.'

* * *

It seemed, to Warren, an eternity before Raqi returned. The minutes ticked by and he contemplated the sort of man he was becoming under the stress of this crazy adventure. Not only was he guilty of blackmailing Follet, but he had assisted in the corruption of a young man who had hitherto been blameless. It was all right for Follet to preach that you can't cheat an honest man; the men who offer the thirty pieces of silver are just as guilty as he who accepts them.

Again there was the expected knock at the door and Follet went to open it. Raqi had pulled himself together a little and did not seem so woebegone; there was more colour in his cheeks and he did not droop as he had when he left.

Follet said, 'Well, kid; did you get it?'

Raqi nodded. 'I took it from the ledgers in English – I thought that would help.'

'It surely would,' said Follet, who had forgotten that problem. 'Let me have it,'

Raqi gave him three sheets of paper which he passed to Tozier. 'You'll see it gets to the right place, Andy.' Tozier nodded, and Follet gave Raqi a bundle of money. 'There's your fifty thousand, Javid. You'd better put it back in the safe real fast.'

Raqi was just putting the money into his pocket when the door burst open. A man stood there, his face concealed by a scarf, and holding an automatic pistol. 'Stay still, everyone,' he said indistinctly. 'And you won't get hurt.'

Warren looked on unbelievingly as the man took a step forward. He wondered who the devil this was and what he thought he was doing. The stranger wagged the gun sideways. 'Over there,' he said, and Raqi and Follet moved under the threat to join Warren at the other side of the room.

'Not you,' said the man, as Tozier began to obey. 'You stay there.' He stepped up to Tozier and plucked the papers from his hand. 'That's all I want.'

'Like hell!' said Tozier and lunged for him. There was a sharp crack and Tozier stopped as though he had hit a brick wall. A stupid expression appeared on his face and his knees buckled. Slowly, like a falling tree, he toppled, and as he dropped to the ground a gush of blood spurted from his mouth.

There was a bang as the door closed behind the visitor, and a faint reek of gunsmoke permeated the atmosphere.

Follet was the first to move. He darted over to Tozier and knelt down beside him. Then he looked up in wonder: 'Good Christ – he's dead!'

Warren crossed the room in two strides, his professional instincts aroused, but Follet straight-armed him. 'Don't touch him, Nick; don't get any blood on you.' There was something odd in Follet's tone that made him stop.

Raqi was shaking like an aspen in a hurricane. A moaning sound came from his lips – not words, but the mere repetition of his vocalized gasps – as he stared in horror at the blood spattered on the cuff of his jacket. Follet took him by the arm and shook him. 'Javid! Javid, stop that! Do you hear me?'

Raqi became more coherent. 'I'm . . . I'm all . . . right.'

'Listen carefully, then. There's no need for you to be mixed up in this. I don't know what the hell it's all about, but you can get clear if you're quick about it.'

'How do you mean?' Raqi's rapid breathing was slowing.

Follet looked down at Tozier's body. 'Nick and I will get rid of him. Poor guy; he was a bastard if ever there was one, but I wouldn't have wished this on him. That information his friend wanted must have been really something.' He turned to Raqi. 'If you know what's good for you you'll get out of here and keep your mouth shut. Go to the office, put the dough back in the safe, go home and say nothing. Do you understand?' Raqi nodded.

'Then get going,' said Follet. 'And walk – don't run. Take it easy.'

With a choked cry Raqi bolted from the room and the door slammed behind him.

Follet sighed and rubbed the back of his neck. 'Poor Andy,' he said. 'The chivalrous son-of-a-bitch. Okay, you can get up now. Arise, Lazarus.'

Tozier opened his eyes and winked, then leaned up on one elbow. 'How did it look?'

'Perfect. I thought Ben had really plugged you.'

Warren stepped over to Follet. 'Was that play-acting really necessary?' he asked coldly.

'It was really necessary,' said Follet flatly. 'Let's suppose we hadn't blown him off that way. Some time in the next few days he'd start to think and put things together, and it wouldn't take an egghead to figure he'd been conned. That boy's not stupid, you know; it's just that we rushed him – we didn't give him time to think straight.'

'So?'

'So now he'll *never* be able to think straight about what happened. The fact of sudden death does that to people. As long as he lives he'll never be able to figure out what really happened; he'll never know who shot and killed Andy – or why. Because it doesn't tie in with anything else. So he'll keep his mouth shut in case he's implicated in murder. That's why we had to blow him off with the cackle bladder.'

'With the *what?*'

'The cackle bladder.' Follet gestured. 'Show him, Andy.'

Tozier spat something from his mouth into his hand. 'I nearly swallowed the damn' thing.'

He held out his hand to disclose a reddened piece of limp rubber. Follet said, 'It's just a little rubber bag filled with chicken blood – a cackle bladder. It's used quite often to dispose of the chumps when they're no longer needed around.' He sniggered. 'It's the only other good use for a contraceptive.'

Ben Bryan came in, grinning. 'How did I do, Johnny?'

'You did fine, Ben. Where are those papers?' He took them from Bryan and slapped them into Warren's limp hand. 'Those are what you wanted.'

'Yes,' said Warren bitterly. 'These are what I wanted.'

'You wanted them – you've got them,' said Follet tensely. 'So use them. But don't come the big moral act with me, Warren. You're no better than anyone else.'

He turned away abruptly and walked out of the room.

SIX

They drove again among the ochre-red mountains of Kurdistan along the winding and precipitous roads. Warren was thankful to be in the lead; somewhere behind and hidden in the cloud of dust were Tozier and Follet in the second Land-Rover and he did not envy them. Bryan was driving and Warren navigating, trying to find his way to a spot pinpointed on the map. This was more difficult than had at first appeared; at times Warren felt as though he were in Alice's Looking Glass Land because the roads, unmarked on the map, twisted and turned sinuously and often it seemed that the best way to approach a given point was to drive in the opposite direction.

And again, it was only by a considerable stretch of the imagination that these scratch marks in the mountains could be called roads. Ungraded, stony, washed-out and often on the living rock, these tracks had been worn by the pads of thousands of generations of camels over hundreds, possibly thousands of years. Alexander had marched through these mountains, riding among his *hetaeroi* to the conquest of Persia and the penetration of India, and Warren judged that the roads had not been repaired since.

Several times they passed groups of the nomadic Kurds who were presumably in search of greener pastures, although where those pastures could possibly be Warren did not know. The whole land was a wilderness of rock and eroded bare earth with minimal hardy vegetation which sprouted in crevices in the bare hillsides, sparse and spindly but with the clinging tenacity of life. And it was all brown and burnt and there was no green at all.

He checked the map again, then lifted it to reveal the three sheets of paper which Javid Raqi had abstracted from his office at so much expense of the spirit. The information had been a constant worry to Warren ever since he had seen it. He had been prepared for a reasonable amount of chemicals – enough to extract, at most, a hundred pounds of morphine from the raw opium. But this was most unreasonable.

The quantities involved were fantastic – enough methylene chloride, benzene, amyl alcohol, hydrochloric acid and pharmaceutical lime to extract no less than two tons of morphine. *Two tons*! He felt chilled at the implications. It would provide enough heroin to saturate the United States illicit market for a year with plenty left over. If this amount got loose then the pushers would be very busy and there would be an explosion of new addicts.

He said, 'I've checked the figures again, Ben – and they still don't make sense.'

Bryan slowed as he approached a difficult comer. 'They are startling,' he admitted.

'Startling!' echoed Warren. 'They're damned nearly impossible. Look, Ben; it calls for twenty tons of raw opium – twenty tons, for God's sake! That amount of opium would cost nearly a million pounds on the illegal market. Do you think the Delorme woman has that much capital to play with?'

Bryan laughed. 'If I had that much money I'd retire.' He twisted the wheel. 'I've just had a thought, though. Perhaps Raqi fudged the figures in his excitement. He was translating from an oriental script into western notation, remember. Perhaps he made the identical mistake throughout, and uprated by a constant factor.'

Warren chewed his lip. 'But what factor? Let's say he made an error of a factor of ten – that brings us to about four hundred pounds of morphine. That's stall a hell of a lot, but it's much more reasonable.'

'How much would that be worth to Delorme?' asked Bryan.

'About twenty million dollars, landed in the States.'

'Yes,' said Bryan judiciously. 'I think I'd call that reasonable.' He slammed into low gear as they breasted a rise. 'How much longer before we get to whosit's place – what's his name?'

'Sheikh Fahrwaz.' Warren checked the map. 'If everything goes well – which it won't on past form – we should be there in an hour.'

The Land-Rover roared up to the top of the mountain pass, and Bryan slowed as they reached the crest. Warren, looking through the dusty windscreen, suddenly tensed. 'Reverse, Ben,' he said sharply. 'Quickly, now – get off the skyline.'

Bryan crashed the gears, infected by the excitement transmitted by Warren, and the Land-Rover lurched backwards in a series of jerks and came to a halt. 'Run back down the road,' said Warren. 'Run as far as you can and flag Andy to stop. Ask him to join me on foot. And don't slam that door when you get out.'

He opened the door and jumped to the ground, and as he ran up to the rest of the pass he veered to one side and headed for a clump of rocks which would give cover. When he arrived at the top he was panting, but more with excitement than exertion. He crouched behind the rocks and then slowly raised his head to get a view of the valley below.

Against a background of the usual arid hills on the other side of the valley there was a smear of green, cultivated land, chequer-boarded into fields, and in the middle was a cluster of buildings, low and flat-topped – either a small village or a biggish farm. This was the settlement of Sheikh Fahrwaz, the man who had ordered vast quantities of non-agricultural chemicals, and it was where Warren hoped to find Speering.

He heard a stone clatter behind him and turned his head to see Tozier approaching with Follet close behind. He waved them down and they came up more cautiously and joined him in looking down upon the valley. 'So this is it,' said Tozier after a while. 'What now?'

Follet said suddenly, 'Those people have been in big trouble.'

Warren looked down. 'How do you make that out?'

'Haven't you got eyes?' asked Follet. 'Look at those bomb craters. There's a line of them right across the valley – one bomb just missed that big building. Someone's had a crack at these boys from the air.'

It appeared that Follet was right. The line of craters stretched across the valley, starting from just below them and arrowing straight towards the settlement and beyond. Tozier reached behind for his binoculars. 'Who would want to bomb them unless it was the Iranian Air Force?' He juggled with the focusing. 'It was a poor attempt, though. That building hasn't been touched; there's no sign of repair work on the wall near the crater.'

'Are you sure they're bomb craters?' asked Warren. Something niggled at the back of his mind.

'I've seen plenty of them in Korea,' said Follet.

'Yes, they're bomb craters,' confirmed Tozier. 'Not very big bombs.'

This was a new element in the situation and something else for Warren to worry about. He put it on one side, and said, 'So what do we do?'

Bryan joined them. 'We just go down there,' he said, and jerked his head back at the vehicles. 'Our cover's good enough to carry it off. Even these people will have heard of motion pictures.'

Tozier nodded. 'Half of us go down,' he corrected. 'One vehicle. The other stays up here out of sight and keeps a listening watch on the radio.'

'What's the general procedure?' asked Warren. He had no illusions about himself, and he knew that Tozier, the professional, knew more than he about an operation of this sort. He was quite prepared to take orders.

Tozier squinted at the valley. 'I've searched many an innocent-looking village in my time, looking for arms caches mostly. But then we went in as an open operation – bristling with guns. We can't do that here. If the people down there are innocent, they'll be hospitable; if they're guilty, they'll *seem* to be hospitable. We've got to get a look into every building, and every one we're barred from is a black mark against them. After that we play it as it comes. Let's go.'

'So it'll be you and me,' said Warren. 'While Ben and Johnny stay up here.'

The road wound down to the fertile oasis of the valley where the green vegetation looked incredibly refreshing. Some of the fields were bare and had the shallow lines of primitive ploughing, but most of them were under crops. Tozier, who was driving, said, 'Would you recognize an opium poppy if you saw one? You might find them here.'

'There's none that I can see,' said Warren. 'Wait a minute – can you go across there?' He pointed.

'I don't see why not.' Tozier twisted the wheel and the Land-Rover left the road and bumped across open country. It did not make any appreciable difference to the bounce and jolt – the road was purely symbolic. 'Where are we going?'

'I want to have a look at those craters,' said Warren. 'The idea of bombing worries me – it doesn't make sense.'

Tozier drove to the nearest crater and left the engine idling. They got out and looked across the valley floor towards the settlement. The line of craters stretched out towards the buildings, equally spaced at fifty-yard intervals. Tozier looked at the nearest and said, 'If that's not a bomb crater then I'm a duck-billed platypus. You can see how the earth has been thrown up around the edge.'

'Let's have a closer look,' said Warren, and started walking. He climbed over the soft earth at the crater's edge, looked inside and started laughing. 'You're a duck-billed platypus, Andy. Look here.'

'Well, I'm damned!' said Tozier. 'It's just a hole.' He stepped inside the crater, took a pebble and dropped it into the hole. There was a long pause and then a very faint splash. He straightened up and looked along the line of craters – of holes – with a puzzled expression. 'This is even crazier. Who'd want to dig a hell of a lot of deep wells at fifty-yard intervals and in a dead straight line?'

Warren snapped his fingers. 'I've got it! I nearly had it when Follet pointed them out, but I couldn't pin it down. This is a *qanat.*'

'A who-what?'

'A *qanat* – an underground canal.' He turned and looked back at the hills. 'It taps an aquifer in the slopes over there, and leads water to the village. I was studying Iran before we came out here and I read about them. Iran is pretty well honeycombed with the things – there's a total of nearly two hundred thousand miles of *qanats* in the country.'

Tozier scratched his head. 'Why can't they build their canals on the surface like other people?'

'It's for water supply,' said Warren. 'They lose less by evaporation if the channel is underground. It's a very old system – the Persians have been building these things for the last three thousand years.' He grinned with relief. 'These aren't bomb craters – they're ventilation shafts; they have to have them so the workmen aren't asphyxiated when they're doing repairs.'

'Problem solved,' said Tozier. 'Let's go.'

They set off again and drove back to the road and then towards the settlement. The buildings were of the common sort they had seen elsewhere – walls made of rammed earth, flat roofs, and all of them single storey which would conveniently make a search easier. As they got nearer they saw goats grazing under the watchful eye of a small boy who waved as they passed, and there were scrawny chickens which scattered as they approached the courtyard of the largest building.

Tozier drew up inside. 'If you want to tell me anything let it wait until we're alone. These people might have more English than they'll admit to. But I must say everything looks peaceful.'

It did not seem so to Warren because a crowd of small boys rushed forward towards the unexpected visitors and were capering about in the dust, their shrill voices raised high. The women who had been about were vanishing like wraiths, drawing their shawls about their faces and hurrying out of sight through a dozen doors. He said, 'There are a hell of a lot of rooms to look into; and if Fahrwaz has a harem that will make things difficult.'

They descended to the ground and the small boys engulfed them. Tozier raised his voice. 'Better lock up or we'll be missing a lot of gear.'

Another voice was raised in harsh command and the boys scattered, running across the courtyard as though the devil were at their heels. A tall man stepped forward, richly dressed and straight-backed, though elderly. The haft of the curved knife in his sash glinted with jewels, a stone shone in his turban and others from the rings on his fingers. His face was thin and austere, and his beard was grey.

He turned and spoke in a low voice to his companion, who said – astonishingly in English – 'Sheikh Fahrwaz welcomes you. His house is yours.' He paused, then added sardonically, 'I wouldn't take that too literally – it's just a figure of speech.'

Warren recovered enough to say, Thank you. My name is Nicholas Warren and this is Andrew Tozier. We're looking for locations to make a film.' He indicated the inscription on the side of the Land-Rover. 'We work for Regent Films of London.'

'You're off the beaten track. I'm Ahmed – this is my father.' He spoke to the old man and the Sheikh nodded his head gravely and muttered a reply. Ahmed said, 'You're still welcome, although my father cannot really approve. He is a good Moslem and the making of images is against the Law.' He smiled slightly. 'For myself, I couldn't give a damn. You need not lock your truck – nothing will be stolen.'

Warren smiled. 'It's . . . er . . . unexpected to find English spoken in this remote place.'

Ahmed smiled a little mockingly. 'Do you think I should have a big sign put up there on the Djebel Ramadi – "English Spoken Here"?' He gestured. 'My father wishes you to enter his house.'

Thank you,' said Warren. 'Thank you very much.' He glanced at Tozier. 'Come on, Andy.'

'The room into which they were led was large. Sheepskin rugs were scattered on the floor and the walls were hidden behind tapestries. Several low settees surrounded a central open space which was covered by a fine Persian carpet, and coffee was already being brought in on brass trays.

'Be seated,' said Ahmed, and sank gracefully on to one of the settees. Warren tactfully waited until Sheikh Fahrwaz had settled himself and then sat down, doing his best to imitate the apparently awkward posture of Ahmed, which Ahmed did not seem to find awkward at all. Tozier followed suit and Warren could hear his joints crack.

'We have had European visits before,' said Ahmed. 'My father is one of the old school, and I usually instruct visitors in our customs. It pleases my father when they do what is right in his eyes, and does no harm to anyone.' He smiled engagingly. 'Afterwards we will go to my quarters and drink a lot of whisky.'

'That's very kind of you,' said Warren. 'Isn't it, Andy?'

'I could do with a stiff drink,' admitted Tozier.

Ahmed spoke to his father, then said, 'We will now have coffee. It is a little ceremonious, but it will not take long. My father wishes to know how long you have been in Kurdistan.'

'Not very long,' said Warren. 'We came in from Gilan two days ago.'

Ahmed translated this to his father, then said, 'You take the brass coffee cup in your right hand. The coffee is very hot and already sweetened – perhaps too sweet for your palate. Is this your first time in Kurdistan?'

Warren thought it better to tell the truth; unnecessary lies could be dangerous. He picked up the cup and cradled it in the palm of his hand. 'We were here a few weeks ago,' he said. 'We didn't find just what we wanted so we went back to Tehran to rest for a while.'

'No,' said Ahmed. 'Kurdistan is not a restful place.' He turned to Sheikh Fahrwaz and ripped off a couple of sentences very fast, then he said, 'You drink the coffee all at once, then you put the cup on the tray – upturned. It will make a sticky mess, but that doesn't matter. What is this film you are going to make, Mr Warren?'

'I'm not going to make the film,' said Warren. 'I'm just an advance man scouting locations as called for by the script.' He drank the coffee; it was hot and sickly sweet, and the cup was half full of grounds which he pushed back with his tongue. He brought the cup down and turned it over on the tray. Old Sheikh Fahrwaz smiled benevolently.

'I see,' said Ahmed. 'Just the other two cups and then we are finished. You make my father very happy when you understand our Kurdish hospitality.' He drank his coffee apparently with enjoyment. 'Are you the . . . er . . . the man in charge, Mr Warren?'

'Yes.' Warren followed Ahmed's example and picked up the second cup. 'Andy – Mr Tozier, here – is more of a technician. He concerns himself with camera angles and things like that.' Warren did not know how a unit like this was supposed to operate, and he hoped he was not dropping too many clangers.

'And there are just the two of you?'

'Oh, no,' said Warren blandly. 'Four of us in two vehicles. The others had a puncture and stopped to change the wheel.'

'Ah, then we must extend our hospitality to your friends. Night is falling.'

Warren shook his head. 'It is not necessary. They are fully equipped for camping.'

'As you say,' said Ahmed, and turned to his father.

They got through the third and last cup of the coffee ceremony and Sheikh Fahrwaz arose and uttered a sonorous and lengthy speech. Ahmed said briefly, 'My father extends to you the use of his house for the night.'

Warren gave Tozier a sideways glance and Tozier nodded almost imperceptibly. 'We'll be delighted. I'd just like to get some things from the Land-Rover – shaving kit and so forth.'

'I'll get it,' said Tozier promptly.

'Why, Mr Tozier,' said Ahmed chidingly, 'I was beginning to think the cat had got your tongue.' He brought out the English idiom triumphantly.

Tozier grinned. 'I leave the talking to the boss.'

'Of course you may leave,' said Ahmed. 'But *after* my father – that is the custom.'

Sheikh Fahrwaz bowed and disappeared through a doorway at the back of the room, and Tozier went out into the courtyard. He reached into the cab, unhooked the microphone and tossed it carelessly into the back. Luckily it had a long lead. He climbed into the back and, as he was unstrapping his case, he pressed the switch, and said in a low voice, 'Calling Regent Two; calling Regent Two. Come in – come in. Over.'

Follet's voice from the speaker in front was a bit too loud for comfort. 'Johnny here. Are you okay? Over.'

'We'll be all right if you speak more softly. We're staying the night. Keep listening in case anything happens. Over.'

'I can't keep the set alive all night without moving,' said Follet more quietly. 'It'll run the batteries flat. Over.'

'Then keep a listening watch every hour on the hour for ten minutes. Got that? Over.'

'Got it. Good luck. Out.'

Tozier unpacked everything he and Warren would need and then stowed the microphone away out of sight. When he went back into the house he found Warren and Ahmed chatting. 'Ahmed has just been telling me how he came by his English,' said Warren. 'He lived in England for seventeen years.'

'Oh,' said Tozier. 'That's interesting. How come?'

Ahmed waved gracefully. 'Let us talk about it over a drink. Come, my friends.' He led them from the room, across the courtyard and into what were unmistakably his own quarters, which were furnished completely in European style. He opened a cabinet. 'Whisky?'

'Thank you,' said Warren civilly. 'It's very kind of you.'

Ahmed poured the drinks and Warren noted he drank Chivas Regal. 'My father does not approve, but I do as I

wish in my own rooms,' He handed a glass to Warren.
The Prophet is against alcohol, but would God allow us to
make it if we weren't to use it?' He held up the bottle and
said jocularly, 'And if I sin, at least my sins are of the finest
quality. Mr Tozier, your drink.'

'Thank you.'

Ahmed poured himself a healthy slug. 'Besides, the very
word alcohol is Arabic. I must say I acquired a taste for
Scotch whisky in England. But sit down, gentlemen; I think
you will find those seats more comfortable than those of my
father.'

'How did you get to England?' asked Warren curiously.

'Ah, what a long story,' said Ahmed. 'Do you know
much of our Kurdish politics?'

'Nothing at all. What about you, Andy?'

'I've heard of the Kurdish problem, but I've never
known what it is,' said Tozier.

Ahmed laughed. 'We Kurds prefer to call it the Iranian
problem, or the Iraqi problem, or the Turkish problem; we
don't look upon ourselves as a problem, but that is quite
natural.' He sipped his whisky. 'During the war Iran was
occupied, as you know, by you British in the south and by
the Russians in the north. When the occupying forces left
the Russians played one of their favourite tricks by leaving
a Fifth Column behind. For this purpose they tried to use
the Kurds. The Mehabad Kurdish Republic was set up,
backed by the Russians, but it was short-lived and collapsed
as soon as the new Iranian government moved an army to
the north.'

He waved his glass. 'That was in 1946 when I was five
years old. My father was involved, and with Mullah Mustapha Barzani, he took refuge in Russia.' He tapped his
chest. 'But me he sent to England where I lived until 1963.
My father is a wise man; he did not want all his family in
Russia. You English have a saying about too many eggs in

one basket – so I was sent to England, and my elder brother
to France. That explains it, does it not?'

'This Mullah what's-his-name – who is he?' asked Tozier.

'Mullah Mustapha Barzani? He is one of our Kurdish
leaders. He is still alive.' Ahmed chuckled gleefully. 'He is in
Iraq with an army of twenty thousand men. He causes the
Iraqis a lot of trouble. Me, I am also a Barzani; that is, a
member of the Barzani tribe of which the Mullah is the
leader. And so, of course, is my father.'

'How did your father get back into Iran?' asked Warren.

'Oh, there was a sort of amnesty,' said Ahmed, 'and he
was allowed to return. Of course he is watched; but all
Kurds are watched, more or less. My father is now old and
no longer inclined to politics. As for me – I never was. Life
in England conditions one to be . . . gentle!'

Warren looked at the knife in Ahmed's sash and wondered if it was entirely ceremonial. Tozier said, 'Where do
the Iraqis and Turks come into all this?'

'Ah, the Kurdish problem. That is best explained with a
map – I think I have one somewhere.' Ahmed went to a
bookcase and pulled out what was obviously an old school
atlas. He flicked the pages, and said, 'Here we are – the
Middle East. In the north – Turkey; in the east – Iran; to the
west – Iraq.' His finger swept in a line from the mountains
of eastern Turkey south along the Iraqi-Iranian border.

'This is the homeland of the Kurds. We are a divided
people spread over three countries, and in each country we
are a minority – an oppressed minority, if you like. We are
divided and ruled by the Persians, the Iraqis and the Turks.
You must admit this could lead to trouble.'

'Yes, I can see that,' said Tozier. 'And it's happening in
Iraq, you say.'

'Barzani is fighting for Kurdish autonomy in Iraq,' said
Ahmed. 'He is a clever man and a good soldier; he has
fought the Iraqis to a standstill. With all their war planes,

tanks and heavy artillery the Iraqis have not been able to subdue him – so now President Bakr is reduced to negotiation.' He smiled. 'A triumph for Barzani.'

He closed the atlas. 'But enough of politics. Have more whisky and tell me of England.'

II

Warren and Tozier left rather late the next morning. Ahmed was prodigal in his hospitality, but they did not see Sheikh Fahrwaz again. Ahmed kept them up late at night talking about his life in England and quizzing them about current English affairs. In the morning, after breakfast, he said, 'Would you like to see the farm? It's typically Kurdish, you know' He smiled charmingly. 'Perhaps I will yet see my father's farm on the screen.'

The tour of the farm was exhaustive – and Ahmed was exhausting. He showed them everything and kept up a running commentary all the time. It was after eleven when they were ready to leave. 'And where do you go now?' he asked.

Tozier looked at his watch. 'Johnny hasn't turned up yet; maybe he's in trouble. I think we ought to go back and find him. What do you say, Nick?'

'It might be as well,' said Warren. 'But I bet he's gone back to have another look at that encampment he was so enthusiastic about. I think we'd better chase him up.' He smiled at Ahmed. 'Thank you for your hospitality – it's been most kind.'

'Typically Kurdish,' said Ahmed cheerfully.

They exchanged a few more polite formalities and then departed with a wave from Ahmed and his 'God speed you,' in their ears. As they bumped back along the road to the pass Warren said, 'What did you think of that?'

Tozier snorted. 'Too bloody good to be true, if you ask me. He was altogether too accommodating.'

'He certainly took a lot of trouble over us,' said Warren. ' "Typical Kurdish hospitality",' he quoted.

'Hospitality, my backside,' said Tozier violently. 'Did you notice he took us into every building – into every room? It was as though he was deliberately demonstrating he had nothing to hide. How did you sleep?'

'Like the dead,' said Warren. 'He was very liberal with his Chivas Regal. I felt woozy when I turned in.'

'So was I,' said Tozier. 'I usually have a better head for Scotch than that.' He paused. 'Maybe we were doped with some of that morphine we're looking for. Is that possible?'

'It's possible,' said Warren. 'I must admit I felt a bit dreary when I woke up this morning.'

'I have a vague idea there was quite a bit of movement during the night,' said Tozier. 'I seem to remember a lot of coming and going with camels. The trouble is I don't know if it really happened or if it was a dream.'

They came to the top of the pass and Warren looked back. The settlement looked peaceful and innocent – a pleasant pastoral scene. Typically Kurdish, he thought sardonically. And yet Sheikh Fahrwaz was the consignee for those damned chemicals. He said, 'We saw everything there was to be seen down there, therefore there was nothing to hide. Unless . . .'

'Unless?'

'Unless it's so well hidden that Ahmed knew we wouldn't spot it.'

'How much room would Speering need for his laboratory, or whatever it is?'

Warren considered the ridiculous amount of chemicals that Javid Raqi had come up with. 'Anything from two hundred square feet to two thousand.'

'Then it's not there,' said Tozier flatly. 'We'd have seen it.'

'Would we?' said Warren thoughtfully. 'You said you've searched villages for arms caches. Where did you usually find them?'

'Oh, for God's sake!' said Tozier, thumping the wheel violently. 'Underground, of course. But just in bits and pieces – a few here and there. There was never any big-scale construction like you'd need here.'

'It wouldn't be too difficult. The ground in the valley bottom isn't rocky – it's soil over red clay; quite soft, really.'

'So you think we ought to go back and have a look. That's going to be difficult, as well as being dicey.'

'We'll talk about it with the others. There's Ben now.'

Bryan waved them off the road into a little side valley which was hardly more than a ravine, and jumped on to the running-board as they passed. After two hundred yards the ravine bent at right-angles and they saw the other vehicle parked, with Follet sitting on the ground in front of it. He looked up as they stopped. 'Any trouble?'

'Not yet,' said Tozier briefly. He joined Follet. 'What's that you've got there?'

'A photograph of the valley. I took a dozen with the Polaroid camera.'

'Those could be useful. We have to go in there again – discreetly. Let's have a look at them, Johnny – all of them.'

Follet spread the photographs on the bonnet of the Land-Rover. After a while Tozier said, 'There's not much joy here. Anyone coming down the pass can be spotted in daylight, and you can lay odds that a watch is kept. It's four miles from the bottom of the pass to the settlement – eight miles there and back – that's a long way at night on foot. And when we get there we have to stumble around in the dark looking for something that might not be there. I can't see it.'

'What are you looking for?' asked Follet.

'A secret underground room,' said Warren.

Follet pulled a face. 'How in hell do you expect to find that?'

'I don't know how we're going to find it,' said Warren a little wearily.

Bryan leaned over and picked up a photograph. 'Andy seems more concerned about getting to the settlement unseen,' he said. 'There's more than one way of skinning a cat.' His finger traced the lane of 'craters'. 'Tell me more about this underground channel.'

'The *qanat*? It's just a means of tapping water from the mountains and leading it to the valley.'

'How big is it? Big enough for a man to walk through?'

Warren nodded. 'It must be.' He tried to remember what he had read about them. 'They send men down to keep them in repair.'

There you are,' said Bryan. 'You don't have to go stumbling around. That's an arterial highway pointing straight at the settlement. You can pop down a hole here and pop up another there just like a rabbit.'

Tozier stared at him for a moment. 'You make it sound so easy,' he said with heavy irony. 'What's the slope in these things, Nick?'

'Not much. Just enough to keep the water moving.'

'How deep is the water?'

'I don't think that's very much, either. Maybe a foot.' Warren felt a sense of desperation. 'Look, Andy; I don't know much about this. All I know is what I've read.'

Tozier ignored that. 'What's the footing like? Is it flat?'

Warren closed his eyes, trying to visualize the illustrations he had seen. At last he said, 'Flat, I think.'

Tozier looked at the photographs. 'We go down the pass on foot just after dark. We drop down a shaft into the *qanat*. If the footing is reasonable we ought to make two miles an hour – there's two hours to the settlement. We come up as close as possible and we can search until just before daybreak. Then we pop back down our hole and come back underground and unseen. We take our chances coming up the pass in daylight – there's a reasonable amount of cover. It's becoming practicable.'

Follet snorted. 'Practicable! I think it's crazy. Burrowing underground, for Christ's sake!'

'Supposing the *qanat* route is practicable,' said Warren. 'I doubt it, but let's suppose we can do it. How are we going to search the settlement without being nabbed?'

'You never know your luck unless you try,' said Tozier. 'In any case, can you suggest anything else?'

'No,' said Warren. 'I can't, damn it!'

III

Tozier supervised the preparations. He hauled more rope out of the Land-Rovers than Warren had thought they carried – light nylon rope with a high breaking strain. From a toolbox he took crampons. 'Dropping down a shaft will be easy,' he said. 'We can do that on the end of a rope. Getting up another might be difficult. We'll need these.'

He produced high-powered electric torches and knives to go in their belts, but Warren was surprised when he began to take apart one of the photographic tripods. 'What are you doing?'

Tozier paused. 'Supposing you find this laboratory – what do you intend to do?'

'Destroy it,' said Warren tightly.

'How?'

'I thought of burning it, or something like that.'

'That might not work underground,' said Tozier, and continued to strip the tripod. He took off the tubular aluminium legs and from them shook several brown cylinders. 'This will do it, though. You don't need much gelignite to make a thorough mess of a relatively small installation.'

Warren gaped as he watched Tozier wrap the gelignite into a neat bundle with strips of insulating tape. Tozier grinned. 'You left the fighting preparations to me – remember?'

'I remember,' said Warren.

Then Tozier did something even more surprising. Using a screwdriver he removed the clock from the dashboard. 'This is already gimmicked,' he said. 'See that spike on the back? That's a detonator. All we do is to ram that into one of those sticks of gelignite and we can set the clock to explode it at any time up to twelve hours in advance.' He laughed. 'The art of preparation is the art of war.'

'Got any more surprises?' asked Warren drily.

Tozier looked at him seriously and jerked his thumb in the direction of the settlement. 'Those boys are gangsters and they'll use gangster's weapons – knives and pistols. In these parts maybe rifles, too. But I'm a soldier and I like soldier's tools.' He patted the side of the Land-Rover. 'These aren't the same vehicles that left the factory. The Rover company wouldn't recognize some of the parts I put in, but then, neither would a customs officer.'

'So?'

'So what does a gun look like?'

Warren shook his head in a baffled way. 'It has a barrel, a trigger, a stock.'

'Yes,' said Tozier. He went to the back of the Land-Rover and began to take out one of the struts which held up the canopy. He hauled it out and the canopy sagged slightly but not much. 'There's your barrel,' he said, thrusting it into Warren's hands. 'Now we want the breech mechanism.'

He began to strip the vehicle of odd bits of metal – the cigarette lighter from the dash-board was resolved into its component parts, an ashtray which was apparently a metal pressing turned out to be a finely machined slide, springs were picked out of the toolbox and within ten minutes Tozier had assembled the gun.

'Now for the stock,' he said, and unstrapped the spade from the side of the Land-Rover. With a twist of his wrist it came neatly in half and the handle part was slotted into the gun to form a shoulder rest. 'There you are,' he said. 'An automatic machine-pistol. There's so much metal in a truck that no one recognizes small components for what they are – and the big bits you disguise as something else.' He held out the gun. 'We couldn't just walk into the country with a thing like this in our hands, could we?'

'No,' said Warren, fascinated. 'How many of those have you got?'

'Two of these little chaps and a rather decent air-cooled machine-gun which fits on one of the tripods. Ammunition is the difficulty – it's hard to disguise that as anything else, so we haven't got much.' He jerked his thumb. 'Every one of those sealed cans of unexposed film carries its share.'

'Very ingenious.'

'And then there's the mortar,' said Tozier casually. 'You never know when a bit of light artillery will come in useful.'

'No!' said Warren abruptly. 'Now, that's impossible.'

'Be my guest,' said Tozier, waving at the Land-Rover. 'If you find it you can have my bonus – or as much of it as Johnny Follet leaves me with.'

He went away, leaving Warren to look at the Land-Rover with renewed interest. A mortar was a big piece of equipment, and search as he would he could not find anything remotely resembling one, nor could he find any mortar bombs – sizeable objects in themselves. He rather thought Tozier was pulling his leg.

They made the final preparations and drove up to the top of the pass and parked the Land-Rovers off the road behind some boulders. At sunset they began to descend the pass. Going down into the valley was not too difficult; it was not yet so dark that they could not see a few yards in front of them, but dark enough to make it improbable that they should be seen from a distance. From the top of the pass to the first ventilation shaft of the *qanat* was just over a mile, and when they got there it would have been quite dark but for the light of the newly risen moon.

Tozier looked up at the sky. 'I'd forgotten that,' he said. 'It could make it dicey at the other end. We're damned lucky to have this underground passage – if it works.' He began to uncoil a rope.

'Hold on,' said Warren. 'Not this shaft.' He had just remembered something. 'This will be the head well – the water's likely to be deep at the bottom. Try the next shaft.'

They walked about fifty yards along the line of the *qanat* until they came to the next shaft, and Tozier unslung the rope. 'How deep are these things, Nick?'

'I haven't a clue.'

Tozier picked up a pebble and dropped it down the hole, timing its fall by the ticking of his watch. 'Less than a hundred feet. That's not too bad. We might have to come up this one in a hurry.' He gave one end of the rope to Bryan.

'Here, Ben; belay that around something – and make sure it's something that won't shift.'

Bryan scouted around and found a rock deeply embedded in the earth around which he looped the rope, tying it off securely. Tozier hauled on it to test it, then fed the other end into the shaft. He handed his machine-pistol to Warren. 'I'll go first. I'll flash a light three times if it's okay to come down.' He sat on the edge of the shaft, his legs dangling, then turned over on to his belly and began to lower himself. 'See you at the bottom,' he whispered, the sound of his voice coming eerily from the black hole.

He went down hand over hand using his knees to brace against the wall of the shaft which was about three feet in diameter. One by one he came to the bits of cloth he had tied to the rope at ten-foot intervals and by which he could judge his distance and, at just past the ninety-foot mark, his boots struck something solid and he felt the swirl of water over his ankles.

He looked up and saw the paler blackness of the sky. It flickered a little and he guessed someone was looking down the shaft. He groped for his torch, flashed it three times upwards, then he shone it around and down the *qanat*. It stretched away, three feet wide and six feet high, into the distance, far beyond the range of his light. The bare earthen walls were damp and the water flowed about nine inches deep.

He felt the rope quiver as someone else started down the shaft and a scattering of earth fell on his head. He stepped out of the way downstream and presently Warren joined him, gasping for breath. Tozier took the gun and said, 'This is it, Nick.' He played the light on the earthen roof. 'God help us if that caves in.'

'I don't think it will,' said Warren. 'If there's a danger of that they put in big pottery hoops to retain it. Don't forget that people are working down here pretty regularly to keep the waterway unrestricted. They don't want to get killed, either.' He forebore to tell Tozier that the men who worked in the *qanats* had an aptly descriptive name for them – they called them 'the murderers'.

'How old do you think this is?' asked Tozier.

'I don't know. Could be ten years – could be a thousand, or even more. Does it matter?'

'I don't suppose so.'

Bryan joined them and was soon followed by Follet. Tozier said, 'The shaft we want to go up is the thirty-fifth from here . . .'

'The thirty-fourth,' said Warren quietly.

'Oh, yes; I forgot we skipped the first one. We'll all keep a count just in case. If there's an argument the majority vote wins. And we go quietly because I don't know how sounds carry up the shafts. I go first with a gun, Nick next, then Ben and lastly Johnny with the other gun as rearguard. Let's go.'

It was ridiculously easy and they made far better time than Warren had expected – at least three miles an hour. As Bryan had said, it was a main highway pointing at the farm. The footing was firm and not even muddy or slippery so that it was even easier than walking in the middle of an English stream. The water was not so deep as to impede them unduly and Tozier's powerful torch gave plenty of light.

Only once did they run into a minor difficulty. The water deepened suddenly to two feet and then to three. Tozier halted them and went ahead to kick down a dam of soft earth where there had been a small roof fall. The pent-up water was released and gurgled away rapidly until it fell to the normal nine inches or so.

But still, it was a hard slog and Warren was relieved when Tozier held up his hand for them to stop. He turned and said softly, 'This shaft is thirty-three – are we agreed on that?' They were. He said, 'Now we go canny. Remember that the settlement is just above us. Gently does it.'

They carried on into the darkness with Tozier meticulously checking his paces. Suddenly he stopped so that Warren almost collided with him. 'Do you hear anything?' he asked in a low voice.

Warren listened and heard nothing but the gentle chuckle of the water. 'No,' he said, and even as he said it he heard a throb which rapidly died away. They kept quiet, but heard nothing more.

At last Tozier said, 'Come on – it's only another twenty yards.' He pushed on and stopped under the shaft. Abruptly he turned and whispered, 'There's a light up there. Have a look and tell me what you think it is.'

Warren squeezed past him and looked up the shaft. Far above he saw the pale circle of the sky but there was

another and brighter light shining on the wall of the shaft
not so far up, which seemed to be emanating from the
side of the shaft itself. He estimated that it was about fifty
feet up.

He drew back and said quietly, 'We were looking for
something underground, weren't we? I think this is it. The
place would have to be ventilated somehow so they're
using the *qanat* shaft. And this shaft is the nearest to the
farm.'

Tozier's voice was filled with incredulity. 'You think
we've stumbled across it first crack out of the box?'

Follet said out of the darkness. 'Everybody's lucky some
time. Why not us?'

There was a sound. The distant but distinct noise of
someone coughing. 'Someone's awake,' breathed Tozier.
'We can't do anything yet.' He peered up the shaft. 'If
they ever sleep they'll put the light out. I'll keep watch –
the rest of you go back, say, a hundred yards. And keep
quiet.'

Thus began one of the most uncomfortable periods of
Warren's life. It was nearly three hours before Tozier
flashed for them and he knew what his feet would look like
when he took off his boots; they would be as white as a
fish's belly and as wrinkled as a washerwoman's hands. He
made a mental note to issue surgical spirits when – and if –
they got back, otherwise everyone could become crippled
with blisters.

So he was very glad when Tozier gave the signal and he
was able to move up and to stretch his cramped limbs.
'Everything all right?'

'The light has been off for nearly an hour. I thought I
heard someone snoring a while back, so let's hope he's still
asleep. I think I'll nip up and have a look. You'll have to give
me a boost up to the shaft.'

'Take it easy.'

'I will,' said Tozier with grim humour. 'I was studying the light before it went out. I reckon that's the main entrance to their cubby-hole. Well, here goes – I'll drop a rope for you.'

Warren, Bryan and Follet braced themselves, forming a human stepladder up which Tozier could climb. He hoisted himself up, felt the sides of the shaft with his hands, and then brought up one leg so that the crampons on his boot bit into the clay. He pushed, straightening his leg, and dug in with the other boot. It was not too difficult – he had made worse climbs, but never in such darkness. Slowly he went up, his back braced against the wall and his feet climbing the opposite wall in the chimney technique he had once learned at mountain school.

Half way he stopped, and rested for a couple of minutes and then started again, feeling it easier as he got the rhythm so that the second half of the climb was done much more quickly than the first. And so he came to the ledge, broad enough to stand on, that had been cut into the side of the shaft. He risked a flash of his light and saw a support post, so he uncoiled his rope, tied one end securely to the post, and dropped the rest down the shaft.

Warren came up next with his gun which Tozier took and cocked with a metallic click. Then Bryan came, and Follet soon after, and all four of them were crammed on the narrow ledge. Tozier flashed his light and they saw a door. He pushed it gently and it swung open without a sound, so he passed inside – gun first.

Follet went next because he too had a gun, and Warren and Bryan were close behind. Tozier switched on his light and the beam roved about, striking bright reflections from the glassware set up on benches. The light moved on and settled on a bed where a man lay sleeping. He moved restlessly under the glare, and Tozier whispered, 'Take him, Johnny.'

Follet moved forward into the light. He crossed the room in three strides, his hand came up holding something black, and when it came down there was a dull thump and a muffled gasp.

Tozier searched the room with his light, looking for other sleepers, but he found none. 'Close the door, Ben,' he said. 'Johnny, light that Coleman lamp.'

The bright light from the lamp was enough to show Warren that they had found the right place. There was only the one room, carved out of the alluvial clay, the roof supported by rough timber. It reminded him very much of the dug-outs of the trenches of the First World War which he had seen depicted on the screen. The room was cramped because nearly half of it was filled with boxes, and the rest with benches full of equipment.

Tozier said, 'Take a look, Nick. Is this what you're looking for?'

Warren cast a professional eye on the bench set-up. 'By God, it is!' He sniffed at some of the open bottles, then found some white powder and cautiously put the tip of his tongue to a couple of granules held on his fingertip. He grimaced. 'This is it, all right.'

Bryan straightened up from the bed. 'He's out cold. What did you hit him with, Johnny?'

Follet grinned and held up a stubby, leather-covered cosh.

'It's Speering, all right,' said Bryan. 'He's been growing a beard, but I recognize him.'

'He can't have been working on his own,' said Tozier.

Warren was probing among the benches. 'He'd need a few assistants, but once he'd made this set-up he could get by with unskilled labour as long as he did the supervision. Some of our hospitable Kurds upstairs, I suppose.' He looked about the room, at the coffee-pot and the dirty plates and the empty whisky bottles. 'Ahmed doesn't give him Chivas Regal, I see. He's been living down here all the time,

I think. They couldn't let him give the game away by allowing him to walk around the settlement.'

His gaze settled on the boxes and he investigated one that had been opened. 'Christ Almighty!'

Tozier looked over his shoulder at the cylindrical objects. 'What are they – cheeses?'

'That's opium,' said Warren. 'And it's Turkish opium, by God! Not Iranian at all.'

'How do you know it's Turkish?'

'The shape – only the Turks pack it that way.' He stepped back and looked at the stack of boxes. 'If these are all full there must be ten tons of the stuff here.'

Tozier tested the weight of a couple of boxes at random. 'They're full, all right.'

Warren began to think that the figures supplied by Raqi were correct, after all. He found a corner of the room used for chemical storage and started to check the remaining chemicals against Raqi's list. After a while he said, 'As near as I can get to it he's used about half – but where's the morphine?'

Follet made a muffled exclamation which was covered by Tozier's voice as he held up a rectangular block. 'What's this?'

Warren took it and scratched the surface with his fingernail. 'More opium – wrapped in poppy leaves. From Afghanistan, I'd say. It looks as though they've been getting the stuff from all over the Middle East.' He tossed it on to the bench. 'But I'm not interested in that – I want the morphine.'

'What would it look like?'

'A fine white powder – like table salt or castor sugar. And there ought to be a hell of a lot of it.'

They searched the room carefully and eventually Follet said excitedly, 'What's this?' He hefted a large glass carboy half full of white powder.

Warren sampled it gingerly. 'This is it. This is morphine.'

'Cut or uncut?' asked Follet.

'It's pure – or as pure as you can make the stuff in a slum like this.'

Follet whistled. 'So this is what you were after. You played it close to your chest, didn't you, Warren?' He tested the weight of the carboy. 'Jesus! There must be twenty pounds here. This lot should be worth half a million bucks.'

'Don't get any ideas, Johnny,' said Tozier.

Warren whirled around. 'Twenty pounds! I'm looking for a hundred times that amount.'

Follet stared at him. 'You serious? You must be joking, Doc.'

'This isn't a thing to joke about,' said Warren savagely. He flung out his arm and pointed to the boxes of opium stacked against the wall. 'There's enough opium there to extract a ton of morphine. Speering had used half his chemicals so we can say his job was half done – he's been here long enough to have extracted a ton of morphine with help – and the scale of this laboratory set-up is just about right, too. So where the hell is it?' His voice rose.

'Not so loud,' said Tozier warningly. He nodded to where Speering lay breathing stertorously on the bed. 'We could ask him?'

'Yeah,' said Follet. 'But he might make a noise while we're doing it.'

'Then we'll take him with us,' said Tozier. 'Some of the way.' He turned back to Warren. 'What do you want done with this place?'

'I want it wrecked,' said Warren coldly. 'I want it totally destroyed.'

'Half a million bucks,' said Follet, and tapped the carboy with his foot. 'An expensive bang.'

'Would you have any other ideas?' asked Tozier softly.

'Hell, no,' said Follet. 'It's not my line. I stay on the legal side – although I must say I've been stretching it a bit on this trip.'

'All right; then stick Speering down the shaft. Nick, you can give me a hand with the explosives.'

Follet ripped a sheet into strips and began to truss up Speering, ending by making a gag and stuffing it into his mouth. 'That's in case he comes to half-way down the shaft. Give me a hand with him, Ben.'

They lashed the rope around Speering's slack body, dragged him through the doorway and began to lower him down the shaft. When the strain eased off the rope they knew he had touched bottom, and Follet prepared to follow. He went over to Tozier and said, 'Ben and I are going down now.'

'Okay. Wait for Nick and me at the bottom.' Tozier looked at his watch. 'I'm setting the time of the bang at three hours from now. That should give us time to get out with a bit to spare.'

Follet left and Tozier completed setting the charges. The last thing he did was to set the clock carefully and, very delicately, to push over a small lever. 'She's cocked,' he said. 'An alarm clock to wake up Ahmed. Come on, Nick, let's get the hell out of here. Armed charges always make me nervous.'

Warren launched himself into the darkness of the shaft and went down the rope hand over hand until his feet splashed in water. 'Over here,' whispered Bryan, and Warren splashed up-stream.

Follet said, 'Our friend is coming round.' He flashed his light on Speering who rolled his eyes wildly while choked sounds came from behind the gag. A long knife came into view and highlights slithered along the blade held before Speering's eyes. 'You make a noise and you'll end up with a cut throat.'

Speering became abruptly silent.

There was a muffled thump and a splash from the direction of the shaft. 'All right,' said Tozier. 'Let's move fast. Can Speering walk?'

'He'd better,' said Follet. 'I'll be right behind him with this pig-sticker.' He flashed his light on Speering's feet and cut away the bonds. 'Get on your feet, you son-of-a-bitch; get on your feet and move.'

Despite the encumbrance of Speering they travelled rapidly up the *qanat*. Tozier went first with Speering right behind urged on by the fear of Follet and his knife, while Bryan and Warren brought up the rear. Because Speering's hands were bound he found it difficult to keep his balance – he plunged about from side to side of the *qanat*, ricocheting from one wall to the other, and sometimes fell to his knees, while Follet pricked him mercilessly with the knife and kicked him to his feet.

After three-quarters of an hour of punishing progress Tozier called a halt. 'It's time to have a breather,' he said. 'Besides, we want to talk to Speering, don't we? It should be safe enough here.' He flashed his light upwards. 'We're well between shafts. Take out the gag, Johnny.'

Follet brought up the knife close to Speering's face. 'You keep quiet – you understand?' Speering nodded, and Follet inserted the knife under the cloth that held the gag in place and ripped it free. 'Spit it out, buster.'

Speering coughed and choked as he ejaculated the wad of sheeting that filled his mouth. Blood ran down his cheek and matted his beard from the gash where Follet had cut him in hacking away the gag. He swallowed violently, and whispered, 'Who are you?'

'You don't ask questions,' said Tozier. 'You answer them. Carry on, Nick.'

'How much morphine did you extract, Speering? And where is it now?'

Speering had not yet recovered his breath. His chest heaved as he shook his head. 'Oh boy!' said Follet. 'We're talking to a dead man.'

Tozier moved suddenly and viciously. His hand came up fast and he rocked Speering with a hard double slap. 'My friend is right,' he said softly. 'Answer the questions – or you're dead.'

'How much morphine did you extract, Speering?' asked Warren quietly.

'They'll kill me,' gasped Speering. 'You don't know them.'

'Who?' asked Tozier.

'Fahrwaz and Ahmed.' Speering was terrified. 'You don't know how bad they are.'

'You don't know how bad *we* are,' said Follet reasonably. 'Take your choice – die now or die later.' He pricked Speering's throat with the knife. 'Answer the question – how much morphine?'

Speering arched away in an attempt to get away from the knife. 'A thou . . . thousand kilograms.'

Tozier glanced at Warren. 'You just about hit it. That's twenty-two hundred pounds. All right, Speering; where is it?'

Speering shook his head violently. 'I don't know. I swear I don't know.'

'When did it leave?'

'Last night – they took it away in the middle of the night.'

'That must have been while we were there,' said Tozier thoughtfully. 'They lifted the stuff right out from under our noses. Where did they take it?'

'I don't know.'

'But you can guess,' said Follet, putting a fraction more pressure on the knife. A trickle of blood ran down Speering's neck. 'I bet you can guess real good.'

'Iraq,' Speering burst out. 'They said it was going to Iraq.'

'We're about thirty miles from the Iraqi border,' said Tozier. 'It begins to add up. I'd swear I heard camels last night. Did they take the stuff out on camel back?'

Speering tried to nod but ran his throat on to the knife-point. 'Yes,' he said weakly.

'Why didn't you acetylate the morphine here?' asked Warren. 'Where are they going to turn it into heroin?'

'I was going to do it here,' said Speering, 'but they changed their minds. They took it away last night. I don't know anything more than that.'

Tozier looked at Warren. 'Wouldn't they need Speering for that?'

'Maybe not. It's not too difficult a job. It looks as though we threw a scare into Ahmed. He got the stuff out of the way prematurely as a safety precaution, I'd say.'

'As a safety precaution it worked,' said Tozier grumpily. 'If he hadn't done it we'd have copped the lot. As it is, we've lost it. The stuff will be in Iraq by now.' He turned to Speering. 'Are you sure you don't know where it was going to in Iraq? You'd better tell the truth.'

Speering twitched his eyes back and forth. 'Come on, baby,' said Follet encouragingly. 'It's the last question.'

Speering gave in. 'I don't know exactly – but it's some-where near Sulaymaniyeh.'

Tozier checked the time. 'Gag him again, Johnny. The road to Iraq goes past Fahrwaz's settlement. We have to be on time when the balloon goes up.'

'What can we do with Speering?' asked Warren.

'What can we do with him? We leave him here. With his hands tied and a gag in his mouth he can't do much. Hurry it along, Johnny.'

Three minutes later they were on their way again with-out Speering. As they left Warren turned round and flashed his light down the *qanat*. Speering was slumped against the wall in the position they had left him, but then he turned and stumbled away in the opposite direction. Warren met the eyes of Ben Bryan. 'Come on, Ben; let's go.'

Bryan hesitated fractionally, then fell in behind Warren who was making good time to catch up with the others who had already drawn well ahead.

Warren's mind was busy with the implications of what he had learned. The mountains of Kurdistan formed part of an age-old smuggler's route – Fahrwaz and Ahmed would know them well and he had no doubt that the morphine could be smuggled into Iraq with little difficulty. The writ of the law did not run strongly in any part of Kurdistan and had broken down completely in Iraqi-Kurdistan where the government forces were held at arm's length.

He plugged along mechanically behind Follet and wondered what the devil they were going to do now. It was evident that Tozier had no doubts. 'The road to Iraq goes past Fahrwaz's settlement,' he had said, and had taken it for granted that they were going to Iraq. Warren envied him his stubborn tenacity.

His train of thought was broken by Bryan thumping him on the back. 'Stop,' said Ben. 'Tell Tozier.'

Warren passed the word on and Tozier stopped. 'What is it?'

'Speering is going to die,' said Bryan. 'The last I saw of him he was heading in the other direction. If he doesn't get killed in the explosion the roof of the *qanat* will cave in and he'll be trapped. So he'll die.'

'He can climb a shaft,' said Follet.

'With his hands tied behind his back?'

'He's going to die,' said Tozier flatly. 'So?'

'But to die like that!' said Bryan desperately. 'Tied up and stumbling around in the dark.'

'Don't you think he deserves it?'

'I wouldn't want anyone to die like that. I'm going back.'

'For Christ's sake!' said Tozier. 'We haven't time. We have to get back to the vehicles and be on our way before the big bang. That settlement is going to swarm like an ant heap when that underground room goes off pop, and I want to be on the other side when it happens.'

'You go ahead,' said Bryan. 'I'll catch you up.'

'Hold it, Ben,' said Warren. 'What are you going to do?'

'Untie his hands and turn him round,' said Bryan. 'It gives him a chance.'

'It gives him a chance to raise a goddam squawk,' said Follet sourly.

'To hell with it, I'm going back,' said Bryan, and broke away suddenly. Warren flicked on his light and saw him retreating rapidly into the darkness of the *qanat*.

'The damned fool,' said Tozier in a gravelly voice.

Warren hesitated uncertainly. 'What do we do?'

'I'm getting out of here,' said Follet. 'I'm not risking my life for a guy like Speering.'

'Johnny's right,' said Tozier. 'There's no point in waiting here. We'll bring the trucks down the pass and stand by to pick up Ben. Let's move.'

It seemed the best thing to do. After an initial pause Warren followed, splashing on the heels of Follet. Tozier imposed a back-breaking pace, secure in the knowledge of free passage ahead and spurred by the imminence of the impending explosion behind. They passed shaft after shaft with monotonous regularity and Warren checked each one off in his mind.

Tozier finally stopped. 'This is it.'

'Can't be,' gasped Warren. 'I only make it thirty-one.'

'You're wrong,' said Tozier with certainty. 'I have hold of the rope. The sooner we're all on the surface, the better I'll be pleased.'

He went up the shaft and was followed by Warren, who collapsed gasping for breath on the raised rim. Tozier helped

Follet up, then said, 'Johnny and I will go for the trucks. You stay here and give us a flash when you hear the engines.' He and Follet disappeared into the darkness and there was just the rattle of loose stones to indicate their passage.

Warren looked up at the sky. The moon was setting behind the mountains but still shed a bright and even light over the rocky landscape so that he could see the roofs of the settlement in the distance. He waited for a while in the profound silence then leaned over the shaft and called, 'Ben – Ben, where are you?'

His voice echoed hollowly in the shaft, but there was no reply. He bit his lip. Undoubtedly Ben had acted stupidly – but was he wrong? Warren felt a turmoil within himself, an unaccustomed battle between idealism and self-interest which was something he had not felt before. Hesitantly he grasped the rope and prepared to let himself down the shaft, and then he paused, wondering if this was the right thing to do, after all. What about the others? Would he not be endangering the lives of them all if he went down after Bryan?

He dropped the rope and disconsolately sat on the edge of the shaft, fighting it out within himself. Presently he heard the low rumble of an engine and cautiously flashed his light in that direction, being careful to shield it with his hand so that no glimmer could be seen from the settlement in the distance. A Land-Rover loomed up suddenly and stopped, its engine dropping to the thrum of idling speed. Tozier got out and walked over. 'Any sign of him?'

'Nothing,' said Warren despondently.

'Bloody idealists!' said Tozier. 'They get on my wick.'

'He's in the profession of life-saving,' said Warren. 'It's hard to change suddenly. So what do we do now?'

Tozier peered at the illuminated fingers of his watch which he carried face inward on his wrist. 'She'll blow in thirty minutes. I was hoping to be on the other side of the settlement by then.' He sighed in exasperation. 'That bloody young idiot has cocked everything up.'

'You push off,' said Warren. 'I'll wait for Ben.'

'No,' said Tozier. 'I'll wait. You and Johnny head for the settlement. When the bang goes off make a break for it – you should be able to get through in the excitement. Wait for me on the other side. If you hear any shooting be prepared to come back in and bail us out.'

'I don't know if that's a . . .' began Warren.

'For Christ's sake, move,' said Tozier forcefully. 'I know what I'm doing and I've had more experience. Get going.'

Warren ran for the second Land-Rover and told Follet what was happening. Follet said, 'You'd better drive then.' He lifted his machine-pistol. 'It'll leave me free to shoot.'

Warren got in and drove off, trying to make as little noise as possible. They bumped across the valley floor towards the settlement, making a speed of less than ten miles an hour, while Follet kept glancing at his watch with a worried eye. At last Warren braked gently; ahead he could see the first low, flat-roofed buildings but there was no movement in the moonlight. The only sound was the gentle throb as the engine ticked over.

'Less than a minute to go,' whispered Follet.

Even as he spoke there was a deep thump as though a giant had coughed explosively, and the ground quivered under them. A plume of dust shot into the air from the shaft of the *qanat* nearest the settlement – the shaft which had formed the secret entrance to the underground laboratory. It rose higher and higher in the form of a ring, coiling and guttering in the moonlight as though the giant had blown a smoke ring. There was a brief change in the skyline of roofs, but it was so imperceptible that Warren could not pin it down.

Follet smote him on the shoulder. 'Go, man – go! Lights!'

The Land-Rover bucked ahead under fierce acceleration, its headlamps glaring at the settlement, and the engine roared and roared again as he slammed through the gears. He felt the wheels spin as he accelerated too fast and then they were off in a jolting ride he would never forget.

All was speed and motion and suddenly-seen vignettes caught in the brightness of the lights – a flutter of hens in the road rudely awakened and alarmed by the explosion, a brown face at a window, eyes squinting as they were dazzled, a man flattened against a wall with arms outspread where he sheltered from their mad rush.

Suddenly Follet yelled, 'Watch it !' and Warren slammed on the brakes. Ahead of them a crack in a wall widened slowly and the wall toppled into the road in what appeared to Warren's heightened senses to be slow motion. There was a crash and a billowing cloud of dust into which the Land-Rover lurched and crunched to a halt. The dust swirled into the cab and Warren coughed convulsively as his mouth was filled.

'Goddam jerry-built houses,' grumbled Follet.

Warren rammed the gear lever into reverse and backed out fast. As the dust settled he saw that the road ahead was completely blocked. Somewhere there was the flat report of a gun being fired. 'Better get out of here,' said Follet. 'See if we can find a way around.'

Warren kept going in reverse because there was no room to turn. At the first clear space he swung around and looked for an exit roughly in the direction he wanted to go. More shots were fired but no bullets seemed to come close. Follet pointed. 'Try down there. Move it, for Christ's sake!'

As Warren headed the Land-Rover at the narrow street something thumped against the side. Follet swung his machine-pistol out of the side window and pressed the trigger. There was a sound as of cloth ripping as he emptied half a magazine. 'Just to keep their heads down,' he shouted.

The Land-Rover plunged down the street which seemed to become even narrower and there was a clang as it scraped a wall. Ahead a man ran out and stood pointing a gun at them. Warren ducked involuntarily and stamped harder with his foot. The Land-Rover bucked and drove ahead; there was a soft thump and a last vision of two hands thrown up despairingly and a rifle thrown into the darkness.

Then they were out of the street and on the other side of the settlement with blackness in front of them as far as they could see. Follet tugged at Warren's arm. 'Switch off the lights so they'll lose us.' He looked back. 'I wonder how Andy's doing?'

Tozier was looking towards the settlement when the explosion happened. He saw the dust cloud climb into the air and presently the ground shivered beneath his feet under the transmitted shock and he heard the sound. A sudden breeze drove upward from the mouth of the shaft against his face and then was gone and there was a noise which he could not interpret.

He bent down and shouted, 'Ben!' There was no answer.

He hesitated, biting his lip, and then seized the rope and lowered himself into the shaft. At the bottom he flashed his light around. Everything appeared to be normal so he shouted again. A piece of earth broke from the roof and splashed into the water.

He pointed his lamp downwards and frowned as he estimated the depth of water. Surely it had not been as deep as that before. He pulled out his knife and stuck it into the *qanat* wall just above the water level and his frown deepened as he saw the water level slowly rise to cover the haft of the knife.

His light, pointing down the *qanat,* showed nothing as he went forward. By the time he had gone a hundred yards and passed two shafts the water was swirling about his thighs, and then he saw the roof fall that blocked the *qanat* completely. This primitive tunnel with an unsupported roof had not been able to withstand the hammer blow of the explosion even at this distance, and he wondered how much of the *qanat* had collapsed.

There was nothing he could do, so he turned away and by the time he reached the rope the water was chest high, fed from the underground spring upstream in the mountains.

When he reached the surface he was soaked and shivering in the cold night air, but he ran without a backward glance at the deadly trap that had entombed Bryan and Speering. In his profession death was a commonplace to be accepted. Nothing he could do would now help Bryan and he would be hard put to it to save his own skin.

He drove to the edge of the settlement carefully and stopped, switching off the engine so he could hear better. There was much to hear – shouting and a babble of voices – and there were lights now as Ahmed and his men tried to find the extent of the damage. Tozier grinned coldly as he heard the centre of activity move over to the left towards the *qanat.*

He removed the shoulder-rest from the machine-pistol, cocked it and laid it on the seat next to him, ready to hand. Then he restarted the engine and crept forward in the darkness without switching on his lights – this was a time for cunning, not bravado; Ahmed's men were now roused and he could not tear through the settlement as he had advised Warren to do.

He moved forward steadily past the first buildings, and as he came into an open space he was spotted. There was a shout and somebody fired a gun, and there was a faint response of other and fainter shouts from further away. Even as he manipulated the gear lever there was another shot; he saw the muzzle discharge as a flicker in the darkness ahead so he switched on his lights to see what he was up against.

The Land-Rover gained momentum and he saw three men ahead of him, their hands upflung to shade their eyes against the sudden dazzle. He groped for the gun on the seat and was just in time to raise it as one of the men jumped on to the running-board, wrenching the door open and reaching for him. He lifted the gun and fired twice and there was a choked cry. When he had time to take his eyes from the road he risked a glance sideways and saw that the man was gone.

He looked up to the rear view mirror and saw the flicker of rifle fire in the darkness behind him which disappeared with shocking suddenness as a bullet whipped past his head to shiver the mirror to fragments. He swung the wheel to turn a corner and pawed at his brow to wipe a sticky wetness from his eyes where the blood dripped from a deep cut.

Then he skidded to a halt as he faced the same fallen wall that had confronted Follet and Warren. He cursed as he put the Land-Rover into reverse and ducked as a bullet hit the side of the body. The quick, sharp report of several rifles shooting simultaneously made him grab his machine-pistol, thumb it on to rapid fire and squirt a magazine full of bullets in a deadly spray towards the indistinct figures behind him.

Follet had been listening intently to the rising crescendo of gunfire in the settlement. When he heard the rip of the machine-pistol he said, 'They've cornered Andy. Let's go get him out.'

Warren, who had already turned the vehicle around in preparation for this moment, moved into action, and they started on their way back. Follet said, 'I think they've trapped him in the same place where they nearly got us. You know where to go.'

Warren drove down the narrow street and past the crumpled body of the man he had run down. At the corner, sheltering from the threat of Tozier's gun, was a crowd of Kurds who were taken by surprise by this newly-launched attack in their rear. Follet leaned from the window and pressed the trigger and they ran for cover. One did not make it – he lurched as though he had tripped over something invisible and went head over heels and lay still.

'Straight on,' yelled Follet. 'Then turn round.'

The tyres squealed as Warren pulled the Land-Rover in a too tight turn at too high a speed. His lights illuminated the other vehicle, and Follet leaned out and yelled, 'Come on, Andy, what the hell are you waiting for?'

Tozier's Land-Rover jerked backwards into the clear space and shot up the narrow street with Warren close behind, while Follet squeezed off regular bursts to the rear to discourage pursuit. They broke from the settlement with Warren close on Tozier's tail, and drove a full three miles before pulling to a halt at the top of the high ground above the valley.

Follet looked down at the lights in the valley, but none was moving. 'They're not following us,' he said. 'They wouldn't chase us in the dark without lights.'

Warren felt squeezed and empty. It was the first time anyone had shot at him with intent to kill. He lifted trembling hands, then looked towards the other vehicle. 'I didn't see Ben,' he said.

There was the crunch of boots on gravel and Tozier appeared at his side window, his face blood-smeared. 'Ben won't be coming,' he said quietly. 'He bought it.'

'It was his own goddam fault,' said Follet in a high voice.

'Yes,' agreed Warren sadly. 'It was his own fault. You're sure, Andy?'

'I'm sure,' said Tozier with finality. He looked back at the valley. 'We'd better go. I want to be over the Iraqi border before Ahmed wakes up to what's really happened.'

He walked away and Warren heard a door slam. The two vehicles moved off slowly.

SEVEN

Dan Parker ran his hand lovingly along the smooth flank of the torpedo. It came away sticky with thin oil. 'The old Mark XI,' he said. 'I never really expected to see one o' these again.'

'You'd better make it work,' said Eastman. 'These things cost a lot of dough.'

'It'll cost a lot more before I'm finished,' said Parker equably. 'I'll be needin' some equipment.' He looked around the bare shed. 'There's room enough here.'

'What will you need?' asked Jeanette Delorme,

'Some machine tools to start with; a lathe, a small milling machine – universal type for preference – an' a drill press. An' a hell of a lot o' small tools, spanners an' suchlike – I'll make a list o' those.'

'Get it from him now, Jack,' she said. 'Give him every-thing he wants. I'm going home.'

'What about me?' asked Eastman.

'Take a taxi,' she said, and walked out.

Abbot smiled at Eastman. 'She's the boss all right. I can see that straight away.'

'I can do without any cracks from you,' said Eastman unsmilingly. He turned to Parker. 'Anything else?'

'Oh yes,' said Parker, who was studying the business end of the torpedo. 'This is a warhead; I hope there's nothin' in it.'

'It was ordered empty.'

'That's a relief. Old TNT is bloody unreliable stuff. But this is no good anyway.'

'What the hell . . .?'

'Take it easy,' said Parker. 'No harm done. But if you want a practice run to prove the thing out I'll need a practice head as well as this one. If you shot off this fish now it would sink at the end of the run, an' you wouldn't want that. A practice head has a flotation chamber to keep the torpedo from sinkin' an' a Holmes light so you can find it. You'll be able to get a practice head from the same place you got this.' He slapped the side of the torpedo. 'Wherever that is.'

'Okay, you'll get your practice head. Anything else?'

'The batteries, o' course. They're pretty important, aren't they? I'll put those on the list, too – types an' quantities. They'll set you back a packet.' He studied the torpedo. 'I'll be wantin' to run her in here, so we'd better have some way o' clampin' her down. Two concrete pillars wi' proper clamps.' He looked up. 'These things develop a hell of a torque an' we don't want her jumpin' all over the bloody shed.' He slapped the side of his game leg. 'That's what busted me out o' the Navy.'

Abbot paced out the length of the torpedo. 'It's bigger than I thought. I didn't realize they were as big as this.'

'Twenty-one-inch-diameter,' said Parker. 'Twenty-two-feet, five-an'-four-fifths-inches long. Weight in war trim – thirty-six-hundred an' thirty-one pounds.' He slapped the warhead. 'An' she packs a hell of a punch – seven hundred an' eighteen pounds o' TNT in here.'

'We can pack over seven hundred pounds in there?' asked Eastman alertly.

Parker shook his head. 'Five hundred I said an' five hundred I meant. I'm goin' to put some batteries in the head. Have you thought how you're goin' to launch her?'

'You're the expert,' said Eastman. 'You tell me.'

'There are three ways. From a tube underwater, like from a submarine; from a tube above water, like from a destroyer; from an aeroplane. I wouldn't recommend the last – not if you're carrying valuables. It's apt to bugger the guidance system.'

'Okay,' said Eastman. 'Airplanes are out. What about the other ways?'

'I don't suppose you can lay your hands on a destroyer,' said Parker meditatively. 'An' torpedo tubes look a bit out o' place anywhere else, if you get my meanin'. I think your best bet is underwater launchin'; it's nice an' inconspicuous. But that means a ship wi' a bit o' draught to it.'

Eastman nodded. 'I like your thinking – it makes sense.'

'You should be able to get a submarine-type tube from the same place you got this fish. I can jury-rig air bottles for the launchin'.'

'You'll get your tube,' promised Eastman.

Parker yawned. 'I'm tired,' he said. 'I'll make out your list tomorrow.'

'The boss said now,' Eastman pointed out.

'She'll have to bloody well wait,' snapped Parker. 'I'm too tired to think straight. This is not goin' to be a quick job an' another eight hours isn't goin' to make any difference.'

'I'll tell her that,' said Eastman ironically.

'You do that, mate,' said Parker. 'Let's start as we mean to go on, shall we?' He looked Eastman in the eye. 'If you want a rush job you can have it – but I won't guarantee the result. If I can do it my way you get my guarantee.' He grinned. 'You wouldn't want to lose the fish when it's carryin' a full load of dope, would you?'

'No, goddam it!' Eastman flinched involuntarily at the thought.

'There you are, then,' said Parker with a wave of his hand. 'You push off an' come back in the morning at about ten o'clock an' I'll have your list all ready. We know where to bed down.'

'Okay,' said Eastman. 'I'll be back tomorrow.' He walked away across the shed and up the wooden staircase. At the top he turned. 'Just one thing: you don't leave here – either of you. Ali is here to see you don't. He's a bad bastard when he's aroused, so watch it.'

Abbot said, 'We'll watch him.'

Eastman grinned genially. 'That's not what I said, but you've got the idea.' He opened the door and they heard him speak in a low voice. When he went out the Arab, Ali, came in. He did not descend the stairs but just stood leaning on the rail watching them.

Abbot glanced at Parker. 'You were pushing him a bit, weren't you?'

'Just gettin' meself a bit of elbow room,' said Parker. He grinned. 'I was a petty officer an' I've met that type before. You meet plenty o' snotty officers in the service who try to run you ragged. But a good craftsman has always got 'em by the balls an' the trick is to squeeze just hard enough to let 'em know it. They get the message in no time at all.'

'I hope you can make it stick,' said Abbot. He looked at the torpedo. 'They got hold of this thing in jig time – I wonder how they were able to lay their hands on it so fast. It strikes me that this is an efficient mob. I think we'll have to watch how we go very carefully.' He looked up at the Arab speculatively.

'I wasn't kiddin' when I said I was tired,' said Parker. 'An' I want to get out o' this bloody monkey suit – it's killin' me. Let's go to bed, for God's sake!'

II

Once provided with his list Eastman moved fast. Within two days most of the equipment needed was installed, and while this was being done the torpedo was removed so that no workman would see it. All that was being done, as far as they were concerned, was the establishment of a small machine-shop.

Then the work began on the torpedo itself. Abbot was astonished at the complexity of it and his respect for Parker increased. Any man who could master such a complicated instrument and treat it with the casual insouciance that Parker did was worthy of a great deal of respect.

They took out the lead-acid batteries – fifty-two of them – and piled them in a corner of the shed. 'I'll be needin' those to test the motor later,' said Parker. 'There's no point in usin' the expensive ones. But then they'd better be taken out to sea an' dumped. Any naval man who caught sight o' those would know what they are, an' that might give the game away.'

Eastman made a note of it and Abbot privately thought that Parker was entering into the spirit of things a little too wholeheartedly. He said as much when they were alone and Parker grinned. 'We have to make it look good, don't we? Every little helps. Eastman is gettin' quite matey an' that could be useful.' Abbot had to agree.

Parker took out the motor for cleaning. 'It's in good nick,' he said, and stroked it almost lovingly. 'A beautiful job. Ninety-eight horsepower an' only that big. A really lovely bit of work an' designed to be blown to hell.' He shook his head. 'It's a bloody funny world we live in.'

He stripped the torpedo meticulously while Abbot did the fetching and carrying and the cleaning of the less important pieces. He demanded – and got – special oils and greases to pack the glands, and expensive wiring for his redesigned circuits, while his new mercury batteries cost a small fortune in themselves. He preached like an evangelist, and the word he preached was 'perfection.' 'Nothing is too good,' he proclaimed flatly. 'This is goin' to be the best torpedo that ever took water.'

And it was very likely so. No service torpedo ever had such undivided and loving attention, and Abbot came to the conelusion that only a prototype fussed over by nervous boffins prior to service tests could be compared with this lone torpedo.

Eastman got the point very early in the game under Parker's needling attitude. He saw that Parker was really putting up a magnificent effort and he co-operated wholeheartedly to give him everything he needed. And that was not really to be wondered at thought Abbot, when you considered that riding in the warhead would be dope worth $25,000,000.

Parker spent most time on the guidance system, clucking over it like a mother hen over an errant chick. 'If this thing packs in you've lost the lot,' he said to Eastman.

'It had better not,' said Eastman grimly.

'It won't,' said Parker in a steady voice.

'What does it do?'

'It keeps her running straight – come what may,' said Parker. 'When I quoted you a figure for accuracy o' three inches in a hundred yards I was allowin' meself a bit o' leeway. In the hands of a good mechanic a Mark XI is damned near as accurate as a rifle bullet – say, an inch in a hundred yards. O' course, the ordinary Mark XI has a short range, so even at maximum the point o' strike wouldn't be more than six feet out if she ran well. But this beauty has to run a hell of a long way so I'm aimin' to beat the record. I'm tryin' for a half-inch error in a hundred yards. It's damn' near impossible but I'm tryin' for it.'

Eastman went away very happy.

'You're putting in a lot of time and sweat on something that's going to be sabotaged,' observed Abbot.

Parker shrugged. 'Every torpedoman gets that feelin' from time to time. You take a lovely bit o' mechanism like this an' you work on it to get a performance that even the designer didn't dream of. Then you slam it against the side

of a ship an' blow it to smithereens. That's sabotage of a
kind, isn't it?'

'I suppose it is if you look at it that way. But it's what torpedoes are for.'

Parker nodded. 'I know this one is goin' to be sabotaged
in the end but we still have sea trials to come an' she's got
to work.' He looked at Abbot and said seriously, 'You know,
I haven't been so bloody happy for a long time. I came out
o' the Navy an' got a job tinkerin' wi' other folk's cars an'
all the time I missed somethin', an' I didn't know what
it was.' He waved at the stripped-down torpedo. 'Now I
know – I missed these beauties.'

'Don't get too carried away,' advised Abbot. 'Remember
that when it comes to the final push this thing must fail.'

'It'll fail,' said Parker glumly. His face tightened. 'But it's
goin' to have one bloody good run first.' He tapped Abbot
on the chest. 'If you think this thing is easy, Mike, you're
dead wrong. I'm working on the edge o' the impossible all
the time. A Mark XI was never designed to go fifteen miles
an' to get it to travel the distance is goin' to be tricky. But
I'll do it an' I'll enjoy doin' it because this is the last chance
I'll ever have of handlin' a torpedo. Now, let's get down
to it.'

Every two bits of metal that could be separated were
taken apart, scrutinized carefully and put back together
with meticulous care. Piece by piece the whole torpedo was
reassembled until the time came when it was clamped
down for a bench test and Abbot saw the reason for the
clamps. Even running at a quarter power it was evident that
it would have run wild in the shed had it not been secured.

Parker professed satisfaction and said to Eastman, 'What
about the tube? I've done all I can wi' the fish.'

'Okay,' said Eastman. 'Come with me.'

He took them a little way up the coast to a small shipyard, and pointed to a worn-out coaster of about 3,000 tons.

'That's the ship – the *Orestes;* Greek-owned and registered in Panama.'

Parker looked at her dubiously. 'Are you goin' to cross the Atlantic in that?'

'I am – and so are you,' said Eastman. 'She's done it before and she can do it again; she only has to do it once more and then she'll be lost at sea.' He smiled. 'She's under-insured and we're not even going to press too hard for that – we don't want anybody getting too nosy about what happened to her. If you're going to install an underwater tube you'll have to cut a hole in the hull. How are you going to do that?'

'Let's have a closer look,' said Parker, so they went aboard. He spent a lot of time below, up in the bows, then he made a sketch. 'We'll make a coffer dam. Get that made up and have it welded to the outside of the hull as marked, then I can cut a hole from the inside an' install the tube. Once that's done the thing can be ripped off. You'll have to find a diver who can keep his mouth shut – it isn't a normal shipyard job.'

Eastman grinned. 'We own the shipyard,' he said softly.

So Parker installed the launching-tube which took another week. He spent a great deal of time measuring and aligned the tube exactly fore and aft. 'All you have to do is to point the ship accurately,' he said. 'That's it – we're ready for trials.'

III

Jeanette Delorme had not been around for some time, and it worried Abbot because he wanted to have her under his eye. As it was, he and Parker were virtually prisoners and cut off from the rest of the organization. He did not know what Warren was doing, nor could he contact Hellier to tell him what was happening. With such a breakdown of communications things could go very wrong.

He said to Eastman, 'Your boss doesn't seem to be taking much interest. I haven't seen her around since that first night.'

'She doesn't mix with the working slobs,' said Eastman. 'I do the overseeing.' He fixed Abbot with a sardonic eye. 'Remember what I told you about her. I'd steer clear if I were you.'

Abbot shrugged. 'I'm thinking of the money. We're ready for the trial and I don't think you are authorised to sign cheques.'

'Don't worry about the dough,' said Eastman with a grin. 'Worry about the trial. It's set for tomorrow and she'll be there – and God help you if it doesn't work out.' As an afterthought he said, 'She's been over to the States, arranging things at that end.'

The black Mercedes called early next morning to pick up Abbot, who was wary when he found he was to be separated from Parker. 'Where will Dan be?'

'On the *Orestes,*' said Eastman.

'And me?'

'Why don't you go along and find out?' said Eastman. He seemed disgruntled.

So Abbot went with reluctance in the Mercedes to wherever it was going to take him – which proved to be the heart of Beirut. As the car passed the office of the *Daily Star,* the English-language newspaper, he fingered the envelope in his pocket and wondered how he could get in there without undue attention. He and Hellier had arranged an emergency information service, but it seemed as though he was not going to get the chance to use it.

The car took him to the yacht harbour where he was met by a trimly dressed sailor. 'Mr Abbot?' Abbot nodded, and the sailor said, 'This way, sir,' and led him to a fast-looking launch which was moored at the steps.

As the launch took off smoothly, Abbot said, 'Where are we going?'

'The yacht – the *Stella del Mare*.' The sailor pointed. 'There.'

Abbot studied the yacht as they approached. She was a rich man's toy of the type typically to be found in the Mediterranean. Of about two hundred tons, she would be fully equipped with every conceivable comfort and aid to navigation and would be quite capable of circumnavigating the world. But, also typically, that she would not do – these boats were usually to be found tied up for weeks at a time at Nice, Cannes, Beirut and all the other haunts of the jet-set – the floating mansions of the wealthy. It looked more and more as though heroin smuggling was profitable.

He was met at the top of the companionway by another floating flunkey dressed in a sailor suit and escorted to the sun deck. As he climbed a ladder he heard the clank of the anchor chain and the vibration of engines. It appeared that the *Stella del Mare* had been waiting for him.

On the sun deck he found Jeanette Delorme. She was stretched supine, adding to her tan, and was so dressed that the maximum amount of skin got the benefit; her bikini was the most exiguous he had ever seen – a small triangle at the loins and two nipple covers. He hadn't seen anything like it outside a Soho strip joint, and he doubted if the whole lot weighed more than an eighth of an ounce; certainly less than the dark glasses through which she regarded him.

She waved her hand lazily. 'Hello, Mike; this is Youssif Fuad.'

Abbot reluctantly looked away from her and towards the man sitting near by. The bald head, the brown lizard skin and the reptilian eyes certainly made a change for the worse. He nodded in acknowledgment. 'Morning, Mr Fuad.' He had seen Fuad before. This was the Lebanese banker

with whom Delorme had had lunch, and whom he had
written off as being too respectable. It just went to show
how wrong you could be. Fuad was certainly not taking a
sea voyage on the day of the torpedo trial for his health.

Fuad gave a quick and birdlike jerk of his head. He said
petulantly, 'What is he doing here?'

'Because I want him here,' said Jeanette. 'Take a seat, Mike.'

'I thought I said I was not to be brought into . . .' Fuad
stopped and shook his head again. 'I don't like it.'

Abbot, who was in a half-crouch preparatory to sitting
down, straightened again. 'I know when I'm not wanted. If
you whistle up that launch again, I'll be going.'

'Sit down, Mike,' said Jeanette with a whip-crack in her
voice that automatically bent Abbot's knees. 'Youssif is
always nervous. He's afraid of losing his respectability.'
There was mockery in her voice.

'We had an agreement,' said Fuad angrily.

'So I've broken it,' said Jeanette. 'What are you going to
do about it?' She smiled. 'Don't be so worried, Youssif; I'll
look after you.'

There was something going on between them that Abbot
did not like. Apparently he was not supposed to know about
Fuad, and Fuad did not like to have his cover broken.
Which made it dicey for Mike Abbot if Fuad decided to
bring things back to normal. From the look of him he would
not bat a lizardlike eye at murder. He looked back towards
Delorme – a much more rewarding sight – and had to
remind himself that she would not, either.

Jeanette smiled at him. 'What have you been doing with
yourself, Mike?'

'You know bloody well what I've been doing,' said Abbot
baldly. 'Or else Eastman's been wasting his time.'

'Jack has told me as much as he knows,' she agreed.
'Which isn't much – he's no technician.' Her voice sharpened. 'Will this torpedo work?'

'I'm no technician, either,' said Abbot. 'But Dan Parker
seems confident.' He rubbed the side of his jaw. 'I think you'll
owe us a hundred thousand dollars before the day's out.'

'Youssif has the cheque ready. I hope he'll give it to you –
for your sake.'

This clear warning of the penalty for an unsuccessful trial
made the sweat break out on Abbot's forehead. He thought
of what Parker had said about working on the edge of the
impossible, took a deep breath and forced himself to say
lightly, 'Where are we going? What's the drill?' He turned
his head and looked towards the receding land, more to
avoid Jeanette's hidden gaze than out of interest. In a comparison of these two it was obvious that the female of the
species was more deadly than the male.

She sat up suddenly, and adjusted the minimal bra which
had sagged dangerously under the stress of her movement.
'We are going to join the *Orestes*. She is out there – away from
the shipping routes. We have some fast boats too, to make
sure we are not disturbed. This is like a naval exercise.'

'How long will we take to get out there?'

'Maybe two hours – maybe longer.'

'Say three hours each way,' said Abbot. 'And God knows
how long for the trial. This is going to take all day. I'm
beginning to feel seasick already. I never have liked ships.'

The tip of her tongue played along her top lip. 'I have a
certain cure for seasickness,' she said. 'Infallible, I assure
you. I don't think you will have time to be seasick, Mike
Abbot.'

She put her hands behind her head and pushed her
breasts at him, and he believed her. He glanced at Fuad who
was also watching her with his lizard stare, but there was no
hint of lust in those dead, ophidian eyes.

Not far over the horizon the *Orestes* lumbered through the
calm morning sea on her way to the rendezvous. Parker

climbed the ladder to the bridge and made the thumbs-up sign. 'Everything's under control. I'm bringin' the batteries up to heat now.'

Eastman nodded, then jerked his head towards the officer with the mildewed braid on his battered cap. 'The skipper's not too happy. He says the ship's cranky in her steering.'

'What would he expect with a bloody big hole cut off-centre in the bows?' demanded Parker. 'He'll get used to it.'

'I guess so,' Eastman was thoughtful. 'Would it help to cut another hole on the other side?'

'It might,' said Parker cautiously. 'It would equalize things a bit.'

'What's this about warming up the batteries? I didn't know you did that.'

'A warm battery delivers power quicker an' easier than a cold one. A difference o' thirty degrees Fahrenheit can increase the range by a third – an' we want all the range we can get.' Parker took out his pipe. 'I've set her to run at twelve feet. Any less than that an' she's likely to porpoise – jump in an' out o' the water. An instability like that could throw her right off course. At the end of her run she'll bob up nice an' easy like a cork, an' her Holmes light will go off so you can see her.'

'You'll be there to find the torpedo.'

'I thought you wanted me here to check the firing.'

'You can do both,' said Eastman. 'There'll be a boat waiting to take you to the other end of the course.'

Parker struck a match. 'You'll need a hell of a fast boat to outrun a torpedo.'

'We've got one. Is forty-five knots fast enough?'

'That's fast enough,' admitted Parker, and blew out a wreath of blue smoke.

Eastman sniffed distastefully and moved up wind. 'What's that you're smoking? Old socks?'

Parker grinned cheerfully. 'Feelin' queasy already?' He drew on the pipe again. 'Where did Mike go this mornin'?'

Eastman stared at the horizon. 'The boss wanted to see him,' he said morosely.

'What for?' asked Parker in surprise.

'I'll give you three guesses,' said Eastman sarcastically. 'The little bitch has hot pants.'

Parker clucked deprecatingly. 'That's no way to talk of your employer,' he observed. 'You think . . . er . . . that she an' Mike are . . . er . . . ?'

'I'll bet they're both in the sack now,' said Eastman savagely, and thumped the rail.

'Why, Jack ! I do believe you're jealous.' Parker chuckled delightedly.

'The hell with that,' said Eastman in a hard voice. 'I'm immune to anything that chick does with her flaunty little ass – but she shouldn't mix pleasure with business. It could get us all into trouble. She shouldn't have . . .'

He broke off, and Parker said innocently, 'She shouldn't have what?'

'Nothing,' said Eastman brusquely, and walked away across the bridge where he talked in a low voice to the skipper.

Abbot buttoned his shirt and leaned across the tousled bed to look through the port. The things I do in the line of duty, he thought, and checked his watch. They had been at sea for just over two hours. From the compartment next to the cabin he heard the brisk splash of water as Jeanette showered, and presently she appeared, naked and dripping. She tossed him a towel. 'Dry me,' she commanded.

As he rubbed her down vigorously he was irresistibly reminded of his boyhood when he had haunted his grandfather's stables and had been taught the horseman's lore by old Benson, the chief groom. Automatically he hissed

through his teeth as Benson had done when currying a
horse, and wondered what the old man would have
thought of this filly.

'You haven't been around much,' he said. 'I expected to
see more of you.'

'You couldn't see much more of me.'

'What were you doing in the States?'

She stiffened slightly under his hands. 'How do you
know I was in the States?'

'Eastman told me.'

'Jack talks too much.' After a while, she said, 'I was doing
what you would expect – setting things up.'

'A successful trip?'

'Very.' She twisted free from him. 'I'm going to make a
lot of money.'

Abbot grinned. 'I know. I've been trying to figure out
how to carve myself a bigger share.' He studied her as she
walked across the cabin. Her long-flanked body was evenly
tanned and there were no betraying white patches.
Evidently the minimal bikini she had worn there morning
had been a concession to someone's modesty – but whose
he could not imagine. Fuad's? That was a laugh.

She turned and smiled. 'It is a possibility – if the trial is a
success.' As she stepped into a pair of brief panties, she said,
'What do you think of Jack Eastman?'

'He strikes me as being a tough boy,' said Abbot consideringly. 'He's no cream-puff.'

'Could you get on with him?'

'I might – if he could get along with me.'

She nodded. 'Something might be arranged.' She fastened the bra strap. 'Even if you didn't get along together
something might be arranged – if you are prepared to help
with the arrangements.'

Christ, what a hellcat! he thought. It was quite clear
what was being tentatively offered. He could supplant

Eastman by getting rid of him, and he had no illusions about what that implied. Probably by enlisting his aid in rubbing out her partner she would make even more money. But then he would be in Eastman's seat – the hot seat – a target for the next gun-happy sucker to enter her sexy little life. He thought of the list of murdered men in her dossier and wondered how many of them had been her lovers. The female spider – the eater of males.

He smiled engagingly. 'It's a thought. Where does friend Fuad fit into all this?'

'Now *you* are talking too much,' she said reprovingly as she buttoned her blouse. 'He has nothing to do with you.'

'Oh yes he does. He holds the moneybags, doesn't he?'

She sat at the dressing-table and began to make up her face. 'You jump to a quick conclusion,' she said. 'But you are right.' Her eyes watched him through the mirror. 'You are very clever, Mike; much cleverer than Jack. I don't think you'd have any trouble with him at all.'

'Thanks for the vote of confidence.'

'Since you are so clever, perhaps you can tell me something. What do you know about Regent Films?'

Abbot was aware that she was watching him even though her back was turned, and hoped his expression had not changed. 'It's an English – British – film company. Quite a big one.'

'Who is at the top?'

'A man called Hellier – Sir Robert Hellier.'

She turned to him. 'So tell me – why should an English nobleman – a milord – interfere with me?'

Abbot chuckled – he could not help it. 'I suppose you could call old Hellier a nobleman. *Is* he interfering with you?'

'His company is – very much so. It has cost me a lot of money.'

Abbot kept a straight face even though he wanted to cheer. So Warren and the Iranian team had stabbed her right in the wallet she substituted for a heart. He shrugged. 'I don't know much about Hellier. He wasn't on my beat – I didn't do films or the gossip stuff. For my money it's a respectable outfit he runs. Regent makes pretty good pictures – I've seen some of them.'

She threw down a comb with a clatter. 'These Regent people have cost me more money than you've even heard of. They're . . .' The telephone rang and interrupted her. She picked it up. 'Yes? All right.'

Abbot looked through the port and saw the *Orestes* not very far away. Jeanette said, 'Come on, Mike; we're wanted on deck. We're transferring to the other ship.'

When they arrived on deck Abbot saw a group of seamen busily engaged in lowering a boat. The *Stella del Mare* had stopped and was rolling uneasily in the slight swell, and the *Orestes* was abeam of them about two hundred yards away.

Fuad was not on deck, but Abbot caught sight of him lurking in the saloon. It seemed that Youssif Fuad was intent on concealing his association with these nefarious activities, which was why he had objected when Abbot had come on board. Jeanette, on the other hand, seemed to want Fuad more deeply involved, and Abbot wondered if he could use the issue as a point of attack.

He followed Jeanette down the companionway and stepped into the launch, and it pulled away in a lazy circle and headed for the *Orestes*. When Jeanette climbed up on to the deck of the battered coaster she was suddenly businesslike. 'All right, Jack; let's get on our way. Are you ready, Parker?'

Parker grinned easily. 'As ready as I'll ever be.'

She offered him a small, tight smile. 'You'd better make it good – but Jack's been telling me you do good work.'

The telegraph clanged, the deck vibrated as the engines increased speed, and the *Orestes* began to move. 'What's the drill?' asked Abbot.

'We go another fifteen miles,' said Eastman. 'Then turn and shoot. We have a couple of boats along the course in case the torpedo comes up too soon, but we'll be pacing it anyway. It should surface somewhere near the yacht – if we get the range we need.'

Abbot laughed, and said to Parker, 'You'd better not be *too* good, Dan; it would be a hell of a joke if you slammed the torpedo into the *Stella del Mare.*'

Parker grunted. 'It wouldn't do too much damage without a warhead. But the fish would be a write-off an' I wouldn't like that.'

'Neither would I,' said Eastman. He gave Abbot an unfriendly stare and said coldly, 'I don't like your sense of humour.'

'Neither do I,' said Abbot, still smiling. 'Dan and I have a hundred thousand dollars riding with this torpedo.'

The *Orestes* ploughed on westward. Jeanette took Eastman by the elbow and they walked to the other side of the deck, deep in conversation. Abbot said, 'He's not as friendly as he was.'

Parker shook with laughter. 'Maybe he's jealous. Has he any cause to be, Mike?'

'You mean me and Delorme?' Abbot pulled a sour face. 'I don't know about jealousy, but he ought to be running scared. The bitch wants me to knock him off at an opportune moment. We had a nice friendly chat.'

'I'll bet you didn't stop at taikin',' said Parker pointedly. 'Do you mean to tell me that she asked you to kill Eastman?'

'Not in so many words, but the subject came up. Another thing – Warren's been hitting her hard over in Iran. She's really steamed up about it. She wanted to know about Regent Films.'

'That's good to know,' said Parker. 'What did you tell her?'

'I acted dumb and stuck to generalities. Maybe Warren can pull off the whole trick and let us off the hook here.'

'He can't,' said Parker. 'We're on the hook an' we're wrigglin'. We'll have to get out o' this ourselves. I'm goin' below – I want to check the fish.'

Abbot frowned; he thought he detected a shade of nervousness in Parker – something that now showed itself for the first time. He did not like to think of what might happen if the trial proved a bust, but Parker was worried about something else – the problem of what was going to happen if the trial was a success. It was something to think about.

Very likely he and Parker would be expected to go with the *Orestes* on the final job, clear across the Atlantic to fire the torpedo ashore on some secluded beach. The snag about that was that it would never get there – Parker would see to that. And what Jeanette would do in that case was not at all problematical, although the details were hazy. Probably he and Parker would share the same concrete coffin at the bottom of the Caribbean. It was a nasty thought.

The correct course of action would be to wait until the warhead was filled with heroin and then dump the lot somehow in such circumstances that he and Parker could get away. The trouble with that line of thought was that everything depended on what Delorme did – he had no initiative at all. They would just have to wait and see what happened.

He leaned on the rail and looked gloomily at the sea, and his thoughts were long and deep. Presently he sighed and turned to watch Jeanette and Eastman who had their heads together. She would be telling him of the arrangements she had made in the States, and he would have given a lot to be able to eavesdrop. If he knew where the heroin was going then the gang in the States could be rounded up – a quick closing in on the beach with the capture of the torpedo – and he and Parker would be in the clear.

His train of thought was broken by the clang of the telegraph bell and the sudden easing of vibration. Parker came up from below and looked over the side. 'We've arrived,' he said. 'Look at that thing down there.'

Abbot saw a fast-looking boat riding easily in the water. Eastman came over, and said, 'That's to take us back to the yacht. How are you going to work this, Parker?'

'Can we talk to this ship from that boat?'

'Sure – there's radio communication.'

'Then have a word with the skipper. There's a switch near the binnacle; he presses the tit when the compass points due north magnetic. I'd like to be in that boat to watch the fish when she leaves. All the skipper has to do is to watch the compass and flick the switch. He'd better be on the wheel himself.'

'I'll tell him,' said Eastman, and went up on to the bridge.

The instructions were given and they went down to the boat which had come alongside, Jeanette and Eastman first, then Abbot and Parker. The engines opened up with a muted growl which spoke of reserve power and they moved away from *Orestes* which turned in a wide sweep on a reciprocal course. Parker watched her. 'Give me the glasses an' tell the skipper he can fire when ready. We move off when I give the word a little over thirty knots – course due north magnetic. Everyone keep an eye astern.'

Eastman spoke into the microphone, then said, 'He'll fire when he gets his bearing – any time now.'

Parker had the glasses at his eyes and was gazing at the bows of *Orestes*. There was a pause, then Eastman said, 'He's fired,' and simultaneously Parker yelled, 'She's on her way – get goin'.' He had seen the burst of air bubbles break from the bow of *Orestes* to be swept away in the wake.

The low growl of the engines burst into an ear-shattering roar as the throttles were opened and Abbot was momentarily pinned back in his seat by the sudden acceleration. Parker was staring at the water. 'She didn't porpoise,' he yelled. 'I was a bit worried about that. She should be runnin' true.'

'What do you mean?' shouted Eastman.

'The tube's only six feet underwater an' the fish is set to run at twelve – I thought she might duck down an' then come up again sharply to break surface. But she didn't – the beauty.' Parker leaned forward. 'Tell your helmsman to keep as near to thirty-one knots as he can an' steer a straight course.'

It was a wild ride and seemed to go on for ever as far as Abbot was concerned. Even though the sea was calm there was a minor swell and the boat would ride a crest and seem to fly for a split second before coming down with a jolting crash. He touched Parker on the arm. 'How long does this go on?'

'Half an hour or so. The torpedo is makin' thirty knots so we should be a bit ahead of her. Keep your eyes peeled aft – wi' a bit o' luck you won't see a bloody thing for a while.'

Abbot stared back at the sea and at the rushing wake unreeling itself from the boat at what seemed to be a fantastic speed. After a while he found it hypnotized him and tended to make him feel sick, so he turned his head and looked at the others, blinking as the wind caught his eyes.

Jeanette was sitting as calmly as she had sat in the Paon Rouge, with one hand braced on a chrome rail. The wind streamed her blonde hair and pressed her blouse against her body. Eastman had his teeth bared in a stiff grin. Occasionally he spoke into the microphone he held, but to whom he was talking Abbot did not know. Probably he was telling the *Stella del Mare* that they were on their way. Parker was riding easily and staring aft, a light of excitement in his eyes and a big grin on his face. This was his day.

The boat rushed through the water interminably. After ten minutes they swept past a fair-sized motor launch which was making lazy circles, and Eastman stood up and waved. This was one of the boats which guarded the course. Eastman sat down abruptly as their own boat bounced violently over the wake which crossed their path – and then again. The circling boat receded into the distance behind them as they pressed on.

Abbot thought of the torpedo somewhere below and behind them if Parker was right. Although he had seen it stripped down, it was hard to realize that it was down there driving through the water undeviatingly at this speed. He looked forward at the broad shoulders of the man at the wheel and saw the muscles of his arms and back writhe as he fought to keep the boat on a straight course and that gave him some inkling of Parker's achievement – one half inch error in a hundred yards for mile after mile after mile.

They passed another circling boat and again bounced over its wake to leave it behind. Eastman looked at his watch. 'Another ten minutes,' he shouted and grinned at Parker. 'We've come ten miles – five to go.'

Parker nodded vigorously. 'Ease a knot off the speed if you can – we don't want to overrun her too much.'

Eastman turned and spoke into the helmsman's ear and the roar of the engines altered the slightest fraction. To Abbot it did not seem to make any difference to the speed; the wake streamed away behind them just as quickly in a line so straight it seemed to be ruled on the blue water. He was beginning to feel sicker; the noise was deafening and the motion upset his stomach, and he knew that if they did not stop soon he would vomit over the side. If this was watersport it was not for him.

Presently Jeanette spoke for the first time. She stood up and pointed. *'Stella del Mare.'*

Abbot felt relieved – his ordeal was almost at an end. Parker twisted round and looked at the yacht, then beckoned to Eastman. 'Don't stop here. Run straight past on the same course. We want the torpedo, not the bloody yacht.'

Eastman nodded and spoke to the helmsman again, and they tore past the Stella del Mare and there was nothing ahead but the bouncing horizon. Parker shouted, 'Everyone look astern – you'll see her with her nose in the air like a bloody great pole stickin' out o' the sea, an' there'll be a light an' a bit o' smoke.'

Everyone looked but there was nothing but the Stella del Mare receding into the distance, and Abbot felt depressed as the minutes ticked by. He looked at his watch and noted that it had been thirty-three minutes since they had begun this mad dash across the Mediterranean. He did a mental calculation and figured they had come at least sixteen miles and possibly more. What could have gone wrong?

He remembered what Parker had said about setting the torpedo to run at a depth of twelve feet from a launch of six feet. Parker had been worried about porpoising, but what if the torpedo had just carried on down into the depths of the sea? From what Parker had previously told him, if the torpedo got much below sixty feet the pressure would damage it beyond repair and it would never be seen again.

He looked at Jeanette whose expression had never changed. What would she do about it? He could guess the answer would be violent. Parker was staring aft with a tense look on his face. His grin was gone and the crowsfeet around his eyes were etched deeper.

Thirty-four minutes – and nothing. Thirty-five minutes – and nothing. Abbot tried to catch Parker's eye, but Parker had attention only for the sea. It's a bust, decided Abbot in desperation.

Suddenly Parker was convulsed into movement. 'Thar she blows!' he yelled excitedly. 'On the starboard quarter. Cut these bloody engines.'

Abbot looked over the sea and was thankful to hear the engines die. Away in the distance bobbed the torpedo, just as Parker had described it, and a smoky yellow flame burned dimly in the strong sunlight. The boat turned and headed towards it while Parker literally danced a jig. 'Where's a boat-hook?' he demanded. 'We have to secure her.'

'What's that flame?' asked Eastman.

'The Holmes light,' said Parker. 'It's powered by sodium – the wetter it gets the hotter it burns.'

'A neat trick,' commented Eastman.

Parker turned to him and said solemnly, 'That torpedo bein' there at all is an even neater trick. I reckon she did eighteen miles an' that's not just a trick – it's a bloody miracle. Are you satisfied wi' it?'

Eastman grinned and looked at Jeanette. 'I guess we are.'

'We'll be expecting your cheque,' said Abbot to Jeanette.

She smiled at him brilliantly. 'I'll get it from Youssif as soon as we get back to the yacht.'

IV

They went back to Beirut in the *Stella del Mare*, leaving the *Orestes* to pick up the torpedo from the launch to which it was secured, with Parker vowing eternal vengeance on anyone who was so ham-fisted as to damage it in the process. In the luxurious saloon Eastman broke open the cocktail cabinet. 'I guess we all need a drink.'

Abbot dropped limply into a chair. For once Eastman had expressed exactly his own feelings. In the last hour he had gone through enough emotions to last a man a lifetime and a stiff drink would go down well. It turned into a convivial party – Eastman was jovial, Parker was drunk on success and needed no liquor to buoy him up, Jeanette was gay and sparkling, and even Youssif Fuad unbent enough to allow a fugitive smile to chase quickly across his face. Abbot was merely thankful.

Jeanette clicked her fingers at Fuad who took a folded piece of paper from his pocket and gave it to her. She passed it to Abbot. 'The first instalment, Mike. There'll be more to come.'

He unfolded the cheque and saw that it was drawn on Fuad's own bank for $100,000 American, and wondered what would happen if he attempted to draw it before the final run of the torpedo off the American coast. But he did not comment on it – he was not supposed to know Fuad was a banker. 'I wish us many more,' he said.

Eastman raised his glass. 'To the best goddam mechanic it's been my fortune to meet.'

They drank to Parker, who actually blushed. 'It's too bad they don't have torpedo races,' said Eastman. 'You'd never be out of a job, Dan. I've not seen anything so exciting since I was at Hialeah.' He smiled at Jeanette. 'But I guess there's a lot more riding on this than I ever had on a horse race.'

Parker said, 'That's just the first bit – now we run into more problems.'

Jeanette leaned forward. 'What problems?' she asked sharply.

Parker swished his drink around in his glass. 'Normally a Mark XI torpedo has a short range – a bit over three miles. Anythin' you shoot at you can see, an' any damn' fool can see a ship three miles away. But you're different – you want to shoot at somethin' that's clear over the horizon. You saw the distance we just travelled.'

'That shouldn't be much trouble,' said Eastman. 'Not if you have a good navigator who knows where he is.'

'The best navigator in the world can't tell his position to a quarter-mile in the open sea,' said Parker flatly. 'Not without an inertial guidance system which you couldn't afford even if the Navy would sell you one. You can't buy *those* on the war surplus market.'

'So what's the answer?' asked Jeanette.

'That big derrick on the *Orestes* is about fifty feet above the water,' said Parker. 'If you put a man up there in a sort o' crow's nest he could see a shade over eight miles to the horizon. What you've got to do is to put up a light on shore about the same height or higher, an' if it's bright enough it'll be seen sixteen miles or more out at sea by the chap in the crow's nest. But it needs to be done at night.'

'It's going to be a night job, anyway,' said Eastman.

Parker nodded. 'It needs polishin' up a bit, but that's the general idea.' He paused. 'There might be a few lights along the coast so you'll need to have some way of identifying the right one. You could have a special colour or, better still, put a switch in the circuit an' flash a code. The man in the crow's nest on the *Orestes* should have a telescope – one o' those things target shooters use would do, an' it should be rigidly fixed like a sort o' telescopic sight. As soon as he sees the light through it he presses the tit an' away goes the torpedo. An' it might help if he's on intercom wi' the helmsman.'

'Ideas come thick and fast from you, don't they?' said Eastman admiringly.

'I just try to earn me money,' said Parker modestly. 'I have a stake in this, you know.'

'Yeah,' said Eastman. 'Another two hundred thousand bucks. You're earning it.'

'There might be even more in it for you, Parker,' said Jeanette and smiled sweetly at Fuad. 'Youssif is neither poor nor ungenerous.'

Fuad's face set tight and firm and he hooded his eyes. To Abbot he looked as generous as someone who had just successfully robbed the church poor-box.

Jeanette's car was still awaiting them when they arrived back in the yacht harbour. 'I have something to show you,' she said to Abbot and Parker. 'Get in the car.' To Eastman she said, 'You stay with Youssif and check over with him what I've told you. See if either of you can find any holes in it.'

She got into the car and sat next to Abbot and the car pulled away. Abbot wanted a chance of a private word with Parker who, intoxicated by success, had been shooting his mouth off a little too much. He would have to talk to him about that. He turned to Jeanette. 'Where are we going?'

'Back to where you came from this morning.'

'There are no surprises there,' he said. 'I've seen everything.'

She just smiled at him and said nothing, and the car drifted opulently out of Beirut along the Tripoli road back to the torpedo shed. It turned into the yard, and she said, 'Take a look inside, then come back and we'll talk about it.'

He and Parker got out and walked towards the shed. Just before they opened the door, Abbot said, 'Wait a minute, Dan; I want to talk to you. I don't think you should give them too much – as you were doing on the way back today. If that hellcat gets the idea she doesn't need us we might be in trouble.'

Parker grinned. 'They need us,' he said positively. 'Who is goin' to put new batteries into that torpedo? Eastman wouldn't have a clue, for one. We'll be all right until the end, Mike.' His face sobered. 'But what the hell is goin' to happen then I don't know. Now let's go in an' see what the big surprise is.'

They went into the shed. Parker switched on the lights and stood transfixed at the top of the stairs. 'Bloody hell!' he burst out. 'They need us an' no mistake.'

Lying on trestles below them were *three* torpedoes.

Abbot's mouth was suddenly dry. 'Three more! That's a hell of a lot of heroin.' He was filled with the terrible necessity of getting the information out to where it would do some good. But how the hell could he? Every step he took, every move he made, was under observation.

'If they think I'm goin' to start a bloody one-man production line they can think again,' Parker grumbled.

'Quiet, Dan, for God's sake!' said Abbot. 'I'm trying to think.' After a while he said, 'I'm going to try to pull a fast one on that bitch outside. You back me up. Just remember that you've had a hard day and all you want to do is to go to bed.'

He left the shed and crossed the yard to where the car was waiting. He bent down, and said, 'Quite a surprise. Are all those going to be loaded and shot off at once?'

Jeanette said, 'It's what Jack calls the jackpot. There's more money in it for you, of course.'

'Yes,' said Abbot. 'We'll have to discuss that – but why do it here? Why don't you and me and Dan take the night off to celebrate – say at the Paon Rouge.' He grinned. 'It's on me – I can afford it now.'

Parker said from behind him, 'Count me out, I'm too tired. All I want is me bed.'

'Well, that doesn't really matter, does it? You'll trust me to fix the finance with Jeanette?'

'O' course. You do what's right.' Parker passed his hand over his face. 'I'm goin' to turn in. Good night.'

He walked away, and Abbot said, 'What about it, Jeanette? I'm tired of being cooped up in this place. I want to stretch my wings and crow a bit.' He gestured towards the shed. 'There's a lot of work in there – I'd like to have a break' before we start.'

Jeanette indicated her clothing. 'But I can't go to the Paon Rouge dressed like this.'

'That's all right,' said Abbot. 'Give me two ticks while I change, then I'll come with you to wherever you live. You change, and we go on the town. Simple.'

She smiled thoughtfully. 'Yes, that might be a good idea. How are you as a lady's maid? I gave my girl the day off.'

'That's fine,' said Abbot heartily. 'I'll be as quick as I can.'

Five hours later he swished brandy around his glass, and said, 'You drive a hard bargain, Jeannie, my girl, but it's a deal. You're getting us cheap, I hope you know that.'

'Mike, don't you care about anything except money?' She sounded hurt.

'Not much,' he said, and drank some brandy. 'We're two of a kind, you and me.' He signalled to a waiter.

'Yes, I think we are alike. I feel much closer to you than I do to poor Jack.'

Abbot quirked an eyebrow. 'Why *poor* Jack?'

She sat back in her chair. 'He was annoyed that you were on Stella today. I think he's becoming jealous. If you stay with us – with me – that will have to be settled, and settled for good.' She smiled. 'Poor Jack.'

'He's living with you, isn't he?' said Abbot. 'I think those were his clothes I saw in the wardrobe.'

'Why, I believe you are jealous, too,' she cried delightedly.

He felt a cold shiver at the nape of his neck as he pictured Jeanette and Eastman lying in bed together while she discussed the possibility of one John Eastman knocking off one Michael Abbot. This she-devil was quite capable of playing both ends against the middle. She believed in the survival of the fittest, and the survivor would get first prize – her lithe and insatiable body. It wasn't a bad prize – if you could stand the competition. The trouble was that if you played by her rules the competition would be never-ending.

He forced a smile. 'I like you and money in roughly equal proportions. As for Jack Eastman, I suggest we leave that problem for a while. He still has his uses.'

'Of course,' she said. 'But don't leave it too long.'

He pushed back his chair. 'If you'll excuse me, I have to see a man about a dog. I'll be back in a moment.'

He walked quickly into the foyer and into one of the few rooms in the Phoenicia where he could get away from Delorme. He locked himself in a cubicle, took an envelope from his pocket and checked the wording on the single sheet of paper inside. Then he reinserted the sheet, sealed the envelope and addressed it carefully.

He found an attendant who obligingly brushed his jacket with subservient attention, and said, 'I'd like to have this letter delivered to the *Daily Star* office at once.'

The attendant looked dubious but brightened immediately as he heard the crisp rustle of folding money. 'Yes, sair; I'll 'ave it delivered.'

'It's important,' said Abbot. 'It must get there tonight.' He added another banknote. 'That's to make sure it arrives within the hour.'

Then he straightened his shoulders and went back to where the she-spider was waiting.

V

Sir Robert Hellier sat behind his desk and looked at the newspaper. It was the Beirut English language paper, *Daily Star,* which he had flown to London regularly. He ignored the news pages but turned to the classified advertisements and ran his fingers down the columns. This he had done every morning for many weeks.

Suddenly he grunted and his finger checked its movement. He took a pen and slashed a ring round an advertisement. It read:

Mixed farm for sale near Zahleh. 2,000 acres good land; large vineyard, good farmhouse, stock, implements. Box 192,

He heaved a sigh of relief. He had lost contact with Abbot and Parker many weeks previously and had been worried about it, but now he knew they were still around he felt better. He re-read the advertisement and a frown creased his forehead as he groped for the pen.

Five minutes later he found he was sweating. Surely he had made a mistake in his calculations. Got a few too many noughts mixed in somewhere or other. The 2,000 acres mentioned in the advertisement meant that the Delorme woman intended to smuggle 2,000 pounds of heroin – that was the jumping-off point. He began right again from the start and worked it out very carefully. The end result was incredible.

He looked at the final figure again and it still shattered him. $340,000,000.

That was what 2,000 pounds of heroin would be worth to the final consumers, the drug addicts who would pay their $7.00 and $8.00 a shot. He wrote down another figure. $100,000,000.

That was what Delorme would be paid if the dope could be safely delivered inside the States. He expected the whole thing would be worked out on a credit basis – not even the Syndicate could be expected to raise that much capital at one time. The stuff would be cached and doled out a few pounds at a time at $50,000 a pound, and Delorme would be creaming the lot. She had organized the whole business right from the Middle Eastern poppy fields, had taken all the risks and would take all the profits, which were enormous.

With shaking fingers he picked up the telephone. 'Miss Walden: cancel all my appointments for an indefinite period. Get me a plane reservation for Beirut as soon as possible, and a hotel reservation accordingly – the Saint-Georges or the Phoenicia. All that as soon as possible, please.'

He sat and looked at the advertisement, hoping to God that whoever had set it in type had made a misprint and that he was embarking on a wild goose chase.

He also hoped he could hear from Warren because Warren and the three men with him had also gone missing.

EIGHT

Entry into Iraq was not too difficult. They had visas for all countries in the Middle East into which it had been thought the chase might lead them, and Hellier had provided them with documents and letters of introduction which apparently carried a lot of weight. But the Iraqi officer at the border post expressed surprise that they should enter via Kurdistan and so far north, and showed an undesirable curiosity.

Tozier made an impassioned speech in throat-rasping Arabic and this, together with their credentials, got them through, although at one time Warren had visions of a jail in Iraqi Kurdistan – not the sort of place from which it would be easy to ring one's lawyer.

They filled up with petrol and water at the border post and left quickly before the officer could change his mind, Tozier in the lead and Follet riding with Warren. At noon Tozier pulled off the road and waited for the other vehicle to come up. He pulled out a pressure stove and said, 'Time for a bite to eat.'

As Follet opened cans, he said, 'This isn't much different from Iran. I don't reckon I'm very hungry – I'm full of dust.'

Tozier grinned and looked at the barren landscape. The roads were just as dusty here, and the mountains as bleak as on the other side of the border. 'It's not far to

Sulaymaniyeh, but I don't know what we'll do when we get there. Take it as it comes, I suppose.'

Warren pumped up the pressure stove and put the water to boil. He looked across at Tozier, and said, 'We haven't had the chance of talking much. What happened back there?'

'In the *qanat*?'

'Yes,' said Warren quietly.

'It collapsed, Nick. I couldn't get through.'

'No hope for Ben?'

Tozier shook his head. 'It would have been quick.'

Warren's face was drawn. He had been right when he told Hellier that blood would be shed, but he had not expected this. Tozier said, 'Don't blame yourself, Nick. It was his own choice that he went back. He knew the risk. It was a damn-fool thing to do anyway, it nearly did for us all.'

'Yes,' said Warren. 'It was very foolish.' He bent his head so that the others could not see his face. It was as though someone had stabbed a cold knife into his guts. He and Ben were both medical men, both lifesavers. But who had been the better – Ben Bryan, for all his foolishness and idealism, or Nicholas Warren who had brought him to the desert and his death? Warren did not relish that ugly question.

They were half-way through lunch when Tozier said casually, 'We've got visitors. I'd advise against sudden moves.'

Despite himself Warren hastily looked around. Follet went on pouring coffee with a steady hand. 'Where are they?' he asked.

'There are a couple on the hill above us,' said Tozier. 'And three or four more circling around the other side. We're being surrounded.'

'Any chance of making a break?'

'I don't think so, Johnny. The guns are too hard to get at right now. If these boys – whoever they are – are serious they'll have blocked off the road ahead and behind. And we couldn't get far on foot. We'll just have to wait until we find out the score.' He accepted the cup of coffee from Follet. 'Pass the sugar, Nick.'

'What!'

'Pass the sugar,' said Tozier patiently. 'There's no point in getting into an uproar about it. They might be just curious Kurds.'

They might just be too goddam curious,' said Follet. 'That guy Ahmed is a Kurd, remember.' He stood up slowly and stretched. 'There's a deputation coming down the road now.'

'Anyone we know?'

'Can't tell. They're all wearing nightgowns.'

Warren heard a stone clatter behind him, and Tozier said, 'Easy does it. Just get up and look pleasant.' He stood up and turned, and the first man he saw come into view was Ahmed, the son of Sheikh Fahrwaz. 'Bingo!' said Tozier.

Ahmed stepped forward. 'Well, Mr Warren – Mr Tozier; how nice to see you again. Won't you introduce your companion?' He was smiling but Warren could detect little humour in his face.

Playing along, he said, 'Mr Follet – a member of my team.'

'Pleased to make your acquaintance,' said Ahmed brightly. 'But wasn't there another man? Don't tell me you've lost him?' He surveyed them. 'Nothing to say? I'm sure you're aware that this is no fortuitous encounter. I've been looking for you.'

'Now why should you do that?' asked Tozier in wonder.

'Need you ask? My father has doubts about your safety.' He waved his hand. 'You would not believe what dreadful people roam these hills. He has sent me to escort you to somewhere safe. Your escort, as I am sure you are aware, is all around to . . . er . . . protect you.'

'To protect us from ourselves,' said Warren ironically. 'Aren't you off your beat, Ahmed? Does the Iraqi government know you are in the country?'

'What the Iraqi government does not know would take far too long to detail,' said Ahmed. 'But I suggest we go. My men will put your picnic kit back in your vehicles. My men will also drive your vehicles – to save you from needless fatigue. All part of the service.'

Warren was uncomfortably aware of the rifles held by Ahmed's men and of the wide circle drawn about them. He glanced at Tozier who shrugged, and said, 'Why not?'

'Very good,' said Ahmed approvingly. 'Mr Tozier is a man of few words but much sense.' He snapped his fingers and his men moved forward. 'Let us not waste time. My father is positively aching to . . . interrogate you.'

Warren did not like the sound of that at all.

II

The three of them were crammed into the back of one of the Land-Rovers. In the front seats were a driver and a man who sat half-turned to them, holding a pistol steadily. Sometimes, as the vehicle bounced, Warren wondered if the safety-catch was on because the man kept his finger loosely curved around the trigger, and it would not have taken much movement to complete the final pressure. Any shot fired into the back would have been certain to hit one of the bodies uncomfortably huddled among the photographic equipment.

As near as he could tell their route curved back to the east, almost as far as the Iranian border, and then straightened out in a northerly direction, heading deeper into the mountains. That meant they had circled Sulaymaniyeh, which was now left behind them. They followed a truck, a big tough brute which looked as though it had been designed for army service, and when he was able to look back he saw the other Land-Rover from time to time through the inevitable dust-cloud.

The man with the gun did not seem to object to their talking but Warren was cautious. The fluent Oxbridge accent that had come so strangely from Ahmed had warned him that no matter how villainous and foreign the man appeared it did not automatically follow that he had no English. He said, 'Is everyone all right?'

'I'll be fine as soon as whoever it is takes his elbow out of my gut,' said Follet. 'So that was Ahmed! A right pleasant-spoken guy.'

'I don't think we should talk too much business,' said Warren carefully. 'Those little pitchers might have long ears.'

Follet looked at the pistoleer. 'Long and goddam hairy,' he said distastefully. 'Needing a wash, too. Ever heard of water, bud?'

The man looked back at him expressionlessly, and Tozier said, 'Cut it out, Johnny, Nick's right.'

'I was just trying to find out something,' said Follet.

'You might just find out the hard way. Never make fun of a man with a gun – his sense of humour might be lethal.'

It was a long ride.

When night fell the headlights were switched on and the speed dropped but still they jolted deeper into the mountains where, according to Warren's hazy memory of the map, there were no roads at all. From the way the vehicle rolled and swayed this was very likely true.

At midnight the sound of the engine reverberated from the sides of a rocky gorge, and Warren eased himself up on one elbow to look ahead. The lights showed a rocky wall straight ahead and the driver hauled the Land-Rover into a ninety-degree turn and then did it again and again as the gorge twisted and narrowed. Suddenly they debouched into an open place where there were lights dotted about on a hillside and they stopped.

The rear doors opened and, under the urged commands of the man with the gun, they crawled out. Dark figures crowded about them and there was a murmur of voices. Warren stretched thankfully, easing his cramped limbs, and looked about at the sheer encroaching hills. The sky above was bright with the full moon which showed how circumscribed by cliffs this little valley was.

Tozier rubbed his thigh, looked up at the lights in the cliff side, and said sardonically, 'Welcome to Shangri-la.'

'Very well put,' said Ahmed's voice from the darkness. 'And just as inaccessible, I assure you. This way, if you please.'

And if I don't please? thought Warren sourly, but made no attempt to put it to the test. They were hustled across the valley floor right to the bottom of a cliff where their feet found a narrow and precipitous path which wound its way up the cliff face. It was not very wide – just wide enough to be dangerous in the darkness, but probably able to take two men abreast in full daylight. It emerged on to a wider ledge halfway up the cliff, and he was able to see that the lights came from caves dotted along the cliff face.

As they were marched along the ledge he peered into the caves, which were pretty well populated. At a rough estimate he thought that there could not be very much less than two hundred men in this community. He saw no women.

They were brought to a halt in front of one of the larger caves. It was well illuminated and, as Ahmed went inside, Warren saw the tall figure of Sheikh Fahrwaz arise from a couch. Tozier gave a muffled exclamation and nudged him, 'What is it?' he whispered.

Tozier was staring into the cave, and then Warren saw what had attracted his attention. Standing near Fahrwaz was a short, wiry, muscular man in European clothing. He lifted his hand in greeting at Ahmed's approach and then stood by quietly as Ahmed talked to Fahrwaz. 'I know that man,' whispered Tozier.

'Who is he?'

'I'll tell you later – if I can. Ahmed's coming back.'

As Ahmed came out of the cave he made a sign and they were pushed further along the ledge and out of sight of Fahrwaz. They went about twenty yards and were stopped in front of a door let into the rock face. Someone opened it with much key-jangling, and Ahmed said, 'I trust you won't find the accommodation too uncomfortable. Food will be sent; we try not to starve our guests . . . unnecessarily.'

Hands forced Warren through the doorway and he stumbled and fell, and then someone else fell on top of him. When they had sorted themselves out in the darkness the door had slammed and the key turned in the lock.

Follet said breathily, 'Pushy bastards, aren't they?'

Warren drew up his trouser-leg and felt his shin, encountering the stickiness of blood. A cigarette-fighter clicked and sparked a couple of times and then flared into light, casting grotesque shadows as Tozier held it up. The cave stretched back into the darkness and all was gloom in its furthest recesses. Warren saw some boxes and sacks stacked against one side but not much more because the light danced about and so did the shadows as Tozier moved about exploratively.

'Ah!' said Tozier with satisfaction. 'This is what we want.' The flame grew and brightened as he applied it to a stump of candle.

Follet looked around. 'This must be the lock-up,' he said. 'Store room too, by the look of it, but first a lock-up. Every military unit needs a lock-up – it's a law of nature.'

'Military!' said Warren.

'Yes,' said Tozier. 'It's a military set-up. A bit rough and ready – guerrilla, I'd say – but definitely an army of sorts. Didn't you see the guns?' He set down the candle on a box.

'This is something I didn't expect,' said Warren. 'It doesn't fit in with drugs.'

'Neither does Metcalfe,' said Tozier. 'That's the man who was with Fahrwaz. Now I really am puzzled. Metcalfe and guns I can understand – they go together like bacon and eggs. But Metcalfe and dope is bloody impossible.'

'Why? Who is this man?'

'Metcalfe is . . . well, he's just Metcalfe. He's as bent as they come, but there's one thing he's known for – he won't have anything to do with drugs. He's had plenty of opportunity, mark you, because he's a smart boy, but he's always turned down the chance – sometimes violently. It's a sort of phobia with him.'

Warren sat down on a box. 'Tell me more.'

Tozier prodded a paper sack and looked at the inscription on the side. It contained fertilizer. He pulled it up and sat on it. 'He's been in my game – that's how I met him . . .'

'As a mercenary?'

Tozier nodded. 'In the Congo. But he doesn't stick to one trade; he's game for anything – the crazier the better. I believe he was kicked out of South Africa because of a crooked deal in diamonds, and I know he was smuggling out of Tangier when it was an open port before the Moroccans took over.'

'What was he smuggling?'

Tozier shrugged. 'Cigarettes to Spain; antibiotics – there was a shortage in those days; and I also heard he was smuggling guns to the Algerian rebels.'

'Was he?' said Warren with interest. 'So was Jeanette Delorme.'

'I heard a garbled story that he was mixed up in smuggling a hell of a lot of gold out of Italy, but nothing seemed to come of that. It didn't make him much richer, anyway. I'm telling you all this to show what kind of a man he is. Anything goes, excepting one thing – drugs. And don't ask me why because I don't know.'

'So why is he here?'

'Because it's military. He's one of the best guerrilla leaders I know. He never was any great shakes in a formal military unit – he didn't go in for the Blanco, bullshit and square-bashing – but with guerrillas he's deadly. That's my guess for what it's worth. We know the Kurds are having a bash at the Iraqis – Ahmed told us. They've imported Metcalfe to help them out.'

'And what about the drugs which he's not supposed to like?'

Tozier was silent for a while. 'Maybe he doesn't know about them.'

Warren ruminated over that, wondering how it could be turned to advantage. He was just about to speak when the key clattered in the lock and the door swung open. A Kurd came in with a pistol ready in his hand and stationed himself with his back to the rock face. Ahmed followed. 'I said we don't starve our guests. Here is food. It may not be congenial to your European palates, but it is good food, none the less.'

Two big brass trays were brought in, each covered by a cloth. Ahmed said, 'Ah, Mr Tozier: I believe we have a friend in common. I see no reason why you and Mr Metcalfe should not have a chat later – after you have eaten.'

'I'd be pleased to see Tom Metcalfe again,' said Tozier.

'I thought you would.' Ahmed turned away, and then paused. 'Oh, gentlemen, there is just one other thing. My father needs certain information. Now, who can give it to him?' He studied Warren with a half smile on his lips. 'I don't think Mr Warren could be persuaded very easily – and

Mr Tozier even less so. I regarded you carefully last time we met.'

His gaze switched to Follet. 'Now, you are an American, Mr Follet.'

'Yeah,' said Follet. 'Next time you see the American consul tell him I'd like to see him.'

'A commendable spirit,' observed Ahmed, and sighed. 'I fear you may be as obstinate as your friends. My father wishes to . . . er . . . talk to you himself, but he is an old man and in need of sleep at this late hour. So you are fortunate in that you have a few more hours.' With that he went, followed by his bodyguard, and the door slammed.

Tozier indicated the paraffin lamp on one of the trays. 'He was kind enough to leave that.'

Follet lifted a cloth. 'It's hot food.'

Tozier took the cloth from the other tray. 'I suppose we might as well eat. It's not too bad – cous-cous and chicken with coffee afterwards.'

Follet gnawed on a leg of chicken, then looked at it in disgust, 'This one must have been an athlete.'

Warren picked up a plate. 'Where do you reckon we are?'

'Somewhere up near the Turkish border,' said Follet. 'As near as I can reckon. Not far from the Iranian border, either.'

'In the Kurdish heartland,' commented Tozier. 'That might mean something – or nothing.' He frowned. 'Do you remember what Ahmed was blowing off about back in Iran, Nick? About the Kurdish political situation? What was that name he mentioned? It was someone who had the Iraqi army tied up in knots.'

'Barzani,' said Warren. 'Mullah Mustapha Barzani.'

'That's the man. Ahmed said he had an army. I wonder if this crowd is part of it.'

'It could be. I don't see how it helps us.'

'God helps those who help themselves,' said Follet practically. Still holding the chicken leg, he got up, took the candle, and began to explore the further reaches of the cave. His voice came hollowly. 'Not much here.'

'What do you expect in a jail?' asked Tozier. 'All the same, it's a good idea to see what resources we have. What's in that box you're sitting on, Nick?'

'It's empty.'

'And I'm sitting on fertilizer,' said Tozier in disgust. 'Anything else, Johnny?'

'Not much. More empty boxes; some automotive spare parts – all rusty, half a can of diesel oil; a hell of a lot of nuts and bolts; a couple of sacks of straw – that's about all.'

Tozier sighed. Follet came back, put down the candle, then picked up the lamp and shook it close to his ear. 'There's some kerosene in here and there's that straw over there – maybe we can do something with that.'

'You can't burn a cave to the ground, Johnny. We'd just asphyxiate ourselves.' Tozier went to the door. 'This is going to take some shifting – it must be four inches thick.' He cocked his head on one side. 'There's someone coming. Watch it.' He retreated from the door and sat down.

It opened and the man called Metcalfe came in. He was brushing himself down and turned his head as the door thudded behind him. 'Then he looked at Tozier and said without smiling, 'Hello, Andy; long time no see.'

'Hello, Tom.'

Metcalfe came forward and held out his hand, and Tozier grasped it. 'What in hell are you doing here?'

'That's a long story,' said Tozier. 'This is Nick Warren – Johnny Follet.'

'If I said, "Pleased to meet you," I'd be wrong,' said Metcalfe wryly. He looked Warren up and down with a keen eye, then glanced at Tozier. 'Here on business, Andy?'

'Sort of. We didn't come willingly.'

'I saw the boys hustling you in – I couldn't believe my eyes. It's not like you to be nabbed as easily as that.'

'Take the weight off your feet, Tom,' said Tozier. 'Which will you have – the fertilizer or the box?'

'Yeah, stay and visit with us for a while,' said Follet.

'I'll have the box,' said Metcalfe delicately. 'You're a Yank, aren't you?'

Follet burlesqued a southern accent. 'Them's fightin' words where ah comes from. Ah may have bin bawn in Arizony but ma pappy's from Jawjah.'

Metcalfe looked at him thoughtfully for a long time. 'I'm glad to see high spirits – you're going to need them. You look as though you've seen service.'

'A long time ago,' said Follet. 'Korea.'

'Ah,' said Metcalfe. He grinned and his teeth gleamed white against his sunburnt face. 'A legitimate type. And you Warren?'

'I'm a doctor.'

'So! And what's a doctor doing wandering about Kurdistan with a bad type like Andy Tozier?'

Tozier pulled at his ear. 'Are you in employment at the moment, Tom?'

'Just wrapping something up,' said Metcalfe.

'In command?'

Metcalfe looked blank. 'In command!' His brow cleared and he laughed. 'You mean – am I training these boys? Andy, this crowd could teach us a thing or two – they've been fighting for the last thirty-five years. I've just brought a consignment in, that's all. I'm leaving in a couple of days.'

'A consignment of what?'

'What the blazes do you think? Arms, of course. What else would this lot need?' He smiled. 'I'm supposed to be asking the questions, not you. That's what old Fahrwaz sent me in here for. Ahmed didn't like it – he wanted to carve you up immediately, but the old boy thought I might solve his problem without him going to extreme lengths.' His face was serious. 'You're in a really bad spot this time, Andy.'

'What does he want to know?' asked Warren.

Metcalfe looked up. 'Everything there is to know. You seem to have upset him somehow, but he didn't go into that with me. He thought that since I know Andy here, I might get your confidence.' He shook his head. 'You've come down in the world if you're working for a film company, Andy. So I think it's a cover – and so does Fahrwaz.'

'And what does Barzani think?' asked Tozier.

'Barzani!' said Metcalfe in surprise. 'How in hell do I know what Barzani thinks?' Suddenly he slapped his knee. 'Did you really think that Fahrwaz was one of Barzani's men? That's really funny.'

'I'm laughing my goddam head off,' said Follet sourly.

'It's time for a lesson in Kurdish politics,' said Metcalfe didactically. 'Fahrwaz used to be with Barzani – they were together when the Russkies tried to set up the Mehabad Kurdish Republic in Iran back in 1946. They even went into exile together when it collapsed. They were great chums. Then Barzani came here to Iraq, built up a following, and has been knocking hell out of the Iraqis ever since.'

'And Fahrwaz?'

'Ah, he's one of the *Pej Merga*,' said Metcalfe as though that was a full explanation.

'The self-sacrificing,' translated Tozier thoughtfully. 'So?'

'The *Pej Merga* was the hard core that Barzani could always rely on, but not any more – not since he started to dicker with President Bakr on the basis of an autonomous Kurdish province in Iran. Fahrwaz is a hawk and he thinks the Iraqis will renege on the deal, and he may be right. More importantly, he and most of the *Pej Merga* want none of a Kurdish Republic *in Iran*. They don't want Kurdistan to be split between Iraq, Iran and Turkey – they want a unified Kurdish nation and no half measures.'

'Something like the Irish problem,' observed Tozier. 'With Fahrwaz and the *Pej Merga* doing the IRA bit.'

'You've got the picture. Fahrwaz regards Barzani as a traitor to the Kurdish nation for even listening to Bakr, but Barzani commands respect – he was fighting the Iraqis for years when Fahrwaz was sitting on his rump in Iran. If Barzani makes a deal with the Iraqis then Fahrwaz is out on a limb. That's why he's stock-piling arms as fast as he can.'

'And you're supplying them,' said Warren. 'What do you believe in?'

Metcalfe shrugged. 'The Kurds have been given a rough deal for centuries,' he said. 'If Barzani does a deal with the Iraqis and it goes sour, then the Kurds will need some insurance. I'm supplying it. Bakr came to power by a coup d'état and his regime isn't all sweetness and light. I can see Fahrwaz's point of view.' He rubbed his jaw. 'Not that I like him – he's a bit too fanatical for my taste.'

'Where is he getting his support – his money?'

'I don't know.' Metcalfe grinned. 'As long as I'm paid I don't care where the money comes from.'

'I think you might,' said Tozier softly. 'How did you bring in the arms?'

'You know better than to ask a question like that. A trade secret, old boy.'

'What are you taking out of here?'

'Nothing,' said Metcalfe in surprise. 'I get paid through a Beirut bank. You don't think I wander through the Middle East with my pockets full of gold. I'm not that stupid.'

'I think you'd better tell him all about it, Nick,' said Tozier. 'It's all falling into place, isn't it?'

'I'd like to know something first,' said Warren. 'Who contacted you originally on this arms deal? Who suggested it would be a good idea to take a load of guns to Fahrwaz? Who supplied them?'

Metcalfe smiled and glanced at Tozier. 'Your friend is too nosy for his own good. That also comes under the heading of trade secrets.'

'It wouldn't be Jeanette Delorme?' suggested Warren.

Metcalfe's eyebrows crawled up his forehead. 'You seem to know quite a lot. No wonder Fahrwaz is getting worried.'

'*You* ought to be getting worried,' said Tozier. 'When I asked you if you were taking anything out I had dope in mind.'

Metcalfe went very still. 'And what gave you that idea?' he said in a tight voice.

'Because there's a ton of pure morphine around here somewhere,' said Warren. 'Because Fahrwaz is running drugs to pay for his revolution. Because the Delorme woman is supplying the arms to pay for the drugs, and she's sitting in Beirut right now waiting to ship a consignment of heroin to the States.'

There were harsh lines on Metcalfe's face. 'I don't know that I believe this.'

'Oh, grow up, Tom,' said Tozier. 'We cleaned up Fahrwaz's place in Iran. I personally destroyed ten tons of opium – blew it to hell. He's in it up to his scrawny old neck.'

Metcalfe stood up slowly. 'I have your word on this, Andy?'

'For what it's worth,' said Tozier. 'You know me, Tom.'

'I don't like being used,' said Metcalfe in a choked voice. 'Jeanette knows I don't like drugs. If she's implicated me in this I'll kill the bitch – I swear it.' He swung on Warren. 'How much morphine did you say?'

'About a ton. My guess is that they'll convert it to heroin before shipment. If that amount of heroin gets on the illegal market in one lump I don't like to think of the consequences.'

'A ton,' whispered Metcalfe incredulously.

'It could have been double that,' said Tozier. 'But we wrecked the laboratory. Your lady-friend has been busy getting everything sewn up. This is one of the biggest smuggling operations of all time.'

Metcalfe thought about it. 'I don't think the stuff's here,' he said slowly. 'Just after I arrived a string of camels came in. There was a hell of a lot of palaver about them – all very mysterious. Everyone was kept away while the load was transferred into a truck. It left this morning.'

'So what are you going to do, Tom?' asked Tozier casually.

'A good question.' Metcalfe took a deep breath. 'The first thing is to get you out of here – and that's going to take a miracle.' He smiled wryly. 'No wonder Fahrwaz is all steamed up.'

'Can you get any weapons in to us? I'd feel better with a gun in my hand.'

Metcalfe shook his head. 'They don't trust me that much. I was searched when I came in here. There are a couple of guards outside all the time.'

Tozier stuck out his finger. 'We've got to get through that door – guards or no guards.' He stood up with a quick movement and the sack of fertilizer fell over against his leg. Impatiently he booted it away, and then stopped and gazed at it. Abstractedly he said, 'Could you find us a few bits of coal, Tom?'

'Coal in Kurdistan!' said Metcalfe derisively. He followed the line of Tozier's gaze, then bent down to read the inscription on the sack. 'Oh, I see – the Mwanza trick.' He straightened up. 'Would charcoal do?'

'I don't see why not – we don't need much. How much oil is there in that can you found, Johnny?'

'About a quart. Why?'

'We're going to blow that door off its hinges. We'll need a detonator, Tom. If you nip down to the Land-Rovers you'll find that one has a clock and the others hasn't. Unscrew the clock and bring it with you with the charcoal.'

'How do you expect me to smuggle a clock in here?'

'You'll find a way. Get going, Tom.'

Metcalfe knocked on the door and was let out. As it closed behind him Warren said, 'Do you think he's . . . safe?'

'For us – yes,' said Tozier. 'For Fahrwaz, no. I know Tom Metcalfe very well. He goes off pop if he even hears people talk about drugs. If we get out of this I'll feel bloody sorry for the Delorme woman – he'll crucify her.' He bent down and started to open the sack of fertilizer.

Follet said flatly, 'You're going to blow that door open with fertilizer. You did say that – or am I going nuts?'

'I said it,' said Tozier. 'Tom and I were in the Congo. We were just outside a place called Mwanza and the opposition had blown down a cliff so it blocked the road and we couldn't get our trucks through. We were low on ammunition and had no blasting explosives, but we had a secret weapon – a South African called van Niekerk who used to be a miner on the Witwatersrand.'

He put his hand in the sack and lifted out a handful of the white powder. 'This is agricultural fertilizer – ammonium nitrate – good for putting nitrogen into the soil. But van Niekerk knew a bit more. If you take a hundred pounds of this, six pints of fuel oil, two pounds of coal dust, and mix it all together then you get the equivalent of forty per cent blasting gelignite. I've never forgotten that. Van Niekerk scared the pants off me – he brewed the stuff in a concrete mixer.'

'Is this on the level?' said Follet unbelievingly.

'We won't need as much,' said Tozier. 'And I don't know if our substitute ingredients will work. But we'll give it a bang.' He grinned. 'And that's a hell of a bad pun. Van Niekerk said they do a lot of blasting this way in the South African gold mines. They've discovered it's safer – and cheaper – to mix up the stuff at the work face than to store gelignite in magazines.'

'But we need the charcoal,' said Warren.

'And a detonator. We might as well relax until Tom comes back.'

If he comes back, thought Warren. He sat on the box and looked glumly at the sack of fertilizer. He had said to Hellier back in London that they were going into what was virtually a war – but what a devil of a way to fight it!

III

Metcalfe was back within the hour. He came in smoking a cigar and limping a little. As soon as the door closed he nipped the glowing end and handed it to Tozier. 'A stick of charcoal,' he said. 'I did a bit of sleight of hand with a cigar when they searched me. I have a lot more stuffed in my shoes.'

'The detonator?' asked Tozier urgently.

Metcalfe unfastened his belt and rummaged around in his trousers. From somewhere mysterious he produced the clock and handed it over, the spike of the detonator sticking out at right-angles to the back. Follet said, 'How come they didn't find that when they searched you?' His voice had an edge of suspicion.

Metcalfe grimaced. 'I rammed the detonator up my arse and walked tight. I bet it's started piles.'

'It's all for the cause,' said Tozier with a grin. 'Did you have any trouble, Tom?'

'Not a bit. I spun Fahrwaz a yarn pretty close to the truth, but left a couple of gaps in it. He sent me back to fill them in. We'd better get our plans agreed now. They won't be coming for you for a while; the old boy said he was tired and going to bed.' He looked at his watch. 'Dawn will be in three hours.'

'A night escape might be better,' said Tozier.

Metcalfe shook his head decisively. 'You wouldn't have a chance at night. By the time you found the exit you'd be caught. The best time to make a break is at first light so you can see what you're doing – and it'll give me three hours to set up a few diversions I have in mind. How accurately can you set that clock?'

'To the nearest minute.'

'Good enough. Make it five-thirty. You'll hear a lot of action just at that time.' Metcalfe squatted on his haunches and began to draw on the sandy floor of the cave. 'Your Land-Rovers are here with the ignition keys still in place – I checked that. The exit is here. When you blow off the door you'll either kill the guards or give them a hell of a fright; in either case you needn't worry about them if you move fast. When you leave the cave turn left – *not* the way you were brought. There's a devil of a steep path down to the valley floor about ten yards along the ledge outside.'

'How steep?'

'You'll make it,' assured Metcalfe. 'Now, there's only one way in – or out – of this valley, and that's through the gorge. You make your break for your trucks, drive into the gorge and stop at the first sharp turn. I'll be right behind you in one of Fahrwaz's vehicles which I'll abandon in an immovable condition. If we can block up the gorge behind us we stand a fair chance of getting away. But wait for me, for God's sake!'

'I've got it, Tom.'

Metcalfe took off his shoes and shook a pile of black dust from them and pulled some charcoal sticks from his socks. 'I hope this stuff works,' he said doubtfully. 'If it doesn't we'll all be up the spout.'

'It's all we've got,' said Tozier. 'No use binding about it.' He looked at Metcalfe and said quietly, 'Thanks for everything, Tom.'

'Anything for an old pal,' said Metcalfe lightly. 'I'd better be going now. Remember – five-thirty.'

The guard let him out, and Warren said pensively, 'Andy, supposing there weren't any drugs involved – would Metcalfe help you out on the basis of the Old Pals' Act?'

'I'm glad I don't have to put it to the test,' said Tozier drily. 'A mercenary is like a politician – a good one is one who stays bought. I've fought on the same side as Tom Metcalfe, and I've fought in opposition. For all I know we might have shot at each other some time. I think that if it weren't for the drugs we'd have had to take our own chances. We're damned lucky he considers he's been double-crossed.'

'And that he believed us,' said Follet.

'There's that, too,' admitted Tozier. 'But Tom and I have swapped drinks and lies for a long time. We've never crossed each other up, so there's no reason why he shouldn't believe me. Come on; let's get busy.'

He set Follet and Warren to grinding the fertilizer down into an even finer powder, using plates as mortars and the backs of spoons as pestles. 'I want all those lumps out of it.'

'Is this safe?' asked Follet nervously.

'It's just fertilizer,' assured Tozier. 'Even when it's mixed it will need the detonator to explode it.' He began to figure out quantities and weights, and then began to grind down the charcoal. After a while he went to the back of the cave and rooted about in the box which contained engine spares, and came back with a pipe closed at one end with a plug. 'Just the thing we need – everything for the do-it-yourself anarchist. Ever made bombs before, Nick?'

'It's hardly likely, is it?'

'I don't suppose it is much in your line. But this isn't the first time I've had to make do. When you're on the losing side the money tends to run out and you have to do a lot of patching. I once assembled quite a serviceable tank out of six wrecks.' He smiled. 'But this lot is a little too much the Moses lark for my taste – making bricks without straw.'

He cleaned out the coffee-pot and dried it carefully, then poured in the ground-down fertilizer and added the powdered charcoal a little at a time, keeping the mixture well stirred. When he thought he had the right proportions he gave it to Follet. 'Keep stirring – it'll help pass the time.'

He picked up the can of oil and looked at it dubiously. 'The recipe calls for fuel oil – I don't know if this will be suitable. Still, we won't know if we don't try, so let's do the final mix.' He poured a little of the oil into the out-held coffee pot. 'Keep on stirring, Johnny. It shouldn't get wet enough to form a paste; just damp enough to hold together when you squeeze it in your hand.'

'You can do the squeezing,' said Follet. 'The only thing I squeeze is a dame.'

Tozier laughed. 'They're just as explosive if not handled right. Give it to me.' He tried the squeeze test and added a little more oil. This proved to be too much and the mixture was rebalanced by the addition of fertilizer and charcoal. It was quite a time before he pronounced himself satisfied, but at last he said, 'That's it; now we make the bomb.'

He took the tube, checked that the plug was screwed home firmly, and began to stuff the explosive mixture into the other end, using a long bolt to ram it down. Follet watched him for a while, then said tensely, 'Andy – stop right there.'

Tozier froze. 'What's on your mind?'

'That's a steel tube, isn't it?' asked Follet.

'So?'

'And you're using a steel bolt as a ramrod. *For Christ's sake, don't strike a spark!*'

Tozier eased out his breath. 'I'll try not to,' he said, and used the bolt much more carefully. He crammed the tube full of the mixture, well packed down, took the clock and set it, then pressed the detonator spike into the end. 'There's a few bits of sheet metal back there, and the box Warren is sitting on is screwed together. That's how we fasten it to the door.'

It took a long time because they had to work quietly, fearing to attract the attention of the guards outside. Tozier's small penknife, which they used as a makeshift screwdriver, had all its blades broken by the time they were finished. He regarded the bomb critically, then looked at his watch. 'It took longer than I expected; it's nearly five now – just over half an hour to go.'

'I don't want to appear difficult,' said Follet. 'But we're now locked in a cave with a bomb that's about to explode. Have you thought of that little thing?'

'We should be safe enough lying at the back behind those boxes.'

'I'm glad we have a doctor along,' said Follet. 'You might come in useful, Nick, if that firecracker really works. I'm going to pick me a good safe place right now.'

Warren and Tozier followed him to the back of the cave where they built a rough barricade of boxes, then they lay down using the sacks of straw as improvised mattresses. The next half hour crawled by and Warren was mightily astonished to find himself nodding off to sleep. If anyone had told him this could – or would – happen in such a critical circumstance he would have laughed; yet it was not surprising considering that this was his second night without sleep.

Tozier's elbow jerked him into wakefulness. 'Five minutes – get ready.'

Warren found his mind full of questions. Would Tozier's ridiculous bomb work? If it did, would it work well enough? Or too well? Follet had already expressed his apprehensions on that score.

'Four minutes,' said Tozier, his eyes on his watch. 'Johnny, you go first, then Nick. I'll bring up the rear.'

The seconds ticked by and Warren found himself becoming very tense. His mouth was dry and he had an odd feeling in his stomach as though he was very hungry. In a detached manner one part of his mind checked off the symptoms and he thought – *So this is what it's like to be frightened.*

Tozier said, 'Three minutes,' and as he said it there was a sound from the door. 'Hell's teeth!' he exclaimed. 'Someone's coming in.'

Follet grunted. 'A hell of a time to pick.'

Tozier raised his head cautiously as the door creaked open, and saw men silhouetted against the grey light of dawn. The mocking voice of Ahmed echoed from the stone walls. 'What – all asleep? No guilty consciences here?'

Tozier pushed himself up on one elbow and stretched as though just aroused from sleep. 'What the hell do you want now?' he said in a grumbling voice.

'I want somebody to talk,' said Ahmed. 'Who shall it be? Who do you think we should take first, Mr Tozier?'

Tozier played for time. He looked at his watch and said, 'You start too early for my liking. Come back in an hour. Better still, don't come back at all.' *One and a half minutes to go.*

Ahmed spread his hands. 'I regret I cannot oblige you. My father sleeps lightly – he is an old man – and he is now awake and impatient.'

'All right,' said Tozier. 'Wake up, you two. I'll give you one minute to be on your feet. *One minute,* do you hear?'

Warren heard the emphasis and pressed himself to the floor of the cave. He said, 'What is it, Andy? I'm tired.'

'Ah, Mr Warren,' said Ahmed. 'I trust you slept well.' His voice sharpened. 'Up with you, all of you; or do I have to have you dragged out? My father is waiting to entertain you with some of our typical Kurdish hospitality.' He laughed.

Tozier took one glance at him before throwing himself flat. Ahmed was still laughing when the bomb exploded. It blew the door off its hinges and hurled it bodily at the laughing man and swept him aside to smear him bloodily against the rock wall. Dust billowed and far away someone screamed.

'Move!' yelled Tozier.

Follet was first out of the door as planned. He skidded to the left and stumbled over a body on the ledge and nearly went over the edge of the cliff. Warren, right behind him, shot out his arm and grabbed him before he toppled.

Follet recovered and plunged forward along the ledge. At the top of the path there was a guard, his mouth opened in surprise and desperately trying to unsling his rifle. Follet was on him before he could get the rifle free, and hit him in the face with his closed fist. The fist was wrapped around a big steel bolt and Warren distinctly heard the crunch as the man's jawbone was smashed. The guard gave a choked wail and fell aside and the way down the narrow path was open.

Follet ran down it at a dangerous speed, slipping and sliding, with his boots starting miniature avalanches of dust and pebbles. Warren stumbled over a loose stone and pitched forward and for one blind moment thought he was going to fall, but Tozier's big hand grabbed him by the belt and hauled him back. That was all the trouble they had going down to the valley floor.

Across the valley things were happening. A fusillade of small-arms fire popped off, interspersed with the deeper note of exploding grenades. One of the further caves erupted with an earth-shattering explosion and a part of the ledge on the cliff slid abruptly into the valley. Metcalfe's 'diversion' was taking on all the aspects of a small war.

In the dim light of dawn they ran towards the Land-Rovers. A man lay writhing with a broken back just below the cave in which they had been imprisoned, and Warren surmised he had been blown off the upper ledge by the force of Tozier's bomb. He jumped over the feebly moving body and hurried to catch up with Follet. Behind him he heard the regular thudding of Tozier's boots.

A small herd of camels tethered close by were much alarmed by the sudden noise and some of them plunged wildly and, tearing up their stakes, went careering up the valley ahead of them, adding to the confusion. A bee buzzed past Warren's head and there was the sharp *spaaang* and a whine as a bullet ricocheted from rock, and he realized that someone had recovered enough from the general alarm to shoot at them. But he had no time to worry about that – all his attention was directed to getting to the Land-Rovers in the shortest time possible.

There was a hundred yards to go and the breath rasped in his throat as his lungs pumped hard and his legs pumped even harder. Ahead, in front of the vehicles, three Kurds had materialized from nowhere and one was already on one knee with rifle poised to shoot at point-blank range. It seemed he could not miss but as he fired a camel cut across between them and received the bullet. Follet swerved to the right, using the staggering camel as cover, and the second of the Kurds was bowled over by another maddened beast.

Follet jumped him and put the toe of his boot into his throat with great force. He scooped up the fallen rifle and fired as he ran, rapidly but with no great accuracy. But the unexpected spray of bullets was enough to make the two opposing men duck and run for cover, and the way was clear.

Behind them all was turmoil as the frantic camels plunged and bucked and more of them tugged free of their tethers to run down the valley. Warren thought afterwards that this was the one thing that saved them; none of the Kurds near them could get a clear shot in the confusion and their bullets went wild. He reached the nearest Land-Rover, snatched open the door, and hurled himself inside.

As he twisted the ignition key he saw the other Land-Rover take off with spinning wheels with Tozier still running next to it. Tozier jumped as Follet pushed open the door and bullets sent dust spurting in fountains around where his ankles had been. But he was in the passenger seat, and Warren ground gears as he followed, hoping to God that Follet remembered the direction of the gorge.

He glanced in the wing mirror and saw a big truck wheel in line behind. That would be Metcalfe doing his best to bottle up the gorge. The movable windscreen of the truck was wide open and he saw the tanned blur of Metcalfe's face and the glint of white teeth – the man was actually laughing. In that brief glimpse he also saw that there was something wrong with the truck; it trailed a thick cloud of billowing black smoke which coiled in greasy clouds and drifted across the valley behind. Then there were a couple of quick thumps somewhere at the back of the Land-Rover and abruptly the wing-mirror shivered into fragments.

Warren revved the engine fiercely and plunged after Follet as he entered the gorge. He hazily remembered that there was a sharp bend about a hundred yards along, but it came sooner than he expected and he had to slam on anchors in a hurry to prevent himself running into Follet.

From behind there came a rending crash and he turned his head and looked back. Metcalfe had swerved and driven the truck into the wall of the gorge, jamming the entrance completely. Already he was climbing out through the open windscreen while the oily black smoke coming from the truck eddied in thick clouds. It occurred to Warren that this was deliberate – that Metcalfe had provided a smokescreen to cover their sudden dash to the gorge.

Metcalfe ran up brandishing a sub-machine-gun. He waved to Follet in the front vehicle, and shouted. 'Get going!' Then he jumped in alongside Warren, and said breathlessly, 'There's going to be a hell of a bang any moment now – that truck's full of mortar bombs and it's burning merrily.'

Follet moved off and Warren followed, and even as they turned the corner the first explosion came from the burning truck, accompanied by what sounded like an infantry regiment doing a rapid-fire exercise. 'I burst open a few cases of small arms ammunition and scattered those in, too,' said Metcalfe. 'Getting past that truck will be bloody dangerous for the next half hour.'

Warren found his hands trembling uncontrollably on the wheel and he tried desperately to steady them as he drove along the twisting gorge. He said, 'Are we likely to meet any opposition along here?'

'Too bloody right,' said Metcalfe, and cocked the submachine-gun. He saw the microphone and picked it up. 'Does this thing work? Is it on net?'

'It'll work if it's switched on. I don't know if Andy will be listening, though.'

'He will,' said Metcalfe with confidence, and snapped switches. 'He's too old a hand at this game to neglect his communications.' He lifted the microphone to his lips. 'Hello, Andy; can you hear me? Over.'

'I hear you, Tom,' said Tozier metallically. 'You timed everything very well. Over.'

'All part of the service,' said Metcalfe. 'There may be some opposition. Fahrwaz has an outpost at the other end of the gorge. Not more'n a dozen men, but they've got a machine-gun. Any suggestions? Over.'

There was a muffled exclamation from the loudspeaker and Tozier said, 'How long have we got? Over.'

'About twenty minutes. Half an hour at most. Over.'

The loudspeaker hummed and there was a faint crackle. 'Pull us up short and out of sight.' said Tozier. 'I think we can handle it. Out.'

Metcalfe replaced the microphone on its bracket. 'Andy's a good man,' he said dispassionately. 'He'd better be bloody good this time, though.' He twisted the satchel he was wearing to where he could unfasten it, then jerked his thumb to the rear. 'I'm going back there; I won't be long.'

He climbed into the back of the Land-Rover and Warren, flipping an eye up to the interior mirror, saw his arm move in a rhythmic movement as though throwing something repeatedly. As he came back into his seat he tossed the empty satchel from the window.

'What were you throwing out back there?' asked Warren curiously.

'Caltrops – tyre-busters,' said Metcalfe with a grin. 'Whichever way they land there's always one sharp point sticking up. The Kurds use a lot of them when they're being chased by the Iraqi armoured car patrols. I see no reason why they shouldn't be on the receiving end for once.'

Warren's hands were steadier. This calm, matter-of-fact man was a soothing influence. He slowed for another sharp bend, and said, 'How did you cause all that racket back in the valley?'

'Started a fire in an ammunition dump,' said Metcalfe cheerily. 'And laid a time-fuse in the mortar bomb store. I also tied strings to a hell of a lot of grenades and tied the other end to the truck – when I moved off it pulled out the firing pins and they started popping off. Old Fahrwaz may still have the guns I brought, but he won't have much left to shoot out of them.'

More explosions sounded distantly behind them, the noise deadened by the rock walls of the gorge, and Metcalfe grinned contentedly. Warren said, 'How much further to go?'

'We're about half way.' He picked up the microphone and rested it on his lap. Presently he raised it to his lips and said, 'We're just about there, Andy. Stop round the next corner. Over.'

'Okay, Tom. Out.'

Warren eased to a halt as Follet slowed. Metcalfe jumped out and joined Tozier, who asked, 'What's the situation?'

Metcalfe nodded up the road. 'The gorge ends just round that corner. There's a small rocky hill – what we'd call a *kopje* in South Africa – which commands the entrance. Our boys are on top of there.'

'How far from this spot?'

Metcalfe cocked his head on one side. 'About four hundred yards.' He pointed upwards. 'If you climb up there you'll be able to see it.'

Tozier looked up, then nodded abruptly and turned to Warren. 'Nick, you'll be helping Johnny. The first thing you do is to get out the spare wheel. And do it quietly – no metallic clinks.'

Warren frowned. 'The spare wheel . . .' But Tozier had already walked away and was talking to Follet. Warren shrugged and got out the wheel brace to unfasten the nuts which held the spare wheel in place.

Metcalfe and Tozier began to climb the side of the gorge, and Follet came across to help Warren. The spare wheel came loose and Follet rolled it along the ground as though he was looking for a special place to put it. He laid it down carefully, then went back to Warren. 'Get out the jack,' he said, and surprised Warren by diving under the Land-Rover with a spanner clutched in his hand.

Warren found the jack and laid it on the ground. Follet said in a muffled voice, 'Give me a hand with this,' so Warren dropped to his knees and saw Follet busily engaged in removing the exhaust silencer. When he took hold of it he found it surprisingly heavy and only slightly warm to the touch. They dragged it clear and Follet unfastened a couple of nuts and slid out the baffles which formed an integrated unit. He nodded towards the wheel. 'Take it over there,' he said, and picked up the jack and a toolbox.

Warren dumped the silencer next to the wheel. 'What are we supposed to be doing?'

'This will be a mortar when we've assembled it,' said Follet. 'A mortar needs a base plate – that's the wheel. There's a flange on it so it makes firm contact with the ground. The silencer is the barrel – you didn't think Rover silencers are machined like that, did you?' He began to work rapidly. 'Those lugs fit here, on the wheel. Help me.'

The lugs slid home sweetly into the slots in the wheel and Follet pushed a pin through the aligned holes. 'This screw jack is the elevating mechanism,' he said. 'It fits in here like this. You fit the wheel brace and turn, and the whole barrel goes up and down. Just fasten those nuts, will you?'

He ran back to the vehicles leaving Warren a little numb with astonishment but not so much as to neglect the urgency of the occasion. Follet came back and tossed down an ordinary transparent plastic protractor. 'That screws on to the jack – it already has holes drilled.' Warren screwed the protractor in place and found that he had just installed a simple range scale.

Above his head Metcalfe and Tozier looked across at the small rocky hill. As Metcalfe had said it was about four hundred yards away and he could see quite clearly the half-dozen men standing on top. 'Has Fahrwaz got a telephone line laid on – or anything like it?'

Metcalfe held his head on one side as he heard a distant thud. 'He won't need it in the circumstances,' he said. 'Those boys can hear what's going on. They're getting worried – look at them.'

The men on the hill were gazing at the entrance to the gorge and there was some gesticulating going on. Tozier produced a small prismatic compass and sighted it carefully on the hill. 'We have a mortar,' he said. 'Johnny Follet is assembling it now. We also have a light machine-gun. If we get the machine-gun up here you can hose the top of that hill and draw their fire.' He turned and took another sight on the mortar. 'As soon as we know where their machine-gun is, then we knock it out with the mortar.'

'Andy, you're a tricky bastard,' said Metcalfe affectionately. 'I always said so and, by God, I'm right.'

'Our machine-gun has no belt or drum – just a hopper into which you dump loose rounds. You should be able to handle it.'

'It sounds like the Japanese Nambu. I can handle it.'

'You'll also be artillery spotter,' said Tozier. 'We'll be firing blind from down there. Do you remember the signals we used in the Congo?'

'I remember,' said Metcalfe. 'Let's get that machine-gun up here. I wouldn't be surprised if those boys come down the gorge to see what's happening back there.'

They climbed down and found Warren tightening the last nut on the mortar. Metcalfe looked at it unbelievingly. 'What a crazy lash-up. Does it really work?'

'It works,' said Tozier briefly. 'See how Johnny's getting on with the machine-gun. Time is getting few.'

He dropped on one knee, checked the assembly of the mortar, then began to line it up in conformity with the angles he had taken using the compass. 'We'll set it at four hundred yards,' he said. 'And hope for the best.'

'I didn't believe you when you said we had a mortar,' said Warren. 'What about shells?'

'Bombs,' said Tozier. 'We've got precious few of those. You might have noticed that we're liberally equipped with fire extinguishers. There's one under the bonnet in the engine space, one under the dash and another in the back. Six for the two trucks – and that's all the bombs we have. Help me yank 'em out.'

Metcalfe climbed up to his perch on top of the gorge again, trailing a rope behind him. Once settled he hauled up the machine-gun, filled up the hopper with rounds of ammunition, and pushed it before him so that it rested firmly on its bipod. He sighted in carefully at the little group on the hill then turned his head and waved.

Tozier held up his hand and jerked his head at Follet. 'Take that burp-gun which Tom brought along, and go back along the gorge to the first corner. If anything moves, shoot it.'

Follet indicated the mortar. 'What about this?'

'Nick and I can handle it. We're not out for rapid fire – not with only six rounds. Get going. I like to feel that my back's protected.'

Follet nodded, collected the sub-machine-gun and departed at a trot. Tozier waited two minutes and then waved to Metcalfe.

Metcalfe moved his shoulders to loosen them, set his cheek against the butt and looked through the sights. There were five men clearly in view. Gently he squeezed the trigger and death streaked towards the hill at 2,500 feet per second. At that range he could not miss. Delicately he traversed the gun and a scythe of bullets chopped across the top of the hill and suddenly there was no one to be seen.

He stopped firing and waited for something to happen. Moving very slowly he brought his hand forward and dropped a handful of bullets into the hopper. That first long burst had been ruinously expensive of ammunition. He studied the hill carefully but detected nothing that moved.

A rifle cracked twice but no bullet came near him. It was just random shooting. The outpost's machine-gun was mounted so as to sweep the open ground in front of the entrance to the gorge. Apparently no one had taken into account an attack on the outpost from the rear, so it would take some little time for them to reorganize. He smiled grimly as he thought of the frantic effort that must be going

on behind the hill. There would be quite a bit of consterna-
tion, too.

The rifle fired again, twice in quick succession – two of
them, he judged. He was there to draw fire so he decided to
tickle them up and squeezed the trigger again in a quick and
economical burst of five rounds. This time he was answered
in like manner by the sustained chatter of a machine-gun,
and a hail of bullets swept the rocks thirty yards to his left
and ten yards below.

He could not see where the gun was firing from so he
squirted another short burst and was answered again. This
time he spotted it – they had brought the machine-gun
around the curve of the hill and about half way up, sheltered in a tumbled heap of boulders. He signalled to Tozier
who bent down to adjust the mortar.

Tozier tugged the lanyard and the mortar barked. Warren
saw the thin streak against the sky as the bomb arched in its
trajectory and disappeared from sight, but Tozier was
already looking at Metcalfe to find the result of the first
ranging shot.

He grunted as Metcalfe waved his hand complicatedly.
'Thirty yards short – twenty to the left.' He adjusted the
elevation and traversed the mortar slightly, then reloaded.
'This one ought to be better.' The mortar barked again.

The second bomb exploded dead in line with the
machine-gun position but behind it. A man broke from
cover and Metcalfe coolly cut him down with a short burst,
then signalled to Tozier to reduce the range. The consterna-
tion must be just about complete, he thought, but changed
his mind as the machine-gun rattled again and the earth
just below his position fountained magically and rock splinters whined above his head. He ducked and slipped back
into cover as the leaden hail beat the ground where he had
been, sending his gun flying under the impact of the
bullets.

But by that time the third bomb was in the air. He heard it explode and the machine-gun fire was cut off. He eased himself up and risked a look at the hill. A faint drift of smoke on the still morning air marked where it had fallen – square on the machine-gun position. A flat report sounded from behind him as the mortar fired again, and another bomb dropped in almost the same place.

He turned and yelled, 'Enough – they've had it.' He began to scramble down, slipped, and fell most of the way but landed on his feet like a cat. He ran over to the mortar and said breathlessly, 'Let's get on our way while they're still shaken. That natty little gun of yours is buggered, Andy.'

'It served its turn,' said Tozier, and put two fingers in his mouth and whistled shrilly like an urchin. 'That ought to bring Johnny.'

Warren ran for the Land-Rover and started the engine, and Metcalfe tumbled in beside him. 'Andy's a bloody wonder,' he said conversationally. 'That was a lovely bit of shooting.' His head snapped back as Warren took off with tyre-punishing acceleration. 'Take it easy – you'll do me an injury.'

The two Land-Rovers roared out of the gorge and past the hill which was still faintly wreathed in smoke. Follet in the first vehicle was hanging out of the back, his gun at the ready, but for that there was no need. Nobody shot at them, nor did they see anyone move. All Warren saw were three bundles of rags on the rocky hillside.

Metcalfe unhooked the microphone. 'Andy, let us get in front – I know the way. And we'd better move fast before young Ahmed pulls out the plug back there. Over.'

'He won't do that,' said Tozier. 'He's dead. He bumped into a door. Over.'

'Dear me,' said Metcalfe. 'He was the old man's favourite son. All the more reason for speed – Fahrwaz will be looking for us with blood in his eye. The sooner we clear out of the country the better. That means Mosul and the international airport. Move over – I'm coming through. Out.'

He replaced the microphone, and said, 'Doctor, if you want to get back to curing people instead of killing them you'd better hope that this jalopy doesn't break down this side of Sulaymaniyeh. Now move it, Doctor – move it fast.'

NINE

Two days later they landed at Khaldeh International Airport in the Lebanon and drove into Beirut by taxi. The Land-Rovers had been left in Mosul in the care of one of Metcalfe's disreputable friends; they had outlived their usefulness and were no longer needed. 'Beirut's the place,' Tozier had said. 'It's our last chance.'

They registered at a hotel, and Warren said, 'I'm going to ring London; Hellier should be able to bring us up to date with what's been going on here. He'll know where to find Mike and Dan. Then we can figure out the next step.'

'The next step is that I get my hands around Jeanette's beautiful neck,' said Metcalfe savagely.

Warren looked at Tozier and raised his eyebrows. Tozier said softly, 'Are you still with us, Tom?'

'I'm with you. I told you I don't like being used. I can be bought – like you – but on my terms; and my terms have always meant no dope.'

'Then I suggest you leave Delorme strictly alone,' said Tozier. 'She's not important now – it's the heroin we want. Once that is destroyed, then you can have her.'

'It'll be a pleasure,' said Metcalfe.

'All right,' said Tozier. 'Johnny, hire a car – no, better make it two cars; we must be mobile. After Nick has talked to Hellier then we get down to it.'

But when Warren telephoned London he was told by Miss Walden that Hellier was in Beirut. All it took was a quick call to the Saint Georges and half an hour later they were all sitting in Hellier's suite and he was introducing Metcalfe. 'He joined us at just the right time.'

Hellier looked around. 'Where's Bryan?'

'I'll tell you later – if you really want to know,' said Warren. He was beginning to resent Hellier. Hellier had said he wanted blood but so far he had not risked his valuable skin to get it, and things looked a lot different in the Middle East than they had in London.

Hellier pulled papers from a briefcase. 'Abbot doesn't make sense. He got word to me that the Delorme woman is smuggling two thousand pounds of heroin. I think it's ridiculous, but I can't find Abbot to confirm it or otherwise.'

'I confirm it,' said Warren. 'If it weren't for Andy and Johnny it would have been two tons instead of one.'

'You'd better tell me about that,' said Hellier.

Warren did so, not leaving anything out. When he came to what had happened to Ben Bryan he said bitterly, 'It was a damn' silly thing to do. I blame myself; I should never have let him go back.'

'Nuts!' said Follet. 'It was his own choice.'

Warren completed the tale of their adventures and when he stopped Hellier was pale. 'That's about the lot,' said Warren dispiritedly. 'We missed all along the line.'

Hellier drummed his fingers on the table. 'I don't think we can go any further with this. It's a police matter from now on – let them handle it. We have more than enough evidence for them now.'

Tozier's voice was hard. 'You can't bring the police into this – not the way the evidence was collected.' He swung around on Warren. 'How many men have you killed, Nick?'

'None that I'm aware of,' said Warren, but he knew what Tozier meant.

'No? What about coming through Fahrwaz's place in Iran, the night we blew hell out of the laboratory? Johnny is pretty certain you ran down a man.'

Follet said, 'The way we hit him he wouldn't have a chance. Anyway, I saw him lying in the road when we went back in.'

'The man was shooting at us,' said Warren angrily.

'Tell that to the Iranian police,' said Tozier scornfully. 'As for me, I'm not pussyfooting around the truth. I've killed men on this jaunt. Ahmed was killed with my bomb, which Warren helped to make; we mortared hell out of another group – I think that between us we killed a dozen, all in all.' He leaned forward. 'Normally I'm covered – I'm employed by a government which gives me a killing licence. But this time I'm not and I can hang as high as Haman under the civil law, and so can the rest of us.' He jabbed a stiff finger towards Hellier. 'Including you. You're just as guilty – an accomplice before the act, so think of that before shouting copper.'

Hellier snorted. 'Do you really think we'd be prosecuted because of the death of scum?' he said contemptuously.

'You don't understand, do you?' said Tozier. 'Tell the silly bastard, Tom.'

Metcalfe grinned. 'It's like this. People around here are touchy about their national pride. Take the Iraqis, for instance; I don't suppose President Bakr is going to shed any tears over a few dead Kurds – he's been trying to polish off the lot himself – but no government is going to stand for a crowd of foreigners bursting into their country and shooting the place up, no matter how high the motives. Andy's dead right – you shout copper now and you'll start a diplomatic incident so big that there's no knowing where it will end. Before you know it the Russkies would be accusing Johnny of being a CIA agent and casting you as the secret head of British Intelligence. And, by God, it would take a hell of a lot of explaining away.'

Follet said, 'No cops.' His voice was final.

Hellier was silent for a while, digesting this and finding it hard going. He said at last, 'I see what you mean. Do you honestly think that your activities in Kurdistan could be construed as interfering in the internal affairs of another country?'

'By Christ, I do!' said Tozier forcefully. 'What the hell would you call it?'

'I must admit you've convinced me,' said Hellier regretfully. 'Although I still think we could plead justification.' He stared at Metcalfe. 'Some of us, that is. Smuggling arms is quite another thing.'

'Your opinion of me doesn't matter a fart in a thunderstorm,' said Metcalfe calmly. 'Anything I do I carry the can for myself. And if I'm going to stay with this crowd you'd better keep your fat-headed opinions to your fat self.'

Hellier flushed. 'I don't know that I like your attitude.'

'I don't give a stuff if you like it or not.' Metcalfe turned to Tozier. 'Is this chap real or has someone invented him?'

Warren said sharply, 'That's enough. Shut up, Hellier; you don't know enough about it to criticize. If Metcalfe wanted to take arms to the Kurds that's his business.'

Metcalfe shrugged. 'So I picked the wrong bunch of Kurds – that was a mistake which doesn't alter the principle. Those boys have been having a rough time at the hands of the Iraqis and someone has to help them out.'

'While making money at it,' Hellier sneered.

'The labourer is worthy of his hire,' said Metcalfe. 'I risk my skin doing it.'

Tozier stood up and looked at Hellier with dislike. 'I don't think we can do much more here, Tom – not with this bag of wind around.'

'Yeah,' said Follet, pushing back his chair. 'It's a bit stuffy in here.'

Warren's voice was cutting. 'Sit down, everybody.' He looked at Hellier. 'I think an apology is in order, Sir Robert.'

Hellier subsided and mumbled, 'No offence meant. I'm sorry, Mr Metcalfe.'

Metcalfe merely nodded, and Tozier sat down. Warren said, 'Let's stick to the real issue. How do you suppose we should go about finding Abbot and Parker, Andy?'

'Find Delorme and she'll lead you there,' said Tozier promptly.

'I've been thinking a lot about this woman,' said Warren. 'You know more about her than anyone, Tom. What can you tell us that we don't know?'

'I've been wondering a bit myself,' admitted Metcalfe. 'There are some things about this lark that don't add up. Jeanette is pretty good, but she's never been a smash success. Everything she's pulled off has made money, but the overheads are crippling, and I doubt if she has accumulated a lot of capital. All the time I've known her she's been a big spender.'

'What's the point?' asked Hellier.

'How much opium did Fahrwaz collect in Iran?'

'Twenty tons or more,' said Warren.

'There you are,' said Metcalfe. 'That's worth a hell of a lot of boodle. Where would she get it?'

'She wouldn't need it,' said Tozier. 'Not the way she's been working the deal. It was a straight swap for arms. She didn't have to put up the money for the opium – Fahrwaz would – and it wouldn't cost him a lot on his home ground and with his connections.'

'I agree it was a barter transaction,' said Metcalfe exasperatedly. 'But I delivered half a million quids' worth to Fahrwaz. That wasn't the first consignment I'd pushed into Kurdistan. Where would Jeanette get half a million?'

'Wait a minute,' said Hellier, and scrabbled in his brief-case. 'One of Abbot's early reports said something about a banker.' He flipped pages. 'Here it is. She had lunch with a man called Fuad who was traced back to the Inter-East Bank.' He picked up the telephone. 'I could bear to know something more about him. I have good financial connec-tions here.'

'Don't make it too obvious,' warned Warren.

Hellier favoured him with a superior smile. 'Give me the credit for knowing my own job. This is a perfectly normal financial enquiry – it's done all the time.'

He spoke briefly into the telephone and listened for a long time. Then he said, 'Yes, I'd like that; anything to do with him would be welcome. Directorships and so on espe-cially. Thank you very much. Yes, I think I'll be coming in later this week – we're making a film here. I'll ring you as soon as I'm settled and we must have lunch. You'll send the dossier on Fuad immediately? Good.'

He put down the telephone and smiled broadly. 'I thought Fuad might be the manager of Inter-East, but he's not – he owns it. That makes this interesting.'

'How?' asked Warren.

Hellier smiled jovially. 'You bank with the Midland, don't you? When did you last take the Chairman of the Midland Bank to lunch?'

Warren grimaced. 'I never have. I doubt if he knows I exist. I don't swing the financial weight to create interest in such rarefied circles.'

'And neither does Delorme, according to Metcalfe – and yet she lunches with Fuad who *owns* Inter-East.' Hellier tented his fingers. 'Banking in the Lebanon is conducted along lines which would cause grey hairs in the City of London. Ever since the spectacular fall of Intrabank the Lebanese government has been trying to clean up its finan-cial image, but this man, Fuad, has been playing fast and loose with the proposed Code of Conduct. The rules by which he works are considered normal in the relaxed atmosphere of the Middle East, but it means that anyone who shakes hands with him had better count his fingers afterwards. My friend on the other end of that telephone keeps a permanent dossier on Fuad's doings – just for his own safety. He's sending it up to us.'

'So you think he's financing the whole deal,' said Warren.

'I think it's likely,' said Hellier. 'We'll know better when I study the dossier. It's surprising what a list of directorships tell about a man.'

'That's one angle to be worked on,' said Tozier. 'But there's another. The morphine has still to be converted into heroin. What are your views on that, Nick?'

'They have to do it somewhere. It's my bet they'll do it here in Beirut.'

'Without Speering?'

'There are other chemists, and it's not too difficult – not nearly as difficult as the extraction of morphine from opium. You acetylate the morphine and convert the base to hydrochloride. All you need are a lot of plastic buckets, and it requires as much chemical knowledge as you get in a sixth-form stinks class.'

They discussed it for a while and came up with no positive solution. Heroin could be made practically anywhere, and it was impossible to search the whole of Beirut or, possibly, the entire Lebanon.

Warren brought up the disappearance of Abbot and Parker. 'If Delorme fell for the torpedo scheme, then Parker will be busy. I think that's why they're not in plain sight.'

'Getting torpedoes would be no trouble to Jeanette,' observed Metcalfe. 'She's been running arms all over the Mediterranean for quite a few years. But that brings up something else – she'll need a ship. That cuts down the search area to the coast and the ports.'

'Not much help,' said Follet. 'There are a lot of ships.'

The telephone rang and Hellier picked it up. 'Send him up,' he said. Presently there was a discreet knock at the door which Hellier answered, and he returned with a fat envelope. 'The Fuad dossier,' he said. 'Let's see what we can find.'

He pulled out the sheaf of typescript and studied it. After a while he said in disgust, 'This man has the ethics of a Byzantine bazaar trader – he's making a lot of money. He even runs a yacht – the *Stella del Mare*.' He flipped the pages. 'According to this list of directorships he has a finger in a lot of pies – hotels, restaurants, vineyards, a couple of farms, a shipyard . . .' He looked up. 'That might bear investigation in view of what we've been discussing.'

He made a note and continued. 'A condiment and pickle factory, a garage, a general engineering works, housing developments . . .'

Warren broke in. 'Say that again.'

'Housing developments?'

'No – something about a pickle factory.'

Hellier checked back. 'Yes, sauces and pickles. He bought it quite recently. What about it?'

'I'll tell you,' said Warren deliberately. 'The acetylation of morphine makes a hell of a stink, and it's exactly the same stink you find in a pickle factory. It's the acetic acid; it smells just like vinegar.'

'Now we're getting somewhere,' said Tozier with satisfaction. 'I suggest we split this lot up. Nick investigates the pickle factory – he's the expert there. Johnny keeps tabs on Delorme, and I'll help him with that if necessary. Tom takes the shipyard angle.' He turned to Metcalfe. 'You'd better steer clear of the woman. Fahrwaz will have been screaming blue murder and she must know about it by now, and of your implication.'

'All right,' said Metcalfe. 'But I'll want her later.'

'You'll get her,' said Tozier grimly. 'Sir Robert can keep digging into Fuad because that's already paying dividends and might pay more. He's also HQ staff – he stays here and we telephone in; he correlates the operation.'

II

Parker hummed happily as he prepared to tackle the last torpedo. He had been working long hours, eating bad food, and had been confined to the shed and its immediate vicinity for a long time, but he was supremely happy because he was doing the work he liked best of all. He was sorry the job was coming to an end for two reasons – the pleasurable part would be over and the really dangerous part beginning. But right now he was not thinking of what would happen on the other side of the Atlantic, but concentrating on opening the warhead.

Abbot was becoming increasingly edgy. He had not been able to get out of Jeanette anything concerning the operation on the American side. He badly wanted to know the place and the time, but that valuable information she kept to herself. He did not think that Eastman knew, either. Delorme played her cards very close to her beautiful chest.

Ever since the night he had taken her to the Paon Rouge he had been confined, like Parker, to the shed. He had seen a copy of the newspaper and knew that his advertisement trick had worked, but what good it would do he did not know. He frowned irritably and turned his head to see the Arab, Ali, leaning on the rail at the top of the stairs and watching him with unblinking brown eyes. That was another thing – this sense of being continually watched.

He became conscious of a sudden stillness in the workshop and looked at Parker who had his head down and was looking at the warhead. 'What's the matter?'

'Step over here,' said Parker quietly.

He joined Parker and looked down at the warhead, and at Parker's hands which trembled a little. Parker put down the tool he was holding. 'Don't make a scene,' he said. 'Don't do anything that'll attract the attention of that bloody Arab – but this thing is full.'

'Full of what?' asked Abbot stupidly.

'TNT, you bloody fool. What do you suppose a warhead would be full of? There's enough in here to blow this whole place a mile high.'

Abbot gulped. 'But Eastman said they'd be delivered empty.'

'Then this one got through by mistake,' said Parker. 'What's more – it has a detonator in it which I'm hopin' isn't armed. It shouldn't be armed, but then, it shouldn't be there at all – an' neither should the TNT. You'd better do your walkin' around here very quietly until I take it out.'

Abbot looked at the warhead as though hypnotized, and Parker did the necessary operation very carefully. He laid the detonator on a bench. 'That's a bit better – but not much. I don't know why this hasn't blown before. To leave a detonator in a warhead is criminal, that's what it is.'

'Yes,' said Abbot, and found himself sweating. 'What do you mean – it's not much better?'

'TNT is right funny stuff,' said Parker. 'It goes sour with age. It's not so stable any more. It becomes that sensitive it can explode on its own.' He looked sideways at Abbot. 'It's best you don't go near it, Mike.'

'Don't worry; I won't.' Automatically Abbot took a cigarette packet from his pocket, and then changed his mind at the unspoken look in Parker's eyes. 'No smoking, either, I suppose. What do we do about it?'

'We get it out. In the service they'd steam it out an' flush it away, but I want to hold on to this little lot – it could come in useful. I don't want Ali to know about it, either.'

'It's hardly likely that he'd know,' said Abbot. 'He's not a technical type. But Eastman might if he came in and saw what we were doing. What you want the stuff for, Dan?'

'It's in my mind that a torpedo ought to explode,' said Parker. 'That's what it's made for, an' it don't seem right it shouldn't. When these fish are launched I want them to go off wi' a bang. That this one is full o' TNT is an act o' providence to my way o' thinkin'.'

Abbot thought of four torpedoes, each loaded with heroin worth $25,000,000 and each exploding on the American shore before the unbelieving eyes of the waiting reception committee. It would be a good ploy. 'What about your weights? You've bitched about the difficulties often enough.'

Parker winked. 'Never tell the whole truth. I've been keepin' somethin' in reserve.'

'You have only one detonator.'

'A good artificer can always make do,' pronounced Parker. 'But like as not I'll probably blow us both to hell gettin' the stuff out, so let's leave that problem until later. It may never come up.' He studied the warhead. 'I'll need some brass tools; I'll start makin' those up now.'

He went away, and Abbot, after looking at the warhead for some time, also left – walking very quietly.

Four days later Eastman surveyed the torpedoes with satisfaction. 'So you reckon we're ready to go, Dan,'

'All ready,' said Parker. 'Bar loadin' the warheads. Then you can stick the fish in the tubes an' shoot.'

'Putting that other tube in the *Orestes* improved her handling,' said Eastman. 'The skipper says she's not as cranky.'

Parker smiled. 'It equalized the turbulence. I'm ready to begin loadin' if you've got the stuff.'

'The boss is a bit worried about that,' said Eastman. 'She wants to do it herself – just to make sure.'

'Well, she can't – an' that's flat,' said Parker abruptly. 'It's a tricky job. I have to see that the centre o' gravity comes in the right place because if it doesn't I can't guarantee how the fish will behave. They have to be balanced just right.'

To have someone prying into the warheads was the last thing he wanted. 'She can stand over me an' watch while I do it,' he said at last. 'I don't mind that.'

Abbot said, 'Dan was telling me that if the balance isn't right the torpedo might dive to the bottom.'

'It would affect the steering, too,' said Parker. 'They'd be bloody erratic.'

'Okay, okay,' said Eastman, holding up his hands. 'You've convinced me – as usual. Jeanette will be here pretty soon with the load for one fish. See if you can convince her.'

Jeanette took a lot of convincing but at last she agreed, bowing to the superior weight of technical know-how which Parker dazzlingly deployed. 'As long as I'm here when you do it and the warhead is sealed,' she said.

Abbot grinned. 'You don't trust us very much.'

'Correct,' she said coolly. 'Help Jack to get the stuff in here.'

Abbot helped Eastman to haul a big cardboard box into the shed and down the stairs, and then they went back for another. Jeanette delicately tapped the box with a neatly shod foot. 'Open it.'

Parker took a knife and ripped open the top of the box. It was full of polyethylene bags, all holding a white powder. 'Those bags hold half a kilogram each,' she said. 'There are five hundred of them – one torpedo load.'

Parker straightened. 'That's not on. I said five hundred pounds – not two hundred and fifty kilos. I don't know if I can do it – it's fifty pounds over the odds.'

'Just put it in,' she said.

'You don't understand,' he said exasperatedly. 'I've balanced these torpedoes for a five hundred pound load. If you stick an extra ten per cent right at the nose it's goin' to alter the leverage arm – alter the centre o' balance.' He rubbed the side of his nose. 'It's possible, I suppose,' he said doubtfully.

'For another hundred thousand dollars?' she asked. 'Just for you. I won't tell Abbot.'

'All right,' he said. 'I'll give it a go.' He did not want to leave any heroin behind if he could help it, and it did not really matter a damn about the balance as far as he was concerned. He would make a song and dance about it and go through the motions, baffling her with science, just to avoid suspicion. 'For another hundred thou', you're on.'

'I thought you could do it,' she said, and smiled.

He thought she was getting it cheaply. A further two hundred pounds of heroin worth $10,000,000 for a mere $100,000 – if he was ever paid at all. God, the profits to be made in this business!

Eastman and Abbot came back bearing another load, and Parker began to stow the packets into the warhead very carefully. 'It's a matter o' density, too,' he said. 'This stuff isn't as solid as TNT. It takes up more room, especially in these plastic packets.'

'You're sure the warhead is waterproof?' demanded Jeanette.

'You needn't worry about that,' he assured her. 'It's as tight as a duck's arse.'

She looked mystified and Eastman chuckled. He began to poke about on the bench which was littered with tools and bits of metal. He picked up something and began to examine it, and Abbot froze as he saw it was one of the detonators Parker had been making up. 'What's this?'

Parker looked at it, and said casually, 'Contact breaker for the "B" circuit. That one wasn't working very well, so I made up another.'

Eastman tossed it in the air, caught it, and replaced it on the bench. 'You're pretty good with your hands, Dan. I think I could find you a good job over in the States.'

'I wouldn't mind that,' said Parker. 'Not if it pays as well as this one.' He worked in silence for a long time with Jeanette hovering over him and peering over his shoulder. At last he said, 'That's the last packet. I'm surprised – I really am. I didn't think we'd get 'em all in. I'll screw it down tight an' you can put your seal on if you want to.'

He checked the heavily greased gasket and clamped the small hatch down, then said, 'Get the block an' tackle ready, Mike. We'll couple it to the torpedo body an' then it'll be ready to go to the *Orestes*.'

The warhead was swayed up on the block and tackle and run across to the body where Parker bolted it down firmly. 'There, miss,' he said. 'Are you happy wi' that? I feel I ought to ask for a receipt, but I doubt I'd get it.'

'I'm satisfied,' she said. 'Have it taken to the *Orestes* tonight, Jack. There'll be another load tomorrow, Parker. The *Orestes* sails the morning after.' She smiled at Abbot. 'A nice sea cruise for all of us.'

III

Warren felt dispirited when they met in Hellier's suite to compare notes. He had had an unproductive day. 'The pickle factory is closed up tight as a drum. There's a sign outside saying it's closed for alterations.'

'How do you know that's what it said?' asked Metcalfe. 'Wasn't the sign in Arabic script?'

'I found someone to translate it into French,' said Warren tiredly. 'There was a bit of a vinegary smell, but not much. I didn't see anyone go in or come out. It was a wasted day.'

'I saw somebody go in,' said Follet unexpectedly. 'I followed the Delorme dame and she went in the back way. There was a guy with her – an American, I think – they spent about an hour there.'

'It's all linking up nicely,' said Hellier, regarding Follet with approval. 'This definitely ties up Delorme with Fuad. What about the shipyard?'

'It's not very big,' said Metcalfe. 'Impossible to get into, if you want to be unobtrusive about it. I didn't see Jeanette at all. I hired a boat and had a look at the yard from the sea. Fuad's yacht is anchored there, and there's a scrubby old coaster flying the Panamanian flag – the *Orestes,* she's called. That's all. The yard itself looks run down; not many working types about, but plenty of toughs at the main gate.'

'Perhaps it's closed for alterations, too,' said Tozier ironically. 'If they're ferrying millions of dollars' worth of heroin about Beirut they're going to be damned sure there'll be no prying eyes at the staging points. It's quite possible the *Orestes* is the ship we're looking for. Could she make the Atlantic crossing?'

'I don't see why not,' said Metcalfe. 'She's about three thousand tons. But there's more. This afternoon a truck pitched up hauling a very long trailer. I couldn't see what the trailer carried because it was covered with a tarpaulin, but it could very well have been a torpedo.'

'I'm not so sure of this torpedo bit,' said Warren. 'Parker told me a torpedo can only carry about five hundred pounds, and we know there's a ton to be smuggled.' He frowned. 'Even if Abbot and Parker scupper the first consignment that still leaves another three-quarters of a ton of heroin around. If the torpedo is sabotaged Delorme and her gang will go to ground and we'll be worse off than we are now.'

'If Jeanette can get one torpedo – which she can – then she can get four,' said Metcalfe. 'I know Jeanette – she's a go-for-broke type, and if she's convinced that a torpedo will do the trick she'll go for it wholeheartedly.'

'That's all very well,' said Warren. 'But we don't even know if Parker sold her on the idea.'

'Ah, but I have more,' said Metcalfe. 'When the truck and trailer came out of the shipyard I followed it. It went to another place on the coast which was also locked up tight and the very devil to observe. But I paid a lot of money for the use of an attic from which I could see about a quarter of what's on the other side of the wall. There was an Arab who is apparently some kind of caretaker; there's a shortish man with broad shoulders – very muscular – and who walks with a slight limp . . .'

'Parker!' said Warren.

'. . . and there's a tall young chap with fair hair. Would that be Abbot?'

Warren nodded. 'It matches him.'

'A car came in once, stayed a few minutes and drove away again. It brought a tall man with a beaky nose and hair receding at the temples.'

'That sounds like the guy who was with the Delorme dame,' said Follet. 'Was it a black Mercedes?'

Metcalfe nodded, and Hellier said, 'I think it's quite clear we're all moving in the right direction. The point is – what do we do now?'

'I think Parker and Abbot are in a very dangerous position,' said Warren.

'And that's an understatement.' Metcalfe snorted. 'Suppose the ship sails and the torpedoes don't work because Parker has sabotaged them. Jeanette is going to be as mad as a hornet. Nobody loses that much money and stays civilized, and she's a touchy girl at the best of times. Parker and Abbot will get the chop – they'll go over the side of the *Orestes* and no one will ever hear of them again.' He brooded. 'Come to that, they might get the chop even if the torpedoes are successful. Jeanette has a passion for covering up her tracks.'

Tozier said, 'Nick, I'm very much afraid you've boobed. This torpedo trick is all right as far as it goes, but you didn't think it through. It's all very well being in a position to dump the heroin, but what about Abbot and Parker?'

'I think the point at issue here is very simple,' said Hellier. 'Do we attack the pickle factory or the ship?'

'Not the pickle factory,' said Warren instantly. 'Supposing they've moved some of the heroin out already? Even if we attack the factory there'll still be some of the stuff on the loose. I favour the ship where we'll have a chance of scooping the pool and getting the lot.'

'And of rescuing Parker and Abbot,' pointed out Hellier.

'That means attacking just before she sails,' said Tozier meditatively. 'And we don't know when that will be.'

'Or whether she'll be carrying the whole consignment,' said Metcalfe. 'We still don't know enough.'

'If only I could talk to Abbot for just five minutes,' said Warren.

Metcalfe snapped his fingers. 'You say Parker was in the Navy. Is there any chance he'd understand Morse?'

'It's possible,' said Warren. 'It may even be probable.'

'That attic I was in faces the setting sun,' said Metcalfe, 'I had the devil of a job because the sun got in my eyes. But it opens up possibilities and all I need is a mirror. I could heliograph.'

Warren's lips tightened. 'Unobtrusively, I hope.'

'I'll watch it,' said Metcalfe seriously.

The conference broke up. Warren was to back up Metcalfe, and Tozier and Follet were to concentrate on the shipyard, looking for a weak spot. Hellier stayed behind to coordinate.

Warren discussed the plan with Metcalfe, then said, 'I'd like to ask you a personal question.'

'That's all right, as long as you don't expect an honest answer.'

'You puzzle me, Metcalfe. You don't believe much in law and order, do you? And yet you're dead against dope. Why?'

Metcalfe stopped smiling. 'That's none of your business,' he said stiffly.

'Under the present circumstances I think it is,' said Warren carefully.

'Maybe you have a point,' conceded Metcalfe. 'You're afraid I might run off with the loot and diddle you all.' He smiled faintly. 'I would, too, if it wasn't dope; there's a hell of a lot of money involved. Let's just say that I once had a younger brother and leave it at that, shall we?'

'I see,' said Warren slowly.

'Maybe you do – you're in the business yourself, so Andy tells me. As for law and order, I believe in it as much as the next man, but if the poor bloody Kurds want to fight for the right to live like men then I'm prepared to transport their guns.'

'You seem to have the same point of view as Andy Tozier.'

'Andy and I get along with each other very well,' said Metcalfe. 'But let me give you a bit of advice, Nick; don't go about asking people personal questions – not anywhere east of Marseilles. It's an easy way to get seriously – and permanently – damaged.'

IV

Dan Parker sat on the stool by the bench and contemplated the one remaining torpedo. The late afternoon sun flooded the shed and his work was nearly done. Two torpedoes had been filled and taken away that morning, and this last one was to leave in a very few hours. He felt tired and a little depressed and he was acutely worried about the next stage of the adventure.

Back in London he had left his wife and his sons and he wondered if he would ever see them again. He had no illusions about what would happen on the other side of the

Atlantic when four torpedoes exploded on a quiet shore and a major fortune went to destruction. He would, quite simply, be killed and he could see no way of avoiding it. His life had been at risk before, but in the random way of war; never in the cold-blooded manner which he now faced.

He blinked as a stray beam of light flickered across the bench, and pondered on possible ways out of the gruesome situation he and Abbot found themselves in. They could not attempt to escape in Beirut because that would be an immediate tip-off that there was something wrong with the torpedoes and the whole dangerous operation would have gone for nothing. Delorme would cut her losses and revert to whatever plans she had originally conceived. So there was nothing for it but to board the *Orestes* next day and hope for the best.

Something niggled at the back of his mind, something which was striving to express itself – something to do with himself, with his own . . . name? He frowned and tried to pin it down. What was it? What was it about the name of Parker that should be so important? He tensed as the light flickered again across the bench because he was suddenly aware that it was spelling his name out – over and over again.

He got up casually and walked over to Ali who was squatting at the bottom of the stairs. 'Hey, Ali, you bloody scoundrel; go to the office an' get me some cigarettes. Got that? Cigarettes.' He mimed the action of lighting a cigarette and pointed up the stairs.

Abbot said, 'I've got some here, Dan.'

Without turning, Parker said briefly, 'They're not my brand. Get crackin', you damned heathen!'

Ali nodded and went up the stairs. As soon as he had left the shed Parker whirled around. 'Get up there an' stop him comin' back – I don't care how you do it but keep him out o' this shed. Have an attack o' bellyache in the yard – anythin'!'

Abbot nodded and ran up the stairs, prodded into unques-
tioning action by the authoritative rasp in Parker's voice. He
did not know why Parker wanted this but the tone of
urgency was unmistakable. Parker returned to the bench
Where the light still flickered and studied it for a moment.
Then he traced an imaginary line to the window through
which it struck. He bent down and the light struck him full
in the face and steadied so that he was blinded. He brought
up his hand before his face in the thumbs-up sign and then
stepped aside.

The light remained steady on the bench for a moment
and then began to flicker again and to spell out words in
Morse rather slowly. *Warren here . . . questions coming . . . flash
light one for yes . . . two for no . . . got that . . .*

Parker took the trouble-shooting lamp which was on a
long lead and set it up facing the window. He flashed it once.
The reflected light from outside steadied momentarily on the
bench and began again . . . *is torpedo working* . . .

Parker paused. He took that to mean: Is the method of
smuggling to be by torpedo? He flashed once.

. . . *how many . . . one* . . .

Two flashes.

. . . *four* . . .

One flash.

. . . *by Orestes* . . .

One flash.

. . . *when . . . next week* . . .

Two flashes.

. . . *tomorrow* . . .

One flash.

Metcalfe, up in the attic, checked his prepared question
list into which he had put a great deal of thought. He had
used Warren's name because he himself was unknown to
Parker, and he had to get the maximum information in the
minimum time for Parker's safety. It was rather like playing

the game of Twenty Questions. He flashed the next question
which was all important.

. . . is all dope going . . . repeat . . . all . . .

One flash.

. . . are you and Abbot going . . .

One flash.

. . . do you want rescue . . .

The faint light in the shed flickered wildly and Metcalfe
guessed that Parker was trying to send Morse. It was
unreadable because the light was so faint and the sun in his
eyes so strong. He let his light remain steady until Parker
stopped, then hesitated as he saw the Arab come into view
from the office. He was relieved to see Abbot step forward
and waylay the Arab. Abbot pointed away from the shed
and the two men went back into the office.

Metcalfe steadied the mirror again.

*. . . check where I am . . . can you flash Morse up here at
night . . .*

One flash.

. . . will be here all night . . . good luck . . .

The light steadied on the bench once more and then
abruptly vanished. Parker took his hand from the switch
and sighed. He walked to the window and looked up at the
faraway building from which the signals had come; the setting sun gleamed redly on a single pane of glass set in the
roof. His depression was gone – he and Abbot were no
longer alone.

He climbed the stairs and went to the door of the shed.
'Where are those bloody cigarettes?' he roared.

V

Hellier had chartered a fast cruiser which lay in the yacht
harbour and they gathered there early in the morning for a

conference. Follet helped Metcalfe lift aboard the heavy suitcase he carried, then they all sat around the table in the saloon. Tozier said, 'Are you sure the *Orestes* is due to sail at nine, Tom?'

'That's what Parker signalled. We had quite a long chat.'

'What are his views?' asked Tozier.

'He doesn't want to be rescued from the shed. He and Abbot could get out themselves if they wanted to – just knock that Arab on the head and blow. But that would give the game away.'

Tozier consulted his watch. 'It's seven now. We don't have much time to make up our minds. Do we hit her before she sails – in the shipyard – or when she's at sea?'

'It must be before she sails,' said Metcalfe positively. 'We'd never get aboard her at sea. The skipper isn't going to heave to and roll out a red carpet for us – not with Eastman looking on.'

'Let me get this straight,' said Hellier. 'Eastman is sailing in the *Orestes* with Parker and Abbot. The Delorme woman is staying in Beirut.'

'Not for long,' said Warren. 'Parker says that she and Fuao are following in the yacht – going for a cruise in the Caribbean, that's the story. He reckons they'll scuttle the *Orestes* after getting rid of the torpedoes – those torpedo tubes are evidence and they daren't let the *Orestes* put into port where she'll be given a going over by Customs officers. The *Stella del Mare* will be standing by to take off the crew.'

'Maybe,' said Metcalfe cynically. 'Some of the crew, perhaps. I told you that Jeanette likes to cover up her tracks.'

'So it's the shipyard,' said Tozier. 'I suggest we hit them just before the *Orestes* is due to sail. We take over the ship and get her out to sea where we can dump the torpedoes. After that we beach her somewhere and split up.'

'We ought to surprise them,' said Metcalfe. 'We'll be coming in from the sea. They're typical landlubbers and their guards are on the landward side, at the gates. But it's got to be slick and fast.' He gestured to Follet. 'Open the case, Johnny.'

Follet opened the suitcase and began to lay the contents on the table. 'I contacted some of my pals,' said Metcalfe, as the guns were laid out one by one. 'I thought we'd need these. Jeanette isn't the only one with access to weapons.' He grinned at Hellier. 'You'll get the bills later.'

Tozier picked up a sub-machine-gun. 'This is for me. What's the ammo situation?'

'There'll be enough if you don't pop off into the air, but it'll be best if we don't have to use them at all. Guns are noisy, and we don't want the port police chasing us.' He waved at the table. 'What's your fancy, Nick?'

Warren stared at the collection of pistols. 'I don't think so,' he said slowly. 'I've never used a gun. I don't think I could hit anything.'

Follet picked up a pistol and worked the action. 'You'd better have one, even if it's just to point; otherwise you might find your ass in a sling.'

Hellier reached over. 'I think I'll have this one. Not that I've had much practice. I was in the Artillery and that was too long ago.'

Metcalfe raised his eyebrows. 'Are you coming?'

'Of course,' said Hellier calmly. 'Is there any reason why not?'

Metcalfe shrugged. 'None at all. But I thought you'd be one of the back-room boys.'

Hellier glanced at Warren. 'It's partly my fault that Abbot and Parker are where they are. A long time ago I told Warren I wanted blood; I'm quite prepared to pay for it myself.'

Warren looked at the single pistol on the table. 'I'll show you how to handle it, Nick,' said Follet. 'We'll have time enough for a run-down.'

Slowly Warren stetched out his hand and picked up the pistol, feeling the unaccustomed weight of the blued metal. 'All right, Johnny,' he said. 'Show me how,'

TEN

The making and writing of reports reached a minor crescendo in countries stretching right across the Middle East. In Tehran, Colonel Mirza Davar studied one of these reports. There had been a considerable explosion quite close to the Iraqi border in the province of Kurdistan. Loud bangs were undesirable anywhere in Iran and especially so in that sensitive area. Besides, Fahrwaz seemed to be involved and the colonel did not particularly like the implications of that. Colonel Mirza Davar was Chief Intelligence Officer for the North-West Provinces.

A tap at the door introduced his secretary. 'Captain Muktarri to see you.'

'Show him in immediately.'

Captain Muktarri, by his travel-stained appearance, had evidently travelled hard and fast and in rough country. The colonel looked him up and down, and said, 'Well, Captain: what did you find?'

'There was an explosion, sir – a big one. A *qanat* was thoroughly wrecked.'

The Colonel relaxed in his chair. 'A squabble over water rights,' he said. A minor problem and not in his province; a matter for the civil police.

That's what I thought, sir,' said Muktarri. 'Until I found this.' He put down a small square block on the desk.

The colonel picked it up, scratched it with his finger-nail and then sniffed at it delicately. 'Opium.' Although still not a matter for his own attention this was much more serious. 'And this was found on Fahrwaz's farm?'

'Yes, sir, among the debris left by the explosion. Fahrwaz was not there – nor was his son. The villagers denied knowledge of it.'

'They would,' said the colonel, unimpressed. 'This is a matter for the narcotics people.' He drew the telephone towards him.

In Baghdad another Intelligence colonel was studying another report. Something odd had been going on up near the Turkish border. There had been a battle of sorts, but as he had found by intensive checking, no Iraqi troops had been involved.

Which was very interesting. It seemed very much as though the Kurds had begun to fight among themselves.

He reached for the microphone and began to dictate the last of his comments on to tape. 'It is well known that the rebel leader, Al Fahrwaz, who is commonly resident across the border in Iran, has a stronghold in this area. My tentative conclusion is that Mustapha Barzani has attempted to solve the Fahrwaz problem before continuing negotiations with the Iraqi government. According to an unconfirmed report Ahmed ben Fahrwaz was killed in the fighting. Further reports will follow.'

He did not know how wrong he was.

Not two hundred yards along the same street in Baghdad a senior police officer was checking yet another report against a map. Ismail Al-Khalil had been in the Narcotics Department for many years and knew his job very well. The report told of an explosion in Iran which had wrecked an underground laboratory. Broken glassware had been found, and an immense quantity of opium together with a large amount of chemicals, the details of which were listed. He knew exactly what that meant.

His finger traced a line from Iran into northern Iraq and from thence into Syria. He returned to his desk and said to his companion, 'The Iranians are certain it crossed the border.' He shrugged. 'There's nothing we can do about it – not with the political situation being what it is in Kurdistan right now. I'd better make a report – copies to go to Syria, Jordan and the Lebanon.'

Al-Khalil sat down and prepared to dictate his report, and said in parenthesis, 'The Iranians think there's as much as five hundred kilos of morphine or heroin loose. Somebody has been very lax over there.' He shook his head in regret.

The reports proliferated and one dropped on the desk of Jamil Hassan of the Narcotics Bureau in Beirut. He read it and took action, and life became very difficult for the Lebanese underworld. One of those picked up for questioning was a small-time crook named André Picot, suspected of being involved in narcotics smuggling. He was questioned for many hours but nothing could be got from him.

This was for two reasons; he knew very little anyway, and his interrogators did not know enough themselves to ask him the right questions. So, after an all-night session in front of the bright lights which gave him eyestrain but nothing else, he was released a little before nine in the morning – which was a great pity.

II

At ten minutes to nine the cruiser rocked gently on the blue water of the Mediterranean, one engine ticking over gently so that the boat barely had steerage way. Hellier was sitting in the open cockpit apparently interested in nothing else but the fishing-rod he held, but Tozier was in the saloon and keeping careful watch on the *Orestes* through binoculars. A curl of smoke from the single funnel stained the sky to show that her boilers were fired and she was preparing to move.

Warren sat in the saloon close to the door and watched Metcalfe at the wheel. He thought Metcalfe handled the boat very well, and said so. Metcalfe grinned. 'I learned in a hard school. A few years ago I was running cigarettes out of Tangier into Spain with a Yank called Krupke; we had a big-gish boat – a war-surplus Fairmile – which I had re-engined so she could outrun the Spanish excise cutters. If you can't learn to handle a boat doing that sort of thing you'll never learn.'

He leaned down and looked into the saloon. 'Any change, Andy?'

'No change,' said Tozier, without taking his eyes from the binoculars. 'We go in ten minutes.'

Metcalfe straightened and said over his shoulder, 'We're going to abandon this tub, Sir Robert. The charterers won't like it – you'll have a lawsuit on your hands.'

Hellier grunted in amusement. 'I can afford it.'

Warren felt the hard metal of the pistol which was thrust into the waistband of his trousers. It felt uncomfortable and he shifted it slightly. Metcalfe looked down at him, and said, 'Take it easy, Nick, and you'll be all right. Just follow up the rope and take your cue from me.'

It made Warren uncomfortable that Metcalfe should have seen his nervousness. He said curtly, 'I'll be all right when we start.'

'Of course you will,' said Metcalfe. 'We all get butterflies at this stage.' He sighed. 'I've talked myself into things like this all my life. I must be a damned fool.'

There was a metallic click from behind Warren and he turned his head to see Follet slamming a full magazine into the butt of his pistol. Metcalfe said, 'It takes us different ways. Johnny there is nervous, too; that's why he keeps checking his gun. He can never convince himself that it's ready to shoot – just like the old lady who goes on holiday and is never sure she turned off the gas before she left.'

Warren shifted the gun again, and said quietly, 'We're going on board that ship with guns in our hands, ready to shoot. The crew may be quite innocent.'

'Not a chance,' scoffed Metcalfe. 'You can't fit torpedo tubes aboard a scow that size without the crew knowing it. They're all in on the act. And there'll be no shooting, either – not unless they start first.' He looked across at the *Orestes*. 'It's quite likely she'll have a skeleton crew, so that'll make it easier for us. Jeanette won't let one more person in on this than she has to.'

Tozier said, 'I don't see why we can't go in now. She's as ready as she ever will be, and so are we. We can't wait until she begins to haul anchor.'

'All right,' said Metcalfe, and swung the wheel gently. Over his shoulder he said, 'Make like a fisherman, Sir Robert.' He opened the throttle a fraction and the boat moved more purposefully through the water. With a wink at Warren, he said, 'The whole idea is to be gentle. We don't roar up with engines going full blast – we just edge in nice and easy so that even if they see us coming they won't know what the hell to make of it. By the time they do, it'll be too late, I hope.'

Tozier put down the glasses and got busy. He slung the sub-machine-gun over his shoulder and checked a coil of rope for unwanted kinks. At one end of the rope was attached a three-pronged grapnel, well padded for quietness, and he tested that it was secure. He tapped Warren on the shoulder. 'Stand back and let the dog see the rabbit,' he said, and Warren made way for him.

To an onlooker from the shore it might have seemed that the boat was drifting dangerously close to the *Orestes* which, after all, showed all the signs of getting under way. If the boat were to be caught when the screw began to turn then there could be a nasty accident. It was a thoroughly bad piece of seamanship which could not be excused even if the big, fat Englishman had caught a fish and the helmsman was diverted in his excitement,

Hellier hauled the fish out of the sea. He had bought it that morning in the fish market near the Suq des Orfèvres and a very fine specimen it was. It was a last-minute bit of camouflage devised by Follet, the master of the con game, and Hellier dexterously made it twitch on the line as though still alive. With a bit of luck this by-play would allow them to get ten yards nearer to the *Orestes* without being challenged.

The boat edged in still nearer, and Metcalfe nodded to Tozier. 'Now!' he said sharply, as he opened the throttle and spun the wheel, turning them towards the stern of the *Orestes*, but still keeping the bulk of the ship as a screen between the boat and the quay.

Tozier leaped up into the cockpit and whirled the grapnel twice about his head before casting it upwards to the stern rail. As the grapnel caught, Hellier dropped his fish smartly and grabbed the rope, hauling it taut and swinging the boat in to the side of the ship while Metcalfe put the gears into neutral. Even as he did so Tozier was climbing hand over hand, and Warren heard the light thump of his feet as he landed on deck.

Metcalfe abandoned the wheel and went next, and Warren felt apprehensive as he looked over the side of the boat towards the underhang of *Orestes*'s stern. The screw was only two-thirds submerged, the ship being in ballast, and if the skipper gave the order to move the turbulence would inevitably smash the little boat.

Follet pushed him from behind. 'Get going!' he hissed, and Warren grasped the rope and began to climb. He had not climbed a rope since his schooldays when he had been driven up ropes in the gymnasium by an athletic games master wielding a cricket stump. Warren had never been athletically-minded. But he got to the top and a hand grasped him by the scruff of the neck and hauled him over the rail.

There was no time to rest and, breathlessly, he found himself following Metcalfe. Tozier was nowhere to be seen but when Warren turned his head he found Hellier padding behind and looking ridiculous in the bright floral shirt and the shorts he had chosen as his fisherman's get-up. But there was nothing at all funny about the gun held in Hellier's meaty fist.

The deck vibrated underfoot and Metcalfe held up his hand in warning. As Warren came up, he said in a low voice, 'We just got here in time. She's under way.' He pointed. 'There's the bridge ladder – let's go.'

He ran forward lightly and climbed up on to the bridge.

Even as Warren followed he thought it incredible that they should not yet have been seen; but now it came to the crunch – you don't invade a ship's bridge without the skipper having objections.

Metcalfe arrived on the bridge first and, as though by a preconceived plan, Tozier appeared simultaneously from the other side. There were four men on the bridge; the skipper, two officers and the helmsman. The skipper looked incredulously at the sub-machine-gun cradled by Tozier and whirled around only to be confronted by Metcalfe. As he opened his mouth Metcalfe snapped, 'Arrêtez!' and then, for good measure, added in Arabic, 'Ukaf!'

The gesture he made with the gun was good in all languages and the skipper shut his mouth. A sweeping motion from Tozier's sub-machine-gun herded the officers aside, while Metcalfe motioned the helmsman to stay where he was. Warren stood at the top of the bridge ladder and held his pistol loosely in his hand. He looked down at Hellier who stood guard at the bottom of the ladder; presumably Follet was doing the same on the other side.

The ship was still moving slowly and he could now see the widening gap of water between the *Orestes* and the quay. Metcalfe grasped the brass handle of the engine-room telegraph and rang for half speed, and the telegraph clanged again as the engineer obeyed the order. With the gun in his back the helmsman looked at Metcalfe's pointing finger and nodded vigorously. He spun the spokes of the wheel and the quay receded faster.

Suddenly there was an interruption. Eastman stepped from the bridge house and froze as he saw what was happening. His hand dipped beneath his coat and was magically full of gun. Warren brought up his own pistol to the ready and for the minutest fraction of a second the tableau was held. Then Eastman cried out under the impact of a steel bar which struck his arm from behind. His gun went off and there was a ringing clang and a whine as the bullet ricocheted from metal and away over the sea. But he still held on to the gun and whirled on Dan Parker, who was just behind him with a steel bar gripped in his hand as though it had grown there.

He drove his elbow into Parker's stomach and Parker doubled up in pain, the steel bar clattering to the deck. Then Eastman was gone at a dead run and Warren heard the bang of a door in the distance.

Metcalfe moved first. He ran to the side of the bridge and looked ashore and saw the ripple of movement as heads turned towards the departing ship. 'They heard that,' he said, and raised his voice. 'Johnny, come up here.' He turned to Tozier. 'The crew will have heard it, too. Can you hold the bridge while Johnny and I nail Eastman.'

'Carry on,' said Tozier. 'Nick, get Hellier up here, then look at our friend with the iron bar.' He turned to the officers. 'Who speaks English?' he asked conversationally.

'I speak English good,' said the skipper.

'Then we'll get along together. Get the loudhailer and tell the crew to assemble on the forehatch there. But first, where's the radio shack?'

The skipper took a deep breath as though nerving himself to defiance but stopped short as Tozier's gun jerked threateningly. He nodded his head to where Warren was helping Parker to his feet. 'Through there.'

'Watch him,' said Tozier to Hellier, and went off fast. When he returned he found the skipper bellowing into the loudhailer under the supervision of Hellier and already the crew was assembled. As he had thought, there were few of them; the ship was undermanned.

'I'd give a lot to know if that's all,' he said, looking down at them.

Warren came forward with Parker at his side. 'This is Dan Parker; he might be able to tell us.'

Tozier smiled. 'Glad to know you.'

'I'm even gladder to know you,' said Parker. He looked over the deck. 'That's all – but I don't see the engine-room staff. If they stop the engines we're dead mutton.'

'They couldn't have heard the shot,' said Tozier. 'But we can soon find out.' He rang for full speed on the telegraph and it clanged obediently. 'No one has told them yet.'

'If we get them out of there I can handle the engines,' said Parker. He looked around. 'Where's Mike?'

'I haven't seen him,' said Warren. 'Where was he?'

'In his cabin, I think.'

'We'll find him later,' said Tozier impatiently. 'What can we do with the crew? We have to secure the ship before anything else.'

'There's an empty hold,' said Parker. 'They'll be safe enough in there.'

'Nick, you and Hellier go along with Parker and see to it – and take this lot with you.' Tozier indicated the ship's officers. 'They won't give you any trouble; they look a pretty poor lot to me.' He pulled at his lower lip. 'I hope Tom is doing all right, though.'

III

Warren helped secure the crew and herded them into the hold, and then the three of them took over the engine-room. He left Parker and Hellier down there, put the three engineers with the rest of the crew, and then looked up to the bridge. Tozier leaned over the rail. 'We've got a problem – come up here.'

'What about this lot?'

'I'll send Abbot down – we found him. Leave him your gun.'

Abbot came down and gave Warren a cheery grin. 'A nice bit of fun and games,' he said. 'I was very glad to see the gang.'

Warren gave him the gun. 'What's the problem?'

'That's a beauty – I'll leave your pals up there to tell you.'

Warren went up to the bridge and found Follet on the wheel with Tozier close by. Tozier said quickly, 'We have Eastman bottled up, but it's a stand-off. Tom is keeping the cork in the bottle down there, but it leaves us with a problem. He's down where the torpedoes are, so we can't get rid of the heroin until we winkle him out.'

'He went to protect the loot,' said Follet, 'It's my guess he's expecting to be rescued. The crew can't do it, but Delorme has Fuad's yacht and she might chase us.'

Warren dismissed that eventuality. 'What arrangements have been made for firing the torpedoes?'

Tozier pointed. 'Those two buttons near the helm. Press those and you fire two torpedoes.'

Warren nodded. We can get rid of half the heroin.' He took a step forward.

Tozier grabbed him. 'Steady on. Your man, Parker, has been working too hard. All the torpedoes are live. He found some explosives – each warhead is carrying a hundred and eighty pounds of TNT.'

'Short of a hydrogen bomb it'll be the most expensive bang in history,' said Follet.

Warren was perplexed. 'But what's the problem?'

Tozier stared at him. 'Christ, man; you can't shoot live torpedoes indiscriminately in the Mediterranean – especially these. They have an eighteen-mile range, so Abbot says.' He pointed towards the horizon. 'How the hell do we know what's over there? We can't see eighteen miles.'

Follet laughed humorously. 'Last I heard the US Sixth Fleet was in these parts. If we knock off one of Uncle Sam's aircraft carriers that's as good a way of starting World War Three as I know.'

Warren thought about it. 'Are there any uninhabited islands around here? Or rocks or shoals? Anything we can shoot at without killing anything else except fish?'

'A nice way to cause an international ruction,' said Tozier. 'You fire torpedoes at any rocks in the Arab world and the Israelis are going to be on the short end of the stick. Things are touchy enough now and a few bangs around here could really start something.'

'And we'd still have half the stuff left on our hands,' said Follet. 'Maybe all of it. If Eastman is smart enough he'll have ripped out the firing connections.'

'So we have to get him out of there,' said Warren. 'I think we'd better have Parker in on this – he knows the ship.'

'Just a minute,' said Follet. 'I'm still hanging on to this goddam steering-wheel, so would someone mind telling me where we're going?'

'Does it matter?' said Tozier impatiently.

'Metcalfe reckons it matters,' said Follet. 'He saw Jeanette Delorme on the quay when we left – and she saw him. She'll reckon it's a hi-jacking and Tom says she'll come after us loaded for bear.'

'So?'

'So we can stick to the coast or we can head out to sea. She has the same choice. What do you want to do?'

'I'd sooner stick to the coast,' said Tozier. 'If she caught us at sea where it wouldn't matter how many guns she popped off I wouldn't give much for our chances, especially if that yacht is loaded to the gunwales with her cut-throats.'

'Haven't you thought that she'll think that you'll think that and automatically come along the coast and catch us anyway? I'll bet she can see us right now.'

'How the hell do I know what she'll think?' burst out Tozier. 'Or what any other woman will think?'

'There's a way around that,' said Follet. 'Here, take the wheel.' He stepped on one side and produced a pen and a notebook. 'Now, if we go along the coast and she searches out to sea our survival is one hundred per cent – right?'

'Until she catches on,' said Warren.

'We could get clear away,' argued Follet. 'And the same applies to the situation vice versa – we go to sea and she goes along the coast. Andy, what chance of survival would you give us if she caught us at sea?'

'Not much,' said Tozier. 'Say, twenty-five per cent.'

Follet noted it down. 'And if she caught us on the coast?'

'That's a bit better – she couldn't be as noisy. I think we'd have a good chance of coming out – say, seventy-five per cent.'

Follet started to scribble rapidly and Warren, looking over his shoulder saw that he was apparently working out a mathematical formula. Follet finished his calculation, and said, 'What we do is this. We put four pieces of paper in a hat – one marked. If we pick the marked paper we go to sea; if not, we stick to the coast.'

'Are you crazy?' demanded Tozier. 'Would you leave something like this to chance?'

'I'm crazy like a fox,' said Follet. 'How much have I won from you at the coin-matching game?'

'Nearly a thousand quid – but what's that got to do with it?'

Follet pulled a handful of loose change from his pocket and thrust it under Tozier's nose. 'This. There are eight coins here – three of them dated 1960. When I matched coins with you I pulled one of these at random from my pocket; if it was dated 1960 I called heads – if not, I called tails. That was enough to give me my percentage – my edge; and there wasn't a damned thing you could do about it.'

He turned to Warren. 'It's from game theory – a mathematical way of figuring out the best chances in those tricky situations when it's a case of if I do that you'll know I'll do it but I do the other thing because I know the way you're thinking and so it goes on chasing its goddam tail. It even gives the overall chances – in this case a little over eighty-one per cent.'

Tozier looked at Warren with a baffled expression. 'What do you think, Nick?'

'You *did* lose money consistently,' said Warren. 'Maybe Johnny has a point.'

'You're goddam right I have.' Follet stooped and picked up a uniform cap from the deck into which he dropped four coins. 'Pick one, Nick. If it's dated 1960 we go to sea – if it's one of the others we stick to the coast.'

He held the cap out to Warren, who hesitated. 'Look at it this way,' said Follet earnestly. 'Right now, until you pick a coin, we don't know which way we're going – and if *we* don't know how in hell can Delorme figure it? And the mix of coins in the hat gives us the best chance no matter what she does.' He paused. 'There's just one thing; we do what the coin tells us – no second chances – that's the way this thing works.'

Warren put out his hand, took a coin, and held it on the palm of his hand, date side up. Tozier inspected it. '1960,' he said with a sigh. 'It's out to sea, God help us.'

He spun the wheel and the bows of the *Orestes* swung towards the west.

IV

Tozier left Warren and Follet on the bridge and went down to the engine-room to consult Parker. He found him with an oilcan strolling amid shining and plunging steel piston rods at a seeming risk to life. Hellier was standing by the engine-room telegraph.

He beckoned to Parker, who put down the oilcan and came over to him. 'Can you leave here for a while?' he asked.

'We're a bit short-handed,' said Parker. 'But it wouldn't do any harm for a short time. What do you want?'

'Your friend Eastman has barricaded himself in the torpedo compartment in the bows. We're trying to get him out.'

Parker frowned. 'That'll be a bit dicey. I had a watertight bulkhead put in there in case anythin' went wrong wi' the tubes. If he's behind that it'll be bloody impossible to get him out.'

'Haven't you any suggestions? He's locked himself in and we can't do a damn' thing about the heroin.'

'Let's go an' see,' said Parker briefly.

They found Metcalfe crouched at the end of a narrow steel corridor, at the other end of which was a solid steel door clamped tightly closed. 'He's behind that,' said

Metcalfe. 'You can open it from this side if you care to try but you'll get a bullet in you. He can't miss.'

Tozier looked up the corridor. 'No, thanks; there's no cover.'

'The door's bullet proof too,' said Metcalfe. 'I tried a couple of shots and found it was more dangerous for me than for him the way things ricochet around here.'

'Have you tried to talk him out?'

Metcalfe nodded. 'He either can't hear me or he doesn't care to answer.'

'What about it, Parker?'

'There's only one way into that compartment,' said Parker. 'And it's through that door.'

'So it's a stand-off,' said Tozier.

Metcalfe gave a wry grimace. 'It's more than that. If he can keep us out of there until the ship is retaken then he's won.'

'You seem a bit worried about that. Delorme has to find us first and taking us won't be easy. What have you got on your mind?'

Metcalfe swung round. 'When I took that stuff to Fahrwaz there were a few things left behind – a couple of heavy machine-guns, for instance.'

'That's bad,' said Tozier softly.

'And that's not the worst of it. She tried to flog four 40-millimetre cannons to Fahrwaz, but he wasn't having them at any price. They swallowed ammo too quickly for his liking, so she got stuck with them. If she's had the gumption to stick one of those aboard that yacht, she'd have plenty of time to jack-leg a deck mounting. All she'd need is steel and a welding torch, and mere's plenty of both back in that shipyard.'

'You think she might?'

'That little bitch never misses a trick,' said Metcalfe violently. 'You should have let me get her back in Beirut.'

'And we'd have lost the heroin. We've got to get rid of that dope. We can't let her have it.'

Metcalfe jerked his thumb up the corridor. 'Be my guest –
open that door.'

'I've got an idea,' said Parker. 'Maybe we can flush him
out.'

'You mean flood the compartment,' said Tozier. 'Can it be
done?'

'Not water,' said Parker. He raised his head and looked
upwards. 'On the foredeck just above us there's the anchor
winch. It's run by steam taken from the boiler. I reckon I
could take a tapping off the line an' run it down here.'

'And what would you do with it?'

'There's provision for fumigatin' the ship – gettin' rid
o' rats. There's a gas line goin' into each compartment
an' I'm pretty sure the one leadin' into there is open. I
find the other end an' connect my line to it. A bit o' live
steam will bring Jack Eastman out o' there like a scalded
cat.'

'You've got nice ideas,' said Metcalfe. 'Humane, too. How
long will it take?'

'Dunno; an hour – maybe two. It depends on what I find
topside.'

'Get cracking,' said Metcalfe.

V

Jamil Hassan was a methodical man and it was unfortunate
that the bureaucratic organization he worked for was
unyielding in its procedures and tended to be compartmen-
talized. The news did not reach his office at all and it was
only because he decided to have a mid-morning cup of
coffee that he heard anything about it.

On his way out he passed the duty officer's desk and
automatically asked, 'Anything happening?'

'Nothing much, sir; just the usual. There was one odd

thing – a report of a shooting on board a ship leaving El-gamhûrîa Shipyard.'

A young policeman who was writing a report close by pricked up his ears. Hassan said, 'What was odd about it?'

'By the time it was reported and we got a man down there the ship was outside territorial waters.' The duty officer shrugged. 'There was nothing we could do about it.'

The young policeman sprang to his feet. 'Sir!'

Hassan eyed him. 'Yes?'

'Last night a man called Andre Picot was brought in for questioning – on your instructions, sir.'

'Well?'

The young man fidgeted a little. 'It's . . . it's just that I saw Picot leaving El-gamhûrîa Shipyard three days ago. It may not be . . .'

Hassan waved him quiet, his brain assessing facts like a card-sorter. Heroin – a large quantity of heroin – had left Iran heading westward; Picot, a suspected smuggler, had been questioned – unsuccessfully; Picot had been seen at El-gamhûrîa Shipyard; a shot – or shots – had been fired on a ship in El-gamhûrîa Shipyard; the ship had promptly left Lebanese waters. It was not much, but it was enough.

He picked up the telephone, dialled a number, and said, 'Bring in André Picot for questioning, and get me a car.'

Thirty minutes later he was standing on the quay in the shipyard interrogating the officer who had made the investigation. 'And the ship left after the shot was fired?'

'Yes, sir.'

'What was its name?'

'The *Orestes*.'

Hassan surveyed the deserted quay. 'And it was the only ship here. That's strange.'

'No, sir; there was a yacht. She left only five minutes ago.' He pointed. 'There she is.'

Hassan shaded his eyes against the sun and looked out to sea. 'And you let her go? Was the owner here when the incident happened?'

'Yes, sir. He said he did not hear or see anything. Nor did his crew.'

Hassan peered at the yacht. 'Very convenient for him. Who is he?'

'His name is Fuad, sir. He said he is to cruise in the Caribbean.'

'By the Living God!' said Hassan. 'Did he? What is that at the stern?'

The officer strained his eyes. 'A pile of canvas?' he hazarded.

'A sheet of canvas covering something,' corrected Hassan. 'I want a telephone.'

Two minutes later he was embroiled in an argument with a particularly stupid staff officer of Naval Headquarters, Beirut.

VI

The *Orestes* plugged away on her new course and the loom of land astern had disappeared leaving only a cloudbank to indicate Mount Lebanon. Warren made himself useful by finding the galley and preparing a meal; corned beef from tins and flat loaves of Arab bread to be washed down with thin, acid wine.

As he worked he pondered on the relationship between Metcalfe and Tozier. They were both of the same stripe, both men of strong will, and they seemed to work in harmony, each instinctively knowing that the other would do the right thing when necessary. He wondered, if it ever came to a conflict between them, who would come out on top.

He finally decided he would lay his money on Metcalfe. Tozier was the more conservative and preferred his employment to have at least a veneer of legality. Metcalfe was more the amoral buccaneer, unscrupulous to a degree and adept in the department of dirty tricks. Warren thought that if it ever came to a showdown between them that Tozier might show a fatal flaw of hesitation where Metcalfe would not. He hoped his theory would never be put to the test.

He finished his preparations and took the food to the bridge. Metcalfe, because of his knowledge of ships and the sea, was now in command, while Tozier kept an eye on Eastman. Follet was in the engine-room, having released a couple of the engine-room staff who were tending the engines nervously under the threat of his gun. Parker and Abbot worked on the foredeck by the anchor winch, and Hellier stood guard over the hold.

Metcalfe called up Abbot to collect something to eat, and also brought Hellier up to the bridge. 'All quiet?' he asked.

'No trouble,' assured Hellier. 'They've settled down.'

Metcalfe offered him a sandwich. As Hellier bit into it, he said with a wide grin, 'You've now added piracy to your list of crimes, Sir Robert. That's still a hanging matter in England.'

Hellier choked over the dry bread and spluttered crumbs. Warren said, 'I don't think Delorme will press charges, not with the evidence we have aboard.' He cocked an eye at Metcalfe. 'I wonder what she's thinking now.'

'Evil thoughts – that's for sure,' said Metcalfe. 'But I'm more concerned about what she'll be doing. She certainly won't be sitting on her beautiful bottom. When Jeanette gets mad she becomes active.' He nodded towards the foredeck. 'How is Parker doing?'

'He says he'll need another hour,' said Abbot.

Warren said, 'I'll take him some grub and see if he needs any help.'

Metcalfe steadied the wheel with one hand and held a sandwich with the other. 'What a hooker this is. She might do nine knots if she could go down hill.' He looked up. 'What's that gadget up there on the derrick?'

Abbot said, 'It's one of Dan's tricks.' He explained about the light ashore and the man in the crow's nest.

'Ingenious,' commented Metcalfe. 'Climb up there and see what you can see.'

Abbot went up the derrick and steadied himself at the top by holding on to the sighting telescope which was rigidly fixed. At that height, fifty feet above the water, he felt the breeze which stirred his fair hair, and the slow roll of the *Orestes* was magnified. 'There are two more buttons up here,' he shouted. 'Eastman wanted two sets.'

'Leave them alone. What do you see?'

Abbot looked over the bows. 'There's a ship ahead of us. I can see the smoke.' He turned slowly, scanning the horizon. 'There's one behind us, too.'

Metcalfe clicked into alertness. 'Overtaking us?'

'It's hard to say,' shouted Abbot. He was silent for a while. 'I think she is – I can see a bow wave.'

Metcalfe left the wheel, saying to Hellier, 'Take it.' Without breaking his stride he scooped up a pair of binoculars and went up the derrick like a monkey up a palm tree. At the top he steadied himself against the roll of the ship and focused the binoculars astern. 'It's Fuad's yacht. She's coming like a bat out of hell.'

'How far?'

Metcalfe did a mental calculation. 'Maybe six miles. And she has radar – she'll have spotted us.' He handed the binoculars to Abbot. 'Stay here and keep an eye on her.'

He went down the derrick and back to the bridge where he picked up the bridge telephone and rang the engine-room. 'Johnny, prod your chaps a bit – we want more speed . . . I know that, but Jeanette is on our tail.'

As he slammed down the telephone Hellier gave him a sideways glance. 'How long have we got?'

'This rust bucket might do a little over eight knots if she's pushed. That yacht might do thirteen or fourteen. Say an hour.' Metcalfe walked on to the wing of the bridge and looked astern. 'Can't see her from here; she's still below the horizon.' He turned and there was a grim smile on his face. 'I was in a lark like this once before – over in the Western Mediterranean. Me and a guy called Krupke in a Fairmile. But we were doing the chasing that time.'

'Who won?' asked Hellier.

Metcalfe's smile grew grimmer. 'I did!'

'What can she do if she catches up? She can't board us.'

'She can shoot hell out of us.' Metcalfe looked at his watch. 'This tub isn't going to be too healthy an hour from now.'

Hellier said, 'We have plenty of steel plate to hide behind.'

There was something of contempt in Metcalfe's voice as he said in disgust, 'Steel plate!' He kicked against the side of the bridge and rust fell in large flakes. 'Nickel-jacketed bullets will rip through this stuff like cardboard. You were in the artillery, so you ought to know. Tell me what a 40-millimetre cannon will do to this bridge?'

He left Hellier with that disconcerting thought and went up to the foredeck where Parker and Warren were working on the winch. 'Put a jerk in it – we're being followed. How long, for God's sake?'

Parker did not pause in his steady movements as he screwed in a pipe. 'I said an hour.'

'An hour is all you've got,' said Metcalfe. 'After that keep your head down.'

Warren looked up. 'Dan's been telling me about what you think Delorme will do. Will she really shoot us up?'

That was enough to make Parker stop. 'The first time I laid eyes on that cow I knew she was bad,' he said. 'I dunno how Mike could stand her. She'll kill the lot of us an' then

go back an' dance all night without a second thought.' He
hauled on the pipe wrench again, and said, 'That does it up
here. The rest we do below decks.'

'If there's anything I can do to speed up the job just
shout,' said Metcalfe. 'I'm going below to tell Andy the
score.' He checked with Tozier and with Follet in the
engine-room, and when he arrived back in the open air
he saw that the *Stella del Mare* was visible from the deck, low
on the horizon. He went right to the stern and explored,
then went up on to the bridge and said to Hellier, 'This is
going to be the prime target – anybody standing where you
are is going to get the chop.'

'Someone has to steer,' said Hellier quietly.

'Yes, but not from here. There's an emergency steering
position aft.' Metcalfe looked up at the derrick. 'Mike, come
down from there and take the wheel.'

He and Hellier went aft where they dragged the emergency steering-wheel from the locker and fixed it in place
directly above the rudder. Metcalfe surveyed it. 'A bit
exposed,' he commented. 'It needs some canvas round it. It
won't stop bullets but they might not shoot at the stern if
they don't see anyone here.'

They draped a canvas awning around the wheel. 'Stay
here a while,' said Metcalfe. 'I'll take Abbot off the wheel on
the bridge – I need him. You can con the ship from now on
until I relieve you.'

He dashed forward again, thinking as he went that he
was covering a fair mileage on his own flat feet. He took
Abbot off the wheel and regarded the course of the *Orestes*.
After a preliminary swerve she continued on her way, and
the bridge wheel turned slowly and even back and forth as
though controlled by an invisible man.

'Nip into the officers' quarters,' he said to Abbot. 'Bring
some pillows, blankets, jackets, hats – I want to rig up some
dummies.'

They draped coats over pillows and fastened the uniform caps on top with meat skewers from the galley. They made three dummies and suspended them from the top of the wheelhouse by ropes so that they looked unpleasantly like hanging men. But from a distance they would look real enough, and they swayed lightly to and fro most realistically giving an impression of natural movement.

Metcalfe went out on the wing of the bridge and looked aft. 'She's catching up fast. About a mile to go – say ten minutes. You'd better get the hell out of here, Mike. I'm going to see what Parker's doing.'

'There's a ship over there,' said Abbot, pointing to starboard. She was going the other way and was about two miles on the starboard beam. 'Do you think there's any chance of getting help?'

'Not unless you want to make this a real massacre,' said Metcalfe in a strained voice. 'If we went over to that ship we'd just be adding to the list of the dead.'

'You mean she'd kill the crew of that ship, too?'

'A hundred million dollars has a lot of killing power. The ports around here are stuffed with men who'll kill anyone you specify for five thousand dollars, and I'll bet she has that yacht full of them.' He shrugged irritably. 'Let's move.'

Parker and Warren were tired and grimy. 'Five minutes,' said Parker in answer to Metcalfe's urgent question. 'This is the last bit o' pipe.'

'Where do you turn on the steam?'

'There's a valve on deck near the winch,' said Parker. 'You can't miss it.'

'I'll be up there,' said Metcalfe. 'Give me a shout when you want it turned on. And someone had better go and tell Andy what's going on. He might need some backing up, too, but I doubt it.'

He climbed back on deck to find the *Stella del Mare* coming up on the port beam. She slackened speed to keep pace with the *Orestes* and took station about two hundred yards away. He crouched behind the winch and looked across at her. Abbot said, from behind him, 'Look at the stern. What's that?'

'Keep out of sight,' said Metcalfe sharply. He looked at the unmistakable angles barely disguised beneath the canvas covering, and felt a little sick. 'It's a cannon. That thing can squirt shells like a hosepipe squirts water.' He paused. 'I think there's a machine-gun mounted forrard up in the bows, and another amidships on top of the boatdeck. A floating packet of trouble.'

'What are they waiting for?' demanded Abbot almost petulantly.

'For that other ship to get clear. Jeanette doesn't want any witnesses. She'll wait until it's hull down before she tries anything.' He judged the distance to the valve which was in the open. 'I hope she does, anyway.'

He drummed his fingers against the metal of the winch and waited to be given the word and at last he heard Warren call, 'All right, Tom; Dan says give it a three-minute squirt – that should be enough.'

Metcalfe came from behind the winch, stood over the valve, and gave it a twist. He was very conscious that he was in full view of the *Stella del Mare* and felt an uncomfortable prickling between his shoulder-blades. Steam hissed with violence out of a badly connected joint.

Far below him Tozier waited, the sub-machine-gun ready in his hands. Behind him Parker leaned stolidly against the wall waiting for something to happen. That something would happen he was certain. No man would stay for long in a steel box into which live steam at boiler pressure was being fed. He merely nodded as Tozier whispered, 'The clamp is moving.'

Tozier might have given Eastman a chance out of pity, but Eastman slammed back the door amid a cloud of steam and came out shooting. Tozier squeezed the trigger and the sub-machine-gun roared noisily in the confined space but could not drown the ear-splitting high-pitched whistle of escaping steam. Eastman was cut down before he had gone two steps and was thrown back to lie across the open threshold of the torpedo room.

The shriek of steam stopped. Parker said, 'He stood it for two minutes, longer than I expected. Let's see if he did any damage.'

Tozier lowered the gun. 'Yes, let's get rid of the damned stuff.'

Parker halted abruptly. 'That be damned for a tale,' he said violently. 'Those are weapons we've got in there. We can use 'em.'

Tozier's jaw dropped. 'By God, you're right. I must be crazy not to have thought of it myself. Check the torpedoes, Dan; I must get this organized.' He ran off down the corridor and climbed the vertical ladders to the forecastle. He was just about to step on deck when someone held his arm.

'Take it easy,' said Metcalfe. 'Or you'll run into a bullet. Look out there.'

Tozier cautiously looked past the door frame and saw the *Stella del Mare* very close. He ducked back, and said, 'Hell's teeth! She's right alongside.'

'There's a ship not far away, but it's getting further away every minute. Jeanette's waiting for a clear horizon.'

'Parker's had a thought,' said Tozier. 'He wants to torpedo her.' He grinned at Metcalfe's expression. 'Of course, he was a sailor – the idea came naturally to him.'

'It should have come to me, too,' said Metcalfe. There was a wicked glint in his eye. 'I'd better relieve Hellier – this is going to take better ship handling than he's capable of. Does Parker want help?'

'He will. You'd better tell Hellier to go and help him. I'll give Johnny the word.'

Tozier went below to the engine-room and found Follet sitting by the telegraph, a gun in his hand and his eye on an engineer officer who was inspecting a dial. He had to raise his voice to be heard as he brought Follet up-to-date.

'Son of a bitch!' said Follet admiringly. 'You mean we're going to torpedo her?'

'We're going to try.'

Follet looked at the sweating plates close by. Beyond that thin steel shell lay the sea. 'If anything happens – any trouble – let me know,' he said. 'I'm a good swimmer, but I'd like a chance to prove it.'

A grim smile came to Tozier's lips. 'What odds are you offering now, Johnny?'

'All bets are off,' said Follet. 'But we did the right thing, I *know* that. It's just that even if you have the edge you can't win them all.'

Tozier punched him lightly on the arm. 'Keep this junk pile working. Tom will be wanting to manoeuvre.'

He went forward to the torpedo compartment, and before he entered he dragged the body of Eastman aside. 'Everything seems all right,' said Parker. 'Eastman didn't mess around in here.' He slapped the side of a torpedo. 'I'll need help wi' these. Two are already in the tubes, but I can't slide these in on me own.'

'Hellier's coming down,' said Tozier. 'He's the beefiest.' He turned. 'Here he is now. Dan, let me get this straight. We just punch the buttons – is that it?'

Parker nodded. 'There's one set on the bridge an' another in the crow's nest; you can use either. But you'd do better in the crow's nest – there's a sightin' telescope up there.'

'I'll get back up top,' said Tozier. 'The fun will be starting.'

He nodded to Hellier and went away. Hellier said, 'What do I do?'

'Nothin' yet,' said Parker stolidly. 'We just wait.' He looked up. 'If you're a religious man you could try a prayer.'

Tozier found Abbot and Warren at the stern. Abbot was lying flat on the deck and peering cautiously around the corner of the deckhouse at the *Stella del Mare*. He drew back as Tozier touched him on the shoulder. 'They're doing something with that thing at the stern.'

Tozier took his place. Three or four men were busy on the after deck of the yacht, stripping away the canvas to reveal the elongated barrel of the cannon. One of them sat on a seat and turned a handle and the barrel rose and fell; another seated himself and traversed the gun, then applied his eye to the sight. Tozier would have given his soul for a good rifle; he could have knocked off all of them before they could get away.

Further forward others were preparing the machine-guns for action and he distinctly saw a drum of ammunition being put in place. He withdrew and looked astern. The ship they had passed was a mere blob on the horizon surmounted by a smear of smoke. He stood up and called penetratingly, 'Tom – action stations!'

The reply from behind the canvas awning was muffled. 'Aye, aye, sir!'

Tozier drew Warren and Abbot away. 'The port side won't be too healthy from now on. It'll be best to lie flat on the deck on the starboard side somewhere behind the bridge. We're going to try to torpedo her and Tom's in command; he has to be because he must point the ship at whatever he's shooting at.'

'But the firing buttons are on the bridge,' said Warren.

'Yes,' said Tozier. 'That's where the fun comes in. Mike, you stay back here and keep in touch with Tom – you pass the word forward when he's ready to attack. Nick, you'll be with me. When the word comes you make for the bridge and try to get at the buttons.'

Warren nodded and wondered momentarily what part Tozier had picked for himself. He soon found out because Tozier nodded to the derrick. 'There's another set of buttons at the top of that. That's my job in case you can't make it to the bridge.'

Warren looked up at the horribly exposed crow's nest and moistened his lips. 'Suppose you can't make it up there?'

'I'll be past caring by then,' said Tozier easily. 'Someone else will have to have a go. Let's get set.'

He and Warren crouched in cover on the starboard side and waited. When it happened it came suddenly and shockingly.

From where he sheltered Warren could see the rear of the bridge and, to the accompaniment of a din of rapid explosions, it began to disintegrate. Bright points of light danced all over it as the cannon shells exploded with ferocious violence, and the wheelhouse was, in a moment, reduced to a shattered wreck.

There was a thump above his head and he looked up to see, incredibly, a piece of glass driven into the teak coaming. Flung from the wheelhouse it had spun murderously towards him and struck with its razor sharp edge to sink an inch deep into the hard wood. Had his head been lifted another few inches he would have been decapitated.

He dropped back into safety just in time as the cannon fire swept aft. Shells exploded on the deck and splinters of planking drove all about him, one cutting through the hem of his jacket and tearing a jagged hole. Above the deeper roar of the cannon came the light chatter of the machine-guns and bullets ripped through the deck-house as though the walls were of paper, and he grovelled on the deck as though to dig himself into it.

The firing was heard four miles to the west by the young skipper of the Lebanese patrol boat which carried Jamil Hassan. He turned to Hassan and said, 'Gunfire!'

Hassan made an abrupt gesture. 'Faster – go faster.'

Warren cautiously raised his head as the monstrous noise stopped and everything was as quiet as before, with just the steady beat of the engines and the lapping of the bow wave.

He looked up at the bridge and was horrified at the mass of wreckage. He had a sudden vision of the puppets which Metcalfe had constructed, dancing like marionettes on their strings as the bullets and shells drove through and among them until the roof caved in.

The *Orestes* slowly began to swing to port as though a restraining hand had been removed from the helm. Metcalfe called, 'I'm swinging over to get her athwart my bows as though by chance. We might just get away with it. Tell Andy to get ready.'

Abbot ran forward at a crouch and passed on the message. Tozier looked up at the pulverized bridge and shook his head. 'Up you go, Nick; but take it easy. Wait until she's on target before pressing the tit. If you can't fire at all give me a shout.'

Warren found he was trembling. This was not the sort of work he was cut out for and he knew it. He ran for the bridge ladder and climbed it quickly, ducking his head as he came on to the bridge and sprawling flat. He raised his head and looked at the wheelhouse. The front of it had been blasted off and there was very little left behind it. There was no wheel, no binnacle, no engine telegraph – and no small box with two buttons mounted on it. The bridge had been swept clear.

He shouted, 'No good here, Andy,' and twisted around to go back, afraid of being caught by the next blast of gunfire. He did not bother to climb down the ladder but launched himself into space and fell heavily to the deck in the precious shelter of what remained of the bridge.

He saw Tozier run past him, along the deck and out into the open space of the waist of the ship, zig-zagging so as never to take more than three steps in the same direction. He disappeared behind the donkey-engine casing at the foot of the derrick and Warren looked upwards. It seemed impossible that any man should climb that after what had happened.

Metcalfe had one eye on the derrick and the other on the *Stella del Mare*. He saw Tozier scrambling up and then turned the wheel so as to straighten the *Orestes* on her course. Tozier reached the crow's nest and bent to put his eye to the sight, but the yacht was sheering off, although Metcalfe did his best to keep the bows in line with her.

The sudden change of course of both ships confused the gunners on the yacht. The forward machine-gun could not be brought to bear at all, while the one amidships fired but the aim was wild. However, the cannon was perfectly positioned and it traversed smoothly and opened fire. A hail of shells drove past Tozier and it seemed impossible that he should not be hit. Astern of the *Orestes* the sea erupted in fountains for a mile as the shells overshot the ship and exploded harmlessly.

Tozier stabbed at the buttons and two torpedoes, worth the combined sum of $50,000,000 were on their way.

Then he scrambled down the derrick as fast as he could. He got within ten feet of the bottom and fell the rest of the way. The cannon stopped firing and Warren heard someone cheering from the stern and wondered what Metcalfe had to be so glad about. One thing was certain – the torpedoes had missed. There was no explosion from the sea and a machine-gun still continued its staccato conversation.

Metcalfe had tried to emulate a tortoise as the cannon shells whipped overhead, hunching his neck into his shoulders as though that would save his head from getting knocked off. If the cannon had been depressed a fraction lower the stern of the *Orestes* would have been swept clear and Tom Metcalfe with it. When the cannon fire stopped he looked through a hole in the awning and began to cheer loudly.

Things had gone wrong on the *Stella del Mare*; there was confusion on her poop deck and the long barrel of the cannon was canted upwards at an unnatural angle. The

improvised mounting had not been able to withstand the
incessant hammering as the cannon had pumped out shells
and it was now out of action. From the yacht came a thin
and distant wail, sounding as though someone had been
hurt.

So Metcalfe cheered.

Below, in the bows, Parker and Hellier heard the hiss of
compressed air as the torpedoes left the tubes. Hellier was
disposed to wait to hear if they struck, but Parker was
already closing the outer doors of the tubes in preparation
for reloading. He swung open the inner doors and stepped
aside as the water gushed out, and then pulled smartly on
the handles of the clamps which held the racked torpedo
on the port side. 'Come on,' he yelled. 'Get the bastard
in!'

He and Hellier heaved on the torpedo which moved
slowly on its rollers towards the open tube. It was very
heavy and moved a fraction of an inch at a time, but it
picked up speed as they pushed harder, and finally went in
sweetly. Parker slammed the door home and spun the
locking wheel. 'Now the other one,' he gasped.

'Do you think the first lot hit?' asked Hellier.

'Dunno,' said Parker, his hands busy. 'Shouldn't think so.
Must have been point-blank range judgin' by the racket
goin' on up there. Let's get this one in, for God's sake!'

Warren looked to see if he could see Tozier but there was
no sign of him. He stuck his head around the side of the
bridge and looked across at the *Stella del Mare*. She had
turned as the *Orestes* had turned and was still on the port
side keeping a parallel course. The midships machine-gun
was still firing in short bursts and now the one in the bows
could be brought to bear again and it also opened up, but
both seemed to be concentrating on the forward deck.

He saw why. Tozier was sheltering in the break of the
forecastle, just sitting there with one leg trailing behind

him and oddly bent in a place where there should have been no joint. Even at that distance Warren could tell that the leg was broken. He saw Dan Parker dash from the doorway of the forecastle in an attempt to get to Tozier. He had not gone two steps when he stopped a bullet which flung him round and sent him crashing to the deck where he lay feebly moving.

It was too much for Warren. He broke from cover and ran up the deck, careless of whether he was in danger or not. Simultaneously there was a stentorian bellow from the stern. 'She's coming around to strafe us on the starboard side. She'll be crossing our bows – get ready to shoot.'

Warren heard the words but they made no sense to him; he was intent on getting to Parker and Tozier. But he was thankfully aware that the machine-gunning had stopped as the *Stella del Mare* began to swing ahead of the *Orestes* and firing became unprofitable. Thus he was able to reach Parker without a scratch.

He bent down and took Parker under the arms and dragged him into the forecastle. He was ruthless about it because he had no time to waste, but mercifully Parker was unconscious. Then he went back for Tozier who looked up and gave a weak grin. 'Busted leg,' he said.

'You can stand on the other,' said Warren, and helped him up.

'For Christ's sake!' yelled Metcalfe. 'Someone get up that bloody derrick.'

Warren looked back and hesitated as he felt Tozier's weight lean on him. He saw Abbot make a run for it, disappearing behind the donkey engine as Tozier had done to reappear half way up the derrick, climbing as though the devil were at his heels.

Metcalfe, on the poop, had a grandstand view. The *Stella del Mare* crossed his bows three hundred yards ahead. At the sight of Abbot on the derrick the machine-guns opened up again, hosing the *Orestes* unmercifully. Abbot did not bother to use the sight. He slammed his hand on the buttons just as a burst of machine-gun fire stitched bloody holes across his chest. He spread his arms as he was flung backwards to crash thirty feet to the deck below.

But then the yacht shivered and checked her stride as the torpedoes hit her, and she erupted as over three hundred and fifty pounds of TNT exploded in her guts. She was no warship built to take punishment, and the explosions tore her apart. Her mid-section was ripped and destroyed utterly, thus cutting her in half; her bows floated for a few seconds only, leaving the stern filling with water fast.

Several small figures jumped from the stern just before it went under in a boil of swirling water, and Metcalfe's teeth bared in a humourless smile. The *Orestes* ploughed on towards the bits of wreckage floating on the surface, and he saw a white face under long blonde hair and an arm waving desperately.

Slowly, and with intense care, he turned the wheel so that the stern of the *Orestes* slid sideways towards Jeanette Delorme and she was drawn into the maelstrom of the churning screw. With equal precision he straightened the *Orestes* on her course and did not look back at what might appear in the wake.

VII

Metcalfe leaned on the rail and looked into the gaping muzzle of the second quick-firing gun he had seen that day. It was trained on the *Orestes* from the Lebanese patrol boat which ticked over quietly a hundred yards to port in exactly the same position the *Stella del Mare* had held. Everything was the same except that the engines of the *Orestes* were stopped, the companion was lowered and a small motor boat containing two ratings and a junior officer of the Lebanese Navy lay close at hand.

'Give me a hand, Tom,' called Warren.

Metcalfe turned and went over to where Warren was bandaging Parker's shoulder. He bent down and held the dressing so that Warren could tie it off. 'How are you feeling?' he asked.

'Not bad,' said Parker. 'It could have been worse – mustn't grumble.'

Metcalfe squatted and said to Warren, 'That civilian who came aboard didn't look like a Navy man to me.'

'I didn't even know the Lebanon had a navy,' said Warren.

'It doesn't; just a few coastal defence vessels.' Metcalfe nodded to the patrol boat. 'I've given those boys the slip many a time.' He frowned. 'What do you suppose Hellier's nattering about all this time? Those two must have been talking for an hour.'

'I wouldn't know,' said Warren shortly. He was thinking about Mike Abbot and Ben Bryan – two dead of the original team of five. Forty per cent casualties was a high price to pay, and that did not count the wounded – another forty per cent.

Tozier lay close by, his leg in splints, while Follet talked to him. 'Goddam it!' said Follet. 'I'll explain it again.' He jingled the coins in his hands.

'Oh, I believe you,' said Tozier. 'I have to, don't I? After all, you took the money from me. It's a neat trick.' He looked across the deck at the canvas-shrouded body which lay at the head of the companion way. 'It's a pity the idea didn't work later.'

'I know what you mean, but it was the best thing to do,' said Follet stubbornly. 'As I said – you can't win 'em all.' He looked up. 'Here comes Hellier now.'

Hellier walked across the deck towards them. Metcalfe stood up and asked, 'Is that a Navy man?' He nodded to Hassan who waited by the rail.

'No,' said Hellier. 'He's a policeman.'

'What did you tell him?'

'Everything.' said Hellier. 'The whole story.'

Metcalfe blew out his cheeks. 'That puts us right in the middle,' he said. 'We'll be lucky if we're not in the nick for another twenty years. Have you ever been in a Middle East jail, Sir Robert?'

Hellier smiled. 'I was a bit vague about your gun-running activities. He wasn't interested in that, anyway. He wants to talk to us.'

He turned to Hassan, who walked over to them, his hands in his pockets. He surveyed them with tight lips and said abruptly, 'My name is Jamil Hassan; I am a police officer. You gentlemen appear to have been conducting a private war, part of which was on Lebanese territory. As a police officer I find that most irregular.'

Some of the sternness softened from his face. 'However, as a police officer I find myself helpless since the high seas outside Lebanese territorial waters do not come within my jurisdiction – so what am I to do?'

Metcalfe grinned. 'You tell us, chum.'

Hassan ignored the interjection. 'Of course, as well as being a police officer I am also a private citizen of the Lebanon. In that capacity let me offer you my thanks for what you have done. But I would advise you, in future, to leave such pursuits in the hands of the proper and competent authorities.' His lips quirked in a smile. 'Which in this case were not very competent. But that still leaves unanswered the question – what am I to do with you?'

'We have wounded men,' said Warren. 'They need attention – a hospital. You could take them back to Beirut in that boat of yours.'

'Not mine,' corrected Hassan. 'You, I take it, are Dr Warren?' At Warren's answering nod, he continued, 'Any of you going back to Beirut in that boat would inevitably end in jail. Our small Navy does not have your English tradition of turning a blind eye. No, you will stay here and I will go back to Beirut. I will send someone to pick you up and you will be landed quietly and discreetly. You understand that I am arranging this purely in my capacity of a private citizen and not that of a police officer.'

Metcalfe let out his breath in a long sigh. Hassan looked at him sardonically, and said, 'Our Arab nations work together very closely and extradition is easily arranged. There have been reports of a gang of international thugs roaming the Middle East, killing indiscriminately, using military weapons and – ' he fixed Metcalfe firmly with a gimlet eye – 'indulging in other activities against the state, particularly in Iraq. Owing to these circumstances you will leave the Lebanon at the earliest opportunity. Air tickets will be delivered to your hotel and you will use them. I hope you understand.'

Tozier said, 'What about the crew of this ship? They're still battened down in the hold.'

'You will release the crew just before you leave this ship.' Hassan smiled thinly. 'They will have some awkward questions to answer if the ship ever puts into port. In the circumstances I don't think we will see the ship again.'

'Thank you,' said Hellier. 'We appreciate your understanding of our position.'

Hassan nodded curtly and turned away. He was half way to the companionway when he paused and turned. 'How much heroin was there?'

'One thousand kilos exactly,' said Parker. 'A metric ton.'

Hassan nodded. 'Thank you, gentlemen.' Unexpectedly, he smiled. 'I thought I knew all about smuggling – but torpedoes!' He shook his head and his face turned grave as he saw the shrouded body of Abbot. 'I suggest you bury the body of this brave man at sea,' he said, and went over the side to his waiting boat.

Tozier said, 'Well, Nick; it's over. It was nip and tuck towards the last, but we made it.'

Warren leaned against the hatch coaming. He suddenly felt very tired. 'Yes, we made it. Some of us made it, anyway.'

But Ben Bryan would never be Lord of the Manor, although Warren intended to see that Hellier came through with his promise of a community centre for the treatment of addicts; and Mike Abbot would never again be found waiting on his doorstep for the latest dirt on the drug scene.

He looked up at Hellier – the man who had wanted blood – and hoped he was satisfied. Had the deaths been worth it? There would be an unknown number of people, most of them in the United States, who would live longer and presumably happier lives, quite unaware that their extra years had been purchased by death – and next year, or the year after, another Eastman or another Delorme would arise, and the whole damned, filthy business would start again.

Warren closed his eyes against the sun. But let somebody else stop it, he thought; the pace is too hot for a simple doctor.

JUGGERNAUT

ONE

The telephone call came when I was down by the big circular pool chatting up the two frauleins I had cut out of the herd. I didn't rate my chances too highly. They were of an age which regards any man of over thirty-five as falling apart at the seams; but what the hell, it was improving my German.

I looked up at the brown face of the waiter and said incredulously, 'A phone call for me?'

'Yes, sir. From London.' He seemed impressed.

I sighed and grabbed my beach robe. 'I'll be back,' I promised, and followed the waiter up the steps towards the hotel. At the top I paused. 'I'll take it in my room,' I said, and cut across the front of the hotel towards the cabana I rented.

Inside it was cool, almost cold, and the air conditioning unit uttered a muted roar. I took a can of beer from the refrigerator, opened it, and picked up the telephone. As I suspected, it was Geddes. 'What are you doing in Kenya?' he asked. The line was good; he could have been in the next room.

I drank some beer. 'What do you care where I take my vacations?'

'You're on the right continent. It's a pity you have to come back to London. What's the weather like there?'

'It's hot. What would you expect on the equator?'

'It's raining here,' he said, 'and a bit cold.'

I'd got used to the British by now. As with the Arabs there is always an exchange of small talk before the serious issues arise but the British always talk about the weather. I sometimes find it hard to take. 'You didn't ring me for a weather report. What's this about London?'

'Playtime is over, I'm afraid. We have a job for you. I'd like to see you in my office the day after tomorrow.'

I figured it out. Half an hour to check out, another hour to Mombasa to turn in the rented car. The afternoon flight to Nairobi and then the midnight flight to London. And the rest of that day to recover. 'I might just make it,' I conceded, 'but I'd like to know why.'

'Too complicated now. See you in London.'

'Okay,' I said grouchily. 'How did you know I was here, by the way?'

Geddes laughed lightly. 'We have our methods, Watson, we have our methods.' There was a click and the line went dead.

I replaced the handset in disgust. That was another thing about the British – they were always flinging quotations at you, especially from *Sherlock Holmes* and *Alice in Wonderland*. Or *Winnie the Pooh*, for God's sake!

I went outside the cabana and stood on the balcony while I finished the beer. The Indian Ocean was calm and palm fronds fluttered in a light breeze. The girls were splashing in the pool, having a mock fight, and their shrill laughter cut through the heated air. Two young men were watching them with interest. Goodbyes were unnecessary, I thought, so I finished the beer and went inside to pack.

A word about the company I work for. British Electric is about as British as Shell Oil is Dutch – it's gone multi-national, which is why I was one of the many Americans in its employ. You can't buy a two kilowatt electric heater from British Electric, nor yet a five cubic foot refrigerator, but if you want the giant-sized economy pack which produces current measured in megawatts then we're your boys. We're at the heavy end of the industry.

Nominally I'm an engineer but it must have been ten years since I actually built or designed anything. The higher a man rises in a corporation like ours the less he is concerned with purely technical problems. Of course, the jargon of modern management makes everything *sound* technical and the subcommittee rooms resound with phrases drawn from critical path analysis, operations research and industrial dynamics, but all that flim-flam is discarded at the big boardroom table, where the serious decisions are made by men who know there is a lot more to management than the mechanics of technique.

There are lots of names for people like me. In some companies I'm called an expeditor, in others a troubleshooter. I operate in the foggy area bounded on the north by technical problems, on the east by finance, on the west by politics, and on the south by the sheer quirkiness of humankind. If I had to put a name to my trade I'd call myself a political engineer.

Geddes was right about London; it was cold and wet. There was a strong wind blowing which drove the rain against the windows of his office with a pattering sound. After Africa it was bleak.

He stood up as I entered. 'You have a nice tan,' he said appreciatively.

'It would have been better if I could have finished my vacation. What's the problem?'

'You Yanks are always in such a hurry,' complained Geddes. That was good for a couple of laughs. You don't run an outfit like British Electric by resting on your butt and Geddes, like many other Britishers in a top ranking job, seemed deceptively slow but somehow seemed to come out ahead. The classic definition of a Hungarian as a guy who comes behind you in a revolving door and steps out ahead could very well apply to Geddes.

The second laugh was that I could never break them of the habit of calling me a Yank. I tried calling Geddes a Scouse once, and then tried to show him that Liverpool is closer to London than Wyoming to New England, but it never sank in.

'This way,' he said. 'I've a team laid on in the board-room.'

I knew most of the men there, and when Geddes said, 'You all know Neil Mannix,' there was a murmur of assent. There was one new boy whom I didn't know, and whom Geddes introduced. 'This is John Sutherland – our man on the spot.'

'Which spot?'

'I said you were on the right continent. It's just that you were on the wrong side.' Geddes pulled back a curtain covering a notice board to reveal a map. 'Nyala.'

I said, 'We've got a power station contract there.'

'That's right.' Geddes picked up a pointer and tapped the map. 'Just about there – up in the north. A place called Bir Oassa.'

Someone had stuck a needle into the skin of the earth and the earth bled copiously. Thus encouraged, another hypodermic went into the earth's hide and the oil came up driven by the pressure of natural gas. The gas, although not altogether unexpected, was a bonus. The oil strike led to much rejoicing and merriment among those who held on to the levers of power in a turbulent political society. In modern times big oil means political power on a world scale, and this was a chance for Nyala to make its presence felt in the comity of nations, something it had hitherto conspicuously failed to do. Oil also meant money – lots of it.

'It's good oil,' Geddes was saying. 'Low sulphur content and just the right viscosity to make it bunker grade without refining. The Nyalans have just completed a pipeline from Bir Oassa to Port Luard, here on the coast. That's about eight hundred miles. They reckon they can offer cheap oil to ships on the round-Africa run to Asia. They hope to get a bit of South American business too. But all that's in the future.'

The pointer returned to Bir Oassa. 'There remains the natural gas. There was talk of running a gas line paralleling the oil line, building a liquifying plant at Port Luard, and shipping the gas to Europe. The North Sea business has made that an uneconomical proposition.'

Geddes shifted the pointer further north, holding it at arm's length. 'Up there between the true desert and the rain forests is where Nyala plans to build a power station.'

Everyone present had already heard about this, but still there were murmurs and an uneasy shifting. It would take more than one set of fingers to enumerate the obvious problems. I picked one of them at random.

'What about cooling water? There's a drought in the Sahara.'

McCahill stirred. 'No problem. We put down boreholes and tapped plenty of water at six thousand feet.' He grimaced. 'Coming up from that depth it's pretty warm, but extra cooling towers will take care of that.' McCahill was on the design staff.

'And as a spin-off we can spare enough for local irrigation and consumption, and that will help to put us across to the inhabitants.' This from Public Relations, of course.

'The drought in the Sahara is going to continue for a long time yet,' Geddes said. 'If the Nyalans can use their gas to fuel a power station then there'll be the more electricity for pumping whatever water there is and for irrigating. They can sell their surplus gas to neighbour states too. Niger is interested in that already.'

It made sense of a kind, but before they could start making their fortunes out of oil and gas they had to obtain the stuff. I went over to the map and studied it.

'You'll have trouble with transport. There's the big stuff like the boilers and the transformers. They can't be assembled on site. How many transformers?'

'Five,' McCahill said. 'At five hundred megawatts each. Four for running and one spare.'

'And at three hundred tons each,' I said.

'I think Mister Milner has sorted that out,' said Geddes.

Milner was our head logistics man. He had to make sure that everything was in the right place at the right time, and his department managed to keep our computers tied up rather considerably. He came forward and joined me at the map. 'Easy,' he said. 'There are some good roads.'

I was sceptical. 'Out there – in Nyala?'

He nodded thoughtfully. 'Of course, you haven't been there yourself, have you, Neil? Wait until you read the full specs. But I'll outline it for you and the others. After they got colonial rule their first president was Maro Ofanwe. Remember him?'

Someone made a throat-slitting gesture and there was a brief uneasy laugh. Nobody at the top likes to be reminded of coups of any sort.

'He had the usual delusions of grandeur. One of the first things he did was to build a modern super-highway right along the coast from Port Luard to Hazi. Halfway along it, here at Lasulu, a branch goes north to Bir Oassa and even beyond – to nowhere. We shouldn't have any trouble in that department.'

'I'll believe that road when I see it.'

Milner was annoyed and showed it. 'I surveyed it myself with the boss of the transport company. Look at these photographs.'

He hovered at my elbow as I examined the pictures, glossy black-and-white aerial shots. Sure enough, there it was, looking as though it had been lifted bodily from Los Angeles and dumped in the middle of a scrubby nowhere.

'Who uses it?'

'The coast road gets quite a bit of use. The spur into the interior is under-used and under-maintained. The rain forest is encroaching in the south and in the north there will be trouble with sand drifts. The usual potholes are appearing. Edges are a bit worn in spots.' This was common to most African tarmac and hardly surprised me. He went on, 'There are some bridges which may be a bit dicey, but it's nothing we can't cope with.'

'Is your transport contractor happy with it?'

'Perfectly.'

I doubted that. A happy contractor is like a happy farmer – more or less nonexistent. But it was I who listened to the beefs, not the hirers and firers. I turned my attention back to Geddes, after mending fences with Milner by admiring his photographs.

'I think Mister Shelford might have something to say,' Geddes prompted.

Shelford was a political liaison man. He came from that department which was the nearest thing British Electric had to the State Department or the British Foreign Office. He cocked an eye at Geddes. 'I take it Mr Mannix would like a rundown on the political situation?'

'What else?' asked Geddes a little acidly.

I didn't like Shelford much. He was one of the striped pants crowd that infests Whitehall and Washington. Those guys like to think of themselves as decision makers and world shakers but they're a long way from the top of the tree and they know it. From the sound of his voice, Geddes wasn't too taken with Shelford either.

Shelford was obviously used to this irritable reaction to himself and ignored it. He spread his hands on the table and spoke precisely. 'I regard Nyala as being one of the few countries in Africa which shows any political stability at the present time. That, of course, was not always so. Upon the overthrow of Maro Ofanwe there was considerable civil unrest and the army was forced to take over, a not atypical action in an African state. What was atypical, however, was that the army voluntarily handed back the reins of power to a properly constituted and elected civil government, which so far seems to be keeping the country on an even keel.'

Some of the others were growing restive under his lecturing, and Geddes cut in on what looked like the opening of a long speech. 'That's good so far,' he said. 'At least we won't have to cope with the inflexibility of military minds.'

I grinned. 'Just the deviousness of the political ones.'

Shelford showed signs of carrying on with his lecture and this time I cut in on him. 'Have you been out there lately, Mister Shelford?'

'No, I haven't.'

'Have you been there at all?'

'No,' he said stiffly. I saw a few stifled smiles.

'I see,' I said, and switched my attention to Sutherland. 'I suggest we hear from the man on the spot. How did you find things, John?'

Sutherland glanced at Geddes for a nod of approval before speaking.

'Well, broadly speaking, I should say that Mister Shelford seems correct. The country shows remarkable stability; within limits, naturally. They are having to cope with a cash shortage, a water shortage, border skirmishes – the usual African troubles. But I didn't come across much conflict at the top when we were out there.'

Shelford actually smirked. Geddes said, 'Do you think the guarantees of the Nyalan Government will stand up under stress, should it come?'

Sutherland was being pressed and he courageously didn't waver too much. 'I should think so, provided the discretionary fund isn't skimped.'

By that he meant that the palms held out to be greased should be liberally daubed, a not uncommon situation. I said, 'You were speaking broadly, John. What would you say if you had to speak narrowly?'

Now he looked a little uncomfortable and his glance went from Geddes to Shelford before he replied. 'It's said that there's some tribal unrest.'

This brought another murmur to the room. To the average European, while international and even inter-county and intercity rivalries are understandable factors, the demands of tribal loyalties seem often beyond all reason; in my time I have tried to liken the situation to that of warring football clubs and their more aggressive fans, but non-tribal peoples seemed to me to have the greatest difficulties in appreciating the pressures involved. I even saw eyebrows raised, a gesture of righteous intolerance which none at that table could afford. Shelford tried to bluster.

'Nonsense,' he said. 'Nyala's a unified state if ever I saw one. Tribal conflict has been vanquished.'

I decided to prick his balloon. 'Apparently you haven't seen it, though, Mister Shelford. Conflict of this sort is never finished with. Remember Nigeria – it happened there, and that's almost next door. It exists in Kenya. It exists throughout Africa. And we know that it's hard to disentangle fact from fiction, but we can't afford to ignore either. John, who are the top dogs in Nyala, the majority tribe?'

'The Kinguru.'

'The President and most of the Cabinet will be Kinguru, then? The Civil Service? Leading merchants and businessmen?' He nodded at each category. 'The Army?'

Here he shook his head. 'Surprisingly enough, apparently not. The Kinguru don't seem to make good fighters. The Wabi people run the military, but they have some sort of tribal affiliation with the Kinguru anyway. You'll need a sociologist's report if you want to go into details.'

'If the Kinguru aren't fighters they may damn well have to learn,' I said, 'Like the Ibo in Nigeria and the Kikuyu in Kenya.'

Someone said, 'You're presupposing conflict, Neil.'

Geddes backed me. 'It's not unwise. And we do have some comments in the dossier, Neil – your homework.' He tapped the bulky file on the table and adroitly lightened the atmosphere. 'I think we can leave the political issues for the moment. How do we stand on progress to date, Bob?'

'We're exactly on schedule,' said Milner with satisfaction. He would have been pained to be behind schedule, but almost equally pained to have been ahead of it. That would show that his computers weren't giving an absolutely optimum arrangement, which would be unthinkable. But then he leaned forward and the pleased look vanished. 'We might be running into a small problem, though.'

There were no small problems in jobs like this. They were all big ones, no matter how small they started.

Milner said, 'Construction is well advanced and we're about ready to take up the big loads. The analysis calls for the first big haul to be one of the boilers but the government is insisting that it be a transformer. That means that the boiler fitters are going to be sitting around on their butts doing nothing while a transformer just lies around because the electrical engineers aren't yet ready to install it.' He sounded aggrieved and I could well understand why. This was big money being messed around.

'Why would they want to do that?' I asked.

'It's some sort of public relations exercise they're laying on. A transformer is the biggest thing we're going to carry, and they want to make a thing of it before the populace gets used to seeing the big flat-bed trundling around their country.'

Geddes smiled. 'They're paying for it. I think we can let them have that much.'

'It'll cost us money,' warned Milner.

'The project is costing them a hundred and fifty million pounds,' said Geddes. 'I'm sure this schedule change can be absorbed: and if it's all they want changed I'll be very pleased. I'm sure you can reprogramme to compensate.' His voice was as smooth as cream, and it had the desired effect on Milner, who looked a lot happier. He had made his point, and I was sure that he had some slack tucked away in his programme to take care of such emergencies.

The meeting carried on well into the morning. The finance boys came in with stuff about progress payments in relationship to cash flow, and there was a discussion about tendering for the electrical network which was to spread after the completion of the power plant. At last Geddes called a halt, leaned over towards me and said quietly, 'Lunch with me, Neil.'

It wasn't an invitation; it was an order. 'Be glad to,' I said. There was more to come, obviously.

On the way out I caught up with Milner. 'There's a point that wasn't brought up. Why unship cargo at Port Luard? Why not at Lasulu? That's at the junction of the spur road leading upcountry.'

He shook his head. 'Port Luard is the only deep water anchorage with proper quays. At Lasulu cargo is unshipped in to some pretty antique lighters. Would you like to trans-ship a three hundred ton transformer into a lighter in a heavy swell?'

'Not me,' I said, and that was that.

I expected to lunch with Geddes in the directors' dining room but instead he took me out to a restaurant. We had a drink at the bar while we chatted lightly about affairs in Africa, the state of the money market, the upcoming by-elections. It was only after we were at table and into our meal that he came back to the main topic.

'We want you to go out there, Neil.'

This was very unsurprising, except that so far there did-n't seem to be a reason. I said, 'Right now I should be out at Leopard Rock south of Mombasa, chatting up the girls. I suppose the sun's just as hot on the west coast. Don't know about the birds though.'

Geddes said, not altogether inconsequentially, 'You should be married.'

'I have been.'

We got on with the meal. I had nothing to say and let him make the running. 'So you don't mind solving the problem,' he said eventually.

'What problem? Milner's got things running better than a Swiss watch.'

'I don't know what problem,' Geddes said simply. 'But I know there is one, and I want you to find it.' He held up a hand to stop me interrupting. 'It's not as easy as it sounds, and things are, as you guessed, far from serene in Nyala under the surface. Sir Tom has had a whisper down the line from some of the old hands out there.'

Geddes was referring to our Chairman, Owner and Managing Director, a trinity called Sir Thomas Buckler. Feet firmly on the earth, head in Olympus, and with ears as big as a jack rabbit's for any hint or form of peril to his beloved company. It was always wise to take notice of advice from that quarter, and my interest sharpened at once. So far there had been nothing to tempt me. Now there was the merest breath of warning that all might not be well, and that was the stuff I thrived on. As we ate and chatted on I felt a lot less cheesed off at having lost my Kenya vacation.

'It may be nothing. But you have a nose for trouble, Neil, and I'm depending on you to sniff it out,' Geddes said as we rose from the table. 'By the way, do you know what the old colonial name for Port Luard used to be?'

'Can't say that I do.'

He smiled gently. 'The Frying Pan.'

TWO

I left for Nyala five days later, the intervening time being
spent in getting a run down on the country. I read the rele-
vant sections of *Keesing's Archives* but the company's own
files, prepared by our Confidential Information Unit, proved
more valuable, mainly because our boys weren't as deterred
by thoughts of libel as the compilers of *Keesing*.

It seemed to be a fairly standard African story. Nyala was
a British colony until the British divested themselves of
their Empire, and the first President under the new constitution was Maro Ofanwe. He had one of the usual qualifications for becoming the leader of an ex-British colony; he
had served time in a British jail. Colonial jails were the
forcing beds of national leaders, the Eton and Harrow of
the dark continent.

Ofanwe started off soberly enough but when seated
firmly in the saddle he started showing signs of megalo-
mania and damn near made himself the state religion. And
like all megalomaniacs he had architectural ambitions,
pulling down the old colonial centre of Port Luard to build
Independence Square, a vast acreage of nothing surrounded by new government offices in the style known as
Totalitarian Massive.

Ofanwe was a keen student of the politics of Mussolini,
so the new Palace of Justice had a specially designed balcony

where he was accustomed to display himself to the stormy cheers of his adoring people. The cheers were equally stormy when his people hauled up his body by the heels and strung it from one of the very modern lampposts in Independence Square. Maro Ofanwe emulated Mussolini as much in death as in life.

After his death there were three years of chaos. Ofanwe had left the Treasury drained, there was strife among competing politicians, and the country rapidly became ungoverned and ungovernable. At last the army stepped in and established a military junta led by Colonel Abram Kigonde.

Surprisingly, Kigonde proved to be a political moderate. He crushed the extremists of both wings ruthlessly, laid heavy taxes on the business community which had been getting away with what it liked, and used the money to revitalize the cash crop plantations which had become neglected and run down. He was lucky too, because just as the cocoa plantations were brought back to some efficiency the price of cocoa went up, and for a couple of years the money rolled in until the cocoa price cycle went into another downswing.

Relative prosperity in Nyala led to political stability. The people had food in their bellies and weren't inclined to listen to anyone who wanted a change. This security led outside investors to study the country and now Kigonde was able to secure sizeable loans which went into more agricultural improvements and a degree of industrialization. You couldn't blame Kigonde for devoting a fair part of these loans to re-equipping his army.

Then he surprised everybody again. He revamped the Constitution and announced that elections would be held and a civil government was to take over the running of the country once again. After five years of military rule he stepped down to become Major General Kigonde, Commander in Chief of the Armed Forces. Since then the government had settled down, its hand greatly strengthened by the discovery of oil in the north. There was the usual amount of graft and corruption but no more so, apparently, than in any other African country, and all seemed set fair for the future of Nyala.

But there were rumours.

I read papers, studied maps and figures, and on the surface this was a textbook operation. I crammed in a lot of appointments, trying to have at least a few words with anybody who was directly concerned with the Nyala business. For the most part these were easy, the people I wanted to see being all bunched up close together in the City; but there was one exception, and an important one. I talked to Geddes about it first.

'The heavy haulage company you're using, Wyvern Haulage Ltd. They're new to me. Why them?'

Geddes explained. British Electric had part ownership of one haulage company, a firm with considerable overseas experience and well under the thumb of the Board, but they were fully occupied with other work. There were few other British firms in the same field, and Geddes had tendered the job to a Dutch and an American company, but in the end the contract had gone to someone who appeared to be almost a newcomer in the business. I asked if there was any nepotism involved.

'None that I know of,' Geddes said. 'This crowd has good credentials, a good track record, and their price is damned competitive. There are too few heavy hauliers about who can do what we want them to do, and their prices are getting out of hand – even our own. I'm willing to encourage anyone if it will increase competition.'

'Their price may be right for us, but is it right for them?' I asked. 'I can't see them making much of a profit.'

It was vital that no firm who worked for us should come out badly. British Electric had to be a crowd whom others

were anxious to be alongside. And I was far from happy
with the figures that Wyvern were quoting, attractive
though they might be to Milner and Geddes.

'Who are they?'

'They know their job, all right. It's a splinter group from
Sheffield Hauliers and we think the best of that bunch went
to Wyvern when it was set up. The boss is a youngish chap,
Geoffrey Wingstead, and he took Basil Kemp with him for
starters.'

I knew both the names, Wingstead only as a noise but
Kemp and I had met before on a similar job. The difference
was that the transformer then being moved was from the
British industrial midlands up to Scotland; no easy matter
but a cake-walk compared with doing any similar job in
Africa. I wondered if Wyvern had any overseas experience,
and decided to find out for myself.

To meet Wingstead I drove up to Leeds, and was mildly
startled at what I found when I got there. I was all in favour
of a new company ploughing its finances into the heart of
the business rather than setting up fancy offices and shop
front prestige, but to find Geoff Wingstead running his show
from a prefab shed right in amongst the workshops and
garaging was disturbing. It was a string-and-brown-paper
setup of which Wingstead seemed to be proud.

But I was impressed by him and his paperwork, and
could not fault either. I had wanted to meet Kemp again,
only to be told that he was already in Nyala with his load
boss and crew, waiting for the arrival of the rig by sea.
Wingstead himself intended to fly out when the rig was
ready for its first run, a prospect which clearly excited him:
he hadn't been in Africa before. I tried to steer a course mid-
way between terrifying him with examples of how different
his job would be out there from anything he had experienced
in Europe, and overboosting his confidence with too much
enthusiasm. I still had doubts, but I left Leeds and later

Heathrow with a far greater optimism than I'd have thought possible.

On paper, everything was splendid. But I've never known events to be transferred from paper to reality without something being lost in the translation.

Port Luard was hot and sweaty. The temperature was climbing up to the hundred mark and the humidity was struggling to join it. John Sutherland met me at the airport which was one of Ofanwe's white elephants: runways big enough to take jumbos and a concourse three times the size of Penn Station. It was large enough to serve a city the size of, say, Rome.

A chauffeur driven car awaited outside the arrivals building. I got in with Sutherland and felt the sweat break out under my armpits, and my wet shirt already sticking to my back. I unbuttoned the top of my shirt and took off my jacket and tie. I had suffered from cold at Heathrow and was overdressed here – a typical traveller's dilemma. In my case was a superfine lightweight tropical suit by Huntsman – that was for hobnobbing with Cabinet ministers and suchlike – and a couple of safari suits. For the rest I'd buy local gear and probably dump it when I left. Cheap cotton shirts and shorts were always easy to get hold of.

I sat back and watched the country flow by. I hadn't been to Nyala before but it wasn't much different from Nigeria or any other West African landscape. Personally I preferred the less lush bits of Africa, the scrub and semi-desert areas, and I knew I'd be seeing plenty of that later on. The advertisements for Brooke Bond Tea and Raleigh Bicycles still proclaimed Nyala's British colonial origins, although those for Coca-Cola were universal.

It was early morning and I had slept on the flight. I felt wide awake and ready to go, which was more than I could

say for Sutherland. He looked exhausted, and I wondered
how tough it was getting for him.

'Do we have a company plane?' I asked him.

'Yes, and a good pilot, a Rhodesian.' He was silent for a
while and then said cautiously, 'Funny meeting we had last
week. I was pulled back to London at twelve hours' notice
and all that happened was that we sat around telling each
other things we already knew.'

He was fishing and I knew it.

'I didn't know most of it. It was a briefing for me.'

'Yes, I rather guessed as much.'

I asked, 'How long have you been with the company?'

'Seven years.'

I'd never met him before, or heard of him, but that was-
n't unusual. It's a big outfit and I met new faces regularly.
But Sutherland would have heard of me, because my name
was trouble; I was the hatchet man, the expeditor, sometimes the executioner. As soon as I pitched up on anyone's
territory there would be that tightening feeling in the gut as
the local boss man wondered what the hell had gone wrong.

I said, to put him at his ease, 'Relax, John. It's just that
Geddes has got ants in his pants. Trouble is they're invisible
ants. I'm just here on an interrupted vacation.'

'Oh quite,' Sutherland said, not believing a word of it.
'What do you plan to do first?'

'I think I'd like to go up to the site at Bir Oassa for a
couple of days, use the plane and overfly this road of theirs.
After that I might want to see someone in the Government.
Who would you suggest?'

Sutherland stroked his jaw. He knew that I'd read up on
all of them and that it was quite likely I knew more about
the local scene than he did. 'There's Hamah Ousemane – he's
Minister for the Interior, and there's the Finance Minister,
John Chizamba. Either would be a good starting point. And
I suppose Daondo will want to put his oar in.'

'He's the local Goebbels, isn't he?'

'Yes, Minister for Misinformation.'

I grinned and Sutherland relaxed a little more. 'Who has the itchiest palm? Or by some miracle are none of them on the take?'

'No miracles here. As for which is the greediest, that I couldn't say. But you should be able to buy a few items of information from almost anyone.'

We were as venal as the men we were dealing with. There was room for a certain amount of honesty in my profession but there was also room for the art of wheeling and dealing, and frankly I rather enjoyed that. It was fun, and I didn't ever see why making one's living had to be a joyless occupation.

I said, 'Right. Now, don't tell me you haven't any problems. You wouldn't be human if you didn't. What's the biggest headache on your list right now?'

'The heavy transport.'

'Wyvern? What exactly is wrong?'

'The first load is scheduled to leave a week from today but the ship carrying the rig hasn't arrived yet. She's on board a special freighter, not on a regular run, and she's been held up somewhere with customs problems. Wyvern's road boss is here and he's fairly sweating. He's been going up and down the road checking gradients and tolerances and he's not too happy with some of the things he's seen. He's back in town now, ready to supervise the unloading of the rig.'

'The cargo?'

'Oh, the transformers and boilers are all OK. It's just that they're a bit too big to carry up on a Land Rover. Do you want to meet him right away?'

'No, I'll see him when I come back from Bir Oassa. No point in our talking until there's something to talk about. And the non-arrival of the rig isn't a topic.'

I was telling him that I wasn't going to interfere in his job and it made him happier to know it. We had been travelling up a wide boulevard and now emerged into a huge dusty square, complete with a vast statue of a gentleman whom I knew to be Maro Ofanwe sitting on a plinth in the middle. Why they hadn't toppled his statue along with the original I couldn't imagine. The car wove through the haphazard traffic and stopped at one of the last remaining bits of colonial architecture in sight, complete with peeling paint and sagging wooden balconies. It was, needless to say, my hotel.

'Had a bit of a job getting you a room,' Sutherland said, thus letting me know that he was not without the odd string to pull.

'What's the attraction? It's hardly a tourist's mecca.'

'By God, it isn't! The attraction is the oil. You'll find Luard full of oil men – Americans, French, Russians, the lot. The Government has been eclectic in its franchises.'

As the car pulled up he went on, 'Anything I can do for you right now?'

'Nothing for today, thanks, John. I'll book in and get changed and cleaned up, do some shopping, take a stroll. Tomorrow I'd like a car here at seven-thirty to take me to the airport. Are you free this evening?'

Sutherland had been anticipating that question, and indicated that he was indeed available. We arranged to meet for a drink and a light meal. Any of the things I'd observed or thought about during the day I could then try out on him. Local knowledge should never be neglected.

By nine the next morning I was flying along the coast following the first 200 miles of road to Lasulu where we were to land for refuelling before going on upcountry. There was more traffic on the road than I would have expected, but far less than a road of that class was designed to carry. I took out the small pair of binoculars I carried and studied it.

There were a few saloons and four-wheel drive vehicles, Suzukis and Land Rovers, and a fair number of junky old trucks. What was more surprising were the number of big trucks; thirty- and forty-tonners. I saw that one of them was carrying a load of drilling pipe. The next was a tanker, then another carrying, from the trail it left, drilling mud. This traffic was oil-generated and was taking supplies from Port Luard to the oilfields in the north.

I said to the pilot, a cheerful young man called Max Otterman, 'Can you fly to the other side of Lasulu, please? Not far, say twenty miles. I want to look at the road over there.'

'It peters out a mile or so beyond the town. But I'll go on a way,' he said.

Sure enough the road vanished into the miniature build-up around Lasulu, reemerging inland from the coast. On the continuation of the coastal stretch another road carried on northwards, less impressive than the earlier section but apparently perfectly usable. The small harbour did not look busy, but there were two or three fair-sized craft riding at anchor. Not easy to tell from the air, but it didn't seem as though there was a building in Lasulu higher than three storeys. The endless frail smoke of shantytown cooking fires wreathed all about it.

Refuelling was done quickly at the airstrip, and then we turned inland. From Lasulu to Bir Oassa was about 800 miles and we flew over the broad strip of concrete thrusting incongruously through mangrove swamp, rain forest, savannah and the scrubby fringes of desert country. It had been built by Italian engineers, Japanese surveyors and a mixture of road crews with Russian money and had cost twice as much as it should, the surplus being siphoned off into a hundred unauthorized pockets and numbered accounts in Swiss banks – a truly international venture.

The Russians were not perturbed by the way their money was used. They were not penny-pinchers and, in fact, had worked hard to see that some of the surplus money went into the right pockets. It was a cheap way of buying friends in a country that was poised uncertainly and ready to topple East or West in any breeze. It was another piece laid on the chessboard of international diplomacy to fend off an identical move by another power.

The road drove through thick forest and then heaved itself up towards the sky, climbing the hills which edged the central plateau. Then it crossed the sea of grass and bush to the dry region of the desert and came to Bir Oassa where the towers of oil rigs made a newer, metal forest.

I spent two days in Bir Oassa talking to the men and the bosses, scouting about the workings, and cocking an ear for any sort of unrest or uneasiness. I found very little worthy of note and nothing untoward. I did have a complaint from Dick Slater, the chief steam engineer, who had been sent word of the change of schedule and didn't like it.

'I'll have thirty steam fitters playing pontoon when they should be working,' he said abrasively to me. 'Why the bloody hell do they have to send the transformers first?'

It had all been explained to him but he was being wilful. I said, 'Take it easy. It's all been authorized by Geddes from London.'

'London! What do they know about it? This Geddes doesn't understand the first damn thing about it,' he said. Slater wasn't the man to be mealy-mouthed. I calmed him down – well, maybe halfway down – and went in search of other problems. It worried me when I couldn't find any.

On the second day I had a phone call from Sutherland. On a crackling line full of static and clashing crossed wires his voice said faintly, '. . . Having a meeting with Ousemane and Daondo. Do you want . . . ?'

'Yes, I do want to sit in on it. You and who else?' I was shouting.

'. . . Kemp from Wyvern. Tomorrow morning . . .'

'Has the rig come?'

'. . . Unloading . . . came yesterday . . .'

'I'll be there.'

The meeting was held in a cool room in the Palace of Justice. The most important government man there was the Minister of the Interior, Hamah Ousemane, who presided over the meeting with a bland smile. He did not say much but left the talking to a short, slim man who was introduced as Zinsou Daondo. I couldn't figure whether Ousemane didn't understand what was going on, or understood and didn't care: he displayed a splendid indifference.

Very surprising for a meeting of this kind was the presence of Major General Abram Kigonde, the army boss. Although he was not a member of the government he was a living reminder of Mao's dictum that power grows out of the muzzle of a gun. No Nyalan government could survive without his nod of approval. At first I couldn't see where he fitted in to this discussion on the moving of a big piece of power plant.

On our side there were myself, Sutherland, and Basil Kemp, who was a lean Englishman with a thin brown face stamped with tiredness and worry marks. He greeted me pleasantly enough, remembering our last encounter some few years before and appearing unperturbed by my presence. He probably had too much else on his plate already. I let Sutherland make the running and he addressed his remarks to the Minister while Daondo did the answering. It looked remarkably like a ventriloquist's act but I found it hard to figure out who was the dummy. Kigonde kept a stiff silence.

After some amiable chitchat (not the weather, thank God) we got down to business and Sutherland outlined some routine matters before drawing Kemp into the discussion. 'Could we have a map, please, Mister Kemp?'

Kemp placed a map on the big table and pointed out his bottlenecks.

'We have to get out of Port Luard and through Lasulu. Both are big towns and to take a load like this through presents difficulties. It has been my experience in Europe that operations like this draw the crowds and I can't see that it will be different here. We should appreciate a police escort.'

Daondo nodded. 'It will certainly draw the crowds.' He seemed pleased.

Kemp said, 'In Europe we usually arrange to take these things through at extreme off-peak times. The small hours of the night are often best.'

This remark drew a frown from Daondo and I thought I detected the slightest of headshakes from the Minister. I became more alert.

Kigonde stirred and spoke for the first time, in a deep and beautifully modulated voice. 'You will certainly have an escort, Mister Kemp – but not the police. I am putting an army detachment at your service.' He leaned forward and pressed a button, the door of the room opened, and a smartly dressed officer strode towards the table. 'This is Captain Ismail Sadiq who will command the escort.'

Captain Sadiq clicked to attention, bowing curtly, and then at a nod from Kigonde stood at ease at the foot of the table.

Daondo said, The army will accompany you all the way.'

'The whole journey?' Sutherland asked.

'On all journeys.'

I sensed that Sutherland was about to say something wrong, and forestalled him. 'We are more than honoured, Major General. This is extremely thoughtful of you and we appreciate it. It is more of an honour than such work as this usually entails.'

'Our police force is not large, and already has too much work. We regard the safekeeping of such expeditions as these of the greatest importance, Mister Mannix. The army stands ready to be of any service.' He was very smooth, and I reckoned that we'd come out of that little encounter about equal. I prepared to enjoy myself.

'Please explain the size of your command, Captain,' Daondo said.

Sadiq had a soft voice at odds with his appearance. 'For work on the road I have four infantry troop carriers with six men to each carrier, two trucks for logistics purposes, and my own command car, plus outriders. Eight vehicles, six motorcycles and thirty-six men including myself. In the towns I am empowered to call on local army units for crowd control.'

This was bringing up the big guns with a vengeance. I had never heard of a rig which needed that kind of escort, whether for crowd control or for any other form of safety regulations, except in conditions of war. My curiosity was aroused by now, but I said nothing and let Sutherland carry on. Taking his cue from me he expressed only his gratitude and none of his perturbation. He'd expected a grudging handful of ill-trained local coppers at best.

Kigonde was saying, 'In the Nyalan army the rank of captain is relatively high, gentlemen. You need not fear being held up in any way.'

'I am sure not,' said Kemp politely. 'It will be a pleasure having your help, Captain. But now there are other matters as well. I am sorry to tell you that the road has deteriorated slightly in some places, and my loads may be too heavy for them.'

That was an understatement, but Kemp was working hard at diplomacy. Obviously he was wondering if Sadiq had any idea of the demands made by heavy transport, and if army escort duty also meant army assistance. Daondo picked him

up and said easily, 'Captain Sadiq will be authorized to nego-
tiate with the civil bodies in each area in which you may find
difficulty. I am certain that an adequate labour force will be
found for you. And, of course, the necessary materials.'

It all seemed too good to be true. Kemp went on to the
next problem.

'Crowd control in towns is only one aspect, of course,
gentlemen. There is the sheer difficulty of pushing a big
vehicle through a town. Here on the map I have outlined a
proposed route through Port Luard, from the docks to the
outskirts. I estimate that it will take eight or nine hours to
get through. The red line marks the easiest, in fact the only
route, and the figures in circles are the estimated times at
each stage. That should help your traffic control, although
we shouldn't have too much trouble there, moving through
the central city area mostly during the night.'

The Minister made a sudden movement, wagging one
finger sideways. Daondo glanced at him before saying, 'It
will not be necessary to move through Port Luard at night,
Mister Kemp. We prefer you to make the move in daylight.'

'It will disrupt your traffic flow considerably,' said Kemp
in some surprise.

'That is of little consequence. We can handle it.' Daondo
bent over the map. 'I see your route lies through
Independence Square.'

'It's really the only way,' said Kemp defensively. 'It would
be quite impossible to move through this tangle of narrow
streets on either side without a great deal of damage to
buildings.'

'I quite agree,' said Daondo. 'In fact, had you not suggested it we would have asked you to go through the
Square ourselves.'

This appeared to come as a wholly novel idea to Kemp. I
could see he was thinking of the squalls of alarm from the
London Metropolitan Police had he suggested pushing a

300-ton load through Trafalgar Square in the middle of the rush hour. Wherever he'd worked in Europe, he had been bullied, harassed and crowded into corners and sent on his way with the stealth of a burglar.

He paused to take this in with one finger still on the map. 'There's another very real difficulty here, though. This big plinth in the middle of the avenue leading into the Square. It's sited at a very bad angle from our point of view – we're going to have a great deal of difficulty getting around it. I would like to suggest –'

The Minister interrupted him with an unexpected deep-bellied, rumbling chuckle but his face remained bland. Daondo was also smiling and in his case too the smile never reached his eyes. 'Yes, Mister Kemp, we see what you mean. I don't think you need trouble about the plinth. We will have it removed. It will improve the traffic flow into Victory Avenue considerably in any case.'

Kemp and Sutherland exchanged quick glances. 'I . . . I think it may take time,' said Sutherland. 'It's a big piece of masonry.'

'It is a task for the army,' said Kigonde and turned to Sadiq. 'See to it, Captain.'

Sadiq nodded and made quick notes. The discussion continued, the exit from Port Luard was detailed and the progress through Lasulu dismissed, for all its obvious difficulties to us, as a mere nothing by the Nyalans. About an hour later, after some genteel refreshment, we were finally free to go our way. We all went up to my hotel room and could hardly wait to get there before indulging in a thorough postmortem of that extraordinary meeting. It was generally agreed that no job had ever been received by the local officials with greater cooperation, any problem melting like snowflakes in the steamy Port Luard sunshine. Paradoxically it was this very ease of arrangement that made us all most uneasy, especially Basil Kemp.

'I can't believe it,' he said, not for the first time. 'They just love us, don't they?'

'I think you've put your finger on it, Basil,' I said. 'They really need us and they are going all out to show it. And they're pretty used to riding roughshod over the needs and wishes of their populace, assuming it has any. They're going to shove us right down the middle in broad daylight, and the hell with any little obstacles.'

'Such as the plinth,' said Sutherland and we both laughed.

Kemp said, 'I think I missed something there. A definite undercurrent. I must say I haven't looked at this thing too closely myself – what is it anyway – some local bigwig?'

Sutherland chuckled. 'I thought old Ousemane would split his breeches. There's a statue of Maro Ofanwe still on that plinth: thirty feet high in bronze, very heroic. Up to now they've been busy ignoring it, as it was a little too hefty to blow up or knock down, but now they've got just the excuse they want. It'll help to serve notice that they don't want any more strong men about, in a none too subtle sort of way. Ofanwe was an unmitigated disaster and not to be repeated.'

THREE

During the next few days I got on with my job, which mainly consisted of trying to find out what my job was. I talked with various members of the Government and had a special meeting with the Minister of Finance which left us both happy. I also talked to journalists in the bars, one or two businessmen and several other expatriates from Britain who were still clinging on to their old positions, most of them only too ready to bewail the lost days of glory. I gleaned a lot, mostly of misinformation, but slowly I was able to put together a picture which didn't precisely coincide with that painted by Shelford back in London.

I was also made an honorary member of the Luard Club which, in colonial days, had strictly white membership but in these times had become multi-racial. There were still a number of old Africa hands there as well, and from a couple of them I got another whiff of what might be going bad in Nyala.

In the meantime Kemp and Sutherland were getting on with their business, to more immediate ends. On the morning the first big load was to roll I was up bright and early, if not bushy tailed. The sun had just risen and the temperature already in the eighties when I drove to the docks to see the loaded rig. I hadn't had much chance to talk to Kemp and while I doubted that this was the moment, I had to pin him down to some time and place.

I found him and Sutherland in the middle of a small slice of chaos, both looking harassed as dozens of men milled around shouting questions and orders. They'd been at it for a long time already and things were almost ready to go into action. I stared in fascination at what I saw.

The huge rig wasn't unfamiliar to me but it was still a breathtaking sight. The massive towing trucks, really tractors with full cab bodies, stood at each end of the flat-bed trailer onto which the transformer had been lowered, inch by painful inch, over the previous few hours. Around it scurried small dockside vehicles, fork-lift trucks and scooters, like worker ants scrambling about their huge motionless queen. But what fascinated and amused me was the sight of a small platoon of Nyalan dock hands clambering about the actual rig itself, as agile and noisy as a troop of monkeys, busy stringing yards of festive bunting between any two protruding places to which they could be tied. The green and yellow colours of the Nyalan flag predominated, and one of them was being hauled up a jackstaff which was bound to the front tractor bumpers. No wonder that Kemp looked thunderstruck and more than a little grim.

I hurried over to him, and my arrival coincided with that of Mr Daondo, who was just getting out of a black limousine. Daondo stood with hands on hips and gazed the length of the enormous rig with great satisfaction, then turned to us and said in a hearty voice, 'Well, good morning, gentlemen. I see everything is going very well indeed.'

Kemp said, 'Good morning, Mister Daondo – Neil. May I ask what –'

'Hello, Basil. Great day for it, haven't we? Mister Daondo, would you excuse us for just one moment? I've got your figures here, Basil . . .'

Talking fast, waving a notebook, and giving him no time to speak, I managed to draw Kemp away from Daondo's side, leaving the politician to be entertained for a moment by John Sutherland.

'Just what the hell do they think they're doing?' Kemp was outraged.

'Ease off. Calm down. Can't you see? They're going to put on a show for the people – that's what this daylight procession has been about all along. The power plant is one of the biggest things that's ever happened to Nyala and the Government wants to do a bit of bragging. And I don't see why not.'

'But how?' Kemp, normally a man of broad enough intelligence, was on a very narrow wave length where his precious rig was concerned.

'Hasn't the penny dropped yet? You're to be the centre-piece of a triumphal parade through the town, right through Independence Square. The way the Ruskies trundle their rockets through Red Square on May Day. You'll be on show, the band will play, the lot.'

'Are you serious?' said Kemp in disgust.

'Quite. The Government must not only govern but be seen to govern. They're entitled to bang their drum.'

Kemp subsided, muttering.

'Don't worry. As soon as you're clear of the town you can take the ribbons out of her hair and get down to work properly. Have a word with your drivers. I'd like to meet them, but not right away. And tell them to enjoy themselves. It's a gala occasion.'

'All right, I suppose we must. But it's damn inconvenient. It's hard enough work moving these things without having to cope with cheering mobs and flag-waving.'

'You don't have to cope, that's his job.' I indicated Daondo with a jerk of my thumb. 'Your guys just drive it away as usual. I think we'd better go join him.'

We walked back to where Daondo, leaning negligently against the hood of his Mercedes, was holding forth to a small circle of underlings. Sutherland was in the thick of it, together with a short, stocky man with a weathered face. Sutherland introduced him to me.

'Neil, this is Ben Hammond, my head driver. Ben, Mister Mannix of British Electric. I think Ben's what you'd call my ranch foreman.'

I grinned. 'Nice herd of cattle you've got there, Ben. I'd like to meet the crew later. What's the schedule?'

'I've just told Mister Daondo that I think they're ready to roll any time now. But of course it's Mister Kemp's show really.'

'Thank you, Mister Sutherland. I'll have a word with Daondo and then we can get going,' Kemp said.

I marvelled at the way my British companions still managed to cling to surnames and honorifics. I wondered if they'd all be dressing for dinner, out there in the bush wherever the rig stopped for the night. I gave my attention to Daondo to find that he was being converged upon by a band of journalists, video and still cameras busy, notebooks poised, but with none of the free-for-all shoving that might have taken place anywhere in Europe. The presence of several armed soldiers nearby may have had a bearing on that.

'Ah, Mister Mannix,' Daondo said, 'I am about to hold a short press conference. Would you join me, please?'

'An honour, Minister. But it's not really my story – it's Mister Kemp's.'

Kemp gave me a brief dirty look as I passed the buck neatly to him. 'May I bring Mister Hammond in on this?' he asked, drawing Ben Hammond along by the arm. 'He designed this rig; it's very much his baby.'

I looked at the stocky man in some surprise. This was something I hadn't known and it set me thinking. Wyvern Haulage might be new as an outfit, but they seemed to have gathered a great deal of talent around them, and my respect for Geoff Wingstead grew fractionally greater.

The press conference was under way, to a soft barrage of clicks as people were posed in front of the rig. Video camera-men did their trick of walking backwards with a buddy's hand on their shoulder to guide them, and the writer boys ducked and dodged around the clutter of ropes, chain, pulleys and hawsers that littered the ground. Some of the inevitable questions were coming up and I listened carefully, as this was a chance for me to learn a few of the technicalities.

'Just how big is this vehicle?'

Kemp indicated Ben Hammond forward. Ben, grinning like a toothpaste advertisement, was enjoying his moment in the limelight as microphones were thrust at him. 'As the transporter is set up now it's a bit over a hundred feet long. We can add sections up to another eighteen feet but we won't need them on this trip.'

'Does that include the engines?'

'The tractors? No, those are counted separately. We'll be adding on four tractors to get over hilly ground and then the total length will be a shade over two hundred and forty feet.'

Another voice said, 'Our readers may not be able to visualize that. Can you give us anything to measure it by?'

Hammond groped for an analogy, and then said, 'I notice that you people here play a lot of soccer – football.'

'Indeed we do,' Daondo interjected. 'I myself am an enthusiast.' He smiled modestly as he put in his personal plug. 'I was present at the Cup Final at Wembley last year, when I was Ambassador to the United Kingdom.'

Hammond said, 'Well, imagine this. If you drove this rig onto the field at Wembley, or any other standard soccer pitch, it would fill the full length of the pitch with a foot hanging over each side. Is that good enough?'

There was a chorus of appreciative remarks, and Kemp said in a low voice, 'Well done, Ben. Carry on.'

'How heavy is the vehicle?' someone asked.

'The transporter weighs ninety tons, and the load, that big transformer, is three hundred tons. Add forty tons for each tractor and it brings the whole lot to five hundred and fifty tons on the hoof.'

Everybody scribbled while the cameras ground on. Hammond added, airing some knowledge he had only picked up in the last few days, 'Elephants weigh about six tons each; so this is worth nearly a hundred elephants.'

The analogy was received with much amusement.

'Those tractors don't look big enough to weigh forty tons,' he was prompted.

'They carry ballast. Steel plates embedded in concrete. We have to have some counterbalance for the weight of the load or the transporter will overrun the tractors – especially on the hills. Negotiating hill country is very tricky.'

'How fast will you go?'

Kemp took over now. 'On the flat with all tractors hooked up I dare say we could push along to almost twenty miles an hour, even more going downhill. But we won't. Five hundred and fifty tons going at twenty miles an hour takes a lot of stopping, and we don't take risks. I don't think we'll do much more than ten miles an hour during any part of the journey, and usually much less. Our aim is to average five miles an hour during a ten hour day; twenty days from Port Luard to Bir Oassa.'

This drew whistles of disbelief and astonishment. In this age of fast transport, it was interesting that extreme slowness could exert the same fascination as extreme speed. It also interested me to notice that Nyala had not yet converted its thinking to the metric unit as far as distances were concerned.

'How many wheels does it have?'

Hammond said, 'Ninety-six on the ground and eight spares.'

'How many punctures do you expect?'

'None – we hope.' This drew a laugh.

'What's the other big truck?'

'That's the vehicle which carries the airlift equipment and the machinery for powering it,' said Kemp. 'We use it to spread the load when crossing bridges, and it works on the hovercraft principle. It's powered by four two hundred and forty-hp Rolls Royce engines – and that vehicle itself weighs eight tons.'

'And the others?'

'Spares, a workshop for maintenance, food and personal supplies, fuel. We have to take everything with us, you see.'

There was a stir as an aide came forward to whisper something into Daondo's ear. He raised his hand and his voice. 'Gentlemen, that will be all for now, thank you. I invite you all to gather round this great and marvellous machine for its dedication by His Excellency, the Minister of the Interior, the Right Honourable Hamah Ousemane, OBE.' He touched me on the arm. 'This way, please.'

As we followed him I heard Hammond saying to Kemp, 'What's he going to do? Crack a bottle of champagne over it?'

I grinned back at him. 'Did you really design this thing?'

'I designed some modifications to a standard rig, yes.'

Kemp said, 'Ben built a lot of it, too.'

I was impressed. 'For a little guy you sure play with big toys.'

Hammond stiffened and looked at me with hot eyes. Clearly I had hit on a sore nerve. 'I'm five feet two and a half inches tall,' he said curtly. 'And that's the exact height of Napoleon.'

'No offence meant,' I said quickly, and then we all came to a sudden stop at the rig to listen to Ousemane's speech. He spoke first in English and then in Nyalan for a long time in a rolling, sonorous voice while the sun became hotter and everybody wilted. Then came some ribbon cutting and handshakes all round, some repeated for the benefit of the press, and finally he took himself off in his Mercedes. Kemp mopped his brow thankfully. 'Do you think we can get on with it now?' he asked nobody in particular.

Daondo was bustling back to us. In the background a surprising amount of military deployment was taking place, and there was an air of expectancy building up. 'Excellent, Mister Kemp! We are all ready to go now,' Daondo said. 'You will couple up ail the tractors, won't you?'

Kemp turned to me and said in a harassed undertone, 'What for? We won't be doing more than five miles an hour on the flat and even one tractor's enough for that.'

I was getting a bit tired of Kemp and his invincible ignorance and I didn't want Daondo to hear him and blow a gasket. I smiled past Kemp and said, 'Of course. Everything will be done as you wish it, Minister.'

'Good,' he said. 'I must get to Independence Square before you arrive. I leave Captain Sadiq in command of the arrangements.' He hurried away to his car.

I said to Kemp, putting an edge on my voice, 'We're expected to put on a display and we'll do it. Use everything you've got. Line 'em up, even the chow wagon. Until we leave town it's a parade every step of the way.'

'Who starts this parade?'

'You do – just tell your drivers to pull off in line whenever they're ready. The others will damn well have to fall in around you. I'll ride with you in the Land Rover.'

Kemp shrugged. 'Bunch of clowns,' he said and went off to give his drivers their instructions. For the moment I actually had nothing to do and I wandered over to have another look at the rig. It's a funny thing, but whenever a guy looks at a vehicle he automatically kicks a tyre. Ask any second-hand auto salesman. So that's what I did. It had about as much effect as kicking a building and was fairly painful. The tyres were all new, with deep tread earthmovers on the tractors. The whole rig looked brand new, as if it had never been used before, and I couldn't decide if this was a good or a bad thing. I squinted up at it as it towered over me, remembering the one time I had towed a caravan and had it jackknife on me, and silently tipped my hat to the drivers of this outfit. They were going to need skill and luck in equal proportions on this trip.

Kemp drew up beside me in the Land Rover with a driver and I swung in the back. There was a lot of crosstalk going on with walkie-talkies, and a great deal of bustle and activity all around us.

'All right, let's get rolling,' Kemp said into the speaker. 'Take station on me, Ben: about three mph and don't come breathing down my neck.' He then said much the same thing into his car radio as drivers climbed into cabs and the vast humming roar of many engines began throbbing. Captain Sadiq rolled up alongside us in the back of an open staff car and saluted smartly.

'I will lead the way, Mister Kemp. Please to follow me,' he said.

'Please keep your speed to mine, Captain,' Kemp said.

'Of course, sir. But please watch me carefully too. I may have to stop at some point. You are all ready?'

Kemp nodded and Sadiq pulled away. Kemp was running down a roster of drivers, getting checks from each of them, and then at last signalled his own driver to move ahead in Sadiq's wake. I would have preferred to be behind the rig, but had to content myself with twisting in the rear seat of the car to watch behind me. To my astonishment something was joining in the parade that I hadn't seen before, filtering in between Kemp and the rig, and at my sharp exclamation he turned to see for himself and swore.

The army was coming in no half measures. Two recoilless guns, two mortars and two heavy machine guns mounted on appropriate vehicles came forward, followed by a tank and at least two troop carriers. 'Good God,' said Kemp in horror, and gave hasty orders to his own driver, who swung us out of the parade and doubled back along the line of military newcomers. Kemp was speaking urgently to Sadiq on the radio.

'I'll rejoin after the army vehicles, Captain. I must stay with the rig!'

I grinned at him as he cut the Captain off in mid-sentence.

'They're armed to the teeth,' he said irritably. 'Why the hell didn't he warn me about all this?'

'Maybe the crowds here are rougher than in England,' I said, looking with fascination at the greatly enhanced parade streaming past us.

'They're using us as an excuse to show what they've got. They damn well know it's all going out on telly to the world,' Kemp said.

'Enjoy the publicity, Basil. It says *Wyvern* up there in nice big letters. A pity I didn't think of a flag with *British Electric* on it as well.'

In fact this show of military prowess was making me a little uneasy, but it would never do for me to let Kemp see that. He was jittery enough as it was. He gave orders as the tanks swept past, commanders standing up in the turrets, and we swung in behind the last of the army vehicles and just in front of the rig, now massively coupled to all its trac-tors. Ben Hammond waved down to us from his driving cab and the rig started rolling behind us. Kemp concentrated on its progress, leaving the other Wyvern vehicles to come along in the rear, the very last car being the second Land Rover with John Sutherland on board.

Kemp was watching the rig, checking back regularly and trying to ignore the shouting, waving crowds who were gathering as we went along, travelling so slowly that agile small boys could dodge back and forward across the road in between the various components of the parade. There was much blowing of police whistles to add to the general noise. We heard louder cheering as we came out onto the coastal boulevard leading to the town centre. The scattering of people thickened as we approached.

Kemp paid particular attention as the rig turned behind us into Victory Avenue; turning a 240-foot vehicle is no easy job and he would rather have done it without the extra towing tractors. But the rig itself was steerable from both ends and a crew member was spinning a ship-sized steering wheel right at the rear, synchronizing with Ben Hammond in the front cab. Motorcycle escorts took up flanking positions as the rig straightened out into the broad avenue and the crowd was going crazy.

Kemp said, 'Someone must have declared a holiday.'

'Rent-a-crowd,' I grinned. Kemp sat a little straighter and seemed to relax slightly. I thought that he was beginning to enjoy his moment of glory, after all. The Land Rover bumped over a roughly cobbled area and I realized with a start that we were driving over the place where Ofanwe's plinth had been only a few days before.

We entered the Square to a sea of black faces and colourful robes, gesticulating arms and waves of sound that surged and echoed from the big buildings all around. The flags hung limply in the still air but all the rest was movement under the hard tropical sun.

'Jesus!' Kemp said in awe. 'It's like a Roman triumph. I feel I ought to have a slave behind me whispering sweet nothings in my ear.' He quoted, *'Memento mori* – remember thou must die.'

I grunted. I was used to the British habit of flinging off quotations at odd moments but I hadn't expected it of Kemp. He went on, 'Just look at that lot.'

The balcony of the Palace of Justice was full of figures. The President, the Prime Minister, members of the

Government, Army staff, some in modern dress or in uniforms but some, like Daondo, changed into local costume: a flowing colourful robe and a tasselled hat. It was barbaric and, in spite of my professed cynicism, a touch magnificent.

The tanks and guns had passed and it was our turn. Kemp said to me, 'Do we bow or anything?'

'Just sit tight. Pay attention to your rig. Show them it's still business first.' Off to one side of the parade, Sadiq's staff car was drawn up with the Captain standing rigidly at the salute in the back seat. 'Sadiq is doing the necessary for all of us.'

The vast bulk of the rig crept slowly across Independence Square and the troops and police fought valiantly to keep the good-humoured crowd back. As soon as our car was through the Square we stopped and waited too for the rig to come up behind us, and then set off again following Sadiq, who had regained his place in the lead. The tanks and guns rumbled off in a different direction, and the convoy with its escort of soldiers crept on through narrower streets and among fewer and fewer people.

The town began to thin out until we were clear of all but a few shanties and into the beginning of the croplands, and here the procession came to a halt, with only an audience of goats and herd boys to watch us.

Sadiq's car came back. He got out and spoke to Kemp, who had the grace to thank him and to congratulate him on the efficiency of his arrangements. Clearly both were relieved that all had gone so well, and equally anxious to get on with the job in hand. Within minutes Kemp had his men removing the bunting and flags; he was driving them hard while the euphoria of the parade was still with them.

'This is all arsey-versey,' I heard him saying. 'You've had your celebration – now do something to earn it.'

'I suppose they'll do their celebrating tonight,' I remarked to him.

Kemp shook his head.

'We have a company rule. There's no hard liquor on the journeys: just beer, and I control that. And they've got a hell of a few days ahead of them.'

'I guess they have,' I said.

'A lot of trips,' Kemp said. 'Months of work. Right now it's a pretty daunting prospect.'

'You only have this one rig?'

I still felt I didn't know as much about Wyvern as I ought to. Having seen a tiny slice of their job out here, I was in a fever to talk to Geddes back at home, and to get together with Wingstead too. Reminded of him, I asked Kemp when he was due to come out.

'Next week, I believe,' Kemp said., 'He'll fly up and join us during the mid-section of the first trip. As for the rig, there's a second one in the making and it should be ready towards the end of the job. It'll help, but not enough. And the rains start in a couple of months too: we've a lot of planning to do yet.'

'Can you keep going through the wet season?'

'If the road holds out we can. And I must say it's fairly good most of the way. If it hadn't existed we'd never have tendered for the job.'

I said, 'I'm frankly surprised in a way that you did tender. It's a hell of a job for a new firm – wouldn't the standard European runs have suited you better to begin with?'

'We decided on the big gamble. Nothing like a whacking big success to start off with.'

I thought that it was Wingstead, rather than the innately conservative Kemp, who had decided on that gamble, and wondered how he had managed to convince my own masters that he was the man for the job.

'Right, Basil, this is where I leave you,' I said, climbing down from the Land Rover to stand on the hard heat-baked tarmac. 'I'll stay in touch, and I'll be out to see how you're getting on. Meanwhile I've got a few irons of my own in the fire – back there in the Frying Pan.'

We shook hands and I hopped into John Sutherland's car for the drive back to Port Luard, leaving Kemp to organize the beginning of the rig's first expedition.

FOUR

We got back to the office hot, sweaty and tired. The streets were still seething and we had to fight our way through. Sutherland was fast on the draw with a couple of gin and tonics, and within four minutes of our arrival I was sitting back over a drink in which the ice clinked pleasantly. I washed the dust out of my mouth and watched the bubbles rise.

'Well, they got away all right,' Sutherland said after his own first swallow. 'They should be completely clear by nightfall.'

I took another mouthful and let it fizz before swallowing. 'Just as well you brought up the business of the plinth,' I said. 'Otherwise the rig would never have got into the Square.'

He laughed. 'Do you know, I forgot all about it in the excitement.'

'Sadiq damn nearly removed Independence Square. He blew the goddamn thing up at midnight. He may have broken every window in the hotel: I woke up picking bits of plate glass out of my bed. I don't know who his explosives experts are but I reckon they used a mite too much. You said it wouldn't be too subtle a hint – well, it was about as subtle as a kick in the balls.'

Sutherland replenished our glasses. 'What's next on the programme?'

'I'm going back to London on the first possible flight. See to it, will you? And keep my hotel room on for me – I'll be back.'

'What's it all about? What problems do you see?'

I said flatly, 'If you haven't already seen them then you aren't doing your job.' The chill in my voice got through to him and he visibly remembered that I was the trouble-shooter. I went on, 'I want to see your contingency plans for pulling out in case the shit hits the fan.'

He winced, and I could clearly interpret the expressions that chased over his face. I wasn't at all the cheery, easy-to-get-along-with guy he had first thought: I was just another ill-bred, crude American, after all, and he was both hurt and shocked. Well, I wasn't there to cater to his finer sensibilities, but to administer shock treatment where necessary.

I put a snap in my voice. 'Well, have you got any?'

He said tautly, 'It's not my policy to go into a job thinking I might have to pull out. That's defeatism.'

'John, you're a damned fool. The word I used was contingency. Your job is to have plans ready for any eventuality, come what may. Didn't they teach you that from the start?'

I stood up. 'When I get back I want to see those plans laid out, covering a quick evacuation of all personnel and as much valuable equipment as possible. It may never happen, but the plans must be there. Get some guidance from Barry Meredith in the Zambian offices. He's had the experience. Do I make myself clear?'

'You do,' he said, clipped and defensive, hating my guts.

I finished my drink. 'Thanks for the life-saver. Send the air tickets to the hotel, and expect me when you see me. And keep your ears open, John.'

He couldn't quite bring himself to ask me what he was supposed to listen for, and I wasn't yet ready to tell him. I left him a sadder and a none the wiser man.

* * *

I got back to London, spent a night in my own apartment, which God knows saw little enough of me, and was in to see Geddes the next morning. It was as though time had stood still; he sat behind his desk, wearing the same suit, and the same rain pattered against the windows. Even the conversation was predictable. 'You're looking very brown,' he said. 'Good weather out there?'

'No, I've picked up a new suntan lamp. You ought to try it some time. How's your prickly feeling?'

'It's still there. I hope you've brought some embrocation.'

'I haven't.' I crossed the room, opened the discreet executive bar and poured out a neat Scotch.

'You've picked up some bad habits,' Geddes said. 'Early morning drinking wasn't your line.'

'It's almost noon, and this isn't for me, it's for you – you'll need it. But since you invite me I'll join you.' I poured another, took the drinks to the desk and sat down.

Geddes looked from the glass to me. 'Bad news?'

'Not good. At the same time, not certain. It's one of those iffy situations. I've looked over the Nyala operation, and there's nothing wrong with our end of it. It's running like a well-oiled machine, and I'm mildly impressed by Wyvern, with reservations. But I put my ear to the ground, talked some and listened more, and I didn't like what I was hearing. Do you want it now or should I save it for a board meeting?'

'I'll have it now, please. I like to be ahead of any committee.'

'OK. A few years ago, after Ofanwe, there was military rule and Abram Kigonde was top dog. When he pulled out and allowed elections there were two basic parties formed, one rather grandly called the Peoples' Agrarian Party and one with the more prosaic name of the Nationalist Peoples' Party. The Agrarians won the first election and set out to reform everything in sight, but in a rather middle-of-the-road fashion; they were not particularly revolutionary in their thinking.'

I sipped some whisky, 'Times change. Because of the political stability, quite a lot of investment money came in, and then with the oil strikes there was still more. After a while the moderates were squeezed out and the Nationalists took over at the next elections. They are a lot more industry orientated. And of course by now Nyala had become self-financing and there were a lot of pickings to be had. And that's the nub – had by whom?'

'We know a lot of pockets have been lined, Neil. That's fairly common. Damn it, we've done it ourselves.'

'As common as breathing. But I think too much of it has gone into the wrong pockets – or wrong from one point of view anyway.'

'Whose point of view?'

'Major General Abram Kigonde.'

Geddes pursed his lips and nodded thoughtfully. 'What's he got to do with all this?'

'Everything. He's having trouble keeping the army in line. When he handed over power to the civil authority there were grumbles from some of his officers. A few senior types thought the army should hang on; they'd had a taste of power and liked it. But then nothing much happened, because there wasn't much power, or much loot, to divide. Then came industrialization and finally, to top it all, the oil strikes. Now there's a hell of a lot of loot and the army is split down the middle. They know the Government lads are creaming it off the top and some of those senior officers are licking their lips. Of course what they're saying is that the country which they saved from the evils of Maro Ofanwe is now being sold down the river by other equally evil politicians, but that's just for public consumption.'

'Yes, it sounds highly likely. Who's the main trouble-maker?'

'A Colonel Sagundisi is at the bottom of it, the word says. He hasn't put a foot wrong, his popularity with the younger officers is increasing, and he's preaching redemption. If Kigonde lets him he'll go right out on a limb and call for army reforms again.'

'With what results?'

'Could be a *coup d'éetat.*'

'Um,' said Geddes. 'And the timetable? The likelihood?'

'That's hard to guess, naturally. It depends partly on the Air Force.'

Geddes nodded tiredly. 'The usual complications. They're playing both ends against the middle, right?'

'Right now the army is split in two; half for Kigonde and the *status quo,* half for Sagundisi and the quick takeover. Word is that they're level pegging with Sagundisi making points and Kigonde losing them. The influence of their so-called Navy is negligible. But the Air Force is different. If it comes to open conflict then the side that has air power is going to win.'

'A poker game.'

'You're so damned right. The Air Force Commander is a wily old fox called Semangala and he's playing it cool, letting each side of the army raise the ante alternately. The Government is also bidding for support in all this, naturally, tending to Kigonde's angle but I wouldn't be surprised if they jumped whichever way would get them into the cream pot.'

'It seems to come down to Semangala, the way you see it. When he makes his mind up you expect a crack down one way or the other.'

'There are other factors, of course. Student unrest is on the increase. The pro-Reds are looking for a chance to put their oar in; and in the north – where the oil is – the country is largely Moslem and tends to look towards the Arab states for support and example. Oh yes, and when all else fails there's always the old tribal game: all of the lesser tribes are ready to gang up on the too successful Kinguru, including their cousins the Wabi, who make up the army backbone. Take your pick.'

Geddes picked up his glass and seemed surprised to find that he'd drained it. 'All right, Neil. When do you think it will blow open?'

'The rains will come in nearly two months if they're on schedule which they may not be. They've been erratic the last few years. But if they do come they will effectively put a damper on any attempted *coup* —'

Geddes smiled without mirth at my unintended pun.

'Anyway, no army commander will take that chance. I'd say that if it happens, it will be within the month or not for another six months.'

'And if you had to bet?'

I tapped the table with my forefinger. 'Now.'

'And us with a three year contract,' mused Geddes wryly. 'What the hell's happened to Shelford and his department? He should know about all this?'

'How could he when he doesn't take the trouble to go and find out? I'd kick him out on his ass if I had my way.'

'We don't do things that way,' said Geddes stiffly.

I grinned. No, Geddes would shaft Shelford in the well-bred British fashion. There'd be a report in the *Financial Times* that Mr Shelford was going from strength to strength in the hierarchy of British Electric and his picture would smile toothily from the page. But from then on he'd be the walking dead, with his desk getting emptier and his phone more silent, and eventually he'd get the message and quit to grow roses. And wonder what the hell had hit him. A stiletto under the third rib would be more merciful.

'But Sutherland should have known,' Geddes was saying. 'He should have told us.'

Although I had put the frighteners into John Sutherland myself I did not think he ought to share Shelford's imagined fate – he had much to learn but a great deal of company potential and I wanted him kept on the job. So I let him down lightly.

'He tried, back in that boardroom, but Shelford shouted him down. He's a good man and learning fast. It's just that he works too hard.'

'Oh yes?' Geddes was acidly polite. 'Is that possible?'

'It surely is. He should take out more time for his social life. He should get around more, do some drinking: drinking and listening. How the hell do you think I got all the dope I've just given you? I got it by damn near contracting cirrhosis of the liver drinking with a lot of boozy old colonial types who know more about what makes Nyala tick than the President himself. They're disillusioned, those men. Some have lived in Nyala all their lives but they know they'll always be on the outside because their skins are white. They're there by grace and favour now, discounted by the country's new masters, but they look and listen. And they *know*.'

'That's a précis of a Somerset Maugham story,' said Geddes sardonically. 'Does Sutherland know all this? Has he got the picture now?'

I shook my head. 'I thought I'd have a word with you first. Meantime I wouldn't be too surprised if he doesn't put some of it together for himself, while I'm away. I jumped on him a bit to frighten him but I don't think he's the man to panic.'

Geddes pondered this and clearly approved. Presently he said, 'Is there anything else I ought to know?'

'Kigonde's used half the army to help the rig along its first journey. I'll tell you more about that later; it's off to a good start. And I believe he's moved an infantry brigade up to Bir Oassa.'

'Quite natural to guard an oilfield. Does he expect sabotage?'

'The Government is leaning heavily on our operation for propagation purposes, as you'll see in my full report. There was the damnedest celebration you ever did see when the

first transformer left Port Luard. If it should *not* get to Bir
Oassa, or if anything happened to it up there, the
Government would be discredited after all the hoopla they've
made. Which makes it a prime target for the opposition.'

'Christ!' Geddes was fully alert for the first time. 'Have
you told Kemp all about this?'

'No, I haven't. The guy is under a lot of strain. I had a
feeling that if any more piled up on him he might fall apart.
The man to tell, the man who can take it, I think, is
Geoffrey Wingstead.'

'He'll be down here tomorrow, to hear your report to the
board, Neil. Then he's flying out to Nyala.'

'Good. I want time with him. In fact, I'd like to fix it so
that we can go out together. Why the hell did you pick this
shoestring operation in the first place?'

Geddes said, 'They could do very well. Geoff has a good
head on his shoulders, and a first-rate team. And their figures
tally: they've cut it to the bone, admittedly, but there's still a
lot in it for them. They're building more rigs, did you know
that?'

'One more rig. I met the guy who developed their prototype. He seems fast enough on the ball, but what happens if
something goes wrong with Number One? Collapse of the
entire operation, for God's sake.'

'Wingstead has a second rig on lease from a Dutch company which he's planning to send out there. He and Kemp
and Hammond have been pushing big loads all their lives.
They won't let us down.'

He thought for a moment, then said, 'I'll arrange things
so that you go back out with Wingstead, certainly. In fact,
I'll give both of you the company jet. It's at Stansted right
now, and you can get away tomorrow, after the briefing.'

It was the speed of his arrangements that made me
realize that the prickle at the back of his mind had turned
into a case of raging hives.

FIVE

Port Luard was cooler when we got back – about one degree cooler – but the temperature went down sharply when I walked into John Sutherland's office. It was evident that he'd been hoping I'd disappear into the wide blue yonder never to return, and when he saw me you could have packaged him and used him as a refrigeration plant.

I held up a hand placatingly and said, 'Not my idea to turn around so fast – blame Mister Geddes. For my money you could have this damn place to yourself.'

'You're welcome, of course,' he said insincerely.

'Let's not kid each other,' I said as I took a can of beer from his office refrigerator. 'I'm as welcome as acne on a guy's first date. What's new?'

My friendly approach bothered him. He hadn't known when to expect me and he'd been braced for trouble when he did. 'Nothing, really. Everything has been going along smoothly.' His tone still implied that it would cease to do so forthwith.

It was time to sweet-talk him. 'Geddes is very pleased about the way you're handling things here, by the way.'

For a moment he looked almost alarmed. The idea of Geddes being pleased about anything was odd enough to frighten anybody. Praise from him was so rare as to be nonexistent, and I didn't let Sutherland know that it had

originated with me. 'When you left you implied that all
was far from well,' Sutherland said. 'You never said what
the trouble was.'

'You should know. You started it at the meeting in
London.'

'I did?' I saw him chasing around in his mind for exactly
what he'd said at that meeting.

'About the rumours of tribal unrest,' I said helpfully. 'Got
a glass? I like to see my beer when I'm drinking it.'

'Of course.' He found one for me.

'You were right on the mark there. Of course we know you
can't run the Bir Oassa job and chase down things like that at
the same time. That was Shelford's job, and he let us all down.
So someone had to look into it and Geddes picked me – and
you proved right all down the line.' I didn't give him time to
think too deeply about that one. I leaned forward and said as
winningly as I knew how, 'I'm sorry if I was a little abrupt just
before I left. That goddamn phoney victory parade left me a
bit frazzled, and I'm not used to coping with this lot the way
you are. If I said anything out of line I apologize.'

He was disarmed, as he was intended to be. 'That's quite
all right. As a matter of fact I've been thinking about what
you said – about the need for contingency plans. I've been
working on a scheme.'

'Great.' I said expansively. 'Like to have a look at it sometime. Right now I have a lot else to do. I brought someone
out with me that I'd like you to meet. Geoff Wingstead, the
owner of Wyvern Haulage. Can you join us for dinner?'

'You should have told me. He'll need accommodation.'

'It's fixed, John. He's at the hotel.' I gently let him know
that he wasn't the only one who could pull strings. 'He's
going to go up and join the rig in a day or so, but I'll be
around town for a bit longer before I pay them a visit. I'd
like a full briefing from you. I'm willing to bet you've got a
whole lot to tell me.'

'Yes, I have. Some of it is quite hot stuff, Neil.'

Sutherland was all buddies again, and bursting to tell me what I already knew, which is just what I'd been hoping for. I didn't think I'd told him too many lies. The truth is only one way of looking at a situation; there are many others.

For the next few days I nursed Sutherland along. His contingency plan was good, if lacking in imagination, but it improved as we went along. That was his main trouble, a lack of imagination, the inability to ask, 'What if . . .?' I am not knocking him particularly; he was good at his job but incapable of expanding the job around him, and without that knack he wasn't going to go much further. I have a theory about men like Sutherland: they're like silly putty. If you take silly putty and hit it with a hammer it will shatter, but handle it gently and it can be moulded into any shape. The trouble is that if you then leave it it will slump and flow back into its original shape. That's why the manipulators, like me, get three times Sutherland's pay.

Not that I regarded myself as the Great Svengali, because I've been manipulated myself in my time by men like Geddes, the arch manipulator, so God knows what he's worth before taxes.

Anyway I gentled Sutherland along. I took him to the Luard Club (he had never thought about joining) and let him loose among the old sweaty types who were primed to drop him nuggets of information. Sure enough, he'd come back and tell me something else that I already knew. 'Gee, is that so?' I'd say. 'That could put a crimp in your contingency plans, couldn't it?'

He would smile confidently. 'It's nothing I can't fix,' he would say, and he'd be right. He wasn't a bad fixer. At the end of ten days he was all squared away, convinced that it was all his own idea, and much clearer in his head about the politics around him. He also had another conviction – that this chap Mannix wasn't so bad, after all, for an American that is. I didn't disillusion him.

What slightly disconcerted me was Geoff Wingstead. He stayed in Port Luard for a few days, doing his own homework before flying up to join the rig, and in that short time he also put two and two together, on his own, and remarkably accurately. What's more, I swear that he saw clear through my little ploy with Sutherland and to my chagrin I got the impression that he approved. I didn't like people to be that bright. He impressed me more all the time and I found that he got the same sense of enjoyment out of the business that I did, and that's a rare and precious trait. He was young, smart and energetic, and I wasn't sorry that he was in another company to my own: he'd make damned tough opposition. And I liked him too much for rivalry.

Getting news back from the rig was difficult. Local telephone lines were often out of action and our own cab radios had a limited range. One morning, though, John Sutherland had managed a long call and had news for me as soon as I came into the office.

'They're on schedule. I've put it on the map. Look here. They're halfway in time but less than halfway in distance. And they'll slow up more now because they have to climb to the plateau. Oh, and Geoff Wingstead is flying back here today. He has to arrange to send a water bowser up there. Seems the local water is often too contaminated to use for drinking.'

I could have told Geoff that before he started and was a little surprised that he had only just found out. I decided that I wanted to go and see the rig for myself, in case there was any other little detail he didn't know about. I was about due to go back to London soon, and rather wanted one more fling upcountry before doing so.

I studied the map. 'This town – Kodowa – just ahead of them. It's got an airstrip. Any chance of renting a car there?'

He grimaced. 'I shouldn't think so. It's only a small place, about five thousand population. And if you could get a car there it would be pretty well clapped out. The airstrip is privately owned; it belongs to a planters' cooperative.'

I measured distances. 'Maybe we should have a company car stationed there, and arrange for use of the airstrip. It would help if anyone has to get up there in a hurry. See to it, would you, John? As it is I'll have to fly to Lasulu and then drive nearly three hundred miles. I'll arrange to take one of Wyvern's spare chaps up with me to spell me driving.' I knew better than to set out on my own in that bleak territory.

I saw Wingstead on his return and we had a long talk. He was reasonably happy about his company's progress and the logistics seemed to be working out well, but he was as wary as a cat about the whole political situation. As I said, he was remarkably acute in his judgements. I asked if he was going back to England.

'Not yet, at any rate,' he told me. 'I have some work to do here, then I'll rejoin the rig for a bit. I like to keep a finger on the pulse. Listen, Neil . . .'

'You want something?' I prompted.

'I want you to put Basil Kemp completely in the picture. He doesn't know the score and he may not take it from me. Why should he? We're both new to Africa, new to this country, and he'll brush off my fears, but he'll accept your opinion. He needs to know more about the political situation.'

'I wouldn't call Kemp exactly complacent myself,' I said.

'That's the trouble. He's got so many worries of his own that he hasn't room for mine – unless he can be convinced they're real. You're going up there, I'm told. Lay it on the line for him, please.'

I agreed, not without a sense of relief. It was high time that Kemp knew the wider issues involved, and nothing I had heard lately had made me any less uneasy about the

possible future of Nyala. The next morning I picked up
Ritchie Thorpe, one of the spare Wyvern men, and Max
Otterman flew us up to Lasulu. From there we drove inland
along that fantastic road that thrust into the heart of the
country. After Ofanwe had it built it had been underused
and neglected. The thick rain forest had encroached and the
huge trees had thrust their roots under it to burst the concrete. Then came the oil strike and now it was undergoing
a fair amount of punishment, eroding from above to meet
the erosion from below. Not that the traffic was heavy in the
sense of being dense, but some damn big loads were
being taken north. Our transformer was merely the biggest
so far.

The traffic varied from bullock carts with nerve-wracking
squeaking wheels plodding stolidly along at two miles an
hour to sixty-tonners and even larger vehicles. Once we
came across a real giant parked by the roadside while the
crew ate a meal. It carried an oil drilling tower lying on its
side, whole and entire, and must have weighed upwards of
a hundred tons.

I pulled in and had a chat with the head driver. He was a
Russian and very proud of his rig. We talked in a mixture of
bad English and worse French, and he demonstrated what
it would do, a function new to me but not to Ritchie.
Apparently it was designed to move in soft sand and he
could inflate and deflate all the tyres by pushing buttons
while in the cab. When travelling over soft sand the tyres
would be deflated to spread the load. He told me that in
these conditions the fully loaded rig would put less pressure
on the ground per square inch than the foot of a camel. I
was properly appreciative and we parted amicably.

It was a long drive and we were both tired and dusty
when we finally came across Wyvern Transport. By now we
had passed through the rainforest belt and were entering
scrubland, the trees giving way to harsh thorny bush and

the ground strewn with withering gourd-carrying vines. Dust was everywhere, and the road edges were almost totally rotted away; we slalomed endlessly to avoid the potholes. We found the rig parked by the roadside and the hydraulics had been let down so that the load rested on the ground instead of being taken up on the bogie springs. They had obviously stopped for the night, which surprised us – night driving at their speed was quite feasible and much cooler and normally less of a strain than daywork.

I pulled up and looked around. Of the men I could see I knew only one by name: McGrath, the big Irishman who had driven the lead tractor in the parade through Port Luard. Ritchie got out of the car, thanked me for the ride up and went off to join his mates. I called McGrath over.

'Hi there. Mister Kemp around?' I asked.

McGrath pointed up the road. 'There's a bridge about a mile along. He's having a look at it.'

'Thanks.' I drove along slowly and thought the convoy looked like an oversized gypsy camp. The commissary wagon was opened up and a couple of men were cooking. A little further along were the other trucks, including the big one with the airlift gear, and then the camp of Sadiq and his men, very neat and military. Sadiq got to his feet as I drove up but with the light fading I indicated that I would see him on my return from the bridge, and went on past. I saw and approved of the fact that the fuel truck was parked on its own, well away from all the others, but made a mental note to check that it was guarded.

The road had been blasted through a low ridge here and beyond the ridge was a river. I pulled off the road short of the bridge and parked next to Kemp's Land Rover. I could see him in the distance, walking halfway across the bridge, accompanied by Hammond. I waved and they quickened their pace.

When they came up to me I thought that Kemp looked better than he had done in Port Luard. The lines of his face fell in more placid folds and he wasn't so tired. Obviously he was happier actually doing a job than arranging for it to be done, Ben Hammond, by his side, hadn't changed at all. He still had his gamecock strut and his air of defensive wariness. Some little men feel that they have a lot to be wary about.

'Hello there,' I said. 'I just thought I'd drop by for a coffee.'

Kemp grinned and shook my hand, but Hammond said, 'Checking up on us, are you? Mr Wingstead's just been up here, you know.'

Clearly he was saying that where Geoff had gone, no man need go after. His voice told me that he thought a lot of his boss, which pleased me. I sometimes wondered if I was as transparent to other people as they appeared to me.

I jerked my thumb back up the road. 'Sure I'm checking. Do you know what that transporter is worth? Landed at Port Luard it was declared at one million, forty-two thousand, nine hundred and eighty-six pounds and five pence.' I grinned to take the sting out of it. 'I still haven't figured out what the five pence is for. If it was yours, wouldn't you want to know if it was in safe hands?'

Hammond looked startled. Kemp said, 'Take it easy, Ben,' which I thought was a nice reversal of roles. 'Mister Mannix is quite entitled to come up here, and he's welcome any time. Sorry if Ben's a bit edgy – we have problems.'

I wasn't a bit surprised to hear it, but dutifully asked what they were. Kemp held out a lump of concrete. 'I kicked that out with the toe of my boot. I didn't have to kick hard, either.'

I took the lump and rubbed it with my thumb. It was friable and bits dropped off. 'I'd say that someone used a mite too much sand in the mix.' I pointed to the bridge. 'Milner said the bridges would prove dicey. Is this the worst?'

Kemp shook his head. 'Oh no. This isn't too bad at all. The really tricky one is way up there, miles ahead yet. This one is run-of-the-mill. Just a little shaky, that's all.' He and Hammond exchanged rueful smiles. 'It's too risky to move in the dark and there's only half an hour of daylight left. We'll take her across at first light. Anyway it will be our first full night stop for nearly a week, good for the lads.'

I said, 'I came just in time to see the fun. Mind if I stick around? I brought Ritchie Thorpe up with me.'

'Good show. We can use him. We'll rig a couple of extra bunks after we've eaten,' Kemp said, climbing into his car. Hammond joined him and I followed them back to camp, but stopped to say a few polite and appreciative things to Sadiq on the way. He assured me that any labour necessary for strengthening the bridge would be found very quickly, and I left him, marvelling at the self-assurance that a uniform lends a man.

My mind was in top gear as I thought about the bridge. Someone had made a bit of extra profit on the contract when it was built, and it was going to be interesting to watch the passage of the rig the next day. From a safe vantage point, of course. But if this bridge was run of the mill, what the hell was the tricky one going to be like?

I laid my plate on one side. 'Good chow.'

There was humour in Kemp's voice. 'Not *haute cuisine*, but we survive.'

Two of the tractors were parked side by side and we sat under an awning rigged between them. Kemp was certainly more relaxed and I wondered how best to take advantage of the fact. We weren't alone – several of the others had joined us. Obviously Kemp didn't believe in putting a distance between himself and the men, but I wanted to get him alone for a chat. I leaned over and dropped my voice. 'If you can find a couple of glasses, how about a Scotch?'

He too spoke quietly. 'No thanks. I prefer to stick to the camp rules, if you don't mind. We could settle for another beer, though.' As he said this he got up and disappeared into the night, returning in a moment with a four-pack of beer. I rose and took his arm, steering him away from the makeshift dining room. 'A word with you, Basil,' I said. 'Where can we go?'

Presently we were settled in a quiet corner with our backs up against two huge tyres, the blessedly cool night wind on our faces, and an ice cold can of beer apiece.

'You've got it made,' I said, savouring the quietness. 'How do you keep this cold?'

He laughed. 'There's a diesel generator on the rig for the lights. If you're already carrying three hundred tons a ten cubic foot refrigerator isn't much more of a burden. We have a twenty cubic foot deepfreeze, too. The cook says we're having lobster tails tomorrow night.'

'I forget the scale of this thing.'

'You wouldn't if you were pushing it around.'

I drank some beer. It was cold and pleasantly bitter. A little casual conversation was in order first. 'You married?'

'Oh yes. I have a wife and two kids in England: six and four, both boys. How about you?'

'I tried, but it didn't take. A man in my job doesn't spend enough time at home to hang his hat up, and women don't like that as a rule.'

'Yes, indeed.' His voice showed that he felt the same way.

'How long since you were home?'

'About two months. I've been surveying this damned road. I reckon it'll be a while before I'm home again.'

I said, 'Up at Bir Oassa the government is just finishing a big concrete airstrip, big enough for heavy transports. It's just about to go into operation, we've been told, though we're not sure what "just about" means.'

Kemp said, 'No parades up there though, with no-one to see them.'

'Right. Well, when it's ready we'll be flying in the expensive bits that aren't too heavy, like the turbine shafts. There'll be quite a lot of coming and going and it wouldn't surprise me if there wasn't room for a guy to take a trip back to England once in a while. That applies to your crew as well, of course.'

'That's splendid – we'd all appreciate it. I'll have to make up a roster.' He was already perking up at the thought, and I marvelled all over again at what domesticity does for some men.

'How did you get into heavy haulage?' I asked him.

'It wasn't so much getting into it as being born into it. My old man was always on the heavy side – he pushed around tank transporters in the war – and I'm a chip off the old block.'

'Ever handled anything as big as this before?'

'Oh yes. I've done one a bit bigger than this for the Central Electricity Generating Board at home. Of course, conditions weren't exactly the same, but just as difficult, in their way. There are more buildings to knock corners off in Britain, and a whole lot more bureaucracy to get around too.'

'Was that with Wyvern?'

'No, before its time.' He knew I was pumping him gently and didn't seem to mind. 'I was with one of the big outfits then.'

I drank the last of my beer. 'You really *are* Wyvern Transport, aren't you?'

'Yes. Together with Ben and Geoff Wingstead. We'd all been in the business before, and when we got together it seemed like a good idea. Sometimes I'm not so sure.' I saw him wave his hand, a dim gesture in the darkness, and heard the slight bitter touch in his voice. I already knew that financially this was a knife edge operation and I didn't want to spoil Kemp's mood by raking up any economic dirt, but I felt I could get a few more answers out of him without pressing too hard.

He carried on without my prompting him. 'We each came into a little money, one way or another – mine was an inheritance. Ben had ideas for modifying current rigs and Geoff and Ben had worked together before. Geoff's our real ideas man: not only the financial end, he's into every angle. But if we hadn't landed this contract I don't think we'd have got off the ground.'

I had had my own doubts about giving this enormously expensive and difficult job to a firm new to the market but I didn't want to express them to Kemp. He went on, though, filling me in with details; the costly airlift gear, which they only realized was necessary after their tender had been accepted, was rented from the CEGB. Two of the tractors were secondhand, the others bought on the never-never and as yet not fully paid for. The tender, already as low as possible to enable them to land the job, was now seen to be quite unrealistic and they did not expect to make anything out of the Nyalan operation: but they had every hope that a successful completion would bring other contracts to their doorstep. It was midsummer madness, and it might work.

I realized that it was late, and that I hadn't yet broached the subject of security or danger. Too late in fact to go into the whole thing now, but I could at least pave the way; Kemp's practical problems had rendered him oblivious to possible outside interference, and in any case he was used to working in countries where political problems were solved over the negotiation table, and not by armies.

'How are you getting on with Captain Sadiq?' I asked.

'No trouble. In fact he's quite helpful. I'll make him into a good road boss yet.'

'Had any problems so far? Apart from the road itself, that is.'

'Just the usual thing of crowd control through the villages. Sadiq's very good at that. He's over-efficient really;
puts out a guard every time we stop, scouts ahead, very
busy playing soldiers generally.' He gestured into the night.
'If you walk down there you'll stand a chance of getting a
bullet in you unless you speak up loud and clear. I've had to
warn my chaps about it. Road transport in the UK was
never like this.'

'He's not really here just as a traffic cop,' I said. 'He is
guarding you, or, more to the point, he's guarding the rig
and the convoy. There's always a possibility that someone might try a bit of sabotage. So you keep your eyes
open too, and pass that word down the line to your men,
Basil.'

I knew he was staring at me. 'Who'd want to sabotage
us? No-one else wanted this job.'

He was still thinking in terms of commercial rivalry and
I was mildly alarmed at his political naivety. 'Look, Basil,
I'd like to put you in the picture, and I think Ben
Hammond too. But it's late and you've a major job to do in
the morning. It's nothing urgent, nothing to fret about.
Next time we stop for a break I'll get you both up to date,
OK?'

'Right you are, if you say so.' I sensed his mind slipping
away; mention of the next day's task had set him thinking
about it, and I knew I should leave him alone to marshall
his ideas.

'I'll say good night,' I said. 'I guess you'll want to think
about your next obstacle course.'

He stood up. 'We'll cross that bridge when we come to it,'
he said sardonically. 'Sleep well. Your bunk is rigged over
there, by the way. I sleep on top of one of the tractors: less
risk of snakes that way.'

'I know how you feel,' I grinned. 'But with me it's scor-
pions. Good night.'

I strolled in the night air over to the rig and stood looking up at the great slab of the transformer. Over one million pounds' worth of material was being trundled precariously through Africa by a company on the verge of going bankrupt, with a civil war possibly about to erupt in its path, and what the hell was I going to do about it?

I decided to sleep on it.

SIX

Everybody was up early in the dim light before dawn. I breakfasted with the crew, standing in line at the chuck wagon. The food was washed down with hot, strong, sweet, milky tea which tasted coppery and which they called 'gunfire'.

'Why gunfire?' I queried.

'That's what they call it in the British Army. The Army fights on this stuff,' I was told.

I grinned. 'If they could stomach this they'd be ready to face anything.'

'It's better than bloody Coca-Cola,' someone said, and everybody laughed.

After breakfast there was a great deal of activity. I went in search of Captain Sadiq, and found him sitting in his command car wearing earphones. He saw me approaching and held up his hand in warning as he scribbled on a notepad he held on his knee. Then he called to a sergeant who came trotting over. Sadiq took off the earphones and handed them to the sergeant. Only then did he come around the car to meet me. 'Good morning, Mister Mannix.'

'Good morning, Captain. Sorry I was in a hurry last night. Any problems? Mister Kemp says he is very gratified by all your help.'

He smiled at that. 'No problems at all, sir,' he said, but it was a brushoff. He looked deeply concerned and abstracted.

The sun was just rising as I heard an engine start up. It had a deep roar and sounded like one of the big tractors. A small crowd of curious onlookers had materialized from nowhere and were being pushed back by Sadiq's men. Small boys skylarked about and evaded the soldiers with ease.

I indicated the crowd. 'These people are up early. Do you have much of this kind of thing?'

'The people, they are always with us.' I wondered for a moment whether that was an intended parody of a biblical quotation. He pointed. 'These come from a small village about a mile over there. They are nothing.'

One of the military trucks fired up its engine and I watched it pull out. Mounted on the back was a recoilless gun. The range of those things wasn't particularly great but they packed a hell of a wallop and could be fired from a light vehicle. One thing you had to remember was not to stand behind when they fired. 'Nice piece of artillery,' I said. 'I haven't seen one of those since Korea.'

Sadiq smiled noncommittally. I sensed that he was itching for me to be off.

'Is there anything I can do for you, Captain?' I wanted to see how far he'd let me go before he pulled rank on me, or tried to. But outside influences had their say instead.

'Nothing at all, Mister Man . . .'

His words were drowned as three jets streaked overhead, making us both start. They were flying low, and disappeared to the south. I turned to Sadiq and raised my eyebrows. 'We are quite close to a military airfield,' he said. His attempt at a nonchalant attitude fooled neither of us.

I thanked him and walked away, then turned my head to see him already putting on the earphones again. Maybe he liked hi-fi.

I wanted to relieve myself so I pushed a little way into the bushes by the side of the road. It was quite thick but I came across a sort of channel in the undergrowth and was able to push along quite easily. What bothered me was that it was quite straight. Then I damn near fell down a hole, teetered for a moment on the edge and recovered by catching hold of a branch and running a thorn into my hand. I cursed, then looked at the hole with interest. It had been newly dug and at the bottom there were marks in the soil. The spoil from the hole had been piled up round it and then covered with scrub. If you had to have a hole at all this was one of the more interesting types, one I hadn't seen since I was in the army.

I dropped into it and looked back the way I had come. The channel I had come along was clearly defined right up to the road edge, where it was screened by the lightest of cover, easy to see through from the shady side. Captain Sadiq was clearly on the ball, a real professional. This was a concealed machine gun pit with a prepared field of fire which commanded a half mile length of road. Out of curiosity I drummed up what I had been taught when Uncle Sam tried to make me into a soldier, and figured out where Sadiq would have put his mortars. After a few minutes of plunging about in the scrub I came across the emplacement and stared at it thoughtfully. I didn't know if it was such a good idea because it made out Sadiq to be a textbook soldier, working to the rules. That's all right providing the guys on the other side haven't read the same book.

When I got back to the rig Kemp hailed me with some impatience, shading into curiosity. I was dusty and scratched, and already sweating.

'We're ready to move,' he said. 'Ride along with anyone you like.' Except me, his tone added, and I could hardly blame him. He'd have enough to do without answering questions from visiting firemen.

'Just a minute,' I said. 'Captain Sadiq appears to be cemented to his radio. How long has that been going on?'

Kemp shrugged. 'I don't know – all morning. He does his job and I do mine.'

'Don't you sense that he's uneasy?' I asked with concern. I'd seldom met a man so oblivious to outside events as Kemp. 'By the way, what did you make of those planes?'

'They say there's an airfield somewhere about. Maybe they were just curious about the convoy. Look, Neil, I have to get on. I'll talk to you later.' He waved to Hammond, who drove up in the Land Rover, and they were off in a small cloud of dust. During my absence the rig and most of the rest of the convoy including my car had moved off, so I swung myself on to the chuck wagon and hitched a lift down to where the others were grouped around the approach to the bridge.

The scene was fascinating. Kemp was using only one tractor to take the rig across the bridge and it was already in place. Another tractor had crossed and waited on the far side. The rig was fitted with its airlift skirts and looked rather funny; they seemed to take away the brute masculinity of the thing and gave it the incongruous air of one of those beskirted Greek soldiers you see on guard in Athens. Though no doubt Kemp, who had been outraged by the bunting in Port Luard, saw nothing odd about it. Behind it was the airlift truck to which it was connected by a flexible umbilicus. Through this the air was rammed by four big engines.

If Kemp was nervous he didn't show it. He was telling the crew what they were to do and how they were to do it. He was sparing of words but most of this team had worked with him before and needed little instruction. He put the Irishman, McGrath, in the tractor and Ben Hammond and himself on the rig.

'No-one else on the bridge until we're clear across,' he said. 'And keep that air moving. We don't want to fall down on our bums halfway across.' It brought a slight ripple of amusement.

McGrath revved the tractor engine and there came a roar from the airlift truck as one after another the engines started up. A cloud of dust erupted from beneath the rig as the loose debris was blown aside by the air blast. I knew enough not to expect the rig to become airborne, but it did seem to rise very slightly on its springs as the weight was taken up from the axles and spread evenly.

The noise was tremendous and I saw Kemp with a micro phone close to his lips. The tractor moved, at first infinitesimally, so that one wasn't sure that it had moved at all, then a very little faster. McGrath was a superb driver: I doubt that many people could have judged so nicely the exact pressure to put on an accelerator in order to shift a four hundred and thirty-ton load so smoothly.

The front wheels of the tractor crossed the bitumen expan sion joint which marked the beginning of the bridge proper. Kemp moved quickly from one side of the control cab to the other, looking forwards and backwards to check that the rig and the tractor were in perfect alignment. Behind the rig the air umbilicus lengthened as it was paid out.

I estimated that the rig was moving at most a quarter of a mile an hour; it took about six minutes before the whole length of the combine was entirely supported by the bridge. If you were nervous now was the time to hold your breath. I held mine.

Then above the uproar of the airlift engines and the rush of air I heard a faint yell, and someone tugged at my arm. I turned and saw Sadiq's sergeant, his face distorted as he shouted something at me. At my lack of comprehension he pulled my arm again and pointed back along the road leading up to the bridge. I turned and saw a column of vehicles coming up: jeeps and motorcycles at the front and the looming, ugly snouted silhouettes of tanks behind them.

I ran towards them with the sergeant alongside me. As soon as the volume of noise dropped enough to speak and be heard I pulled up and snapped, 'Where's Captain Sadiq?'

The sergeant threw out his hand towards the river. 'On the other side.'

'Christ! Go and get him – fast!'

The sergeant looked dismayed. 'How do I do that?'

'On your feet. Run! There's room for you to pass. Wait. If Mister Kemp, if the road boss sees you he may stop. You signal him to carry on. Like this.' I windmilled my arm, pointing forwards, and saw that the sergeant understood what to do. 'Now go!'

He turned and ran back towards the bridge and I carried on towards the armoured column, my heartbeat noticeably quicker. It's not given to many men to stop an army single-handed, but I'd been given so little time to think out the implications that I acted without much reflection. A leading command car braked to a stop, enveloping me in a cloud of dust, and an angry voice shouted something in Kinguru, or so I supposed. I waved the dust away and shouted, 'I'm sorry, I don't understand. Do you speak English, please?'

An officer stood up in the passenger seat of the open command car, leaning over the windscreen and looking down at the bridge with unbelieving eyes. When he turned his gaze on me his eyes were like flint and his voice gravelly. 'Yes, I speak English. What is going on there?'

'We're taking that load across the bridge. It's going up to the new power plant at Bir Oassa.'

'Get it off there!' he shouted.

'That's what we're doing,' I said equably.

'I mean move it faster,' he shouted again, convulsed with anger. 'We have no time to waste.'

'It's moving as fast as is safe.'

'Safe!' He looked back at his column, then again at me. 'You don't know what that word means, Mister Englishman.' He shouted a string of orders to a motorcyclist who wheeled his bike around and went roaring back up the road. I watched it stop at the leading tank and saw the tank commander lean down from the turret to listen. The tank cut out of the column and ground to a rattling halt alongside the command car. The officer shouted a command and I saw the turret swivel and the barrel of the gun drop slightly.

I was sweating harder now, and drier in the mouth, and I wished to God Sadiq would show up. I looked round hopefully, but of Sadiq or any of his military crowd there was no sign.

'Hey, Captain,' I shouted, giving him as flattering a rank as possible without knowing for sure. 'What are you doing? There are four hundred and thirty tons on that bridge.'

His face cracked into a sarcastic smile. 'I will get it to go faster.'

I sized him up. He was obviously immune to reason, so I would have to counter his threat with a bigger one. I said, 'Captain, if you put a shell even near that rig you'll be likely to lose it and the whole bridge with it. It's worth a few million pounds to your government and Major General Kigonde is personally handling its wellbeing. And I don't think he'd like you to wreck the bridge either.'

He looked baffled and then came back with a countermove of his own. 'I will not fire on the bridge. I will fire into the trucks and the men on the river bank if that thing does not go faster. You tell them.'

His arm was upraised and I knew that if he dropped it fast the tank would fire. I said, 'You mean the airlift truck? That would make things much worse.'

'Airlift? What is that?'

'A kind of hovercraft.' Would he understand that? No matter: at least I could try to blind him with science. 'It is run by the truck just off the bridge and it's the only way of getting the rig across the bridge. You damage it, or do anything to stop our operation and you'll be stuck here permanently instead of only for the next half-hour. Unless you've brought your own bridge with you.'

His arm wavered uncertainly and I pressed on. 'I think you had better consult your superior about this. If you lose the bridge you won't be popular.'

He glared at me and then at last his arm came down, slowly. He dropped into his seat and grabbed the microphone in front of him. The little hairs on the back of my neck lay down as I turned to see what was happening at the bridge.

Sadiq's troops had materialized behind our men and trucks, but in a loose and nonbelligerent order. They were after all not supposed to protect us from their own side, assuming these troops were still their own side. Beyond them the rig still inched its way painfully along as Kemp stuck to the job in hand. Sadiq was standing on the running board of one of his own trucks and it roared up the road towards us, smothering me in yet another dust bath on its arrival. Before it had stopped Sadiq had jumped down and made straight for the officer in the command car. Captain Whoosit was spoiling for a fight and Sadiq didn't outrank him, but before a row could develop another command car arrived and from it stepped a man who could only have been the battalion commander, complete with Sam Browne belt in the British tradition.

He looked bleakly around him, studied the bridge through binoculars, and then conferred with Sadiq, who was standing rigidly to attention. At one point Mr Big asked a question and jabbed a finger towards me. I approached uninvited as Sadiq was beginning to explain my presence. 'I can speak for myself, Captain. Good morning, Colonel. I'm Neil Mannix, representing British Electric. That's our transformer down there.'

He asked no further questions. I thought that he already knew all about us, as any good commander should. 'You must get it out of our way quickly,' he said.

'It's moving all the time,' I said reasonably.

The Colonel asked, 'Does the driver have a radio?'

'Yes, sir,' said Sadiq. A pity; I might have said the opposite.

'Talk to him. Tell him to move faster. Use my radio.' He indicated his own command car, but as Sadiq moved to comply I said, 'Let me talk to him, Colonel. He will accept my instructions easier.'

'Very well, Mister Mannix. I will listen.'

I waited while Sadiq got on net with Kemp and then took the mike. 'Basil, this is Neil Mannix here. Do you read me? Over.'

'Yes, Neil. What's going on back there? Over.'

'Listen and don't speak. There is an army detachment here which needs to use the bridge urgently. I assume you are moving at designated speed? It will be necessary for you to increase to the –'

The Colonel interrupted me. 'What is this designated speed?'

'Hold it. Over. It works out about a mile an hour, Colonel.' I ignored his stricken face and went on into the mike, 'Basil? Increase if necessary. How long do you estimate as of now? Over.'

'Fifteen minutes, perhaps twenty. Over.'

Taking his cue, Kemp was giving answers only. He could pick up clues pretty smartly. There was no such thing as a designated speed and Kemp knew this. I went on, 'Get it down to no more than fifteen, ten if possible. Over.'

I was praying for an interruption and for once I got lucky. Sadiq's military unit had got restless and several vehicles, including those carrying the guns, started down the road towards us. The commander turned alertly to see what was going on. In that moment, with nobody listening except the

Colonel's driver, I said hastily, 'Basil, if you don't get the hell off that bridge we'll have shells coming up our ass. These guys are trigger-happy. Go man go. Acknowledge formally. Over.'

It was all I had time for, but it was enough. The Colonel was back, looking more irritated than ever, just in time to hear Kemp's voice saying, 'Message understood, Neil, and will be acted upon. Going faster. Out.'

I handed the microphone back to the driver and said, 'That's it, Colonel. He'll do the best he can. You should be on your way in a quarter of an hour. I'll arrange to hold all the rest of our stuff until you're through.'

The muscles round his jaw bunched up and he nodded stiffly, casting a quick glance skywards, and then began snapping orders to his Captain who got busy on the radio. All down the line there was a stir of activity, and with interest and some alarm I noted that machine guns were sprouting from turret tops, all pointing skywards. I remembered the jets that had gone over and wondered what Air Chief Marshal Semangala, or whatever his title might be, was doing just at that moment. Away in the distance I saw the four barrels of a 20-millimetre AA quickfirer rotating.

I said, 'Has a war broken out, Colonel?'

'Exercises,' he said briefly. 'You may go now.'

It was a curt dismissal but I wasn't sorry to get it. I joined Sadiq and we drove back to our lines. I passed the word for everyone to remain clear of the bridge and to let the army through, once the rig was safely on the other side and uncoupled from its umbilicus. Everyone was bursting with curiosity and the tension caused by the rig's river passage had noticeably increased, which wasn't surprising. But I had little to tell them and presently everyone fell silent, just watching and waiting.

Seventeen minutes later the rig was clear of the bridge and safe on firm land again. Things are comparative, and after the bridge even the most friable and potholed road would seem like a doddle, at least for a time. The airlift truck was uncoupled, its hoses stowed, and it was moved back from the bridge approach. The Colonel came towards us in his staff car.

'Thank you,' he said abruptly. Graciousness was not a quality often found out here and this was the nearest we'd get to it. He spoke into the mike and his leading motorcycles roared off across the bridge.

I said, 'Mind a bit of advice, Colonel?'

He speared mc with dark eyes. 'Well?'

'That bridge really isn't too safe: it's been cheaply made. I'd space out my tanks crossing it, if I were you.'

He nodded shortly. 'Thank you, Mister Mannix.'

'My pleasure.'

He peered at me uncertainly and then signed to his driver to go ahead. As he drove off already talking into his microphone, I sighed for the days of the mythical bush telegraph. The battalion that followed was mostly armour, tanks and a battery of self-propelling guns, with a few truckloads of infantry for close defence work. Even as small a unit as a battalion takes up an awful lot of road space and it was twenty dusty minutes before the rearguard had crossed. I watched them climb the hill on the other side of the river and then said, 'Right, you guys. Let's go and join Mister Kemp, shall we?'

As the convoy started I turned to Sadiq. 'And then, Captain, perhaps you'll be good enough to find out from your driver, and then tell me, what the hell is going on. I know you'll have had him radio-eavesdropping right from the beginning.'

And then for some reason we both glanced quickly skywards.

SEVEN

Both Kemp and Hammond looked shaken. I couldn't blame them; nobody likes being at the wrong end of a big gun. Hammond, as could be expected, was belligerent about it. 'This wasn't allowed for in any contract, Mannix. What are you going to do about it?'

'It's hardly Neil's fault,' said Kemp.

'I am going to do something about it,' I said. 'Something I should have done before this. I'm going to put you two properly in the picture.'

'Was that what you said you wanted to talk about?' Kemp asked, giving me a chance to cover myself. I nodded. 'Overdue,' I said. 'But first I want another word with Captain Sadiq. Want to come along?'

Kemp and Hammond conferred briefly, then Kemp said, 'Yes. Everyone's a bit jittery still. We shouldn't move on until we know the situation. I wish to God Geoff was here.'

'We'll try to contact him,' I said. I didn't see what he could do but if his presence was enough to calm his partners' fears it would be a big bonus. We found Sadiq, as expected, glued to his earphones in his car, and according to the usual ritual he handed them to his sergeant before joining us. I said, 'All right, Captain. What's the story?'

His voice was neutral. 'You heard Colonel Hussein. The Army is holding manoeuvres.'

I stared at him. 'Don't give us that crap. No army captain is going to threaten to shell a civilian vehicle during war games. He'd be scrubbing latrines next. And that was damn nearly more than a threat.'

Kemp said, 'You'll have to do better than that, Captain.'

I jerked my thumb towards the sergeant. 'You've been monitoring the wavebands pretty constantly. What have you heard?'

Sadiq shrugged. 'It's difficult to tell. There's a lot of traffic, mostly in code. There seems to be much troop movement. Also a lot of aircraft activity.'

'Like those jets this morning.' I had plenty of ideas about that but I wanted his version. 'What do you *think* is happening?'

'I don't know. I wish I did,' he said.

'What does Radio Nyala have to say?'

'Nothing unusual. Much music.' Kemp and I glanced at one another. 'There was a little about us, news of the new power plant at Bir Oassa. And other talk as well . . .'

He was getting closer to the real thing. His voice had become very careful. I said nothing but waited, out-silencing him. He went on at last, 'There was other news from Bir Oassa. The new airfield was opened today, with a ceremony.'

I gaped at him. 'But it isn't meant to be ready for a couple of months at least. Who opened it?'

'The Air Chief Marshall.'

My first irrelevant thought was that I'd guessed his title right after all. Then I said, 'Semangala. Right?'

'Yes, sir.'

Kemp said, 'Isn't he the chap who was in France when we left Port Luard? The only military bigwig who couldn't attend?'

'Yes,' I said grimly. 'And what's more, he's meant to be in Switzerland right now. He left two days ago with his family. I saw him at the airport when I left for Lasulu. He got all the usual military sendoff, except that he was in civvies. Are you *sure*, Sadiq?'

'Yes, sir.' His eyes were sad now. 'He made a speech.'

'Who exactly is Semangala?' asked Hammond. 'Is he that important?'

'He's the Air Force boss and right now he's the most important man in Nyala. Wouldn't you say so, Sadiq?'

I was pushing him and he hated it. 'I don't know what you mean, sir.'

'Oh yes, you do. You're not stupid, Sadiq, and remember, neither am I. I know the score as well as you or anyone else in your army. Listen, you two; I'm going to have to make this short and sharp. This country is on the verge of civil breakdown and military takeover, and if you didn't guess that it's only because you're new here and you've had your hands full with that giant of yours. The Army is split; half supports the Government and half wants a military junta to take over. It's complex but don't worry about the reasons for now. Both sides need the Air Force to give them a victory, and up to now Semangala has been playing one side against the other. Am I right so far, Sadiq?'

'I am not a politician,' he said.

I smiled. 'Just a simple soldier, eh? That's an old chestnut, my friend. Now, Semangala has been in France, probably buying planes or missiles. He comes back and decides he needs a holiday: a funny time to choose but he's his own boss. He flies out openly with his wife and kids, but he's back the next day. He probably had a plane on standby in Zurich. My guess is that he's made up his mind and has parked his family out of the way. Now he's bulldozed through the opening of the Bir Oassa airfield, which means that it's squarely in his hands instead of being run by the civil aviation authority. The only question that needs answering is, which side did he come down on?'

Hammond and Kemp were listening carefully. Hammond said, 'I'll be damned. Usually I just read about this stuff in the press.'

Kemp asked, 'Just how much does it matter to us which side he's on? Either way they'll still want the power plant.'

'Don't be naïve. Of course they do, but that doesn't mean we can go on trundling through the country with a shield of invincibility around us. This is going to be a shooting war.'

Sadiq nodded. 'Very bad for you. I do not know how to protect you.'

He meant that he didn't know which side to protect us from.

I said, 'If there's a war, whoever wins will want us. But they have to win first. Meantime we're going to be up to our necks in it, and accidents happen all the time. If the Air Force is against the Government they might decide to take us out, simply to help topple the economy. And what the hell could we do about it?'

'But you're talking about civil war!' Kemp said.

'What else? Captain Sadiq, which side will you be on?'

He looked aghast, 'I do not know. I told you I know nothing of these affairs. I must obey my orders from Major General Kigonde.'

'And if you get no orders? Confucius he say that man who walks down middle of road gets run over. You'll have to make up your own mind sometime. Now that Colonel Hussein – whose side is he on, do you think?'

'He is Kigonde's man.'

'Where's he heading for, and why?'

Sadiq showed a flash of irritation. 'He didn't tell me. Colonels don't make a habit of telling captains their orders.'

Kemp asked, 'What did he tell you concerning us?'

'To stay with you. To protect you. To watch out for sabotage.'

'And you'll do that – even if your own army buddies start shooting at you?'

He didn't answer and I couldn't blame him. For the moment my mind had ground to a halt, and I felt that without a great deal more data to work on I couldn't begin to make any decisions regarding our mission. Then to my surprise and my considerable relief the matter was taken firmly out of my hands. Basil Kemp had become inattentive during the last few exchanges, and was drawing patterns in the dust with his toe. I was starting to think that he was in the grip of the same uncertainty as held me, when he suddenly straightened up and spoke with decision.

'We've work to do. I think we're wasting time, Neil. We have to get on the road at once. We can discuss things as we go.'

'Go where?' I asked.

'To Bir Oassa. While you've been jabbering I've been thinking. The war hasn't started yet and we don't know that it ever will. All this is speculation so far. If there is no war we're still in business. But if there is I would like to be a good deal closer to Bir Oassa than we are now. Sadiq has told us that the new airfield is open, so there's one escape route for us at least. Here there's nothing – we're like sitting ducks. And we can't go back. If there is a war the two main towns will be worst hit and the docks a shambles.'

His words made sense and his voice was firm.

Ben Hammond was almost jubilant. 'Right, let's get on with it. We've got pretty good fuel reserves, water too. We were supposed to be restocked with food but we're not short yet.' His mind was into top gear, sorting out the priorities and he was obviously glad to have something positive to do.

Kemp went on, 'Captain Sadiq thinks there may be shooting. We must talk this over with the men. Ben, call them all together for me, please. I still wish to God Geoff was with us. He's better at this sort of thing.'

'You're doing fine,' I said. 'Better than me. I agree that we can't just sit here, and there's another good reason for pressing on.' My mind was working again.

'And what's that?'

'Tell you in a moment. You go on ahead; I want another word with the Captain first.' I stared hard at him, and as before, he picked up my cue and said at once, 'Right. See you soon.' He went off, taking Ben with him. I turned to Sadiq.

'This is a hell of a mess, Captain. I'm glad you intend to stick with us. I've been admiring your foresight. The gun emplacements, for example.'

He expanded. 'You noticed that? I was told to be aware of possible danger.'

'What do you really think is going on?'

He took off his cap and scratched his head, and the smart soldier became an ordinary, slightly baffled man. 'Colonel Hussein is going to meet the Seventh Brigade, which is stationed at Bir Oassa. Then they will all come south. Back here, unfortunately.'

'Won't they stay there to protect the oilfields?'

'No-one will attack the oilfields. Both sides will need them. But here at Kodowa . . .' He took out a map. Kodowa was about thirty miles north of us, sprawled across the great road, and the only sizeable town in the vicinity. We had reckoned on using it as a major restocking depot.

'From Kodowa a road also goes east and west,' Sadiq was saying. 'So it is a crossroad. Also the heart of Kinguru country. If it was taken by rebels there would be little Kinguru resistance left. So the Seventh Brigade must come down here to protect it, to hold this bridge as well. Hussein will meet them somewhere north of Kodowa.'

'Christ! We're right in the thick of it, then. What about the air force base near here?'

'It is just outside Kodowa. It makes it very difficult to take the town, if the Air Force has really gone with the rebels. That is why Hussein will not stop there.'

'And do you think the Air Force has gone over – or will?'

He shrugged. 'Very hard to say, Mister Mannix. But I think . . .'

'Yes. So do I.' We were silent for a moment, and then I went on. 'I thank you for your frankness. It is very necessary that we keep each other aware of all that we know, Captain. I think I must go and join Mister Kemp now.'

I had a hundred questions still. For one thing, I would very much like to have asked his personal convictions. As a Moslem he might well be against the Kinguru rule; he already had one Moslem superior and the head of the Seventh Brigade might be another. But there was a limit to what I could ask him, and for the moment I had to rely on the fact that our convoy might be felt worthy of protection by both sides, so that Sadiq's loyalty would not affect his usefulness to us. But it was one hell of a nasty situation.

I joined Kemp just as his meeting broke up. There was much talk as the crew went about its business, and Kemp turned to me with relief. 'They're all a bit shocked, naturally, but they're willing to bash on,' he said. There's been some talk of danger money, though.'

'Good God! There's not a shot been fired yet – and may never be.'

'It's just one man. A trade union smart boy.'

'You'd better remind him he's in darkest Africa, not home in dear old England. The guy who comes at him with a rifle won't ask if he believes in the brotherhood of man, or look at his union card. Who is he?'

'Look, he hasn't –'

'Basil, I must know *all* the factors. Who is he? I'm not going to say or do anything, just keep an eye open.'

'His name's Burke, Johnny Burke. He's a damned hard worker and a good crewman. For God's sake don't make much of this.'

'Okay, I promise. But if he starts making waves I have to know. Now, I want to fill you in.' I quickly told him of my conversation with Sadiq and some of my own speculations. He said, 'You wanted to tell me something else, presumably out of Sadiq's hearing.'

'Yes. I think the less Sadiq hears of our plans or discussions the better. You've got a map of Nyala? Let's have it.'

We both bent over the map. From Kodowa our road continued in a more or less northerly fashion, through increasingly sparse scrubland and into the semi-desert regions where Bir Oassa's oil derricks were pumping out the country's newly discovered lifeblood. The river we had just crossed, like two others before it and one more to come, were all fairly major tributaries of the huge Katali, which ran up from the coast north of Lasulu to form the boundary with Manzu, Nyala's neighbouring state. And from Kodowa another road, not as massive as the one we were travelling on, ran right across the country from the east to the western boundary, towards the Katali river. Here there was no bridge, but a ferry carried goods and people over the river from one country to the other, doing desultory trade and forming a second route to the oilfields.

I pointed to this road. 'Do you know anything about this route?'

'Not much. I saw it, of course, when I did the survey. But I didn't go and look at it. There was a fair amount of small traffic using it. Why?'

'If we get to Kodowa and this damned war has started, you're right in saying that we can't turn back to the coast. But I'm not happy about going on to Bir Oassa either.

There's nothing up there that isn't brought in: no food supplies, no water –'

'Not even fuel,' he said with a wry smile. 'It's all crude.'

'Exactly. The desert is a godawful place to be stranded in. And if the rebels have the airfield, they won't simply let us fly out. They'll hold all personnel in what the press calls a hostage situation. So I don't think we want to go there, do you?'

He looked at me in horror. All his careful plans were being overturned, and now here I was about to suggest the whackiest scheme imaginable.

'You want me to take a three hundred ton load on a multi-artic trailer over an unsurveyed route into the depths of nowhere? What for, for God's sake?' he asked.

'Look at the road going west. It goes back towards the rainforest. There are several villages, lots of chances to find food and water. And fuel, both gas and diesel. It may not be a good road, but it exists. At the Katali it follows the water course down to Lasulu and the coast. I saw the beginning of that road beyond Lasulu and it wasn't too bad. We would meet the river here – at Lake Pirie.' It wasn't really a lake but a considerable widening of the river. 'There's even a moderately sized town there, Fort Pirie, as big as Kodowa apparently.'

'Yes, I see all that. I take your point about the food, and water, and possibly fuel. But there's something else, isn't there?'

'Yes indeed. There's Manzu.'

'The Republic of Manzu? But we can't get there by crossing the river with the rig. There's no bridge. And it's another country, Neil. We don't have the necessary papers to enter. We've got no business with Manzu.'

I felt a wave of exasperation. 'Basil, use your head! If necessary we abandon the rig. Yes, abandon it. I know it's valuable, but the crew matters more. We can get them across the river, and they're safe in a neutral country. And as refugees, and whites at that, we'll get plenty of help and plenty of publicity. I bet nobody would dare touch the rig or the rest of the convoy with a bargepole; they'd be valuable assets for negotiations to either side.'

Actually I didn't believe this myself. I thought that without our expertise to handle it the rig, abandoned in the rainforest, would be so much junk and treated as such by all parties. But I had to convince Kemp to see things my way. I knew what the priorities were, and they didn't include taking a team of men into the desert to become hostages to either side in a shooting war. Or food for the vultures either.

'I'll have to think about it.'

'Naturally. There's a lot we need to know. But keep it in mind. Nothing will happen until we get to Kodowa, and we're not there yet. And by then the whole picture may have changed.'

'Right you are. Can we get back to here and now, please? Are you staying with us?'

'I sure am. I'd hate to try and drive back to the coast without knowing what's going on there. When do you plan to get started?'

'Immediately. We should get to Kodowa tomorrow morning. I won't stop too close to the town, though, not in these circumstances. Will you ride with me in the Land Rover? We can plan as we go. I'll get someone else to bring your car.'

A little later we were on the move once more. Rumbling along in the dust, the rig and its attendants were left behind as we set off to find out what was happening in Kodowa. Yesterday Kemp had expected to be buying fresh fruit and vegetables in the marketplace; today his expectations were entirely different.

EIGHT

As Kemp pulled ahead of the convoy I saw with approval that two of Sadiq's motorcyclists shot past us and then slowed down, holding their distance ahead, one at about a quarter of a mile, one at half a mile. Kemp drove fairly slowly, carefully scrutinizing the road surface and checking the bends. Once or twice he spoke over the car phone to the rig but otherwise we drove in silence for some time. He was deeply preoccupied.

After we had gone a dozen miles or so he said, 'I've been thinking.'

The words had an ominous ring.

'Pull over and let's talk.'

He asked me to flesh out the political situation and I added my speculations concerning the Air Force and Sadiq's attitude, I sensed his growing truculence, but when the reason for it finally surfaced I was dismayed. If I had thought of John Sutherland as lacking in imagination he shrank into insignificance beside Kemp.

'I don't think much of all this,' he said. 'There's not one solid bit of evidence that any of it is happening.'

'A while ago back up the road there was a guy who wanted to shoot up the convoy,' I said. 'What do you call that?'

'All they did was threaten, get excited. They may well have been on exercises. The jets that came over – we've seen others before. I'm not sure I believe any of this, Neil. And that army detachment is way ahead of us by now.'

'How do you know? They may have stopped round the next corner. And there are others, not all necessarily as friendly.' But I knew I wasn't getting through to him. Something had set his opinions in concrete, and I had to find out what it was and chip it out fast.

I said, 'As soon as we get to Kodowa I'm going to have a try at getting back to Port Luard. I may be able to get a plane, or at least an army escort. I want to get the gen from headquarters, and not on the air. Before I go I'll want the names of every man you've got with you.' I took out a notebook and pen. Kemp looked at me as if I were going crazy.

'Why do you want to know that?'

I noticed he didn't query my intention to return to base. Perhaps he'd be pleased to see the back of me. 'Just tell me,' I said.

'I insist on knowing why.'

I thought it wise to be brutal.

'To tell their next of kin, and the company, if they get killed. That goes for you too, of course.'

'My God! You're taking this seriously!'

'Of course I am. It is serious, and I think you know it. Let's have those names.'

He was reluctant but complied. 'There's Ben Hammond; the drivers are McGrath, Jones, Grafton and Lang. Bert Proctor, on rig maintenance with Ben. Two boys on the airlift truck, Sisley and Pitman – both Bob, by the way. Thorpe, who came with you. Burke and Wilson. In the commissary truck we've got Bishop and young Sandy Bing. Fourteen with me. I don't know their addresses.' This last was said sarcastically but I treated it as a straight fact.

'No, we can get those from head office if necessary. You might want to write a message for me to take back to Wingstead – assuming I get back.'

'You really mean to try? It could be –'

'Dangerous? But I thought you said there wasn't any danger?'

He fiddled with the car keys. 'I'm not totally stupid, Mannix. Of course I realize there could be trouble. But your plan –'

At last we were getting to the root of his problem. Something about my hastily formulated escape plan had touched a nerve, and now I could guess what it was. 'I'll leave you a written letter too, if you like. If there is danger and the rig looks like holding up any chances of your all getting clear, you're to abandon it immediately.'

I had guessed right. His face became set and stubborn. 'Hold on a minute. That's the whole thing. I'm not abandoning this job or the rig just on your say-so, or for any damned local insurrection. It's got too much of our sweat in it.'

I looked at him coldly. 'If you're the kind of man who would trade a pile of scrap metal for lives you can consider yourself fired as of now.'

His face was pale. 'Wyvern has a contract. You can't do that.'

'Can't I? Go ahead and sue the company; you'll be stripped naked in public. Christ, man, the transformer is worth ten times as much as the rig and yet I'm prepared to drop it like hot coal if it hinders getting the men out alive. I can order you to leave the rig and I'm doing it. In writing, if you like. I take full responsibility.'

He couldn't find words for a moment. He was outraged, but perhaps at himself as much as at me. He had seen the chasm under his feet: the moment when a man puts property before life is a crisis point, and as a normally ethical man he had realized it.

'Come on, Basil.' I softened. 'I do understand, but you've got to see reason. Damn it, British Electric will have to make good if you abandon your rig on my say-so. You'd have your money back in spades one day.'

'Of course the chaps' lives come first – my own too. It's just that I . . . I can't get used to the idea of –'

'Leaving it to rot? Of course not. But war does funny things to men and equipment alike, assuming there is going to be a war. And we dare not assume otherwise. Think again.'

He sat silent, pale and shaken. Then at last he said, 'All right, if we have to do it, we will. But not unless we absolutely must, you hear me?'

'Of course not. And in any case, you don't have to throw it off a mountain top, you know. Just park it in some nice lay-by and you can come and pick it up when the shooting's over.'

He gave me a wan smile.

'I'd like to drive back to the rig,' he said. 'I want a word with Ben. And we could do with something to eat.' It was a truce offering, and I accepted.

The rig was crawling along into the growing heat of the day, moving so slowly that it disturbed relatively little dust. Strung out ahead and behind were the rest of the convoy and the military vehicles. There was a timeless, almost lulling atmos phere to the whole scene, but I wondered how much of it I could take. The rig drivers must be specially trained in patience and endurance.

Kemp signalled the chuck wagon out of line and Bishop started a brew up and a dispensing of doorstep sandwiches. My hired car had suddenly come into its own as a delivery wagon, to Kemp's pleasure freeing the Land Rover from that chore. 'We'll keep this car on,' he said. 'We should have had an extra one all along.'

'I'm sure Avis will be delighted.'

Sadiq reported that he had sent scouts ahead to find out how things were on the Kodowa road. He had stationed a similar escort well behind the convoy lest anything else should come up from the direction of the bridge. He was working hard and doing quite well in spite of the unexpected pressures.

Over tea and sandwiches Hammond and Kemp had a long conversation which seemed to be entirely technical, something to do with the rig's performance since the air bags had been removed. It wasn't a major problem but one of those small hitches which enthrall the minds of technicians everywhere. Presently Kemp said that he wanted to drive alongside the rig for a while, to watch her in action, and invited me to join him.

Just as we were starting we heard a whisper from the air and looked up to see the contrails of jets flying northwards high up. There were several of them, not an unusual sight, and nobody mentioned it. But our eyes followed them thoughtfully as they vanished from sight.

The rest of that morning moved as slowly as though the mainspring of time itself had weakened. We were entering the foothills of the escarpment which separated the scrubland from the arid regions ahead, and there were a series of transverse ridges to cross so that the road rose and dipped like a giant roller coaster. We would crawl up a rise to find a shallow valley with the next rise higher than the last. At the crest of every rise the dim, blue-grey wall of the escarpment would become just that little more distinct. Kemp now had three tractors coupled up to haul on the hills and control the speed on the down slopes. When he got to the escarpment proper he would need all four.

Curiously enough the vegetation was a little lusher here and the country seemed more populous. There was a village every mile or so and a scattering of single huts in between. The huts were made of grass thatched with palm leaves, or double walls of woven withies filled with dried mud. If one burnt down or blew over it could be replaced in a day.

The villagers grew corn, which the British called maize, and sweet potatoes, and scrawny chickens pecked among the huts. They herded little scraggy goats and cows not much bigger, and thin ribby dogs hung about looking for scraps. The people were thin too, but cleanly clothed and with a certain grave dignity. They lined the route to watch us go by, clearly awed and fascinated but not in a holiday mood. In one village a delegation took Sadiq away to talk to their headman, and the men of the village seemed a little threatening towards the troops. No women or children were to be seen which was unusual.

Sadiq came back with bad news. 'Hussein's battalion went through here very fast and a child was killed. Nobody stopped and the people are all very angry.'

'My God, that's awful.' Suddenly Kemp looked much more as though he believed in our talk of civil war. I thought of what Napoleon had said about eggs and omelettes, but people weren't eggs to be smashed. If there were much of this sort of thing going on there would be scant support from the rural populace for either side, not that the local people had any say in what went on.

Kemp asked if we could do anything to help, but was told that it would be best to keep going. 'They know it wasn't you,' Sadiq said. 'They do not want you here but they have no quarrel with you. You cannot help their grief.'

We moved out again to catch up with the rig and I asked to ride with Sadiq. I had some more questions to ask him, and this seemed like a good moment. As we pulled away I began with an innocuous question. 'How come there are so many people living here? There seem to be more than at the coast.'

'It is healthier country; less fever, less heat. And the land is good, when the rains come.'

Then the radio squawked and Sadiq snatched up the earphones and turned up the gain. He listened intently, replied and then said to me, 'Something is happening up the road. Not so good. I'm going to see. Do you want to come?'

'I'd like to.' I hadn't the slightest desire to go hurtling into trouble, but the more I could learn the better.

He eased out of the line and barrelled up the road. Behind us his sergeant crouched over the earphones though I doubt that he could have heard anything. Several miles ahead of the place where Kemp and I had previously stopped and turned back we came across one of Sadiq's troop trucks parked just below the top of a rise; the motor-cyclists were there too. The corporal who headed the detachment pointed along the road, towards a haze of smoke that came from the next valley or the one beyond.

'A bush fire, perhaps?' I asked. But I didn't think so.

'Perhaps. My corporal said he heard thunder in the hills an hour ago. He is a fool, he said he thought the rains were coming early.'

'No clouds.'

'He has never heard gunfire.'

'I have. Have you?' I asked. He nodded.

'I hope it is not Kodowa,' he said softly. 'I think it is too near for that. We shall go and see.' He didn't mention the planes we'd all seen earlier.

We went off fast with the cyclists about a mile ahead and the truck rattling along behind. There was nothing abnormal in the next valley but as we climbed the hill a cyclist came roaring back. Sadiq heard what he had to say and then stopped below the crest of the hill. He went back to the truck and the men bailed out, fanning into a line.

He signalled to me and I followed him as he angled off the road, running through the thick scrub. At the top of the ridge he bent double and then dropped flat on his belly. As I joined him I asked, 'What is it?'

'There are tanks on the other side. I want to know whose they are before I go down.'

He snaked forward and fumbled his binoculars out of their case. He did a quick scan and then stared in one direction for some time. At last he motioned me to come forward and handed me the glasses.

There were four tanks in the road. One was still burning, another was upside down, its tracks pointing to the sky. A third had run off the road and into a ditch. There didn't seem to be much the matter with the fourth, it just sat there. There were three bodies visible and the road was pitted with small, deep craters and strewn with debris.

I'd seen things like that before. I handed him back the glasses and said, 'An air strike with missiles. Hussein?'

'His tanks, yes. They have the Second Battalion insignia. I see no command car.'

He looked around to where his corporal waited, made a wide sweeping motion with one hand and then patted the top of his own head. That didn't need much interpretation: go around the flank and keep your head down.

In the event there was no need for caution; there were no living things on the road except the first inquisitive carrion birds. Sadiq had the vehicles brought up and then we examined the mess. The three bodies in the road had come out of the burning tank. They were all badly charred with their clothing burnt off, but we reckoned they had been killed by machine gunfire. The tank that seemed intact had a hole the size of an old British penny in the turret around which the paint had been scorched off until the metal showed. That damage had been done by a shaped charge in the head of a stabilized missile. I knew what they'd find in the tank and I didn't feel inclined to look for myself. Anyone still inside would be spread on the walls.

Sadiq gave orders to extinguish the fire in the burning tank, and the dead bodies were collected together under a tarpaulin. There was no sign of the rest of the men except for some bloodstains leading off into the bush. They had scarpered, wounded or not.

I said, 'Nothing is going to get past here until this lot is shifted. We need one of Kemp's tractors. Shall I go back and tell him what's happened? Someone can bring one along. He's only using three.'

'Yes, you can ride on the back of one of the motorcycles. I do not think there is any danger – now.' But we both scanned the sky as he spoke. There wasn't much that needed discussion, but it seemed evident to me that the civil war had finally erupted, and the Air Force had gone with the opposition. I felt a wave of sickness rise in my throat at the thought of what the future was likely to hold.

We returned to the convoy and the cyclist dropped me without ceremony at Kemp's car, then shot off to pass orders to the rest of the military escort. Kemp stared and I realized that for the second time in that long day he was seeing me dusty and scratched from a trip through the bush.

'That war you didn't like to think about is just a piece up the road,' I told him. 'We can't get through for wrecked tanks. There are four of them, stragglers from Hussein's out-fit. All kaput. We need the spare tractor and a damn good driver. I'd like it to be McGrath. And a couple of other guys. And you, too; you are in the heavy haulage business, aren't you?'

I may have sounded just a touch hysterical. Kemp certainly looked at me as if I were.

'You're not kidding me?'

'Jesus, maybe I should have brought one of the bodies as evidence.'

'Bodies?'

'They happen in a war.'

I looked along the road. The rig was crawling towards us, but ahead of it was the extra tractor, driven by Mick McGrath. I waved him down and he stopped alongside, alive with curiosity. Everyone had seen the sudden activity of our military escort and knew something was up.

'Basil, get the rig stopped. Better here than too close,' I said.

Kemp looked from me to the rig, then slowly unhooked the microphone from the dashboard of the Land Rover. Stopping the rig was a serious business, not as simple as putting on a set of car brakes, more like stopping a small ship. For one thing, all three tractor drivers had to act in concert; for another the rig man, usually either Hammond or Bert Proctor, had to judge the precise moment for setting the bogie brakes, especially on a hill. Although they were all linked in a radio circuit, they were also directed by a flag waved from the control car; a primitive but entirely practical device. Now Kemp poked the flag out of the car window, and followed his action with a spate of orders over the mike. McGrath got out of his tractor and strode over. 'What's going on, Mister Mannix?'

'A war.'

'What does it look like over there?'

'Like any old war. Hussein got shot up from the air and lost four tanks. One of them should be no trouble to move, but three are blocking the road. We'll need your help in clearing the way.'

By now several of the men were milling around talking. McGrath overrode the babble of conversation.

'Any shooting up there now, Mister Mannix?'

'No, and I don't think there will be. We think that both sides will leave us alone. We're precious to them.'

McGrath said, 'Any bad corners on the way there?'

'None that matter. It's pretty easy going.'

'Right you are then. I'll take Bert from the rig. Barry, you whip a team together and follow us up. Tell the fuel bowser boys to stay back, and leave the airlift team behind too. We could do with your car, Mister Mannix. OK? Sandy, go and send Bert to me, then you stay up there and tell Mister Hammond what's going on.'

He issued this stream of orders with calm decision, then strode off back to the tractor. I was impressed. He had taken the initiative in fine style and seemed to be dependable. It would be interesting seeing him in action if things got tough, as I was certain they would.

Kemp rejoined me and I briefed him and saw that he approved. 'He's a good organizer, is Mick. A bit hot-headed but then what Irish rigger isn't? Ben will stay here with the rig and the rest of the crew. A detachment of the escort can hold their hands. I'm coming with you. Get in.'

He made no apology for doubting that this might happen. The tension that had gripped him in Port Luard was returning, and I realized with something between horror and exasperation that what was bothering him wasn't the prospect of an entire country devastated by civil war, but the sheer logistic annoyances of any delays or upsets to his precious transportation plans. He was a very single-minded man, was Kemp.

As we pulled out to overtake the tractor Kemp said, 'You mentioned bodies. How many?'

'I saw three, but there'll be more in the tanks. The rest have scarpered.'

'God damn it, as though we didn't have enough problems of our own without getting mixed up in a bloody war,' he grumbled.

'It could be worse.'

'How the hell could it be worse?'

'The planes could have shot up your rig,' I said dryly.

He didn't answer and I let him drive in silence. I was thankful enough myself to sit quietly for a while. I felt drained and battered, and knew that I needed to recharge my batteries in a hurry, against the next crisis.

The scene of the air strike hadn't changed much except that the bodies had been moved off the road and the fire was out. Sadiq was waiting impatiently. 'How long to clear it, sir?' he asked at once.

Kemp looked dazed.

'How long, please?' Sadiq repeated.

Kemp pulled himself together. 'Once the tractor arrives, we'll have the tanks off the road in an hour or so. We don't have to be too gentle with them, I take it.'

I wasn't listening. I was looking at the ridge of hills ahead of us, and watching the thick black haze of smoke, several columns, mingling as they rose, writhing upwards in the middle distance. Sadiq followed my gaze.

'My scouts have reported back, Mister Mannix. Kodowa is burning.'

'Still reckoning on buying fresh vegetables there?' I couldn't resist asking Kemp. He shook his head heavily. The war had happened, and we were right in the middle of it.

McGrath and Proctor were experts in their field and knowledgeable about moving heavy awkward objects. They estimated angles, discussed the terrain, and then set about connecting shackles and heavy wire ropes. Presently McGrath shifted the first of the stricken tanks off the road as though it were a child's toy. The rest of us, soldiers and all, watched in fascination as the tank ploughed to a halt deep in the dust at the roadside, and the team set about tackling the next one.

Sadiq went off in his command car as soon as he was satisfied that our tractor could do the job, heading towards Kodowa with a cycle escort. The work of clearing the road went on into the late afternoon, and Kemp then drove back to the convoy to report progress and to bring the rig forward. He had decided that we would stop for the night, a wise decision in the aftermath of an exhausting and disturbing day, but he wanted to cover as much ground as possible before total nightfall.

McGrath and Proctor were resting after moving the up-turned tank, which had been a tricky exercise, and gulping down the inevitable mugs of hot tea which Sandy had brought along for everyone. I went over to them and said, 'Got a spade?'

McGrath grinned. 'Ever see a workman without one? We use them for leaning on. It's a well-known fact. There's a couple on the tractor.'

Proctor, less ebullient, said quietly. 'You'll be wanting a burial party, Mister Mannix?'

We buried the bodies after giving the soldiers' identity tags to Sadiq's corporal. Afterwards everyone sat around quietly, each immersed in his own thoughts. McGrath had vanished, but presently I heard him calling.

'Hey, Mister Mannix! Bert!'

I looked around but couldn't see him. 'Where are you?'

'In here.' His voice was muffled and the direction baffling. I still couldn't see him, and then Bert pointed and McGrath's head appeared out of the turret of the tank that he hadn't needed to shift, the one that had run into the ditch. He said cheerily, 'I don't think there's anything wrong with this one.'

'You know tanks too?'

'The army taught me. There isn't anything on wheels I don't know,' he said with simple egotism. Proctor, alongside me, nodded in his grave fashion.

I said, 'Can you drive it out?'

'I'm pretty sure so. This thing never got a hit. The crew just baled out and she piled herself up in the dust here. Want me to try?'

'Why not?'

His head bobbed down and after a lot of metallic noises the engine of the tank burst into noisy song. It moved, at first forward and digging itself deeper into the ditch, and then in reverse. With a clatter of tracks and to spattered applause it heaved itself out of the gulley and onto the road. There was a pause and then the turret started to move. The gun traversed around and depressed, pointing right at us.

'Stick 'em up, pal!' yelled McGrath, reappearing and howling with laughter.

'Don't point that thing at me,' I said. 'Once a day is enough. Well, it looks as though we've just added one serviceable tank to the Wyvern fleet. Captain Sadiq will be delighted.'

NINE

It was an uneasy night. Nothing more happened to disturb us, but very few of us got a full night's sleep; there was a great deal of coming and going to the chuck wagon, much quiet talking in the darkness, a general air of restlessness. The day had been packed with incident, a total contrast to the normal slow, tedious routine, and nobody knew what the next day would bring except they could be sure that the routine was broken.

The rig had reached the valley where the tanks had been hit, and was resting there. Kemp had no intention of moving it until we knew much more about what had happened in Kodowa, and Sadiq had taken him off at first light to look at the road. I had elected to stay behind.

Talk over breakfast was sporadic and I could sense the crew's tension. Certainly I knew they had been discussing their own safety and the chances of their coming through the conflict unscathed, with less than full confidence, and I suspected that Johnny Burke and Bob Sisley were pushing the shop floor angle rather hard. That could bear watching. I began to put some words together in my mind, against the time when I'd have to give them reasoned arguments in favour of doing things my way. They weren't like Sadiq's army lads, trained to obey without question.

Ben Hammond had gone with Kemp to look at the road. McGrath and three or four of the men were still playing with the tank, which they had cheerfully but firmly refused to turn over to the military until they had tinkered with it for a while longer. The others, including myself, were doing nothing much; everything looked remarkably peaceful and normal if one ignored the three tanks piled up in the gulley by the roadside.

When the interruption came it was heart-stopping.

There was a mighty rush of air and a pounding roar in our ears. Men sprang to their feet like jack-in-the-boxes as five air force jets screamed overhead at low altitudes, hurtling up over the ridge beyond us.

'Christ!' A pulse hammered in my throat and my coffee spilled as I jerked to my feet.

'They're attacking!' someone yelled and there was a dive for cover, mostly under the shelter of the rig itself, which would have been suicidal if an attack had followed. But no missiles or bombs fell. The formation vanished as suddenly as it had appeared. Men resurfaced, staring and chattering. Soldiers grabbed belatedly for their rifles.

'Was it an attack?' Ritchie Thorpe asked me. Having driven up with me he'd been tacitly appointed the position of spokesman.

'No. They were going much too fast. I'm not sure they were even aware of us.'

'Where do you think they're going?'

'God knows.' I felt as if we were on a desert island, with no news getting through. 'Are you sure you can't raise anything on the radios? Any local station?'

'Sorry, Mister Mannix. It's all static. Everything's off the air, I think. Mister Kemp said he'd call in on the half-hour, so I'll be listening in then. Maybe he'll have some news for us.'

There was a distant roar and our faces snapped skywards again. One of the jets was returning, but flying much higher, and as we watched it made a big sweeping circle in the sky and vanished in the direction of the rest of the formation. For a moment it seemed to leave a thin echo behind, and then I stiffened as I recognized what I was hearing.

'Bert. There's another plane. A small one. Can you see it?'

He too stared round the sky.

'No, but I can hear it.' He raised his voice to a shout. 'Any of you see a light plane?'

Everyone stared upwards, and three or four of them scrambled up onto the rig for a better vantage point. It was Brad Bishop on top of the commissary truck who first shouted, 'Yes, over there!' and pointed south.

A moment later I'd seen it too, a small speck of a plane flying low and coming towards us. Longing for binoculars, I kept my eyes glued to the approaching plane and felt a jolt of recognition. I'd never been a flier myself, and though I'd logged hundreds of hours in small company planes as well as in commercial liners I had never developed an eye for the various makes, but this one I definitely knew.

'It's the BE company plane,' I called out. 'We've got visitors.'

'Where can they land?' Thorpe asked me.

'Good question. Kodowa's got a town strip somewhere but I don't know if it's going to be usable. He can't land here, that's for certain.'

But that was where I was wrong.

It wasn't an intentional landing, though. As the plane came nearer we recognized signs of trouble. It was flying in a lopsided, ungainly fashion. A thin trail of smoke came from it, and the full extent of the damage became visible. Part of the undercarriage was missing, and the tailfin was buckled out of alignment.

'She's going to crash.'

'Do you think the jets attacked her?'

I said, 'No – too high, too fast. That was a ground attack. Damn it, she's not a fighter plane, not even armed!'

We watched in alarm as it began a wobbly circle over the bush country, slowly spiralling downwards.

'Bring up the water carrier!' I shouted, and sprinted for the hire car. Three or four others flung themselves in beside me. The car was ill-equipped for bouncing off the road into the bush but with the Land Rover gone there wasn't much choice. The water tanker and some of the military stuff followed. I concentrated on charting the course of the stricken plane and on avoiding the worst of the rocks and defiles in front of me. The others clung on as they were tossed about, leaning out of the car windows in spite of the choking dust clouds to help keep track of the aircraft.

Soon it dipped to the horizon, then went below it at a sharp angle. I tried to force another fraction of speed out of the labouring car. The plane reappeared briefly and I wondered if it had actually touched down and bounced. Then it was gone again and a surge of dust swirled up ahead.

My hands wrenched this way and that to keep the car from slewing sideways in the earth. I brought it joltingly through a small screen of thorn bushes and rocked to a halt, and we looked downhill towards the misshapen hulk that had been airborne only moments before.

We piled out and started running. The danger of fire was enormous. Not only would the plane erupt but the bush was likely to catch fire, and we all knew it. But there was no fire as yet, and the plane was miraculously upright.

As we got to the plane a figure was already beginning to struggle to free himself. The plane was a six-seater, but there were only two men visible inside. Our men clambered up onto the smashed wing and clawed at the pilot's door. The water tanker was lumbering towards us and Sadiq's troops were nearer still; I waved the oncoming vehicles to a halt.

'No further! Stay back! If she burns you'll all be caught. No sparks – don't turn your ignition off,' I shouted. 'Wilson, you and Burke start laying a water trail down towards her.'

As one of the big hoses was pulled free and a spray of water shot out, the door was pulled open and the two men inside were helped out. I ran back to the car and brought it closer. One of the plane's occupants seemed to be unhurt; two of our men were steadying him but he appeared to be walking quite strongly. The second was lolling in unconsciousness, carried by Grafton and Ron Jones. As they came up to my car I recognized both new arrivals.

The unconscious man was Max Otterman, our Rhodesian pilot. The other was Geoffrey Wingstead.

Max Otterman was in a bad way.

He'd done a brilliant job in bringing his plane down in one piece, upright and more or less intact, but at a terrible cost to himself. His left arm was broken, and he had contusions and cuts aplenty, especially about the face in spite of goggles and helmet. But there was something more drastic and this none of us was able to diagnose for certain. He recovered consciousness of a sort in the car as we drove him and Geoff Wingstead back to the rig site, moving as gently as possible. But he was obviously in great pain and kept blacking out. We got him bedded down in the rig's shade eventually, after letting Bishop have a good look at him. Bishop had first aid training and was pretty useful for day-to-day rig accidents, but he didn't know what was wrong with Otterman, apart from being fairly sure that neither his neck nor his back was broken.

It was the most worrying feature so far of a very worrying situation.

Wingstead was in good shape apart from one severe cut on his left shoulder and a selection of bruises, but nevertheless both Bishop and I urged him to take things very carefully. He saw Otterman bedded down, then sank into a grateful huddle in the shade with a cold beer to sustain him.

The men tended to crowd around. They all knew Geoff, naturally, and it was apparent that they thought a great deal of their boss. Their astonishment at his unorthodox arrival was swamped in their relief at his safety, and curiosity overrode all.

Presently I had to appeal to them to leave him for a while.

'Come on, you guys. He doesn't exactly want to give a press conference just this minute, you know,' I said. I didn't want to speak too sharply; it would be unwise to trample on their good will. But they took my point and most of them moved a little way off.

Wingstead said, 'I'll have to thank everybody properly. You all did a damned good job, back there.' His voice was a little shaky.

'None better than Max,' I said. 'There's plenty of time, Geoff. Time for questions later too. Just rest a bit first.'

In fact I was aching to know what had brought him up to us, what he knew and what the situation was that he'd left behind him. Kemp and Sadiq should hear it too, though, and one account from Wingstead would tax him quite sufficiently. So I went a little way off, and saw Wingstead's head droop forward as he surrendered to the sleep of exhaustion. I was anxious for Kemp to rejoin us. He seemed to have been gone for ever, and I was eager to give him our latest piece of dramatic news. But it wasn't until nearly noon that we saw Sadiq's escorted car returning, and I walked down the road to intercept them.

'Neil. There's a pack of problems up ahead of us,' said Kemp.

'We haven't done too badly ourselves.'

Kemp's eyes immediately flashed to the rig. 'Problems? Have you been having trouble?'

'I wouldn't quite put it that way. Look, I'm damned keen to hear what you've got to tell, but I guess our news has priority. We've got visitors.'

'Who – the army?'

Sadiq had got out of the car and already had his glasses unslung, scanning the road. I knew he wouldn't see the plane from where we were standing, though. I'd have preferred to discuss the latest developments with Kemp alone, but Sadiq had to be told: he'd find out fast enough in any case.

'No. We were overflown by some air force planes but I don't think they were looking for us or had any business with us. But a small plane came up a while ago. It crashed – over there.' I waved my hand. 'It had been shot up, I think. There were two men on board and we got them both out, but one's badly hurt.'

'Who the hell are they?'

'You're going to like this, Basil. One's your boss. And he's in pretty fair shape.'

'Geoffrey!' As with the men, astonishment and relief played over Kemp's face, and then alarm. 'Who was with him – who's hurt?'

'It's our pilot, Max Otterman. He made a damn good landing, probably saved both their necks, but he's in a bad way. The plane's a write-off.'

It was sensational stuff, all right. They were both suitably impressed, and had more questions. After a while I managed to get rid of Sadiq by suggesting that the guarding of the plane was probably not being done to his satisfaction. He went away at once, to go and see for himself. Kemp would have gone along too but I detained him.

'You can look at the wreckage later.'

'I want to see Geoff and the pilot.'

'One's sleeping and the other's damn near unconscious. You can't do a thing for either just yet awhile. I'd rather you briefed me on what you've found out down there.'

Kemp said, 'The road is in good shape right up to the environs of Kodowa. The town is in a hell of a mess. It's been strafed and it's almost completely burnt up. The people are in shock, I'd say, and they certainly won't be much use to us, and there's not enough of us to be much use to them. It's a pretty ghastly situation. You're right it is a war.'

It was as much of an apology as I'd get.

'We didn't go right in because we got a lot of opposition. They felt ugly about anyone in uniform, and Sadiq didn't have enough force with him to do much about it. But we'll have to go back in eventually. Look, did Geoff say anything to you?'

'Not yet. I didn't let him. I want to hear his story as much as you do, but I thought he should rest up and wait for you to come back. Where's Ben Hammond, by the way?'

Kemp made a despairing gesture. 'You'll never believe it, but the damned troop truck broke down on the way back. String and cardboard army! Nobody knew what to do about it except Ben, so he's still out there doing a repair job. Should be along any moment, but Sadiq said he's sent some men back to give them support if they need it. There's nobody on the road. They shouldn't have any trouble.' But I could see that he was worried at having been persuaded to leave Ben out in the middle of the bush with a broken down truck and a handful of green soldiers. I didn't think much of the idea myself.

'He'll be OK,' I said hopefully. 'You'd better get yourself something to eat – and drink.'

'By God, yes. I could do with a beer.' He thought for a moment and then said, 'On second thoughts, no. We'd better go gently on our supplies from now on. I'll settle for a mug of gunfire.'

We exchanged humourless smiles. The slang term for camp tea had suddenly become alarmingly appropriate.

*   *   *

Ben turned up two hours later, hot, sticky and desperate for sustenance. Kemp broke into the newly-rationed beer stores for him; we hadn't yet told the men about this particular form of hardship and Kemp was not enjoying the prospect. Wingstead had slept steadily, and we didn't want to waken him. Otterman, on the other hand, seemed worse if anything. He tossed and muttered, cried out once or twice, and had us all extremely worried.

'There must be doctors in Kodowa, but God knows how we'll find them, or whether they'll be able to help,' Kemp said fretfully. He was concerned for Max, but he was also disturbed by the increasing rate of entropy about us. The rapid breakdown from order to chaos was something he seemed ill-equipped to cope with.

'What do you plan to do?' Hammond asked Kemp.

'Go on into Kodowa this afternoon, with enough chaps of my own and of Sadiq's to make a reasonable show of solidarity. We have to locate their officialdom, if any, and find out the precise facts. And we're going to need food, and water – they ran a hell of a lot out of the tanker – and medical help. I'd like you both to come and I'll choose a few of the others.'

We were interrupted by Sandy Bing, coming up at the run.

'Brad says will you come, Mister Kemp. Mister Wingstead's awake.'

'Be right there.'

The awning had been strung up at the rig's side and under it Geoff Wingstead was sitting up and seemed a lot brighter. He reached up to pump Kemp's hand with obvious pleasure.

'You're all OK, then?' he said.

'Yes, we're fine. Problems, but no accidents,' said Kemp.

'I had to come up here and see for myself how you were doing. But I can't fly a plane and Max . . .' He broke off for a moment, then went on. 'Well, he's quite a fellow. They tell me he's in a bad way. Can we get help for him?'

Briefly, Kemp put him in the picture concerning the situation up ahead at Kodowa, or as much of it as we ourselves knew. Wingstead looked grave as we recapped the events of the past couple of days.

Finally he said, 'So we're OK for fuel, not too good for water, food or doctors. Well, you may not know it all, but you can probably guess that you're a damn sight better off here than if you had stayed in Port Luard. At least you're all alive.'

'Is it that bad?' I asked.

'Bloody bad. Riots, strife, total breakdown of authority. Shooting in the streets. Looting. Docks burning, police helpless, military running amok in every direction. All the usual jolly things we see on the nine o'clock news.'

'Oh, great. No getting out for us benighted foreigners, I suppose?'

'In theory, yes. But the airport's in rebel hands and the commercial planes aren't coming in. Kigonde's off somewhere trying to rally his army. I heard that Ousemane was dead, and that Daondo's managed to slip out of the country – which figures. He's a smart one, that lad. But none of the news is certain.'

Kemp, Hammond and I stared at him as he reeled off the grim facts.

'It's a shambles, and I don't quite know what we're going to do about it. I had to get up here, though. Guessed you'd not be getting regular news bulletins and might feel a bit lonely without me.'

Too true, Geoff. We all feel *much* better now,' I said sardonically, and he grinned at me. 'Yes, well, it didn't seem too difficult at first. I asked Max if he was game and he couldn't wait to give it a bash. And we'd have done all right, too, only . . .'

He paused for a moment.

'We'd seen the air force types streaking about here and there, taking no notice of us. And quite a lot of ground movement, tank troops, armoured columns and so on, but no actual fighting once we were clear of Port Luard.'

'How did you achieve that, by the way?'

'Oh, real *Boy's Own* stuff. It'll make a good tale one day. Anyway we figured we'd catch up with you about Kodowa. You're nicely to schedule, Kemp, by the way. My congratulations.'

Kemp snorted.

'We reckoned to land there and cadge a lift back to you. There hadn't been any sign of the insurrection, you see, so we thought it was quieter up here. And then . . . it all happened at the same moment. I saw you, saw the rig parked and we started to come in for a closer look . . . there were some military trucks quite close and I wasn't sure if it was your official escort or not. And then there was this almighty slam and jerk and Max said we'd been hit. Christ, I . . . still can't really believe it. We hadn't *seen* any planes, couldn't believe we were being attacked. Max was superb. I think he was hit by a bit of metal, because he was already bleeding when he decided he had to put us down. It was a marvellous show, wasn't it, Neil? You saw it happen, didn't you?'

'Yes. It was great.'

He lay back against the pillow. 'I can fill you in with lots of detail about what's going on back in Port Luard, but I'm afraid I've come up here without a thought in my head about getting you all out,' he said apologetically. He was looking a little faded, I thought. I decided to let him rest, but perhaps in a more optimistic frame of mind.

'We've got a plan, haven't we, Basil?'

'You have?'

'Oh, yes,' Kemp said, playing along stoutly. 'Neil's idea really, and it's a very good one. We've every reason to think

it may work. Look, I think you'd better rest up a bit. We're
not going anywhere for what's left of today, not with the rig
anyway. And the more rest you have now the more use
you'll be to us tomorrow.'

Out of Wingstead's earshot we stopped and took a simul-
taneous deep breath.

'Do you think what I think?' Kemp asked.

'I do,' I said grimly. 'What I'd like to know is whether
half of our gallant captain's men are rebels, or whether it
was all nicely official from the start. Sadiq couldn't have
known that Geoff was coming, but he may have left blan-
ket orders to stop anyone who tried to get to us. He's
inclined to be over-protective. Alternatively, he's got traitors
in his ranks and doesn't know it.'

'Or he's one himself.'

'I don't think so. In that case he'd have immobilized us
quite easily, long before this.'

'Are you going to ask him?' Hammond asked.

'Not yet. I think we should string him along a little. I suggest that we say nothing of this to anyone, and go ahead
with the plan to inspect Kodowa a little more closely. We
need Sadiq for that, and as long as we keep alert, we may as
well make the most use of him we can.'

When we breasted the rise and looked down, my first
thought was that the problem was not that of getting beyond
Kodowa but *into* it. Much of the town was still burning.

The central core of Kodowa consisted of two short streets
running north and south and two intersecting streets running east and west. None of them was as wide or as well
made as the great road on which we'd been travelling so far.
This was the modern, 'downtown' area. The biggest building was three storeys high, or had been. Now it and most of
the others lay in rubble on the streets.

The rest of the town had been of the local African
architecture. But palm thatch burns well, and mud walls

crumble with ease, and it looked as though a little section of hell had been moved into that valley. I don't know if the local authorities ever had any fire regulations, but if so they hadn't worked. Flames, driven by a wind which funnelled up the valley, had jumped across the streets and there wasn't going to be much left when the fires finally died.

Sadiq said, 'They have killed this place.' His voice sounded bitter.

I twisted in my seat. I was driving with Sadiq because Kemp and I had planned it that way. Kemp had packed the Land Rover and the car with his own men so that there was no room for me. The idea was that I should be at hand to keep an eye on Sadiq.

Where the road narrowed as it entered the town it was blocked by a slow moving line of ramshackle traffic, beat up old cars and pick-up trucks, bullock carts and bicycles, all moving outwards, and slowed even more by one large limousine which had stalled right across the road. Sadiq drove off the road and unhooked his microphone. I got out and went towards the stalled car. The hood was up and two men were poking about under the bonnet, one a Nyalan and the other one of the Asiatic merchants who seem to monopolize so much of small retail business all over Africa. In this case he was a Syrian.

I tapped him on the shoulder. 'Get this car off the road. Push it.'

He turned a sweaty face to me and grimaced uncomprehendingly. I made gestures that they should shift the car and he shook his head irritably, spat out a short sentence I didn't understand, and turned back to the car. That was enough. I leaned over his shoulder, grabbed a handful of wiring and pulled. The only place that car could go now was off the road.

The Syrian whirled furiously and grabbed my shoulder. I let him have a fist in the gut, and he sprawled to the ground. He tried to scramble to his feet and clawed under his coat for some weapon so I kicked him in the ribs and he went down again just as Sadiq came up, unfastening the flap of his pistol holster.

'You have no right to attack citizens, Mister Mannix,' he said angrily.

I pointed to the ground. A heavy cosh had spilled out of the Syrian's jacket and lay near his inert hand.

'Some guys need a lot of persuading,' I said mildly. 'Let's get this thing out of here.' The other man had vanished.

Sadiq's pistol was a better persuader than my voice. He grabbed four able-bodied men out of the milling throng and within three minutes the road was cleared. As he re-holstered his pistol he said, 'You believe in direct action, Mister Mannix?'

'When necessary – but I'm getting too old for brawling.' In fact the small display of aggression had done me the world of good. I'd really been needing to let off steam and it had been the Syrian merchant's bad luck to have been a handy target.

'I would prefer you do no more such things. For the moment please stay with your own men. Tell Mister Kemp I will meet him in the central square soon.' He was off before I had a chance to respond.

I pushed through the crowds and found our Land Rover parked at the intersection of the two main roads. Dozens of distressed, battle-shocked people milled about and smouldering debris lay everywhere. Our eyes watered with the sting of acrid smoke. Broken glass crunched under our boots as we picked our way through the rubble. The Nyalans shrank away from us, weeping women pulling their bewildered children from our path. It was incredibly disturbing.

It became obvious pretty soon that there was no one in charge; we saw no policemen, no soldiers apart from Sadiq's own troops, and no sign of a doctor, a hospital or even a Red Cross post. Attempts to get sensible answers from passers-by proved useless. Presently, utterly dispirited, we decided to withdraw.

The stream of refugees thinned out as we left the town but there were still a lot of them, going God knows where. But I was interested and pleased to see that on the outskirts Sadiq had set up the rudiments of a command post, and slowly his troops were beginning to bring order out of the chaos, reuniting families and doing a little crude first aid of their own. A makeshift camp was already taking shape and people were being bedded down, and some sort of food and drink was being circulated. It made me feel more confident about Sadiq.

We left him to get on with it. Our men were ready enough to give assistance, but we were not welcome and what little we had to offer wouldn't go nearly far enough. Kemp was anxious to keep our unit together; the crew were his responsibility and he was still thinking in terms of the safety of the rig. We drove back to our camp site in the dusk feeling very depressed.

Kemp went to give Wingstead an edited version of what we'd found. I settled down for a quiet cigarette while waiting for the meal that Bishop was preparing for us, and into the silence McGrath and Ron Jones settled down alongside me. Two cigarettes and one foul pipe glowed in the dusk.

'A hell of a thing, this,' Ron Jones said presently. The Welsh lilt in his voice seemed more pronounced than in full daylight. 'Shouldn't we be back there helping?'

'We can't do much,' I said. 'And I don't think Captain Sadiq really wants us. If he needs us he knows where we are.'

'We could spare them a bit of food, though.'

McGrath snorted.

'There could be five thousand people out there, Ron, and none of us is Jesus Christ. Five French loaves and two lobster tails?' I asked.

McGrath said, 'They get wind of our food stocks and they'll mob us, as like as not. I'd be happier with a gun in my fist, myself.'

'I don't know if you're right. Nyalans are peaceable folk. A gun may not be such a good idea. People tend to get the wrong impression when armed foreigners wander about taking part in someone else's war.'

'I'd still be happier with a gun in my cab,' he said. 'One of those Russian Kalashnikovs that the black lads carry, maybe. Better still, a Uzi like Sadiq has in his car.'

I glanced at him. 'You're observant.'

'It pays. I told you I was in the army once myself.'

'What rank?'

He grinned. 'Never more than sergeant. But I made sergeant three times.'

Ron Jones laughed, 'I never had the pleasure of army life,' he said. 'This is my idea of something to watch on the telly, not be caught in the middle of.'

Wingstead had said something similar. I reflected that a lot of men of my age were comparative innocents, after all.

McGrath said, 'Not this mess, maybe. But there are worse lives.' In the twilight he seemed even bigger than he looked by day, a formidable figure. He tamped down his pipe and went on, 'I've seen sights like this before though, many times, in other countries. It's all right for the soldiers but for the civilians it's very sad indeed. But there's nothing you or I can do about it.'

I had seen it before too. I thought back to my young days, to Pusan and Inchon, to the wrecked towns and refugee-lined roads, the misery and the squalor. I didn't want to see it ever again.

McGrath suddenly dug his elbow into my ribs.

'There's someone out there – with a white face. I think it's a woman!'

He scrambled to his feet and ran into the growing darkness.

TEN

Her name was Sister Ursula and she was a nun, and how in hell McGrath had detected that she had a white face in the semi-darkness I'll never know because it was blackened and smudged with smoke and wood ash. Her habit was torn and scorched, and slashed down one side showing that she wore long pants to the knee. She managed it so decorously that it didn't show most of the time.

She was tired but very composed, and showed few signs of strain. I once knew a man who was an atheist; he was also a plumber and had done a week's stint in a convent fixing the water system. He'd gone in with the firm conviction that all religious types were nutters of some sort. When he finished I asked him what he now thought about the contemplative life. He said, 'Those women are the sanest lot of people I've ever met,' and seemed baffled by it.

I went to my gear and fetched out a bottle of whisky. This was no time to be following Kemp's camp rules. When I got back she was sitting on a stool surrounded by our men. They were full of curiosity but polite about it, and I was pleased to see that they weren't badgering her with questions. McGrath's eyes gleamed when he saw the whisky. 'A pity it's only Scotch,' he said. 'Irish would be better, wouldn't it, Sister?'

Her lips curved in a small, tired smile. 'Right now, whisky is whisky. Thank you, Mister – Mannix, is it?'

I'd have said that she was about thirty-five, maybe forty, but she could well have been older; it's never easy to tell with nuns. When Hollywood makes movies about them they pick the Deborah Kerrs and Julie Andrews, but Sister Ursula wasn't like that. She had a full jaw, her eyebrows were thick black bars which gave her a severe and daunting look, and her face was too thin, as though she didn't eat enough. But when she smiled she was transformed, lovely to look at. We found out that she didn't use that radiant smile very often; and with reason, just at that time.

I said, 'Someone get a glass, please.'

'From the bottle is good enough,' she said, and took it from me. She swallowed and coughed a couple of times, and handed it back to me. The men watched transfixed, though whether this was the effect of the nun or the bottle I wasn't sure.

'Ah. It tastes as good as it did last time – some six years ago.'

'Have some more.'

'No, thank you. I need no more.'

Several voices broke in with questions but I overrode them. 'Pipe down, you guys, and quit crowding.' Obediently they shuffled back a pace. I bent over Sister Ursula and spoke more quietly. 'You look pretty beat; do you want to sleep somewhere?'

'Oh no, but I would dearly like a chance to clean up.' She put her stained hands to her face and then brushed at her skirts. Although she was a nun, she was vain enough to care about her appearance.

I said, 'Sandy, see there's some hot water. Ben, can the lads rig a canvas between the trucks to make a bathroom? Perhaps you'll join us for a meal when you're ready, Sister.'

Young Bing sped off and Hammond set the men to putting up a makeshift tent for her. McGrath was helping her to her feet and hovering like a mother hen; presumably as a Catholic he regarded her in some especially proprietorial light. Eventually she thanked us all and disappeared into the tent with a bowlful of water and a spare kettle and someone's shaving mirror.

Kemp had been with Wingstead and Otterman and had arrived a little late for all this excitement. I filled him in and he regarded the tent thoughtfully.

'I wonder where the others are?' he said.

'Others?'

'There'll be at least one more. Nuns are like coppers – they go around in pairs. Most likely there's a whole brood of them somewhere. With any luck they're a nursing sisterhood.'

I was being pretty slow, perhaps simply tired out, but at last the penny dropped. 'You mean they'll come from a hospital or a mission? By God, perhaps you're right. That means they may have a doctor!'

She came out half an hour later, looking well-scrubbed and much tidier. We were ready to eat and I asked her if she wished to join us, or to eat on her own. Someone must have lent her a sewing kit for the rip in her habit had been neatly mended.

'I'll join you, if I might. You're very kind. And you'll all be wanting to hear what I have to say,' she said rather dryly.

I noticed that she said a short, private grace before actually coming to the table, and appreciated her courtesy: doing it publicly might well have embarrassed some of the men. She sat between Kemp and me and I quickly filled her in on our names and business, of which she said she had heard a little on the radio, in the far-off days of last week before the war broke out. We didn't bother her while she was eating but as soon as was decent I asked the first question. It was a pretty all-embracing one.

"What happened?'

'It was an air raid,' she said. 'Surely you know.'

'We weren't here. We were still further south. But we guessed.'

'It was about midday. There had been some unrest, lots of rumours, but that isn't uncommon. Then we heard that there were tanks and soldiers coming through the town, so Doctor Katabisirua suggested that someone should go and see what was happening.'

'Who is he?' Kemp asked.

'Our chief at the hospital.' There was an indrawing of breath at the table as we hung on her words. Kemp shot me a look almost of triumph.

'Sister Mary sent me. It wasn't very far, only a short drive into town. When I got there I saw a lot of tanks moving through the town, far too quickly, I thought. They were heading north, towards Ngingwe.'

Ngingwe was the first village north of Kodowa, which showed that Sadiq had probably been right when he said that Hussein's lot would go northwards to join forces with his superior.

'They got through the town but some soldiers stayed back to keep the road clear. We heard that there were more tanks still coming from the south of the town.' Those would be the tanks that we had seen shot up. 'There were still a lot of people in the town square when the planes came. They came in very fast, very low. Nobody was scared at first. We've seen them often, coming and going from the Air Force base out there.' She pointed vaguely westward.

'How many planes, Sister?' Kemp asked.

'I saw seven. There may have been more. Then things happened very quickly. There was a lot of noise – shooting and explosions. Then the sound of bombs exploding, and fires started everywhere. It was so sudden, you see. I took shelter in Mister Ithanga's shop but then it started to fall to pieces and something must have hit me on the head.'

In fact she had no head wound, and I think she was felled by the concussion blast of a missile. She couldn't have been unconscious long because when I saw the shop next day it was a fire-gutted wreck. She said that she found herself coming to in the street, but didn't know how she got there. She said very little about her own part in the affair after that, but we gathered that eventually she got back to the hospital with a load of patients, her little car having escaped major damage, to find it already besieged by wailing, bleeding victims.

But they were not able to do much to help. With a very small staff, some of whom were local and only semi-trained, and limited supplies of bedding, food and medicines they were soon out of their depth and struggling. Adding to their problems were two major disasters: their water supply and their power had both failed. They got their water from a well which ran sweet and plentiful normally, but was itself connected to other local wells, and somewhere along the line pipes must have cracked, because suddenly the well ran dry except for buckets of sludgy muck. And horrifyingly, shortly after the town's own electricity failed, the hospital's little emergency generator also died. Without it they had no supply of hot water, no cooking facilities bar a small backup camping gas arrangement, and worst of all, no refrigeration or facilities for sterilizing. In short, they were thrown back upon only the most basic and primitive forms of medication, amounting to little more than practical first aid.

It was late afternoon and they were already floundering when the hospital was visited by Captain Sadiq. He spent quite a time in discussion with the doctor and Sisters Mary and Ursula, the leading nuns of the small colony, and it was finally decided that one of them should come back with him to the convoy, to speak to us and find out if our technical skills could be of any use. Sister Ursula came as the doctor couldn't be spared and Sister Mary was elderly.

Kemp asked why Captain Sadiq hadn't personally escorted her to the camp and seen her safe. He was fairly indignant and so was I at this dereliction.

'Ah, he's so busy, that man. I told him to drop me at the military camp and I walked over. There's nothing wrong with me now, and walking's no new thing to us, you know.'

'It could have been damned dangerous.'

'I didn't think so. There were a score of people wishing to speak to the Captain, and no vehicles to spare. And here I am, safe enough.'

'That you are, Sister. You'll stay here tonight? I'm sure you could do with a night's sleep. In the morning we'll take you back to the hospital, and see what we can do to help.'

Kemp had changed quite a lot in a short time. While not inhumane, I'm fairly sure that as little as three days ago he would not have been quite so ready to ditch his transportation job at the drop of a hat to go to the rescue of a local mission hospital. But the oncome of the war, the sight of the burnt out town with its hapless population, and perhaps most of all the injury to one of his own, our pilot, had altered his narrow outlook.

Now he added, 'One of our men is badly hurt, Sister. He was in a plane crash and he needs help. Would you look at him tonight?'

'Of course,' she said with ready concern.

Ben Hammond had left the table, and now came back to join us with a stack of six-packs of beer in his arms.

'We've relaxed the rationing for tonight,' he said. 'Everybody deserves it. Sister, you wouldn't take a second shot of whisky, but maybe you'll settle for this instead?' He handed her a can from the pack.

She tightened her fist around the can.

'Why, it's ice cold!'

Hammond smiled. 'It just came out of the fridge.'

'You have a refrigerator? But that's marvellous. We can preserve our drugs then, praise be to God!'

Kemp and Hammond exchanged the briefest of glances, but I could guess what they were thinking. There was no way that refrigerator could be left at the hospital, urgent though its need might be; it was run by the generator that was solidly attached to the rig, and without which nothing could function.

Things looked better the next morning, but not much. No smoke wreathed up from the distant town but I suspected that this was because there was nothing left there to burn. We were greatly cheered when Sam Wilson told us that he had located a source of clean water, a well at a nearby village which hadn't been affected by the bombing, and which seemed to have a healthy supply. He intended to fill the water tanker and top up drinking containers. When he learned about the water shortage at the hospital he said that there should be enough for them too, assuming they had some sort of tank in which to store it.

Geoff Wingstead joined us for breakfast and met Sister Ursula for the first time. She had been to see Otterman but wanted him taken to the hospital for the doctor to see, and now looked professionally at Wingstead's gash and bruises and approved of what had been done for them. Wingstead insisted that he was now perfectly well and was eager to see the town and the hospital for himself. In spite of his heavy financial commitment, he seemed far less anxious about the rig and Wyvern Transport's future than Kemp did. Perhaps it was just that he was younger and more adventurous.

I drove back to the town in the Land Rover with Kemp, Wingstead, Sister Ursula, and Hammond. Sadiq came over just before we left and said that he would see us at the hospital a little later. He looked drawn and harassed. The lack

of communication from his superiors and the consequent
responsibility was taking its toll, but even so he was bearing
up pretty well. Kemp and I still had a nagging doubt as to
his loyalty, but we'd seen nothing to prove the case one way
or the other, except that he was still with us, which probably counted for something. As for the shooting down of our
plane, nothing whatever had been said about it and I was
content to let the question lie.

The fires had burnt themselves out and the heavy pall of
smoke of yesterday was replaced by a light haze fed by ash
and still smouldering embers. Kodowa had nothing left
worth destroying. A few isolated buildings still stood, but
most of the centre was gone, and it was by no means sure
that when we cleared the rubble we would find an intact
road surface beneath it.

People wandered about still, but very few of them. Many
had simply melted back into the bush, others had gone to
cluster round the hospital or the army encampment, and
we'd seen pathetic faces hovering near our own camp during the early hours of the morning. We didn't spend much
time in the town, but asked Sister Ursula to direct us to the
hospital which stood slightly apart and to the east. The road
getting there was not in good condition.

The hospital looked exactly like the casualty station it
had become. We threaded our way through the knots of
Nyalans who were already setting up their makeshift homes
in the grounds, avoiding the little cooking fires and the live-
stock which wandered about underfoot, and the small
naked children. People stared at us but there was none of
the crowding round that usually happened in the villages in
happier times. Sister Ursula, though, was accosted and
hailed by name as we left the car and made our way
indoors.

We met Sister Mary, who was elderly and frail, and two
younger nuns, all fully occupied. I noticed that none of

them seemed surprised to see Sister Ursula back with a team of British men, or even particularly relieved at her safe return from what might have been regarded as a dangerous mission; the impression I got was that they all had the most sublime faith in her ability to take care of herself, and to turn up trumps in any eventuality. I could see their point of view.

She led us into an office, asked us to wait and vanished, to return very soon with the surgeon in tow.

Kemp said, 'We're very pleased to meet you, Doctor –'

He was a tall, saturnine Nyalan with a strong Asian streak, grey-haired and authoritative. He wore tropical whites which were smudged and blood-streaked. He put out a hand and took Kemp's, and smiled a mouthful of very white teeth at all of us.

'Katabisirua. But here everyone calls me Doctor Kat. It is a pleasure to have you here, especially at this moment.'

'Doctor – Doctor Kat, I'm Basil Kemp of Wyvern Transport. You probably know what we're doing here in Nyala. This is my partner, Mister Wingstead. Mister Hammond, our chief mechanic. Mister Mannix is from our associated company, British Electric.' He ran through the introductions and there were handshakes all round, very formal. Ben hid a smile at the man's nickname.

'Gentlemen, I can offer you little hospitality. Please forgive me.'

Wingstead brushed this aside.

'Of course you can't, and we don't expect it. There's work to be done here. Let me say that I think we have got your water problem sorted out, thanks to some of my lads, provided you've got tanks or somewhere to store the stuff.'

Dr Kat's eyes lit up. 'Thank God. Water is a pressing need. We have a storage tank which is almost empty; I have been trying to take nothing from it until we knew about replacement, but naturally everyone is in need of it.'

'We'll get the tanker up here as soon as we can. We expect Captain Sadiq to join us soon; he's the officer of the military detachment here. When he comes, I'll get him to send a message to our camp,' Wingstead said. He and Dr Kat were on the same wavelength almost immediately, both men of decision and determination. Basil Kemp's tendency to surrender to irritation and his stubborn inability to keep his plans flexible would be easily overridden by these two.

'Now, what about the electricity? We cannot make our generator work. We have bottled gas, but not much. What can you do to help us there?' Dr Kat asked. He had another attribute, the calm assurance that every other man was willing to put himself and his possessions completely at the service of the hospital at any time. Without that self-confidence no man would have been capable of even beginning to run such a project, for the obstacles Katabisirua must have had to overcome in his time would have been enormous.

'Hammond and I are going to have a look at your generator. We've some experience at that sort of thing. I can't make any promises but we'll do our best,' Wingstead said.

Sister Ursula interrupted. 'What about your refrigerator?' she asked.

Dr Kat's head came up alertly. 'What refrigerator?'

Wingstead hadn't known about last evening's conversation and Kemp, for whatever motives I didn't quite like to think about, hadn't referred to it. Sister Ursula said firmly, 'Doctor Kat, they have a working fridge on their transporter. We should send all the drugs that must be kept cold and as much food as possible down there immediately. We can save a lot of it.'

His face beamed. 'But that's wonderful!'

Sister Ursula went on inexorably, 'And also they have electricity. Lights, cooking, even a deepfreeze. I saw all this last night. Isn't that so, gentlemen?'

'Of course we have,' Wingstead concurred. 'We're going to do what we can to use our power supply to restart yours. We'll have to get the rig up here, though, and that isn't going to be at all easy.'

Kemp looked troubled. 'I've been studying the road up here. What with the refugees and the condition of the road itself, I'd say it's going to be damn near impossible, Geoff.'

The nun interrupted, her jaw set at its firmest. 'But all we want is your generator. We don't need that huge thing of yours. We could do with your deepfreeze too; and with the generator our own refrigerator will run. You gentlemen can manage without cold beer, but we need that facility of yours.'

The Wyvern team exchanged looks of despair.

'Ma'am, Doctor Kat, that just isn't possible,' Hammond said at last.

'Why not, please?' The surgeon asked.

Sister Ursula showed that she'd picked up a bit of politics during her evening at our camp. 'Mister Mannix,' she said, 'you represent a very wealthy company. Please explain to your colleagues that it is imperative that we have this facility! I am sure your board of executives will approve. It is of the highest importance.'

I was dumbfounded and showed it. 'Sister, that just isn't the problem. British Electric would give you anything you asked for, but they're not here. And the reason you can't have the generator isn't economic, it's technical. Explain, someone.'

Hammond took up a pad of paper lying on the desk, and his pen began to fly over the paper as he sketched rapidly.

'Look here, ma'am. You too, Doctor.'

They bent over the sheet of paper and I peered over Ben's shoulder. He had produced a lightning and very competent sketch of the entire rig. He pointed to various parts as he spoke, and it must have been obvious to his whole audience that he was speaking the truth.

'Here's the generator. To drive it you have to have an engine, and that's here. The actual generator is really a part of the engine, not a separate section. If you looked at it, just here, you'd see that the engine casting and the generator casting are one and the same; it's an integral unit.'

'Then we must have the engine too,' said Sister Ursula practically.

Kemp choked.

Hammond shook his head. 'Sorry. The engine has much more to do than just drive this generator. Sure, it provides the electricity to power the fridge and freezer, and light the camp at night and stuff like that, but that's just a bonus.'

He pointed to the illustration of the transformer.

'This big lump on its trailer is now resting on the ground, practically. Before we can move off we have to lift three hundred and thirty tons – that's the load plus the platform it's resting on – through a vertical distance of three feet. It's done hydraulically and it needs a whole lot of power, which comes from the engine. And when we're moving we must have power for the brakes which are also hydraulically operated. Without this engine we're immobile.'

'Then you must – '

Hammond anticipated the nun's next demand.

'We can't ditch our load. It took a couple of pretty hefty cranes to get it in place, and it'd need the same to shift it off its base. Some flat-bed trucks have the mobility to tip sideways, but this one hasn't, so we can't spill it off. And any attempt to do so will probably wreck the entire works.'

It was stalemate. Kemp tried to hide his sigh of relief.

Into the disappointed silence Wingstead spoke. 'Don't be too downhearted. We *can* refrigerate your drugs and a lot of your food too, if you think it's safe to do so, at least while we're here. And we can probably get the whole rig up here so that we can couple up with your lighting and sterilizing units.'

Sister Ursula did look thoroughly downcast.

Katabisirua said gently, 'Never mind, Sister. It was a good idea, but we will have others.'

'But they're going to be moving along. Then what can we do?'

Wingstead said, 'We won't be moving anywhere for a bit, not until we know a little more about the general situation and have a decent plan of action. Let's take this one step at a time, shall we? I think we should go back to our camp now. Would you like to make a pack of all your drugs that need to go into the refrigerator, Sister? We'll take them with us. If you need any in the meantime we can arrange for the Captain to put a motorcyclist at your disposal. What do you suggest we do for our wounded pilot?'

'I will come with you. I think I should see him. They must spare me here for a little while,' the Doctor said. After a quick conference, Sister Ursula went off to supervise the packing of drugs and other items that could do with refrigeration, while Dr Kat collected the ubiquitous little black bag and said that he was ready to go.

We found a soldier standing guard over the Land Rover, and parked nearby was Sadiq's staff car. The Captain was speaking to a knot of Nyalan men, presumably the elders of Kodowa, but left them to join us.

'Good morning, sir. You are better now?' This was addressed to Wingstead, who nodded cheerfully.

'I would like to know what your plans are, sir. There is much to do here, but do you intend to continue up-country?' Sadiq asked.

'We're not going immediately,' Wingstead said. I noticed how easily he took over command from Kemp, and how easily Kemp allowed him to do so. Kemp was entirely content to walk in his senior partner's shadow on ail matters except, perhaps, for the actual handling of the rig itself. I

wasn't sorry. Geoff Wingstead could make decisions and
was flexible enough to see alternative possibilities as he
went along. He was a man after my own heart.

Now he went on, 'I'd like to discuss plans with you,
Captain, but we have to sort ourselves out first. We are going
to try and help the doctor here, but first we're going back to
camp. Can you join me there in a couple of hours, please?'

At this moment Sadiq's sergeant called him over to the
staff car, holding out earphones. Sadiq listened and then
turned dials around until a thin voice, overlaid with static,
floated out to us as we crowded round the car. 'Radio Nyala
is on the air,' Sadiq said.

It was a news broadcast apparently, in Nyalan, which
after a while changed into English. The voice was flat and
careful and the words showed signs that they had come
under the heavy hand of government censorship.
Apparently 'dissident elements' of the Army and Air Force
had rioted in barracks but by a firm show of force the
Government had checked the rebels. The ringleaders were
shortly to stand trial in a military court. There was no need
for civil unease. No names or places were given. There was
no mention of Kodowa. And there was no other news. The
voice disappeared into a mush of palm court music.

I smiled sourly as I listened to this farrago. Next week, if
the Government survived, the 'dissident elements' would
be plainly labelled as traitors. The news broadcasts would
never refer to a state of war, nor give more than the most
shadowy version of the truth. Of course, all that depended
on whether the broadcast station remained in government
hands. If the rebels took it there would be an entirely different version of the 'truth'.

None of us made much comment on what we'd heard,
all recognizing it for the fallacy that it was. We piled into the
Land Rover with Dr Kat and drove back in silence to the
convoy camp.

ELEVEN

Three hours later after a short discussion with Wingstead I gathered the people I wanted for a conference. But I had decided that this wasn't going to be a committee meeting; I wasn't going to put up my proposals to be voted on. This was to be an exchange of ideas and information, but the only person who was going to have the final say was me.

I had found McGrath shaving in front of his tractor. 'Mick, you've just got your old rank back.' He looked a bit blank while the lather on his chin dried in the hot sun. 'You're back to sergeant. We might be going through a tough time in the next few days, and I want someone to keep the crew whipped in line. Think you can do it?'

He gave a slow grin. 'I can do it.'

'Hurry up with your shaving. I want you to sit in on a conference.'

So we had McGrath, Hammond, Kemp, Wingstead, Captain Sadiq and me. Katabisirua had been joined at our camp by Sister Ursula and they were included as a matter of courtesy; any decisions would affect them and in any case I didn't think I had the power to keep them out. I had already realized they made a strong team: just how strong I was shortly to find out.

Firstly I outlined the geographical position, and gave them my reasons for changing our direction. Instead of

going on up to the arid fastness of Bir Oassa we would turn
at right angles and take the secondary road to the Manzu
border at Lake Pirie on the Katali River. Here we had two
options whereas at Bir Oassa we had only one, or slightly
less than one; we could turn back along the coast road to
Lasulu and the capital if the country had by then settled its
internal quarrel and things were judged safe, or we could
get the men at least across the Katali into Manzu and diplomatic immunity.

Wingstead had already heard all this from me and was
resigned to the possibility of losing his rig and convoy, and
of not being able to fulfil the terms of his contract with the
Nyalan Government. He did not contest my arguments. I
had already spoken to Kemp, and Hammond had heard it
all from him. Kemp was still obviously fretting but
Hammond's faith in Wingstead was all-encompassing. If his
boss said it was OK, he had no objections. I asked McGrath
what he thought the men's reactions might be.

'We haven't got much choice, the way I see it. You're the
boss. They'll see it your way.' He implied that they'd better,
which suited me very well.

Sadiq was torn between a sense of duty and a sense of
relief. To take the long hard road up to the desert, with all
its attendant dangers, and without any knowledge of who
or what he'd find waiting there, was less attractive than
returning to a known base, in spite of the unknown factors
waiting in that direction as well. But there was one problem
he didn't have that we did; any decision concerning the
moving of the rig.

We discussed, briefly, the possible state of the road back.
It was all guesswork which Kemp loathed, but at least we
knew the terrain, and there was a bonus of the fact that it
was principally downhill work, redescending the plateau
into the rainforest once more. We would not run short of
water; there were far more people and therefore more

chance of food and even of fuel. And we wouldn't be as exposed as we would be if we continued on through the scrublands. I hadn't discounted the likelihood of aerial attack.

Hammond and Kemp, with an escort of soldiers, were to scout ahead to check out the road while McGrath and Bert Proctor began to organize the convoy for its next stage forward, or rather backward. Wingstead asked McGrath to call a meeting of the crew, so that he could tell them the exact score before we got down to the business of logistics. Everything was falling nicely into place, including my contingency plans to help the hospital as much as possible before we pulled out.

Everything didn't include the inevitable X factor. And the X factor was sitting right there with us.

The moment of change came when I turned to Dr Katabisirua and said to him, 'Doctor Kat, those drugs of yours that we have in refrigeration for you; how vital are they?'

He tented his fingers. 'In the deepfreeze we have serum samples and control sera; also blood clotting agents for our few haemophiliac patients. In the fridge there is whole blood, plasma, blood sugars, insulin and a few other things. Not really a great deal as we try not to be dependent on refrigeration. It has been of more use in saving some of our food, though that is being used up fast.'

I was relieved to hear this; they could manage without refrigeration if they had to. After all, most tropical mission hospitals in poor countries work in a relative degree of primitiveness.

'We'll keep your stuff on ice as long as possible,' I said. 'And we're going to have a go at repairing your generator. We'll do all we can before leaving.'

Dr Kat and Sister Ursula exchanged the briefest of glances, which I interpreted, wrongly, as one of resignation.

'Captain Sadiq,' the Doctor said, 'Do you have any idea at all as to whether there will be a measure of governmental control soon?'

Sadiq spread his hands. 'I am sorry, no,' he said. 'I do not know who is the Government. I would do my best for all civilians, but I have been told to stay with Mister Mannix and protect his convoy particularly, you see. It is very difficult to make guesses.'

They spoke in English, I think in deference to us.

'The people of Kodowa will scatter among the smaller villages soon,' Kat said. 'The area is well populated, which is why they needed a hospital. Many of them have already gone. But that solution does not apply to my patients.'

'Why not?' Kemp asked.

'Because we do not have the staff to scatter around with them, to visit the sick in their homes or the homes of friends. Many are too sick to trust to local treatment. We have many more patients now because of the air raid.'

'How many?'

'About fifty bed patients, if we had the beds to put them in, and a hundred or more ambulatory patients. In this context they could be called the "walking wounded",' he added acidly.

'So it is only a matter of extra shelter you need,' said Sadiq. I knew he was partly wrong, but waited to hear the Doctor put it into words.

'It is much more than that, Captain. We need shelter, yes, but that is not the main problem. We need medical supplies but we can manage for a while on what we have. But our patients need nursing, food and water.'

'There will be dysentery here soon,' put in Sister Ursula. 'There is already sepsis, and a lack of hygiene, more than we usually suffer.'

'They also are vulnerable to the depredations of marauding bands of rebels,' said Dr Kat, a sentence I felt like cheering for its sheer pomposity. But he was right for all that.

'As are we all, including the younger nurses,' added the Sister. It began to sound like a rather well-rehearsed chorus and Wingstead and I exchanged a glance of slowly dawning comprehension.

'Am I not correct, Mister Mannix, in saying that you consider it the safest and most prudent course for your men to leave Kodowa, to try and get away to a place of safety?'

'You heard me say so, Doctor.'

'Then it follows that it must also be the correct course for my patients.'

For a long moment no-one said anything, and then I broke the silence. 'Just how do you propose doing that?'

Katabisirua took a deep breath. This was the moment he had been building up to. 'Let me see if I have everything right that I have learned from you. Mister Hammond, you say that the large object you carry on your great vehicle weighs over three hundred tons, yes?'

'That's about it.'

'Could you carry another seven tons?'

'No trouble at all,' said Hammond.

'Seven tons is about the weight of a hundred people,' said Katabisirua blandly.

Or one more elephant, I thought with a manic inward chuckle. The silence lengthened as we all examined this bizarre proposition. It was broken by the Doctor, speaking gently and reasonably, 'I am not suggesting that you take us all the way to the coast, of course. There is another good, if small, hospital at Kanja on the north road, just at the top of the next escarpment. It has no airfield and is not itself important, so I do not think it will have been troubled by the war. They could take care of us all.'

I doubted that and didn't for a moment think that Dr Kat believed it either, but I had to hand it to him; he was plausible and a damned good psychologist. Not only did his proposition sound well within the bounds of reason and capability, but I could tell from the rapt faces around me that the sheer glamour of what he was suggesting was beginning to put a spell on them. It was a *Pied Piper* sort of situation, stuffed with pathos and heroism, and would go far to turn the ignominious retreat into some sort of whacky triumph. The Dunkirk spirit, I thought – the great British knack of taking defeat and making it look like victory.

There was just one little problem. Kanja, it appeared, was on the very road that we had already decided to abandon, heading north into the desert and towards the oilfields at Bir Oassa. I was about to say as much when to my astonishment Wingstead cut in with a question which implied that his thinking was not going along with mine at all.

He said, 'How far to Kanja?'

'About fifty miles. The road is quite good. I have often driven there,' the Doctor said.

Hammond spoke up. 'Excuse me, Doctor. Is it level or uphill?'

'I would say it is fairly flat. There are no steep hills.'

McGrath said, 'We could rig awnings over the bogies to keep off the sun.'

Hammond asked, his mind seething with practicalities, 'Fifty odd patients, and a staff of – ?'

'Say ten,' said Sister Ursula.

'What about all the rest, then?'

'They would walk. They are very hardy and used to that, and even those who are wounded will manage. There are a few hospital cars but we have no spare petrol. I believe you do not go very fast, gentlemen.'

'We could take some up on top of the trucks. And we've got your car, Mister Mannix, and Mister Kemp's Land Rover, and perhaps the military could give up some space,' Hammond said.

'And the tractors?' the Sister asked.

'No, ma'am. They're packed inside with steel plates set in cement, and the airlift truck is full of machinery and equipment we might need. But there's room on top of all of them. Awnings would be no problem?'

McGrath said, 'There'd be room for a couple of the nippers in each cab, like as not.'

'Nippers?' the Doctor asked.

'The children,' McGrath said.

I looked from face to face. On only one of them, and that predictably was Basil Kemp's, did I see a trace of doubt or irritation. Minds were taking fire as we talked. Geographical niceties were either being entirely overlooked or deliberately avoided, and somehow I couldn't bring myself to dash cold water on their blazing enthusiasm. But this was madness itself.

Dr Kat regarded the backs of his hands and flexed his fingers thoughtfully. 'I may have to operate while we are travelling. Would there be room for that?'

'Room, yes, but it would be too bumpy, Doctor. You'd have to work whenever we were stopped,' said Hammond. He had a notebook out and was already making sketches.

Sadiq spoke. 'I think my men can walk and the wounded will ride. They are our people and we must take care of them.' He squared his shoulders as he spoke and I saw the lifting of a great burden from his soul; he had been given a job to do, something real and necessary no matter which side was winning the mysterious war out there. It called for simple logistics, basic planning, clear orders, and he was capable of all that. And above all, it called for no change in the route once planned for him and us by his masters. It was perfect for him. It solved all his problems in one stroke.

Sister Ursula stood up.

'Have you a measuring tape, Mister Hammond?'

'Yes, ma'am. What do you want it for?' he asked.

'I want to measure your transport. I must plan for beds.'

'I'll come with you,' he said. 'Tell me what you want.'

McGrath lumbered to his feet. 'I'll go round up the lads, Mister Wingstead,' he said. 'You'll be wanting to talk to them yourself.' The Doctor too rose, dusting himself off fastidiously. He made a small half-bow to Geoff Wingstead. 'I have to thank you, sir,' he said formally. 'This is a very fine thing that you do. I will go back now, please. I have many arrangements to make.'

Sadiq said, 'I will take the Doctor and then prepare my own orders. I will come back to advise you, Mister Mannix. We should not delay, I think.'

Around us the conference melted away, each member intent on his or her own affairs. Astonishingly, nobody had waited to discuss this new turn of events or even to hear from the so-called bosses as to whether it was even going to happen. In a matter of moments Kemp, Wingstead and I were left alone. For once I felt powerless.

Kemp shrugged his shoulders. 'It's all quite mad,' he said. 'We can't possibly get involved in this – this – '

'Stunt?' Wingstead asked gently. 'Basil, we *are* involved. I've never seen a piece of manipulation more skilfully done. Those two have run rings round the lot of us, and there isn't any way that we could put a stop to this business. And what's more,' he went on, overriding Kemp's protests, 'I don't think I'd want to stop it. It is crazy, but it sounds feasible and it's humanely necessary. And it's going to put a lot of heart into our lads. None of them likes what's happened, they feel frustrated, cheated and impotent.'

I finally got a word in. 'Geoff, we'd already decided that we shouldn't carry on northwards. This would be a very fine thing to do, but –'

'You too, Neil? Surely you're not going to fight me on this. I think it's damned important. Look, it's fifty miles.

Two, maybe three days extra, getting there and back here to Kodowa. Then we're on our own again. And there's something else. The news that we must turn back is one they were going to take damned hard. This way they'll at least have the feeling that they've done something worthwhile.'

He stretched his arms and yawned, testing the stiffness in his side.

'And so will I. So let's get to it.'

Down near the commissariat truck McGrath had called all hands together. Wingstead and I went to meet them. On the way I stopped and called Bishop over to give him an instruction that brought first a frown and then a grin to his face. He in turn summoned Bing and they vanished. 'What did you tell him?' Wingstead asked.

'Bit of psychology. You'll see. Don't start till he's back, will you?'

Bishop and Bing returned a few moments later, lugging a couple of cardboard boxes. To the assembled men I said, 'Here you go, guys. A can apiece. Send them around, cookie.'

Bishop began handing out six-packs of beer. 'Management too,' I reminded him. 'And that includes the Doctor and Sister Ursula.' There was a buzz of conversation as the packs went out, and then I held up a hand in silence.

'Everybody happy?'

Laughter rippled. Cans were already being opened, and Barry Lang paused with his halfway to his mouth. 'What are we celebrating, chief? The end of the war?'

'Not quite. We're celebrating the fact that this is the last cold beer we're all going to get for a while.' At this there was a murmur of confusion. I held up an open can. 'Some of you may know this already. We're using the fridge to store the hospital's drugs and as much food as possible for the patients, especially the kids. From now on, it'll be warm beer and canned food for the lot of us. My heart bleeds for you.'

This brought another laugh. Grafton said, 'We're staying here, then?'

This was Wingstead's moment, and he jumped lightly onto the top of the cab. He had recovered well from his shake-up in the air crash, unlike Max Otterman, who still lay unconscious in the shade of the water tanker and was a constant source of worry to all of us.

Wingstead said, 'No, we're not staying here. We're moving out, maybe today, more likely tomorrow. But we're not going much further north.'

Into an attentive silence which I judged to be not hostile he outlined the geographical picture, the political scene such as we knew it, and the reasons for abandoning the contract. The crew accepted everything without argument, though there was a lot of muted discussion, and I was impressed again by Wingstead's air of command and his control over his team. I'd had my eye on Sisley and Lang as being the two most likely hard liners, but there was no opposition even from them. The argument in favour of saving their own skins was a strong one, and unlike Wyvern's management they had no direct stake in the outcome of the job.

Wingstead went on to the second half of the story, and now their astonishment was obvious. There was a burst of talking and signs of excitement and enthusiasm beginning to creep into their voices. It was almost like giving a bunch of kids a dazzling new game to play with.

'So there it is, chaps. We move out as soon as we can, and we're taking a whole lot of sick and injured people and all the hospital staff with us, and everybody who can walk will be tailing along for their daily bandage changes. We're going to pack the badly injured onto the rig and carry as many of the rest as we can on the trucks. We're going to need every ounce of your energy and good will. Are we agreed?'

There was a ready chorus of assent. Wingstead went on, 'Any bright ideas you may have, pass them along to Mick or Mister Hammond or me. Any medical questions direct to the Sister.' I smiled briefly at the division between those who were 'Mister' and those who were not, even in these fraught moments; another example of the gulf between their country and mine.

'When we've seen them safe at the hospital in Kanja, we'll turn round and set off towards the Katali. We reckon on only two extra days for the mission. Thank you, chaps.'

Mick McGrath rose and bellowed.

'Right, lads! Five minutes to finish your beer and then let's be at it. There's plenty to be done.'

As Wingstead and I walked off, well pleased with the way our bombshell of news had gone down, Sister Ursula way-laid us, having, no doubt got all she wanted from Ben Hammond.

'Mister Mannix, I want transport back to the hospital, please.'

'No you don't,' I said. 'You're wanted here. The crew is going to be pestering you with questions and ideas, and Geoff and I have got quite a few of our own.'

'I'll be needed at the hospital.'

'I'm sure you will. But Sister Mary is there with the others and you're the only one here. And the rate your Doctor Kat works, there'll probably be a first load of patients arriving within the hour. The lads will work under your direction, yours and Ben's that is. They've got awnings to rig up, bedding to get cut, all sorts of stuff. And you have to choose a spot for your operating theatre.'

'I've done that already.' But she wasn't stubborn when faced with plain good sense, and agreed readily enough to stay and get on with her end of the job, for which I was grateful. If it came to the crunch I didn't think I would ever win out against her.

We all worked hard and the rig was transformed. Sadiq's men rounded up some of the local women who knew how to thatch with palm leaf fronds and set them to work, silently at first and then as the strangeness and the fear began to wear off, singing in ululating chorus. As it took shape the rig began to look pretty strange wearing a selection of thatched umbrellas. I was amused to think what Kemp would have to say: he had gone off to check the road leading northwards out of town.

Awnings were being made for the tops of each of the trucks as well, and reeds from the river were beginning to pile up to make bedding for each of the patients as we found places for them. All four tractors were similarly bedecked. Even the tank McGrath had salvaged was to carry its share of patients, perched in the turret. The gun had been ditched once it was clear that there was no ammunition for it. I doubt if you could see anything in the world more incongruous than a thatched tank.

Sadiq had unearthed a couple of old trucks which Ben Hammond pronounced as serviceable and we thatched one of those. The other already had a canvas awning. There were few other vehicles in Kodowa that had escaped either the strafing or the fires.

There was moderately good news about fuel. Outside the town we found a full 4000-gallon tanker. It must have been abandoned by its driver at the onset of the air attack. Both it and our own tanker escaped thatching because I jibbed at carrying bedridden patients on top of potential bombs. The water tanker wasn't thatched either, being the wrong shape for carrying people.

Sister Ursula was endlessly busy. She supervised the cutting of bedding, to make sure that none was wet and that the worst of the insect life was shaken out of it, checked through our food supplies and made a complete inventory, rounded up towels and sheets from everybody, and selected a place on the rig for Dr Kat's mobile surgery, the top of the foremost tractor cab, as being the only really flat surface and the one least likely to get smothered in the dust we would stir up in our progress. It was, she pointed out, very exposed but in our supplies we had a couple of pup tents and one of these, after some tailoring, made a fairly passable enclosed space. The other formed a screen for the patients' toilet, a galvanized iron bucket.

It was all quite astonishing.

The Sister then proceeded to go through the camp like a one-woman locust swarm, sweeping up everything she thought might be of any use. Every pair of scissors she could find she confiscated; she almost denuded the commissary wagon of knives; and she kept young Bing on the run, setting him to boil water to sterilize the things she found.

Once done, they were wrapped in sheets of polythene. Everything as sterile as she could make it. And then they were stored in a corner of our freezer, to slow down bacterial activity. She confiscated packets of paperclips and went through Kemp's Land Rover, removing clips from every piece of paper in sight, garnering sticky tape, elastic bands and string. Our several first aid boxes all went into her hoard.

Military trucks began arriving from the hospital carrying, not people yet, but goods; food, medications, bandaging, implements, dishes and hardware of all sorts. Among other things was a contraption on a trolley that Sister Ursula dismissed with annoyance.

'That thing doesn't work. Hasn't for a long time. It's a waste of space.'

'What is it, Sister?' It was Ben Hammond who asked, and who seemed to be in constant attendance, not in Mick

McGrath's proprietorial fashion but as head gofer to a factory foreman. Her demands fascinated and challenged him.

'It is, or was, a portable anaesthetic machine.'

'If it were fixed, would it be of use?' She nodded and he fixed it. He was a damned good mechanic.

The Sister found a place for Max Otterman and he was gently lifted onto his pile of bedding; Wyvern Transport Hospital's first inmate. He'd been showing some signs of recovering consciousness in the past few hours but the portents were not good; he looked and sounded awful.

I kept busy and tried not to think about him, putting him in the same mental folder in which lurked other worries: the state of the nation, the progress of war, the possibility of aircraft bombing us as we sat helpless. Our fuel or water might run out, there could be sickness or mechanical breakdowns. There was no communication with the world apart from the unreliable and sporadic messages received on the Captain's radio. I kept going, knowing that when I stopped the problems would close in.

It was a long, complex and exhausting day. There was little talking as evening fell and we ate thoughtfully and turned in. I lay fighting off despair, and even coined a phrase for it: Mannix' Depression. But I couldn't raise a laugh at my own joke. The odds against us seemed to be stacked far too high.

TWELVE

There was another change of plan that afternoon. We were to move the rig to the hospital rather than risk moving the patients before it was necessary. At daybreak we got going, the oddly transformed convoy passing slowly through the town that wasn't a town any more, to Katabisirua's head-quarters beyond. The command car bumped over rubble as we passed the remains of the shattered tanks which we had laboured to shift and crunched through cinders and debris in what had been the main street of Kodowa. The place still stank of death and burning.

We passed a truncated and blackened telegraph pole from which a body dangled. Sadiq said laconically, 'A looter, sir.'

'Have you had many?'

'A few. He was one of the first. He discourages the others, as they say.'

Every now and then Sadiq's obviously broader than average education showed through. For a locally trained lower echelon officer of a somewhat backward country he was surprisingly well-read in military matters. It seemed a pity that he had been given so little room to do his own thinking, but was still tied by the bonds of discipline.

I saw a sign on a blackened but still standing shop front and a soldier who stood in front of the door, cradling a gun. 'Will you stop a minute, Captain? May I go in there?'

'It is off limits, Mister Mannix.' Again the flash of an unexpected phrase.

'Yes, and we both know why.'

I got out of the car without waiting for any more objections and gestured to the soldier to let me by. Sadiq entered the ruined premises behind me. I picked my way through a jumble of fallen stock, farm implements, clothing, magazines, household stuff, all the usual clutter of an upcountry store, to a locked glass-fronted cupboard towards the back. The glass was shattered now, and the doors buckled with heat. I took a hunting knife from a display rack, inserted the point just below the lock, and pushed smartly sideways. There was a dry snap and the doors sagged open. There wasn't much of a choice, just six shotguns; four of them double-barrelled which the British still favour, and two pump action. Four were fire-damaged.

I picked up a Mossberg Model 500, twelve-gauge with six shot capacity, and laid it on the counter. Then I started to attack the warped drawers below the gun rack, praying that I'd find what I wanted, and did so; two packs of double-o buckshot, magnum size. Each shell carried nine lead pellets, a third of an inch in diameter, and capable of dropping a 200-pound deer. And a deer is harder to kill than a man.

I dumped the shells next to the gun, added a can of gun oil, then as an afterthought searched for a scabbard for the hunting knife and put that with the rest. Sadiq watched without comment. Then I tore a piece of paper from a singed pad on the counter, scribbled a note, and dropped it into the open till. I slammed the till drawer shut and walked out of the store with my collection.

'Are you going to hang me for a looter, Captain? That was an IOU I put in the cash till. The owner can claim from British Electric.'

'If he is still alive,' said Sadiq dryly.

He watched as I ripped open a packet of shells and started to load the gun. 'Are you expecting trouble at the hospital, Mister Mannix?'

'You're a soldier. You ought to know that an unloaded gun is just a piece of junk iron. Let's say I may be expecting trouble, period. And you may not be around to get me out of it.'

'Please do not wave it about, then. I will not ask you for a licence; I am not a policeman. I authorize you to hold it. I would feel the same, myself.'

He surprised me by his acquiescence. I had expected him to make it hard for me, but I was determined to go no further without any sort of personal weapon. I made sure the safety catch was on and then laid the gun down by the side of my seat. 'You have some pretty fine weapons yourself,' I said. 'One of my men was casting an envious eye on your Uzi. Keep a close check on all your guns, Captain; I don't want any of them to go missing.' It was Mick McGrath I was thinking of. Something had made me think quite a while back that I'd always be happier if he remained unarmed.

'I will take care. Take your own precautions, please,' Sadiq said, and we drove on to catch up with the rest of the convoy.

I suppose you could call the setup at Katabisirua's a field hospital. Everyone seemed to have been moved out of the buildings into a field, and nurses scurried about their business. To me it just looked like a lot of people dying in the open air. Last time I'd only seen the offices, and all this was pretty horrifying.

After a while I began to see order in the apparent chaos. Way over at one end were a lot of people, sitting or walking about, some supported by friends. Scattered cooking fires sent plumes of smoke into the air. In the field were rows of makeshift beds with friends or families in attendance. Hastily erected frond screens hid what I assumed to be the worst cases, or perhaps they were latrines. In the middle of the field were tables around which moved nurses in rumpled uniforms. A stretcher was being lifted onto a table presided over by Dr Katabisirua. At another Sister Mary, frail and leaning on a stick, was directing a nurse in a bandaging operation. I couldn't see Sister Ursula anywhere.

Away from this area were two newly filled in trenches and a third trench standing open. Slowly I walked across to look at it. It had been half filled with loose earth and stones and scattered with lime. A single naked foot protruded and I choked on the acridity of the chloride of lime which did not quite hide the stench of decay.

I turned away with sweat banding my forehead, and it had nothing to do with the morning sun.

Sadiq's car had gone but a man was standing waiting for me. He was white, smallish and very weathered, wearing shorts and a torn bush jacket; his left arm was in a sling and his face was covered with abrasions.

'Mannix?' he said huskily.

'That's right.'

'You might remember me if I were cleaner. I'm Dan Atheridge. We met in the Luard Club not long ago.'

I did remember him but not as he was right now. Then he had been a brisk, chirpy little man, dapper and immaculate, with snapping blue eyes that gave a friendly gleam in a walnut face. Now the skin was pasty under the surface tan and the eyes had become old and faded. He went on, 'Perhaps I'd have been better off if I'd stayed there . . . and perhaps not. What exactly is going on here? I understand you're moving everybody out. That right?'

I said, 'I could say I was glad to see you, but they're not quite the right words under the circumstances.'

He moved his arm and winced. 'Got a broken flipper –
hurts like hell. But I survived.' He nodded towards the open
grave. 'Better off than those poor buggers.'

'How come you're here?'

'I run beef on the high ground up past Kanja. I brought
a truck down here for servicing three days ago. I was standing on what was the hotel balcony watching the troops go
by when all hell let loose. I say, are you *really* going to
evacuate the hospital up to Kanja?'

'We're going to try.'

'Can I come along? My home's up that way. My wife will
be worrying.'

I tried to imagine what it would be like to be a woman
on a remote farm in the Nyalan uplands with a war breaking out and a husband vanished into a bombed out town,
and failed. Then I had another, more practical thought. He'd
know the Kanja route backwards.

'You'd be more than welcome. We can find you a meal,
perhaps – and a warm beer.'

'Great!' His warm smile lit the weary eyes.

'Mister Mannix!'

I turned to see Dr Kat approaching. 'Damned good chap,
that,' Atheridge muttered.

The doctor looked wearier than ever; his eyes were
sunken deep into his head and his cheeks were hollow. I
judged he was driving himself too hard and made a mental
note to see if Sister Ursula could get him to slow down.
Come to that, she probably needed slowing down herself.

'We lost fifteen in the night,' Dr Kat said. 'The worst
cases, of course.'

'Triage?' Atheridge murmured.

I knew about that. Triage was a grisly business used in
many armies, but perfected by the French at Dien Bien Phu.
The idea was that the wounded were sorted into three
categories; lightly wounded, medium but salvageable, and

hopeless. The lightly wounded were the first to get treatment so they could be pushed back into action quickly. And it saved on badly needed medical supplies. But it also meant that a lot of others died who might have been saved; a coldly logical, strictly military solution to a medical problem.

'Nothing of the sort,' snapped Katabisirua. 'They had the best attention but they still died. This is not an army. Even you, Mister Atheridge, waited your turn.'

'I'm sorry. You're quite right, of course.'

Dr Kat turned to me. 'I see you have prepared the convoy for us, Mister Mannix.' We glanced over to the distant, thatch-draped rig. 'I have seen what you have done and am most grateful.'

'Have you seen your new operating theatre? You'd be amazed at how much Sister Ursula has achieved.'

'I would not be amazed in the least. I know her.'

I asked, 'What is your worst problem right now, Doctor?'

'All those who had extensive burns or severe wounds are already dead or will die soon – later today, I should think. Now the death rate will fall rapidly. But it will rise again in two days?'

'Why?'

'Sepsis. I would give a fortune for ten gallons of old-fashioned carbolic. We have no disinfectants left, and we are running out of sterile bandaging. Operating on a patient in these conditions is like signing his death warrant. I cannot heal with my knife in times like this.'

I felt helpless; I had absolutely no medical knowledge and sympathy seemed a pretty useless commodity. I offered the only thing I had. 'We'll get you all to Kanja as quickly as possible, Doctor. We can start in the evening, when it's cooler, and travel through the night. Mister Atheridge will be invaluable, knowing the road so well.'

The doctor nodded and went back to work.

* * *

I'd never make a doctor, not even a bad one, because I guess I'm too squeamish. Medical friends have told me it's something you get used to, but I doubt if I ever could. I'm tough enough at boardroom and even field politics, but blood and guts is another matter. What we loaded onto the rig weren't people but cocooned bundles of pain. The burn cases were the worst.

It was a long and bitter job but we did it, and when we had got everyone aboard somewhere or other, and as comfortable as possible, I went in search of Katabisirua. I found him with Sister Ursula, and as I approached she was saying in a stern voice, 'Now don't argue, Doctor Kat. I said I'll stay. It's all arranged.' She turned to me and said in no less stern a tone, 'Try and get him to have some rest, Mister Mannix. And you too. All of you.' She marched off across the field without waiting for an answer, heading for one of Sadiq's trucks which stood isolated from the rest in the comparative shade of a couple of palms. Two soldiers leaned casually against it and close by three white bundles lay on the ground. A couple of Nyalans squatted over them, waving palm fronds to keep off the flies.

I said, 'What's all this about?'

'Those are the last of the bad burn cases, three of them. Two men and a woman. They can't be moved. Sister Ursula will stay with them and comfort them in their dying. When they are dead the soldiers will bury them. Then they'll bring her to join us. I cannot persuade her otherwise.'

I looked at the stiff-backed figure walking away. 'She's quite a lady.'

'Yes. Very stubborn.'

Coming from him that was ridiculous, almost enough to make me smile but not quite. I said, 'We're all set to move. I'm about to check with Basil Kemp. Are you ready to board, Doctor?'

'Yes, I suppose so.' We both glanced briefly round at the desolation, the bloodstained earth, the abandoned beds and fireplaces, the debris and impedimenta of human living strewn all about. There had been no time to tidy up, and no reason either. The vultures could have it all.

I went in search of Basil Kemp. He had been very quiet all day, looking punch-drunk like a concussed boxer after a losing fight. He did his job all right but he did it almost as though by memory. Ben Hammond was forming a perfect backup for him, covering up whatever weaknesses he sensed in his boss, though he was doubtless motivated more by his faith in Geoff Wingstead.

'Doctor Kat's coming on board,' I told him. 'That's the last of it. We're ready to roll any time you say.'

He had planned to push on well into and maybe right through the night. He had not had time to reconnoitre the road very far ahead, but he had the previous surveys to go by, and there were no very sharp bends or steep gradients in the next twenty miles or so. Up as far as the next river course there were no foreseeable problems. That river lay between us and Kanja which was a pity, but all things being equal we shouldn't have too much trouble. All things weren't equal, of course; somewhere a war was probably still being fought, but in the total absence of any news on that score the only rational thing to do was to ignore it. We'd heard no further aircraft activity and the airport itself, a mile or so outside the town, was reported by Sadiq to be completely deserted.

'Right, we'll get moving. I hope to God these damn thatch roofs don't become a nuisance.' He didn't say it, but I could hear in his voice the phrase, 'Or the people either'. Not the man to depend on for kindness, but at least his concern for his precious rig would keep him attentive.

I drove the hire car. Atheridge and I were in front and between us a Nyalan nurse. She was not on the rig as she had injured a leg. In the back were four of the walking, or rather riding, wounded, three of them teenage children.

As I pulled out to drive to my allocated place, ahead of the rig and among the troop trucks, I said to the girl, 'You do speak English, don't you?'

'Oh yes.'

'Will you tell these people behind to yell out if I do anything to hurt them? I'll try to drive smoothly.'

She half-turned and spoke in Nyalan over her shoulder.

'What's your name, honey?'

'Helen Chula,' she said.

'Can you drive a car, Helen?'

'Yes, I can. But my leg – I would have to go slowly.'

I laughed briefly. 'Don't worry, slowly is what we'll all be doing. If necessary you can take over. Mister Atheridge can't do much with that arm of his, though I guess he could stand on a foot pedal if he had to.'

Sadiq's staff car passed us and I remembered something. I hooted and when he stopped I jumped out and ran over to retrieve the shotgun and pack of shells from his car. Walking past us towards his tractor, Mick McGrath stopped dead and looked at the gun with interest.

'Hey, Mister Mannix. You got yourself a shooter. Now what about me?'

'Who do you want to kill, Mick?'

He shrugged. 'Oh hell, nothing like that. It's just that I feel naked being in a war and me without a gun.'

I grinned. 'Get your own fig leaves.'

He went on and I got back into my car, feeling another slight ripple of unease. Atheridge also eyed the weapon quizzically but said nothing as I stowed it with some difficulty, down alongside the driving seat. Behind us the whole convoy was breaking into the guttural growls that signified engines churning to life, blue smoke belching from exhaust pipes, I stuck my head out of the car window and listened.

My imagination was irrational. Had there really been cries of pain from the sick and wounded people on the rig, I would never have been able to hear them over the rumbling of the transports. But my stomach clenched in sympathy as I visualized the shuddering, lurching torment of the rig's movement under their bodies. I caught Helen Chula's eyes and knew that she was thinking exactly the same thing.

It had to be done. I shrugged, put the car in gear, and moved out. Vehicle by vehicle, the entire procession pulled away from the hospital and the ruins of Kodowa.

THIRTEEN

The road beyond Kodowa continued to switchback but the gradients were slightly steeper and the hills longer. The average speed of the rig dropped; it was slow enough downhill but really crawled up the long reverse slopes. In general the speed was about a walking pace. Certainly the flock of Nyalans in our wake, injured though some of them were, had no difficulty in keeping up. They were a hardy people, inured to the heat, and well used to walking those dusty roads.

But we worried about these refugees. We had discussed the need to provide them with food and Sadiq had told us that it would have to be gathered on the way. But there were too many women carrying babies or helping toddlers, old men, and wounded of all ages. It wasn't really our responsibility but how else could we look upon it?

As we got going Helen Chula said, 'If I sleep will you wake me in an hour, please?' and promptly did fall asleep, her head pillowed on Atheridge's good arm. I checked on the four Nyalans behind me; two were asleep and the others stared with wary brown eyes. All were silent.

We travelled for nearly two hours, incredibly slowly, and the morning heat began to give way to the fierce sun of noonday. Atheridge and I didn't talk much because we didn't want to wake the girl. Around us dust billows clouded the little groups of Nyalans into soft focus, and here and there among them walked soldiers. I began to worry about the car engine overheating.

Suddenly I realized that I was being the biggest damn fool in creation; the heat must have fried my brains. I tapped the horn, cut out of the column and nosed through the refugees who were walking ahead of the rig to avoid the worst of the dust. I caught up with Sadiq's command car at the head of the column and waved him down. He had two Nyalan women in the back of his car, but his sergeant was still up front beside him.

I said, 'Captain, this is crazy. There's no law which says that we all have to travel at the same speed as the rig. I could get up to Kanja in under two hours, dump my lot at their hospital and come back for more. What's more, so can all the other faster transport. We could get them organized up there, alert them to what's coming.'

Sadiq shook his head. 'No, Mister Mannix, that would not be a good thing.'

'In God's name, why not?'

He looked up and for a moment I thought he was scanning the sky for aircraft. Then I realized that he had actually looked at a telegraph pole, one of the endless line that accompanied the road, and again I cursed my slow brains. 'Damn it, you've got a handset, Sadiq. We can telephone ahead from here.'

'I have tried. That is what is worrying me – there is nothing. I can understand not being able to reach back to Kodowa, but the line to Kanja is also dead.'

'There'll be a lot of people dead if we keep this pace. There seem to be a hell of a lot more than Doctor Kat reckoned on, and most of them aren't injured at all.'

'I cannot stop them, Mister Mannix. They are simply coming with us.'

I felt nonplussed. More mouths to feed? Surely we weren't obliged to lead the entire remaining population of Kodowa to safety.

'Well, how about some of us pushing on? There's my car, the two trucks we found plus your four. Even the tank can move faster than this, and there are six people on board her. The Land Rover has to stay with the rig, but even you –'

'I stay with the convoy. Also my trucks,' said Sadiq flatly. 'Mister Mannix, have you noticed that there is no traffic coming southwards? Have you thought that Kanja might be just like Kodowa?'

I had, and the thought was unnerving. 'If so, now's the time to find out,' I said.

'I am finding out. I have sent a motorcycle patrol on ahead.' He checked his watch. 'They should be back soon with news, perhaps with help too.'

I mentally apologized to Sadiq. I thought he'd been as stupid as me. He went on, 'If they are not back within the hour then I think it will mean bad trouble at Kanja. They will at least be able to warn us, though; they have one of the radio sets.'

I sighed. 'Sorry. You win on all points.'

He acknowledged my apology with a grave nod. 'It is very difficult, sir. I appreciate that you are doing all you can for my people.'

I returned to my car to find Atheridge standing beside it and Helen Chula stretching herself awake. 'Captain Sadiq's on the ball,' I said. But he wasn't listening to me. Slowly, out of the dust and the crowd, another car was pulling ahead to join us. It was a battered Suzuki. I hadn't seen it before.

'Good God, Margretta,' Atheridge breathed. The car stopped alongside us and a woman climbed out stiffly. She was tall, fiftyish and clad in workman-like khaki shirt and pants. Her grey hair was pulled back in a loose bun. She looked as though she was ready to collapse.

'Gretta, my dear girl, how did you get here?' Atheridge asked.

'You're not hard to follow, Dan.' Her voice wasn't much more than a whisper.

'Gretta, this is Neil Mannix – Mannix, I'd like you to meet Doctor Marriot,' Atheridge said formally.

There were deep wrinkles round her eyes and her skin was leathery; she had the look of a woman who'd had too much sun, too much Africa. I turned and opened the passenger door of my car.

'Good morning, doctor. I think you'd better sit down.'

She nodded faintly. 'Thank you. I think it will be better,' she said. Her voice sounded Scandinavian.

'Are you a doctor of medicine?' I asked.

'Medical missionaries, from outside Kodowa,' Atheridge said. He bent over her and said gently, 'Where's Brian, Gretta? We all thought you two were in Port Luard.'

Which explained why nobody had mentioned them before. She spoke to Atheridge for some time in a low voice, and then started crying softly. Helen Chula got out of the car and came round to stay with Dr Marriot while I drew Atheridge aside.

'What is it, Dan?'

'Pretty bloody, I'm afraid. They drove up from the coast to Kodowa just when the air strike hit us. Brian, her husband, was killed outright. She must have been in shock for over a day, you know. She came out to the hospital and found Sister Ursula still there, and insisted on catching up with us.'

'Christ, that's a lousy deal.' We turned back to her.

'You look as though you could do with a drink, ma'am. How about a lukewarm Scotch?' I said.

'It wouldn't be unwelcome.'

I got a bottle from the trunk and poured a measure into a dusty glass. Atheridge glanced wistfully at the bottle but made no comment as I screwed the cap firmly back on. From now on this was strictly a medical reserve.

'I have come to help Doctor Kat,' she said after downing the Scotch in strong swallows. 'The Sister says he will need all the help he can get, and we have often worked together. Where is he, please?'

'Never mind where he is. Right now you need some sleep. Helen, tell her how much better she'll feel for it.'

Helen smiled shyly. 'Indeed the gentleman is right, Doctor Marriot. Sleep for an hour, then Doctor Kat will be most happy to have you with him. I am going to help him now.' She gently lowered the doctor's head onto the back of the seat.

'How's your leg?' I asked her.

'I will be all right up there,' she said, pointing towards the rig. 'I will wait here until it comes.'

In the car Dr Marriot was already sagging into sleep.

'Hop in, Dan. We'll move on slowly. At least moving creates a draught,' I said. The crawling pace was more frustrating than ever but I had to content myself with the thought that Captain Sadiq was coping very efficiently, better than I had done, and that in Dr Margretta Marriot we had a very useful addition to our staff. The Wyvern Travelling Hospital ground on through the hot African day. The sooner we got to Kanja, the better.

Half an hour later the whole pattern changed again. We seemed to be living inside a kaleidoscope which was being shaken by some gigantic hand. A motorcyclist, one of Sadiq's outflankers, roared up and said that Captain Sadiq would like to see me. I pulled out of line hoping not to disturb Dr Marriot, though I doubted if anything short of an earthquake would waken her.

Kemp and Wingstead were already with Sadiq, talking to two white men, more strangers. Behind them was a big dreamboat of an American car which looked as out of place

in that setting as an aircraft carrier would on Lake Geneva.
Atheridge and I got out and joined them.

One of the men was tall, loose-limbed and rangy, wearing denim Levis and a sweat-stained checked shirt, and
unbelievably he was crowned by a ten-gallon hat pushed
well back on his head. I looked at his feet; no spurs, but he
did wear hand-stitched high heeled boots. He looked like
Clint Eastwood. I expected him to produce a pack of
Marlboros or a sack of Bull Durham tobacco.

By comparison the other guy was conventional. He was
shorter, broad-shouldered and paunchy, and dressed in a
manner more suitable for Africa; khaki pants and a bush
jacket. Both looked dusty and weary, the norm for all of us.

I said, 'Hello there. Where did you spring from?'

The tall man turned round. 'Oh, hi. Up the road a way.
You folks got the same trouble we have.'

Kemp's face was more strained than usual.

'Neil, there's a bridge down further along the road.'

'Christ! The one you were worried about, way back?'

Kemp nodded. 'Yes. It's completely gone, they've just
told us. It spans a ravine. And it's this side of Kanja. It
would be.'

Wingstead looked more alert than worried, ready to hurl
himself at the next challenge. He was a hard man to faze.

I said, 'I'm Neil Mannix, British Electric. I guess it's a
pleasure to meet you, but I'm not sure yet.'

The tall man laughed. 'Likewise. I'm Russ Burns and this
is Harry Zimmerman. We're both with Lat-Am Oil. There
are some other guys up the road too, by the way – not our
lot; a Frenchman and a couple of Russki truckers.'

'What happened? Did you see the bridge go down?'

Burns shook his head. 'We were halfway to the bridge
when the planes hit Kodowa. Mind you, we didn't know for
sure what the hell was happening but we could guess. We'd
seen a lot of troop movement a few days before, and there

were stories going round about a rebellion. We couldn't see the town itself but we heard the bombing and saw the smoke. Then we saw the planes going over.'

His hand went to his shirt pocket. 'We didn't know what to do, Harry and me. Decided to push on because we didn't fancy turning back into all that, whatever it was. Then we met up with the Russkies.'

'A convoy, like ours?' I watched with fascination as he took out a pack of cigarettes. By God, they *were* Marlboros. He even lit one the way they do in the ads, with a long, appreciative draw on the first smoke. He didn't hand them round.

'No, just one big truck. The Frenchman's driving a truck too. He had a buddy he'd dropped off in Kodowa. I guess he must have got caught in the raid. You didn't see him?'

Nobody had. Write off one French trucker, just like that.

'I was shoving my foot through the floorboards the first ten miles after that raid,' Burns said. 'Even though I knew we couldn't outrun a jet. Maybe thirty miles from here we turned a corner and damn near ran into this pipe truck. The Soviets. They hadn't seen or heard anything. Then the Frog guy turned up, him and a nig . . . a Nyalan assistant.' He glanced at Sadiq as he said this.

Zimmerman spoke for the first time. 'We four camped together that night, and the next day we pushed on in our car with one of the Russians. I speak Russian a little.' He said this almost apologetically. 'Ten miles on there's this bridge.'

'*Was* this bridge. By God, it's just rubble at the bottom of that ravine now. Took a real hammering.'

'Was it bombed?' I asked.

'Yeah, I reckon so. We could see the wreckage, five hundred feet down the hillside.'

'Any chance of getting across?' I asked, even though I could already guess the answer.

'No chance. Not for a truck. Not for a one-wheel circus bicycle. There's a gap of more than two hundred feet.'

Burns inhaled deeply. 'We all just stuck around that day. Nobody wanted to make a decision. Our radios only picked up garbage. We couldn't go on, and we didn't feel like coming back into the middle of a shooting war. The Soviets had quite a store of food and the Frenchie had some too. All *we* had to put in the pool was some beer, and that didn't last long, believe me. Then this morning we decided we'd go two ways; the Frenchie was to have a try at Kodowa with the two Reds, and Harry and me said we'd have a go at getting through the gorge on foot and make for Kanja.'

'Can't say I was hankering for the experience,' put in Harry.

'Then just as we were about to get going, up comes these two guys.' Burns indicated Sadiq's riders. 'We thought at first the rebels had caught up with us. Hell of a note, and us with just a couple of popguns between us. Then they told us what was going on back here. It didn't sound real, you know that?'

I made mental note. They had weapons.

'Travelling circus,' Kemp muttered.

'Wish it was, buddy. Elephants now, they'd be some use. Anyway, we changed our plans, left the truckers to wait up ahead, and Harry and me came back to see for ourselves.'

I asked, 'Is it possible to cross on foot?'

'I reckon so, if you're agile.'

I looked at Sadiq. 'So?'

Wingstead said, 'What's the use, Neil? We can't send the wounded and sick that way and even if the Kanja hospital is still in business they can't send help to us. You know what we have to do.'

I nodded. One problem out of a thousand raised its head.

'Basil,' I said, 'how do you turn your rig around?'

'We don't need to,' Kemp said. 'It'll go either way. We just recouple the tractors.' His mind was shifting up through the gears and his face looked less strained as he started calculating. There was nothing better for Basil Kemp than giving him a set of solid logistics to chew on.

Sadiq said, 'What will you do now, Mister Mannix?' He too looked as though the ground had been pulled from under his feet.

I studied our two new arrivals. 'What we're going to do first is get these two gentlemen a beer and a meal apiece. And we have a lady who joined us recently who'd also be glad of something to eat. Geoff, could you get Bishop to organize that? As long as the convoy's stopped, we may as well all stoke up. We'll have a conference afterwards. Captain Sadiq, could you pass the word around that we are no longer going towards Kanja? Everyone must rest, eat if they can, and then be ready to move.'

Wingstead said, 'Who's the lady?'

'She's a medical doctor. She was widowed in the raid on Kodowa, and right now she's asleep in my car. I'm going to have a word with Doctor Kat and I'll take her along. As a matter of fact, Dan knows her quite well . . .'

I tailed off. Behind us, standing quietly, Dan Atheridge looked pasty grey over his tan. During our briefing from the Lat-Am men Atheridge had been listening and their news touched him more closely than any of us. His wife was waiting for him, somewhere beyond Kanja. He was cut off from his home.

'Dan –'

'It's OK. Susie's going to be perfectly safe, I know. You're quite right though, you can't get the patients across the gorge. But I know a way over, a few miles downstream. Perhaps you'll lend me an escort, Captain, and take me there?' He spoke in a flat, controlled voice.

'Don't worry, Dan. We'll get you across,' I said, hoping like hell I could keep my word. 'Come on, you guys, let's get you outside that beer and hear the rest of it.' We got back into my car and turned back towards the rig, Kemp following with the two newcomers. As we drove past the stream of refugees the little huddled groups were preparing for the long drowsy wait. The bush telegraph was way ahead of modern communication.

FOURTEEN

Dr Margretta Marriot and I stood looking up at the rig. It was an extraordinary sight, covered here and there with windblown thatching, piled with sheet-covered bodies lying on lumpy reed bedding, draped with miscellaneous bits of cloth, towels and pillowcases hung from anything handy to give shade. Figures clambered about the rig carrying bandaging and other necessities. Sister Mary had been forbidden to travel on the rig because of her own precarious health and was standing at the base of the huge wheels shouting instructions to her nurses. Several of our men were helping by supporting those of the wounded who could move about, taking them to and from the makeshift latrines. The chuck wagon was in action as Bishop and young Bing prepared a canned meal for us and our visitors.

During the day Sister Ursula had arrived. She saw me and waved, then lit up on catching sight of Dr Marriot.

'Doctor Gretta! What are you doing here?'

Mick McGrath was at her side instantly to give her a hand down. She knew at once that all was not well, and gently led the doctor away to the far side of the rig.

McGrath said, 'Why have we stopped, Mister Mannix? Rumour is there's more trouble.'

'That there is. There's a bridge down between us and Kanja, and no way we can get there. We haven't made the decision official yet, but I can tell you we're going to have to turn back.'

'Take the east-west road, then, like you planned? With all this lot?'

'Maybe. Ask Doctor Kat to come down, would you.'

'He won't come.'

'Why not?'

'He's busy,' McGrath said. 'Soon as we stopped he went into action at the operating table. Right now I think he's lifting off the top of someone's skull.'

I said, 'All right, don't bother him yet. But when you can, tell him that Doctor Marriot is here. I think it will please him. Tell him her husband was killed at Kodowa, though. And I'd like a word with him as soon as possible.'

I walked back to where the Wyvern management and the Lat-Am men were sitting in the shade of the trucks. Atheridge was not with them. As I approached, Wingstead said, 'Neil, I've put Harry and Russ in the picture geographically. They travelled the east-west road, a few months ago and say it's not too bad. The two rivers come together at a place called Makara. It's very small, not much more than a village, but it may be of some strategic importance. It's a crossroads town, the only way up from the coast used to be from Lasulu and Fort Pirie through Makara to here, before Ofanwe's government built the new road direct.'

'Is there a bridge there?'

'Yes, apparently quite good but narrower than the new bridge that you crossed when you met the army. Assuming it's still there. We'll send outriders ahead to find out; if our gallant Captain's on the ball they've already gone. And someone's gone to fetch down Lat-Am's friends to join us.'

'The army might be there. If I were commanding either side I'd like to hold Makara, if it hasn't been bombed into oblivion.'

Wingstead stood up. 'We don't have to make up our minds until we hear the report. Where's Doctor Kat?'

'Operating. He'll join us when he can, and I expect he'll have something to say about all this.'

I too stood up, and as I did so Mick McGrath came over. We knew instantly that something was wrong; he looked like thunder.

'Mister Wingstead, there's trouble,' he said. 'You're about to receive a deputation.'

Five other men were approaching with the dogged stomping walk you see on TV newscasts featuring strikers in action. They appeared to be having an argument with a couple of soldiers in their way, and then came on to face us. I wasn't surprised to see that the ringleader was Bob Sisley, nor that another was Johnny Burke, the man who'd been heard to speak of danger money some time past. The others were Barry Lang, Bob Pitman, and the fifth, who did surprise me, was Ron Jones. They walked into a total silence as we followed Wingstead's lead. I'd handled industrial disputes in my time but here I was an outsider, unless the Wyvern management invoked my aid directly.

Sisley, naturally, was the spokesman. He said, ignoring Wingstead for an easier target, 'Mister Kemp, these Yanks say that the bridge up north has gone, right?'

'That's right.'

I wondered how Burns liked being called a Yank, though he was free enough with derogatory nicknames himself.

'Seems we can't take the rig on, then. You planned for us to go down to Lake Piric, before we ran into all this crap with the sickies. What's to stop us going there now? You said we could get across the border into a neutral country.'

I felt a wash of disgust at the man, and I saw my thoughts echoed on other faces. The odd thing was that one of those faces belonged to Ron Jones. Kemp still said nothing and Sisley pressed on.

'You've broken your own contract so you can't hold us to ours. We say it's getting dangerous here and we didn't sign on to get involved in any nignog's bloody political duff-ups. We're getting out of here.'

'With the rig?' Kemp asked coldly.

'To hell with the rig. We're in a jam. A war's something we didn't bargain for. All we want is out. It's your duty to see us safe, yours and the boss's here.' He indicated Wingstead with an inelegant jerk of his thumb. He may have been a good transport man, Wyvern wouldn't hire less, but he was a nasty piece of work nonetheless.

Wingstead took over smoothly.

'We're taking the rig and all transport back to Kodowa,' he said. 'Including the hospital patients. Once there, we'll reassess the situation and probably, all being well, we'll start back on the road to Port Luard. If we think that unsafe we'll take the secondary road to Fort Pirie. We are all under a strain here, and cut off from vital information, but we'll do the best we can.'

But calm, reasoned argument never did work in these affairs. Sisley made a face grotesque with contempt. 'A strain! Oh, we're under a strain all right. Playing nursemaid to a bunch of blacks who can't take care of themselves and baby-sitting a rig that's worthless junk while the food runs out and the country goes to hell in a handcart. Christ, we haven't even been paid for two weeks. You can fart-arse up and down this bloody road as much as you like, but you'll do it without us.'

'What exactly is it you want?' Wingstead asked.

'We want to get the hell back to Fort Pirie as we planned. With or without the rig – it makes no difference.'

'*You* didn't plan anything, my friend.' I knew I should stay out of this but I was livid. 'Your boss has run a hell of a risk coming up here to join you, and he's the man who does the planning around here.'

'You keep out of this, Mister Bloody Mannix.'

Wingstead said, 'Bob, this is crazy talk. How far can any of us get without the whole group for support?'

'The group! Christ, old men and babies and walking dead, mealy-mouthed nuns and God knows who else we're dragging around at our heels! Now we hear you're bringing a bunch of damned foreigners into it too. Well, we won't stand for it.'

None of the others said a word. They stood behind him in a tight wall of silent resentment, as Sisley gave full rein to his foul mouth and fouler thoughts. At his reference to the nuns McGrath's breathing deepened steadily. I suspected that an outbreak was imminent and tried to forestall it.

'You can argue shop floor principles all you want with your boss, Sisley,' I said. 'But leave out the personalities, and don't foul-mouth these people like that.'

He rounded on me. 'I told you to shut up, you bigmouth Yank. Keep the hell out of this!' He cocked his arm back like a cobra about to strike. I took a step forward but McGrath grabbed my arm in a steel grip. 'Now, hold it, Mister Mannix,' he said in a cool, soft voice, and then to Sisley, 'Any more lip from you, my lad, and you'll be shitting teeth.' I think it was the matter-of-fact way he said it that made Sisley step back and drop his arm.

For a moment the whole tableau froze; the two groups facing each other, the Lat-Am men and several other Wyvern people crowding up to listen, Atheridge behind them, and myself, McGrath and Sisley in belligerent attitudes front and centre. Then from nowhere Ben Hammond's voice broke in.

'Right, you've had your say, and very well put it was, Bob. Now you'll give Mister Wingstead and Mister Kemp five minutes to talk it over, please. Just you shift along, you chaps, nothing's going to happen for a while. Sandy! Where's that grub you were getting ready? Go on, you lot, get it while it's there. Bert, we've got a spot of bother with the rear left axletree.'

It was masterly. The tableau melted like a spring thaw and I found myself alone with Kemp and Wingstead, shaking our heads with relief and admiration. Hammond's talents seemed boundless.

Wingstead said, 'Sisley and Pitman run the airlift truck. It's obvious they'd be in this together, they've always been buddies and a bit bloody-minded. Johnny Burke is what the Navy would call a sea lawyer, too smart for his own good. He's a fair rigger, though. And Lang and Jones are good drivers. But Sisley and Pitman are the specialists, and we'll need that airlift again. Who else can run it?'

Kemp shook his head but Hammond, who had rejoined us after some skilful marshalling of the men, said, 'I can. I can run any damned machine here if I have to. So could McGrath, come to that.'

'We'll need you both on the rig,' said Kemp.

'No you won't. You're as good on the rig as I am,' Hammond said. 'I could work with Sammy Wilson though.'

'I suppose we must assume that Sisley's had a go at everyone,' I said. 'So whoever wasn't with him is on your side?'

'I have to assume that. I'm surprised about Ron Jones, I must say,' said Wingstead. 'So we've still got Grafton and Proctor, and Ritchie Thorpe too. Thank God you brought him up here, Neil.'

'He might not thank me,' I said.

Our rueful smiles brought a momentary lightening of tension.

'I wouldn't like an inexperienced man on a tractor when it's coupled to the rig,' Kemp said. 'We can get along with three tractors at some expense to our speed. And we can ditch that damned tank. I don't suppose you can drive a tractor, Mannix?' I smiled again, but to myself, at Kemp's single-mindedness. There were times when it came in handy. Right now he was too busy juggling factors to get as fully steamed up at having a mutiny on his hands as any good executive should.

'No, but I might find someone who can.'

Wingstead and Kemp conferred for a while and I left them to it. The breakaway group had taken their food well away from the others, and a huddle of shoulders kept them from having to look at their mates while they were eating. The faithful, as I mentally dubbed them, were laughing and talking loudly to demonstrate their camaraderie and freedom from the guilt of having deserted. It was an interesting example of body language at work and would have delighted any psychologist. The Nyalans, sensing trouble, were keeping well clear, and there was no sign of any of the medical people.

Presently Wingstead called me over.

He said, 'We're going to let them go.'

'You mean *fire* them?'

'What else? If they don't want to stay I can hardly hold them all prisoner.'

'But how will they manage?'

Wingstead showed that he had become very tough indeed.

'That's their problem. I've got . . . how many people to take care of, would you say? I didn't ask for it, but I'm stuck with it and I won't weasel out. I can't abandon them all for a few grown men who think they know their own minds.'

Suddenly he looked much older. That often talked of phenomenon, the remoteness of authority, was taking visible hold and he wasn't the boyish, enthusiastic plunger that he'd seemed to be when we first met in the workshop garage in England. He had taken the whole burden of this weird progression on his own shoulders, and in truth there was nowhere else for it to lie. I watched him stand up under the extra load and admired him more than ever.

'Tell them to come over, Basil.'

The rebels came back still wary and full of anger. This time, at Wingstead's request, McGrath stayed a little way off and exerted his own powerful authority to keep bystanders back out of earshot. Wingstead said, 'Right, we've had our chat. Are you still sure you want out?'

'Bloody sure. We've had it, all of this.'

'Do you speak for everyone?' Wingstead looked past him to the other four, but no-one spoke. Sisley said, 'You can see that.'

'Right you are then. You can buzz off. All five of you. You're fired.'

The silence this time was almost comical.

Sisley said at last, 'All right then, just you try that. You can't just bloody well fire us! We're under contract, aren't we, Johnny?'

'That's right,' Burke said.

'You said yourself that if our contract with Nyala was broken, which it is, then so was yours. Hop it,' Wingstead said.

'Then what about our pay? We missed two weeks, plus severance. We want it now.'

I stared at him in astonishment.

'Go on, give them a cheque, Geoff,' I said sarcastically. 'They can cash it at the bank in Kodowa.'

'I'll write vouchers for the lot of you. You can be sure that Wyvern will honour them,' Wingstead said. 'You can collect them from Mister Kemp in one hour's time.'

'We'll do that,' said Sisley. 'But we want some security against them too. We'll take one of the trucks.'

Hammond said, 'The hell you will, Bob!'

'Or the airlift truck. There's room for all of us at a pinch, and it's worth more. Yes, that's what we'll do.'

Hammond was beginning to lose his temper. 'Over my dead body!'

Wingstead held out a hand to calm him. 'There'll be no arguments. I forbid you to touch the transports, Sisley,' he said.

'And just how are you going to stop us?'

This had gone far enough. It was time I intervened. 'You're not taking that airlift truck anywhere. Or any other vehicle. Wyvern Transport is heavily in debt to British Electric and I'm calling that debt. In lieu of payment I am sequestering all their equipment, and that includes all vehicles. Your vouchers will come from me and my company will pay you off, when you claim. If you live to claim. You've got one hour and then you can start walking.'

Sisley gaped at me. He said, 'But Fort Pirie is –'

'About two hundred and fifty miles away. You may find transport before then. Otherwise you can do what the people you call nignogs are doing – hoof it.'

He squared himself for a fight and then surveyed the odds facing him. Behind him his own men murmured uneasily but only Burke raised his voice in actual protest. Hearing it, McGrath came across, fists balled and spoiling for a fight once again, but still with the matter-of-fact air that made him all the more dangerous. The mutineers subsided and backed away.

Sisley mouthed a few more obscenities but we ignored him. Soon they moved off in a tightknit, hostile group and disappeared behind one of the trucks.

'Keep an eye on them, Mick, but no rough stuff,' Hammond said.

Wingstead let out a long steady breath.

'I'd give a lot for a pull from that bottle of Scotch of yours. Or even a warm beer. But I'll settle for a mug of gunfire very gladly indeed.'

'Ditto,' I said, and we grinned at one another.

'You're my boss now, do you know that?'

'Sure I am. And that's my first order: a cup of that damned hellbrew of Bishop's and a plateful of whatever mess he's calling lunch,' I said. 'You too, Basil. Save the figuring for afterwards.'

Later that afternoon I had my chance to talk to Dr Katabisirua. The defection of five of our men troubled him little; they were healthy and capable, and he felt that having taken their own course it was up to them to make it in safety. The addition to our number of two more Americans and the expected arrival of a Frenchman and two Russians also meant little to him, except in so far as he hoped they might have some medical stores in their vehicles. The arrival of Dr Marriot he saw as pure gold.

He fretted about malnutrition, about sepsis, and was more perturbed than he liked to admit about the jolting his patients were receiving. For me, his worst news concerned Max Otterman, who was sinking into unconsciousness and for whom the future looked very grave.

He'd heard about the bridge, of course.

'There is no way to get to Kanja, then? No way at all?'

'Only for fit men on their own feet, Doctor. I'm sorry.'

'Mister Atheridge said he knew a way, I am told.'

'Yes,' I said, 'but he's wounded, over fifty, and in some shock. He's driven up there with some soldiers and one of our men to have a look but they won't be back before nightfall, I reckon. I don't think for a moment that they'll find any feasible way of getting across that ravine.'

He sighed. 'Then you are going to turn back.'

'To Kodowa, yes. And then south or west. Probably west. Do you know the town of Makara? Is there a medical station there?'

But he said that Makara patients had always been brought to him at Kodowa. There wasn't even a trained nurse, only a couple of midwives. Then he brightened. 'There is the cotton factory,' he said. 'They have very large well-built barns but I have heard that they stand almost empty and the factory is idle. It would make a good place to put all my patients.'

'If it's still intact, yes.' And, I thought, if some regiment or rebel troop hasn't turned it into a barracks first.

Shortly afterwards the two Russians and the Frenchman arrived. The Russians were as alike as peas in a pod, with broad Slavic features and wide grins. They had polysyllabic unpronounceable names and neither spoke more than ten words of English. God knows how they'd managed in earlier days. Zimmerman, who had worked alongside Russians laying pipelines in Iran, was able to interpret reasonably well. Later they became known as Brezhnev and Kosygin to everybody, and didn't seem to mind. Probably the way we said the names they couldn't even recognize them. They were hauling a load of pipe casing northwards to the oilfields.

The Frenchman spoke fair English and was called Antoine Dufour. He was carrying a mixed load for Petrole Meridional. They were all glad of company and resigned to a return journey, but they were unwilling to quit their trucks, especially when they found we had a store of reserve fuel. After a lot of trilingual palaver, Wingstead's French being more than adequate, they agreed to stick with us in a policy of safety in numbers.

So did Russ Burns and Zimmerman. But they had a different problem.

'I hear you have gas,' Burns said. 'We're about dry.'

'We've got gas,' I told him. 'But not to burn up in your goddam air-conditioning, or hauling all that chrome around Africa.' I walked over to look at their car. The overhang behind the rear wheels was over five feet and the decorations in front snarled in a savage grin. 'Your taste in transport is a mite old-fashioned, Texas?'

'That's a good American car. You won't find me driving one of those dinky European models. Hell, I can't get my legs under the wheel. Anyway, it's a company car. It wouldn't look good for an oilman with Lat-Am to drive an economy car; that would show lack of confidence.'

'Very interesting,' I said, 'but so far you've been on the blacktop. Suppose we have to take to the country roads. That thing will lose its exhaust in the first mile, and the sump in the next. It'll scrape its fanny every ten yards.'

'He's right, Russ,' said Zimmerman.

'Oh hell,' Burns said sadly, unwilling to give up his status symbol.

I pointed to a tractor. 'Can either of you drive one of those?'

'I can,' said Zimmerman promptly, 'I started my working life as a trucker. I might need a bit of updating tuition, though.'

'Well, you know our problem. Five guys walked out and two of them were drivers. You won't be asked to drive it coupled up, Kemp wouldn't buy that. I'm leaving the hire car here because it's never going to make the dirt roads. You'll have to do the same, because you get no gas from me. You drive the tractor uncoupled, and take care of the sick folk up on the roof.' I turned to Burns. 'And you can drive with me in the Land Rover. There's plenty of leg room there.'

He sighed and patted his car on the hood. 'So long, baby. It's been nice knowing you.'

It was dark as I'd guessed it would be before Atheridge and his party returned, quiet and dispirited. The ravine crossing which he remembered from many years before was now overgrown, the ledges crumbled and passage impossible. Thorpe told me privately that they had had quite a job persuading Atheridge to return with them; he was passionately determined to try crossing on his own, but he was quite unfit to do so.

Eventually the entire camp settled down to an uneasy night's sleep. The five mutineers, strikers, whatever one wanted to call them, had vanished, their gear gone. Wingstead and I felt itchy with unease about them, both for their safety and for our own future without their expertise. I'd had a guard of soldiers put around every vehicle we possessed, just in case any of them decided to try to collar one. There wasn't much left to say, and at last we all turned in and slept, or tried to, and awaited the coming of morning.

FIFTEEN

The morning brought the usual crises and problems attendant on any normal start of a run, plus of course the extra
ones imposed by our status as a mobile hospital.
Somewhere in the middle of it, while Kemp was supervis-
ing the recoupling of the tractors to the other end of the rig
it was discovered that McGrath was missing. The air was
lively with curses as both Kemp and Hammond sought their
chief driver. At about the same time Sadiq's sergeant came
to tell us that the hire car was missing too.

And then suddenly there was McGrath, walking into our
midst with one arm flung round the shoulders of a cowed
and nervous Ron Jones. Tailing up behind them were Lang
and Bob Pitman, looking equally hangdog, pale and
exhausted.

'Mister Kemp,' McGrath called out in a cheerful, boister-
ous voice, 'these lads have changed their minds and want to
come with us. Would you be taking them back onto the
payroll? I promised I'd put in a word for them.'

Kemp wasn't sure what to do, and glanced at me for
guidance. I shook my head. 'I don't hire and fire around
here, Basil. Have a word with Geoff.'

But of course there wasn't any doubt about it really; the
hesitation was only for form's sake. After a long private talk
Geoff announced that the three delinquents were to be

taken back into the fold, and a reallocation of driving jobs ensued, somewhat to Harry Zimmerman's relief.

It was impossible to find out exactly what had happened; McGrath kept busy and enquiries would have to wait until later. Wingstead did tell me that according to all of them, Bob Sisley and Johnny Burke had refused point blank to return when McGrath caught up with them. It seemed that he had taken the car and gone off at first light. The other three were less committed to Sisley's cause and Jones in particular had been a most unwilling mutineer. The three of them would bear careful watching but there was no doubt that we were greatly relieved to have them back.

We camped that night back near Kodowa, but not at the hospital, where Dr Kat decreed that there would be too much danger of infection from the debris left behind. Instead a cleaner site was found further west on the road we were to take. It had been a day wasted. We arrived in the late afternoon and buried our dead, four more, and then began the laborious process of settling in for the night, and of planning the start for Makara in the morning.

At the end of it I had had a gutful. I was weary of talking and of listening, settling arguments, solving problems and doling out sympathy and advice. The only good news we heard all evening was from Dr Marriot, who told us that Max Otterman seemed to be making progress towards recovery.

Eventually I went off for a walk in the warm night. There were refugees everywhere and I had to go a long way to put the camp behind me. I had no fear of meeting wild animals, the noise and stench of our progress had cleared both game and predators for miles around, and as I looked back at the cooking fires glowing like fireflies I wondered where the food was coming from.

I'd been tempted to take the dwindling bottle of whisky with me but had resisted, and now I regretted my self-denial. I stopped well out of sight and earshot of the camp and sat down to soak in the solitude for a spell. Finally, feeling rested, I started back. I'd gone about ten paces when something ahead of me crunched on dry vegetation and my heart thudded. Then a voice said softly, 'Mister Mannix – can I talk to you?'

It was Ron Jones. For a moment I felt a fury of hot resentment at not being left alone even out here. Then I said, 'Jones? What do you want?'

He was still downcast, a shadow of his cheery former self. 'I'm sorry to intrude, Mister Mannix. But I must talk. I have to tell *somebody* about what happened. But you must promise me not to tell anyone who told you.'

'I don't know what you're talking about.'

'I'll tell you, if you promise first.'

'Be damned to that, Jones. Tell me or not as you please. But I make no bargains.'

He paused, thinking about this, and then said, 'It's about Bob Sisley. He's dead.'

'Dead? What the hell do you mean?'

'He's dead, I tell you. Mick McGrath shot him.'

Christ, I thought. I'd been right. All along I'd had an uneasy feeling about McGrath, and this news came as less of a shock than a grim confirmation of my thoughts. 'You'd better tell me all about it. Let's sit down.'

'But you really mustn't let on who told you,' Jones said again. He sounded terrified and I could hardly blame him.

'All right, I promise. Now tell.'

'It was like this. When we left we took as much of our kit as we could carry and went off towards Kodowa. Bob wanted to nick a truck but they were all guarded. Then he said we'd be sure to find transport in Kodowa. After all, there were lots of cars left behind there.'

He said nothing about the events which had led up to the mutiny, nor about his own reasons for going along with it, and I didn't ask. All that was past history.

'We didn't get very far. Walking, it's not like being in a motor, not out here especially. It was bloody hot and hard going. Those Nyalans, they're pretty tough, I found out . . . anyway we pushed on for a while. We'd nicked some food and beer, before we left. Brad Bishop didn't know that,' he put in, suddenly anxious not to implicate the cook in their actions. It was things like that which separated him from Bob Sisley, who wouldn't have cared a damn.

'Then we heard a car and up comes Mick on his own. He tried to talk us into going back, but pretty soon it turned into an argument. He and Bob Sisley got bloody worked up. Then Bob went for him but Mick put him down in the dust easy; he's the bigger man by a long chalk. None of the rest of us wanted a fight except maybe Johnny Burke. But he's no match for Mick either and he didn't even try. To be honest, Barry and Bob Pitman and me, we'd had enough anyway. I really wanted to go back.'

He hesitated and I sensed that the tight wound resolution was dying in him. 'Go on. You can't stop now. You've said too much and too little.'

'Then Mick took us off the road and –'

'How do you mean, took you? You didn't have to go anywhere.'

'Yes we did. He had a gun.'

'What kind of gun?'

'An automatic pistol. He took us off the road and down into the bush, where nobody else could see us. Then he said we had to go back or we'd die out there. He said he could beat us into agreeing, one at a time. Starting with Bob Sisley. Bob had some guts. He said Mick couldn't keep us working, couldn't hold a gun on us all the time. He got pretty abusive.'

'Did they fight?'

'Not again. Sisley said a few things he shouldn't and . . . then Mick shot him.'

'Just like that?'

'Yes, Mister Mannix. One second Bob was standing there, and the next he was on the ground. That bloody Irishman shot him through the head and didn't even change his expression!'

He was shivering and his voice wavered. I said, 'Then what happened?'

'Nobody said anything for a bit. Someone upchucked – hell, it was me. So did Barry. Then Mick said again that we were to go back. He said we'd work the rig, all right. And if any of us talked about what had happened he'd get kneecapped or worse.'

'Kneecapped – that was the word he used?'

'Yes. Bob Pitman got down to look at Sisley and he was stone dead, all right. And while we were all looking. Johnny Burke he took off and ran like hell, through the bush. I thought Mick would shoot him but he didn't even try, and Johnny got clean away.'

'Do you know what happened to him?'

'Nobody does.'

'What happened next?'

'Well, we said OK, we'd go back. And we'd shut up. What else could we do? And anyway we all wanted to come back by then. Christ, I've had this bloody country.'

'What happened to Sisley's body?'

His voice shook again. 'Mick stripped it and him and Barry put it down in a gulley and covered it up a little, not buried. Mick said the wildlife would get him.'

'He was right about that,' I said grimly. 'You did the right thing, telling me about this. Keep your nose clean and there'll be no more trouble out of it for you. I'll do something about McGrath. Go back to the camp now, and get a good night's sleep. You're out of danger, or at least that sort of danger.'

He went, thankfully, and I followed more slowly. I had one more lousy job to do that night. Back at camp I strolled across to the Land Rover and got into it on the passenger side, leaving the door open. There was still some movement here and there and as one of the men walked past I called out to him to find McGrath and tell him I wanted to see him.

I switched on the interior light, took the shotgun I had liberated, emptied and reloaded it. Previously, when I'd tried to put in a fourth shell it wouldn't go, and I had wondered why, but now I had the answer; in the States pump and automatic shotguns are limited to a three-shot capacity when shooting at certain migratory birds. To help remind hunters to keep within the law the makers install a demountable plug in the magazine, and until it's removed the hunter is limited to three fast shots. I guessed the gun makers hadn't bothered to take out the plugs before exporting these weapons.

Now I began to strip the gun. When McGrath came up I was taking the plug out of the magazine. He looked at it with interest. 'That's a fine scatter-gun,' he said easily. 'Now, how many shots would a thing like that fire before reloading, Mister Mannix?'

'Right now, three. But I'm fixing it to shoot six.' I got the plug out and started to reassemble the gun.

McGrath said, 'You've done that before.'

'Many times.' The gun went together easily. I started to put shells into the magazine and loaded the full six. Then I held the gun casually, not pointing at McGrath but not very far away from him, angled downwards to the ground. 'Now you can tell me what happened to Bob Sisley,' I said.

If I'd hoped to startle him into an admission I was disappointed. His expression didn't change at all. 'So someone

told you,' he said easily. 'Now I wonder who it could have
been? I'd say Ronnie Jones, wouldn't you?'

'Whoever. And if anything happens to *any* of those
men you'll be in even more trouble than you are now – if
possible.'

'I'm in no trouble,' he said.

'You will be if Sadiq strings you up the nearest tree.'

'And who'd tell him?'

'I might.'

He shook his head. 'Not you, Mister Mannix. Mister
Kemp now, he might do that, but not you.'

'What makes you say that?' I hadn't meant the interview
to go this way, a chatty debate with no overtones of nervousness on his part, but the man did intrigue me. He was
the coolest customer I'd ever met.

He grinned. 'Well, you're a lot tougher than Mister
Kemp. I think maybe you're nearly as tough as me, with a
few differences, you might say. We think the same. We do
our own dirty work. You're not going to call in the black
captain to do yours for you, any more than I did. We do the
things that have to be done.'

'And you think Sisley had to be killed. Is that it?'

'Not at all. It could have been any one of them, to
encourage the others as the saying goes, but I reckon Sisley
was trouble all down the line. Why carry a burden when
you can drop it?'

The echo of Sadiq, both of them using Voltaire's aphorism
so glibly and in so similar a set of circumstances, fascinated
me against my will. 'I don't need lessons in military philosophy from you, McGrath,' I said. 'What you did was murder.'

'Jesus Christ! You're in the middle of a war here and
people are dying all around you, one way or the other.
You're trying to save hundreds of lives and you worry about
the death of one stinking rat. I'll tell you something. Those
other bastards will work from now on. I'll see to that.'

'You won't touch them,' I said.

'I won't have to. You found out; the word will spread to everyone, you'll see. Nobody else is going to turn rat on us, I can promise you . . . and nobody is going to touch me for it.'

'Why did you really do it, McGrath? Loyalty to Wyvern Transport?'

'Be damned to that, Mannix. I want out of this and I want out alive and unhurt. And the more we've got pulling for us, the better chance each man has. You have to have unity on this. You owe it to your people, and they to you.'

There at last was the political undertone I'd been expecting. I said, 'All right, what are you, McGrath? IRA or Ulster Loyalist?'

'Do I have to be either.'

'Yes, you do. Unity in face of oppression, casual shooting, kneecapping threats – it's all there. And I'm not one of your American pseudo-Irish sympathizers. As far as I'm concerned, both of your bloody so-called movements can fall into the nearest bog and the sooner the better.'

As I'd hoped, this sort of talk did get some rise out of him. He shifted one hand instinctively to his right-hand coat pocket, arresting the movement almost instantly. But it was a dead giveaway.

'All right,' I said, having achieved what I wanted. 'We won't talk politics. Let's change the subject. Where did you get the gun?'

'I found it in the tank we salvaged.'

'And where is it now?'

'In my cab.'

I shook my head gently, hefting the shotgun very slightly.

He actually laughed. 'You're in no danger from me, Mister Mannix. You're one man I look to to get us all out of this mess.'

I said, 'I'll have that gun, McGrath – now.'

With no hesitation he dipped into his pocket, produced the pistol and tossed it onto my lap. 'There'll be others,' he said.

'And from now on, you can consider yourself under open arrest.'

Now he gave me a belly laugh. 'Ah, it's the military ways you're picking up, Mister Mannix. Just like old times.'

'Old times in what army, McGrath? And just by the way, I suppose that isn't your real name. No doubt you're on a good few wanted lists, aren't you?'

He looked pensive. 'They were the days, all right. Well, the name now, that's something of a convenience. I've had several, and passports to match in my time. All this –' He waved at the darkness around us, '– this was going to be a bit of a holiday for me. Things were getting a little hot at home so I thought I'd take a sabbatical. Now I find it's a working holiday.'

I wondered what to do. Keeping McGrath around would be like leading a tiger on a length of string. He was a killing machine, proficient and amoral; a most dangerous man, but extremely useful in times of war. I couldn't trust him, but I found that I couldn't quite dislike him, which troubled my conscience only a little. And I felt we could work together for the moment at all events. There would be a showdown one day, but not yet.

I could hand him over to Sadiq, and he might be strung up from the next telegraph post; but quite apart from my liking the man, it would be a course of action very deleterious to our morale. The crew were civilians and nothing scares a civilian more than summary military law. I thought about McGrath's views on our relative toughness, and said abruptly, 'How old are you, McGrath?'

He was mildly surprised. 'Forty-nine.'

So was I; and only an accident of birth had prevented me from being even more like him than he realized. In spite of what I'd said about Irish politics, I could to a degree understand the motives that drove him, and saw that they might have been my own. It was only chance that my weapon had become a boardroom rather than a gun. 'Listen carefully,' I said. 'If you don't keep in line from now on you won't make your half-century. You were right, McGrath – we *do* think the same. But from now on even more so. Your thoughts and your actions will be dictated by me. You won't do one single goddamn thing without my say-so. And I'll pull the plug on you any time I feel it's better that way. Am I understood?'

He gazed at me steadily, 'I said you were a tough man. I know what you're thinking, Mannix. You're thinking that I'd be a good man to have around if things get tougher. You're thinking that you can point me like a weapon and I'll go off, aren't you? Well, I won't argue with you about that, because I feel much the same myself. And speaking of guns –'

'You're not getting it back.'

'Oh, that's all right,' he said. 'There's nothing so easy to come by in a war as a gun. All I was going to say was that I've not had a chance to clean it up yet. Careless of me, I know. You'll want to do it yourself, I imagine.'

I secured the safety catch on the shotgun and lowered it to the floor of the Land Rover. 'Just remember this, McGrath. I'm never going to stop watching you.'

'On probation, am I?'

'Not at all. You're awaiting trial. Be sure and stay around. Don't go jumping bail, will you?'

'Out there on my own? You have to be joking, Mannix. Now what did you think I went to all this trouble for, if not to prevent that very thing from happening with my lads . . . and I still wish I knew for sure which one came running to you. It wasn't really necessary now, was it?'

I waved a hand in dismissal. I felt no sense of danger from McGrath for the moment, and he must have had the same feeling about me, for he raised a hand and ambled away.

'We'll all be needing a bit of sleep, I think. See you in the morning, Mannix. Thanks for the chat,' he said and was gone.

I sat for a while longer wondering if I was doing the right thing.

SIXTEEN

Early next morning I did a check round the camp. There seemed to be more Nyalans than ever camped some little distance from where we were sited, and the soldiers' camp was further off still, so that we covered a pretty vast area. Lights still burned on the rig, because full daylight had not yet arrived, and there was movement as the medical staff tended their patients, the skeleton night watch making way for the full team. I found Sister Ursula tidying up in the makeshift operating theatre.

'Morning, Sister. Everything all right?'

She offered a wry smile. 'Not exactly all right, but as well as we can expect.' She bustled about just as she would in a regular hospital, and probably saw nothing incongruous in her newly acquired methods; habit skirts tucked into her belt, one hand free to grasp at holds as she swung expertly about the rig.

'No deaths last night, thanks be to God. It's a pity about Kanja, but no doubt we'll manage.'

I told her about the cotton warehouses and she nodded. 'Cool and spacious, much easier for my nurses, certainly.' We had reached the fridge and she opened it, checked the contents against a list, reshuffled the dwindling stores and closed it swiftly, to let as little cold air escape as possible. 'This has been a Godsend,' she commented.

She somehow pronounced the word with an audible uppercase G.

'From God via Wyvern Transport,' I said a little more harshly than was kind. I sometimes tired of the religious habit of thanking God for strictly man-made assistance. She took me up on it at once.

'Don't you believe in God, Mister Mannix? Or in thanking Him?'

Having spent some time the night before in a short seminar on the philosophy of terrorism from McGrath, I didn't feel in the least like getting into another on religion. 'We'll debate it some other time, Sister. We've both got enough else to do at the moment. Where are the doctors?'

'Doctor Marriot's having coffee and Doctor Kat is still asleep.' She smiled. 'He didn't know it but last night I put a sleeping draught in his tea. It knocked him out.'

She showed all the signs of being a very bossy woman. 'Don't ever try that on me, Sister,' I said, smiling back, 'or there'll be trouble. I like to make my own decisions.'

'You have enough sense to know when to stop. But the Doctor was out on his feet and wouldn't admit it.'

'But what happens if there's an emergency? He'd be no good to us doped to the eyebrows.'

She raised one at me. 'I know my dosage. He'll wake up fresh as a daisy. In the meantime there is Doctor Marriot, and me. By the way, Sister Mary is still not to be allowed up here, please. She can travel in the truck again, with the children. Don't listen to anything she says to the contrary.'

She was indeed a bossy woman. She went on, 'I've got Nurse Mulira and Nurse Chula who are both well-trained, and the others are doing well too. Sister Mary doesn't realize how frail she is.'

'Point taken, ma'am. By the way, how much sleep did you get last night?'

'Mind your own business.' Before I could object to that blunt statement she went on, 'I've just been with Mister Otterman. He's not too well again . . .' She looked down past me. 'Someone wants you. I think it's urgent.'

'It always is. Be ready to move in about an hour, Sister.'

I swung down off the rig. Sadiq's sergeant looked harassed. 'The captain wants you, please. It is very urgent.'

I followed him to the command car and found Sadiq examining a battered map. He had an air of mixed gloom and relief. He said, 'The radio is working. I have just had new orders. I have been reassigned.'

I leaned against the car and suddenly felt terribly tired.

'Good God, that's all we need. What orders? And where from?'

'I have heard from a senior officer, Colonel Maksa. I am to take my troops and join him at Ngingwe.' This was on the nearside of the blocked road to Kanja.

'Ngingwe! Sadiq, does this make sense to you?'

'No, sir. But I am not to query orders from a superior.'

The sergeant returned with Geoff Wingstead. I recapped what Sadiq had told me, and Wingstead looked as puzzled as I had. 'I can't see how this Colonel Maksa got to Ngingwe, or why he wants Captain Sadiq there,' he said.

The only good thing in all this was that the radio was working again. If someone had got through to us, we could perhaps get through to others. And we were desperate for news.

'Tell me what Colonel Maksa's politics are,' I asked Sadiq.

'I don't know, Mister Mannix. We never spoke of such things. I don't know him well. But – he has not always been such an admirer of the President.'

'So he could be on either side. What will you do?'

'I cannot disobey a direct order.'

'It's been done. What did you say to him?'

'We could not answer. The lines are still bad, and perhaps we do not have the range.'

'You mean he spoke to you but you couldn't reply. So he doesn't know if you heard the order. Did it refer directly to you or was it a general call for assembly at Ngingwe?'

'It was a direct order to me.'

'Who else knows about this?' I asked.

'Only my sergeant.'

Wingstead said, 'You want him to put the headphone to a deaf ear, to be a modern Nelson, is that it?' We both looked at Sadiq, who looked stubborn.

'Look, Captain. You could be running into big trouble. What if Colonel Maksa is a rebel?'

'I have thought of that, sir. You should not think I am so stupid as to go off without checking.'

'How can you do that?' Wingstead asked.

'I will try to speak to headquarters, to General Kigonde or someone on his staff,' he said. 'But my sergeant has tried very often to get through, without any luck. Our radio is not strong enough.'

Wingstead said abruptly, 'I think we can fix that.'

'How?' I knew that his own intervehicle radios were very limited indeed.

He said, 'I've got reason to think we're harbouring a fairly proficient amateur radio jockey.'

'For God's sake, who?' I asked.

Wingstead said, 'Sandy Bing. A few days ago we caught him in your staff car, Captain, fiddling with your radio. There was a soldier on duty but Bing told him he had your permission. We caught him at it and I read him the riot act. But I let it go at that. We're not military nor police and I had other things on my mind besides a bored youngster.'

'Did you know about this talent of his?' I asked.

'I'd caught him once myself fiddling with the set in the Land Rover. That's really too mild a word for what he'd

been doing. He had the damn set in pieces. I bawled him out
and watched while he put the bits back together. He knew
what he was doing and it worked as well as ever afterwards.
He's damned enthusiastic and wants to work with radio one
day. Sam Wilson told me that he's for ever at any set he can
get his hands on.'

'What do you think he can do? Amplify this set?'

'Maybe. Come along with me, Neil. I'll talk to Bing, but I
want a word with Basil first. This will delay our start again,
I'm afraid.'

Sadiq agreed to wait and see if Bing could get him
through to his headquarters before taking any other action.
My guess was that he wanted to stay with us, but right now
he was torn by a conflict of orders and emotions, and it was
hard to guess which would triumph.

Less than an hour later we stood watching as Sandy Bing
delved happily into the bowels of a transmitter. Sadiq
allowed him access to his own car radio, which Bing wanted
as he said it was better than anything we had, though still
underpowered for what he wanted. He got his fingers into
its guts and went to work, slightly cock-a-hoop but determined to prove his value. He wanted to cannibalize one of
Kemp's radios too, to build an extra power stage; at first
Kemp dug his heels in, but common sense finally won him
round.

'We'll need a better antenna,' said Bing, in his element.
'I'll need copper wire and insulators.'

Hammond managed to find whatever was needed. The
travelling repair shop was amazingly well kitted out.

Our start was delayed by over four hours, and the morning was shot before Bing started to get results. Eventually he
got the beefed-up transmitter on the air which was in itself
a triumph, but that was just the beginning. General
Kigonde's headquarters were hard to locate and contact,
and once we'd found them there was another problem; a

captain doesn't simply chat to his commander-in-chief whenever he wants to. It took an hour for Sadiq to get patched through to the military radio network and another hour of battling through the chain of command.

I'll give Sadiq his due; it takes a brave and determined man to bully and threaten his way through a guard of civilian sec-retaries, colonels and brigadiers. He really laid his neck on the block and if Kigonde hadn't been available, or didn't back him, I wouldn't have given two cents for his later chances of promotion. When he spoke to Kigonde the sun was high in the sky and he was nearly as high with tension and triumph.

'You did OK, Sandy,' I said to Bing, who was standing by with a grin all over his face as the final connection came through. Wingstead clapped him on the shoulder and there were smiles all round.

Sadiq and Kigonde spoke only in Nyalan, and the Captain's side of the conversation became more and more curt and monosyllabic. Sadiq looked perturbed; obviously he would like to tell us what was going on, but dared not sever the precious connection, and Kigonde might run out of patience at any moment and do his own cutting off from the far end. I was sick with impatience and the need for news. At last I extended a hand for the headphones and put a whipcrack into my own voice.

'Tell him I want to speak to him.'

Before Sadiq could react I took the headphones away from him. There was a lot of static as I thumbed the speak button and said, 'General Kigonde, this is Mannix. What is happening, please?'

He might have been taken aback but didn't close me out.

'Mister Mannix, there is no time for talk. Your Captain has received orders and he must obey them. I cannot super-vise the movement of every part of the army myself.'

'Has he told you the situation at Ngingwe? That it is a dead end? The road goes nowhere now. We *need* him,

General. Has he told you what's happening here, with your people?'

Through the static, Kigonde said, 'Captain Sadiq has orders to obey. Mister Mannix, I know you have many people in trouble there, but there is trouble everywhere.'

That gave me an idea. I said, 'General Kigonde, do you know who gave Captain Sadiq his orders?'

'I did not get the name. Why do you ask?'

'Does the name Colonel Maksa mean anything to you?' It was taking a gamble but I didn't think the chances of Maksa or anyone on his staff overhearing this conversation were strong. It was a risk we had to take.

Static crackled at me and then Kigonde said, 'That is . . . perhaps different. He was in command of forces in the north. I have not heard from him.'

Doubt crept into Kigonde's voice.

I said urgently, 'General, I think you do have doubts about Colonel Maksa. If he were against you what better could he do than draw off your troops? Captain Sadiq is completely loyal. Where would you get the best use out of him? Here with us, or cut off upcountry? If I were you I'd cancel those orders, General.'

'You may be right, Mister Mannix. I must say the Captain would be better off for my purposes further west. I will send him to Makara instead.'

'But we're going to Makara ourselves. Can he stay with us until we get there?'

I was really pushing my luck and I wasn't surprised when he demanded to speak to Sadiq again. It was a long one-sided conversation, and when he rang off we could all see that he had been told something that had shaken him badly.

He remembered his manners before anything else, turned to Bing and said, 'Thank you very much. I am grateful to you,' which pleased Bing immensely. But Sadiq didn't look grateful, only distressed.

'Let's go and sit down, Captain,' I said. 'Geoff, you, me and Basil only, I think. Move it out, you guys. Find something to do.'

Sadiq filled us in on the conversation. He was to move westwards to Makara with us, but once there he was to push on towards Fort Pirie, leaving us to cope. It was as much as we could have expected. But it occurred to me that the General must be in a bad way if he was calling such minor outfits as Sadiq's to his assistance.

'The General says that the Government is in power in Port Luard once again. The rebellion is crushed and almost all the rebels are rounded up,' Sadiq said. That was what Kigonde would say, especially on the air, and none of us put too much faith in it. But at least it meant that the Government hadn't been crushed.

'The rebellion was premature, I think,' Sadiq said. 'The opposition was not ready and has been beaten quite easily in most places.'

'But not everywhere. Does he know where this Colonel Maksa is? I think we have to assume he's on the wrong side, don't you?' I said.

'Yes, the Colonel's politics are suspect. And he is known to be hereabouts. There are planes looking for him and his force.'

'Planes?' said Wingstead in alarm. 'Whose planes?'

'Ah, it is all most unfortunate, sir. We were wrong, you see. The Air Force, Air Chief Marshall Semangala is on the side of the Government.'

'Ouseman's *allies*?' My jaw dropped. 'Then why was Mister Wingstead's plane shot down, for God's sake?'

'I don't know, Mister Mannix, But perhaps the Air Force expected that any civilian planes flying in the battle area belonged to the rebels,' Sadiq said unhappily. I thought of Max Otterman, fighting for his life somewhere on the rig, and rage caught in my throat.

Geoff Wingstead was ahead of me. 'What about the bombing of Kodowa, then? The troop moving through the town at the time was Kigonde's own Second Battalion. Are you going to tell us that was a mistake, too?'

'Ah, that was very bad. Air Force Intelligence thought that the Second Battalion was already with the Seventh Brigade at Bir Oassa. When they saw troops moving north they thought it was the enemy trying to cut off the Seventh Brigade from coming south. So they attacked.' Sadiq looked anguished.

A mistake! They'd bombed their own men thinking they were the enemy. It wouldn't be the first time that had happened in a war. But they'd bombed them in the middle of a town when they could easily have waited to catch them out in the open. So would somebody eventually apologize for this colossal, tragic mistake? Apologize for the pits full of corpses, the ruined town, the wrecked and tortured people on the rig or hobbling through the wasted country? To Sister Ursula and Dr Kat, to Dr Marriot for the killing of her husband? To Antoine Dufour for the death of his partner?

Somebody ought to say they were sorry. But nobody ever would.

SEVENTEEN

We left Kodowa again.

We went north-west this time, descending from the scrubland to the rainforest country of the lower plains, the same sort of terrain that we'd moved through on our journey northwards. The people in the little villages we passed through came out to see us but they weren't laughing this time. They gazed at the great rig and the strange load it carried and their faces were troubled. Even the children were subdued, catching the uneasiness of their elders.

The rig's passengers varied. Some improved and were allowed to ride in one of the trucks, others collapsed and were given a place on the bedding. Two women gave birth on the rig, and Dr Kat removed a swollen appendix from a ten-year-old boy. The medical supplies dwindled steadily.

At each village Sadiq sent his men out to forage. A couple of beat-up trucks were added to the convoy as well as provisions. Occasionally they found petrol and it was added to our store. Our own food became more basic and the beer had long since run out. But we managed.

In one village we found a small cache of clothing and bartered food for it, and it did feel wonderful to be wearing something clean for a while. The men were beginning to look shaggy as beards sprouted.

With each few hours the make-up of the flock of Nyalans that trailed along after us subtly altered. The convoy was behaving much like a comet in space, picking up and losing bits of its tail as it went along. Groups of Nyalans would arrive at some village where they had kin or were too weary to walk further, and would leave us there. Others would follow along. There may have been several hundred in our wake, and there was something of a ritual, almost mystic, quality in their behaviour. Often one or more would approach the rig and reach up to touch it wonderingly before dropping behind again.

It was Dan Atheridge who explained it to me. He'd lived here for many years, and spoke a little Nyalan. His arm troubled him and he had to be restrained from doing too much; but I knew that he was deliberately driving himself into exhaustion in an attempt to numb the pain and horror of leaving his wife Susie somewhere behind him in the hills beyond Kanja. He had begged to be allowed to go off and try to find her, but had finally been persuaded not to.

I asked him about the Nyalans.

'Your rig's turning into a juggernaut, Neil,' he said.

'That's an Indian thing, isn't it? A sort of God-mobile?'

That got a smile from him. 'You could put it that way. Actually it's one of the names of the god Krishna. It became applied to a huge idol that's dragged through the streets in a town in India annually in his honour. In the olden days sacrificial victims were thrown under it to be crushed to death. A rather bloodthirsty deity, I fear.'

'It isn't inappropriate,' I said. 'Except that nobody's been run down by the rig yet, which God forbid.'

'It's followed in procession by thousands of devotees, who regard it as a sacred symbol of their wellbeing. That's the similarity, Neil. This rig of yours has become a fetish to the Nyalans. You're leading them to the promised land, wherever that is. Out of danger anyway.'

'I hope that's true, Dan. Still, I guess they have to believe in something.'

I mentioned the parallel with the Pied Piper and he smiled again. 'I hope you think of them as children rather than as rats, Neil.'

I got precisely the other viewpoint from Russ Burns some time later that day, when we stopped at last, more than halfway to Makara.

Several of us were waiting for whatever Brad Bishop could offer as an evening meal. Making idle conversation, I mentioned Atheridge's theory about the new role of the rig as a fetish, and Wingstead was fascinated. I could see him formulating an article for some truckers' magazine. Burns' attitude was very different and typical of him.

'More like rats,' he said when I invoked the Pied Piper image. 'Little brown bastards, eating up everything that isn't nailed down. Probably carrying disease too.' I felt a strong desire to hit him. Wingstead got up and walked away.

After a strained silence Burns spoke again. 'How come you work for a limey outfit?' He seemed to enjoy baiting me.

'Good pay,' I said briefly.

He snorted. 'For pushing this thing along?'

'Good enough,' I said. He seemed to have got the notion that I was a transport man and I didn't bother to disillusion him. It wasn't worth the trouble, and in any case right now it was nearer the truth than otherwise.

'What do you do with Lat-Am?' I asked him.

'I'm a tool pusher. Harry here's a shooter.'

'Come again? I don't know oil jargon.'

Zimmerman laughed. 'Russ is a drilling superintendent. Me, I make loud bangs in oil wells. Blasting.'

'Been in Nyala long?' I didn't take to Burns but Zimmerman was a much more likeable man. They made an odd pair.

'A while. Six months or so. We were based in Bir Oassa but we went down to the coast to take a look. The desert country's better. We should have stayed up there.'

'You can say that again,' Burns said, 'then we'd be out of this crummy mess.'

'I was up in Bir Oassa earlier this month,' I said. 'Didn't have much time to look at the oilfields, though. How you doing there?'

'We brought in three,' Zimmerman said. 'Good sweet oil, low sulphur; needs no doctor at all. Lat-Am isn't doing badly on this one.'

'What about the war, though?'

Burns shrugged. 'That's no skin off Lat-Am's ass. We'll stop pumping, that's all. The oil's still in the ground and we've got the concession. Whoever wins the war will need us.'

It was a point of view, I suppose.

They talked then between themselves for a while, using oilfield jargon which I understood better than I'd let on. Burns appealed to me less and less; he was a guy for whom the word chauvinist might have been invented. Texas was Paradise and the Alamo was the navel of the earth; he might grudgingly concede that California wasn't bad, but the East Coast was full of goddamn liberals and Jews and longhaired hippies. You might as well be in Europe, where everyone was effete and decadent. Still, the easterners were at least American and he could get along with them if he had to. The rest of the world was divided between commies, niggers, Ayrabs and gooks, and fit only for plundering for oil.

The next day we arrived at Makara. It was no bigger than other villages we'd passed through, but it earned its place on the map because of the bridge which spanned the river there. Further west, near Lake Pirie where the river joined the huge Katali there was a delta, and building a bridge would not have been possible. Our first concern was to find out whether the river was passable, and Sadiq, Kemp and I went ahead of the convoy to take a look. To our relief the bridge stood firm and was fit for crossing.

We halted outside the village and sent off another scouting party to investigate the cotton warehouses. Word came back that they were intact, empty and serviceable as a hospital, and so we moved to the cotton factory and camped there. Apart from the grave faces of the local people there was no sign of trouble anywhere.

That was the last good thing that happened that day. Dr Katabisirua came to look at the warehouses and arranged for some Nyalan women to give the largest a clean through before bringing in the patients, which he wouldn't do until the next day. 'My nurses are tired from the journey,' he said, 'and that is when mistakes are made.'

He was very despondent. Two more burn patients had died and he feared for one of the new born babies. Some of the wounded were not improving as he would wish. 'And now Sister Ursula tells me we have no more Ringer's lactate.'

'What's that?'

'A replacement for lost plasma. We have no substitute.' There was no hospital closer than Lasulu, and that was as far away as the moon. He also fretted about Sister Mary who was sinking into frail senility under the stress.

By the end of our talk I was even more depressed than he was. There wasn't a thing I could do for him or his patients, and I was profoundly frustrated by my helplessness. Never before in my adult life had I been unable to cope with a situation, and it galled me.

Burns, passing by, said casually, 'Hey, Mannix, the coon captain wants you,' and walked on.

'Burns!'

He looked back over his shoulder. 'Yes?'

'Come here.'

He swung back. 'You got a beef?'

I said, 'This morning Captain Sadiq persuaded his superior officer to let him stay with this convoy. He put his career on the line for us. What's more, over the past few days he's worked harder than you could in a month, and a damned sight more willingly. Around here you'll speak respectfully of and to him. Got the idea?'

'Touchy, aren't you?' he said.

'Yes I am. Don't push me, Burns.'

'What the hell do you want from me?' he asked.

I sighed, letting my neck muscles relax. 'You will not refer to the Captain as a coon or a nigger. Nor his soldiers, nor any other Nyalans, come to that. We're fed up with it.'

'Why should I take orders from you?' he asked.

I said, 'Because right now I'm top man around here. As long as you're with us you do what I say, and if you don't toe the line you'll be out on your can. And you won't hold a job with Lat-Am or any other oil company after this is over. If you don't think I can swing that then you just ask Mister Kemp.'

I turned my back and walked away, seething. If I'd been near him much longer I couldn't have kept my hands off him, which wouldn't have solved any problems. I passed a couple of staring men and then McGrath was beside me, speaking softly.

'Need any help, Mannix?'

'No,' I said curtly. McGrath stuck in my craw too.

'I'll be around if you do.' He returned to his job.

I recalled that the reason for this outburst had been that Captain Sadiq wanted a word, and I set about finding him. It was a routine matter he wanted settled. After our business was over I pointed to the milling flock of Nyalans around the camp.

'Captain, how many of them are there?' I asked.

'Perhaps two hundred, Mister Mannix. But they do not stay with us for long. It is only that there are always more of them.'

'Yes, I've noticed that. I understand they've attached themselves to the rig, made some sort of mascot of it. Do you know anything about it?'

'I am of Islam,' he said. 'These people have different ideas from you and me. But they are not savages, Mister Mannix. Perhaps it is no more than the thing Mister Lang hangs in the cab of his tractor. It is a lucky charm.'

'That's a rabbit's foot. I see what you mean,' I said, impressed by his logic. 'Just a bigger talisman than usual. But I'm worried about them. Are they getting enough food and water? What if a real sickness strikes among them? What can we do to stop them, make them return to their homes?'

'I do not think anything will stop them, sir. They manage for food, and none will walk further than he can achieve. For each of them, that is enough.'

One thing it ensured was a redistribution of the local population, a reshuffle of families, genes and customs; perhaps not altogether a bad thing. But it was a hell of a way to go about it. And suppose ill fortune should fall on these people while they were tailing us. Would they see their erstwhile lucky talisman becoming a force of evil instead, and if so what might they take it into their collective heads to do about it, and about us?

I reflected on the crusades. Not all of them were made by armed and mailed men; there was the Peasants' Crusade led by Peter the Hermit, and the Children's Crusade. If I remembered my history, terrible things happened to those kids. And come to think of it, Hamelin's rats and children didn't do too well either.

I didn't much relish the role of a twentieth century Peter leading a mad crusade into nowhere. A whole lot of people could die that way. The thought of an armoured column ploughing through this mob chilled my blood.

The run-in with Burns later that day was inevitable, a curtain-raiser to the real drama that followed. The men who work the oil rigs are a tough bunch and you don't get to boss a drilling crew by backing down from a fight. Maybe I should have handled Burns more tactfully, maybe I was losing my touch, but there it was. I had threatened him and I might have known he wouldn't stand still for it.

But that was yet to come. First we had to set up the cotton warehouse for Dr Kat to move in to the next day, and we parked the rig close by in order to run a cable from its generator. Ben Hammond, as usual, provided ideas and the equipment to put them into action, and his goody box included a sizeable reel of cable and several powerful lamps.

While this was being done I had a look around the warehouse. It was just a huge barn about a quarter full of cotton stacked at the far end. The bottom stacks were compressed but the upper layers were soft and would provide comfort for everybody soon, including myself. I intended to sleep there that night. The biggest mattress in the world, but better not smoke in bed.

Late in the afternoon I saw Harry Zimmerman sitting on an upturned box near the Land Rover, smoking and drinking a mug of tea. I sensed that he was waiting for me, though his opening remark was casual enough.

'Been a busy day,' he said.

'Sure has. And it'll be a busy night. I've got another job for you, anytime you're ready.' I dropped down beside him. 'Trade you for a mouthful of that gunfire, Harry.'

'What have you got to trade?' he asked as he handed over the mug. I took a swig and passed it back.

'Good soft bed for tonight.'

'Now you're talking. Anyone in it?'

'Sorry, only me – and probably all the rest of the crew. We may as well doss down in comfort for one night before handing the warehouse over to the medics.'

He was silent for a spell and then said, 'Seen Russ about?'

'No. Why?'

'Just thought I'd mention it. He's spoiling for a fight. Can be nasty, once he's off and flying.'

It was a fair warning and I wasn't particularly surprised. I nodded my thanks and crossed to the Land Rover. Zimmerman seemed to be waiting for something to happen. It did. As I opened the door an object rolled off the seat and smashed at my feet. It was my bottle of Scotch, and it was quite empty.

'Russ did this, Harry?'

'I'm afraid so.'

He'd left the bottle where I'd find it; it was a direct challenge. There would have been just enough in it to put an edge on his appetite for supper, or for a brawl.

'Where is he?'

'Neil, Russ is one tough guy to tangle with. Be careful.'

I said, 'He's not going to hurt me. I'm going to straighten your buddy out.'

'Hell, he's not my buddy,' Zimmerman said, and there was an edge to his normally placid voice. 'We just work together. I've seen this before and I don't have a taste for it. He's having a game of poker with some of your guys.'

I picked up the pieces of glass and ditched all but the largest which had the label still attached, and closed the car door. Zimmerman added, 'Watch his left. He has a sneaky curve punch there.'

'Thanks.'

I knew where to find Burns. One of the lamps leading from the generator cable had been looped over a tree so that the light shone on the ground below. Five men were sitting playing cards, using a suitcase as a table. I didn't notice who they were; I had eyes only for Burns. He played a hand casually but I knew he'd seen me arrive and his back had stiffened.

I stopped just outside the circle of light and said, 'Burns, come here. I want you.'

He looked up and shaded his eyes. 'Why, it's our top man,' he said. 'What can I do for you, Mannix?'

Cards went down all round the circle. I said, 'Come over here.'

'Sure. Why not?' He uncoiled his lean length from the ground.

I watched him come. He was younger, taller, heavier and probably faster than I was, so I'd have to get in first. It's a stupid man who starts a fight without reckoning the odds. Burns knew that too; he was spoiling for a fight, as Zimmerman had warned me, and he had set up the time and place. It was years since I'd done much fighting except with words, while he was probably well in practice.

I was aware of figures forming the inevitable spectators' ring, but I couldn't afford to take my eyes off Burns. Witnesses were in any case going to be more on my side than on his, so long as I could hold my own.

I held up the bottle shard. 'Did you drink my whisky?'

'Sure I drank it. What's wrong with borrowing a little booze? It was good stuff while it lasted.'

I controlled my anger, and was so intent that when the interruption came I couldn't quite credit it. A hand came over my shoulder and took the broken glass from me. 'Do you mind if I have a look at that?' a voice said.

McGrath stepped out beside me and peered at the label. Everyone else stood motionless.

'I've seen this before. Isn't it the bottle you were keeping for medical emergencies, now?'

Then without warning the hand not holding the shard connected with Burns just at the angle of his jaw and the

Texan grunted, staggered and dropped as though poleaxed. Only afterwards did I see the cosh.

I grabbed McGrath by the arm. 'God damn it, McGrath, I told you not to go off half-cocked!'

He said so that only I could hear, 'You couldn't have whipped this bucko and we both know it. He'd take you to pieces. I've had my eye on him; he's dangerous.' Coming from McGrath that was a ludicrous statement. 'Now if I don't defuse him he'll come looking for both of us and he might have a gun by then. He has to be made harmless. That OK with you?'

'Christ, no! I don't want him killed,' I said.

'I wouldn't kill him. I said made harmless. Now, have I your leave?'

I didn't have much choice. 'Don't hurt him,' I said.

'Not really hurt, no,' McGrath said. He pushed his way through the knot of men who had gathered round Burns. They made way instantly, though none faster than Jones and Bob Pitman. Neither Wingstead nor Kemp were present.

McGrath took Burns by his shirtfront, hauled him to his feet and shook him. 'Are you all right, Texas?' he asked.

Burns' eyes looked fogged. He put a hand up to his jaw and mumbled, 'You son of a bitch – you busted it!'

'Not at all,' said McGrath, 'Or you couldn't be saying so. I didn't hit you all that hard, did I now? And I don't think that's the language for someone in your position to be using.'

The hand that had held the cosh came up again and this time there was a knife in it. McGrath was a walking armoury. He pressed the sharp edge against Burns' throat and a ribbon of blood trickled down. He pushed Burns until the Texan's back was against a truck.

'Now listen,' McGrath said in a matter-of-fact voice, 'You can have your throat cut fast, slow or not at all. Take your pick.'

Burns choked. 'Not – not at all.'

'Well, then, you can answer a couple of questions, and if you give the right answers you get a prize, your life. Here comes the first question. Are you ready?'

'Yes,' whispered Burns.

McGrath said, 'Right, this is it. Name one boss in this camp.'

'Y-you.'

'Wrong,' said McGrath pleasantly. 'You're losing points, sonny. But I'll give you another go. Guess again.'

Burns hesitated and the knife shifted. More blood soaked into his shirt. 'Mannix?'

'Mister Mannix, yes. But a little more respect with it, please. Now here comes the next question. Are you ready for it?'

'Christ, yes.' Burns face was running with sweat.

'Then here goes. Name another boss.'

'Wing . . . Mister Wingstead.'

'Oh, very good. See how well you can do when you try. So from now on when Mister Mannix or Mister Wingstead says for you to jump, you jump. Got that?'

'Yes.'

'And if you give either of them any trouble, guess what? Third question.'

'You bastard –'

McGrath's hand moved once more. Burns gasped, 'I won't give them any trouble. Let go of me, damn you!'

McGrath did just that and Burns sagged against the truck. His hand went to his throat and came away covered with blood. He stared at McGrath and then appealed to me. 'He's crazy! You keep him away from me.'

'He'll never touch you again. Not if you do what he's just told you,' I said. Then I pressed the lesson home. 'You said you'd borrowed that Scotch. I want it returned.'

He gaped at me. 'You're as crazy as he is! You know I can't do that.'

'In my book a man who takes what he can't return is a thief.'

He said nothing and I let it go at that. I turned to the others. 'All right, the show is over. There's no –'

I was interrupted by a distant commotion of voices.

'Mannix! Ben Hammond, you there?'

It was Kemp calling. Hammond shouted back, 'We're both here. What is it?'

Kemp came out of the dark at a jog trot, looking strained. Burns was forgotten in the face of a new crisis.

'Come up to the rig. Geoff wants you.'

'What the hell is it?'

'It's Max. He's gone into convulsions. We think he's dying.'

There was a murmur around us. To most of the crew Otterman was not well-known but he was the man who'd saved Wingstead's life at risk to his own. They were taking a close interest in his progress, and at that moment were no more free of superstition than the Nyalans who followed their talisman through the countryside: Otterman's sudden turn for the worse was a bad omen. As for me, I'd flown with him, liked him, and felt a stab of sorrow at Kemp's news.

And then the quiet of the night was shattered again. To the east there was thunder. There followed noises like Fourth of July rockets, and the earth shook underfoot. It was the sound of heavy gunfire and small arms. The war was catching up with us at last.

EIGHTEEN

Things began to happen fast.

From the military camp soldiers came running towards the warehouse. People milled about in the darkness and shouted questions. The men around me were galvanized into agitation which could become panic.

I shouted for attention. 'That was gunfire. Keep together and stay quiet. Let the soldiers do their job. Hammond, you there?'

'Yes, I'm here.'

'Set guards round all the transports, especially the trucks and cars. The rig can't be shifted so it's reasonably safe. Basil, go tell the doctors and staff to stay put whatever happens. I'm sorry about Max, but tell Geoff I need him here fast.'

He ran off and I went on, 'Zimmerman – if Russ Burns isn't fit get him to the medics. I'm going to find the Captain.'

I heard Burns mumble, 'I'll be OK, Harry,' and turned away. I wondered what had become of McGrath; at the very first sound of battle he had disappeared, cat-like, into the night. I headed off towards the military area, stumbling over camp litter. I heard guns firing again before I found Captain Sadiq.

He was at his staff car, and inevitably on the radio. He spoke for some time, looking alarmed, and then ripped off the headphones.

'What's happening?' I asked.

'Army units coming from the east, from Kodowa. They ran into a patrol of men and started shooting.'

'We heard a big gun.'

'I think they shelled a truck.'

'They must be the rebels,' I said.

'Maybe, Mister Mannix. Men become nervous in the dark.'

'How many?'

'I don't know yet. My corporal reported many vehicles coming this way. Not in battalion strength but not far short. Then the transmission stopped.'

So a whole platoon of Sadiq's men was possibly wiped out. I asked if he knew how far off they were.

'Six miles, maybe. They could be here in half an hour or less.'

This could be a nasty mess. With the Nyalan civilians strung out all the way to the bridge, with our sick and wounded, and with a small bunch of virtually unarmed white rig-pushers, there could be a massacre. And to prevent it a handful of soldiers armed with rifles and one or two light mounted guns.

Sadiq said, 'If we stand and fight it will be useless. We couldn't combat a company, let alone this strength. Sergeant! Get the men ready to pull out. There must be no shooting under any circumstances. We'll be moving that way.' He pointed away from Makara. This had been in English and was clearly for my benefit, but he carried on in Nyalan. The sergeant went off at a run.

I said, 'So you're pulling out – leaving us? What the hell are we supposed to do on our own?'

He raised a hand to silence me. Danger had increased his authority and he knew it. 'No, Mister Mannix. There are tracks beyond the warehouses which lead into the bush. I'm going to hide my men there. If I am to be of any use it can only be from a position of surprise. I suggest that you make your camp look as peaceful as possible. And that means hiding all weapons, including your shotgun. And anything that Mister McGrath may have.'

'You know about him?'

'I am *not* a fool, Mister Mannix. You took a pistol from him, but he may have some other weapon. When the soldiers come act peacefully. As soon as possible give me a signal. If they are loyal troops you fire this.'

He handed me a Very pistol and a couple of cartridges.

'The white star will signal no danger. If there is trouble, fire the red. Try not to provoke them.'

Sadiq could simply vanish into the bush and desert us but I felt that he would do no such thing. I said, 'Thank you, Captain. And good luck.'

He saluted me, jumped into his car, and was gone into the night.

'Remarkable,' said a voice behind me. Wingstead had been listening. I nodded briefly, then called Bing. 'Get back to the rig, Sandy. Tell the men to gather round quietly and wait for us. And take the guards off the trucks. Tell Mister Hammond I said so.' I debated giving instructions to immobilize the transports but reflected that it might do us as much harm as our enemy.

Zimmerman was beside me. I said to him, 'Please go fetch Mister Kemp. He'll be at the rig, And get Doctor Kat as well. Tell him he must leave his patients for a few minutes.'

Wingstead said, 'I gather we aren't sure if it's the goodies or the baddies who are coming along, right?'

'Exactly right. So we play it as cool as we can. What's happened with Otterman?'

'He was having some sort of convulsion. God knows what it is; the medics have nothing left to sedate him with. I feel responsible but I can't do him one bit of good. I've never had a man working for me die before.'

'Well, he's not dead yet. They'll pull him through if they can,' I said, but it was hollow comfort. We hurried back to the rig, and I noticed that the Nyalan refugees had vanished; like the soldiers, they had dissolved back into the land. It had needed no bush telegraph to pass the word. They had heard and recognized the gunfire.

Back at the rig Hammond had got my message and gathered the men together. 'The army's pulling out,' someone said.

'Who's doing the shooting?'

'Hold it! Just shut up and listen. Harry, you translate for our Russian friends, please. This is the position as far as we know. There's a force coming down from Kodowa. They ran into one of Sadiq's patrols and we think they shot them up, so it's likely that they're rebels. But we can't be sure yet. Mistakes happen in the dark.'

And in broad daylight too, I thought, remembering the bombing raid on Kodowa.

'If they are rebels they'll be too much for Sadiq to handle, so he's done a little disappearing act with his men. We'll signal to let him know if the new arrivals are friendly or otherwise. If they want to know where Sadiq is, he's gone off with his men. It's important that everybody tells the same story. He left us as soon as we got here. Right?'

Kemp asked, 'Why this flimflam? He's supposed to stay and guard the rig, isn't he?'

Not for the first time I despaired of Kemp's single-mindedness. I said, 'I'll explain later,' and turned back to the men.

'When they get here I want the camp to look normal. Remember, we know nothing about their politics and care less. We're paid to push the rig, that's all. We're a crowd of foreigners in the middle of a shooting war, trying to keep our noses clean, and we're scared.'

'None of us will have to be Laurence Olivier to act that part,' someone said.

'Let Mister Wingstead or me answer any questions. And no rough stuff, no opposition, no matter what.' This wouldn't be easy. Men like this wouldn't willingly allow themselves to be pushed around. But it was essential. Opposition could only bring reprisal.

A voice said, 'Why stay here? Why don't we scarper and hide out in the bush till they've gone, same as the army?'

Dr Kat said sharply, 'I am not leaving my patients.'

'I don't think it'd wash, or I'd be the first to go,' Wingstead put in. 'If there's no-one here they'll get suspicious and come looking for us.'

His calm decisiveness was what was needed. There wasn't a man amongst them who didn't respect him.

I said, 'Right, let's get this camp looking peaceful.'

I left Wingstead to organize things and went to the Land Rover to get the shotgun and its shells. I took them into the warehouse and hid them deep inside a bale of cotton, hoping that nobody had seen me do it. Then I went back to rejoin Wingstead at the rig.

He had persuaded the doctors and Sister Ursula to accept our need for deception, and to brief the nurses. I had a quick look at Otterman and was not reassured. He looked desperately ill.

Geoff and I made a quick tour of the camp, checking to make sure that everything looked reasonably normal. Of the Nyalans there was no sign whatsoever, and Sadiq had taken off his platoon complete with all their transport. Camp fires had been extinguished and there was nothing to show that his departure had been anything other than orderly.

We settled down around the rig, tense and nervous, to wait for our visitors. They took about an hour to reach us, and it was probably the longest wait of our lives.

NINETEEN

We heard them before we saw them.

Bert Proctor cocked his head at the distant rumble, then settled at the table and picked up his cards. 'Just go on with the game,' he said quietly.

Ron Jones got up. 'Count me out, Bert. I'm too nervous,' he said.

I took his place. 'Deal me in. Just take it easy, Ron. No sweat.'

As Proctor dealt I noticed that Russ Burns was one of my fellow players. To my surprise he spoke to me directly.

'You play goddamn rough, Mannix,' he said. The 'Mister' had disappeared. 'Where did you get that goon you set on me?'

'I didn't get him. I inherited him. He's one of Wyvern's best rig hands,' I said. I didn't expect friendship from Burns but he sounded easy enough.

'I really thought he was going to cut my throat. He's pretty dangerous,' Burns said.

'I'll try to keep him on a leash,' I said casually. 'By the way, anyone seen Mick lately?'

There were headshakes all round.

Burns looked at his cards and cursed them. 'We've got a few things to sort out, you and me, after this is over,' he said, 'but if there's trouble in the meantime, I'm with you. What say?'

'Suits me.' We played a round or two with less than full attention. The engine noises were louder and there were voices shouting. Soon we put our cards down to watch the arrival of the army.

A few motorcyclists came first. They roared to a halt just over the crest of the hill that led down to Makara and the camp, and there was a glow in the sky behind them as the rest followed. Soldiers came through the bush on each side of the road. I hoped they wouldn't fan out far enough to find Sadiq's team.

The minutes ticked by and there were rustling sounds in the undergrowth. They were being cautious, not knowing what they were getting into, and nervous men could do stupid things. We stood fully illuminated while they closed in around us, and felt terrifyingly vulnerable.

Wingstead said loudly, 'I'm going to bed. We've got a busy day ahead. Goodnight, everyone.'

I followed his lead. 'Me too. That's enough poker for one night.'

Hammond, in a flash of inspiration, said equally loudly, 'What about all the activity out there, Mister Wingstead? Anything we should know about?'

'No, I don't think so,' he replied. 'Just manoeuvres, I should guess. They won't bother us.'

Truck after truck was coming over the crest towards us. I couldn't see any tanks but the trucks' headlights began to light up the whole camp in a glaring display. A ring of armed soldiers was gathered on the fringes of the camp, and we knew we were surrounded.

I shouted to carry over the engine roar, 'We've got company. Let's hope they can spare us some food and medical stuff.'

Into the light came a command car. In the back was a captain, his uniform identical to Sadiq's except that he wore a red brassard on his right arm. He was unlike Sadiq in looks too; where Sadiq had a distinctly Arabic cast and a light skin this was the blackest man I had ever seen. He was huge and burly and most unnervingly wearing enormous dark glasses; in combination with his dark skin and the night the effect was weird.

He stood up in the back of the car and looked from us to the rig and then back. He said in English, 'Who are you?'

I answered. 'The rig team of Wyvern Transport. Who are you?' But my counterattack didn't work; I hadn't thought it would.

'Are you in charge of – of this?' He indicated the rig.

'No,' I said, 'that's Mister Wingstead here. I am his associate. We were taking a transformer up to the oilfields. But now we have to head back westward.'

'Where is Captain Sadiq?' he asked abruptly.

I'd been expecting that question.

'He should be well on the road to Fort Pirie by now. He left at first light with his men.'

'You're lying,' the captain said. 'Where is he?'

One of his men hitched his rifle. We were in the hands of a military power, and an unfriendly one at that. I hadn't been accustomed to shutting up at anyone else's say-so for a long time and it was an unpleasant sensation. I put an edge on my voice. 'Now wait a minute, captain. You're not dealing with soldiers now. You'd better consult your superior officer before you start dictating to civilians. I told you that Captain Sadiq left this morning and pushed on. He had orders reassigning him. I don't know where he is now and I can't say I care. He left us flat.'

All this rolled off his back without touching. 'I do not believe you,' he said. 'There is much that is strange here. Who are all the people we found on the road as we came up?'

'Women and children? They're local folk, following us for food, and they're in a bad way. I think you should be doing something to help them.'

He regarded the rig again. 'What is that stuff up there?' He'd recognized the incongruity of the thatching.

'That's a long story,' I said. 'You've been in Kodowa lately? Then you'll know what it was like there. The hospital wasn't usable so we turned the rig into a travelling hospital. We're trying to get the patients to Fort Pirie. Perhaps you can help us, Captain.'

He looked at me unbelievingly. 'Why didn't you take them to Kanja? There's a hospital there and it's closer.'

'We tried. But there's a bridge down in between.'

Apparently he hadn't known that, because he fired questions at me about it and then called a couple of messengers and rattled off orders to them. Then he turned to me and said curtly, 'I am leaving soldiers on guard here. You will stay until I return or until the Colonel arrives.'

'We're going no place, Captain,' I said. 'Not until morning, at any rate. Then perhaps you can help us get the rig across the bridge.'

He gave another order and the car swung round and drove off. A circle of soldiers, rifles at the ready, stood around us. The guns they held were Kalashnikovs.

I sighed and sat down.

'Well done. You're quite a con man,' Wingstead said.

'Cool it, Geoff. God knows how many of them understand English.'

Then we realized that the soldiers had orders to do more than just stand around watching us. A sergeant was doing what sergeants do, and corporals were doing what corporals do; passing orders from top to bottom. They began to swarm over our camp and vehicles and I heard the sound of breaking glass.

'Hold on! What are you doing there?' Kemp asked angrily.

'We follow orders. You go back,' a sullen voice answered.

I turned to a sergeant. 'What's the name of your colonel?'

He considered the question and decided to answer it. 'Colonel Maksa,' he said. 'He will be here soon. Now you go back.'

Reluctantly we retreated away from the vehicles. I hoped to God the soldiers wouldn't try clambering over the rig too, and that they'd respect the doctors and nurses.

We stood around helplessly.

'What the hell do they want?' Kemp asked.

'You could try asking Colonel Maksa when he arrives, but I don't recommend it. I bet he's another man who asks questions and doesn't answer them. I'm pretty sure these are rebel troops; the regulars would be more respectful.' But I remembered Hussein and doubted my own words.

'Are you going to send that signal to Sadiq?'

'Not yet. Let's keep that ace in the hole for when we really need it.'

Kemp said, 'Bloody terrorists. Don't they know they can't win?'

'I wouldn't be too sure of that,' Wingstead said. 'And I wouldn't use that word too freely. One man's terrorist is another man's freedom fighter. No doubt they see themselves as glorious liberators.'

The doors of the warehouse opened and light streamed out. Soldiers were manhandling two men into the open; they were Dan Atheridge and Antoine Dufour, who had retired to sleep on the cotton bales. Atheridge was writhing as someone wrenched his broken arm clear of its sling.

'Good God, what are they doing to them?' Kemp asked in horror.

'I'd like to know,' I said grimly. 'Those two are about the most pacifist of the lot of us.' I wondered if it had anything to do with the shotgun I'd hidden.

Into this scene drove two staff cars; in one was our black-goggled Captain and in the other a large, impressive man who must have been Colonel Maksa. He had the Arabic features of many of his countrymen, marred by a disfiguring scar across his face. His uniform looked as though it had just been delivered from the tailors, in marked contrast to the bedraggled appearance of his Captain and men. He stood up as his car stopped and looked at us coldly.

I tried to take the initiative.

'I must make a formal protest, Colonel Maksa,' I said.

'Must you?' This was a more sophisticated man than the Captain, and just those two words warned me that he could be very dangerous.

'We are a civilian engineering team. Your soldiers have been interfering with our camp and assaulting our men. I protest most strongly!'

'Have they?' he asked indifferently. He alighted from his car and walked past me to look at the rig, then returned to confer with his Captain.

At last he turned back to us.

'Line up your men,' he ordered. Wingstead gestured to the crew and they came to stand with him in a ragged line. The soldiers brought Dufour and Atheridge and dumped them among us. Both looked dazed. I glanced down the line. The two Lat-Am men were there, Burns at his most belligerent and being restrained by a nervous Zimmerman. So were both the Russians, and I hoped that Zimmerman would remember that if they were slow in obeying orders because they couldn't understand them there might be trouble. It would be ironic if they were killed by Moscow-made weapons.

All our own men were there save Mick McGrath, and on him I had begun to pin absurd hopes. None of the medical people were present. There were soldiers in front and behind us, and paradoxically the very fact they were behind us made me feel a little better, because otherwise this would look too much like an execution.

Maksa spoke to his Captain, who barked an order.

'Go into the warehouse.'

'Now wait a goddamn –' began Wingstead.

The Captain thrust his black-visored face alarmingly close. 'I would not argue. Do what the Colonel wishes,' he said. 'He doesn't like arguments.'

I didn't know if this was a warning or a threat. We walked forward between a line of guards and entered the warehouse.

We crowded towards the rear where the cotton was piled. Atheridge collapsed to the floor. Dufour looked dazed still but was on his feet. The doors were closed and a line of Maksa's troops stood just inside them, holding sub-machine-guns.

I had to know about the shotgun. I said to Hammond, keeping my voice low, 'Drift over to the corner behind you, to the left. Get some of the others to do the same. I need a diversion at the door. I want their attention away from that corner for a few seconds.'

Russ Burns said softly, 'I'll do it.'

'Right. Just keep them talking for a few moments.'

He nodded curtly and edged away. I passed Bishop as I moved slowly towards the corner and said to him, 'Brad, keep Sandy out of this if you can.'

He moved in the opposite direction, taking Bing by the arm as he did so. Zimmerman followed Burns and the two Russians went with him as though connected by magnets. We were spread about, and the five soldiers couldn't watch all of us.

Burns went up to the soldiers and started talking. They converged on him threateningly and their voices rose. As all eyes were on them I slipped away into the corner, shielded by the little knot of men around Ben Hammond.

I scrabbled at the cotton searching for the exact spot, and my fingers encountered nothing. The sweat on my forehead was an icy film. The shotgun was gone. I rejoined the others as the warehouse doors opened again.

We were being joined by the whole of the medical staff. They were upset and angry, both Sister Ursula and Dr Kat boiling with rage.

'What's happening out there?' Wingstead asked.

'They made us leave our patients,' Dr Kat said hoarsely. 'They turned guns on us. *Guns*! We are medical people, not soldiers! We must go back.'

The black bars of Sister Ursula's eyebrows were drawn down and she looked furious. 'They are barbarians. They must let us go back, Mister Mannix. There's a baby out there that needs help, and Mister Otterman is dangerously ill.'

'Where's Sister Mary?' someone asked, and Sister Ursula looked more angry still. 'She's ill herself. We *must* make their leader see reason!'

Until the Colonel came there was nothing to do but wait. I considered the two missing factors: McGrath and the shotgun. It was inevitable that I should put them together. When I hid the shotgun, I had thought I wasn't seen but there was no knowing how much McGrath knew. He was used to acting independently, and sometimes dangerously so, and I knew him to be a killer. I hoped that he wasn't going to do anything bull-headed: one wrong move and we could all be dead.

I was still brooding when the warehouse doors opened and Maksa walked in. When I saw the shotgun in his hands I felt as though I'd been kicked in the teeth.

He stared at us then said, 'I want to talk to you. Get into a line.' A jerk of the shotgun barrel reinforced the order. He gave a curt command and the soldiers filed out except for one sergeant and the doors closed behind them. We shuffled into a line to face our captor.

He said, 'I am Colonel Maksa, commander of the fifteenth Infantry Battalion of the Nyalan Peoples' Liberation Army. I am here in pursuit of an unfriendly military force under the command of Captain Sadiq. I have reason to think you are shielding them in an act of aggression against the Nyalan Peoples' Republic and I intend to have this information from you.'

'Colonel, we really don't –' Wingstead began.

'Be silent! I will ask you in due course. I will begin by knowing all your names and your business, starting with you.' He thrust the shotgun in the direction of Ritchie Thorpe, who was at the far end of the line.

'Uh . . . Mister Wingstead?'

Wingstead nodded gently. 'As the Colonel says, Ritch. Just tell him your name.'

'I'm Richard Thorpe. I work for Mister Wingstead there. For Wyvern Transport.'

The gun's muzzle travelled to the next man. 'You?'

'Bert Proctor. I drive a rig for Wyvern. I'm English.'

'Me too. Derek Grafton, Wyvern Transport.'

'Sam Wilson. Driver . . .'

The roll call continued. Some were sullen, one or two clearly terrified, a couple displayed bravado, but no-one refused to answer. The nurses, clustered together, answered in Nyalan but Dr Kat refused to do so, speaking only English and trying to get in a word about his patients. Maksa brushed him aside and went on down the line. Once the flow of voices stopped Maksa said icily, 'Well? Do you refuse to name yourself?'

Zimmerman raised his voice.

'Colonel, they don't understand you. They don't speak English.'

'Who are they?'

'They're Russians: truck drivers. Their names are –' and he supplied the two names which the rest of us could never remember. Maksa's brows converged and he said, 'Russians? I find that most interesting. You speak Russian, then?'

'Yes, a little.'

'Who are you?'

'Harry Zimmerman. I'm a blaster for Lat-Am Oil, and I'm an American. And I don't have anything to do with your war or this captain you're after.'

Maksa looked at him coldly. 'Enough! Next?'

As he looked along the line his sergeant whispered to him. The next man was Russ Burns.

'Russell Burns, Lat-Am Oil, a good Texan, and one who doesn't like being shoved around. What are you going to do about it?'

Burns was looking for trouble once again.

'My sergeant tells me he has already had trouble with you. You insulted my soldiers. Is this true?'

'You're damn right I did! I don't like being pushed around by a bunch of bastards like you.'

He stepped out of the line-up.

'Burns, cut it out!' I said.

Zimmerman added, 'For God's sake, Russ, take it easy.'

The shotgun rose in the Colonel's hand to point straight at the Texan. Burns gave way but was already too late. The Colonel stepped forward and put the muzzle of the shotgun under Burns' chin and tilted his head back.

'You are not very respectful,' Maksa said. 'What is this – has someone tried to kill you already?'

The shotgun rubbed against the bandage round Burns' throat, and he swallowed convulsively. But some mad bravado made him say, 'That's none of your damn business. I cut myself shaving.'

Maksa smiled genially. 'A man with a sense of humour,' he said, and pulled the trigger.

The top of Burns' head blew off. His body splayed out over the floor, pooled with blood. The line scattered with shock. Maksa backed up near the door and his sergeant flanked him with his own gun at the ready. Someone was puking his guts out, and one of the nurses was down on the warehouse floor in a dead faint. The bloody horror of war had caught up with us.

TWENTY

Horror gave way to anger. The men started to voice their outrage. I looked down at Burns' body. Nine one third inch lead slugs, together weighing over an ounce, driven with explosive force from close range had pretty well demolished him. It was the quickest of deaths and quite painless for him; but we felt it, the bowel-loosening pain of fear that sudden death brings.

Maksa's voice rose over the babble.

'Be silent!' he said. He hefted the shotgun and his eyes raked us. 'Who owns this?'

Nobody spoke.

'Who owns this shotgun?' he demanded again.

I was debating what to do when Maksa forced my hand. He stepped forward, scanning us, and then pointed. 'You – come here.' The person he had indicated was Helen Chula. After a moment's hesitation she walked slowly towards him, and he grabbed her by the arm, swung her round to face us and jammed the shotgun against her back. 'I ask for the third time, and there will not be a fourth. Who owns this gun?'

I had never found violence of much use in solving my problems, but it seemed to work for Maksa. He could give McGrath pointers in terrorism. I said, 'It's mine,' and stepped forward.

thrust Helen away. I heard her sobbing but could
ing but the muzzle of the shotgun as it pointed at
my body. It loomed as large as a fifteen inch navy gun.

'So,' said Maksa. 'We have an American civilian, wandering around with a weapon during an armed conflict. A
dangerous thing to do, would you not agree?'

'It's a sporting gun,' I said with a dry mouth.

'Can you produce your licence?'

I swallowed. 'No.'

'And I suppose you will also tell me that you do not work
for your CIA.'

'I don't. I work for a British firm, and no-one else.'

'Backing the corruption of our so-called Government?'

'Not at all.'

'A man can have two masters,' he said thoughtfully. 'You
Americans and the British have always worked in double
harness. You imperialists stick together, don't you? You give
up your colonies and tell the United Nations that now Nyala
is self-governing. But you don't leave my country alone
after that.'

I kept silent.

He went on, 'You say we are independent, but you keep
the money strings tight. You choke us with loans and reap
the profits yourselves; you corrupt our politicians; you
plunder us of raw material and sell us the so-called benefits
of Western civilization in return, to take back the money
you gave us. And now you have been joined by the dogs of
Moscow: the old Czarist imperialists ally themselves with
you to loot our oil and ruin our country.'

He drew a long breath, controlling himself, and then
changed tack.

'Now, about Captain Sadiq. Where is he and what are his
plans?'

I said, 'Colonel Maksa, the Captain pulled his men out
early today and went away. We know no more than that.'

He said, 'I have talked enough to you. You weary me. I can get more from the others.'

I stood frozen. The Colonel slid his hand down the gun barrel, and then a new voice cut in from high up and behind me. It wasn't very loud but it was very firm.

'If you lift that shotgun I'll cut you in half, colonel.'

Maksa glared over my shoulder. I spun round to see a big black-faced man aiming a sub-machine gun at the Colonel: I turned swiftly and took Maksa's gun away from him.

The man on the cotton stack swung the machine gun in a slow arc to point it at the Nyalan sergeant. Without a word the soldier put his gun down and backed away. Hammond picked it up and we held both men under guard. The man with the black face and McGrath's voice swung himself down to the floor. Voices murmured in recognition and relief, and then fell silent again. The atmosphere had changed dramatically, despite Russ Burns' body sprawling at our feet.

I said, 'Maksa, you've seen what this gun can do. One twitch from you and I'll blow your backbone out.'

'If you shoot me you'll bring the soldiers in. They'll kill you all.'

'No they won't,' Hammond said. 'They didn't come in when you shot Russ there.'

McGrath, his face and arms covered with blacking, slung the gun over his shoulder. 'Raise your hands and turn round, Maksa,' he said. Trembling with anger, the Colonel turned as McGrath's hand came out of his pocket holding the cosh. He hit Maksa behind the ear and the Colonel dropped solidly.

McGrath turned to the sergeant. 'Now you, son. Turn round.'

He obeyed unwillingly. Again there was a surge of movement and McGrath said, 'Keep it down, you flaming fools. We'll have the guards in if they hear that going on. Just you keep quiet now.'

Relief made my tone edgy. 'Where the hell have you been, McGrath?'

'Out and about.' He began to strip off the colonel's uniform jacket with its red brassard on one sleeve. 'Give me a hand. Tie him up and dump him back there in the cotton. Same with his sergeant.'

'Goddamnit, we're taking one hell of a risk, McGrath. We might have been able to talk our way out of that jam, but there's no chance now.'

'You weren't going to be given much more time to talk, Mr Mannix,' he said mildly. He was right but I hated to admit it; to be that close to death was hard to accept.

McGrath went on, tugging on a pair of trousers. 'Do you know what they're doing out there? They're piling up petrol drums. They were going to burn down the warehouse.'

'With us in it?' Kemp asked in horror.

Someone said, 'For God's sake, we've got to get out of here.'

'Take it easy,' said McGrath. 'They won't strike a match before the Colonel's out.' He was dressing in the Colonel's uniform. 'Who's for the other outfit? Who fits?'

As we considered this he went on, 'I'm sorry, but I've got a bit more bad news for you.'

'What now?'

'Max Otterman's dead.'

Dr Kat said, 'I should have been with him.'

McGrath said gently, 'He was murdered.'

We stood rigid with shock.

'I saw the soldiers going over the rig after they brought you in here. They were pretty rough on everybody, even their own sick people. Then Max started convulsing and calling out, the way he's been doing, and they . . . Well, they booted him off the rig. I think his neck's broken.'

'Oh my God!' Wingstead whispered.

'I think the fall may have killed him. But one of the troops put a bullet in him as well. I'm sorry to have to tell you.'

The change in everyone's attitude was almost tangible. Neither the war, the bombing in Kodowa, our own capture, nor the death of Russ Burns had had this effect. It had come closer with the news of the intended burning of our prison. But the callous murder of our pilot had done the trick; it had roused them to fighting pitch.

Wingstead said, 'You've got a plan, McGrath, haven't you?'

'Carry on as though the Colonel were still here.' McGrath adjusted his uniform. Sam Wilson was getting into the other. Dr Kat bent over Burns' body.

McGrath said, 'Leave Russ where he is. He's evidence if anyone comes in. They know there was a shooting.' He picked up the sergeant's Uzi. 'Anyone know how to use this?'

'I do,' Wilson and Zimmerman both said. McGrath tossed it to Wilson. 'That's fine. It fits your image. Here, add this.' He tossed Wilson a small pot of blacking. 'It stinks but it'll do.' Wilson started to smear the stuff on his face and hands.

I held on to the shotgun, and Wingstead took the Colonel's pistol. That made four guns plus McGrath's cosh and God knows what else he had in the way of knives or other lethal instruments. It wasn't much to start a war with.

Wingstead said, 'Mick, how did you get in here?'

He pointed upwards. 'Easy. Through the roof. It's corrugated iron but some of it's so old it's soft as butter. But we're not going out that way. There's a door at the back of this shed. I couldn't open it from the outside, it's bolted. And from the inside it's hidden behind the cotton. But we can leave that way.'

Hammond said eagerly, 'Then let's go.'

'Not yet, Ben. We can reduce the odds out there a bit first. Now listen. When I saw what was likely to happen I ducked out; didn't like the idea of waiting to be rounded up.

I went into the bush to look for Sadiq. I damn near got shot by his lads. They're trigger-happy.'

'How far away is he?' Wingstead asked.

'Not far. He's been scouting and these are his conclusions. This Fifteenth Battalion has been in action, probably against the loyalist Seventh Brigade, and came off worst. There are about two hundred men, a quarter of the battalion.'

'It's a hell of a lot more than we can handle,' Zimmerman said.

'Will you wait a minute, now,' McGrath said irritably. 'Maksa has sent most of them across the bridge, leaving about fifty men and a few vehicles on this side. Many of them are wounded. There are only two officers outside. Sadiq's ready to attack. His mortars can drop bombs on them like confetti at a wedding when he gets the signal.'

'Let's hear your plan,' I said.

'It goes like this. We take out the officers first. That way the men have nobody to direct them, and they'll run or surrender.'

'Just how do we do that?' Hammond asked.

'Well, as you see, I borrowed a dab or two of boot polish from the Captain, and here I am like a bloody nigger minstrel in the Colonel's uniform. If I put his cap on I reckon I can get away with it for as long as it takes to call them in here, one by one.'

'It won't work,' said Zimmerman. 'You haven't the voice for it.'

Lang said, 'We've got Doctor Kat though.'

McGrath took a piece of paper from his old jacket. 'Most of the officers are on the other side of the water. The ones here are Captain Mosira, that's the laddie in the dark glasses, and Lieutenant Chawa. We get them in here and deal with them. Then we go out the back way, smuggle the nurses back onto the rig, it's got a light guard but they'll be no problem, and then signal to Sadiq to start his action.'

Wingstead had a tough time of it with Katabisirua. The Doctor was concerned about violating his noncombatant status as a medical man.

'For Christ's sake, Doctor, we're not asking you to kill anyone. Just talk to them,' McGrath said. Eventually Dr Kat agreed to do what we wanted.

I said to McGrath, 'What happens after we knock off the officers?'

McGrath took out a knife and squatted on the floor. 'When Sadiq makes his attack he doesn't want any interference from across the bridge. So our job is to hold the bridge.' He scratched lines in the dirt floor. 'Here's the river and here's the bridge. On it near the other side they've stationed a Saracen armoured troop carrier. We have to stop it coming across and at the same time block the bridge somehow.'

'What's it armed with?'

'A heavy machine gun in a turret, and twin light machine guns on a Scarfe ring.'

Hammond blew out his cheeks. 'How in hell do we stop a thing like that? Bullets will bounce off. It'll be moving as soon as Sadiq attacks.'

'I stop it,' said McGrath. 'With Barry Lang's help.'

Lang stared at him.

'Look, here's the rig. All our tractors bar one have been coupled, ready to take it across the river. The free tractor is here, near the bridge. We take it onto the bridge and ram that bloody Saracen with it.'

Wingstead said sharply, 'You won't have a chance, Mick. The heavy machine gun will shoot hell out of you.'

'Not if we go backwards,' said McGrath simply.

Lang's face lit up.

'Behind that cab are twenty tons of steel plate set in cement. The thing's armoured like a tank. Nothing they've got will penetrate it and it outweighs the Saracen by a long chalk. What we need is covering fire. The cab windows aren't armoured and we'll have to lean out to see our way backwards. The rebels on this side will be busy but there may be some shooting and it'll be up to the rest of you to give us protection.'

Kemp said, 'With what?'

I said, 'We've already got three guns and a pistol and we'll get more from each officer. And there are four or five guards out there with sub-machine-guns that we can pick up too. I think the time for talking is over.'

'I agree,' McGrath said briskly, standing up. 'I want everybody lined up again, except for a couple of you behind the doors.'

'What about me?' I asked.

'When an officer walks through that door he'll expect to see Maksa, you and Mister Wingstead, because you're the boss men. So you'll be right there in line, under the guns.' He gave his knife to Lang and the cosh to Bert Proctor. 'You two take anyone coming through that door but only after the doors are closed. Harry, you take the other machine-gun and go stand up there where I was. If the guards do come in you can fire over our heads, and if that happens everyone ducks fast. Doctor Kat, you're in line too. Think your voice can carry outside?'

The doctor nodded reluctantly.

'I'll take the shotgun, Mister Mannix, if you don't mind,' McGrath said. I handed it over to him with some hesitation, but he was right, he had to look the part. It left me feeling vulnerable again.

We stood like actors waiting for a curtain to rise. Facing me was McGrath looking surprisingly like Maksa even from where I stood. Just as I had taken over from Kemp and Wingstead in one crisis, so now McGrath had as easily taken over from me. He was a natural leader and afterwards he would be damned hard to control. If there was an afterwards.

TWENTY-ONE

McGrath went and opened one of the doors. He put his arm through the narrow opening, holding the shotgun at the ready. Dr Kat stood immediately behind him out of sight, so that the voice should seem to come from the bogus colonel. McGrath's head was averted as though he were keeping an eye on his prisoners, but light fell on his shoulder tabs and brassarded arm. When Dr Kat spoke it didn't sound much like Maksa but we could only hope that the soldiers would accept it. McGrath closed the door and breathed a sigh of relief.

'Right,' he said. 'Two officers are coming in. You ready, you three?'

The attack team nodded silently, and at the rear of the warehouse Zimmerman waved his machine-gun and dropped out of sight behind the topmost stack of cotton. McGrath strode across to Burns' body and stood beside it with his back to the doors. His legs were apart and he held the shotgun so that it pointed down towards the shattered skull. It was a nice piece of stage setting; anyone entering would see his back and then their eyes would be drawn to Burns, a particularly nasty sight.

McGrath judged it was too quiet.

'Say something, Mister Mannix,' he said. 'Carry on your conversation with the Colonel.'

'I don't want your bloody oil,' I improvised. 'I'm not in the oil business. I work for a firm of electrical engineers.' Behind McGrath Proctor had his ear to the door and the cosh raised. I carried on, 'We're certainly not responsible for how you run your country . . .'

The door opened and two officers walked in, Mosira still wearing his dark glasses and a much younger officer following him. I went on speaking. 'Colonel Maksa, I demand that you allow our medical people to see their . . .'

Proctor hit the lieutenant hard with the cosh and he went straight down. Captain Mosira was putting up a struggle, groping for his pistol. Lang had an arm round the Captain's neck but his knife waved wildly in the air. Mosira couldn't shout because of the stranglehold but it was not until McGrath turned and drove the butt of the shotgun against his head that he collapsed.

Outside all was quiet, and in the warehouse nobody spoke either. McGrath turned to Barry Lang and held out his hand for the knife. 'I said, don't be squeamish,' he said coldly.

Lang gave him the knife. 'I'm sorry, Mick, I just –'

'Who can use this?'

'I can,' said Hammond.

McGrath instantly tossed him the knife. 'Right, lads, let's pick up our loot and get this lot out of the way.'

Both officers had worn pistols and the lieutenant had a grenade at his belt. In the distribution I got one of the pistols. We looked to McGrath for guidance.

'Let's get those guards, lads. There are only six or seven of them. It'll be easy.'

It was entirely McGrath who made it work, his drive and coolness that kept the exercise moving. But paradoxically Maksa's own personality also helped us. He was clearly a martinet and no enlisted man was going to question his orders. The guards entered on demand and were easy to deal with.

We looked round the warehouse. The soldiers were laid in a row behind the cotton bales, together with the body of Russ Burns. The door in the rear was opened with ease and we were ready to leave.

McGrath said, 'As soon as possible we get that signal off. You know the drill, Mister Mannix?'

I nodded. The back of the warehouse faced away from our camp so we'd have to go around it and might run into enemy soldiers at any moment. One group was to get the medical team and Dan Atheridge to the rig and then rejoin the rest of us, who'd be in cover as close to the bridge as we could get. We'd leapfrog one another to get in place, ready to protect McGrath and his tractor team-mate. There had been some doubt as to who that would be.

McGrath looked at Barry Lang speculatively. He had jibbed at knifing Mosira and this made McGrath uncertain of his mettle. But they usually teamed up, and it was safer to work with a man one knew, so McGrath said to him, 'Right then, Barry, you're with me in the cab. Just stick close, you hear me?'

'What's the signal for Sadiq to attack? The Very pistol?' I asked.

'Yes, a red flare the way you planned.'

'The Very pistol's still in a suitcase by the rig, unless they found it.'

He grinned, swarmed up on top of the cotton and came down again with the Very pistol in his hand. 'Full of surprises, aren't I?' he said.

I didn't ask him how he knew where it was. He'd obviously been hiding nearby when I hid the thing. He might have seen me go off with the shotgun too, and I wondered again how Maksa had come by it.

'You take it,' McGrath said, handing me the signal pistol. 'You'll be in charge of this exercise, Mister Mannix.'

I said, 'Just what are you going to do?'

He grinned. 'I'm going to march Barry out of here at gunpoint. I still look like the Colonel, and I've got Sam as my sergeant. We're going to take Lang down to the bridge and when we're near enough we'll make a break for the tractor. Sam will get into cover and wait for you to come up, if you're not there already.'

It was audacious but it could work. Wingstead said, 'You'll have every eye on you.'

'Well, it's a chance, I'll grant you. But it should get us to the cab. You get off the signal the instant we make our break, so that Sadiq can keep those laddies too busy to think for a bit.'

As quietly as possible we barricaded the front doors with cotton bales, and were ready to go. I opened the rear door a crack and looked out. There was some moonlight, which would help McGrath in the tractor later on, and the night was fairly quiet. We left cautiously.

As we rounded the warehouse we could see the fires from the rebels' camp, and brighter lights around our rig. I could see soldiers in the light near the rig but there weren't many of them. There was plenty of cover all the way to the bridge, just as we had visualized.

'OK, Mick, start walking,' I whispered.

We moved away from the warehouse according to plan. McGrath and his party stepped out, Lang first with a submachine-gun jammed into his spine. Next was Wilson, his sergeant's cap pulled well down over his face. McGrath followed with the shotgun. It looked pretty good to me. I paced myself so that I was not too far ahead of McGrath, and the rest passed me to fan out ahead.

The marchers were almost opposite the rig when a soldier called out. I heard an indistinguishable answer from McGrath and a sharp retort, and then the soldier raised his gun. He didn't fire but was clearly puzzled.

Then there came the rip fire of an Uzi from beyond the rig. Someone had been spotted. The soldier turned uncertainly and McGrath cut him down with the shotgun. Then he and Lang bolted for their tractor. Wilson disappeared into the roadside cover. The shotgun blasted again and then gunfire crackled all around us, lighting up the night with flashes. I pointed the Very pistol skywards and the cartridge blossomed as I ran for cover, Bert Proctor at my side.

Soldiers tumbled out everywhere and guns were popping off all over the place. Then there was an ear-splitting roar as engines churned and a confusion of lights as headlamps came on. The night was split by the explosions of mortar bombs landing in the rebels' camp.

We left the cover of the bushes and charged towards our convoy. The nearest vehicle was Kemp's Land Rover and we flung ourselves down beside it. An engine rumbled as a vehicle came towards us and when I saw what it was I groaned aloud. It was a Saracen. Maksa's men must have already got it off the bridge. It moved slowly and the gun turret swung uncertainly from side to side, seeking a target.

'It's coming this way!' Proctor gasped.

Behind us the deeper voice of our tractor roared as McGrath fired its engine. The Saracen was bearing down on it. We had to do something to stop its progress. The Uzi wouldn't be much good against armour but perhaps a Very cartridge slamming against the turret would at least startle and confuse the driver. As the Saracen passed us, already opening fire on the tractor, I took aim and let fly. The missile grazed the spinning turret and hit the armoured casing behind it, igniting as it landed. I must have done something right; there was a flash and a vast explosion which threw us sideways and rocked the Land Rover. When we staggered up the Saracen was on fire and inside someone was screaming.

I groped for my pistol but couldn't find it, and watched the burning Saracen run off the road into the bushes as our tractor passed it. McGrath leaned out and yelled at me.

'Lang's bought it. Get him out of here!'

I ran to the passenger side of the cab. The Saracen had set bushes burning and in the flaring light I saw blood on Lang's chest as I hauled him out of his seat. Proctor took him from me as we ran alongside the tractor.

McGrath yelled at me, 'Stay with me. Get in!' I clung onto the swinging cab door, hooked a foot over the seat and threw myself inside.

'Welcome aboard,' McGrath grunted. 'Watch our rear. Say if anything gets in our way.' He looked rearwards out of his own window. I followed suit.

Driving backwards can be tricky on a quiet Sunday morning in the suburbs, In these conditions it was terrifying. The tractor swayed from side to side, weaving down the road and onto the bridge. In the rear mirror I could see the second Saracen at the far end. There were heavy thumps on the tractor casing; we were being fired on by the Saracen as it retreated ahead of us. The driver had decided that he'd have more room to manoeuvre and fight off the bridge. We wanted to ram him before he could leave. We made it by a hair.

The Saracen's driver misjudged and reversed into the parapet; his correction cost him the race. The tractor bucked and slammed with an almighty wrench into the front of the Saracen, and there was a shower of sparks in the air. Our engine nearly stalled but McGrath poured on power and ground the tractor into the Saracen.

'Go, you bastard, go!' McGrath's face was savage with joy as he wrestled with wheel and accelerator.

There wasn't much doubt that we'd won. The armoured car was a solid lump of metal but it didn't weigh much over ten tons to the tractor's forty. The impact must have knocked the Saracen's crew out because the shooting stopped at once. The turret was buckled and useless.

McGrath kept up a steady pressure and the tractor moved remorselessly backwards, pushing the armoured car.

He judged his angle carefully and there was a grinding crunch as the Saracen was forced against the coping wall of the bridge. But we didn't want the bridge itself damaged and McGrath stopped short of sending it into the river, which would have shattered the wall.

The Saracen's engine was ground into scrap and wasn't going anywhere under its own power. The bridge was effectively blocked to the enemy, and Sadiq was free to get on with the job.

McGrath put the tractor gently into forward gear. There was no opposition as we travelled back across the bridge and stopped to form a secondary blockade. We tumbled out of the cab to an enthusiastic welcome.

'Where's Barry?' I asked.

'We've got him back to the rig. He's with the medics,' Proctor said.

McGrath stirred and stretched hugely. I said, 'That was damn good driving, Mick.'

'You didn't do too badly yourself. What the hell did you use on that first Saracen – a flame-thrower?'

'I fired the Very gun at it. It shouldn't have worked but it did.'

Looking around, we could see figures heading off towards the river downstream from the bridge. There was some scattered shooting. The remains of Maksa's force were intent only on escaping back to their own side. More mortars fired and the shooting stopped.

We tensed up at this renewal of hostilities but it was happening a long way off from us, to our relief.

Geoff Wingstead was beside me. 'I've had it. This is Sadiq's war. Let him fight it from now on. I'm all for going back to being a truck driver.'

'Me too – only I'll be happy just to ride that desk of mine.'

McGrath said, 'I'll be happier when we've got a detachment down here; they still might try to rush that bridge and Sadiq isn't nearby. We might still be wanted.'

'I hope to God not. We've had one casualty and we don't want any more.'

Wingstead said, 'I'm afraid we've had more than one.'

I said, 'Who else, then?'

He pointed to a group of men at the foot of the water tanker, consisting of Harry Zimmerman, a Russian, and Brad Bishop.

'One of the Russians bought it,' Wingstead told me. Together we walked over to Zimmerman, who was looking sadly at the huddled body. 'I'm sorry about this, my friend,' I said to his fellow countryman, standing impassively by, then to Zimmerman, 'Who was he – Brezhnev or Kosygin?' I never could tell them apart.

Zimmerman sighed. 'His name was Andrei Djavakhishkili and he came from Tbilisi in Georgia. He was a nice guy when you got to know him.'

The remaining two hours to dawn were quiet. Sadiq had joined us, and we sat in the cover of our vehicles, waiting for the morning light. We didn't expect the enemy to try anything; their only passage was blocked off and the decisiveness of Sadiq's action, and our own, must have rocked their morale.

With the rising of the sun we could see no sign of movement from across the river. The scene was one of destruction; burnt out vegetation still smouldered, the camp site littered with debris, and the wreckage of the first Saracen huddled in a ditch. We found the bodies of three men near it, one shot and two who had died of burns. There were more bodies up the hill at the soldiers' camp but Sadiq's men were taking care of them and we didn't want to see the site of that battle.

Our tractor blocked the nearside of the bridge and at the far end the second Saracen lay canted over diagonally across the road and forced up hard against the coping. There was no sign of men or vehicles beyond.

I said to Sadiq, 'What now, Captain?'

He studied the opposite bank carefully through binoculars, holding them one-handed as his left arm was in a sling. He was no longer the immaculate officer whose pants were creased to a knife edge and whose shoes gleamed. He'd lost his boot polish to McGrath. His uniform was scorched and rumpled.

There were lines of strain about his eyes and mouth. Presently he said, 'We watch and wait for one, two hours maybe. If everything is still quiet I will send scouts across the river.'

'Risky.'

'Would you expect anything else in war, Mister Mannix?'

'You did well last night, Captain. It was a fine operation.'

He nodded gravely. 'Yes, we did well. But you all did well, especially Mister McGrath. He is very efficient. Without him it might not have come about.'

I knew that and didn't want to dwell on it. I would have liked to admire McGrath whole-heartedly but found it impossible. I was pleased to hear that Sadiq had sustained no losses among his men, and only a couple were wounded.

Our losses were worse.

The Russian was dead. Lang was in a bad way and lay on Dr Kat's operating table. Proctor had a bullet graze on the leg and Kemp on the shoulder, and others had an assortment of bruises and abrasions. But a roll call proved one man missing. After a search we found the body of Ron Jones, shot through the head and stomach by machine-gun bullets.

TWENTY-TWO

It was ten o'clock before Sadiq took his chance on the bridge. First he wanted the tractor shifted so that if necessary he could get troops across fast, and we were wary of sending anyone out of cover to do that until we felt fairly sure, it was safe. Sadiq would not send scouts across, as being too dangerous. He was going to cross first himself in the Scorpion tank, which was a brave thing to do because even a lone infantryman might have a tank-killing weapon. He was taking three men with him, a driver, a gunner and a radio operator, and he left instructions that nobody was to move until he came back or sent a coded all clear signal.

Before that we'd cleaned up the camp, repairing what was possible and listing what needed repair when we could spare the time. Luckily Maksa's men had not destroyed much of importance, though there were two car windows shattered and sundry minor damage done here and there. Bishop and Bing, with help from the others, got a food supply moving, and on the rig the medical people were kept very busy.

Max Otterman's body had been found at the foot of the rig with a bullet in his back and two ribs broken, presumably by the fall though the damage could have been done by a boot. It was an appalling death. We organized a digging party off the road and held a mass funeral service.

Otterman, Burns, Ron Jones and Andrei Djavakhishkili, a Rhodesian, an American, a Welshman and a Russian, shared one grave, though we gave them each separate headboards. In another grave were two of Sadiq's men and with them four rebels, all with the common bond of being Nyalans.

Both the ailing infant and the hospital's other serious patient, Sister Mary, had survived the night. But the two doctors and the nursing staff were under great strain and an urgent discussion on ways and means was long overdue.

Astonishingly, during the early hours of the morning we had visitors.

Sandy Bing, carrying a bucket of hot water towards the rig, stopped and said, 'I'll be damned, Mister Wingstead! Just look at them.'

In the distance, quietly and almost shyly, little clumps of Nyalans were reappearing, still mostly women and children, to stand in respectful yet wary homage to their travelling talisman. Some of them spoke to the soldiers, and Dr Kat and two of the Nyalan nurses went down among them, to return with news that the vast majority had melted away just far enough to be within earshot of the fight, and close enough to come back if they felt all was safe again. It was truly extraordinary.

'I think it may mean that the other soldiers have all gone,' Dr Kat told us. 'They speak of them as evil, and they would not come back if they were still close by.'

'But they'd be across the river, Doctor Kat. How could these people know?'

'I think you call it the bush telegraph,' the surgeon said with his first smile for a long time. 'It really does work quite well. You will see, the Captain will return to give us an all clear. In the meantime, they have brought me a woman who broke her leg last night. I must go back and see to her.'

I went to have a look at the Saracen that had caught fire.
I was curious to see why it had happened; an armoured car
isn't a paper bag to be burned up by a Very flare.

It was simple enough when we reconstructed what had
occurred. At the time that the shooting started someone
must have been filling the gas tank and in the hurry to get
things moving the fuel tank cap hadn't been screwed back
on properly. When the Very ignited, a spark must have gone
straight into the tank, blowing up the vehicle in fine style.
We found the cap still on its hinge, military fashion, but
hanging loose.

I had another job to do that I didn't relish, and that was
to speak to McGrath alone. I started by telling him about the
Saracen and he grinned approval.

'Dead lucky. We have to have some of it,' he commented.

I said, 'McGrath, there's something bothering me.'

'Why then, let's have it,' he said calmly.

'In the warehouse you told us that Maksa was getting
ready to burn it down with us inside. But I found no petrol
drums anywhere near the warehouse, and there's no fuel of
theirs this side of the river. Our tanker is still locked and
nobody took the keys.'

'Well, maybe they were going to do it another way,' he
said easily.

'Don't mess with me, McGrath. Did you actually hear
them say anything like that?'

'Oh for Christ's sake,' he said, driven out of his normal
calm, 'I had to say *something* to get you lot moving! You
were just going to stand there and take it. Or try talking
your way out, I suppose.'

'You were safe enough, free and armed. Why the hell did
you bother to come back for us?'

'If I thought I could have got away through this benighted
country on my own, Mannix, I'd have done so. I need you,

that's why.' He crowned this casually selfish statement with one more shocking. 'I must say Otterman's death came in handy. That really did the trick.'

I felt disgusted, and then had another appalling idea.

'McGrath, did you kill Ron Jones?'

He looked amused rather than alarmed. 'Why should I do that?'

'You know why. And you had time to do it. In God's name, how can I believe you even if you say you didn't?'

'Well now, you can't, Mannix, so if I were you I'd stop worrying about it. I didn't as a matter of fact, though he's no great loss for all that. In fact he was more dangerous to you than I've ever been.'

I couldn't help rising to the bait. 'What do you mean?'

'Well, he was a bit of a sniveller, wasn't he? You know that, the way he came babbling things to you that he shouldn't. He saw you take the shotgun into the warehouse, Mannix, and it was he who told the Colonel about it. I heard him myself.'

Quite suddenly I knew that this was the truth. I recalled Jones's fear in the warehouse, the way he hung back from Maksa as he'd always hung back from McGrath, perhaps fearing lest he be unmasked before us all for Maksa's pleasure. Any regret I had for his death ebbed away, and despite myself I felt a nagging touch of understanding of McGrath and his ruthlessness. He'd manoeuvred us into doing the one thing he knew best; fighting and killing. He'd done it all for the most selfish of reasons, and without compunction. And yet he was brave, efficient and vital to our cause; and perhaps justified as well.

I walked away from him in silence. I would never know if he had killed Ron Jones, but the worst of it, and the thing that filled me with contempt for myself as well as for him, was that I didn't care. I prayed that I wouldn't become any more like him.

McGrath was a maverick, intelligent, sound in military thinking and utterly without fear. I felt that he might be a useful man to have about in a war, but perhaps on the first day of peace he ought to be shot without mercy, and that was one hell of an assessment.

Sadiq had decided that it was time to go.

'Mister Mannix, if I do not return I have told my sergeant to take command of the soldiers,' he said. 'And they are to stay with you unless given alternative orders in person by a superior.'

'Thank you. I wish you good luck.'

He saluted and climbed up into the Scorpion, dropping down through the command hatch and dogging it shut. He was taking no chances. The tank trundled slowly across the bridge. Sadiq had reckoned he could pass the wrecked Saracen but might have to nudge it aside and he proved right. Once past it he picked up speed and the driver did not bother to avoid the scattered bodies. I remembered being told back in Korea that if one wanted to sham dead on a battlefield better not to do it with tanks around.

Not a shot was fired as the tank left the bridge. It began to climb the hill beyond, then swerved and entered the bush and was lost to view. We settled down to wait in the hopeful expectation of hearing nothing. It was a long hour before the Scorpion rumbled back up the hill towards us. Sadiq got out and said, 'There is nothing. They have pulled out and gone.'

There was a ragged cheer from soldiers and civilians alike.

'Which way, do you think?' Wingstead asked.

'Their vehicles must have gone on up the road.' This wasn't good news because it was to be our route too. He went on, 'We found two of them damaged and off the road, and there are many uniform jackets lying there.

I think the Fifteenth Battalion has disbanded. They were nearly finished anyway, and the fight with us has destroyed them.

'Now that I am certain the bridge is clear I will send scouts further ahead. I will place men to form a holding force while we decide what must be done next.'

And so the next item on the agenda was a council of war.

Sadiq's active force was down to twenty-two. There were sixteen of us and a medical staff of nine including three semitrained nurses. On the rig were fifteen Nyalans, including the mother and her sick baby. So we totalled some seventy odd people, many of whom could not take care of themselves. We couldn't stay where we were nor could we turn back, which left us with an obvious conclusion. We had to carry on towards Lake Pirie and possible freedom in Manzu if we couldn't travel on to Port Luard.

Food and medical supplies were in shorter supply than ever, and our stock of petrol was dwindling fast. The only thing we had in plenty was water. The soldiers had run short of ammunition and had no mortar bombs left. We were ragged, weary and uncomfortable. But morale was high.

We reckoned that we could make Fort Pirie in three days or less, and it would be downhill all the way, with villages scattered along the route. We debated yet again leaving the rig but there were still too many sick people to accommodate in the other vehicles, and by now the contraption was beginning to take on a talisman-like quality to us as well as to the Nyalans. We'd got it this far: surely we could get it the rest of the way.

Kemp and Hammond went to inspect the bridge. Though well constructed it had taken a battering and they were concerned for its integrity. They decided that it was sound enough to get the rig across but with nobody on board except for the drivers. That meant that the invalids must be carried across, and Dr Kat set Sister Ursula to organize this with her usual barnstorming efficiency. We had little rest for the remainder of that day. At last we settled down for a final night in the Makara camp, a guard of soldiers on watch, ready to move out at first light.

Kemp and Hammond drove the rig, McGrath had charge of the towing tractor, and Thorpe joined Bob Pitman in running the airlift truck to give the rig its necessary boost. There was a large audience as Nyalans emerged to stare as the rig inched its way across; the Saracen had been towed clear and someone had had the mangled bodies removed. After an hour of tension it was across, and the job of transferring the sick on improvised stretchers began.

It was mid-morning before we really got going. We had quite a selection of vehicles to choose from, our inheritance from the Fifteenth Battalion. In spite of possible fuel problems Sadiq insisted on taking the remaining Saracen, but we ditched some of the trucks. We left the Russian pipe truck but took Dufour's vehicle with us, at the Frenchman's insistence. Brad Bishop said that he had so little cooking to do that the chuck wagon might as well be ditched too, but he didn't mean it.

Kemp, who had been a passenger on the rig because of his shoulder wound, had joined Wingstead and me in the Land Rover. Atheridge drove with Dufour. Their common ordeal at the hands of Maksa's men had forged a bond between them, just as one now existed between Harry Zimmerman and the Russian, Vashily Kirilenko; with his partner's death the nicknames had disappeared.

Wingstead said, 'Ben Hammond can move the convoy out. Let's drive on. We have to talk about McGrath.'

'I think he's psychopathic,' Wingstead went on. 'He's been with you more than with anyone else lately, Neil. What do you think?'

Kemp intervened, 'He's an unscrupulous bastard, and it was me who hired him. If you think I've made a mistake for God's sake say so.'

'Don't take this personally,' Wingstead said. 'If you want my candid opinion, he's the best bloody truck man you've ever hired. He's a damned marvel with that tractor.'

'Amen to that,' I said.

Kemp was still on the defensive. 'Well, I knew that. I couldn't afford to turn him down, Geoff. I knew we'd need the top men for this job. But his papers weren't in order. I advertised for heavy haulage drivers and he applied. He could do the job and had the necessary certificates, but I found discrepancies. I think he's travelling on a false passport.'

Kemp had come a long way on his own.

I told them what I knew, both fact and speculation. At the end there was silence before either spoke.

Then Kemp said, 'He *killed* Sisley? But why should he?'

'He has only one answer to every problem – violence. I think he's a hard line gunman on the run from Ireland. He's dangerous. To look at he's a big amiable Mick straight from the bog. He works at that image.'

Wingstead asked, 'Do you think he could have killed Burke too?'

'Not the way Jones told it.'

'And you're not sure about Ron Jones' death.'

'No, that's only a gut feeling. But four men saw McGrath gun Sisley down. Burke ran off and is very likely dead by now. Jones is dead. Lang is gravely wounded, though thank God I know that one isn't at McGrath's door. That leaves Bob Pitman and if I were he I'd be walking carefully right now. Whatever we know or suspect about McGrath I suggest we keep it buttoned up, or we could find ourselves in deep trouble.'

We turned our attention to the future.

'There's a biggish town, Batanda, not far across the Manzu border,' Wingstead said. 'I haven't found anyone who's been there, but the country itself is known to be relatively stable. There must be a road from Batanda to the ferry on Lake Pirie, because a lot of trade goes on between the two countries at that point. If we can take the ferry to Manzu and drive to Batanda we should be safe.'

'What's Fort Pirie like?' Kemp asked.

'Another Makara, not much there at all. And there may have been military activity there, so God knows what we'll find.'

Kemp asked, 'What are Sadiq's plans?'

'He'll stay with us as far as Fort Pirie, and help us cross the ferry if the road to Lasulu isn't clear. He won't cross himself, of course. He'll keep his men inside his own border. But I think he'll welcome our departure.'

'Not half as much as I will,' Kemp said fervently.

The bush country was left behind and the rainforest began to close in, green and oppressive. The exuberant plant life had eroded the road surface, roots bursting through the tarmac. The trees that bordered the road were very tall, their boughs arched so that it was like driving through a tunnel. There was more bird life but the game, which had been sparse before, was now nonexistent.

In the days before Maro Ofanwe improved matters this road had been not much more than a track, only one car wide for miles at a stretch. Traffic was one way on Mondays, Wednesdays and Fridays, and the other way on Tuesdays, Thursdays and Saturdays. Sundays you stayed home or took your chances and prayed to God. A lot of other roads in Nyala were still like that.

Occasionally there was a hard won clearing, usually with a scattering of grass huts clustered about a warehouse. These were the collection points for the cotton, coffee and cacao beans from the plantations hewed out of the forest. There were people in all these villages but little in the way of food or goods, and hardly anyone spoke English. We asked for news but it was scanty and the people ill-informed.

One or two villages were larger and we were able to drain storage tanks and pumps of available petrol. It was a good sign that there was some, as it meant that there'd been little traffic that way. Somehow enough food was found to keep us going, though it was pretty unpalatable. Behind and around us, our escort of Nyalans swelled and diminished as people joined in for a few miles, dropped out and were replaced by others. The train was growing, though; Sadiq told us there were several hundred people now, coming as remorselessly as a horde of locusts, and with consequences for the countryside nearly as disastrous. There was nothing we could do about it.

Two days passed without incident. On the rig, Lang's condition worsened and one of the soldiers died of his wounds. Sister Ursula nursed with devotion, coming among us to do spot checks on our continuing health and bully us into keeping clean, inside as well as out. If she could she'd have dispensed compulsory laxatives all round.

Margretta Marriot did the rounds too, changing bandages and keeping a watch for infection. There was little for her to do on the rig now except basic nursing, and sometimes she rode with one or other of us. A dour woman at best, I thought, and now she had retreated into a pit of misery that only work could alleviate. Sister Ursula, for all her hectoring, was more of a tonic.

On the morning of the third day Sadiq's scouts returned with news that they'd reached the Katali river and seen Lake Pirie shining in the sun. From where we were camped it was only a couple of hours' drive in a car, and spirits lifted; whatever was going to happen there, we'd reached another of our goals with the convoy still intact.

I'd travelled for most of the previous day in the cab of the water tanker with Sam Wilson (we each gave one another a turn in the comparative comfort of the Land Rover) and now I was with Thorpe in the travelling workshop when a messenger came asking me to join Captain Sadiq.

'I am going ahead, Mister Mannix,' he told me. 'I wish to see for myself what the situation is. There is a village ahead with petrol pumps. Would you and Mister Kemp drive there with us to look at it, please?'

I said, 'Harry Zimmerman told me there was a fuel depot hereabouts, one of his own company's places. We'll take him with us.'

Zimmerman, Kemp and I pushed on behind the soldiers, glad of the release. Soon enough we saw a welcome bottle-green expanse spreading out between the trees, and the road ran down through them to emerge on the shore of a large body of water, a sight quite astonishing after the endless days of bush and forest, and incredibly refreshing to the eye. It stretched away, placid in the blazing sun.

For a while we just sat and stared at it. Then we drove along the lakeside road for another mile or two.

Eventually we arrived at what might have passed for civilization. The place consisted of a roadside filling station with a big, faded Lat-Am fascia board; it was obviously a gas and oil distribution centre. Behind it was an extensive compound fenced in by cyclone netting, which contained stacks of drums. I supposed the gas and oil would be hauled along the road by tankers, transferred to ground tanks here and then rebottled in the drums for distribution to planters and farmers.

If anyone spoke English we were likely to find him here, though I did curse my lack of foresight in not bringing an interpreter with us. It proved not to be necessary.

At first there was nobody to be seen and few sounds; a water pump chugging somewhere, scrawny chickens pecking about, the monotonous tink of some wild bird. I eyed the chickens speculatively, then blew a blast on the horn which scattered them, though not very far. They were used to traffic. A hornbill rose lazily from a tree and settled in another, cocked its head and looked down with beady eyes, as unconcerned as the chickens. At the sixth blast the door of the cabin behind the pumps opened, and a brown face peered warily at us through the crack.

We'd had this sort of nervous reaction before and could hardly blame the locals for being cautious, but at least our non-military car and clothing should prove reassuring. I called out cheerfully, 'Good morning. Are you open for business?'

The door opened wider and a Nyalan stepped out into the sun. He wore a tired overall on which the logo of Lat-Am was printed, a travesty of the livery which they inflicted on their gas station attendants in more affluent places.

'I am not open,' he said. 'I got no custom.'

I got out of the car into the scorching morning air. 'You have now,' I told him. Through the open door I saw a familiar red pattern painted on an ice box. 'You got cold Coca-Cola in there?'

'How many?' he asked cautiously.

'I could drink two. Two each – six of them. I'll pay.' I pulled out a handful of coins, wondering as I did so how he managed to keep them cold. He thought about it, then went in and returned with the Cokes, blissfully chilling to the touch in the narrow-waisted bottles that were still used in this part of the world. I sank half of my first in one swallow. 'Quiet around here, is it?'

He shrugged. 'There is trouble. Trouble come and the people they stop coming.'

'Trouble meaning the war?'

He shook his head. 'I don't know about no war. But there are many soldiers.'

Kemp asked, 'Soldiers where – here?' It certainly didn't look like it. Our untapped mine of information doled out another nugget. 'Not here. In Fort Pirie they are come.'

I swallowed air this time. Soldiers in Fort Pirie could be bad news if they were rebels, and I wondered how Sadiq was getting on.

'Has there been any fighting here at all?' Kemp asked.

A headshake. 'Not here.'

'Where then?'

This time we got the shrug again. 'Somewhere else. I do not know.'

This was like drawing teeth the hard way. I downed some more Coke in silence and tried to keep my impatience under control. Then, surprisingly, the attendant carried on unasked. 'Two tanks come two days ago from Fort Pirie. Then they go back again. They not buy nothing.'

'Did they threaten you? I mean, were they bad people?'

'I think not so bad. Gov'ment people.'

They might or might not be, but it sounded a little better. At least they weren't hellbent on destruction like the last lot we'd met up with.

The attendant suddenly went into his cabin and returned with another opened Coke, which he began to drink himself. I recognized a social gesture; he must have decided that we were acceptable, and was letting his guard down a little by drinking with us. I wondered with amusement how much of his stock vanished in this way, and how he fiddled his books to account for it. I didn't yet know him very well.

'Soldiers come by now, one half-hour ago. Not many. They go that way. Also they go that way this morning, then come back. They not stop here.'

He indicated the direction of the river and I realized that he was talking about Sadiq, but we weren't in a hurry to enlighten him about our association with any military force. We exchanged a few more generalities and then, noticing the wires leading down to the cabin from a pole across the road, I said, 'Do you mind if we use your telephone?'

'No use. It dead.'

That would have been too easy. 'It's the trouble that caused it, I suppose. What about your radio?'

'It play dance music, long time only music. Sometimes nothing at all.' He decided that it was his turn to ask questions. 'You people. Where you from?'

'We've come from Kodowa.'

'A man said that Kodowa is not there no more. Is bombed, burnt. Is that true?'

'Yes, it's true. But Makara is all right. Was Fort Pirie bombed?'

Now we were trading information. 'No bombs there. No fighting, just many soldiers, the man he say. Where you go?'

'We are going to Fort Pirie, if it's safe there. We have more people waiting back there for us, men and women. We are not soldiers.'

'White women? Very bad for them here. They should stay in city, here is dangerous.' He seemed genuinely anxious.

'Believe me, my friend, they'd like nothing better. We are going to go back and get them, tell them it's safe here. When we come back we would like to buy gas, OK?'

'I not sell gas.'

'Sorry, I mean petrol. Petrol and other things if you have them to sell. Meantime, how many Cokes have you got in that ice box in there?'

'Many. Maybe twenty, twenty-four.'

'I'll buy the lot. Find a box and if you've got any more, put them in the cold right away. We'll buy them when we come back.'

He seemed bemused by this but was quite ready to deal with me, especially as I produced the cash at once. Kemp said, 'Do you have many people living here? Could we get food for our people, perhaps?'

The attendant thought about this. He was careful with his answers. 'Not so many people. Many of them go away when trouble comes, but I think maybe you can get food.'

Kemp had noticed the chickens, and caught a glimpse of a small field of corn out behind the cabin. Even his mind, running mainly to thoughts of fuel, road conditions and other such technicalities, could spare a moment to dwell on the emptiness of our stomachs. The station hand was back with us now with some twenty icy bottles in a cardboard box, for which he gravely accepted and counted my money and rung it into his little till. Zimmerman, who'd said nothing, watched with interest as he filled our tank with gas and rung up that sale as well. After we drove off he said, 'He runs a pretty tight ship. That's good to see. We're both on the same payroll, him and me. We've got to give him a square deal when we bring the convoy in.'

Zimmerman was a Lat-Am man and he regarded the station in a rather proprietorial manner.

'Don't worry, Harry,' I said to him, feeling unwarranted optimism rising inside me. 'We won't rip him off, I promise you.' I patted the box of Cokes. 'This is going to make them sit up, isn't it? Something tells me that it's going to be easy all the way from now on.'

It wasn't quite like that.

TWENTY-THREE

There was some restrained rejoicing when we got back to camp with the news and the Cokes, which hadn't yet lost all their chill. Geoff Wingstead decided that unless we heard anything to the contrary from Sadiq within an hour, he'd move the rig on as far as the filling station, thus saving some valuable time. I suggested that he leave Kemp in charge of this phase of the operation and come on ahead again with me. I'd had a couple of ideas that I wanted to check out.

He agreed and we left taking Zimmerman with us and adding Ben Hammond to the Land Rover complement. Proctor was quite able to take Hammond's place for this easy run. This time I bypassed the gas station and we carried on for a little way, with the forest, which was still quite dense at the station, now thinning away until there was only a narrow screen between the road and the gleam of sunlight on water. When we had a clear view I pulled off and stopped. At this point Lake .Pirie was about five miles wide, broadening out to our right. We were told that where the ferry crossed it was a couple of miles across, with the far bank visible, but I wasn't sure how far downwater that would be from where the road came out; local maps were not entirely accurate, as we had often discovered.

Wingstead said, 'It doesn't look like a river.'

It wouldn't, to an Englishman to whom the Thames was the Father of Waters, but I recalled the Mississippi and smiled. 'It's all part of the Katali,' I said. 'It would have been better if they hadn't put the word Lake into it at all. Think of it as the Pirie Stretch and you'll have a better mental picture.' It was a long stretch, being in fact about thirty miles from where it broadened out to where it abruptly narrowed again, a pond by African standards but still a sizeable body of water.

'It's a pity it isn't navigable, like most of the European rivers,' Kemp said, his mind as ever on transport of one sort or another.

'It's the same with most African rivers,' I said. 'What with waterfalls, rapids, shoals, rocks and crocodiles they just aren't very cooperative.' Zimmerman laughed aloud. We sat for a while and then heard the rumble of traffic and a moment later a Saracen came into view, moving towards us from the river. There wasn't much we could do except hope that it was ours, and it was; a couple of Sadiq's men waved and the armoured car stopped alongside us.

'We came back to look for you, sir. To stop you going any further,' one of them said.

'What's wrong?'

It was bad news. The ferry crossing was about six miles downstream, and the Nyalan ferrypoint and the road to it were occupied by a rebel force, not a large one but probably a guard detachment. There was no ferry movement at all. All this Sadiq had seen from far off, which was bad enough, but what was worse was that he had picked up radio conversations, thanks to Bing's expertise; and it was apparent that Kigonde had not told him the whole truth. The opposition was stronger than we'd been led to believe. A large part of the army had defected and the countryside through to Fort Pirie and perhaps as far down as Lasulu was in rebel hands.

From what the soldiers told us, there was even some doubt as to whether they should be called rebels or military

representatives of a new ruling Government; all news from
Port Luard had ceased. There was no indication as to which
way the Air Force had gone, but no doubt that whichever
side they started on they'd find a way of ending up on the
side of the victors.

'Thank you for the news,' I said, though I didn't feel at
all thankful. 'Tell Captain Sadiq that we will bring the convoy no further than the filling station along the road there.
We'll wait there until we hear from him.'

Sadiq would probably regard even this as dangerously
close to the enemy. The Saracen turned back and so did we,
bearing a cargo of gloom to the gas station. Wingstead said,
'Christ, can't anything go right?' It wasn't like him to be
dejected and I hoped it was caused by nothing more than
exhaustion.

'Why couldn't they have been government troops?'
Zimmerman asked plaintively.

'You think that would make much difference? In a civil
war the best bet for a foreigner is to stay clear of all troops
whichever side they're on. There'll be bastards like Maksa
on both sides.'

We arrived at the station and I took the Land Rover
round the back of the cabin out of sight of the road. The
Nyalan attendant popped out with a disapproving face, then
relaxed when he saw who we were, 'I got more Cokes getting cold, like you said,' he announced proudly.

'You know the trouble we talked about? Well, it's not far
away, my friend. There are soldiers down at the ferry and
they are not friends of your Government.'

The others got out of the car and joined me. I said, 'We
would like to look around here. I think there is going to be
more trouble, and it may come this way. If I were you I'd go
tell your people in the village to go away until it's over, and
that means you too.'

He said, 'Other people, they already go. But not me.'

'Why not?'

'I leave and Mister Obukwe, he kill me,' he said very positively.

'Who's he?'

'My boss in Fort Pirie.'

I thought that Mr Obukwe must be quite a terrifying guy to instil such company loyalty, and exchanged a grin with Harry Zimmerman. He came forward and said, 'What's your name?'

The attendant thought about answering him. 'Sam Kironji,' he said at last. Zimmerman stuck out his hand.

'Pleased to meet you, Sam. My name is Harry Zimmerman. Call me Harry. And I work for Lat-Am same as you. Look here.' He opened a wallet and produced a plastic identification badge, to which Kironji reacted with delight.

'Very good you come. You tell Mister Obukwe I got no trade except I sell Coca-Cola.'

'Sure, I'll tell him. But if you want to leave, Sam, it'll be OK. Neil here is right, there could be trouble coming this way.'

Kironji thought about it and then gave him a great smile.

'I stay. This is my place, I take care of it. Also I not afraid of the soldiers like them.' He waved a contemptuous hand at his departed fellow inhabitants. 'You want Cokes, other things, I got them maybe.'

I said, 'Sure, we want Cokes and food and all sorts of things. Soon our trucks will come here and we'll want lots of petrol too.' Probably more than you've ever seen sold in a year, I thought. I pointed to a hard-surfaced track which led away from the road. 'Tell me, Sam, where does that track go to?'

'The river.'

'But you're already at the river.'

'It go compound, back there,' he said, waving a vague hand.

'How far is it?'

'Not far. Half an hour walking maybe.'

I said, 'We're going to take our car down there and have a look. If any white men come by here, tell them to wait for us.'

'Hey, man,' he said, 'that company property. You can't drive there.'

I looked at him in amusement and wondered if Lat-Am knew how lucky they were. 'Harry?'

Zimmerman persuaded him that we were going on company business and Kironji finally gave way to our demands.

The track was better surfaced than I had expected and showed signs of considerable use. Wherever it was rutted the ruts had been filled in with clinker and the repair work was extensive and well done. Presumably Mr Obukwe of Lat-Am Oil had need of this track and we wondered why.

It wasn't all that wide, just enough to take a big truck through the trees. On the right they pressed in thickly but on the left they barely screened the water. The trees showed signs of continual cutting back, the slash marks ranging from old scars to new-cut wood still oozing sap.

The track ran parallel to the main road to the lake shore. We emerged into a clearing to see the sun striking hard diamond reflections from the water and to find yet another fenced compound full of drums. There was also a landing stage, a rough structure consisting of a wooden platform on top of empty oil drums making a floating jetty about ten feet wide and eighty feet long.

There was even a boat, though it was nothing much; just a fifteen-foot runabout driven by an outboard. I walked out onto the landing stage which swayed gently and looked closely at the boat. It was aged and a bit leaky, but the outboard looked to be well maintained. I turned my attention to the lake itself.

The distance to the far side was about four miles and through binoculars I thought I could see the shore and a ribbon of track leading up from it. That was Manzu, a country

blessedly free of civil war and as desirable as Paradise. But
as far as we were concerned it might as well have been the
far side of the moon. It was ironic to think that if we had
no-one to worry about but ourselves we four could have
crossed this stretch of water to safety in no time.

'Pretty sight, isn't it,' Wingstead murmured as he took his
turn with the binoculars. He was thinking my thoughts.

I turned back to the clearing. It was easy now to see the
reason for the good road. Delivery to and from this petrol
dump was made by water, probably from Fort Pirie to this
and other drop points along the shore. It would be easier
than road transport especially if the fuel came prepacked in
drums.

There was a locked wooden shed standing nearby. By
peering through the boards we could see that it was a workshop and toolroom. There was every sign that it was used
regularly for maintenance work, though everything was
tidy. I walked back along the pontoon and prowled around
the perimeter of the compound I found a gate which was
also locked and there was a palm-thatched hut just inside it.
It crossed my mind that the clearing, which was very long,
would be a good place to put the rig and the rest of the convoy off the road and out of sight. The road down was rough
but I had learned enough from Kemp to judge it would
stand the traffic, and Wingstead confirmed this.

'It's not a bad idea. And it brings us at least within sight
of our goal,' he said when I put the proposition to him.

On the far shore we could make out a cluster of buildings
where there was possibly another landing stage. On the
water itself there were no boats moving. Traffic on Lake
Pirie might simply be infrequent or it may have been
brought to a halt by the advent of war.

When we got back to the station we arranged for Kironji
to load the balance of his Cokes and a few other items into
the car. The cabin wasn't exactly a shop but there was some

tinned foodstuff for sale and a few bits of hardware that
might be useful. He also had a little first aid kit but it wasn't
worth ransacking. As Kironji closed the cooler lid on the last
load of Cokes I saw something else down there.

'Are those beer cans, Sam?'

'Mine.' He closed the lid defiantly.

'OK, no sweat.' A ridiculous statement in this scorching
weather. This train of thought made me wipe my forehead.
Kironji watched me, hesitated, and then said, 'You want a
beer?'

'You'd be a hero, Sam.'

He grinned and handed me a cold can. 'I got a few. Only
for you and your friends. I not sell them.'

It tasted wonderful. Our warm beer had long been
finished.

I looked around as I drank. The interior of the cabin was
neat and tidy. It was a combination of office and store, with
a few tyres in racks and spare parts on shelves. I thought
that Hammond could make something of all this, and in fact
he had already been browsing through the stock. At the
back was a door which led to Kironji's living quarters; he
was a bachelor and preferred to live where he worked, presumably to protect his precious Lat-Am property. There was
a supply of tools here too, and a small workbench.

'Do you do all your own repair work, Sam?'

'I got plenty tools, sir, and much training. But mostly I
work by the lake.' The shed we had seen housed a fair
amount of stuff, a well-equipped workshop for boats as well
as vehicles.

'Who does the boat belong to?' I asked.

'To me. I go fishing sometime.'

'I'd like to hire it from you. I want to have a look at the
lake.'

He shook his head at my folly but we agreed on a hire
fee, and he jotted it down on what was becoming a pretty

healthy tab. He wasn't going to be done out of a penny, either by way of business or personally.

Wingstead came in and to his great delight Kironji handed out another beer. He disposed of it in two swallows.

Kironji asked, 'You say you have other people coming. What you doing here, man?'

'We were going to Bir Oassa with parts for the oilfields,' Wingstead said. 'We met the war and had to turn back. Now we must try to get back to Lasulu.' He said nothing of the Manzu border. Kironji pondered and then said, 'You know this hospital?'

'Which hospital?' I asked, thinking he meant that there was one in the vicinity. But his reply only proved the efficiency of the bush telegraph once again.

'I hear it go travel on a big truck, lots of sick people. The other they follow where it go, all through the country.'

'By God,' Wingstead exclaimed. 'The juggernaut's famous! If Sam here has heard about it it'll be all over the damn country by now. I don't know if that's good news or bad.'

I said, 'Yes, Sam, we are travelling with that hospital. The sick people are on a big trailer, all the way from Doctor Katabisirua's hospital in Kodowa.'

He brightened. 'Doctor Kat! I know him. He very good doctor. One day he fix my brother when he break a leg.' That was good news; if our doctor was well thought of his name was a reference for the rest of us.

'He'll be here later today, Sam,' Wingstead said.

Kironji looked only mildly incredulous.

Hammond came to the doorway. 'The Captain's here, Mister Mannix. He's asking for you.'

I tossed him two beers. 'One for you and one for Harry,' I said, 'but don't go back and boast about it. There isn't any more.'

'You said no soldiers,' said Kironji reproachfully as I passed him.

'Not many, and they are friends. Doctor Kat knows about them.'

Sadiq was waiting outside. I thanked him for his message, and went on, 'I've suggested to Mister Wingstead that we stop here, and he's agreed. There's a good road down to the lake and it's well hidden. We can put the whole convoy there, including the rig, and your men too if you think fit.'

Sadiq liked the idea and went to see for himself. Kironji watched him go from the cabin doorway.

'Sam,' I said, 'have you ever used the ferry?'

'Me, no. What for? I not go Manzu, I work here.'

'Who does use the ferry?'

He considered. 'Many truck from Manzu go to oilfields. Farmers, Government people. Many different people go on ferry.'

In happier times the international border here was obviously open and much-used. It was the only route to the Bir Oassa fields from countries north of Nyala. Kironji's information that trucks crossed on it suggested that it was larger than I would have expected, which was encouraging news.

Geoff Wingstead beckoned to me.

'When the rig gets here we will get it off the road. We're a little too close to Fort Pirie for comfort, and there's no point in buying trouble. There's plenty of room at the lakeside and it can't be seen from up here. But we'll have to widen the turn-off.'

For the next hour he and I together with Zimmerman and Hammond laboured. Widening the turn for the rig involved only a few modifications. We heaved rocks and equipment to one side, uprooted vegetation and chopped down a small spinney of thorn bushes, and generally made a mess of Sam Kironji's carefully preserved little kingdom.

If it hadn't been for the fact that Zimmerman was from Lat-Am Kironji would never have allowed us to do it. As it was he could barely bring himself to help.

Four hours later the rig was bedded down in the clearing by the lake, its load resting on the ground and the weight taken off the bogies. The clearing held most of the vehicles and those that couldn't be fitted in were scattered off the road where they could leave in a hurry, or be used to block the way to the rig. We might have been bypassed and remain invisible if it wasn't for the Nyalans who were still doggedly following us. They camped in the trees all about us, chattering, cooking, coming and going endlessly. According to Sam Kironji many lived nearby but preferred our company to their homes.

Sadiq set his men to try and persuade them to leave us but this was a wasted effort. The rig was a magnet more powerful than any of us could have imagined, and politely but obstinately its strange escort insisted on staying. The countryside was steadily pillaged for whatever food could be found, and Sam Kironji's chickens disappeared before we could bargain for them.

I found Sister Ursula tearing a little pile of bedding she'd found in Kironji's cabin into bandaging strips and said to her, 'Let me do that. You've got more important things to do.'

'Thank you.' She had discarded her coif and her hair, cut close to the scalp, was sheened with sweat.

'How are things, Sister?'

'Not too bad,' she said briskly. 'We've lost no more patients and I really think the infant is going to make it, thanks be to God. We worry about Mister Lang, though.' He had taken Max Otterman's place as their most serious case. 'Doctor Marriot says that Sister Mary is a little better. But she shouldn't exert herself in the slightest. We do need to get to a hospital soon though. What are our chances?' she asked.

I put her in the picture. 'Do you know of any hospitals in Manzu?' I then asked.

She didn't, and hadn't heard that we intended to try and reach the neighbouring country. Few people had as yet, for the sake of security, but now I told her.

'It's a fine idea, and just what we need. All these poor people who are following us, they do need a place to settle down in peace once more.'

'But they're Nyalans. They'd be in a foreign country without papers.'

She laughed. 'You're naïve, Mister Mannix These people think of it simply as land, Africa. They haven't much nationalistic fervour, you know. They cross borders with little fear of officialdom, and officialdom has better things to do than worry about them. They just go where the grazing and hunting is good.'

I wished it was as simple for us, but we had a lot to do first. I left the Sister to her bandages and went to find Hammond, McGrath and Sam Wilson.

We walked down to stand at the pontoon, looking out over the water. Hammond said, 'I don't see many possibilities. If there was a bridge we could at least fight for it.'

'The ferry point is swarming with rebels,' I said. 'I don't think we've got the force we'd need.'

'You know, I was getting really worried about fuel,' Hammond said. 'It's ironic that now, when we can't go anywhere, we've got all we want and more.'

'I've been thinking about that,' said McGrath. 'We could float petrol down to the ferry and set it alight, construct a fire ship.'

Wilson said, 'Pleasant ideas you have, Mick,' and I caught an undertone I recognized; here was someone else who mistrusted the Irishman.

Hammond said, 'We can get people across Manzu in threes and fours, with this little boat . . . or perhaps not,' he added as he crossed the pontoon to look down into it. He hopped up and down, making the pontoon bobble on the water, then came back ashore looking thoughtful.

'I wonder why they have a pontoon instead of a fixed jetty,' he said.

'Does it matter?' I was no sailor and the question wouldn't have occurred to me, but Wilson took up Hammond's point. 'A fixed jetty's easier to build, unless you need a landing stage that'll rise and fall with the tide,' he said. 'Only there's no tide here.'

'You can see the water level varies a little,' Hammond said. He pointed out signs that meant nothing to me, but Wilson agreed with them. 'So where does the extra water come from?' I asked. 'It's the dry season now. When the rains come the river must swell a lot. Is that it?'

'It looks like more than that. I'd say there was a dam at the foot of the lake,' Hammond hazarded. McGrath followed this carefully and I could guess the trend of his thoughts; if there was a dam he'd be all for blowing it up. But I didn't recall seeing a dam on the maps, faulty though they were, and hadn't heard one mentioned.

But this wasn't Hammond's line of thinking at all.

'They have level control because the lake rises and falls at times. That's why they need a floating jetty,' he said.

'So?'

'The point is that the jetty is a tethered raft.' He pointed to the dinghy. 'That isn't very seaworthy but if we cut the pontoon loose it could be towed across the lake with people on it.'

Now he was giving me ideas. 'Only a few at a time,' I said.

'But we could build a bigger one. We might find other outboards,' Hammond went on, growing interested in his own hypothesis.

'Supposing you could do it. What does everyone do at the other side without transport? It's a long way to Batanda.'

'I hadn't got that far,' he admitted glumly.

I looked around. One boat, one pontoon, one outboard motor, plenty of fuel, a workshop . . . a work force . . . raw materials . . . my mind raced and I felt excitement rising. I said, 'All of you go on thinking about this. But don't share your ideas with anyone else for the time being.'

I got into the Land Rover and shot off up the road to the filling station and went up to Sam Kironji's cabin, which was latched. He let me in with some reluctance.

He said bitterly, 'You come, now they all come. Stealers! You didn't tell me this big crowd come. They steal everything I got. They steal things I don't got.' He was hurt and angry.

'Relax, Sam. We didn't bring them, they followed us. You said yourself you heard the travelling hospital was big magic.'

'That not magic. That *theft*. How I relax? How I explain to Mister Obukwe?'

'You won't have to. Mister Zimmerman will explain and Lat-Am Oil will be very pleased with you. You'll probably get a bonus. Got another beer?'

He stared at the desk top as I opened the cooler, which was empty, and then looked along his shelves which were as bare as Mother Hubbard's cupboard. Kironji looked up sardonically. 'Stealers! I tell you. Here.' He reached under the desk and came up with a beer can which he thrust out at me as if ashamed of his own generosity. I took it thankfully and said, 'There's still lots of stuff here, Sam.'

'Who eat tyres? Who eat batteries? You tell me that.'

I sat down on the edge of his desk. 'Sam. You know all those petrol drums you've got outside and down by the lake?'

'Why? You want to steal them?'

'No, of course not. How big are they?'

He addressed the desk top again. 'Forty-two gallon.'

'Imperial?'

'What you mean? Gallons, man – that what they are.'

Forty-two imperial gallons, which is what they probably were, equalled about fifty American. I had tried to decipher the marks on one but they were pretty rusty.

'Sam,' I said, 'please do me a big favour. Give me some paper and a pen or a pencil, let me borrow your office, and go away for a bit. I have to do some calculating, some planning. I'll be really grateful.'

He reluctantly produced a pad of paper with Lat-Am's logo on it and a ballpoint pen. 'I want my pen back,' he said firmly and began to retreat.

'Wait a moment. What's the weight of an empty drum?'

He shrugged. 'I dunno. Plenty heavy.'

It didn't matter too much at this stage. 'How many empty drums have you got here?'

Again his shoulders hunched. 'Too many. No supplies come, I use 'em up. Many empty now.'

'For Christ's sake, Sam, I don't want a long story! How many?'

'Maybe a thousand, maybe more. I never count.'

I jotted down figures. 'Thanks. Sam, that cooler. Where do you get your power from?'

'Questions. You ask too much questions.' He jerked his thumb. 'You not hear it? The generator, man!'

I had got so accustomed to hearing the steady throb of a generator on the rig that it hadn't penetrated that this one was making a slightly different sound. 'Ah, so you do have one.'

'Why? You want to steal it?' He flapped his hand dejectedly. 'You take it. Mister Obukwe, he already mad at me.'

'Don't worry,' I told him. 'Nobody will steal it, or anything else. But buying would be different, wouldn't it? My company is British Electric. Perhaps we can buy your generator from you.'

'You pay cash?'

I laughed aloud. 'Not exactly, but you'll get it in the end. Now let me alone for a while, Sam, would you?'

Before he left he went and wrote down one can of beer on my tab.

TWENTY-FOUR

I had a bit of figuring to do. For one thing, while we Americans think our way of doing things is always best, the European metric system is actually far better than our own multi-unit way, even the conservative British are adopting it, and oddly enough an imperial gallon is a better measure than our American gallon because one imperial gallon weighs exactly ten pounds of fresh water. It didn't take much figuring to see that a drum would hold four hundred and twenty pounds of water.

There was some other reckoning to be done and I persevered, even to cutting shapes out of paper with a rusty pair of scissors. At last I stretched, put Kironji's pen safely back in a drawer, took a hopeful but useless look in the cooler and set off down to the lakeside on foot. It was only a short distance and I used the walk to do some more thinking. I went straight down to look at the pontoon once again.

It was a rickety enough contraption, just a few empty oil drums for flotation with a rough log platform bolted on top. It was very weathered and had obviously stood the test of time, but it was as stable as a spinning top just about to lose speed and I wouldn't have cared to cross Central Park Lake on it.

I yelled for anybody and Bob Pitman responded.

'Bob,' I said, 'go round up a couple of people for me, will you? I want Kemp, Hammond, and Geoff Wingstead. Oh, and Mick McGrath. Ask them to meet me here.'

'Will do,' he said and ambled off. When they had all arrived I found that Zimmerman had got wind of the conference and had made himself part of it, though without his Russian mate. I looked around at them and drew a deep breath.

'I have a nutty idea,' I started.

This drew a couple of ribald comments and I waited until they died down before I carried on. 'It's crazy and dangerous, but it just might work. We have to do something to get ourselves out of this fix. You gave me the idea, Ben. You and Mick.'

'We did?' Hammond asked.

'Yes. I want us to build a raft.'

'I know I mentioned that but you shot that idea down in flames. You had a point too.'

'I've developed your idea. We don't use this thing as a basis, we build our own. I've done some figuring on paper and I think it will work. The trouble is that the lake isn't made of paper.' I filled in for the benefit of the others. 'Ben suggested that if we towed the landing stage it could form a raft on which we could get people over to Manzu. The pontoon isn't big or stable enough and we'd need transport on the far shore. But I think I've worked something out.'

'Build a bigger raft?' asked Wingstead.

'How could you power it?'

'What do we make it of?'

'What do you think this is, a navy shipyard?'

I held up my hand. 'Hold it. Give me a chance and I'll explain.' There were two phases to my scheme and I thought it wiser to introduce them one at a time, so I concentrated on the concept of the raft first. 'To start with, every one of these drums in the compound, when empty,

has a flotation value of four hundred pounds, and there are
hundreds of them. We won't need more than say one hundred for my plan to work.'

'Sounds idiotic to me,' said Kemp. 'A hundred of these
drums won't make a raft big enough to take anything anywhere.' I knew he was trying to visualize the rig floating
across the lake on a bed of oil drums and failing, and had
indeed done that myself.

'Building a raft is the first part of my plan. And it'll do to
go on with, unless someone has a better one. We can't stay
here indefinitely.'

'It sounds like you have a pretty big job lined up,'
Wingstead said. He didn't sound encouraging. 'Let's hear it.'

'Think about the raft. To make it we need material and
muscle. And brains, I guess. We've got the brains between
us and there's a hell of a lot of suitable raw material lying
about. As for the muscle, that's how the pyramids were
built, and the Great Wall of China. God knows we've got
enough of that.'

'The Nyalans?' Hammond asked. He was beginning to
kindle with excitement. I wanted them all to feel that
way.

'We'll need a work force. The women to plait lianas to
make a lot of cordage, and some of the men to cart stuff
about. I've got the basic blueprints right here.' I held up the
pad of paper.

Zimmerman and Hammond looked ready for any challenge. Kemp had a stubborn set to his jaw and I knew that
he was thinking about the rig to the usual exclusion of
everything else, and ready to oppose any plan that didn't
involve saving it.

Geoff Wingstead was oddly lacklustre, which disappointed
me. I'd hoped to enrol his enthusiasm first of all, and wondered why he was hanging fire. McGrath had said nothing
and was listening intently in the background. With the odd,

unwanted rapport that I sometimes felt between us I knew
he was aware that I had something tougher yet to propose,
and he was waiting for it.

Hammond said, 'How do we persuade the Nyalans to
cooperate? We can't pay them.'

'Sister Ursula gave me the answer to that. We can take as
many of them across to Manzu as want to go. When the
war's over they'll probably drift back again, but right now
they're as threatened as we are. I think they'll help us.'

Kemp had been drawing in the sand, and now he said,
'Look, Neil, this is ridiculous. To build a raft big enough to
take maybe a couple of hundred people is crazy enough, but
to take vehicles across on them is beyond belief. Good God,
each tractor weighs forty tons. And how do we embark and
disembark them?'

I said, 'You're thinking the wrong way. I agree with you,
and I've already rejected that idea. We don't build a raft to
get people to Manzu.' It was time to drop the bombshell.

'What? Then what's all this about?'

I said, 'We're going to use it to capture the ferry.'

They stared at me in total silence. McGrath's face
warmed into a broad grin of appreciation.

Wingstead said at last, 'You're out of your mind, Neil.'

'OK, what the hell do we do? Sit here and eat ants until
the war goes away? We have to do something. Any immunity as foreigners and civilians we might have had was
shattered when we met up with Maksa's force. We played
soldiers then. And I have a bad feeling about this war; if the
Government forces were going to win they'd have done so
by now. The rebels are gaining strength and if they take
over they aren't going to be exactly lenient.'

Wingstead said, 'You're right. It just seems so far-
fetched.'

'Not at all,' said McGrath. 'It's a lovely idea, Mannix.
Lovely. How did I give you the idea, if I might ask?'

'You mentioned fire ships,' I said shortly. I needed him desperately but I was damned if I could make myself at ease with him. 'We're going to attack the ferry from the water, the one thing they won't expect.'

I had him with me, naturally. I thought I had Hammond too. He was fully aware of the danger but absorbed by the technical challenge. Kemp might disapprove but couldn't resist putting his mind to the problem.

Hammond said, 'I think at this stage you want to keep this rather quiet, don't you, Mister Mannix?'

'Yes. Why?'

'I'd like Bert Proctor in on it from the start. He's got a good head, and I've worked with him on projects so often –'

I said, 'Yes, of course. Go get him.'

He went off at the double and Wingstead smiled. 'They really are quite a team, you know.' I was still worried about his lack of enthusiasm. He was the kingpin of the team and they looked to him for direction.

Proctor, grave and attentive as always, listened as I recapped. He calmly accepted the idea of Wyvern Transport men turning into privateers, and I understood why Hammond wanted him.

I showed them my idea for building the raft. I hadn't yet calculated the load but I reckoned on as many men as we could muster, at least one or maybe two trucks and whatever we could develop in the way of weapons – a formidable prospect. They were dubious but fascinated and the engineers among them could see the theoretical possibilities. We had to build a raft before considering the rest of the plan.

To Kemp I said, 'Basil, I've got an idea about the rig too. I know how important it is. We'll talk about that later.' This was a sop; I had no ideas about the rig but I couldn't afford to let him know it.

McGrath asked, 'How many men do you think we'll have?'

I said, 'All of Sadiq's men, that's twenty-three. We can't conscript our crew but I don't think anybody will want to be left out. I make that sixteen. Thirty-nine in all.'

'Say thirty-five, allowing for accidents,' said McGrath.

'Fair enough.'

'What did Sadiq have to say about the ferry?'

'They have a guard detachment there. Exactly how many we don't know, but it doesn't sound formidable. If we come out of the dark yelling at them they'll probably scatter like autumn leaves.'

Faces brightened. It didn't sound quite so bad put that way.

McGrath said, 'We'd need much more accurate information than that, Mannix.'

'Oh, I agree. By the way, I haven't spoken to Sadiq yet, but we will soon. I want to propose an expedition, using Sam Kironji's boat. You, McGrath, Geoff, Sadiq and myself. It won't take any more. Down river by night.'

Wingstead said, 'Oh my God, Neil, I don't think we should do that.'

I was dumbfounded. 'What the hell's the matter with you, Geoff? I'm depending most of all on you. For God's sake stop being such a damned pessimist.'

I'd never let fly at an executive in front of his men before. But it was vital to keep morale high and a waverer at the top of the command line could ruin all our plans. He made a strangely listless gesture and said, 'I'm sorry, Neil. Of course I'm with you. Just tired, I guess.'

Zimmerman broke into the embarrassed silence. 'I don't think Geoff should go anyway, Neil. He's got enough on his plate already. Let me come instead.'

I was relieved. Damn it, I wanted Wingstead with me, and yet in his present mood he might be a liability. I wished I knew what was eating him.

'Suppose we succeeded, took the ferry. What then?' Hammond asked. 'Wouldn't their main force get to know about it?'

'Very likely, but they're at Fort Pirie and we'd silence radios and prevent getaways,' I said. 'The only thing we have to pray for is that the ferry is operative, and from what Kironji told me it's been in regular use recently so it ought to be.'

'Then what?' Wingstead asked.

'We bring up the rig and get all the invalids on board the ferry, cram it full of people and shoot it across to Manzu. When it comes back we pile on as many vehicles as it can take, trucks for preference, and the last of the people. Once in Manzu it's a doddle. Get to Batanda, alert the authorities and send back transport for the stragglers. I bet they've got cold beer there.'

They chewed on this for a while. I had painted a rosy picture and I knew they wouldn't entirely fall for it, but it was important to see potential success.

Hammond stood up and rubbed out the sketch marks in the sand with his foot. 'Right – how do we start?' he asked practically.

Wingstead looked up, absurdly startled. His face was pale under its tan and I wondered fleetingly if he was simply afraid. But he hadn't been afraid back in the warehouse at Makara.

'I don't know,' he said uncertainly. 'I'd like to think about it a bit, before we start anything. It's just too –'

The hesitation, the slack face, were totally unfamiliar. Doubt began to wipe away the tentative enthusiasm I had roused in the others. Wingstead had cut his teeth on engineering problems such as this and he was deeply concerned for the safety of his men. I had expected him to back me all the way.

The problem solved itself. He stood up suddenly, shaking his head almost in bewilderment, took a dozen paces away from us and collapsed in the dust.

We leapt up to race over to him.

'Go and get a doctor!' Kemp barked and Proctor ran to obey. Gently Kemp cradled Wingstead whose face had gone as grey as putty, sweat-soaked and lolling. We stood around in shocked silence until Dr Kat and Dr Marriot arrived.

After a few minutes the surgeon stood up and to my amazement he looked quite relieved. 'Please send for a stretcher,' he said courteously, but there was one already waiting, and willing hands to carry Wingstead to the mobile hospital. Dr Marriot went with him, but Dr Kat stayed behind.

'I should have seen this coming,' he said. 'But you may set your minds at rest, gentlemen. Mister Wingstead will be perfectly all right. He is not dangerously ill.'

'What the hell is it then?' I asked.

'Overstrain, overwork, on top of the injuries he suffered in the plane crash. He should have been made to take things more easily. Tell me, did you notice anything wrong yourselves?'

I said, feeling sick with anger at myself, 'Yes, I did. I've seen him losing his drive, his energy. And I damned well kept pushing at him, like a fool. I'm sorry –'

Kemp cut me off abruptly.

'Don't say that. I saw it too and I know him better than anyone else here. We must have been crazy to let him go on like that. Will he really be all right?'

'All he needs is sleep, rest, good nourishment. We can't do too much about the last but I assure you I won't let him get up too soon this time. I might tell you that I'm very relieved in one respect. I have been afraid of fever – cholera, typhoid – any number of scourges that might strike. When I heard that Mister Wingstead had collapsed I thought it was the first such manifestation. That it is not is a matter of considerable relief.'

The Doctor's report on Wingstead was circulated, and the concern that had run through the convoy camp like a brush fire died down.

I found Hammond. 'I want to talk to all the crew later this evening. The medical staff too. We'll tell them the whole plan. It's risky, but we can't ask people to work in ignorance.'

Then I went to find Sam Kironji.

'Sam, what's in that little hut inside the compound?' I asked him.

He looked at me suspiciously. He'd already found the compound gate unlocked and Harry Zimmerman and two others counting empty drums, much to his disgust. 'Why you want to know?'

I clung to my patience. 'Sam, just tell me.'

There was nothing much in it. The hut held a miscellany of broken tools, cordage, a few other stores that might be useful, and junk of all sorts. It was where Sam put the things he tidied away from everywhere else.

I made a space in the middle of it, had Kironji's desk brought in, and established it as my headquarters. The roadside cabin was too far from the camp and too exposed. Some wag removed a Pirelli calendar from the cabin wall and hung it in the hut, and when Kironji saw this I think it hurt him most of all.

'Stealers! Now you take my women,' he said tragically.

'Only to look at, same as you. You'll get them back, I promise. Thank you for the desk and the chair, Sam.'

He flapped his hand at me. 'Take everything. I not care no more. Mister Obukwe, he fire me.'

Hammond was listening with amusement. 'Never mind, Sam. If he does I'll hire you instead,' I said and hustled him outside. I sat down and Hammond perched on the end of the desk. We each had a pad of paper in front of us.

'Right, Ben. This is what I've got in mind.'

I began to sketch on the pad. I still have those sketches; they're no masterpieces of the draughtsman's art, but they're worth the whole Tate Gallery to me.

Take an empty drum and stand it up. Place around it, in close contact, six more drums, making damn sure their caps are all screwed home firmly. Build an eight-sided wooden framework for them, top, bottom and six sides, thus making a hexagon. No need to fill the sides solidly, just enough to hold the drums together like putting them in a cage. This I called the 'A' hexagon, which was to be the basic component of the raft. It had the virtue of needing no holes drilled into the drums, which would waste time and effort and risk leaks.

How much weight would an 'A' hexagon support?

We got our answer soon enough. While we were talking Sandy Bing reported breathlessly to the office. 'Mister Mannix? I got forty-three and a half gallons into a drum.' He was soaking wet and seemed to have enjoyed the exercise.

'Thanks, Sandy. Go and see how many empties Harry Zimmerman has found, please.' Zimmerman and his team were getting very greasy out in the compound.

The drums were forty-two gallons nominal but they were never filled to brimming and that extra space came in handy now. We figured that the natural buoyancy of the wooden cage would go some way to compensate for the weight of the steel drums, and Bing had just handed me another few pounds of flotation to play about with. We decided that my 'A' hexagon should support a weight of 3,000 pounds: one and a half tons.

But there wouldn't be much standing room. And a floating platform about six by five feet would be distinctly unstable. So my next lot of figures concerned the natural development upwards.

All this would take a little time to produce but it shouldn't be too difficult. Testing the finished product as a floating proposition would be interesting, and finding a way to push it along would stretch a few minds, but I didn't really doubt that it could be done. And the final result, weird of shape and design, was going to win no prizes for elegance. I jiggled with a list of required materials; some of them were going to be hard to find if not impossible. All in all, I couldn't see why on earth I was so confident that the plan would work.

'We have to go up a stage, Ben,' I said, still sketching. 'Look at this.'

The hexagon is a very useful shape, ask any honey bee, but I doubt if it has been used much in naval architecture.

'Start off assuming we've built an "A"-gon,' I told Ben. That was how new words came into a language, I guess, though I didn't think this one would last long enough to qualify for *Webster's Dictionary.* Ben caught on and grinned in appreciation. 'Here's what comes next.'

Take an 'A'-gon and float it in shallow water so that a man could stand on the bottom and still handle equipment. Float another six 'A'-gons round it and fasten together the hexagons of the outer ring. There is no need to fasten the inner one because, like the first drum, it is totally surrounded and pressed in from all sides.

The result is a 'B' hexagon, a 'B'-gon in our new nomenclature, with a positive buoyancy of ten and a half tons, enough to carry over a hundred people or a medium sized truck. We decided to make two of them, which is why we needed a hundred drums.

Hammond was impressed and fascinated. 'How do we make the cages?' he asked.

'We'll have to find timber and cut pieces to the exact size,' I said. 'That won't be too difficult. I'm more concerned about finding planking to deck it, otherwise it'll be unsafe to walk on. Nyalan women make good cordage, and we can lash the "A"-gon frames together, which will save nails. But I'm worried about the fastening of the larger "B"-gons. Rope and fibre won't help us there. We need steel cable.'

'I've got some,' he offered, a shade reluctantly.

'I don't want to have to use that yet. We'll figure out something else.'

I stood up. 'It's only four o'clock and I need some exercise. There's two hours of daylight yet. Let's go build us an "A"-gon.'

We were just leaving the office when Bing arrived back.

'Mister Zimmerman says they've only found sixty-seven drums,' he said.

At the compound we found Zimmerman, Kirilenko and Derek Grafton looking mucky with old oil and somewhat bad-tempered. It appeared that there were not many empty drums. Kironji seldom got them back, and these had not been placed neatly away from the full drums but stood all over the place. Here Kironji's normal tidiness had deserted him, to our detriment. It didn't help that neither Grafton nor Kirilenko knew why they had to find empty drums, and of the two only the Russian was equable about taking unexplained orders.

I commiserated with them and sent them off for a breather, after we'd rolled eight or nine drums down to the lake shore. Zimmerman stayed with us. Hammond left in search of Kironji, to get the workshop unlocked; he would cut some timber frameworks and we decided to use rope, which we knew was available, for the prototype 'A'-gon.

'I don't see how we're going to find enough empties,' Zimmerman grumbled.

'Ever hear about the guy who went into a store to buy some eggs? There was a sign up saying "Cracked Eggs Half Price", so he asked them to crack him a dozen eggs.'

Zimmerman smiled weakly.

'You mean empty out full drums?'

'Why not? To start with we'll fill every fuel tank we can with either gas or diesel, and all our spare jerrycans too. If there are still not enough drums we'll dig a big pit somewhere well away from the camp and ditch the stuff. And put up a "No Smoking" notice.'

He realized I wasn't joking and his jaw dropped. I suppose that as an oil man he was more used to getting the stuff out of the earth than to putting it back in. Then we were interrupted by Sam Kironji in his usual state of high indignation.

'You cut trees! You use my saw. You never stop make trouble.'

I looked enquiringly at Sandy Bing who had raced in behind him. 'Yes, Mister Mannix. Mister Hammond found a chain saw in the workshop. But it won't be good for long. The teeth are nearly worn out and there's no replacement.'

Kironji shook his head sadly. 'You use my saw, you welcome. But you cut tree, you get in big trouble with Mister Nyama.'

'Who's he, Sam?'

'Everybody know Mister Nyama. Big Government tree man. He cut many tree here, with big machine.'

I said, 'Are you telling us that there's a government logging camp near here?'

'Sure.'

'Well where, for God's sake?'

Sam pointed along the lake. 'One, two mile. They use our road.'

I recalled that the road led on past the compound, but I hadn't given any thought as to where it went. A bad oversight on my part.

'Chain saws,' Zimmerman was saying, his voice rising to a chant of ecstasy, 'Axes, felling axes, trimming axes, scrub cutters.'

'Fantastic. Get off there right away. We've got enough drums to be going on with. Take some men, some of Sadiq's if you have to. I'll clear it with him. And Harry, plunder away; we'll make everything good some time. Break in if you have to. My bet is that there'll be nobody there anyhow.'

Zimmerman went off at a run and Kironji said dolefully, 'You steal from Government, you steal from *anybody*.'

Hammond rejoiced at the good news and had some himself. 'Found an oxyacetylene welding kit in there with a few bottles. And a three-and-a-half inch Myford lathe that'll come in handy.'

'Bit small, isn't it?'

'I'll find a use for it. There's another outboard engine, too, and some other useful bits and pieces.'

'Take them,' said Kironji hysterically. 'No need you steal. I give.'

I chuckled. When he saw us pouring his precious gasolene into a hole in the ground he'd be a broken man. 'Come on, let's build our "A"-gon.'

It took six of us nearly two hours to build the prototype 'A'-gon but then we were inventing as we went along. From the middle distance the Nyalans watched us and wondered. Our people came to watch and make comments. At last we wrestled it down to the water and to our relief it floated, if a trifle lopsidedly. We dragged it ashore again as the light was fading and Bing arrived to say that a meal was ready. I felt tired but surprisingly contented. This had been a fruitful day, I was careful not to dwell on the possible outcome of my plans.

After an unsatisfying meal everybody gathered round, and between us Hammond and I explained the basics of the scheme. We said little about the military side of the operation and discouraged questions. We concentrated on the more immediate goal, the building of the 'B'-gons.

Grafton was sceptical, possibly because he'd had first-hand experience of the labour involved.

'It took you two hours to make that thing. How many do you need?'

'Fourteen for two "B"-gons. Possibly more.'

He looked appalled. 'It'll take days at that rate.'

'Ever hear about Henry Ford's biggest invention?'

'The Model T?'

'No, bigger than that. The assembly line.'

Hammond said at once. 'Ford didn't invent that. The Royal Navy had one going in Chatham in seventeen ninety-five for making ships' blocks.'

'I think the Egyptian wall paintings show something like an assembly line,' put in Atheridge.

'We won't be chauvinistic about it,' I said. 'But that's what we're going to do. We build simple jigs, stakes driven into the sand will do, one at each corner to give the shape. Then the teams move along the rows. That's the difference between this line and those in Cowley or Chicago. Each man goes along doing just one job. They lay down the bottom planking, put the drums on top, drop the side members between the stakes and make them fast. Then they put on a top and do likewise.'

They listened intently, and then Antoine Dufour spoke up. His English was good but heavily accented.

'I have worked in such a place. I think it is better you take the Japanese model, piecework is no good here. You will have too many people moving about, getting confused perhaps. You want teams each in one place.'

It took very little rethinking to see that he was right, and I said so.

'Great going, Antoine. It will be better that way. Each team builds one "A"-gon from the bottom up, complete. Another team to go along doling out material. Another one rolling the drums to them. And a couple of really strong teams to shift the finished "A"-gons to the water, probably towing them on mats. We've got rubber matting in the trucks.'

I looked at Dufour. 'You say you've had some experience at this. How would you like to be in charge of the work teams, you and Dan?'

He considered and then nodded. 'Yes. I will do it.'

His matter-of-fact acceptance of the feasibility of the programme did a lot to encourage the others. Questions and
ideas flew about, with me taking notes. At last I held up a
hand for silence.

'Enough to go on with. Now let's hear from Doctor Kat.'

The Doctor gave us a brief report on Lang and on
Wingstead, who was sleeping soundly and would be none
the worse as long as he was restrained for a few days. 'Sister
Mary is much better, and taking care of Mister Wingstead is
the perfect job for her. She will keep him quiet.'

I hadn't seen much of the senior nun but if she was anything like Sister Ursula there was no doubt that Geoff
Wingstead would shut up and obey orders.

Of the other invalids, he said that as fast as they got one
person on their feet so another would go down with
exhaustion, sickness or accident. The rickety thatched
wards were as busy as ever.

I turned to Harry Zimmerman.

'Harry's got some good news he's been saving,' I said.

'We found a logging camp,' he reported cheerfully. 'We
brought back two loads of equipment, in their trucks.
Chain saws, axes, hammers, nails and screws, a whole lot
of stuff like that. The big power saws are still there but they
work.'

'But you did even better than that, didn't you?' I
prompted.

'Yeah. Planks,' he breathed happily.

'We'll be bringing in a load in the morning. That means
our decking is sorted out, and that's a big problem solved.
And we can get all the struts for the cages cut to exact measurements in no time.' The assembly responded with more
enthusiasm than one might have thought possible, given
how weary they all were.

'It's amazing,' said Dr Marriot. 'I saw your "A"-gon. Such
a flimsy contraption.'

'So is an eggshell flimsy, but they've taken one tied in a bag outside a submarine four hundred feet deep and it didn't break. The "A"-gon's strength lies in its stress factors.'

She said, 'It's your stress factors we have to think about,' and got a laugh. Morale was improving.

The meeting over, we dispersed without any discussion about the proposed attack on the ferry for which all this was merely the prologue, and I was grateful. Those who were to be my fellow travellers in the boat stayed on to talk. We decided to move out by first light and return upriver in time to get cracking on the coming day's work. Sadiq had been briefed and while not exactly enthusiastic he had agreed to come with us, to see the enemy for himself.

Later I lay back looking at the dark shape of the rig looming over us, a grotesque shape lit with the barest minimum of light. I wondered what the hell we were going to do with it. I had enough thinking to keep me awake all night long.

But when I hit the sack I didn't know a thing until I felt Hammond gently awakening me, three hours before dawn.

TWENTY-FIVE

In the raw small hours we assembled at the pontoon, keeping our torches hooded and trying to keep quiet as we crossed the scrubby clearing. We couldn't leave totally unobserved but this was a practice run for later on, when keeping quiet would be vital.

Overnight Hammond had had the boat baled out and the outboard tested and found to run as sweetly as any outboard does, which is to say fitfully and with the occasional lurch and stutter to give you a nervous leap of the pulse. There was ample fuel, a small fluke anchor and a rond anchor for digging into an earth bank if necessary, some water canteens and a couple of long coils of line.

We had found oars for the dinghy but only one rowlock so someone had cobbled up another out of a piece of scrap iron bent to shape in the lathe; this and its more shapely companion were wrapped in cloth to minimize noise. The best we could do for balers were old beer cans with the tops cut out.

The five of us made a pretty tight fit. Hammond and McGrath took the centre thwart to row us out, we'd only start the engine well away from shore, I as the lightest sat forward, and Zimmerman and Sadiq crowded onto the after thwart. It was going to be no pleasure jaunt.

'What about crocodiles?' Hammond asked.

Zimmerman, who'd had years in Africa, snorted. 'Not a chance, Ben. They like shoaling water and they'll be sluggish before dawn anyway. Lazy brutes. Why bother with a boat when the bank's swarming with breakfast?'

Sadiq said gravely, 'Mister Hammond, we need not fear the crocodiles. They seldom attack boats with an engine.'

McGrath said, grinning, 'No, it's the hippos we have to think about,' giving Hammond another direction in which to cast his fears. I told him to lay off. What I didn't say was that, being no sailor even of the Sunday-in-the-park variety, I had a strong conviction that this frail craft was likely to tip us out and drown us at any moment. When we pushed off and the chill water lapped at the gunwales I was certain of it.

We didn't sink, of course, but we did get pretty wet about the feet and the face. After some time Hammond suggested that we start the outboard. This was achieved with only a few curses and false alarms. The little boat rocked wildly before the motor settled down to a welcome steady purr and we began to pick up some pace. We hugged the shoreline though not too close for fear of reed beds, and the light was beginning to allow us to distinguish details.

We were travelling with the current and so moved along swiftly. Hammond had calculated that we should arrive within sight of the ferry at about five o'clock, an hour before dawn. We would shut off the engine and slip along under oars until we could see the ferry point, then pull back upriver to find a concealed landing place. From there we'd reconnoitre on land.

'What happens if the ferry's on the far shore?' Zimmerman asked.

'We can cross in this thing and collect it. No sweat,' Hammond said. 'Come right a little, Mick.'

'What about the ferry people?' I said. 'They aren't simply going to lend us their craft, are they?'

'No, more likely they'll run it for us themselves, at a price.'

I'd been wondering who was going to handle the ferry. There would be a lot of local knowledge involved apart from familiarity with the craft itself. I said, 'Good thinking. Once we've taken the ferry point here we send a delegation and get the ferry back in business – just for us.'

'Well, it might work,' said McGrath dubiously. His form of payment would probably be a gun at the pilot's belly.

'First let's take the ferry,' I said. Perhaps it would be held by about five men whom we could capture or rout with a minimum of fuss, but I doubted that it would be that easy.

There was no further talk as we cruised steadily on until we saw the shapes of man-made buildings along the bank. We had arrived, and it still lacked half an hour to dawn.

'There it is,' I whispered, pointing. Instantly Zimmerman cut the engine and we used the oars to hold us stemming the tide. Shapes were emerging but confusingly, all detail obscured. There was a huge dark shape in the water a hundred yards offshore that we couldn't identify as yet. An island, perhaps? Hammond and McGrath back watered to keep us upstream while we scanned the shore anxiously for movement.

As all dawns do in central Africa, this one came in minutes. The air became grey and hazy, a shaft of early sunlight sprang out across the water and it was as if a veil had been lifted. Several voices whispered together.

'It's the ferry!'

She was anchored offshore, bobbing gently, a marvellous and welcome sight. She was big. Visions of a hand-poled pontoon, one-car sized and driven by chanting ferrymen, not at all an uncommon sight in Africa, receded thankfully from my mind. Kironji had said it took trucks, and trucks he meant. This thing would take several vehicles at one crossing.

And there was something else about her profile in the
watery light which nagged at me: a long low silhouette, bow
doors slanted inwards to the waterline and a lumpy deck
structure aft. She was a far cry from the sleek and sophisticated modern ferries of Europe.

We slid out from under the shadow of her bow and made
rapidly for shore. Hammond rowed us out of sight of the
ferry point and tucked into the bank in as secretive a spot as
we could find, setting both anchors. We disembarked into
the fringe of vegetation.

I looked to McGrath. He and Sadiq were the experts now,
and I wasn't sure which of the two was going to take command. But there wasn't any doubt really; with assurance
Sadiq started giving instructions, and McGrath took it with
equanimity. I think he'd approved of Sadiq as a fighting
man and was prepared to take his orders.

'Mister Mannix, you and Mister Zimmerman come with
me, please,' Sadiq said. 'Mister McGrath will take Mister
Hammond. We are going towards the buildings. We three
will take the further side, Mister McGrath the nearer.
Nobody is to make any disturbance or touch anything.
Observe closely. We must know how many men and officers
are here, and what weapons they have. Where they keep
the radio and telephone. What transport they have. The lay-
out of the terrain. Whether there are people on the ferry,
and what other boats there are.'

I whistled silently. It was a tall order. All he wanted to
know was absolutely everything.

'If you are caught,' he went on, 'make as much outcry as
you can, to alarm the others. But try not to reveal that they
exist. If the opportunity arises for you to steal weapons do
so, but do not use them.'

He looked intently at McGrath who showed no reaction
but that of careful attention. Sadiq said, 'I think that is all.
Good luck, gentlemen.'

The astounding thing was that it worked exactly as he planned it. In my imagination I had seen a hundred things going drastically wrong: ourselves captured, tortured, shot, the site overrun with soldiers armed to the teeth, the ferry incapacitated or nonexistent . . . every obstacle under the sun placed between us and success. In fact it was all extremely easy and may well have been the most fruitful reconnaissance mission in the annals of warfare.

This was because there were so few men there. Our team made a count of fifteen, McGrath said seventeen, and the highest-ranking soldier we could spot was a corporal. They had rifles and one light machine-gun but no other weapons that we could see. There was a radio equipped with head-phones and another in one of the cars, but it was defunct; Hammond reported having seen its guts strewn about the passenger seat. There were two trucks, one with a shattered windscreen, a Suzuki four-wheel drive workhorse and a beat-up elderly Volvo.

This was a token detachment, set there to guard some-thing that nobody thought to be of the least importance. After all, nobody from Manzu was going to come willingly into a neighbouring battle zone, especially when the craft to bring them was on the wrong side of the water.

The two teams met an hour and a half later back at the dinghy and compared notes. We were extremely pleased with ourselves, having covered all Sadiq's requirements, and heady with relief at having got away with it. Perhaps only McGrath was a little deflated at the ease of the mis-sion.

I would have liked another look at that ferry but anchored as she was out in midstream there was no way we could approach her unseen. Whatever it was about her that bothered me would have to wait.

We did some energetic baling with the beer cans and set off upriver, again keeping close to the bank and using oars until we were out of earshot of the ferry point. It was harder work rowing upstream, but once the outboard was persuaded to run we made good time. It was midday when we got back.

We reported briefly on our findings which cheered everyone enormously. We had discovered that the landing point was called Kanjali, although the joke of trying to call it the Fort Pirie Ferry, a genuine tongue twister, had not yet palled. But we didn't know if the ferry itself was in good running order. It might have been sabotaged or put out of action officially as a safeguard. And the problem of who was to run it was crucial.

After a light meal we went to see the raft builders at work.

Dufour had a dry, authoritative manner which compensated for his lack of Nyalan, which was supplemented by Atheridge. With Sadiq's men as interpreters they had rounded up a number of Nyalans who were willing to help in return for a ride to Manzu, and some who didn't want even that form of payment. These people were free in a sense we could hardly understand, free to melt back into the bush country they knew, to go back to their villages where they were left to get along unassisted by government programmes, but also untrammelled by red tape and regulations. But the rig had come to mean something extra to them, and because of it they chose to help us. It was as simple as that.

One of our problems was how to fasten the outer ring of 'B'-gons together. We'd not got anywhere with this until Hammond gave us the solution.

'You'd think we could come up with something,' he said, 'with all the friends we've got here pulling for us.'

'Friends,' I murmured. 'Polonius.'

'What?'

'I was just thinking about a quote from Hamlet. Polonius was giving Laertes advice about friendship.' I felt rather pleased with myself; it wasn't only the British who could play literary games. 'He said, "Grapple them to thy soul with hoops of steel." I could do with some hoops of steel right now.'

Hammond said, 'Would mild steel do?'

'You mean you've got some?' I asked incredulously.

He pointed to an empty drum. 'Cut as many hoops as you like from one of these things.'

'By God, so we can! Well done, Ben. Is there a cutting nozzle with the oxyacetylene outfit?'

'Hold on, Neil,' he said. 'Those drums will be full of petrol vapour. You put a flame near one and it'll explode. We have to do it another way.'

'Then we need a can opener.'

'You'll have one,' he promised.

Hammond's idea of a can opener was interesting. If you can't invent the necessary technology then you fall back on muscle. Within an hour he had twenty Nyalan men hammering hell out of the empty drums, using whatever they could find in the way of tools, old chisels, hacksaw blades, sharp-edged stones. They made the devil of a row but they flayed the drums open, cutting them literally into ribbons.

At the 'A'-gon construction site Dufour had assembled four teams and it took each team about one hour to make one 'A'-gon. In a factory it would have been quicker, but here the work force chatted and sang its way through the allotted tasks at a pace not exactly leisurely but certainly undemanding. Dufour knew better than to turn martinet and try to hurry them.

In some of the old school textbooks there were problems such as this; if it takes one man six hours to dig a pit seven feet long by six feet deep by two feet wide, then how long will it take three men to perform the same task? The text-book answer is two hours, which is dead wrong. Those who have done the dismal job know that it's a one-man operation

because two men get in each other's way and three men can
hardly work at all.

Dufour, knowing this, had seen to it that nobody could
get in each other's way and not one motion was wasted. For
an inexperienced work force it was miraculous, any efficiency expert would have been proud of it. Altogether it
was a remarkable operation.

It started at the sawmill where a team cut timber into
precise measurements, and the wood was hauled down to
the shore. Sufficient pieces were doled out to the construction groups, each one a fair way from the next along the
shore. Each team consisted of one Wyvern man, three
Nyalan men and a few women, including even those with
babies on their backs or toddlers at their sides.

The four men would each lay a beam on the ground, setting them between pegs driven into the sand so that they
would be in exactly the right place. Meantime another force
was rolling empty, tight-bunged drums along the shore
from the compound and stacking them at each site, seven at
a time. The four men would stand the drums on the cross-
beams inside the circle of vertical stakes which formed the
primitive jig. Little pegs were being whittled by some of the
elderly folk, and these went into holes drilled in the ends of
each crossbeam. The sidebeams would then be dropped to
stand at right angles to the bases, the pegs slotting into holes
drilled close to the bottom. Another set of pegs at the top of
each side beam held the top cross-members in position, and
halfway up yet another set of horizontal struts completed
the cage.

At this stage the 'A'-gon was held together only by the
pegs and the jig in which it rested. Now the women bound
it all together with cordage. This was the longest part of the
operation so the men would move to a second jig.

Once the 'A'-gon was finished a strong-arm team would
heave it out of the jig. It was here that the binding sometimes

failed and had to be redone. They would dump it on a rubber car mat and drag it the short distance to the water to be floated off. Then the whole process started again. The guy called Taylor who pioneered the science of time and motion study would have approved.

In the water a bunch of teenagers, treating the whole thing as a glorious water carnival, floated the 'A'-gons to the 'B'-gon construction site. Four teams took about an hour to make enough basic components for one 'B'-gon. I reckoned that we'd have both 'B'-gons, plus a few spare 'A'-gons, finished before nightfall.

I went to visit Wingstead on the rig during the early afternoon. I filled him in on progress. He was wan but cheerful, and that description also precisely suited his nurse, Sister Mary, of whom he seemed in some awe. I also looked in on Lang and was saddened by his deterioration. All the nursing in the world couldn't make up for the lack of medical necessities. I found Grafton on the rig as well. He had broken his ankle slipping between two 'A'-gon drums, and this accentuated the need for decking our extraordinary craft.

This was solved by a trip to the logging mill. There were tall young trees which had been cut and trimmed for use as telegraph poles, and it was a fairly easy job to run them through the cutters so that the half-sections would form perfect decking. Getting them back proved simple, with so many hands available. This operation was in the hands of Zimmerman and Vashily, who had emptied enough empty drums for both 'A'-gons and the steel lashings. Zimmerman said that he never wanted to have anything more to do with oil for the rest of his life.

The day wore on. The Nyalan foragers had found some food for everybody. Teams of swimmers were lifting floating planks onto the deck of the first completed 'B'-gon. It was an ungainly structure, with odd scalloped edges and splintery sides, but it floated high and lay fairly steadily in the water. On measuring we found that we could get one truck of not more than an eight foot beam on to it. Provided it could be driven on board.

Zimmerman, still scrounging about the camp for useful materials, came to me for a word in private.

'Neil, you'd better know about this,' he said. 'I checked all the trucks including the Frog's.' Dufour had been careful with his truck, always driving it himself and parking it away from the others at camp stops.

'He's carrying a mixed cargo of basic supplies. Ben will be happy to know that there is some oxygen and acetylene and some welding rods. But that's not all. The guy is breaking the law. He's carrying six cases of forty per cent blasting gelignite and they aren't on his manifest. That's illegal, explosives should never be carried with a mixed cargo.'

'We ought to stop him carrying it, but what the hell can we do with it? Dump it?'

'Must we?' he asked wistfully. Explosives were his profession.

'OK, not yet. But don't let Dufour know you're on to him. Just make sure nobody smokes around his truck. No wonder he parks it way off.' It was a possible weapon with Zimmerman's expertise to make the best use of it.

Progress on the second 'B'-gon was going well, but I called a halt. We were getting tired and this was when accidents were most likely to occur.

It was time for a council of war.

After the evening meal the crew gathered round and I counted and assessed them. There were fifteen men but I discounted two at once.

'Geoff, you're not coming.' Wingstead had been allowed to eat with us and afterwards he must have given his watchdog nurse the slip. He was very drawn but his eyes were brighter and he looked more like the man I'd first met.

He said ruefully, 'I'm not quite the idiot I was a couple of days ago. But I can sit on your council, Neil. I have to know what you plan to do, and I might be able to contribute.'

'Fair enough,' I said. Just having Wingstead there was a boost.

'And Derek's also out of it. He can't walk, ankle's swollen like a balloon,' Wingstead said. 'He's pretty mad.'

'Tell him I'll trade places,' offered Thorpe.

I said, 'Not a chance, Ritchie – you're stuck with this. You should never have been around in Port Luard when I needed a co-driver.'

'Wouldn't have missed it for the world,' he said bravely.

I turned to the next lame duck.

'Dan,' I said gently, 'it's not on, you know.'

He glanced down at his still splinted arm and heaved a sigh. 'I know. But you take bloody good care of Antoine here, you hear me?' He and the Frenchman exchanged smiles.

'Bert, how's your leg?'

Proctor said, 'Good as new, Mister Mannix. No problem, I promise you,' for which I was grateful. He was one of the stalwarts and we needed him. Kemp's shoulder would not hamper him, and there were no other injuries among us.

I said, 'Sadiq has got twenty-one men. There's one down with dysentery. With twelve of us that makes thirty-four to their seventeen: two to one. With those odds, I don't see how we can fail.'

A figure slid into the circle and I made room for him to sit beside me. It was Captain Sadiq.

I said, 'Basically what we have to do is this. We're going downriver on the "B"-gon. We get there before first light. We try to overpower them without much fighting. We've got a few weapons and we'll be able to get theirs if our surprise is complete. Ideally we don't want any shooting at all.'

'Squeamish, Mannix?' asked McGrath.

'Not at all,' I said coldly. 'But we don't know how near any reinforcements might be. We keep this as quiet as possible.'

There was a slight stir around the circle at our exchange.

'We have to get their radio under control, don't we?' Bing asked.

I had refrained, against my first instincts, from forbidding him to join the expedition. He was nineteen and by medieval standards a grown man ripe for blooding, and this was as near to medieval warfare as you could get. He was fit, intelligent and fully aware of the danger.

'Yes, that's going to be your baby,' I said. 'Your group's first priority will be to keep it undamaged and prevent their using it. The one in the car looks out of action but you'll make sure of that too. Brad, you run the interference for Sandy, OK?' He may not know American football terms, but the inference was obvious and he nodded fervently. Bing was his responsibility.

'Captain?' I turned to Sadiq.

'My men will make the first sortie,' he said. 'We have weapons and training which you do not have. We should be able to take the whole detachment without much trouble.'

Zimmerman whispered hasty translations to Kirilenko,

'Bert, you and Ben and Antoine immobilize all the transport you can find,' I said. 'Something temporary, a little more refined than a crowbar through the transmission.'

'Not a problem,' Bert said, his usual phlegmatic response.

'Mick, you cover Bing in the radio room and then check their weapon store; pile up everything you can. Use . . .' I was about to assign Bob Pitman to him, but remembered that Pitman had no reason to trust McGrath. 'Use Harry and Kirilenko.' They would make a good team.

I waited to see if McGrath was going to make any suggestions of his own but he remained silent. He didn't make me feel easy but then nothing about McGrath ever did.

I turned to Pitman.

'Bob, you stick with me and help me secure the raft. Then we cover the ramp where they load the ferry, you, me and Kemp. We'll want you to look at it from a transportation point of view, Basil.' If he thought for one second that he could get his rig on board the ferry he'd be crazy but he needed to be given at least some faint reason for hope in that direction. I looked round.

'Ritchie, I need a gofer and you're the lucky man. You liaise between me, Captain Sadiq and the other teams. I hope you're good at broken field running.'

'Me? Run? I used to come last at *everything*, Mister Mannix,' he said earnestly. 'But I'll run away any time you tell me to!'

Again laughter eased the tension a little. I was dead tired and my mind had gone a total blank. Anything we hadn't covered would have to wait for the next day. The conference broke up leaving me and Sadiq facing one another in the firelight.

'Do you think we can do it, Captain?' I asked.

'I think it is not very likely, sir,' he said politely. 'But on the other hand I do not know what else we can do. Feeding women and pushing oil drums and caring for the sick – that is not a soldier's work. It will be good to have a chance to fight again.'

He rose, excused himself and vanished into the darkness, leaving me to stare into the firelight and wonder at the way different minds worked. What I was dreading he anticipated with some pleasure. I remembered wryly a saying from one of the world's lesser literary figures, Bugs Bunny: Humans are the craziest people.

TWENTY-SIX

By late afternoon the next day the lakeside was in a state of barely controlled turmoil. Tethered to the shore as close as possible without grounding lay the first 'B'-gon. It was held by makeshift anchors, large rocks on the end of some rusty chains. A gangplank of half-sectioned logs formed a causeway along which a truck could be driven on to the raft. Beyond it lay the second raft, just finished.

Nyalans clustered around full of pride and excitement at seeing their home-made contraptions being put to use. A few had volunteered to come with us but Sadiq had wisely vetoed this idea. I don't think he was any happier about us either but here he had no choice.

From the rig patients and nurses watched with interest. Our intention was to have the truck ready on board rather than manoeuvre it in the dark of the following morning.

'Why a truck at all?' Wingstead had asked. 'If you take Kanjali there'll be transport in plenty there for you. And there'll be no means to unload this one.'

'Think of it as a Trojan Horse, Geoff,' I'd said. 'For one thing it'll have some men in it and the others concealed behind it If the rebels see us drifting towards them then all they'll see is a truck on a raft and a couple of men waving and looking helpless. For another, it'll take quite a bit of equipment, weapons and so on. They'll be safer covered up. It's not a truck for the time being, it's a ship's bridge.'

Hammond approved. He was the nearest thing to a naval man we had, having served in a merchant ship for a short time. I had appointed him skipper of the 'B'-gon. 'Inside the cab I've a much better view than from deck.'

There was a fourth reason, but even Hammond didn't know it.

The gangplank was ready. Kemp as load master beckoned the truck forward. The driver was Mick McGrath. It was going to be a ticklish operation to get the thing safely on board and he was the best we had, apart from Hammond himself. Zimmerman disappeared behind the truck as McGrath started to drive down the shore.

There was a sudden high grinding scream from the truck's engine and the vehicle lurched, bucked and came to a standstill. McGrath's face, looking puzzled and annoyed, appeared at the cab window. Voices shouted simultaneously.

'Christ, watch out! The rear wheel's adrift!'

McGrath jumped down and glared at the damage. One tyre was right off its axle and the truck was canted over into the dust, literally stranded.

'Fetch the jacks!' he called.

I said, 'No time – get another truck. Zimmerman, go drive one down here! You men get cracking and unload the gear.' I gave them no time to think and Kemp, always at his best in a transport crisis, was at my elbow. Considering that I'd anticipated the accident and he hadn't, he coped very well. Swiftly he cleared a path through the littered beach so that a second truck could get around the stranded one and still be able to mount the causeway. An engine roared as Zimmerman returned with the replacement.

Antoine Dufour sprang forward, his face suddenly white.

'No! Not that one – that's *my* truck!' he yelled.

His vehemence startled the men around him.

'Come on, Frenchie, any damn truck'll do,' someone said.

'Not that one!'

'Sorry, Dufour; it must have been the nearest to hand,' I said crisply. Dufour was furious but impotent to stop the truck as it passed us and lined up precisely at the causeway. Zimmerman leapt out of the cab for McGrath to take his place, but Dufour was on top of him.

'You not take my truck, by God!' He lapsed into a spate of French as he struggled to pass Zimmerman who held him back.

'Pack it in!' Kemp's voice rose. 'Dufour, ease off. This truck's part of the convoy now and we'll damn well use it if we have to.'

I said urgently, 'McGrath – get in there and drive it on fast.'

He looked at me antagonistically.

'There are other trucks, Mannix. Let the Frenchy alone.'

'Will you for God's sake obey an order!' I hadn't expected opposition from anyone but Dufour himself. McGrath's eyes locked with mine for a moment and then he pushed his way past Dufour and Zimmerman, swung himself aboard and gunned the motor. He slammed the truck into gear and jerked it onto the causeway. Then common sense made him calm down to inch the truck steadily onto the oddly-shaped 'B'-gon raft. The thing tipped under the weight but to our relief did not founder, and although water lapped about the truck's wheels it was apparent that we had a going proposition on our hands. The cheer that went up was muted. The onlookers were still puzzled by Dufour's outburst.

Kemp got men to put chocks under the truck's wheels and make lashings fast. The gear was loaded. Then the raft was hauled further out to lie well clear of the bank.

I turned my attention to Dufour.

He had subsided but was pale and shaken. As I passed Zimmerman I gave him a small nod of approval, then took Dufour's arm.

'Antoine,' I said, 'come with me. I want a word.'

As we walked away he stared over his shoulder at his truck where it rode on our ridiculous raft offshore and out of his reach.

We stopped out of earshot of the others.

'Antoine, I apologize. It was a dirty trick to play.'

'Monsieur Mannix, you do not know what you have done,' he said.

'Oh yes I do. You are thinking of your secret cargo, aren't you?'

His jaw dropped. 'You *know?*'

'Of course I know. Zimmerman found it and told me. It's his trade, don't forget. He could probably sniff out gelignite at a mile.'

Dufour stared at me appalled. I had to reassure him on one point at once.

'Now, listen. I don't care a damn why you have the stuff. Or where you got it. It's no bloody business of mine. But right now that stuff you've got is the best weapon in our whole arsenal, and to get ourselves and everyone else out of this mess we need it.'

'Oh, my God.' As he looked at me and I saw a bitter smile on his face. 'Gelignite. You want to use my truck to blow up the enemy, yes?'

'I hope not. But it's a damn good threat. Harry Zimmerman will pass the word around, and the assault team will know that we've got a bomb out there. It'll be like pointing a cannon. The rebels have no weapon that can reach us, and we've got one that can devastate them. That's why we have the second "B"-gon along; if we need to we evacuate the first, aim it at the landing point and let her rip. Now do you understand?'

'Suppose I told you the gelignite was worthless.'

DESMOND BAGLEY

'Don't try. We need it.'

He sat down as if his knees had given way. After a couple of minutes he raised his face and said, 'Yes, I understand. You are a clever man, Monsieur Mannix. Also a bastard. I wish us all luck.'

Back at the camp I put my affairs in order. I wrote a personal letter to leave with the Doctor, and gave Sam Kironji an impressive-looking letter on British Electric notepaper, promising that my company would reimburse him for all expenses and recommending him for a bonus. This I implemented with a cash bonus of my own which impressed him even more.

Wingstead and I discussed the rig. If we took the ferry the convoy would move to Kanjali so that the patients could be transferred. And there the rig would have to be abandoned.

'We have to be careful of Kemp, though,' Wingstead said. 'The rig means a lot more to him than to me. It's extraordinary; personally I think he's been bitten by the juggernaut bug as hard as any of the Nyalans.'

'I wonder what they'll do when it grinds to a halt and we abandon it,' I said idly.

'Go home again. It'll probably end up in their mythology.'

'And the rig itself?'

'Whoever gets into power will engage someone to drive it up to Bir Oassa, I suppose. It'll be an interesting exercise in international finance, sorting out the costs and legalities involved. But I'll tell you one thing, Neil, whoever takes it it won't be me. I've had it here. I'll sell it to the best offer.'

'And what then?'

'Go back home with Kemp and Hammond and build a better one. We've learned a hell of a lot out here.'

'Stick to hydroelectric schemes in Scotland, will you?'

He laughed. 'That's the way I feel now. As for later, who knows?'

* * *

For the second day running we embarked in the chill small hours to sail down the Katali River to Kanjali. I felt very apprehensive. Yesterday had been an unnerving experience for anyone untrained in guerrilla warfare. Today was terrifying.

The two 'B'-gons were barely visible. We used the run-about as a tender, poling it over the dark water to lie along-side the 'B'-gon on which stood the darker bulk of the truck. We scrambled aboard, passing our weapons up to be stowed in the truck.

Hammond and his work team had lashed the two 'B'-gons together, slotting hexagon shapes into one another, adding a couple of 'A'-gons here and there and assembling the thing like a child's toy.

The truck barely fitted on the after section, a foot of space to spare around it. With its high rear section and flat for-ward deck it was a travesty of the ferry at Kanjali. Aft on a crossbeamed structure Hammond had mounted Sam Kironji's outboard motors; one was a seven horsepower job and one six, which meant they were close enough in motive power not to send us in a circle. He had a man on each throttle and would control their speed and direction from the cab of the truck.

We were all very quiet as we set off.

We'd made our farewells, temporary ones I hoped. Dr Kat said that Lang might not live to see Manzu. I wondered how many of us would.

I had one curious experience on the journey. I hadn't forgotten McGrath's belligerence on the beach, and twice since he'd jibbed at instructions in a way that I could only think of as petulant. He wasn't just important to the success of our mission, he was vital. I had to find out what was bothering him.

'McGrath, I want to talk to you.'

He turned away.

'Now!'

I moved crouching away from the others and felt some relief that he followed me. We made our way forward, where small waves broke coldly over our faces.

'Mick, what the hell is eating you?' I asked.

He looked sullen. 'Nothing. I don't know what you mean,' he said. He didn't look at me.

'If you've got a gripe for God's sake say so.'

'We're not in the army, Mannix. You're not my officer and I'm not your bloody sergeant.'

'Oh Jesus!' I said. 'A goddamn prima donna. What's your beef?'

'Stop bloody ordering me about. I'm fed up with it.'

I took a deep breath. This was crazy.

I said, 'Mick, you're the best driver we've got. You're also the nearest thing we've got to a soldier, and we're going to need your know-how more than anyone else's, even Sadiq.'

'Now don't think I'll jump when you say so, Mannix, just for a bit of flattery,' he said. To my disbelief his tone was one of pique.

'OK, McGrath, no flattery. But what's really eating you?'

He shrugged. 'Nothing.'

'Then why go temperamental on me? You've never been afraid to speak your mind before.'

He made a fist with one hand and banged it into the other. 'Well, you and me were friendly, like. We think the same way. But ever since Makara and that bit of a fight at the bridge, you've hardly said a word to me.'

I regarded him with profound astonishment. This tough and amoral man was behaving like a schoolboy who'd been jilted in his first calf love.

'I've been goddamn busy lately.'

'There's more to it than that. I'd say you've taken a scunner to me. Know what that means, Yank?'

'I don't know what the hell you're talking about. If you don't take orders I can't trust you and I won't let this whole operation fall apart because of your injured feelings. When we arrive at Kanjali you stay back on the raft. Damned if I'll entrust Bing or anyone else to your moods!'

I rose abruptly to go back to the shelter of the truck. He called after me, 'Mannix! Wait!'

I crouched down again, a ludicrous position in which to quarrel, and waited.

'You're right. I'm sorry. I'll take your orders. You'll not leave me behind, will you?'

For a moment I was totally lost for words.

'All right,' I said at last, wearily. 'You come as planned. And you toe the line, McGrath. Now get back into shelter or we'll both freeze.'

Later I thought about that curious episode.

During his stint in the army and presumably in Ireland too he had never risen in rank; a man to take orders, not quite the loner he seemed. But the man whose orders he obeyed had to be one he respected, and this respect had nothing to do with rank or social standing. He had no respect for Kemp and not much for Wingstead. But for me, perhaps because I'd had the nerve to tackle him directly about Sisley's murder, certainly because he'd sensed the common thread that sometimes linked our thoughts and actions, it seemed that he had developed that particular kind of respect.

But lately I had rejected him. I had in fact avoided him ever since we'd found the body of Ron Jones. And he was sensitive enough to feel that rejection. *By God, Mannix*, I thought. *You're a life-sized father figure to a psychopath*!

Once again as we neared Kanjali dawn was just breaking. The sky was pinkish and the air raw with the rise of the morning wind. Hammond instructed the engine handlers to throttle back so that we were moving barely faster than the run of the current. Before long the two bulky outlines, the ferry and the buildings on the bank, came steadily into view, Sadiq gave quiet orders and his men began handing down their rifles from the truck.

Hammond brought us close to the bank some way upstream from where he intended to stop, and the raft nuzzled into the fringing reeds which helped slow its progress. A dozen men flung themselves overboard and splashed ashore carrying mooring lines, running alongside the raft until Hammond decided to go no further. I thought of his fear of crocodiles and smiled wryly. The noise we were making was enough to scare off any living thing and I could only pray that it wouldn't carry down to the men sleeping at Kanjali.

We tied up securely and the weapons were handed ashore. Hammond set his team to separating the two parts of the raft into their original 'B'-gon shapes and transferring the two outboards to a crossbeam on the section without the truck. This was to be either our escape craft or our means of crossing to Manzu to seek help in handling the ferry.

Once on shore I had my first chance to tell Hammond privately about Dufour's truck. 'Harry saw six cases of the stuff, and checked one to be sure. If we have to we're going to threaten to use it like a fire ship. Harry's got a firing mechanism worked out. He'll come back here, set it and cut the raft free.'

'It might float clear before it goes off, Neil,' Hammond said. His horror at this amateurish plan made me glad I hadn't told him about it sooner. 'Or run aground too soon. The firing mechanism might fail. Or blow itself to smithereens and never touch Kanjali at all!'

'You know that and I know that, but will they? We'll make the threat so strong that they won't dare disbelieve it.'

It was a pretty desperate plan but it was all we had. And it didn't help that at this point Antoine Dufour approached us and said, 'Please, Monsieur Mannix, do not put too much faith in my cargo, I beg of you.' He looked deeply troubled.

'What's the matter with it? If it's old and unstable we'll have to take our chances,' I said brusquely.

'Aah, no matter.' His shrug was eloquent of distress. I sensed that he wanted to say more but my recent brush with McGrath had made me impatient with other men's problems. I had enough on my plate.

Sadiq and his men moved out. The rest of us followed, nervous and tense. We moved quietly, well down in the cover of the trees and staying far back enough from Sadiq's squad to keep them in sight until the moment they rushed the buildings. We stopped where the vegetation was cut back to make way for the landing point. I had a second opportunity to look at the moored ferry where it was caught in the sun's first rays as though in a searchlight beam.

This time I recognized what had eluded me before.

This was no modern ferry. It was scarred and battered, repainted many times but losing a battle to constant rust, a valiant old warhorse now many years from its inception and many miles from its home waters. It was an LCM, Landing Craft Mechanized, a logistics craft created during the war years that led up to the Normandy landings in 1944. Developed from the broad-beamed, shallow-draughted barges of an earlier day, these ships had carried a couple of tanks, an assortment of smaller vehicles or a large number of men into action on the sloping European beaches. Many of them were still in use all over the world. It was about fifty feet long.

What this one was doing here on an inland lake up an unnavigable river was anybody's guess.

I turned my attention to Kanjali, lying below us. There were five buildings grouped around the loading quay. A

spur from the road to Fort Pirie dropped steeply to the
yards. Running into the water was a concrete ramp, where
the bow of the ferry would drop for traffic to go aboard. A
couple of winches and sturdy bollards stood one to either
side. Just beyond was a garage.

The largest building was probably the customs post, not
much bigger than a moderate-sized barn. Beyond it there
was a larger garage, a small shop and filling station, and a
second barn-like building which was probably a warehouse.

Sadiq's men fanned out to cover the customs post front
and rear, the store and warehouse. Our team followed more
hesitantly as we decided where to go. Kemp, Pitman and I
ran to our post, the landing stage, and into cover behind the
garage. Thorpe was at my heels but I told him to go with
McGrath and he veered away.

We waited tensely for any sounds. Kemp was already
casting a careful professional eye on the roadway to the
landing stage and the concrete wharf beside it on the shore.
It was old and cracked, with unused bollards along it, and
must have been used to ship and unship goods from smaller
craft in the days before the crossing had a ferry. But it made
a good long piece of hard ground standing well off the road,
and Kemp was measuring it as another staging post for the
rig. The steep spur road might be a problem.

We heard nothing.

'Shall I go and look?' Pitman asked after several inter-
minable minutes. I shook my head.

'Not yet, Bob.'

As I spoke a voice shouted and another answered it.
There were running footsteps and a sudden burst of rifle
fire. I flattened myself to peer round the corner of the
garage. As I did so an unmistakably male European voice
called from inside it, 'Hey! What's happening out there?'

We stared at one another. Near us was a boarded-up
window. I reached up and pounded on it.

'Who's in there?'

'For God's sake, let us out!'

I heaved a brick at the window, shattering glass but not breaching the boards that covered it. The doors would be easier. We ran round to the front to see a new padlock across the ancient bolt. Then the yard suddenly swarmed with figures running in every direction. There were more rifle shots.

I struggled vainly with the padlock.

Kemp said, 'They're on the run, by God!'

He was right. A few soldiers stood with their arms raised. Some slumped on the ground. Others were streaking for the road. Someone started the Volvo but it slewed violently and crashed into the side of the warehouse. Sadiq's men surrounded it as the driver, a Nyalan in civilian clothing, staggered out and fell to the ground. The door to the main building was open and two of our soldiers covered as men ran across the clearing and vanished inside, Bishop, Bing, McGrath and I thought Kirilenko, en route I hoped for the radio.

Sadiq's men were hotfoot after stragglers.

Neither Kemp, Pitman nor I were directly involved and within five minutes from the first shout it was all over. It was unnerving; the one thing my imagination had never dared to consider was a perfect takeover.

Hammond came away from one of the trucks grinning broadly and waving a distributor cap. Sadiq was every-where, counting men, posting sentries, doing a textbook mopping up operation. We went to join the others, leaving whoever was in the locked garage to wait.

'Christ, that was fantastic. Well done, Captain! How many were there?'

Hammond said, 'We reckon not more than fourteen, less than we expected.'

'Any casualties?'

McGrath was beside me, grinning with scorn. 'Not to us and hardly to them. A few sore heads, mostly. Those laddies were half asleep and didn't know what hit them. A few ran off, but I don't think they'll be telling tales. They thought we were demons, I reckon.'

I looked around. Several faces were missing.

'Bing?' I asked.

'He's fine, already playing with that dinky radio set of theirs. Brad and Ritchie are with him,' McGrath said.

'The Volvo's had it,' said Hammond, 'but the other vehicles are fine. We can use them any time we want to. They didn't even have a sentry posted.'

It wasn't too surprising. They had no reason to expect trouble, no officer to keep them up to the mark, and probably little military training in the first place. I said, 'We've found something interesting. There's someone locked in the garage by the landing. There's a padlock but we can shoot it off.'

We gathered round the garage door and I yelled, 'Can you hear us in there?'

A muffled voice shouted back, 'Sure can. Get us out of here!'

'We're going to shoot the lock off. Stand clear.'

One of Sadiq's men put his gun to the padlock and blew it and a chunk of the door apart. The doors sagged open.

I suppose we looked as haggard and dirty to the two men who emerged as they looked to us. Both were white, one very large and somewhat overweight, the other lean and sallow-skinned. Their clothing was torn and filthy, and both were wounded. The big man had a dirtily bandaged left arm, the other a ragged and untreated scabby gash down the side of his face. The lean man took a couple of steps, wavered and slid gently to his knees.

We jumped to support him.

'Get him into the shade,' Kemp said, 'Fetch some water. You OK?'

The big man nodded and walked unaided. I thought that if he fell it would take four of us to carry him.

I left Kemp to supervise for a moment, and took Sadiq aside.

'Are you really in full command here?' I asked. 'What about the men who ran off?'

'They will probably run away and not report to anyone. But if they do I hope it will be a long time before others get here.'

'Do you think it's safe to bring the convoy here? If we can work the ferry we won't have any time to waste.' Already hope was burgeoning inside me. Sadiq thought in his usual careful way before replying.

'I think it is worth the chance.'

I called to Kemp. 'Basil, take your team and get back to Kironji's place. Start shifting the convoy. Leave the fuel tanker and the chuck wagon. Bring the rig and tractors, and cram the rest into a truck or two, no more.'

The two newcomers were being given some rough and ready first aid. Bishop had found the food stores and was preparing a meal for us, which was welcome news indeed.

I went back to squat down beside the recent prisoners.

'I'm Neil Mannix of British Electric, and this mob works for Wyvern Transport. We're taking stuff to the oilfields . . . or were when the war started. The soldiers with us are loyal to Ousemane's government. We're all in a bit of a fix, it seems.'

The big man gave me a smile as large as his face.

'A fix it certainly is. Bloody idiots! After all I've done for them too. You're American, aren't you? I'm pleased to meet you – all of you. You've done us a good turn, pitching up like this. My name's Pete Bailey, and it's a far cry from Southampton where I got my start in life.' He extended a vast hand to engulf mine. Good humour radiated from him.

His hand bore down on the shoulder of his companion. 'And this here is my pal Luigi Sperrini. He talks good English but he doesn't think so. Say hello, Luigi, there's a good lad.'

Sperrini was in pain and had little of his friend's apparently boundless stamina but he nodded courteously.

'I am Sperrini. I am grateful you come,' he said and then shut his eyes. He looked exhausted.

'Tell the lads to hurry with that food,' I said to Bishop, and then to Bailey, 'How long were you two guys locked in there?'

'Four days we made it. Could have been a little out, mark you, not being able to tell night from day. Ran out of water too. Silly idiots, they look after their bloody cattle better than that.' But there didn't seem to be much real animosity in him, in spite of the fact that he and his companion seemed to be a fair way to being callously starved to death.

I braced myself for the question I most wanted to ask.

'Who are you guys anyway? What do you do?'

And I got the answer I craved.

'What do you think, old son? We run the bloody ferry.'

TWENTY-SEVEN

'Will she run?'

Bailey carne close to being indignant at the question.

'Of course she'll run,' he said. 'Luigi and I don't spend a dozen hours a day working on her just for her looks. *Katie Lou* is as sweet a little goer as the girl I named her for, and a damn sight longer lasting.'

The time we spent between taking Kanjali and waiting for the convoy to arrive was well spent. We found a decent store of food and set about preparing for the incoming convoy. We found and filled water canteens, tore sheets into bandaging, and checked on weapons and other stores. We seemed to have stumbled on a treasure house.

The radio was a dead loss; even with parts cannibalized from the other Bing couldn't make it function, which left us more frustrated for news than ever. Bailey and Sperrini could tell us little; we were more up to date than they were. We were fascinated to learn, however, that the juggernaut had already been heard of.

'The hospital that goes walkabout,' said Bailey. 'It's true then. We thought it just another yarn. They said it had hundreds of sick people miraculously cured, magic doctors and the like. I don't suppose it was quite like that.'

'Not quite,' I said dryly, and enlightened them. Bailey was glad that there were real doctors on the way, not for himself but for Sperrini, whose face looked puffy and inflamed, the wound obviously infected.

'One of their laddies did that with his revolver,' Bailey said. 'First they shot me in the arm, silly buggers. If they'd been a little more polite we might have been quite cooperative. As if I could run away with *Katie Lou* – I ask you! She can't exactly go anywhere now, can she?'

'Except to Manzu,' I said, and told him what we wanted. 'I'm surprised you didn't think of it yourselves.'

'Of course we could have taken her across,' he said tolerantly, 'but I didn't know we were supposed to be running away from anything until it was too late. The war didn't seem to be bothering us much. One minute we're unloading a shipment and the next the place is swarming with laddies playing soldiers. The head man demanded that we surrender the ferry. Surrender! I didn't know what he was talking about. Thought he'd got his English muddled; they do that often enough. Next thing they're damn well shooting me and beating up poor old Luigi here. Then they locked us both in.'

His breezy style belied the nastiness of what had happened.

'We tried to break out, of course. But I built that garage myself, you see, and made it good and burglar-proof, more fool me. They didn't touch *Auntie Bess* but the keys weren't there and I couldn't shift her. Tried to crosswire her but it wouldn't work. Must say I felt a bit of an idiot about that.'

'Who, or more likely what, is *Auntie Bess*? 'I asked. We hadn't been to look in his erstwhile prison yet.

'I'll show you but I'll have to find her keys. And to be honest I'd really rather get *Katie Lou* back into service first.'

Getting the ferry into service proved quite simple. There was a small runabout which Bailey used to get out to it, and in lieu of his trusty Sperrini he accepted the aid of Dufour, Zimmerman and Kirilenko. 'Parkinson's Law, you see,' he said with easy amusement. 'Three of you for one of him.

She only needs a crew of two really, but it's nice to have a bit of extra muscle.'

He took his crew out to *Katie Lou* and with assured competence got her anchors up, judged her position nicely and ran her gently up onto the loading ramp, dropping the bay door on the concrete with a hollow clang. He directed the tying up procedure and spent some time inspecting her for any damage. He found none.

Sperrini waited with resignation.

'He very good sailor,' he said. 'He never make mistake I ever see. For me, first rate partnership.'

Bailey was like Wingstead, engendering respect and liking without effort. I never had the knack; I could drive men and direct them, but not inspire them, except maybe McGrath, which didn't please me. I'd never noticed it before. The difficult journey we'd shared had opened my eyes to some human attributes which hadn't figured very strongly in my philosophy before now. On the whole I found it an uncomfortable experience.

I complimented Bailey on *Katie Lou's* performance and he beamed.

'She's a bit rusty but by God she can do the job,' he said. 'I knew we were on to a good thing from the start.'

'How the hell did she come to be here anyway?' I asked.

'Luigi and I used to run the old ferry. We've been in this trade for donkey's years, the two of us. The old ferry was a cow to handle and very limiting; only deck cargo and passengers and not too many of them. I saw that cars and trucks would want to cross as trade improved and the oilfields opened up. Manzu hasn't got any oil itself but it's got a damn sight better port for off-loading heavy gear.'

I made a mental note to remember this for later, assuming there would be a later.

'The two countries negotiated a traffic agreement. At a price, of course. We started to look for something better, and

I'd always had these old bow loaders in mind. Saw them in action on D-Day and never forgot them. Remember, I've been in this trade all my life. Started in Southampton docks as a nipper.'

'Me too, I sail with my father from a boy,' Sperrini put in.

'Don't ask us how we got her down to Nyala, laddie. It's a long tale and I'll tell it one day over a cold beer. But the long and short of it is that I got wind of this old LCM lying beached up on the North African coast and bought her for a song. Well, a whole damn opera really. Then we sailed her down the coast to Manzu and arranged to bring her over-land to Lake Pirie.'

I whistled. With the first-hand knowledge of large rig transport that I'd gained lately I knew this to be possible, but a hell of a job all the same. I said as much and he swelled with pride.

'A lovely operation, I tell you. Not a scratch on her – well, not too many. And has she ever paid off! Luigi and me, we're doing just fine.' He became pensive. 'Or we were. But when things get back to normal we might go looking for something bigger.'

Sandy Bing was prowling back and forth from the ferry yards up to the main road. His failure to get the radio going had niggled him and he was restless and anxious. Suddenly he ran towards us, interrupting Bailey's story with news of his own. The convoy was on the way.

I said to Bailey, 'We'll start to load invalids onto the ferry at once, plus any other Nyalans who want to go. I'd like one vehicle on board. The Land Rover, say.'

'No problem there.'

'How long will it take to unload and return? On the sec-ond run we'll want a couple of trucks. The more transport we have the better. Would there be time for a third trip?'

He said, 'I usually cross twice a day but that's not push-ing it. With luck I can be back in two hours, I doubt if there'll be anybody to help at the other side, it'll take time to get your sick folk unloaded. But we'll be back as soon as we can make it.'

Sperrini pushed himself up.

'Me, I come too,' he announced firmly. 'I maybe not work so good, but I watch out for you.'

Bailey said, 'Of course you'll come, mate. Couldn't do it without you. We'll need some of your lads, Neil.'

'You'll have them.'

He said, 'If there's trouble before I get back, what will you do?'

'We've got the transport we came here with. And by God, Pete, that's something you'd have to see to believe!' But I had my doubts about the 'B'-gon. It was moored too far away to be of use in a crisis. Bailey gave me one of his great smiles.

'Well, I've got the very thing if you need it. In fact I'd appreciate it if you'd bring it across anyway. You can use *Auntie Bess.*'

'Just what is *Auntie Bess*?'

'A duck,' he said, and laughed at my expression.

'A *duck*?' I had a sudden vision of Lohengrin's swan boat. 'We're going to float across the lake on a giant mutant muscovy, is that it?'

'Come and see,' he said. 'You'll love this.'

Zimmerman, Kirilenko and I followed him to the garage. We pulled the double doors wide and stared into the gloom. A long low shape sat there, puzzling for a moment and then marvellously, excitingly explicit.

'A DUKW!'

Bailey patted its hood lovingly.

'Meet *Auntie Bess*. Named for the most adaptable lady I've ever known. Nothing ever stopped her. I've found the keys and she's ready to go.'

We gathered round the thing, fascinated and intrigued. It was a low-profiled, topless vehicle some thirty feet in length, one set of tyres in front and two more pairs not quite at the rear, where dropping curved metal plates protected a propeller. It had a protruding, faintly boat-shaped front and was hung about with tyres lashed around what in a boat would be called the gunwale. The body was made of tough, reinforced metal, flanged down the sides, and the headlamps were set behind heavy mesh grilles. An old-fashioned windscreen provided all the cover the driver would get on land or water, though there were points along the sides where a framework could be inserted to carry a canvas awning.

Odds and ends of equipment for both elements on which it could travel were strapped about it; an anchor and line, a life belt, a couple of fuel cans, a tyre jack, shovel and spare tyres. Like the *Katie Lou* it was rusty but seemed in good repair. Bailey swung himself in and the engine came to life with a healthy rattle as it slid into the sunlight. He slapped its side with heavy-handed self-approval.

'I did think of calling her *Molly Brown*,' he said, 'but after all she might sink one of these days. She's got a tendency to ship a little water. But she's crossed this pond often enough and she'll do it once more for you, I promise.'

It could carry so many men that to bring off a dozen or so would be no problem. 'How hard is she to drive?' I asked.

Zimmerman said, 'I handled one on land once. Nothing to it. Don't know about the performance on water, though.'

Bailey said, 'Come on, let's go for a swim. I'll show you.'

Zimmerman swung himself on board and in front of an admiring audience the DUKW pounded down the causeway into the water. Pete Bailey was careful with *Katie Lou* but with his DUKW he was a bit of a cowboy. It chugged away throwing up an erratic bow wave to make a big circle on the lake.

The rig was arriving as we walked up the curving spur road from the ferry yard. Kemp and Hammond brought it to a stop on the main road that overlooked Kanjali. We got busy transferring the invalids into trucks to take them on board the ferry. Bailey and Sperrini came to see the rig and get medical attention.

The rig was as impressive as ever, its massive cargo still hulking down between the two trailers. The tractors coupled up fore and aft added power to its bulk. The modifications we had imposed made it look quite outlandish. By now the thatching had been blown away and renovated so often that it appeared piebald as the palm fronds weathered. A workmanlike canvas wall framed the operating theatre but the canvas itself was mildewed so that it looked like the camouflaging used during war to disguise gun emplacements. Sturdy rope ladders hung from every level and the faces of the patients peered out from their straw beds.

'Well, I'll be damned,' Bailey marvelled. 'Worth going a mile to see, that is – good as a circus any day. Hello, who's this?'

'This' was the Nyalan escort still following their fetish, overflowing the road and looked down at the ferry yard with curiosity. Sperrini put into words what we had been feeling about this strange parade for so long.

'It is a *processione sacra*,' he said solemnly. 'As is done to honour a saint.'

I told Kemp and Hammond about *Auntie Bess*. Hammond was delighted and regretted that he would probably have no time to play with the DUKW himself.

'We may have to use it as a getaway craft,' I said.

'What about the raft and Dufour's truck?'

'We might need it yet, if there's trouble,' I said. 'Ben, you and Harry and Kirilenko could slope off and bring the raft downriver closer to Kanjali. Still out of sight but where we can fetch it up bloody fast if we have to. This is strictly a volunteer assignment, though – what do you think?'

Hammond said, 'I'll do it. It would be a shame not to have a weapon like that handy should we need it.'

Zimmerman spoke rapidly to Kirilenko, then said, 'We're both on.'

'Off you go then. I'll cover for you. Try and make it quick.'

'Very funny, Neil,' Zimmerman said. I grinned and left them.

Unloading had begun. Wingstead and the rest had heard of the taking of Kanjali from Kemp; but none were ready for the sight of the ferry resting majestically on the causeway, the ramp down to form a welcome mat. Bishop and Bing were on board handing out food and water. The invalids were laid on straw mattresses.

Dr Kat was strict about rations. 'They can feed for a month on the other side,' he said. 'But too much too soon is dangerous. Nurse, tell them that the crossing will be less bumpy than the rig and not dangerous; some of them have never been on water before. And say there will be proper food and beds for them in Manzu. Sister Mary! What are you doing carrying that child! Put her down at once. Helen, take over there, please.' His eyes were everywhere, considering a hundred details. The excitement in the air and the prospect of salvation so close made him more cheerful than I'd ever seen him.

'How do you feel, leaving Nyala?' I asked during a lull. He regarded me with astonishment.

'How do you think I feel? Only relief, Mister Mannix. At last I see a hope of saving these poor people. I am tired, sad at our losses, infuriated by this senseless wasteful war and what is happening to my country. But I will come back soon enough. I intend to rebuild the hospital at Kodowa.'

He was a man dedicated and inspired. I said, 'You'll get all the help I can muster, and that's not peanuts.'

He hesitated, then said, 'Mister Lang is not going to live, I fear.'

'But we're so close to safety.'

He shook his head.

Impulsively I took his hand. 'We're all deeply in your debt, Doctor Katabisirua. I hope that will be recognized officially one day.'

He seemed pleased by my words as he went off to supervise the rest of the changeover with vigour.

Sister Ursula upbraided me for allowing Bing to go into battle, and for letting Bert Proctor so neglect his bullet-grazed leg as to risk a major infection. There was no pleasing that woman. She was efficient over Sperrini's face but couldn't get near enough to Bailey to administer to his arm. He was jovial but dismissive and I wondered why she let him get away with it.

By now all the invalids and the Land Rover were on board. The last of the Nyalans who wanted to cross were hurrying on, full of excitement. Those who were familiar with the ferry were explaining it to others.

Hammond, Thorpe and Kemp remained, as well as McGrath, Zimmerman, Kirilenko and Dufour. Bishop and Bing went with the first shipment. So did Pitman and Athebridge and Proctor, to act as crew and help unload at the far end. Only two need have stayed, to drive on the trucks, but there was some reluctance to leave the rig until necessary.

The bow ramp of the *Katie Lou* lifted, and we watched as she backed off the causeway, her temporary crewmen warping her out to her stern anchor, aided by a gentle reverse thrust of engines. As the anchor came up the current swung her round and the engines carried on the momentum. She pirouetted lazily to face away from us. Bailey waved from the bridge and the *Katie Lou* moved steadily into midstream, bearing its cargo of refugees away from us and the danger zone to freedom, we hoped, on the other side.

A burden lifted from us. Whatever happened to us now we were responsible for nobody but ourselves. We gave vent to our feelings with cheers of relief.

And then the air exploded. There was a whistling roar and a missile plummeted into the water well astern of the *Katie Lou*. A fountain of water jetted high into the air, followed by a second which was no closer. A dull thump followed as another missile slammed into the earth just behind the causeway, flinging debris and dust into the air. There was the staccato rattle of machine-gun fire from behind us, and a scream from the roadway.

'Oh Christ, the ferry!' Thorpe gasped.

'She's clear – she's out of range,' I said sharply.

Soldiers boiled out from behind the rig and ran down the spur road. Others erupted from the bush beyond the buildings much as we ourselves had done earlier. Sadiq's men were fighting against huge odds.

Zimmerman said, 'The raft. It's our only chance.'

He and Kirilenko hurtled down the causeway. They plunged into the water and vanished under the churned-up wake from the ferry. Hammond dropped into the fringing bushes along the lakeside. McGrath, using the dust cloud from the third explosion to mask his disappearance, slipped behind the garage in which *Auntie Bess* was parked. Dufour, Kemp, Ritchie Thorpe and I stood our ground. The rebels came running towards us and it took a lot of discipline to stand and face them. In a moment we were surrounded.

TWENTY-EIGHT

They were everywhere, poking into the warehouses and garages, examining the rig and the other vehicles of the convoy, beating the bushes for fugitives. On one side of the yard those of Sadiq's men whom they'd rounded up stood under guard. There were more guards around the four of us. We'd seated ourselves on crates to appear as innocuous as possible. I was grateful that they didn't bring *Auntie Bess* out of her garage, though there was some interest shown by those who went in to look at it. I guessed that Zimmerman had the keys.

It was satisfying that the ferry had got clean away. Whatever weapons they had didn't reach far over the water, and by now the *Katie Lou* was out of sight and very likely already at her destination. I hoped Bailey would not bring her back; we had discussed this eventuality and he had reluctantly agreed that if he got wind of trouble he was to stay away.

I felt angry with myself. If I hadn't insisted on a second cargo of trucks going across we'd all be safe by now.

There was no sign of the raft team, nor of McGrath. His disappearance was entirely typical, and I could only wish him luck in whatever he might be planning. That he had deserted us I felt was unlikely, as long as we had the DUKW as a means of escape.

After a nerve-racking wait we had more company. The inevitable staff car came down the spur road with two others trailing it, a motorcycle escort and a truckload of soldiers with a 76 mm gun mounted. We stood up slowly as the leading car stopped short of the causeway.

The man who got out of it was a tall, well-turned out officer with the colonel's insignia that I had come to recognize. Like Sadiq, he had an Arabic cast of feature but in his case it reminded me of the nomadic Tuareg I had seen in North Africa, fine-boned, carrying no spare flesh and insufferably haughty of expression. He wore a side arm and carried a swagger stick in gloved hands. He recalled irresistibly to mind my first senior officer in my army days; I'd hated that bastard too.

'Who are you?' he barked.

I glanced at Kemp and then took the role of spokesman. 'I'm Neil Mannix of British Electric,' I said. I was relieved that he seemed not to have heard of us by name, even if the bush telegraph had passed the word about the rig.

'The others?' he snapped impatiently.

'This is Mister Basil Kemp and this is Mister Thorpe, both of Wyvern Transport. And this is Monsieur Antoine Dufour, a friend. Who are you?'

'What?'

'Now you tell us who *you* are.'

He glowered at me but I was through with servility. I was going to stand by our rights as civilians, foreigners and employees of his country.

He nodded thoughtfully. 'You are angry. Well, Mister . . . Mannix, in your place so perhaps would I be. But I have no quarrel with you personally. You have been ill-advised and manipulated by the corrupt forces of the recent government and its military tyranny, but being ignorant of the destiny of Nyala and of your moral responsibilities towards it, your folly will have to be overlooked. I will redirect you in a more useful and productive fashion. It will be in your best interests to cooperate with good will.'

I suppose I looked as thunderstruck as I felt, and I could see from the faces of the others that they shared my amazement. This was less like Colonel Maksa's approach than anything we could have imagined.

I said, 'That all sounds most interesting, Colonel. What does it mean?'

'For you, very little. We wish you to undertake some work for us which is not beyond your scope or ability. Though I am afraid something more drastic may be called for in this case.' He indicated one of the cars behind his own. I saw with dismay that it was Sadiq's staff car, and that Sadiq was sitting in it. He was in the back seat between two guards, and he was handcuffed.

'You can't treat a prisoner of war like that. What the hell do you think you're doing?' I asked harshly. Sadiq was a good soldier and had stood by us; we had to stand up for him now.

The officer ignored this and said, 'I am Colonel Wadzi, of the army of the Peoples' Liberated Republic of Nyala. I have certain instructions for you. Are these all of your men?'

'Let Captain Sadiq go and then we'll talk about us.'

He spoke briefly, and the car in which Sadiq was being held pulled out of line and drove up the spur road and stopped at the top.

'Captain Sadiq is not the issue here. He will be tried for his offences,' Wadzi said. 'Now – which of you is in charge of this transporter?'

Kemp stepped forward, his face white.

'Don't you do anything to damage that rig,' he said with the courage of his deepest belief.

Wadzi smiled tautly. 'I would not dream of harming it. My superiors are well aware of its value, I promise you. In fact we wish to offer you an equitable financial return for bringing it safely back to the capital, Mister Kemp, in order to renegotiate with your company for its hire in the immediate future. We intend to carry on with the project at Bir Oassa, and naturally you and your company's expertise are vital.'

As he said all this Kemp's face changed. Incredibly enough he believed all this cant. The rig was to be miraculously saved, driven in triumph to Port Luard, refitted and taken once again upcountry to the oilfields, all in perfect safety and with the blessing of financial security, under the benevolent protection of whoever claimed to be the rightful government of Nyala. And he, Basil Kemp, was the man chosen for the task. It was a daydream coming true, and nothing would free him from his delusion.

Goddamn, Wingstead ought to have been here! He was the only man who could have made Kemp see reason. Me he would ignore; the others he would override; and my disadvantage was that it was only a shadow of suspicion that made me distrust all this fine talk, these promises and inducements. What Wadzi said might be true. He too was only a pawn in a political game. But I believed that there wasn't a word of validity in anything he said. We'd seen too much, been too involved. We were doomed men.

Kemp was afire with anticipation.

'Yes, I'm in charge of the rig,' he said.

'Can you drive it back to Port Luard for us?'

Kemp looked round for Hammond and McGrath. I held my breath lest in his one-track minded folly he should betray them.

'Yes, of course we can. We'll have to get fuel. We need diesel and petrol, and water. I'd have to go ahead to check the road conditions. The starter engine needs servicing, perhaps a complete overhaul. I think we need –'

His brain went into overdrive as he reviewed the most important of the many priorities facing him. Thorpe opened his mouth but caught my eye and subsided. As long as Kemp was in full spate he wouldn't mention the vital fact of the missing drivers.

Wadzi interrupted. 'It can all be arranged. I am pleased that you are willing to help us. What about you, Mister Mannix? Not so well-disposed?' The silky menace was overt and I felt a pulse thud in my neck.

'I'm damned if I'm well-disposed. Do you know who was in that ferry, Wadzi?'

He said, 'I believe you liberated the ferryman and have been so misguided as to send a number of Nyalans, including medical people of the utmost value to the country, across to Manzu. We must take steps to extradite them; that will be a nuisance. I am not pleased about it.'

'Then you know it was a hospital ship. You damned well fired on a boatload of invalids, women and kids. In my book that makes you a war criminal. You're not fit to walk the earth, Wadzi. You'd disgrace any damned uniform you put on.'

My companions stared at me in horror at this reckless baiting of our captor, but it seemed to be the only way to keep his attention. The 'B'-gon team had to have a chance to get here with our only weapon, though I wasn't clear what we could do with it. Wadzi was a vain man and rose readily to my lure to justify his cause. Under the same circumstances Colonel Maksa would simply have blown my head off.

'You forget yourself! You are in no position to make such accusations, Mannix, nor question my authority. You do yourself a grave injury in this obstruction and you will pay for it!'

'I've no doubt,' I said grimly.

'I would be within my rights if I were to exercise summary justice in your case, Mannix,' Wadzi said. I wondered sickly if he was so very different to Maksa after all.

Ritchie Thorpe protested bravely.

'You can't just shoot him, Colonel, for God's sake!'

Two soldiers stepped forward, their rifles raised to enforce the threat, and I thought numbly that I'd finally gone too far. But he held them back with a cut of his stick in the air, glowered at Thorpe and said to Kemp, 'This man Mannix – is he necessary to your transport arrangements? Mister Kemp! I am speaking to you.'

Kemp was miles away, planning the rig's forthcoming journey. He was recalled with a start at hearing his own name, and looked with puzzlement from Wadzi to me. I wasn't breathing too well.

'What's that? Oh, Neil? Yes, of course I need him,' he said abstractedly. 'Turned out to be very useful on this trip. Need everyone we've got,' he went on, gazing around the yard, 'Thorpe, where's Ben Hammond? I need him right now.'

In reprieving me he had raised another bogey.

'Hammond? Who is this?' Wadzi demanded, instantly on the alert.

'Mister Kemp sent him on an errand,' Thorpe said the first thing that came into his head.

And at the same moment a babble of voices rose and we all turned to look at the lake. Coming downriver towards the ferry slip, moving extremely slowly, half awash with water and canted over at an acute angle, were the recoupled 'B'-gons. On the front section Dufouf's truck stood uneasily, its lashings removed but the chocks still in place under the wheels. Zimmerman and Kirilenko were each handling an outboard on the after section, with Hammond giving steering instructions.

The soldier's voices died down. Wadzi stared silently.

Handled with great delicacy and precision the raft nuzzled its way onto the ferry slip and the two outboards pushed it inexorably forward until it could go no further. With a grating sound it grounded itself with the forward section half out of the lake, resting firmly on the causeway. Our floating bomb had arrived.

Kemp looked as astonished as the Colonel.

'Neil, what the devil is this?' he asked testily. 'You know we don't need the raft any more –'

'Ah, Hammond!' I shouted to the new arrivals, drowning Kemp's voice with my own. 'Well done! That's the last truck, is it? You'll see that we have company. This is Colonel Wadzi, who's going to take the rig back to Port Luard with our help. He's asked Mister Kemp to take charge of the operation and Mister Kemp is very keen to do so.'

I was trying to give Hammond as much information as possible while at the same time preventing Kemp from saying anything to further rouse Wadzi's suspicions. The Colonel stepped forward and rapped me sharply on the arm. 'Just what is all this about?' he demanded.

'Stores for the convoy, or some of them,' I said rapidly. 'The last of our transport vehicles. We've been waiting for it to arrive.'

'Arrive? Like that?'

'Well, yes, we bought some of them down by water . . .'

Hammond had come ashore and was tying up the raft calmly as if the presence of armed soldiers were commonplace. Now he chipped in and said easily, 'To save fuel, Colonel. Two seven horsepower outboard engines use a lot less than one truck over long distances, so we've ferried them down this way. I suppose you'll want it added to the rest of the convoy, Mister Mannix?'

The implication appalled me. He was prepared to drive the gelignite-filled truck up among the troops and, presumably, explode it where it would cause maximum alarm and destruction. Whether it would save our lives was doubtful, but it would certainly end his.

And he was waiting for me to give him the go-ahead.

'Not just for the moment, Ben,' I said. 'Have a word with Mister Kemp first about moving the rig. He . . . needs your advice.'

Hammond looked at Kemp and at once took in his tense, barely controlled anxiety. He gave a reassuring nod.

'We'll want to plot the mileage charts afresh, Mister Kemp, won't we?' he asked calmly.

Kemp said curtly, 'I've been looking for you. Where are the maps?'

They started talking, ignoring the armed men around them. I hoped that Hammond could keep Kemp occupied. He was in a state of dangerous hypertension, and if not controlled he could be as great a threat as the enemy.

Zimmerman and Kirilenko came ashore cautiously, saying nothing. Zimmerman's hands at his side made a curious twisting gesture reminiscent of turning a key, and then he brushed his wristwatch casually. I realized what this implied: he had set a timing mechanism on the lethal truck.

'How long? Harry, how long did the trip take?' I asked loudly.

'Only fifteen minutes, Neil.'

Christ. A quarter of an hour to get us all out of range before Dufour's truck went sky-high; call it ten minutes because no hastily home-made timer could be all that accurate. Or it might never go off at all. Frantically I juggled possibilities while at the same time continuing to face up to Wadzi.

He was disconcerted by my change in attitude. Before I had defied him; now I was cooperating. He said, 'Mister Mannix, are these all your men now?'

'Yes, that's it.' I mentally subtracted McGrath.

'You will all accompany us with your transporter to Fort Pirie. There we will make further arrangements,' he said briskly. 'I understand that you are not one of the drivers. Is that correct?'

I wondered just how much else he knew about us.

'That's right, Colonel. But of course I can drive a truck.'

I glanced round for inspiration. The ferry yard was full of troops and transport. Soldiers surrounded the rig up on the main road and Wadzi had placed guards on our other vehicles. Sadiq still sat in the rear of his own car at the top of the spur road. *Auntie Bess* crouched hidden in the garage. Of the ferry there was no sign.

Hammond had led Kemp to the far side of the causeway, well clear of the grounded raft, produced a map from his pocket and spread it on the ground so Kemp would have to squat down to study it. It kept his eyes off us, though it meant we would have to manage without Hammond.

Zimmerman stood near the raft-borne truck, hands in his pockets. Kirilenko was behind him, impassive as always. Next to me Thorpe stood rigid and beyond him Dufour, stiff and haggard; his eyes flickered from me to his truck and back, signalling some incomprehensible message.

This is easy, I told myself. You get into the truck, drive it among the soldiers, stall it and fiddle about until the whole damn thing goes sky-high. In the mêlée, during which with any luck quite a few of the enemy get killed including their gallant leader, your men make a dash for the dukw and drive it off into the sunset. Nothing to it. The only small problem was that our own gallant leader was most certainly not going to survive the experience either, and I was rooted by something I frantically hoped wasn't cowardice. Surely it was only sensible to await the play of the card we still had up our sleeve?

Surely McGrath would come up trumps once again?

He had ten minutes at the outside to do so. I swallowed, sucked in my gut and took two steps towards Dufour's truck.

'I'll take it up to join the others, shall I?' I asked Wadzi.

There was a stir among our men. Dufour's gasp was clearly heard and Wadzi reacted instantly. His revolver was

out of its holster and held at arm's length pointing straight
at me.

'Don't move!' Wadzi snapped.

I didn't.

'Where are the keys to that truck?' he demanded.
Zimmerman clenched his fist instinctively and Wadzi saw
the movement; his eyes were lynx-sharp. 'I'll have them,'
he said, extending a hand with a snap of his fingers.

'Do it,' I said.

Zimmerman put the truck keys into the Colonel's hand
and without taking his eyes off me Wadzi flipped them to
one of his men. 'Bring that truck ashore,' he said. The words
were in Nyalan but the meaning all too clear. The soldier
ran down the causeway and swung himself into the cab. I
closed my eyes; bad driving might be fatal.

Two soldiers removed the chocks and the truck inched its
way onto the causeway, leaving the raft rocking, all but submerged and even closer to disintegration. It was certainly
beyond use as an escape device. It was the DUKW or nothing
now.

The truck drove slowly up the spur road. Wadzi rammed
his revolver back into its holster.

'I advise you to be very careful, Mister Mannix,' he was
saying. 'Do nothing without my permission . . . what is it?'

But none of us were listening to him. He whipped round
to see what was holding our enthralled attention.

'Christ, it's Mick!' Thorpe shouted.

From behind one of the buildings a man came running,
weaving through the troops. The sub-machine-gun in his
hands spouted fire in all directions. McGrath closed rapidly
in on the slowly travelling truck, hurtling past men too
stunned to react.

There was a crack of gunfire. High up on the spur road
Sadiq rose in the back seat of the open staff car, his manacled
hands clutching a rifle. One of his guards toppled backwards

out of the car. He fired again among the soldiers who were closing in on McGrath and they fell back in disarray. One man fell to the ground.

Zimmerman yelled, 'No, Mick – don't take it!' He straight-armed a soldier and at the same moment Kirilenko whirled on another and floored him with a massive kick to the groin. In horror I stared at Dufour's truck. McGrath stumbled just as he reached it and lost his grip on the sub-machine-gun.

'He's hit!'

McGrath heaved himself up and into the cab and hurled the driver out with a violent effort. The truck picked up speed and raced up the spur road towards the rig.

Beside me Wadzi opened his mouth to shout an order.

I threw myself at him and we went down in a tangle of arms and legs. I clawed for the revolver at his belt as Thorpe threw himself down to pin Wadzi's legs. As I scrambled to my feet with the gun I saw Sadiq arch out of the staff car, the rifle flying from his hands. He crashed in a sprawling mass onto the roadway. Kirilenko used his boot again on Colonel Wadzi's breastbone and the officer subsided, coughing and writhing. His men scattered.

I gasped, 'Harry, does Mick know?'

'Yes. I told him! Oh my God – it'll go any second!'

And then Dufour had hold of my arm, gripping it like a vice and shaking me violently. 'Mannix – I tried to tell you, I *tried*! It will not explode!'

'Of course it will. I've wired it!' Zimmerman snapped.

Dufour stammered, 'Only four bottles of gelignite . . . right in front . . .'

'What?'

As we spoke the truck rocketed up the slope, fired on from all sides. If the timing mechanism failed the bullets would do the job for us. But what in God's name was Dufour trying to say?

'Not . . . gelignite! Mother of God, Mannix, it's *gin*!'

A blinding light of understanding hit me. Spirits were illegal and therefore precious in Bir Oassa, a predominantly Arab community. The gelignite was a double bluff, to prevent officials from probing further into Dufour's illicit cargo. Few would tamper with such a load. He had been smuggling alcohol to the oilfields.

And now, instead of the shattering explosion that we'd hoped for there would be at most a small thump, a brief shock. The damage would be to the truck itself. McGrath's heroic, insane act would be all for nothing.

'Oh dear God.'

We stood frozen. Wadzi was hurt but alive and he'd be on his feet again any moment. We were still surrounded by armed men, and there was no path to freedom; nowhere to go. The revolver hung loosely in my hand and I felt sick and stunned. We had gambled and lost.

The truck veered off course, clawing its way across the dirt shoulder of the upper road. It was alongside the rig by now. Its erratic steering could only mean that McGrath was badly wounded or perhaps even already dead. It rocked and shuddered to a halt, dwarfed by the enormous structure of the rig. It half tilted off the shoulder and hung over the edge of the sheer drop to the ferry yard. My heart hammered as I saw a figure inside the cab – my last sight of Mick McGrath.

The truck exploded.

It was not, indeed, a very great event. The truck blew apart in a sheet of flame. The men and other vehicles nearby were sheltered from damage by the rig itself, an object too massive to be affected.

But under the truck was the roadway. Years old, carelessly maintained, potholed and crumbling; at this spot it clung to the hillside over a drought-dry, friable crust of earth knitted together with shallow-rooted vegetation. The road had no more stability than a child's sandpit.

The exploding truck tore this fragile structure like a cobweb.

A cracking fissure ran along the ancient tarmac just where the full weight of the rig already bore down too heavily for safety. There was a gigantic roar, a rolling billow of dust, and the entire hillside gave way under the terrible pressure of the rig.

With its load of the three hundred ton transformer and the coupled tractors the rig began to roll and tumble down the slope towards the ferry yard, dreadful in its power. With it came huge chunks of tarmac, earth, boulders and debris. It thundered downwards, gaining momentum, the air split with the tortured scream of metal and the roar of the landslide that came with it.

Men scattered like ants and fled in horror from the monstrous death racing down towards them. Engines screamed into life, rifles clattered to the ground as the soldiers dashed frantically for safety. The rig crashed with appalling, ponderous strength into the first of the outbuildings, crushing them to matchwood. The paving of the yard crumbled under the onslaught.

We stood in shock and terror as the animal we had led about so tamely turned into a raging brute trumpeting destruction. And then there was a scream wilder than any I'd yet heard.

'No! No! Stop it – don't let it happen – '

Kemp burst between us, his face contorted, his eyes bulging in horror, and ran straight towards the rig. We took a couple of steps after him and stopped, helpless to prevent the awful thing Kemp was about to do.

While all other men fled from the oncoming monster, Kemp held his hands out in front of him in a futile, terrible gesture and ran straight into its path. The juggernaut claimed many bloody sacrifices but one went willingly.

Losing momentum on the flat, the rig halted abruptly. From among crushed and unrecognizable fragments the bulk of the transformer rose twisted but identifiable.

Billowing dust mercifully hid details of the trail of carnage. Remnants of one of the ferry buildings leaned drunkenly, ripped open and eviscerated.

My knees were as weak as grass stems and the skin of my face was drawn taut and painful. Hammond was sobbing in a hard, dry fashion that wrenched the breath from his body. Kirilenko was on his knees, gripping a rifle in both hands; the barrel was buckled under the strength he had exerted.

Zimmerman had his hands to his face and blood trickled down where some flying debris had cut him. Dufour and Thorpe stood in total silence; Dufour's arms were wrapped around Ritchie Thorpe's shoulders in a grip of iron. Everyone was white and shattered.

The noise of screams and moaning, voices crying for help, buckling metal and splintering wood were all around us, but we stood in a small oasis of silence. There were no soldiers anywhere near us except Colonel Wadzi himself, who was rocking slightly on his feet, his uniform ripped and dirty, his face haggard with shock.

I took a deep gasp of air.

'Let's get the hell out of here.'

Wadzi raised his face to mine, his eyes bewildered.

'My men . . .' he said uncertainly, and then more firmly, 'I have much to do. You people, you must go. We do not want you here.'

His voice was drained of every emotion. We were bad news. He had done with us for ever.

Hammond said, 'My God, that poor bloody man.'

I knew he meant Kemp, but it was McGrath I thought of.

Thorpe said softly, 'There's nothing to keep us here now.'

I nodded in complete understanding. Safe from the path of destruction the DUKW was unscathed in its waterside garage.

'*Auntie Bess* is waiting,' I said. 'Let's go and join the others.'

THE HOUSE OF THE LIONS

This unpublished short story was written to entertain
Christmas house guests at Hay Hill, the Bagleys' home
in Totnes, Devon, in December 1966.

In the year 1887, in the town of Totnes in the County of Devonshire, a man bought a house. His name was William Cooper Johnson and he was a retired clergyman; the house was called Mount Elwell.

William Johnson was in his middle age and he had spent much of his life in Africa as a missionary. The climate of that continent and the agues induced thereby had, however, caused his early retirement and encouraged him to dwell in a more salubrious environment, of which none better can be found in Devonshire. And so he bought the house known as Mount Elwell in the ancient borough of Totnes.

The house was in the style of the last century, having been built in 1791, and was but a simple dwelling and sorely lacking in that elegance of ornamentation which has become the pride and hallmark of our civilisation. Yet the rooms were large and stood foursquare, the walls were thick and the house was warm, there was a small wing attached for the housing of an abigail, and so William Johnson was content.

He had married young and his children were adult and gone into the world, except for his youngest daughter, Alice. And so there dwelt in Mount Elwell William Johnson; his wife, Elizabeth; his daughter, Alice; and the abigail, one Susan Beer who was but a poor half-witted girl, the only child of a farm labourer who was the best servant Mrs Johnson could obtain because there seemed to be a curious reluctance on the part of the lower classes of Totnes to offer themselves or their daughters in the service of this kind and holy man. The Johnsons found this unaccountable and, at first, put it down to the natural conservatism of an isolated folk to whom a traveller from even the next county was a foreigner. It was only later that the truth was to be made terribly apparent.

William Johnson was determined in his early retirement to write an account of his experiences in Africa which he believed would be of use to his fellow men. However, he discovered that the room most natural to use as a study and library was to the rear of the house and faced north, thus being very cold. His wife insisted that, due to his precarious state of health, it would be impossible for him to work in that room, and it was decided to adapt the dining room as his work place. It faced to the south and on to the walled garden and was flooded with sunshine for many hours of the day, both in summer and winter.

There were odd features about this room. It had only three corners – as we generally regard the corners of a room. The fourth corner swept in a curve which Mrs Johnson found to be a nuisance since it inhibited the placing of furniture. Next to this architectural curiosity was a tall cupboard which was even more curious, since its doors opened, not to the room, but to a passage off the hall. It was a tall and unusually narrow cupboard with split doors of the Dutch or stable variety, and it projected inconveniently into William Johnson's new study. He was in half a mind to tear it down but let it stand because his wife found it convenient to have such a cupboard close to the kitchen.

Being a prudent man Johnson decided to insure the house against fire or other disasters and so he made the journey to

Exeter where he consulted Mr Frederick Milford of the West of England Fire and Life Assurance Society, obtaining very good terms – thirteen shillings and sixpence premium against a capital sum of £800. It was in the course of this transaction that Mr Milford remarked, 'Ah! Mount Elwell! I believe the property has been standing vacant for some time.'

'That is so,' said Mr Johnson. 'I cannot understand why, because it is a very good property.'

'Just so,' said Mr Milford and said no more on that score, but a little while later he said apparently apropos of nothing, 'The last owner of the house was Captain Hampson, a military man. He died four years ago. Captain Hampson was a very strange man – or so I am led to understand.'

'Would it be he who extended the house – who built the servants' wing?'

'That is so.' Mr Milford paused. 'His servants were black.'

'Black!' echoed Mr Johnson in astonishment.

'Just so,' said Milford. 'Captain Hampson had a great deal to do with Africa, so I believe. He was an explorer and when he retired to England he brought his own servants – heathen black fellers from the jungle. It caused quite a bit of talk, I must say.'

'So I can imagine,' said Mr Johnson. 'I wonder if it was he who was responsible for the lions?'

Milford started nervously and his eyebrows crawled up his scalp. 'Lions?' he said doubtfully.

'Yes. Each bracket supporting the roof guttering is decorated with the head of a lion.'

'Hampson did a lot of reconstruction on Mount Elwell,' said Milford cautiously. 'Lions, eh! A curious man was Hampson – in every way, including his death. There was a lot of talk about that too.'

'In what way?'

Milford shrugged. 'Just a lot of gossip. I didn't listen closely.'

He said no more about it, and Johnson did not pursue the matter although he was curious. All the long journey home the next day he pondered over it and decided to consult the Reverend Burrough, the Vicar of St Mary the Virgin, which was the fine church in Totnes. Johnson was a man who did not like mysteries.

Over the teacups that evening his wife said, 'I'm sure there's a cat in the house, William; although I can't find it. I have heard it mewing and thought it was locked in the cellar – or the attic, perhaps; but although I have searched, I cannot find it anywhere.'

'But I've seen it,' said Alice unexpectedly. 'It was in the garden – and a very strange animal it was.'

'How was it strange, my dear?'

Alice frowned. 'It had a curious colouring; light brown with a black – or dark brown – head and paws. What was most startling were the eyes – they were a bright sapphire blue.'

Johnson smiled tolerantly. 'Your imagination is running away with you,' he said. 'Whoever heard of a blue-eyed cat? It was probably an ordinary tom-cat – a stray.'

He thought no more about it, but that night he was awakened by a whispered conversation at the door of his bedroom and discovered his wife and daughter in the midst of an agitated argument.

'What is the matter?' he demanded.

'Nothing, dear,' replied his wife. 'Alice had a bad dream, that is all.'

'It was not a dream,' protested Alice . 'A cat did run over my bed. I felt the paws distinctly.'

Johnson calmed down his daughter and they all returned to bed, but just before falling asleep he thought he heard the mew of a cat, although whether that was his imagination or not he was afterwards unable to tell.

* * *

Two days later Johnson went to the vicarage of St Mary the Virgin and saw the Reverend Burrough who was an old man, failing in health and not long for this world as Johnson judged. After a few minutes of small-talk he said, 'I've been hearing some strange tales about my predecessor at Mount Elwell. I understand that he was in Africa.'

'That is correct,' said Burrough. 'He was an Army man in East Africa, engaged in putting down the slave trade, and was invalided out of the Army because of a recurring ague of the kind the Italians call the malarin.'

'I know the disease,' said Johnson grimly.

Burrough said, 'What tales have you heard?'

'Nothing definite. How did he die?'

'Dreadfully!' said Burrough somewhat forcibly. 'He was killed by an animal.'

'Thrown from his horse?' queried Johnson.

Burrough appeared hesitant. 'No,' he said at last. 'He was deliberately killed by a . . . a predatory animal.'

'My dear sir,' said Johnson in astonishment, 'This is nineteenth-century England. What kind of predators have we here capable of killing a man?'

Burrough shook his head. 'We could but go by the evidence of his body. I have never seen anyone die so bloodily. The whole of his torso was ripped open and there were dreadful claw marks on all limbs.' His voice wavered. 'It was as though . . . '

'As though . . . ?' prompted Johnson.

'As though he had been killed by a . . . let us say, a large cat or member of the cat family such as a tiger or a leopard.'

'Or a lion,' mused Johnson.

'Just so . . .a lion,' agreed Burrough. He appeared ill at ease.

'And was such an animal found and destroyed?'

Burrough shook his head. 'No,' he said sombrely.

Johnson smiled. 'I really cannot believe that in this day and age such a thing could happen. Cats and lions indeed!

Even my daughter is seeing cats and feeling and hearing them when they are not there.'

Burrough sat up straight. 'Your daughter saw a cat! Tell me, did it have blue eyes?'

'Why, yes,' said Johnson. 'Don't tell me there is such an impossible animal hereabouts.'

Burrough seemed disturbed. 'So it has been seen again,' he said softly and then looked Johnson straight in the eye. 'We are both churchmen – do you believe in the physical power of evil?'

'I doubt if the Devil moves among us in physical shape,' said Johnson. 'But that he has spiritual power cannot be denied.'

'I think you are wrong,' said Burrough, folding his lean hands together. 'Captain Hampson was the most evil man I have ever met in my stewardship of this parish – and I have been vicar for nearly fifty years. I am certain he dabbled in the Black Arts – arts he learned in Africa. And he brought devils to Totnes; his servants were black men of abnormal height, scarcely human in appearance. Not one of them was less than seven feet – all were thin beyond belief.'

Johnson said thoughtfully, 'I have heard of a strange tribe in East Africa in which the natives are of such a nature. I believe they are called Watusi.'

'That is the name!' cried Burrough. 'They worship lions.' He lifted a hand. 'Strange things happened at Mount Elwell; curious sounds – the beating of drums and the roar of savage beasts – and an odd flickering glow used to appear in some of the rooms. None of the townsfolk would go near, nor will they do so to this day.'

'That I have reason to know,' said Johnson, somewhat morosely. 'But you cannot really believe that . . .'

'. . . that Hampson was worshipping the devil as he had been taught by those savages? Indeed I do. I was on the point of writing to the Bishop for guidance when the tragedy happened and Hampson was torn to pieces by the awful Power he had invoked.' Burrough's eyes gleamed fanatically. 'And after it was over none of those black devils were ever seen again. It was as though they disappeared from the face of the earth.'

That was certainly an odd circumstance, thought Johnson; a seven-foot blackamoor would find concealment difficult in South Devon. He cleared his throat nervously. 'And what of the strange blue-eyed cat?'

'It is well known that witches and warlocks have their familiars,' said Burrough slowly. 'And the Devil cannot be stupid. Would he appear in the form of a lion in this quiet English town for all to see? But many people have seen the blue-eyed cat and my parishioners know it for what it is.'

The old man was now becoming excited and it took all of William Johnson's powers of persuasion to calm him. Johnson judged Burrough to be senile and failing in intellectual capacity and dismissed his strange story as the maunderings of an old man. All the same, he did not pass on this odd happening to either his wife or his daughter.

The year 1887 drew near to its close and certain events occurred which weighed heavily on his spirit. Alice saw the cat several times although William Johnson never did, nor did his wife. But Mrs Johnson complained continuously about the animal's incessant mewing, and three times she woke up her husband in the dark of the night to tell him that the cat had jumped on the bed. Yet there was nothing there when he looked.

He worked in his study during the dark evenings and was conscious of a brooding spirit which seemed to hover in and around the house, pervading the atmosphere with a dankness that chilled his bones. There was also a heavy scent which seemed to drift about the place and which, at first, he could not identify, but then he recalled his visits to a zoo and could compare it to the musty smell of the lion house.

He became nervous and was strongly aware of being watched and would glance hastily over his shoulder only to see shadows. Then he would go and turn up the gas lights to their full strength and say a prayer before resuming work on his manuscript.

The Christmas of 1887 was not a happy one for the Johnsons. Since they had spent most of their lives in Africa they had no friends in England, and none of the local people, of high or low degree, would visit the house. Even Susan Beer gave notice just before Christmas, saying that her father forbade her to be in that house at that time of the year. There was no other explanation offered.

It was on Christmas Eve that they began to hear the noises – a faint but persistent drumming sound. 'It seems to come from the attic,' said Mrs Johnson, so William went upstairs, but from the attic the sound appeared to come from the cellar, yet the cellar was quiet apart from that eerie distant rhythmical beat.

'We've heard that before,' said Alice quietly. 'In Africa.'

During the week that followed – between Christmas and New Year – life became very difficult at Mount Elwell. The noise of drums became gradually louder and reverberated through the house. All the Johnsons heard the drums although William Johnson could never determine whether he had actually heard the noise with his ears or whether it was purely in his mind, and when he consulted his wife and daughter he found them in like difficulty.

At last he could bear it no longer. 'You must leave,' he said firmly to his wife. 'You and Alice must stay at the Seven Stars Hotel for a while.'

'And you, William?' asked his wife.

'I will consult the vicar,' said Johnson.

And so he did. Burrough nodded gravely when he heard of the manifestations in the house.

'It is coming time,' he said. 'Hampson died on the first of the year.' He clutched Johnson's arm. 'I tell you, sir; I tell you this house is accursed and must be re-dedicated to God. We are churchmen – and we both know what to do in a situation like this.'

Johnson though of the ancient rituals of exorcism; he had learned them before he had been ordained into the priesthood, but he had never expected to use them. Burrough said briskly, 'I will come and keep vigil with you on New Year's Eve together with Alfred Earle, the arch-deacon. We will drive the Devil from Totnes.'

So it was that on New Year's Eve Johnson, Burrough and Alfred Earle gathered in Johnson's study at Mount Elwell. Burrough lit the two big candles, laid out the brass-bound bible, and placed the brazen bell conveniently to hand. Earle, a normally bluff and hearty Devonian, was subdued and quiet.

He carried with him an axe of which Burrough said, 'You will find no target for that, Alfred. There is no physical enemy here. Put your faith in the Lord God.'

But Alfred Earle stubbornly clutched the haft of the axe and would not be parted from it.

The clamour of the drums almost deafened Johnson so that he had difficulty in hearing what the others said, but strangely they seemed to be unaware. 'Can't you hear them?' he demanded wildly.

Burrough cocked his head on one side. 'I hear nothing – nothing at all. But wait. . . yes, I hear a faint throbbing. Could it be coming from your attic?'

Johnson set his teeth. 'It begins like that. If you stayed in this house as long as I have your ears would resound with nothing else.'

Time crept by and the three men knelt and prayed incessantly but Johnson, distracted by the drumming and the unexpected yowling of a cat, could not get the words right and made many mistakes.

At last the big grandfather clock in the hall struck the first stroke of midnight, and the tremendous racket suddenly stopped. There was the thick animal scent heavy on the still air, and another smell of putrefaction. The three men looked at each other in wonder, and Burrough made the sign of the cross.

At that instant a voice spoke, at once dry and glutinous, and it spoke words in a language none could understand. It came from the strange cupboard that opened on to the hall, and there was a scratching noise as though something were trying to get out. William Johnson uttered an inarticulate cry and, seizing the axe from Alfred Earle, he swung it at the cupboard in a great blow. The wood splintered under his onslaught, and he swung again and again, chopping the cupboard to matchwood.

Something loomed tall in the opening he had made and fell slowly forward. It was the figure of a giant of a man, seven feet tall – a corpse long dead and mummified which had been concealed in the false backing of the cupboard. It fell forward as a tree falls, but with the lips writhing and incoherent words spouting forth – a tall African dressed in skins and feathers and bones.

Alfred Earle shouted in terror but Burrough and Johnson were struck speechless as a cat, a strangely coloured, blue-eyed cat sprang from the cupboard to crouch on the fallen corpse, its ears flattened and spitting in rage. Johnson looked upon it in horror as it began to change. It seemed to grow subtly and fluidly and in no time at all it was transformed into a huge black-maned lion. He stared into those eyes, now lambent and yellow, and had no time to even shout as it sprang directly at him.

They found them the next day. Burrough and Earle were both dead and there was not a mark on them, but their faces were dreadfully contorted. The medical evidence was that they had died from heart failure. William Cooper Johnson, however, had been torn limb from limb as though by a great cat and his blood lay red and thick across the open bible. Lying across the corpse was a barbaric necklace of lions' teeth.

All that happened a long time ago. The house is no longer called Mount Elwell – it is now Hay Hill – and the cupboard has been torn down and the opening bricked up, although its doors are still there as you can see to this day.

And if you talk to the old men of Totnes as they drink their pints of cider in the Kingsbridge Inn they will tell you their reckonings of these strange happenings. They will tell you that the house is quite safe for the normal run of men – but if the blue-eyed cat is seen again, and if the house is again occupied by those who have lived in Africa, then the drums will be heard and the lion will walk again to rend and tear with claws and fangs.

Because no one who has not lived in Africa has been touched – save for dying of fright at the awesome things they have witnessed – but those who have lived in the Dark Continent, and come to Hay Hill at this time of the year . . . beware!

DESMOND BAGLEY

'Tense, heroic, chastening . . . a thumping good story.'
Sunday Express

THE SNOW TIGER

Fifty-four people died in the avalanche that ripped apart a small New Zealand mining town. But the enquiry which follows unleashes more destructive power than the snowfall. As the survivors tell their stories, they reveal a community so divided that all warnings of danger went unheeded. At the centre of the storm is Ian Ballard, whose life depends upon being able to clear his name . . .

NIGHT OF ERROR

When Mark Trevelyan dies on a journey to a remote Pacific atoll, the verdict that it was natural causes doesn't convince his brother, Mike. The series of violent attacks that follows only adds to his suspicions. Just two clues – a notebook in code and a lump of rock – are enough to trigger off a hazardous expedition, and a violent confrontation far from civilization . . .

'The detail is immaculately researched – the action has the skill to grab your heart or your bowels.'   *Daily Mirror*

978-0-00-730481-3

DESMOND BAGLEY

'Bagley is one of the best.'   *The Times*

HIGH CITADEL

When Tim O'Hara's plane is hijacked and forced to crash land in the middle of the Andes, his troubles are only beginning. A heavily armed group of communist soldiers intent on killing one of his passengers – an influential political figure – have orders to leave no survivors. Isolated in the biting cold of the Andes, O'Hara's party must fight for their lives with only the most primitive weapons . . .

LANDSLIDE

Bob Boyd is a geologist, as resilient as the British Columbia timber country where he works for the powerful Matterson Corporation. But his real name and his past are mysteries – wiped out by the accident that nearly killed him. Then Boyd reads a name that opens a door in his memory: Trinavant – and discovers that Bull Matterson and his son will do almost anything to keep the Trinavant family forgotten forever . . .

'Very much of the moment. The characters are sympathetic and believable'   *Sunday Times*

978-0-00-730479-0

DESMOND BAGLEY

'Stories charged with suspense.'   *Financial Times*

WYATT'S HURRICANE

Ferocious Hurricane Mabel is predicted to pass harmlessly amongst the islands of the Caribbean. But David Wyatt
has developed a sixth sense about hurricanes. He is convinced that Mabel will change course to strike the island of
San Fernandez and its capital, St Pierre. But nobody
believes him, and the hurricane is only one of the problems
that threaten San Fernandez . . .

BAHAMA CRISIS

Tom Mangan was a sharply successful entrepreneur who
lured the super-rich to his luxury hotels in the sun-soaked
Bahamas. Then violent tragedy struck: his own family disappeared, and a series of misfortunes, accidents and mysterious epidemics began to drive the tourists away and
wreck Mangan's livelihood. Fatally, he becomes determined to confront his enemy – and the hunt is on . . .

'Tautly written adventure, packed with exhaustive detail.
You will be out of breath when you finish.'

                                    Books And Bookmen

978-0-00-730478-3